—UNTIL THEY CAME AFTER HIS FAMILY....

— Phillip Margolin

"A head rush of a thriller." — Esquire

Nobody does it better." — James Grady

The Dallas Morning News

"One helluva thriller." — The Baltimore Sun

The Orlando Sentinel

ALSO BY STEPHEN HUNTER

FICTION

Black Light
Dirty White Boys
Point of Impact
The Day Before Midnight
Tapestry of Spies
The Second Saladin
The Master Sniper

NONFICTION

*Violent Screen: A Critic's 13 Years on the
Front Lines of Movie Mayhem*

TIME
TO
HUNT

A NOVEL BY

STEPHEN
HUNTER

Island
BOOKS

ISLAND BOOKS
Published by
Dell Publishing
a division of
Random House, Inc.
1540 Broadway
New York, New York 10036

ISBN: 0-440-22645-7

Reprinted by arrangement with Doubleday

Printed in the United States of America

Published simultaneously in Canada

April 1999

10 9 8 7 6 5 4 3
OPM

FOR

CPL John Burke, USMC
KIA, I Corps, RSVN, 1967

If any question why we died,
Tell them, because our fathers lied.

—RUDYARD KIPLING
writing in the voice of his son John,
KIA, the Somme, at the age of sixteen

PROLOGUE

We are in the presence of a master sniper.

He lies, almost preternaturally still, on hard stone. The air is thin, still cold; he doesn't shake or tremble.

The sun is soon to rise, pushing the chill from the mountains. As its light spreads, it reveals fabulous beauty. High peaks, shrouded in snow; a pristine sky that will be the color of a pure blue diamond; far mountain pastures of a green so intense it rarely exists in nature; brooks snaking down through pines that carpet the mountainsides.

The sniper notices none of this. If you pointed it out to him, he wouldn't respond. Beauty, in nature or women or even rifles, isn't a concept he would recognize, not after where he's been and what he's done. He simply doesn't care; his mind doesn't work that way.

Instead, he sees nothingness. He feels a great cool numbness. No idea has any meaning to him at this point. His mind is almost empty, as though he's in a trance.

He's a short-necked man, as so many great shooters are; his blue eyes, though gifted with an almost freakish 20/10 acuity, appear dull, signifying a level of mental activity almost startlingly blank. His pulse rate hardly exists. He has some oddities, again freakish in some men but weirdly perfect for a shooter. He has extremely well developed fast-twitch forearm muscles, still supple and defined at his age, which is beyond fifty. His hands are large and strong. His stamina is off the charts, as are his reflexes and his pain tolerance. He's strong, flexible, as charged with energy as any other world-class athlete. He has both a technical and a creative mind and a will as directed as a laser.

But none of this really explains him, any more than

such analysis would explain a Williams or a DiMaggio: he simply has an internal genius, possibly autistic, that gives him extraordinary control over body and mind, hand and eye, infinite patience, a shrewd gift for the tactical, and, most of all, total commitment to his arcane art, which in turn forms the core of his identity and has granted him a life that few could imagine.

But for now, *nothing:* not his past, not his future, not the pain of lying so still in the cold through a long night, not the excitement of knowing this could be the day. No anticipation, no regret: just nothing.

Before him is the tool of his trade, lying askew on a hard sandbag. He knows it intimately, having worked with it a great deal in preparation for the thirty seconds that will come today or tomorrow or the day after.

It's a Remington 700, with an H-S Precision fiberglass stock and a Leupold 10X scope. It's been tricked up by a custom riflesmith to realize the last tenth of a percent of its potential: the action trued and honed, and bolted into the metal block at the center of the stock at maximum torque; a new Krieger barrel free-floated after cryogenic treatment. The trigger, a Jewell, lets off at four pounds with the crisp snap of a glass rod breaking.

The sniper has run several weeks' worth of load experimentation through the rifle, finding the exact harmony that will produce maximum results: the perfect balance between the weight of a bullet, the depth of its seating, the selection and amount, to the tenth grain, hand measured, of the powder. Nothing has been left to chance: the case necks have been turned and annealed, the primer hole deburred, the primer depth perfected, the primer itself selected for consistency. The rifle muzzle wears the latest hot lick, a Browning Ballistic Optimizing System, which is a kind of screw-on nozzle that can be microtuned to generate the best vibrational characteristics for accuracy.

The caliber isn't military but civilian, the 7mm Remington Magnum, once the flavor of the month in international hunting circles, capable of dropping a ram or a whitetail at amazing distances. Though surpassed by some flashier loads, it's still a flat-shooting, hard-hitting cartridge that holds its velocity as it flies through the thin air, delivering close to two thousand foot-pounds of energy beyond five hundred yards.

But of all this data, the sniper doesn't care, or no longer cares. He knew it at one time; he has forgotten it now. The point of the endless ballistic experimentation was simple: to bring the rifle and its load to complete perfection so that it could be forgotten. That was one principle of great shooting—arrange for the best, then forget all about it.

When the sound comes, it doesn't shock or surprise him. He knew it had to come, sooner or later. It doesn't fill him with doubt or regret or anything. It simply means the obvious: time to work.

It's a peal of laughter, girlish and bright, giddy with excitement. It bounces off the stone walls of the canyon, from the shadow of a draw onto this high shelf from close to a thousand yards off, whizzing through the thin air.

The sniper wiggles his fingers, finds the warmth in them. His concentration cranks up a notch or so. He pulls the rifle to him in a fluid motion, well practiced from hundreds of thousands of shots in practice or on missions. Its stock rises naturally to his cheek as he pulls it in, and as one hand flies to the wrist, the other sets up beneath the forearm, taking the weight of his slightly lifted body, building a bone bridge to the stone below. It rests on a densely packed sandbag. He finds the spot weld, the one placement of cheek to stock where the scope relief will be perfect and the circle of the scope will throw up its image as brightly as a movie screen. His *adductor magnus,* a tube of muscle running through his deep thigh, tenses as he splays his right foot ever so slightly.

Above, a hawk rides a thermal, gliding through the blue morning sky.

A mountain trout leaps.

A bear looks about for something to eat.

A deer scampers through the brush.

The sniper notices none of it. He doesn't care.

"Mommy," shouts eight-year-old Nikki Swagger. "Come *on.*"

Nikki rides better than either of her parents; she's been almost literally raised on horseback, as her father, a retired Marine staff NCO with an agricultural background, had decided to go into the business of horse care at his own lay-up barn in Arizona, where Nikki was born.

Nikki's mother, a handsome woman named Julie Fenn Swagger, trails behind. Julie doesn't have the natural grace of her daughter, but she grew up in Arizona, where horses were a way of life, and has been riding since childhood. Her husband rode as an Arkansas farmboy, then didn't for decades, then came back to the animals and now loves them so, in their integrity and loyalty, that he has almost single-mindedly willed himself into becoming an accomplished saddleman. That is one of his gifts.

"Okay, okay," she calls, "be careful, sweetie," though she knows that careful is the last thing Nikki will ever be, for hers is a hero's personality, built from a willingness to risk all to gain all and a seeming absence of fear. She's like an Indian in that way, and like her father, too, who was once a war hero.

She turns.

"Come *on,*" she calls, replicating her daughter's rhythms. "You want to see the valley as the sun races across it, don't you?"

"Yep," comes the call from the rider still unseen in the shadows of the draw.

Nikki bounds ahead, out of the shadows and into the bright light. Her horse, named Calypso, is a four-year-old thoroughbred gelding, quite a beast, but Nikki handles it with nonchalance. She is actually riding English, because it is part of her mother's dream for her that she will go east to college, and the skills that are the hallmarks of equestrian sophistication will take her a lot farther than the rowdy ability to ride like a cowboy. Her father does not care for the English saddle, which seems hardly enough to protect the girl from the muscles of the animal beneath, and at horse shows he thinks those puffy jodhpurs and that little velveteen jacket with its froth of lace at the throat are sublimely ridiculous.

Calypso bounds over the rocky path, his cleverness as evident as his fearlessness. To watch the slight girl maneuver the massive horse is one of the great joys of her father's life: she never seems so alive as when on horseback, or so happy, or so in command. Now, Nikki's voice trills with pleasure as the horse at last breaks out onto a shelf of rock. Before them is the most beautiful view within riding distance and she races to the edge, seemingly out of control, but actually very much in control.

"Honey," cries Julie as her daughter careens merrily toward disaster, "be careful."

The child. The woman. The man.

The child comes first, the best rider, bold and adventurous. She emerges from the shadow of the draw, letting her horse run, and the animal thunders across the grass to the edge of the precipice, halts, then spins and begins to twitch with anticipation. The girl holds him tightly, laughing.

The woman is next. Not so gifted a rider, she still rides easily, with loping strides, comfortable in the saddle. The sniper can see her straw hair, her muscularity under the jeans and work shirt, the way the sun has browned her face. Her horse is a big chestnut, a stout, working cowboy's horse, not sleek like the daughter's.

And finally: the man.

He is lean and watchful and there is a rifle in the scabbard under his saddle. He looks dangerous, like a special man who would never panic, react fast and shoot straight, which is exactly what he is. He rides like a gifted athlete, almost one with the animal, controlling it unconsciously with his thighs. Relaxed in the saddle, he is still obviously alert.

He would not see the sniper. The sniper is too far out, the hide too carefully camouflaged, the spot chosen to put the sun in the victim's eyes at this hour so that he'll see only dazzle and blur if he looks.

The crosshairs ride up to the man, and stay with him as he gallops along, finding the same rhythm in the cadences, finding the same up-down plunge of the animal. The shooter's finger caresses the trigger, feels absorbed by its softness, but he does not fire.

Moving target, transversing laterally left to right, but also moving up and down through a vertical plane: 753 meters. By no means an impossible shot, and many a man in his circumstances would have taken it. But experience tells the sniper to wait: a better shot will lie ahead, the best shot. With a man like Swagger, that's the one you take.

The man joins the woman, and the two chat, and what he says makes her smile. White teeth flash. A little tiny human part in the sniper aches for the woman's beauty and ease; he's had prostitutes the world over, some quite expensive, but this little moment of intimacy is something that has evaded him completely. That's all right. He has chosen to work in exile from humanity.

Jesus Christ!

He curses himself. That's how shots are blown, that little fragment of lost concentration which takes you out of the operation. He briefly snaps his eyes shut, absorbs the darkness and clears his mind, then opens them again to what lies before him.

The man and the woman have reached the edge: 721 meters. Before them runs a valley, unfolding in the sunlight as the sun climbs even higher. But tactically what this means to the sniper is that at last his quarry has ceased to move. In the scope he sees a family portrait: man, woman and child, all at nearly the same level, because the child's horse is so big it makes her as tall as her parents. They chat, the girl laughs, points at a bird or something, seethes with motion. The woman stares into the distance. The man, still seeming watchful, relaxes just the tiniest bit.

The crosshairs bisect the square chest.

The master sniper expels a breath, seeks the stillness within himself, but wills nothing. He never decides or commits. It just happens.

The rifle bucks, and as it comes back in a fraction of a second, he sees the tall man's chest explode as the 7mm Remington Magnum tears through it.

PART I

THE PARADE DECK

Washington, DC,
April–May 1971

CHAPTER ONE

It was unseasonably hot that spring, and Washington languished under the blazing sun. The grass was brown and lusterless, the traffic thick, the citizens surly and uncivil; even the marble monuments and the white government buildings seemed squalid. It was as though a torpor hung over the place, or a curse. Nobody in official Washington went to parties anymore, it was a time of bitterness and recrimination.

And it was a time of siege. The city was in fact under attack. The process the president called "Vietnamization" wasn't happening fast enough for the armies of peace demonstrators who regularly assailed the city's parks and byways, shutting it down or letting it live, pretty much unchecked and pretty much as they saw fit. This month already, the Vietnam Veterans for Peace had commandeered the steps of the Capitol, showering them with a bitter rain of medals; more action was planned for the beginning of May, when the May Tribe of the People's Coalition for Peace and Justice had sworn to close down the city once again, this time for a whole week.

In all the town there was only one section of truly green grass. Some would look upon it and see in the green a last living symbol of American honor, a last best hope. Others would say the green was artificial, like so much of America: it was sustained by the immense labor of exploited workers, who had no choice in the matter. This is what we are changing, they would say.

The green grass was the parade ground, or in the patois of a service which holds fast to the conceit that all land structures are merely extensions of and metaphorical representations of the ships of the fleet, the "parade deck" of the Marine Barracks, at Eighth and I, Southeast. The young enlisted men labored over it as intensely as any cathedral gardeners, for, to the Jesuitical minds of the United States Marine Corps, at any rate, it was holy ground.

The barracks, built in 1801, was the oldest continuously occupied military installation in the United States. Even the British dared not burn it when they put the rest of the city to the torch in 1814. To look across the deck to the officers' houses on one side, the structures that housed three companies (Alpha, Bravo and Hotel, for headquarters) on the other, and the commandant's house at the far end of the quadrangle was to see, preserved, a pristine version of what service in the Corps and service to the country theoretically meant.

The ancient bricks were red and the architecture had sprung from an age in which design was pride in order. Conceived as a fort in a ruder and more violent age, it had taken on, with the maturity of its foliage and the replacement of its muddy lanes with cobblestone, the aspect of an old Ivy League campus. An unironic flag flew above it at the end of a high mast; red, white, blue, rippling in the wind, unashamed. It had a passionate nineteenth century feel to it; it was somehow an encomium of manifest destiny, built on a little chunk of land that was almost an independent duchy of the United States Marine Corps, stuck a mile and a half from and on the same hill as the Capitol, where the unruly processes of democracy were currently being strained to the utmost.

Now, on a particularly hot, bright April day, under that beating sun, young men drilled or loafed, as the authorities permitted.

In the shade at the corner of Troop Walk and the South Arcade, seven men—boys, actually—squatted and smoked. They wore the uniform called undressed blues, which consisted of blue trousers, a tan gabardine short-sleeved shirt open at the neck, and white hat—"cover," as the Corps called hats—pulled low over their eyes. The only oddity in their appearance, which to the casual eye separated them from other Marines, was their oxfords, which were not merely shined but spit-shined, and gleamed dazzlingly. The spit shine was a fetish in their culture. Now the young Marines were on a break and, naturally, PFC Crowe, the team comedian, was explaining the nature of things.

"See," he explained to his audience, as he sucked on a Marlboro, "it'll look great on a résumé. I tell 'em, I was in this elite unit. I needed a top-secret security clearance. We trained and rehearsed for our missions, and then when we went on them, in the hot, sweltering weather, men dropped all around me. But I kept going, goddammit. I was a hero, a goddamn hero. Of course what I *don't* tell them is, I'm talking about . . . parades."

He was rewarded with appropriate blasts of laughter from his cohorts, who regarded him as an amusing and generally harmless character. He had an uncle who was a congressman's chief fund-raiser, which accounted for his presence in Company B, the body-bearer company, as opposed to more rigorous and dangerous duties in WES PAC, as the orders always called it, or what the young Marines had termed the Land of Bad Things. He had no overwhelming desire to go to the Republic of South Vietnam.

Indeed, in all of Second Casket Team, only one of the seven had seen service in RSVN. This was the noncommissioned officer in charge, Corporal Donny Fenn, twenty-two, of Ajo, Arizona. Donny, a large and almost freakishly handsome blond kid with a year of college behind him, had spent seven months in another B Company, 1/9 Bravo, attached to the III Marine Amphibious Force, in operations near and around An Hoa in I Corps. He had been shot at many times and hit once, in the lungs, for which he was hospitalized for six months. He also had something called, uh, he would mumble, uh, *brnzstr,* and not look you in the eye.

But now Donny was short. That is, he had just under thirteen months left to serve and by rumor, at any rate, that meant the Corps would not in its infinite wisdom ship him back to the Land of Bad Things. This was not because the Corps loved his young ass. No, it was because the tour of duty in 'Nam was thirteen calendar months, and if you sent anyone over with less than thirteen calendar months, it hopelessly muddied the tidiness of the records, so upsetting to the anal-retentive minds of personnel clerks. So for all intents and purposes, Donny had made it safely through the central conflict of his age.

"All right," he said, checking his watch as its second hand hurtled toward 1100 to signify the end of break, "put 'em out and strip 'em. Put the filters in your pockets, that is if you're a faggot who smokes filtered cigarettes. If I see any butts out here, I'll PT your asses until morning muster."

The troops grunted, but obeyed. Of course they knew he didn't mean it; like them, he was no lifer. Like them, he'd go back to the world.

So as would any listless group of young men in so pitiless an institution as the Marine Corps, they got with the program with something less than total enthusiasm. It was another day at Eighth and I, another day of operations on the parade deck when they weren't on alert or serving cemetery duty: up at 0-dark-30, an hour of PT at 0600, morning muster at 0700, chow at 0800, and by 0930, the beginning of long, sometimes endless hours of drill, either of the funeral variety or of the riot-control variety. Then the duty day was done: those who had assignments did them, and otherwise the boys could secure (the married could live off base with wives; many of the unmarried shared unofficial cheap places available on Capitol Hill) or lounge about, playing pool, drinking 3.2 in the enlisted men's bar or going to the movies on the Washington PX circuit or even trying their luck with women in the bars of Capitol Hill.

But the luck was always bad, a source of much bitterness. This was only partially because Marines were thought of as baby killers. The real reason was hair: it was, in the outside world, the era of hair. Men wore their locks long and puffed up, usually overwhelming their ears in the process. The poor jarheads—and all the ceremonial troopers of the Military District of Washington—were expected to be acolytes to the temple of military discipline. Thus they offered nearly naked skulls to the world—white sidewalls, it was called—except for a permitted patch no more than three-quarters of an inch up top. Their ears stood out like radar bowls. Some of them looked like Howdy Doody, and no self-respecting hippie chick would deign spit at them, and since all American girls had become hippie chicks, they were, in Crowe's memorable term, shit out of luck.

"Gloves on," Donny commanded, and his men, as they rose, pulled on their white gloves.

Donny started them through another long fifty minutes of casket drill. As body bearers, all were on the husky side. As body bearers, none could make a mistake. It seemed meaningless, but a few—Donny, for one—understood that they did in fact have an important job: to anesthetize the pain of death with stultifying ritual. They had to hide the actual fact—there was a boy in the box going into the ground of Arlington National Cemetery forever, years before his time, and to what end?—with pomp and precision. And Donny, though an easygoing guy in most respects, was determined that in this one aspect, they would be the best.

So the team turned to, under his guidance and soft but forcefully uttered commands: they walked through the precisely choreographed steps by which a flag-draped box of boy was smartly removed from the hearse, which in the rehearsal was only a steel rack, aligned by its bearers, carried with utter calm dignity to the grave site, laid upon a bier. Next came the tricky flag folding: the flag was snapped off the box by six pairs of disciplined hands and, beginning with the man at the boot of the casket, broken into a triangle which grew thicker with each rigid fold as it passed from man to man. If the folding went right, what was finally deposited in Corporal Fenn's hands was a perfect triangle, a tricorn, festooned on either side with stars, with no red stripe showing anywhere. This was not easy, and it took weeks for a good team to get it right and even longer to break in a new guy.

At this point, Corporal Fenn took the triangle of stars, marched with stiff precision to the seated mother or father or whoever, and in his white gloves presented it to her. An odd moment, always: some recipients were too stunned to respond. Some were too shattered to notice. Some were awkward, some even a little starstruck, for a Marine as good-looking as Donny, with a chestful of medals hanging heavily from his dress tunic, his hair gone, his hat as white as his gloves, his dignity impenetrable, his theater craft immaculate, is indeed an awesome sight—almost like a movie star—and that charisma frequently cut through the grief of the moment. One broken mom even took his picture with an Instamatic as he approached.

But on this run-through, the corporal was not pleased with the performance of his squad. Of course it was PFC Crowe, not the best man on the team.

"All right, Crowe," he said, after the sweat-soaked boys had stood down from the ritual, "I saw you. You were out of step on the walk-to and you were half a beat behind on the left face-out of the wagon."

"Ah," said Crowe, searching for a quip to memorialize the moment, "my damn knee. It's the junk I picked up at Khe Sahn."

This did bring a chuckle, for as close as Crowe had come to Khe Sahn was reading about it in the *New Haven Register.*

"I forgot you were such a hero," Donny said. "So only drop and give me twenty-five, not fifty. Out of commemoration for your great sacrifice."

Crowe muttered darkly but harmlessly and the other team members drew back to give him room to perform his absolution. He peeled off his gloves, dropped to the prone and banged out twenty-five Marine-regulation push-ups. The last six were somewhat sloppy.

"Excellent," said Donny. "Maybe you're not a girl after all. All right, let's—"

But at this moment, the company commander's orderly, the bespectacled PFC Welch, suddenly appeared at Donny's right shoulder.

"Hey, Corporal," he whispered, "CO wants to see you."

Shit, thought Donny, what the hell have I done now?

"Ohhh," somebody sang, "somebody's in trouble."

"Hey, Donny, maybe they're going to give you another medal."

"It's his Hollywood contract, it's finally come."

"You know what it's about?" asked Donny of Welch, who was a prime source of scuttlebutt.

"No idea. Some Navy guys, that's all I know. It's ASAP, though."

"I'm on my way. Bascombe, you take over. Another twenty minutes. Focus on the face-out of the hearse that seems to have Crowe so baffled. Then take 'em to chow. I'll catch up when I can."

"Yes, Corporal."

Donny straightened his starched shirt, adjusted the gig line, wondered if he had time to change shirts, decided he didn't, and took off.

He headed across the parade deck, passing among other drilling Marines. The showboats of Company A, the silent drill rifle team, were going through their elaborate pantomime; the color guard people were mastering the intricacies of flag work; another platoon had moved on to riot control and was stomping furiously down Troop Walk, bent double under combat gear.

Donny reached Center Walk, turned and headed into the barracks proper, only crossing paths with half a dozen officers in the salute-crazed Corps and having to toss up a stiff right hand for their response. He entered the building, turned right and went through the open hatch—

Marine for "door"—and down the hall. It was dark and the gleamy swirls of good buffer work on the wax of the linoleum shone up at him. Along the green government bulkheads were photos of various Marine activities supplied by an aggressive Public Information Office for morale purposes, at which they utterly failed. At last, he turned into the door marked COMMANDING OFFICER, and under that CAPTAIN M. C. DOGWOOD, USMC. The outer office was empty, because PFC Welch was still running errands.

"Fenn?" came the call from the inner office. "In here."

Donny stepped into the office, a kind of ghostly crypt to the joint vanities of Marine machismo and bureaucratic efficiency, to discover the ramrod-stiff Captain Morton Dogwood sitting with a slender young man in the summer tans of a lieutenant commander in the Navy and an even younger man in an ensign's uniform.

"Sir," said Donny, going to attention, "Corporal Fenn reporting as ordered, sir."

As he was unarmed, he did not salute.

"Fenn, this is Commander Bonson and Ensign Weber," said Dogwood.

"Sirs," said Donny to the naval officers.

"Commander Bonson and his associate are from the Naval Investigative Service," said Dogwood.

Oh, shit, thought Donny.

The room was dark, the shades drawn. The captain's meager assembly of service medals hung in a frame on the wall behind him, as well as an announcement of his degree in International Finance from George Washington University. His desk was shiny and almost clear except for the polished 105mm howitzer shell that had been cut down to a paper clip cup and was everybody's souvenir from service in RSVN, and pictures of a pretty wife and two baby girls.

"Sit down, Fenn," said Bonson, not looking up from documents he was studying, which, as Donny saw, were his own jacket, or personnel records.

"Aye, aye, sir," said Donny. He found a chair and set himself into it stiffly, facing the three men who seemed to hold his destiny in their hands. Outside, the shouts of drill came through the windows; outside it was bright and hot and the day was filled with duty. Donny felt in murky waters here; what the hell was *this* all about?

"Good record," said Bonson. "Excellent job in country. Good record here in the barracks. Your hitch is up when, Fenn?"

"Sir, May seventy-two."

"Hate to see you leave, Fenn. The Corps needs good men like you."

"Yes, sir," said Donny, wondering if this was some— no, no, it couldn't be a recruiting pitch. NIS was the Navy and the Corps's own, tinny version of the FBI: they investigated, they didn't recruit. "I'm engaged to be married. I've already been accepted back at the University of Arizona."

"What will you study?" asked the commander.

"Sir, pre-law, I think."

"You know, Fenn, you'll probably get out a corporal. Rank is hard to come by in the Corps, because it's so small and there just aren't the positions available, no matter the talent and the commitment."

"Yes, sir," said Donny.

"Only about eight percent of four-year enlistees come out higher than corporal. That is, as a sergeant or higher."

"Yes, sir."

"Fenn, think how it would help your law career if you made sergeant. You'd be one of an incredibly small number of men to do so. You'd truly be in an elite."

"Ah—" Donny hardly knew what to say.

"The officers have a tremendous opportunity for you, Fenn," said Captain Dogwood. "You'd do well to hear them out."

"Yes, sir," said Donny.

"Corporal Fenn, we have a leak. A bad leak. We want you to plug it."

"A leak, sir?" said Donny.

"Yes. You know we have sources into most of the major peace groups. And you've heard rumors that on May Day, they're going to try to shut the city down and bring the war to a halt by destroying the head of the machine."

Rumors like that flew through the air. The Weather Underground, the Black Panthers, SNICC, they were going to close down Washington, levitate the Pentagon or bury it in rose petals, break into the armories and lead armed insurrection. It just meant that Bravo Company was always on alert status and nobody could get any serious liberty time.

"I've heard." His girlfriend was headed in for the May Day weekend. It would be great to see her, if he wasn't stuck on alert or, worse, sleeping under a desk in some building near the White House.

"Well, it's true. May Day. The communist holiday. They have the biggest mobilization of the war planned. They really mean to close us down and keep us closed down."

"Yes, sir."

"Our job is simple," said Lieutenant Commander Bonson. "It's to stop them."

Such determination in the man's voice, even a little tremble. His eyes seemed to burn with old-fashioned Iwo Jima–style zeal. At the same time, Donny couldn't help notice the lack of an RSVN service ribbon on the khaki of his chest.

"Remember November?" asked Bonson.

"Yes, sir," said Donny, and indeed he did. It stuck in his mind, not the whole thing, really, but one ludicrous moment.

It was late, near 2400, midnight in the American soul, and the Marines of Bravo in full combat gear were filing into the Treasury Building, adjacent to the White House, for protective duties against the possibilities of the next morning in a city where 200,000 angry kids had camped on the mall. A bone-dry moon shone above; the weather was crisp but not yet brutal. The Marines debarked from their trucks, holding their M14s at the high port, bayonets fixed, but still wearing their metal scabbards.

As Donny led his men downward toward the entrance, his eye was caught by light and he looked up. The abutment at the end of the ramp was brick and, being situated between the oh-so-white White House on the left and the oh-so-dark Treasury on the right, yielded a perspective on Pennsylvania Avenue, where the architects of the crusade for peace had organized a silent candlelight vigil.

So one line of young Americans carried rifles into a government building, under tin pots and thirty-five pounds of gear, while twenty-odd feet above them, at a perfect right angle, another line of young Americans filed along the deserted street, cupping candles, the light of which weirdly illuminated and flickered on their tender faces. Donny's epiphany came at that moment: no matter what the fiery lifers said or the screaming-head peaceniks, both groups of Americans were pretty much the same.

"Yes, sir," said Donny. "I remember."

"Were you aware, Corporal, that radical elements anticipated the movements of only one military unit, Company B of Marine Barracks, and that just by the hairiest of coincidences did a Washington policeman discover a bomb that was set to take out the phone junction into the Treasury, thereby effectively cutting off B Company and leaving the White House and the president defenseless? Think of it, Corporal. Defenseless!"

He seemed to get a weird charge out of saying *Defenseless!*, his nostrils flaring, his eyes lit up.

Donny had no idea what to say. He hadn't heard a thing about a bomb in a phone junction.

"How did they know you were there? How did they know *that's* where you'd be?" demanded the lieutenant commander.

It occurred to Donny: There are two buildings next to the White House. One is the Executive Office Building, one is the Treasury. If you were going to move troops in, wouldn't you move them into one of the two buildings? Where *else* could they be?

"I don't—" he stammered and almost ended his career right there by blowing up in a big laugh.

"That's when my team began to investigate. That's when NIS got on the case!" proclaimed the lieutenant commander.

"Yes, sir."

"We've run exhaustive background checks on everyone in the three line companies at the Marine Barracks. And we think we've found our man."

Donny was dumbfounded. Then he began to get pissed.

"Sir, I thought we were already *investigated* for clearances before we came into the unit."

"Yes, but it's a sloppy process. One investigator handles a hundred clearances a week. Things get through. Now, let me ask you something. What would you say if I told you one member of your company had an illegal off-base apartment and was known to room with members of a well-known peace initiative?"

"I don't know, sir."

"This PFC Edgar M. Crowe."

Crowe! Of course it would be Crowe.

Ensign Weber spoke up, reading from documents.

"Crowe maintains an apartment at 2311 C Street, Southwest. There he cohabits a room with one Jeffrey Goldenberg, a graduate student at the Northwestern University Medill Newsroom in Washington. Crowe is no ordinary grunt, you know, Fenn. He's a Yale dropout who only came into the Corps because his uncle had connections to a congressman who could make certain he'd never go to Vietnam."

"Think of that, Fenn," said Commander Bonson. "You're over there getting your butt shot off, and he's back here marching in parades and giving up intelligence to the peace freaks."

Crowe: of course. Perpetual fuck-up, smart guy, goof-off, his furious intelligence hidden behind a burning ambition to be just good enough not to get rotated out, but not really good in the larger sense.

Still, Crowe: he was a punk, an unformed boy, he seemed no different than any of them. He was a kid just out of his teens, mixed up by the temptations and confusions of a tempting, confusing age.

"We know you, Fenn," said the lieutenant commander. "You're the only man in the company who enjoys the universal respect of both the career-track Marines who've done Vietnam and the boys who are just here to avoid Vietnam. They *all* like you. So we have an assignment for you. If you bring it off, and I know in my military mind that there's no possibility you won't, you will finish your hitch in twelve days a full E-5 buck sergeant in the United States Marine Corps. That I guarantee you."

Donny nodded. He didn't like this a bit.

"I want you to become Crowe's new best friend. You're his buddy, his pal, his father confessor. Flatter him with the totality of your attentions. Hang out with him. Go to his peace creep parties, get to know his long-haired friends. Get drunk with him. He'll tell you things, a little at first, then more as time goes on. He'll give up all his secrets. He's probably so proud of himself and his little game he's *dying* to brag about it and show you what a smart boy he is. Get us enough material to move against him *before* he gives up the unit on May Day. We'll send him to Portsmouth for a very long time. He'll come out an old man."

Bonson sat back.

There it was, before Donny. What was most palpable was what had not been said. Suppose he didn't do it? What would happen to him? Where would they send him?

"I don't really—sir, I'm not trained in intelligence work. I'm not sure I could bring this off."

"Fenn is a very straightforward Marine," said Captain

Dogwood. "He's a hardworking, gung-ho young man. He's not a spy."

Donny could see that the captain's interjection deeply irritated Lieutenant Commander Bonson, but Bonson said nothing, just stared furiously at Donny in the dark office.

"You have two weeks," he finally said. "We'll be monitoring you and expect a sitrep every other day. There's a lot at stake, a lot of people counting on you. There's the honor of the service and duty to country to consider."

Donny swallowed and hated himself for it.

"You know, you have it pretty good here yourself," said Bonson, to Donny's silence. "You have a room in the barracks, not in the squad bay, a very pleasant duty station, a very pleasant duty day. You're in Washington, DC. It's spring. You're going back to college, a decorated hero with all those veteran's benefits, plus a Bronze Star and a nice chunk of rank. I'd say few young men in America have it quite as made as you."

"Yes, sir," said Donny.

"What the commander is saying," said Ensign Weber, "is that it can all go away. In a flash. Orders can be cut. You could be back slogging the paddies in Vietnam, the shit flying all around you. It's been known to happen. A guy so short suddenly finds himself in extremely hazardous duty. Well, you know the stories. He had a day to go and he got zapped. Letters to his mother, stories in the paper, the horror of it all. The worst luck in the world, poor guy. But sometimes, that's the way it goes."

More silence in the room.

Donny did not want to go back to Vietnam. He had done his time there, he'd gotten hit. He remembered the fear he felt, the sheer immense, lung-crushing density of it, the first time incoming began exploding the world around him. He hated the squalor, the waste, the sheer murder of it. He hated having his real life so close and then taken from him. He hated the prospect of not seeing

Julie ever, ever again. He thought of some peace nerd comforting her after he was gone, and knew how that one would play out.

Almost imperceptibly, he nodded.

"Great," said Bonson. "You've made the right decision."

CHAPTER TWO

He stood outside, feeling idiotic. Rock music pumped out from inside. Inside it was loud, bright, crowded, festive. He felt so stupid.

He turned. There was Ensign Weber in the Ford, parked across the way on C Street. Weber nodded encouragingly, gave a little whisking motion with his head as if to say, Go on, get going, goddammit.

So now Donny stood outside the Hawk and Dove, a well-known Capitol Hill watering hole, where the young men and women who ran, opposed or chronicled the war tended to gather after six when official Washington closed down, except for the few old men in isolated offices waiting for the latest news on the air strikes or casualty figures.

It was a beautiful night, temperate and soothing. Donny was dressed in cutoffs, Jack Purcells, a madras shirt, just like half the kids who'd entered the place since he'd been standing there, except that unlike them, his ears stood out and his head wore only a little topside platter of hair. It said jarhead all the way.

But it was the Hawk and Dove where PFC Crowe was known to hang, and so it was at the Hawk and Dove he had been deposited.

Christ, Donny thought again, looking back to Weber and getting another of the whisking motions with the head.

He turned and plunged inside.

The place, as expected, was dark and close and jammed. Rock music pummeled against the walls. It sounded like Buffalo Springfield: *There's a man with a gun over there, what it is ain't exactly clear*—something like that, vaguely familiar to Donny.

Everybody was smoking and cruising. There seemed to

be a sense of sex in the air as people eyed one another in the darkness, the pretty young girls from the Hill, the slim young men from the Hill. Nearly all the guys had big puffs of hair, but now and then he spied the whitewalls or at least the very short haired look of the military. Yet there wasn't much tension; it was as if everybody just put it aside, left it outside for a generous helping of tribal bonding, the young not having to show anything at all in here to the murderous, controlling old.

Donny squeezed to the bar, ordered a Bud, forked over a buck and remembered, "Keep all your receipts. You can expense this. Our office will pick it up. But nothing hard. Bonson will fucking freak if you start chugging Pinch."

"I've never even *tasted* Pinch," Donny had replied. "Maybe tonight's the night."

"That's a big negative," said Weber.

Donny sipped his beer. Beside him, a guy was in the middle of a bitter fight with a girl. It was one of those quiet, muttered things, but very intense. The boy kept saying, under his breath, "You *idiot.* You unbelievable *idiot.* How could you let him? *Him!* How could you let him? You *idiot.*"

The girl merely stared ahead and smoked.

The time passed. His instructions were clear. He was not to approach Crowe. That would be a mistake. Sooner or later Crowe would see him, Crowe would approach him, and then it would go where it would go. If he threw himself at Crowe, the whole damned thing would fall apart.

Donny had another beer, checked his watch. He scoped the action. There were some attractive chicks but none as cool as Julie, the girl to whom he was engaged. Man, he smiled, I still got the best.

It was the football hero-cheerleader thing, but not really. Yes, he was a football hero. Yes, she was a cheerleader. But he didn't really like football and she didn't really like cheerleading. They actually were sort of forced together as boyfriend and girlfriend by peer pressure at Pima County High School, found they didn't really like each other very much, and broke up. Once they broke up and started hanging out with other people, they missed each other. One night they went on a double date, he with Peggy Martin, Julie's best friend, and she with Mike Willis, his best friend. And that was the night they really connected. Junior year. The war was far away then, happening on TV. Firefights in places like Bien Hoa and I Drang that he had never heard of. The napalm floating off the Phantoms and wobbling downward to blossom in a huge smear of tumbling fire across the jungle canopy. It meant nothing. Donny and Julie went everywhere that year. They were inseparable. It was, he thought, the best summer of his life, but senior year was better, when he'd led the Southwest Counties League in yardage, averaging close to two hundred a game. He was big and fast. Julie was so beautiful but she was nice, somehow. She was so nice. She was . . . *good* was the only word he could think of, and it was so lame.

"Jesus Christ!"

Donny felt a hand on his shoulder as the words exploded into his ear. He turned.

"What the hell are *you* doing here?"

Of course it was Crowe, in jeans and a work shirt looking very proletariat. He had—where the hell did he get that?—a camouflaged boonie cap on to disguise his hairlessness. He held a beer in his hand and was with three other young men who looked exactly like him except their hair was real, and long. They looked like three Jesuses.

"Crowe," said Donny.

"I didn't know this was your kind of place," said Crowe.

"It's a place. They have beer. What the fuck else would I need?" Donny said.

"This is my corporal," Crowe said to his pals. "He's a genuine USMC hero. He's actually killed guys. But he's a good guy. He only made me drop for twenty-five today instead of fifty."

"Crowe, if you'd learn your shit, you wouldn't have to drop for any."

"But then I'd be *collaborating.*"

"Oh, I see. Fucking up funerals is part of your guerrilla war on the grieving mothers of America."

"No, no, I'm only joking. But the funny thing is, I can't tell my left from my right. I really can't."

"It's port and starboard in the Marine Corps," said Donny.

"I don't know *them* either. Well, anyway. You want to join us? Tell these guys about 'Nam?"

"Oh, they don't want to hear."

"No, really," one of the other kids said. "Man, it must be fucking hairy over there."

"He won a Bronze Star," said Crowe with a surprising measure of pride. "He was a hero."

"I was lucky as shit not to get wasted," Donny said. "No, no war stories. Sorry."

"Look, we're going to a party. We know this guy, he's having a big party. You want to come, Corporal?"

"Crowe, call me Donny off duty. And you're Ed."

"Eddie and Donny!"

"That's it."

"Come on, Donny. Chicks everywhere. It's over on C, right near the Supreme Court. This guy is a clerk. He knew my big brother at Harvard. More pussy in one place than you ever saw."

"You should come, Donny," said one of the boys. Donny could tell that the hero thing had cut through politics and somehow impressed these war-haters, who just a few years back had been worshiping John Wayne.

"I'm engaged," Donny said.

"You can *look,* can't you? She'll let you look, won't she?"

"I suppose," said Donny. "But I don't want any Ho

Chi Minh shit. Ho Chi Minh tried to kill my ass. He's no hero of mine."

"It won't be like that," Crowe promised.

"Trig will like him," one of the boys said.

"Trig will turn him into a peacenik," said the other.

"So who's Trig?" said Donny.

It was a short walk and as soon as they were outside, one of the boys pulled out a joint and lit up. The thing was routinely passed around until it came to Donny, who hesitated for a moment, then took a toke, holding it, fighting the fire. He'd had quite the habit for a few months in 'Nam, but had broken it. Now, the familiar sweetness rushed into his lungs, and his head began to buzz. The world seem to come aglow with possibility. He exhaled his lungful.

Enough, he thought. I don't need more of that shit.

Capitol Hill had the sense of a small town in Iowa, under leafy trees that rustled in the night breeze. Then, through a break in the trees, he suddenly saw the Capitol, its huge white dome arc-lit and blazing in the night.

"They sacrifice virgins in there," one of the boys said, "to the gods of war. Every night. You can hear them scream."

Maybe it was the grass, but Donny had to smile. They did sacrifice virgins, but not in there. They sacrificed them ten thousand miles away in buffalo shit–water rice paddies.

"Donny," said Crowe. "Can you call in artillery? We have to destroy the place to save it."

Again, maybe it was the grass.

" 'Ah, Shotgun-Zulu-Three,' " he improvised, " 'I have a fire mission for you, map grid four-niner-six, six-five-four at Alpha seven-oh-two-five, we are hot with beaucoup bad guys, request Hotel Echo, fire for effect, please.' "

"Cool," one of the kids said. "What's Hotel Echo?"

"High explosive," said Donny. "As opposed to frags or white phosphorous."

"Cool as *shit!*" the boy responded.

Music announced the site of the party far earlier than any visual confirmation. As at the Hawk and Dove, it blasted out into the night, hard, psychedelic rock beating the dark back and the devil away. He'd heard the same stuff over there, though; that was the funny thing. The young Marines loved the rock. It went everywhere with them, and if their tough noncoms hadn't stayed on their asses, they'd have played it on ambush patrols.

"I wonder if Trig is here," one of the boys said.

"You never can tell with Trig," Crowe replied.

"Who's Trig?" Donny asked again.

The party didn't seem at all unlike any other party Donny had attended back at the University of Arizona, except that the hair was longer. Milling people of all sorts. The bar scene, though crammed into smaller, hotter rooms. The smell of grass, sickly sweet, heavy in the air. Ho and Che on the walls. In the bathroom, where Donny went to piss, even an NVA flag, though one manufactured in Schenectady, not downtown Haiphong. He had a rogue impulse to burn it, but that would sure blow the gig now. And really: it was only a flag.

The kids were his own age, some younger, with a few middle-aged men hanging around with that intense, long-haired look that the DC crowd so liked. Judging from the hair, only he and Crowe represented the United States Marines, though Crowe was far from an ambassador. He was telling some people a familiar story of how he almost got out of the draft by playing psycho at his physical.

"I'm nude," he was saying, "except for this cowboy hat. I'm very polite and everybody's very polite to me at first. I do everything they ask me to do. I bend and spread, I carry my underwear in a little bag, I smile and call everybody sir. I just won't take off my cowboy hat. 'Uh, son, would you mind taking off that hat?' 'I can't,' I explain. 'I'll die if I take off my cowboy hat.' See, the key is to stay *polite.* If you act *nuts* they know you're faking. Pretty soon they got majors and generals and colonels and all screaming at me to take off my cowboy hat. I'm nude in this little room with all these guys, but I *will not* take off my cowboy hat. What a fuckin' hero I am! What a John Wayne! They're screaming and I'm just saying, 'If I take off my cowboy hat, I'll die.' "

"So you weren't drafted?"

"Well, they kicked me out. It took weeks for the paperwork to catch up, and by that time, my uncle had cut a deal with the Man to get me into a slot in the Marines that wouldn't rotate to the 'Nam. You know, when this is over, all those charges will be dropped. Nobody will care. We'll write the whole thing off. That's why anybody who lets themselves get wasted is a total moron. Like, for what?"

Good question, Donny wondered. For what? He tried to remember the boys in his platoon in 1/3 Bravo who'd gotten zapped in his seven months with them. It was hard. And who did you count? Did you count the guy who got hit by an Army truck in Saigon? Maybe his number was up. Maybe he would have gotten hit back on the street corner in Sheboygan. Would you count him? Donny didn't know.

But you definitely had to count the kid—what was his name? *what was his name?*—who stepped on a Betty and got his chest shredded. That was the first one Donny remembered. He was such a new dick then. The guy just lay back. So much blood. People gathered around him, exactly in the way you weren't supposed to, and he seemed remarkably calm before he died. But nobody read any letter home to Mom afterward in which he told everybody how great the platoon was and how they were fighting for democracy. They just zipped him up and left him. He remembered the face, not the name. A sort of porky kid. Pancakey face. Small eyes. Didn't have to shave. *What was his name?*

Another one got hit by a rifle bullet. He screamed and

bucked and yelled and nobody could quiet him. He seemed so indignant. It was so unfair! Well, it *was* unfair. Why me, he seemed to be asking his friends, why not you? He was thin and rangy, from Spokane. Didn't talk much. Always kept his rifle clean. Was bowlegged. *What was his name?* Donny didn't remember.

There were a few more, but nothing much. Donny hadn't fought in any big battles or taken part in any big operations with dramatic code names that made the news. Mostly it was walking, scared every day you'd get jumped or you'd trip something off, or you'd just collapse under the weight of it. So much of it was boring, so much of it was dirty, so much of it was debasing. He didn't want to go back. He knew that. Man, if you let them send you back at this late date, when units were being rotated back to the world all the time during "Vietnamization," and you got wasted, you *were* a moron.

Suddenly someone bumped him hard.

"Oh, sorry," he said, stepping back.

"Yeah, you are," someone said.

Where had this action come from? There were three of them, but big like he was. Hair pouring from their heads, bright bands around their skulls, dressed in faded jeans and Army fatigue shirts.

"You're the Marine asshole, right? The lifer?"

"I am a Marine," he said. "And I'm probably an asshole. But I'm not a lifer."

The three fixed him with unsteady glares. Their eyes burned with hate. One of them rocked a little, the team leader, with his fist wrapped tightly around the neck of a bottle of gin. He held it like a weapon.

"Yeah, my brother came back in a little sack because of lifer fucks like you," he said.

"I'm very sorry for your brother," said Donny.

"Asshole lifer got him greased so he could make lieutenant colonel."

"Shit like that happens. Some joker wants a stripe so

he sends his guys up the hill. He gets the stripe and they get the plastic bag."

"Yeah, but it happens mainly 'cause assholes like you let it happen, 'cause you don't have the fuckin' guts to say no to the Man. If *you* had the guts to say no, the whole thing stops."

"Did you say no to the Man?"

"I didn't have to," the boy said proudly. "I was 1-Y. I was out of it."

Donny thought about explaining that it didn't matter what your classification was, if you obeyed it, you were obeying orders and working for the Man. Some guys just got better orders than others. But then the boy took a step toward Donny, his face drunkenly pugnacious. He gripped the bottle even harder.

"Hey, I didn't come here to fight," said Donny. "I just drifted in with some guys." He looked around to find himself in the center of a circle of staring kids. Even the music had stopped and the smoke had ceased seething in the air. Crowe had, of course, totally disappeared.

"Well, you drifted into the wrong fucking party, man," said the boy, and made as if to take another step, as Donny tried to figure out whether to pop him or to cut and run to avoid the hassle.

But suddenly another figure dipped between them.

"Whoa," he said, "my brothers, my brothers, let's not lose our holy cools."

"He's a fucking—" said the aggressor.

"He's another kid; you can't blame the whole thing on him any more than you can blame it on anyone. It's the *system,* don't you get that? Jesus, don't you get *anything*?"

"Yeah, well, you have to start somewhere."

"Jerry, you cool out. Go smoke a joint or something, man. I'm not letting any three guys with booze bottles jump any poor grunt who came by looking to get laid."

"Trig, I—"

But this Trig laid a hand on Jerry's chest and fixed him

with a glare hot enough to melt most things on earth, and Jerry stepped back, swallowed and looked at his pals.

"Fuck it," he finally said. "We were splitting anyhow."

And the three of them turned and stormed out.

Suddenly the music started again—Stones, "Satisfaction"—and the party came back to life.

"Hey, thanks," said Donny. "The last thing I need is a fight."

"That's okay," said his new friend. "I'm Trig Carter, by the way." He put out a hand.

Trig had one of those long, grave faces, where the bones showed through the tight skin and the eyes seemed to be both moist and hot at the same moment. He really looked a lot like Jesus in a movie. There was something radiant in the way he fixed you with his eyes. He had something rare: immediate likability.

"Howdy," Donny said, surprised the grip was so strong in a man so thin. "My name's Fenn, Donny Fenn."

"I know. You're Crowe's secret hero. The Bravo."

"Oh, Christ. I can't be a hero to him. I'm in it till my hitch ends, then I'm gone forever back to the land of the cacti and the Navajo."

"I've been there. Mourning doves, right? Little white birds, dart through the arroyos and the brush, really hard to spot, really fast?"

"Oh, yeah," said Donny. "My dad and I used to hunt them. You've got to use a real light shot, you know, an eight or a nine. Even then, it's a tough shot."

"Sounds like fun," said Trig. "But in my case I don't shoot 'em with a gun but with a camera. Then I paint them."

"Paint them?" This made no sense to Donny.

"You know," Trig said. "Pictures. I'm actually an avian painter. Really, I've traveled the world painting pictures of birds."

"Wow!" said Donny. "Does it pay?"

"A little. I illustrated my uncle's book. He's Roger

Prentiss Fuller, *Birds of North America*. The Yale zoologist?"

"Er, can't say I heard of him."

"He was a hunter once. He went on safari in the early fifties with Elmer Keith."

This did impress Donny. Keith was a famous Idaho shooter who wrote books like *Elmer Keith's Book of the Sixgun* and *Elmer Keith on Big Game Rifles*.

"Wow," he said. "Elmer Keith."

"Roger says Keith was a tiny, bitter little man. He had a terrible burn as a kid and he was always compensating for it. They had a falling out. Elmer just wanted to shoot and shoot. He couldn't see any sense to a limit. Roger doesn't shoot anymore."

"Well, after 'Nam, I don't think I will either," Donny said.

"You sound okay for a Marine, Donny. Crowe was right about you. Maybe you'll join us when you get out." He smiled, his eyes lighting like a movie star's.

"Well . . ." Donny said, provisionally. Himself a peacenik, smoking dope, long hair, carrying those cards, chanting "Hell, no, we won't go"? He laughed at the notion.

"Trig! When did you get here?" It was Crowe and his crowd, now with girls in tow, all leading what seemed to be a kind of electric ripple toward Trig.

And in seconds, Trig was gone, borne away on currents of some sort of celebrityhood that Donny didn't understand.

He turned to a girl standing nearby.

"Hey, excuse me," he said. "Who is this Trig?"

She looked at him in astonishment.

"Man, what planet are *you* from?" she demanded, then ran after Trig, her eyes beaming love.

CHAPTER THREE

"Trig Carter!" Commander Bonson exclaimed.

"Yeah, that was it, I couldn't quite remember the last name," said Donny, who could remember the name very well but couldn't quite bring himself to say it out loud. "Seemed like a very nice guy."

Bonson's office was an undistinguished chamber in a World War II–era tempo still standing in the Washington Navy Yard about a half mile from Eighth and I, where by dim pretext Donny had been sent the next day for his debriefing on his first day as spy hunter.

"You saw Trig Carter and Crowe together. Is that right?"

Why did Donny feel so sleazy about all this? He felt clammy, as if someone were listening. He looked around. President Nixon glowered down at him from the wall, enjoining him to do his duty for God and Country. A degree from the University of New Hampshire added to the solemnity of the occasion. A few ceremonial photos of Lieutenant Commander Bonson with various dignitaries completed the decor; the room was otherwise completely bereft of personality or even much sense of human occupation. It was preternaturally neat; even the paper clips in the little plastic box had been stacked, not dumped.

Lieutenant Commander Bonson bent forward, fixing Donny in his dark glare. He was a thin, dark man with a lot of whiskery shadow on his face and a sense of complete focus. There was something pilgrimlike about him; he should have been in a pulpit denouncing miniskirts and the Beatles.

"Yes, sir," Donny finally said. "The two of them . . . and about one hundred other people."

"Where was this again?"

"A party. Uh, on C Street, on the Hill. I didn't get the address."

"Three-forty-five C, Southeast," said Ensign Weber.

"Did you check it out, Weber?"

"Yes, sir. It's the home of one James K. Phillips, a clerk to Justice Douglas and a homosexual, according to the FBI."

"Were most of the people there homosexuals, Fenn? Was it a homo thing?"

Donny didn't know what to say. It just seemed like a party in Washington, like any party in Washington, with a lot of young people, some grass, some beer, music, and fun and hope in the air.

"I wouldn't know, sir."

Bonson sat back, considering. The homosexual thing seemed to hang in his mind, clouding it for a time. But then he was back on the track.

"So you saw them together?"

"Well, sir, not together, really. In the same crowd. They knew each other, that was clear. But it didn't seem anything out of the ordinary."

"Could Crowe have given him any deployment intelligence?"

Donny almost laughed, but Bonson was so set in his glare that he knew to release the pressure he felt building in his chest would have been a big mistake.

"I don't think so," he said. "Not that I saw. I mean, does Crowe *have* any deployment intelligence? I don't. How would he?"

But Bonson didn't answer.

He turned to Weber.

"We've got to get closer," he said. "We've got to get him *inside* the cell. Trig Carter. Imagine that."

"A wire, sir? Could we wire him?" asked Weber.

Oh, Christ, thought Donny. I'm really not going anywhere with a tape recorder taped to my belly.

"No, not unless we could get time to set it up quickly.

He's got to stay fluid, flexible, quick on his feet. The wire won't work, not under these circumstances."

"It was just a suggestion, sir," said Weber.

"Well, Fenn," said Bonson, "you've made a fine start. But too many times we see fast starters are slow finishers. You've got to really press now. You've got to make Crowe your pal, your friend, do you see? He's got to trust you; that's how you'll crack this thing. Trig Carter, Weber. Isn't that the damndest thing you ever heard?"

"Sir, if I may ask, who is Trig Carter?"

"Show him, Weber."

Weber looked into a file and slid something over to Donny. Donny recognized it at once: he'd seen it a thousand times probably, without really noticing it. It was just part of the living-room imagery of the war, the scenes that were unforgettable.

It was a cover of *Time* magazine late in the hot summer of 1968: Chicago, the Democratic National Convention, the "police riot" outside on the last night. There was Trig, in shirtsleeves, a gush of blood cascading down from an ugly welt in his short, neat hair. He was bent under the weight of another kid he was carrying out of the fog of tear gas and the blurs that were Chicago policemen pounding anything that could be pounded. Trig looked impossibly noble and heroic, impossibly courageous. His eyes were screwed up in the pain of the CS gas, he was bloody and sweaty, and the veins on his neck stood out from all the effort he had invested in carrying the dazed, bloody, traumatized boy out of the zone of violence. He looked like any of a dozen insanely heroic Corpsmen Donny had seen pull the same thing off amid not cops but tracer fire and grenades and Bettys over in the Land of Bad Things, none of whose pictures had ever ended up on the cover of *Time* magazine.

THE SPIRIT OF RESISTANCE, said the cover.

"He's their Lancelot," said Weber. "Was beaten up in Selma by the Alabama State Police, got his picture on the cover of *Time* in sixty-eight at the convention. He's been everywhere in the Movement since then. One of the early peace freaks, a rich kid from an old Maryland family. Just came back from a year in England, studying drawing at Oxford. Harvard grad, some kind of painter, isn't that it?"

"Avian painter, sir. That's what he told me."

"Yes. Birds. Loves birds. Very odd," said Bonson.

"Very smart boy," continued Weber. "But then, that seems to be the profile. It was the profile in England, too. The smart ones, they can figure everything out, see through everything. They'll be the elite after the revolution. Anyhow, he's big in the People's Coalition for Peace and Justice, a kind of glamorous roving ambassador and organizer. Lives here in DC, but works the campus circuit, goes where the action is. The FBI's been monitoring him for years. He'd be *exactly* the kind of man who'd get to Crowe and turn him into a spy. He'd be *perfect.* He's exactly who we're looking for."

"Fenn, I can't emphasize this enough. You've got less than two weeks until the big raft of May Day demonstrations is set. Crowe will be pressed to uncover deployment intelligence, Carter will be on him for results. You've got to monitor them very carefully. If you can't get tape or photos, you may have to testify in open court against them."

Donny felt a cold stone drop in his stomach: he saw an image, himself on the stand, putting the collar on poor Crowe. It made him sick.

"I know you'll make a fine witness," Bonson was saying. "So begin to discipline your mind: remember details, events, chronologies. You might write a coded journal so you can recall things. Remember exact sentences. Get in the habit of making a time check every few minutes. If you don't want to take notes, *imagine* taking notes, because that can fix things in your mind. This is very important work, do you understand?"

"Ah—"

"Doubts? Do I see doubts? You cannot doubt." Bonson leaned forward until he and he alone filled the world.

"Just as you could have no doubters in a rifle platoon, you can have no doubters on a counter intelligence mission. You have to be on the team, committed to the team. The doubts erode your discipline, cloud your judgment, destroy your memory, Fenn. No doubts. That's the kind of rigor I need from you."

"Yes, sir," said Donny, hating himself as the world's entire melancholy weight settled on his strong young shoulders.

Crowe was particularly derelict that afternoon in riot control drill.

"It's so hot, Donny. The mask! Can't we *pretend* we're wearing our masks?"

"Crowe, if you have to do it for real, you'll want to be wearing a mask because otherwise the CS will make you a crybaby in a second. Put the mask on with the other guys."

Muttering darkly, Crowe slid the mask over his head, then clapped his two-pound camouflaged steel pot over his skull.

"Squad, on my command, form *up*!" shouted Donny, watching as his casket team, plus assorted others from Bravo Company assigned riot duty in Third Squad, formed a line. They looked like an insect army: their eyes hidden behind the plastic lenses of the masks, their faces made insectoid and ominous by the mandiblelike filter can, all in Marine green, with their 782 gear, their pistols, their M14s held at the high port.

"Squad, fix . . . *bayonets*!" and the rifle butts slammed into the ground, the blades were drawn from their scabbards and in a single clanking, machinelike *click* locked onto the weapon muzzles. Except one.

Crowe's bayonet skittered away. He had dropped it.

"Crowe, you idiot, give me fifty of the finest!"

Crowe was silenced by his clammy mask, but his body posture radiated sullen anger. He fell from the formation.

"At ease," said Donny.

The squad relaxed.

"One, Corporal, two, Corporal, three, Corporal," Crowe narrated through the mask as he banged out the push-ups. Donny let him go to fifteen, then said, "All right, Crowe, back in line ASAP. Let's try it again."

Crowe shot him a bitter look as he regathered his gear and rejoined the line.

Donny took them through it again. It was an extremely hot day and the darkness of his mood was such that he worked the men hard, breaking them down into standard line formation, flank marching them into an arrowhead riot element, counting cadence to govern their approach to the imagined riot, wheeling them left and right, getting them to fix and unfix bayonets over and over again.

He worked them straight through a break as great wet patches discolored their utilities until finally the platoon sergeant came over and said, "All right, Corporal, you can give them a break."

"Yes, Sergeant!" yelled Donny, and even the sergeant, a shit-together but fairly decent lifer named Ray Case, gave him a look.

"Fall out. Smoke 'em if you got 'em. If you don't got 'em, borrow 'em. If you can't borrow 'em, then get outta town because your buddies can't stand you."

Then, instead of mingling with the silently furious, sweating men, he himself walked over to the shade of the barracks and declared himself off-limits. Let 'em grouse.

But soon Crowe detached himself and came over, cheekily enough, secretly irritating Donny.

"Man, you really put me through it."

"I put the *squad* through it, Crowe, not you. We may have to do this shit for real next weekend."

"Oh, shit, none of those guys is going to march with bayonets into a bunch of kids with flowers in their hair where the girls are showing their tits. We'll just hang here or go sit in some fucking building like the last time. What, you figure, the Treasury again?"

Donny let the question simmer in his mind a bit. Then

he said, "Crowe, I don't know. I just go where they tell me."

"Donny, I got it straight from Trig. They're not even coming into DC. The whole thing's going to the Pentagon. Let the Army handle it. We won't even leave the barracks."

"If you say so."

"I thought we were—"

"Crowe, I had fun last night. But out here, in the daylight, I'm still the corporal and squad leader, you're still a PFC, so you still play by my rules. Don't ever call me Donny in front of the men while we're on drill, okay?"

"Okay, okay, I'm sorry. Anyhow, some of us were going to Trig's tonight. I thought you might want to come. You got to admit, he's an interesting guy."

"He's okay for a peacenik."

"Trig's not like that. He was beat up in Selma; he was a fucking *hero* in Chicago. Man, they say he went out twenty-five times and dragged kids in from the pigs. He saved lives."

"I don't know," said Donny.

"It'll be fun. You need to relax more, Corporal."

Donny actually wished the invitation hadn't come; it was his half plan, dimly formed, just to let his secret assignment peter out, go away in vagueness and missed opportunities. But here it was, big and hairy: a chance to do his job.

Trig, as it turned out, lived off upper Wisconsin, just above Georgetown, in a row house that was one in a tatty block of similar dwellings. The house was crowded; it could be no other way. The furniture was threadbare, almost ascetic. Still, the stench of grass almost levitated the house and made Donny's nostrils flare when he entered. Everything was familiar but unfamiliar: lots of books, a wall full of shelved albums (classical and jazz, though; no Jimi H. or Bob D.). But also, no posters, no NVA flags, no commie posters. Instead: birds.

Jesus, the guy was a freak for birds. Some were his own paintings, and he had a considerable talent for capturing the glory of a bird in flight, all the details perfect, all the feathers precisely laid out, the colors all the hues of miracle. But others were older and darker, muted things that appeared to have been painted in another century.

Somehow he found himself talking to a girl about birds and told her that he, uh, hunted them. It wasn't the right thing to say but she was one of those snooty Eastern ones, who wore her hair long and straight and had a pinched look to her.

"You kill them?" she said. "Those little things?"

"Well, where I'm from they're considered good eating."

"Don't you have *stores*?"

This wasn't going too well. This grouping was smaller and more intimate than last night's and everybody seemed to know everybody. He felt a little isolated, and looked for Crowe, because even Crowe would have been a welcome ally. But Crowe was nowhere to be seen. And on top of that he felt incorrectly dressed: he was in chinos and Jack Purcells, plus a madras sport shirt. Everyone here wore jeans and work shirts, had long, exotic hair, beards, and seemed somehow in some kind of Indian conspiracy against the ways that he felt it was proper for a young man to dress. It made him uncomfortable.

Some spy, he thought.

"Don't give Donny a hard time," said someone—Trig, of course, simply appearing dramatically, an event for which he had a little gift.

Trig was more moderate today, his hair back in a ponytail, which he wore over a blue button-down shirt and, like Donny, a pair of chinos. He also had an expensive pair of decoratively perforated oxfords on, in some exotic, rich color.

"Trig, he shoots little animals."

"Sweetie, men have been hunting and eating birds for a million years. Both the birds and the men are still here."

"I think it's strange."

Donny almost blurted, No, it's really fun, but held himself in.

"Well, anyway," said Trig, drawing Donny away. "I'm glad you could come. I don't know who half these guys are myself. People just hang out here. They drink my beer, smoke grass, get stoned or laid and move on. I'm hardly here, so I really don't care. But it's cool that you came."

"Thanks, I didn't have much to do. Well, actually, I wanted to talk to you."

"Oh? Well, go ahead."

"It's Crowe. You know, he's really borderline in the unit, and he keeps fucking up. I know he's a smart kid. But if he gets booted from the company, his tour is no longer stabilized, and he could go on levy to the 'Nam. And I don't think he'd look too good in a body bag."

"I'll talk to him."

"As he said, anyone who gets wasted this late in a lost war is a moron."

"I'll mention it."

"Cool."

Trig was also cool. Donny could see how he'd be a good man in a firefight, and while everybody wept or cowered, he'd be the one to go out and start bringing the people in from the beatings.

"Can I ask you?" he suddenly said to Donny, fixing him in one of those deep Trig looks. "Do you doubt it? Do you ever wonder why, or if it was worth it? Or are you foursquare the whole way, the whole nine yards?"

"Fuck no," said Donny. "Sure, of course I doubt it. But my father fought in a war and so did his father, and I was raised just to see that as a price for living in a great country. So . . . so I went. I did it, I came back, for better or worse."

They had now wandered into the kitchen, where Trig opened his refrigerator and got a beer out for Donny and then took one for himself. It was a foreign beer, Heineken, from a dark, cold green bottle.

"Come on, this way. We'll get away from these idiots."

Trig took Donny out on a back porch, toward two deck chairs. Donny was surprised to see they were on a little hill and that before him the elevation fell away; across the falling roofs, in the distance he was surprised to see the huddled buildings of Georgetown University, looking medieval in profile.

"I forget what real people are like," Trig said, "that's why it's cool to talk to you. Nobody's more hypocritical and swinish than the pretty boys and the fairies of the peace movement. But I know how important soldiers can be. I was in the Congo in sixty-four—I'd gone with my uncle to paint the Upper Congo swallowtail darter. We were in Stanleyville when some guy named Gbenye declared it a people's republic and took about one thousand of us hostage and set out to 'purify' the population of its imperialist vermin. Murder squads were everywhere. Man, I saw some shit. What people do to each other. So anyhow, we're in this compound, the Congolese Army is fighting its way closer and the rumor is the rebels are going to kill us all. Holy shit, we're going to die and nobody gives a shit about us. It's that simple. But when the door is kicked down, it isn't rebels. It's tattooed, tough-ass, kick-butt Belgian paratroopers. They were the meanest pricks I ever saw in my life and I loved them like you wouldn't believe. Nobody would stand against the Belgian Airborne. And they got us out in a convoy, all the white people from the interior. We would have been butchered. So I'm not one of these assholes who says there's no role for soldiers. Soldiers saved my life."

"Roger that," said Donny.

"But," said Trig, holding it in the air, "even if I admire courage and commitment, I have to make a distinction. Between a moral war and an immoral war. World War II: moral. Kill Hitler before he kills all the Jews. Kill Tōjō before he turns all the Filipino women into whores. Korea? Maybe moral. I don't know. Stop the Chinese from turning Korea into a province. I guess that's moral. I would have fought in that one."

"But Vietnam. Not moral?"

"I don't know. You tell me."

Trig leaned forward. Another of his little, unsung gifts: listening. He really wanted to know what Donny thought and he refused to pigeonhole Donny as a baby killer and Zippo commando.

Donny could not resist this earnest attention. "What I saw was good American kids trying to do a job they didn't quite understand. What I saw was kids who thought it was like a John Wayne movie and got their guts blown out. I was in a place once, a forest or a former forest. All the leaves were gone, but the trees still stood. Only, they shined. It was like they were covered in ice. It reminded me of Vermont. I've never been to Vermont, but it reminded me of it just the same."

"I think I know where you're headed. I saw the same thing on the convoy out of Stanleyville."

"Yeah, well, in this case we called in Hotel Echo, on a stand of trees because we saw movement and thought a unit of gooks was infiltrating through it. We got 'em, but good. Those were their guts. They were just pulverized, turned to shiny liquid, and it plastered the stumps and limbs. Man, I never saw anything like that. Of course it was a platoon of Army engineers. Twenty-two guys, gone, just like that. Hotel Echo. It wasn't very pretty."

"Donny, I think you *know*. Underneath. I can feel you getting there. You're working on it."

"My girl is already there. She's coming in in this Peace Caravan deal they got going."

"Good for her. Do you talk about it with her?"

"She says she decided she'd do her part to stop the war when she visited me in the San Diego Naval Hospital."

"Good for her again. But—are you there?"

Donny couldn't lie. He had no talent for it.

"No. Not yet. Maybe never. It just seems wrong. You

have to do what your country tells you. You have to contribute. It's duty."

Trig was like a confessor: his eyes burned with empathy and drew Donny forward to reveal more.

"Donny, I know you'd never leave or quit or anything. I wouldn't ask you to. But consider joining us after you get out. I think you'll feel much better. And I can't begin to tell you how much it would mean to us. I hate this idea we're all a bunch of chickenshits. A guy who's been there, won a medal, fought, dedicating himself to ending it and bringing his buddies home. That's powerful stuff. I'd be proud to be a part of that."

"I don't know."

"Just think about it. Talk to me, keep in touch. That's all. Just think about it."

"Donny, my God!" a voice called, and he looked up and saw a dream coming onto the porch to him. She was thin, blond, athletic, part tawny cowgirl, part perfect American sweetheart, and he felt helpless as he always did when he saw her.

It was Julie.

CHAPTER FOUR

"What's wrong?" she said.

"Why didn't you call me?"

"I did. And I wrote you, too."

"Oh, shit."

"Can we leave? Can we go someplace? Donny, I haven't seen you since Christmas."

"I don't know. I'm here with this PFC from my squad and I sort of promised I'd, uh, look after him. I can't leave him."

"Donny!"

"I can't explain it! It's very complicated."

He kept looking off, back into the house as if he was trying to keep his eye on something.

"Look, let me go tell Crowe I'm leaving. I'll be right back. We'll go somewhere."

He disappeared back inside the house.

Julie stood there in the Washington dark on a street above Georgetown as the traffic veered along Wisconsin. Pretty soon Peter Farris came out. Peter was a tall, bearded graduate student in sociology at the University of Arizona, the head of the Southwest Regional People's Coalition for Peace and Justice and nominal honcho of the group of kids he and Julie had shepherded out by Peace Caravan from Tucson.

"Where's your friend?"

"He'll be back."

"I *knew* that's what he'd be like. Big, handsome, square."

But then Donny returned, ignoring Peter.

"Hi. It's stupid, but Crowe wants to go to another party and I think I ought to go with him. I can't . . . It's just . . . I'll get in touch with you as soon as . . ."

But then he turned, troubled, and before she could say

a thing, he said, "Oh, shit, they're leaving. I'll get in touch" and ran off, leaving the girl he loved behind him.

The next morning, waking early in his room in the barracks, almost an hour before the 0530 alarm, Donny almost went on sick call. It seemed the only sane course, the only escape from his troubles. But his troubles came looking for him.

It was a boneyard day, he knew. His team was up. He had stuff to do. He skipped breakfast in the chow hall, and instead re-pressed his dress tunic and trousers, spent a good thirty minutes spit-shining his oxfords. This was ritual, almost cleansing and purifying.

You put a gob of spit into the black can of polish, and with a scrap of cotton mixed the black paste and the saliva together, forming a dense goo. Then you applied just a little dab to the leather and rubbed and rubbed. You should get a genie for your troubles, you rubbed so hard. You rubbed and rubbed, a dab at a time, covering the whole shoe, and then the other. You let it fry into a dense haze, then went at it again, with another cotton cloth, went at it like war, snappity-snap. It was a lost military art; they said they were going to bring in patent leather next time because the young Marines couldn't be trusted to put in the hours. But Donny was proud of his spit shine, carefully nursed through the long months, built up over time, until his oxfords gleamed vividly in the sun.

So stupid, he now thought.

So ridiculous. So pointless.

The weather was heavy with the chance of rain and the dogwoods were in full bloom, another brutal Washington spring day. Arlington's gentle hills and valleys, full of pink trees and dead boys, rolled away from the burial site and beyond, like a movie Rome, the white buildings of the capital of America gleamed even in the gray light. Donny could see the needle and the dome and the big white house and the weeping Lincoln hidden in his portico of marble. Only Jefferson's cute little gazebo was out of sight, hidden behind an inoffensive, dogwood- and tomb-crazed hill.

The box job was over. It had gone all right, though everybody was grumpy. For some reason even Crowe had tried hard that day, and there'd been no slipup as they took L/Cpl. Michael F. Anderson from the black hearse to the bier to the slow-time march, snapped the flag off the box, folded it crisply. Donny handed the tricorn of stars to the grieving widow, a pimply girl. It was always better not to know a thing about the boy inside. Had L/Cpl. Anderson been a grunt? Had he been a supply clerk, a helicopter crew member, a military journalist, a corpsman, combat engineer? Had he been shot, exploded, crushed, virused or VD'd to death? Nobody knew: he was dead, that was all, and Donny stood at crisp attention, the poster Marine in his dress blue tunic, white trousers and white cover, giving a stiff perfect salute to the wet-nosed, shuddering girl during "Taps." Grief is so ugly. It is the ugliest thing there is, and he had fucking bathed in it for close to eighteen long months now. His head ached.

Now it was over. The girl had been led away, and the Marines had marched smartly back to their bus and climbed aboard for a discreet smoke. Donny now watched to make certain that if they smoked they took their white gloves off, for the nicotine could stain them yellow otherwise. All complied, even Crowe.

"You want a cigarette, Donny?"

"I don't smoke."

"You should. Relaxes you."

"Well, I'll pass." He looked at his watch, a big Seiko on a chain-mail strap he'd bought at the naval exchange in Da Nang for $12, and saw that they had another forty minutes to kill before the next job.

"You ought to hang your coats up," he told the team. "But don't go outside unless you're buttoned and shined. Some asshole major might see you, put you on report and off you go to the 'Nam. You'd be back for the next box job. Only, you'd be the one in the box, right, Crowe?"

"Yes, Corporal, sir," Crowe barked, ironic and snide, pretending to be the shavetail gung-ho lifer he would never even resemble.

"We love our Corps, don't we, Crowe?"

"We love our Corps, Corporal."

"Good man, Crowe," he said.

"Donny?"

It was the driver, looking back.

"Some Navy guys here."

Shit, thought Donny.

"Donny, are you joining the Navy?" Crowe asked. "You could make a *fortune* giving jelly rolls in the showers of a nuclear sub. You could—"

Everybody laughed. Give it to Crowe, he was funny.

"All right, Crowe," said Donny, "I just may put you on report for the fun of it or kick the shit out of you to save the paperwork. While I talk to these guys, you give every man on the team a blow job. That's an order, PFC."

"Yes, Corporal, sir," said Crowe, taking a puff on his cigarette.

Donny buttoned his tunic, pulled on his cover low over his eyes and stepped outside.

It was Weber, in khakis.

"Good morning, sir," said Donny, saluting.

"Good morning, Corporal," said Weber. "Would you come over here, please?"

"Yes, sir," said Donny.

As they got out of earshot of the men in the bus, Donny said, "Man, what the *fuck* is this all about? I thought I was supposed to be undercover. This really blows it."

"All right, Fenn, don't get excited. Tell them we're from personnel at the Pentagon, verifying your RSVN service preparatory to separation. Very common occurrence, no big deal."

Down the way, in the rear of a tan government Ford,

Lieutenant Commander Bonson sat behind sunglasses, peering ahead.

Donny got in; the engine was running and air-conditioned chill blasted over him.

"Good morning, Fenn," said the commander. He was a tight-assed, scrawny lifer in the backseat, sitting ramrod perfect.

"Sir."

"Fenn, I'm going to arrest Crowe today."

Donny sucked a gulp of dry, painful air.

"Excuse me, sir?"

"At 1600 hours, I'll show up at the barracks with a plainclothes detachment of NIS. We'll incarcerate him at the Navy Yard brig."

"On what charge?"

"Security violation. Naval Penal Code DOD 69-455. Unauthorized possession of classified information. Also, DOD 77-56B, unauthorized transmission or transference of classified information."

"Ah—on what basis?"

"Your basis, Fenn."

"*My* basis, sir?"

"Your basis."

"But I haven't reported anything. He went to a couple of parties where they were flying the NVA flag. Half the apartments in Washington are hanging the NVA flag. I see it everywhere."

"You can place him in the presence of a known radical organizer."

"Well, I can place *myself* in that same guy's presence. And I have no information to suggest he was compromising Marine security or intelligence. I just saw him talking with a guy, that's all."

"You can place him in the presence of Trig Carter. Do you know yet who Trig Carter is?"

"Ah, well, sir, you said—"

"Tell him, Weber."

"This is straight from this morning's MDW-Secret Service-FBI briefing, Fenn," said Weber. "Carter is now suspected of being a member of the Weather Underground. He's not 'merely' a peacenik with a placard and some flowers in his hair, but he's an extreme radical who may be linked to the Weather Underground's bombing campaign."

Donny was dumbstruck.

"Trig?"

"Don't you see it yet, Corporal?" said Bonson. "These two bright boys are hatching up something good and bloody for May Day. We have to stop them. If I collar Crowe, maybe that'll be enough to save some lives."

"Sir, I saw nothing that would—"

"Then get with the fucking program, Corporal!" Bonson bellowed. He leaned forward, fixing Donny with his murderous glare. He seemed to bear a grudge against the known world and was holding Donny responsible for all his disappointments, for all the women who wouldn't sleep with him, for the fraternities that wouldn't pledge him, for the schools that wouldn't accept him.

"You think this is some kind of joke, don't you, Corporal? It's beneath you somehow. So you'll go along to stay out of 'Nam, and just play it cool and cute and rely on your good looks and your charm to drift through? You won't get your hands dirty, you won't do the job. Well, that stops today. You have a job. You have a legal order assigned by higher headquarters and passed down through a legal chain of command, vetted by your commanding officer. You will perform. Now, you stop screwing around and pretending like your feelings matter. You get on this thing and you get inside and you get me what I need, or by God, I will see to it that you're the only U.S. Marine on the DMZ when Uncle Ho sends his tanks south to mop up. We'll get you a Springfield rifle and a campaign hat and see how well you do. Are you reading me?"

"Loud and clear," said Donny.

"Go do your fucking job," said Bonson icily. "I'll hold

off a day, maybe two. But get inside *before* May Day or I'll sweep them all up and off to Portsmouth and you to the 'Nam. Do you copy?"

"I copy, sir," said Donny, blushing at the dressing down.

"Out," said Bonson, signifying the interview was over.

"You okay?"

"I'm fine," Donny said.

"You look not-cool."

"I'm cool."

"Well, a bunch of us were going over to this party in G-town, Donny. I found out about it from Trig."

Oh Christ, Donny thought, as the solicitous Crowe loomed over him in the upstairs barracks room where the off-base men kept their huge gray lockers and were now stripping down after a hot afternoon in the boneyard.

"Crowe, you know we may be on alert at any time. Is your riot gear outstanding? What about steaming and pressing your tunic, washing out your dark socks, and spending an hour or two on that spit shine, which has begun to look a little dim. *That's* what you ought to be doing."

"Yeah, well," said Crowe, "believe me on this one, I know. We're not going on alert till 2400 tomorrow night."

Donny almost pointed out that if you said "2400" you didn't have to say "night," but Crowe wasn't stoppable at that point.

"And we'll just hang around here. We may get on trucks and, probably on Saturday, we'll deploy to a building near the White House. But it'll be a short deployment. All the action's going on across the river. The whole point of this one is to converge on the Pentagon and close it down. Trig told me."

"Trig told you? He told you about the deployment? Man, that's classified. Why the hell would he know?"

"Don't ask me. Trig knows everything. He has entrée everywhere. He probably is having cocktails with J. Edgar himself right as we speak. By the way, did you know Hoover was a fruit? He's a goddamn *fruit*! He hangs out in Y's and shit."

"Crowe, you're not *telling* Trig shit, are you? I mean, it might seem like a joke to you, but you could get into deep, serious green crap that way."

"Man, what do *I* know? Little Eddie Crowe's just a grunt. He knows nothing."

"Crowe, I'm not kidding."

"Is someone asking about me?"

"So where's this party?"

"Shouldn't you be trying to find your girl? She didn't look too happy when you bailed out on her last night to hang out with us. And if I know my horny hippie peace freaks, that bearded guy hanging on her shirttails has a serious case of the please-fuck-mes. You may have to call in a fire mission on *him*. Hotel Echo."

"Nobody's asking about you."

"'Cause if they are, here's my advice: give me up. I ain't worth shit. Seriously, Donny, roll over on me in a second. If it's you or me, buddy, choose you. It would be a shame any other way."

"Eddie, you're full of shit. Now, where's this party? I need a fucking keg of beer."

"Maybe Trig can find your girl."

"Maybe he can."

They showered and dressed, and signed out with a warning from the duty NCO to call in every couple of hours to make sure the company hadn't gone on alert. Sure enough, Crowe's obedient buddies waited just outside the barracks' main gate, on Eighth Street. They climbed in the old Corvair.

"Hey, Donny."

"Cool. Donny, the hero."

He could hardly remember the names. He had a splitting headache. He had told a lie, direct and flat out. *Nobody is asking about you.*

But goddammit, how had Crowe known so much?

Why had he asked Donny the other day where they'd deploy? Why was all this bad shit happening anyway? And what about Julie? She was camping in some muddy field with what's his face, and he hadn't even really *talked* to her. She hadn't called and left a number, either. Man, it was all coming down.

But when they got there, Trig came over and greeted them, and when Crowe told him Donny's situation, he said it would be no problem.

"Sure," he said. "Let me make a call." He went off, and Donny sat among a bunch of turned-out Georgetown kids, dressed like young Republicans, while Crowe, in his hair-hiding boonie cap, worked a girl who didn't work him back. Presently, Trig returned.

"Okay, let's go," he said.

"You found her?"

"Well, I found out where the University of Arizona kids are camping. That's where she'd be, right?"

"Right," said Donny.

"Okay, I'll run you over."

Donny paused. Was he supposed to be looking after Crowe? But now he'd set this thing up, and if he hung with Crowe it would look very strange. And he was supposed to watch Crowe *with* Trig, right? And if he was with Trig, then Crowe couldn't be giving up any secrets, could he?

"Great," said Donny.

"Just let me get my book," said Trig. He disappeared for a second, then came back with a large, really filthy looking sketchbook. It had the sense of a treasured relic. "Never go anyplace without this. I might see an eastern swallowtail mudlark!" He laughed at himself, showing white teeth.

Outside, Trig gestured to the inevitable Trigmobile, a TR-6, bright red, its canvas roof down.

"Cool wheels," said Donny, hopping in.

"I picked it up a little while ago in England," he said. "I got burned out on peace shit. I took a little sabbatical, went to London, spent some time in Oxford. The Ruskin School of Drawing. Bought this baby."

"You must be loaded."

"Oh, I think there's money in the family. Not my father; he doesn't make a penny. He's in State, planning some tiny part of the war, the economic infrastructure of the province of Quang Tri. What does your dad do?" Trig asked.

"My dad was a rancher. He worked like hell and never made a penny. He died poor."

"But he died clean. In our family, we don't work. The money works. We play. Working for something you believe in, that's the best. That's the maximum charge. And if you can have a good time at it, man, that's *really* cool."

Donny said nothing. But a darkness settled on him: he was here as a Judas, wasn't he? He'd sell Trig out for thirty pieces of silver, or rather three stripes and no trip back to the Land of Bad Things. He looked over at Trig. The wind was blowing the slightly older man's hair back lushly, like a cape streaming behind a horseman. Trig wore Ray-Ban sunglasses and had one of those high, beautiful foreheads. He looked like a young god on a good day.

This guy was Weather Underground? This guy would bomb things, blow up people, that sort of stuff? It didn't seem possible. By no reach of his imagination could he see Trig as conspiratorial. He was too much at the center of things; the world had given itself to him too easily and too eagerly.

"Could you kill anyone?" Donny asked.

Trig laughed, showing white teeth.

"What a question! Wow, I've never been asked that one!"

"I killed seven men," Donny said.

"Well, if you hadn't have killed them, would they have killed you?"

"They were *trying* to!"

"So, there you have it. You made your decision. But

no, no, I couldn't. I just can't see it. For me, too much would die. I'd be better off dead myself than having killed anything. That's just what I believe. I've believed it ever since I looked in a house in Stanleyville and saw twenty-five kids cut to pieces. I can't even remember if it's because they were rebels or government. They probably didn't know. Right then: no more killing. Stop the killing. Just like the man says, all we are saying is give peace a chance."

"Well, it's hard to give it a chance when a guy is whacking away at you with an AK-47."

Trig laughed.

"You have me there, partner," he said merrily.

But then he said, "Sure, anybody gets that kind of slack. But you wouldn't have shot into that ditch in My Lai like those other guys did. You would have walked away. Hot blood, cold blood. Hell, you're a cowboy. You were trained to shoot in self-defense. You shot *morally*."

Donny didn't know what to say. He just stared ahead glumly until in the falling light they sped through downtown, past the big government buildings still shiny in the fading sun, along the park-lined river and at last reached West Potomac Park, just beyond Jefferson's classy monument.

Welcome to the May Tribe.

On one side of the street, eight or nine cop cars were parked, and DC cops in riot gear watched in sullen knots. Across the street, equally sullen, knots of hippie kids in jeans and oversized fatigue coats and long flowing hair watched back. It was a stare-down; nobody was winning.

Trig's presence registered immediately and the kids parted, suddenly grinning, and Trig drove the Triumph through them and down an asphalt road that led toward the river, some playing fields, some trees. But it was more like Sherwood Forest than any college campus. The meadows streamed with kids in tents, kids at campfires, kids stoned, playing Frisbee, singing, smoking, eating, necking, bathing topless in the river. Port-a-pots had been put up everywhere, bright blue and smelly.

"It's the gathering of the tribes," said Donny.

"It's the gathering of our generation," said Trig.

Being with Trig was like being with Mick Jagger. He knew everybody, and at least three or four times he had to stop the Triumph and clamber out as protégés came upon him for hugs or advice, for gossip or news, or just to be with him. Astonishing thing: he remembered everybody's name. *Everybody's.* He never fumbled, he never forgot, he never made a mistake. He seemed to inflate in the love that was thrust upon him, by boy and girl, man and woman, even some old bearded, be-sandaled radicals who looked as if they'd probably protested World War I, too.

"Boy, they love you," Donny said.

"I've just been riding this circuit for seven long years. You get to know folks. I am tired, though. After this weekend, I'm going to crash at a friend's farm out in Germantown. Paint some birds, blow some grass, just chill. You ought to bring Julie, if she's still here, and come out. Route thirty-five, north of Germantown. Wilson, the mailbox says. Here, here, I think this is it."

Donny saw her almost immediately. She had camouflaged herself in some kind of Indian full-length dress and wore her hair up, pinned with a Navajo silver brooch. He had given it to her. It cost him $75.

The asshole kid Farris was near her, though he wasn't talking to her. He was just watching her from a ways away, utterly mesmerized.

"Hi," Donny called.

"I brought Young Lochinvar from out of the West," Trig said.

"Oh, Donny."

"Enjoy," said Trig. "Let me know when you want to get out of here. I'll go listen to Peter Farris whine for a while."

But Donny wasn't listening. He looked full into the person that was Julie, and his heart broke all over again.

Every time he saw her was like a first time. His breath came in little spurts. He felt himself lighting up inside. He gave her a hug.

"I'm sorry I wasn't making much sense last night. I couldn't put it together fast enough. You know how slow I am."

"Donny. I called the barracks."

"Sometimes those messages get through, sometimes they don't. I was just all out of joint yesterday."

"What's going on?"

"Ah, it's too complicated to explain. It's nothing I can't handle. How are you? God, sweetie, it's so good to see you."

"Oh, I'm fine. This camping stuff I could do without. I need a shower. Where's the nearest Holiday Inn?"

"When this is all over, don't go back," he suddenly blurted, as if finally seeing a path that made some sense. "Stay here with me. We'll get married!"

"Donny! What about the big church wedding? What about all my mother's friends? What about the country club?"

"I—" and then he saw she was joking, and she saw he was not.

"I want us to get married," he said. "Right now."

"Donny, I want to marry you so much I think I'll die from it."

"We'll do it after this weekend thing."

"Yes. I'll marry you as soon as it's over. I'll move into an apartment. I'll find work. I'll—"

"No, then I want you to go home and finish your degree. I'll go for the early out and I'll move back home. There'll be G.I. Bill money. I can work part-time. We'll get some kind of married-student housing. It'll be great fun! And you can tell your mother we'll have all the parties then, so we'll keep her happy too."

"What brought this on?"

"Nothing. I just realized how important you are to me. I didn't want this getting away from me. I was an asshole last night. I wanted to put us back together as the first priority. When I get out, I'll even help you in this peace stuff. We'll stop the war. You and me. It'll be great."

They walked a bit, amid kids their own ages, but stoned and wild, just celebrating the youthfulness of their lives in a great merry adventure in Washington, DC, stopping the war and getting stoned and laid in the same impulse. Donny felt isolated from it terribly: he wasn't a part of it. And he didn't feel as if he were a part of the Marine Corps anymore.

"Okay," he finally said, "I ought to be getting back. We may be on alert. If not, can I come by tomorrow?"

"I'll try and break off tomorrow if nothing's happening here. We don't even know ourselves what's going on. They say we're going to march to the Pentagon over the weekend. More theater."

"Please be careful."

"I will."

"I'll figure out what we have to do to get married legally. It might be better to hide it from the Corps. They're all assholes. Then after it's done, the paperwork will catch up to us."

"Donny, I love you. Ever since that date when you were with Peggy Martin and I realized I *hated* her for being with you. Ever since then."

"We will have a wonderful life. I promise."

Then he saw someone approaching him swiftly. It was Trig, with Peter Farris and several other acolytes following in his wake.

"Hey," he called, "it just came over the radio. The Military District of Washington has just declared a full alert and all personnel are supposed to report to their duty stations."

"Oh, shit," said Donny.

"It's beginning," said Julie.

CHAPTER FIVE

A flare floated in the night. Lights throbbed and swept. The gas was not so bad now, and the mood was generous, even adventurous. It had the air of a huge campout, a jamboree of some sort. Who was in charge? Nobody. Who made these decisions? Nobody. The thing just happened, almost miraculously, by the sheer osmosis of the May Tribe.

At the Pentagon almost nothing had happened. It was all theater. By the time Julie and Peter and their knot of Arizona crusaders actually got onto government property, the word had come back that the Army and the police weren't arresting anybody and they could stand on the grass in front of the huge ministry of war forever and nothing would happen. It was determined by someone that the Pentagon itself wasn't a choke point, and it made more sense, therefore, to occupy the bridges before the morning rush hour and in that way close down the city and the government. Others would besiege the Justice Department, another favorite target of opportunity.

So now they marched along, past the big Marriott Hotel on the right, toward the Fourteenth Street Bridge just ahead. Julie had never seen anything like this: it was a movie, a battle of joy, a stage show, every pep rally and football game she had ever been to. Excitement thrummed in the moist air; overhead, police and Army helicopters buzzed.

"God, have you ever seen *anything* like this?" she said to Peter.

He replied, "You can't marry him."

"Oh, Peter."

"You can't. You just can't."

"I'm going to marry him next week."

"You probably won't be out of jail next week."

"Then I'll marry him the week after."

"They won't let him."

"We'll do it secretly."

"There's too much important work to be done."

They passed the Marriott, maybe fifty abreast and a half-mile long, a mass of kids. Who led them? A small knot at the front with bullhorns of the People's Coalition for Peace and Justice; but more realistically, their own instincts led them. The professional organizers merely harnessed and marginally directed the generational energy. Meanwhile, the smell of grass rose in the air, and the sound of laughter; now and then a news helicopter would float down from the sky, hover and plaster them with bright light. They'd wave and dance and chant.

> *ONE, TWO, THREE, FOUR*
> *WE DON'T WANT YOUR FUCKING WAR*

or

> *HO, HO, HO CHI MINH*
> *N-L-F IS GONNA WIN*

or

> *END THE WAR NOW*
> *END THE WAR NOW.*

That's when the first tear gas hit.

It was acrid and biting and its overwhelming power to disorient could not be denied. Julie felt her eyes knit in pain, and the world suddenly began to whirl about. The air itself became the enemy. Screams rose, and the sound of panic and confusion spread. Julie dropped to her knees, coughing hard. Nothing existed for a second but the pain searing her lungs and the immense crushing power of the gas.

But she stayed there with a few others, though Peter

had disappeared somehow. The evil stuff curled around them, their eyes now gushing tears. But she thought: I will not move. They cannot make me move.

Suddenly someone arrived with a bucket full of white washcloths soaked in water.

"Breathe through this," he screamed, an old vet of this drill, "and it won't be so hard. If we don't break, they'll fall back. Come on, be strong, keep the faith."

Some kids fell back, but most just stood there, trying to deal with it. Someone—no one could ever say who or why—took a step forward, then another one, and in a second or so those that remained had joined. The mass moved forward, not on the assault and certainly not to charge, but just out of the conviction that as young people nothing could deter them because they were so powerful.

As Julie moved she saw ahead a barricade of DC police cars, their lights flashing, and behind them Army soldiers, presumably a contingent of the 7,500 National Guardsmen called up to much hoo-hah in the newspapers. They had an insect look, their eyes giant, their snouts long and descending, like powerful mandibles, their flesh black. The masks, she realized. They were wearing gas masks, all of them. This infuriated her.

"You are warned to disperse!" came an amplified voice. "You are hereby warned to disperse. We will arrest those who do not disperse. You do not have a parade permit."

"Oh, like *that's* really crucial," said someone with a laugh. "Shit, if I'd realized *that* I never would have come!"

A helicopter floated overhead. To the right, over the Potomac, the sun began to rise. It was about six, Julie saw, looking at her watch.

"Keep moving!" came a cry. "One, two, three, four, we don't want your fucking war!"

Julie hated to curse; she hated it when Donny cursed, but standing there in the astringent aftermath of the gas, her eyes bawling, her heart knotted in anger, she picked it up and was not alone.

ONE, TWO, THREE, FOUR
WE DON'T WANT YOUR FUCKING WAR

It was like an anthem, a battle cry. The kids that were left took their strength from it and began to move more quickly. They came together in the strobing lights of the police cars and the running lights of the circling copters. Those who'd fled regained their heroism, stopped and, moved by the strength of the few who remained, turned and themselves began to march.

Pop! Pop! Pop!

More CS gas canisters came at them from the barricade, evil little grenades spurting viscous clouds of the stuff as they bounced. But the kids now knew it wouldn't kill them and that the wind would come to thin it out and take its sting away.

ONE, TWO, THREE, FOUR
WE DON'T WANT YOUR FUCKING WAR

Julie screamed with all her strength. She cried for pale, poor Donny in his hospital bed, a sack of plasma over him, his face drawn, his eyes vacant because of the death that had passed through him. She screamed for the other boys in that awful place, without legs or hopes, faces gone, feet gone, penises gone; she cried for the girls she knew would be bitter forever because their fiancés or brothers or husbands had come home in plastic bags dumped in wooden boxes; she cried for her father who preached of "duty" but himself had sold insurance through World War II; she cried for all the beaten kids in all the demonstrations in the past seven years; she cried for the little girl running from the napalm cloud, naked and afraid; she cried for the little man with his hands tied behind him who was shot in the head and fell to the ground, squirting blood.

ONE, TWO, THREE, FOUR
WE DON'T WANT YOUR FUCKING WAR

They were all moving forward now, hundreds, thousands. They were at the police cars, they were beyond the police cars, the police were fleeing, the National Guard was fleeing.

"Hold it! Hold it, goddammit!" someone was shouting as the melee halted. Before them was clear bridge, all the way to the Jefferson Memorial. In the rising light, the Capitol stood before them, and over some trees the spire of the Washington Monument and off to the right the Alphaville Blocks of the new HEW complex. But there were no cars anywhere, and no cops.

"We did it," somebody said. *"We did it!"*

Yes, they had. They had taken the bridge, won a great victory. They had driven the state away. They had claimed the Fourteenth Street Bridge for the Coalition for Peace and Justice.

They had won.

"We did it," someone was saying next to her; it was Peter.

"NCOs and squad leaders up front ASAP. NCOs and squad leaders up front ASAP!"

The men milled loosely on the broad esplanade of closed-down Route 95 about a half mile on the DC side of the Fourteenth Street Bridge, behind a barricade of jeeps, police cars, deuce-and-a-halfs. Jefferson watched in marble splendor from the portside, amid a canopy of dogwoods and from behind a cage of marble columns. A pale lemon sky oversaw the scene, and helicopters fluttered through it, making far more noise than their importance seemed to warrant. It looked like a fifties movie, the one where the monster has attacked the city and the police and military set up barricades to impede its progress while in some lab, white-coated men labor to invent a secret weapon to bring it down.

"Napalm," said Crowe helpfully. "I'd use napalm. Kill about two thousand kids. Roast 'em nice and tasty-chewie. Make Kent State look like a picnic. Boy, the war'd be over *tomorrow.*"

"Don't think the lifers haven't thought of it," said Donny, as he left to head for the command conference.

He slipped away from Third Squad, slid through other squads and platoons of young men festooned comically for war, exactly as he was, who seemed to feel equally foolish with the huge pots banging on their heads. That was the odd thing about a helmet: when it's not necessary, it feels completely ludicrous; when it is necessary, it feels like a gift from God. This was one of the former occasions.

Donny reached the informal conclave where the barracks commander stood with three men in jumpsuits that said JUSTICE DEPT on the back, some other officials, cops, firemen and some confused DC Guard officers, of whom it was said their panic had led to the rout on the bridge.

"All right, all right, people," the colonel said. "Sergeant Major, all of 'em here?"

The sergeant major made a quick head count of his NCOs and from each man received a nod to signify that the men under him had arrived; it was done professionally in about thirty seconds.

"All present, sir."

"Good," said the colonel, climbing into a jeep to give him elevation over his subordinates, and speaking in the loud, clear voice of command.

"All right, men. As you know, at 0400 hours a large mass of demonstrators commandeered the right-hand span of the Fourteenth Street Bridge, effectively closing it down. The traffic is tied up back beyond Alexandria. The other bridges have been cleared by this time, but we've got a choke point. The Department of Justice has requested the Marine Corps to assist in clearing the bridge, and we've been authorized by our command structure for that mission. So let me tell you what that means: we *will* clear the bridge, we will do it quickly and professionally and with a minimum of force and damage. Understood?"

"Aye, aye, sir," came the cry.

"I want A Company and B Company formed up line abreast, with Headquarters Company in reserve to go by squads to the line as needed. We do not have arrest powers and I do not want any arrests made. We will advance under cover of moderate CS gas with bayonets fixed but sheathed. Under no circumstances will those bayonets be used to draw blood. We will prevail not by force but by good order and solid professionalism. A DC Police mass-arrest unit will follow behind, detaining and shipping those demonstrators who do not disperse. Our limit of advance will be the far end of the bridge."

"Live ammo, sir?"

"Negative, negative, I say again, negative. No live ammo. Nobody will be shot today. These are American kids, not VC. We will move out at 0900. Company commanders and senior NCOs, I want you to hold a quick meeting and get your best squads into the line at the point of contact. This is a standard DOD anti-riot drill. All right, people, let's be professional."

"Dismissed!"

Donny made it back to his squad, as around him other squad leaders were reaching their people. With the weird sensation of a large herbivore awakening, the unit was picking itself up, beginning to form up as each smaller element got instructions. There was some cheering, moderated by ambiguity, but nevertheless a simple expression of the soldier or Marine's preference for doing anything rather than nothing.

"We'll be in that arrow-formation, platoons-abreast thing," Donny explained. "The sergeant major will be counting cadence."

"Bayonets?"

"On but sheathed. Minimum force. We're moving these people out of here by our presence. No ammo, no clubbing, just solid Marine professionalism, got it?"

"Masks?"

"I *said* masks, Crowe, weren't you listening? Some CS will be fired." He looked about. The sergeant major had set up a hundred yards beyond the trucks and now the Marines were streaming to him to form up at the line of departure. Donny looked at his watch. It was 0850.

"All right, let's assemble and march to position. Form up on me, *now!*" His men rose to him and found their places. He marched them at the double time to a formation that was putting itself together on the broad white band of empty highway.

Peter held her hand. He was pale but determined, his face still teary from the gas.

"It'll be okay," he kept saying, almost more to himself than to her. There was something so sad about him, she had a tender impulse to draw him toward her and comfort him.

"All right," came the amplified voice, "WTOP has a camera in the sky and we've just heard that the Marines are forming up to come and move us."

"Oh, this is going to be merry," said Peter. "The Marines."

"I want to counsel everybody; you don't want to resist or you may get clubbed or beaten. Don't yell at them, don't taunt them. Just go limp. Remember, this is your bridge, it's not theirs. We've liberated it. We own it. Hell, no, we won't go."

"Hell, no, we won't go," repeated Peter.

"That's the evil part," Julie said bitterly. "They don't come themselves, the guys in the offices who make it happen. They send in Donny, who's just trying to do his job. He gets the shitty end of the stick."

But Peter wasn't listening.

"Here they come," he said, for ahead, out of the blur, they could now see them drawing ever closer in a phalanx of rectitude and camouflage: the United States Marine

Corps advancing at the half-trot, rifles at the high port, helmets even, gas masks turning them to insects or robots.

Hell, no, we won't go! came the chant, guttural, from the heart. *Marines, go home!* Then again, *Hell, no, we won't go!*

The unit advanced at the half-trot, to the sergeant major's urgent cadence, *Hup-two-THREE-four, Hup-two-THREE-four,* and Donny's squad stayed tight in the crowd-control formation, a little to the left of the point of the arrow.

Jogging actually helped Donny feel a little better, he settled into a steady rhythm, and the constellation of equipment bounded sloppily on his body. His helmet banged, riding the spongy straps of the helmet liner with a kind of liquid mushiness. He felt the sweat run down inside his mask, catch irritatingly at his eyelashes, then flood into his eyes. But it didn't matter.

Through the lens of his mask the world seemed slightly tarnished, slightly dirty. Ahead, he could see the mass of demonstrators sitting on the bridge as if it were theirs, looking fiercely at them.

Hell, no, we won't go! alternating with *Marines, go home! Marines, go home!* rose to fill the air, but it sounded tinny and idiotic. They closed on the crowd until but fifty yards away, then the sergeant major's yell reached out to stop them.

"Ready, *Halt!*"

The two young Americas faced each other on the bridge. On the one side, about two thousand young people, ages fourteen through possibly thirty, most around twenty, college America, the nonconformism of complete conformism: all wore jeans and T-shirts, all had long, flowing, beautiful hair, all were pale, intense, high on grass or sanctimony, standing and drawing strength from one another under a bristle of placards that proclaimed PEOPLE'S COALITION FOR PEACE AND JUSTICE and other, ruder signs, like GIS, JOIN US! or STOP THE WAR! or FUCK THE WAR! or RMN MUST GO!

The other America, 650 strong, wore the green twill of duty, three companies of Marines, average age twenty also, armed with unloaded rifles and sheathed bayonets. They were earnest and, behind the rubber and plastic of their masks, clean-shaven and short-haired, yet in their way just as conflicted and just as frightened as the kids they faced. They were essentially the same kids, but nobody noticed. Behind them were cop cars, ambulances, fire engines, deuce-and-a-halfs, their own Corpsmen, news reporters, Justice Department officials. But they were the ones out front.

A man in the blue jumpsuit of the Justice Department stepped beyond the Marine formation. He had a bullhorn.

"This is an illegal parade. You do not have a parade permit. You are hereby ordered to disperse. If you do not disperse, we will clear the bridge. You are hereby ordered to disperse."

"Hell, no, we won't go!" came the response.

When it had died down after a sweaty bit, the Justice official reiterated his position, adding, "We will commence with CS gas operations in two minutes and the Marine Corps will move you out. *You are hereby ordered to disperse!"*

A moment of quiet followed and then a young man stepped forward, screamed, *"Here's your fucking parade permit!"* then pivoted smartly, bent, and peeled down his jeans to reveal two white half moons of ass.

"God, he's beautiful," said Crowe through his mask, but loudly enough for the squad to hear. "I want him!"

"Crowe, shut up," said Donny.

The man from the Justice Department departed. The sun was high, the weather sticky and heavy. Overhead, helicopters hovered, their rotors kicking up the only turbulence.

Another amplified voice, this from the demonstrators as the older people warned the kids.

"Do not attempt to pick up tear gas canisters as they will be very hot. Do not panic. The gas is not contained and it will disappear very quickly."

"*Gas!*" came a command.

Six soft *plops* marked the firing of six DC Police gas guns, and the missiles skittered across the pavement leaking white fumes, spun, rolled and slid raggedly along. The point of firing them into the ground was to bounce them into the crowd at low velocity rather than firing them into people at high, possibly killing velocity.

"*Gas!*" the command came again, and six more CS shells were fired.

The sergeant major's scream carried through the air: "Assault *arms*!" and with that the rifles left the cross-chest position of carry and were brought around the right side of the body, stocks wedged under right arms and locked in, muzzles with sheathed bayonets angled outward at forty-five degrees to the ground.

"Prepare to *ad-vance*!" came the command.

Only Crowe's rifle wavered, probably out of excitement, but otherwise the muzzles lanced outward from the formation. Donny could sense the crowd of demonstrators drawing back, gathering somehow, then reinflating with purpose. Tear gas drifted loosely amid their ranks. It was just a crowd, identities lost in the blur and the gas. Was Julie over there?

"*Ad-vance!*" came the final command, and the Marines began to stomp ahead.

Here we go, thought Donny.

They looked like Cossacks. The rank was green, slanted in two angles away from the point, an arrowhead of boys, remorseless and helmeted, their facial features vanished behind their masks.

Julie looked through her tears for Donny, but it was useless. The Marines all looked the same, staunch defenders of whatever, in their sharp uniforms with their helmets and now their guns, which jutted out like threats. A cloud of tear gas washed over her, crunching her eyes in pain; she coughed, felt the tears run hot and fluid down her face, and rubbed at them, then dipped for her wet washcloth and wiped the chemical from them.

"Assholes!" said Peter bitterly, enraged at the troops advancing on him. He was trembling so hard he was locked in place, his knees wobbling desperately. But he wasn't going to move.

"Assholes!" he repeated as the Marines closed in at a steady pace.

Donny was in the lead, solid as a rock; next to him, on the left, Crowe seemed strong. They clomped forward to a steady beat of cadence from the sergeant major, and through the jiggling stain of his dirty lenses, Donny watched as the crowd grew closer. The sergeant major's cadence drove them on; tear gas wafted through the chaos; overhead a helicopter swept low and its turbulence drove the gas more quickly, into whirlwinds and spirals, until it rushed like water across the bridge.

"Steady on the advance!" screamed the sergeant major.

Details suddenly swam at Donny: the faces of the scared kids before him, their scrawniness, their physical weakness and paleness, how many of them were girls, the cool way the leader exhorted them with his bullhorn and that shocking moment when at last the two groups clashed.

"Steady on the advance!" screamed the sergeant major.

Maybe it was like some ancient battle, legionnaires against Visigoths, Sumerians against Assyrians, but Donny sensed a great issue of physical strength, of pure force of will as expressed through bodies, when the two came together. There was no striking; no Marine lifted his rifle and drove through for a butt stroke; no blade came unsheathed and leapt forward into flesh. Rather, there was just a crush as the two masses crunched together; it felt more like football than war, that moment when the lines collide and there are a dozen contests of strength all around you and you lay what you've got against someone else and hope you get full-body weight against him and can lift him from his feet.

Donny found himself hard against not an enemy lineman or a Visigoth but a girl of about fourteen, with freckles and red, frizzy hair and braces, headband, tie-dyed T-shirt, breastless and innocent. But she had more hate on her face than any Visigoth ever, and she whacked him hard on the helmet with her placard, which, he read as it descended, stated MAKE WAR NO MORE!

The placard smacked him, its thin wood broke and it slipped away. He felt his body ramming the girl's and then she was gone, either knocked back or pushed down and stepped over. He hoped she wasn't hurt; why hadn't she just fled?

More tear gas drifted in. Screams arose. Melees had broken out everywhere as demonstrators leaned against Marines, who leaned back. One could feel strain as the two leaned and leaned and tried to press the other into panic.

It only lasted a second, really; then the demonstrators broke and fled and Donny watched as they emptied the bridge, leaving behind port-a-pots and sandals and squashed Tab cans and water buckets, the battlefield detritus of a vanquished enemy. There seemed no point in pursuing.

"Marines, stand easy," the sergeant major yelled. "Masks off."

The masks came off and the boys sucked hard at the air.

"Good job, good job. Anybody hurt?" yelled the colonel.

But before anybody could answer, a considerable ruckus arose to the left. Policemen were clustered around the railing of the bridge and the word soon reached the

Marines that someone had panicked as they had approached, and jumped off. A police helicopter hovered low, an ambulance arrived and paramedics got out urgently. Police boats were called, but it took only a few minutes to make it clear that someone was dead.

CHAPTER SIX

The scandal played out pretty much as expected, depending on the perspective of the account.

GIRL, 17, KILLED IN DEMONSTRATION, the *Post* headlined. The more conservative *Star* said, DEMONSTRATOR DIES IN BRIDGE MIX-UP. MARINES MURDER GIRL, 17, argued the *Washington City Paper*.

No matter, for the Marine Corps the news was very bad indeed. Seven liberal House members demanded an investigation into the matter of Amy Rosenzweig, seventeen, of Glencoe, Illinois, who had evidently panicked in the tear gas and the approach of the Marines and climbed over the railing. Before anybody could reach her, though several young Marines tried, she was gone. Walter Cronkite appeared to generate a small tear in his left eye. Gordon Petersen, of WTOP, developed a catch in his voice as he discussed the incident with his co-anchor, Max Robinson.

WHY MARINES? wondered the *Post* two days later on its editorial page.

U.S. Marines are among the world's most feared fighting forces, an elite who have honored their country and their service in hostile environments since 1776. But what were they doing on the 14th Street Bridge May 1?

Surely, with their esprit de corps and constant immersion in the theory and practice of land warfare at its most savage, they were a poor choice for the Justice Department to deploy against peaceful demonstrators who had taken up a harmless "occupation" of the bridge as an expression of the long-precious tradition of civil disobedience. The D.C. police force, the Park Police, or even Guardsmen from the District's own unit, all riot-trained and all experienced in dealing with demonstrations, would have been preferable to combat infantrymen, who tend to perceive all confrontations as us against them.

The place for the Marines is on the battlefields of the world, and the parade ground of the Eighth and I barracks, not on American streets. If the tragedy of Amy Rosenzweig teaches us anything, it teaches us that.

As for the Eighth and I Marines, in the immediate aftermath they were trucked back to the barracks, where they remained on alert and in isolation for two days. Teams from the FBI and the District Police and the U.S. Park Police worked over the members of Alpha Company, Second Platoon, Second Squad, who'd been on the extreme left wing of the crowd control formation, and who had seen the girl hanging on for dear life. Three of them had actually dropped their rifles, thrown away their masks and helmets and rushed to her, but in the instant before they reached her, she closed her eyes and gave her soul to God, relaxing backward into space. They got to the railing in time to see her hit the water thirty-five feet below; they got DC Police there within seconds, and within minutes a DC rescue boat was on the scene. If they'd had a rope, they would have rappelled down to the water themselves, but a quickly arriving platoon sergeant had forbidden any of them to jump off the bridge in attempts to rescue. It was just too high. And it wouldn't have mattered. When she was located thirteen minutes later, it became quickly apparent that Amy's neck had been broken by the impact of striking the water at an extreme angle. A report later exonerated the Marines and made it clear that no actual force had been applied to Amy. The Marines said she chose to martyr herself; the media said the Marines killed her. Who knew the truth?

On the third day, they arrested Crowe.

Rather, under small arms and under the supervision of two officers from the Naval Investigation Service, Lieutenant Commander Bonson and Ensign Weber, four Marine military policemen marched into the barracks where he and the rest of B company were relaxing while maintaining ready-alert status, and put him in handcuffs. Captain Dogwood and the battalion colonel watched it happen.

Then Lieutenant Commander Bonson came up to Donny and said in a loud voice, "Good job, Corporal Fenn. Damn fine work."

"Good work, Fenn," said Weber. "You got our man."

In the aftermath, a space seemed to spread around Donny. He felt it open up, as if oceans of atmosphere had been vacuumed out of the area between himself and his squad and others in the platoon. Nobody would meet his eyes. Some looked at him in horror. Others merely left the vicinity, went into other squad bays or outside to lounge near the trucks.

"What the hell did he mean?" asked Platoon Sergeant Case.

"Uh, I don't know, Sergeant," Donny said. "Uh, I don't know what the hell they were talking about."

"You had contact with NIS?"

"They talked to me."

"About what?"

"Ah. Well," and Donny swallowed, "they had some security concerns and somehow I got —"

"Let me tell you something, goddammit, Fenn. If it happens in *my* platoon, you come tell me about it! You got that? This ain't a one-man goddamn motherfucking operation. You come tell me, Fenn, or by God I will make your young sorry ass sorry you didn't!"

The man's blazing spit flew into Donny's face and his eyes lit up like flares. A vein throbbed on his forehead.

"Sergeant, they told me—"

"I don't give a monkey's fuck what they told you,

Fenn. If it happens in *my* platoon, I have to know about it, or you ain't worth pig shit to me. Copy that, Corporal?"

"Yes, Sergeant."

"You and me, boy, we got some *serious* talk ahead."

Donny swallowed.

"Yes, Sergeant."

"Now, get these men off their asses. I'm not going to have them sitting around all goddamn day like they just won the fucking war all by themselves. Get 'em on work detail, drill 'em, do something with them."

"Yes, Sergeant."

"And you and I will talk later."

"Yes, Sergeant."

Donny turned in the wake of Sergeant Case's departure, which was more like an ejection from a jet fighter than a normal retrograde adjustment.

"Okay," he said to the squad. "Okay, let's get outside and run through some riot control drills. There's no point just sitting in here."

But nobody moved.

"All right, come on, guys. I'm not shitting around here. You heard the man. We have an order."

They just stared at him. Some looked hurt, the rest disgusted.

"I didn't do *anything*," Donny said. "I talked to some Navy lifers and that's all."

"Donny, if I flash the peace sign in a bar, will you turn me in to NIS?" someone asked.

"All right, fuck that shit!" Donny bellowed. "I don't have to explain *anything* to *anybody*! But if I did, I'd point out I didn't rat *anybody* out. Now, get into your gear and let's get the fuck outside or Case'll have us on a barracks party until 0400 next Tuesday!"

The men got up, but their slow heaviness expressed their bitterness.

"Who'll take Crowe's place?" someone asked.

There was no answer.

Julie was released from the lockup at the Washington Coliseum at 4 P.M. that same day, after forty-eight hours of incarceration with several hundred of the more recalcitrant demonstrators. At least physically, it was almost pleasant being arrested; the cops were old hands by this time and as long as everybody cooperated, the process was all right. She spent two nights on a cot in a field where the Washington Redskins practiced when it was their season. The seats of the junky old place rose above like a Pentecostal cathedral from the twenties, and in the pen, all the kids had a good time and nobody watched them too carefully. Grass was abundant; the portable toilets were cleaner than the ones at Potomac Park. The showers were never crowded and she got a good wash for the first time since leaving Arizona in the Peace Caravan. Some of the boys caught fantasy touchdown passes in what had to have been an end zone.

But no word at all from Donny. Had he been there on the bridge? She didn't know. She'd looked for him, but then it'd all dissolved in confusion and tears as more of the gas flooded in. She remembered crumpling, rubbing her eyes desperately as the gas drifted by, and then there was the shock of the Marines and she found herself looking into the eyes of a boy, a child, really, big and booming behind his lenses; she saw fear in them, or at least as much confusion as she herself felt, and then he was by her and the Marine line moved on, and as she watched, teams of policemen pounced on the demonstrators behind the lines and led them away to buses. It was handled very simply, no big deal at all to anybody concerned.

Only later, in the lockup, did the word come that a girl had somehow died. Julie tried to work it out but could make no sense of it; the Marines had seemed quite restrained, really; it wasn't anything like Kent State. Still, it was an appalling weight. A girl was dead, and for what? Why was it necessary? In the lockup, they had a television, and Amy Rosenzweig's young and tender face, freckled, under sprigs of reddish hair, was everywhere. She looked to Julie like a girl she'd grown up with, though she could not remember seeing Amy amid the crowd, but that wasn't surprising, for there had been thousands, and much confusion on the ground.

They let her out and she went back to the campground in Potomac Park. It was like a Civil War encampment after Gettysburg: mostly empty now that the big week was over and the kids in their multitudes had returned to their campuses and the professional revolutionaries to their secret cabals to plot the next move in the war against the war. Litter was everywhere and the cops no longer bothered. A few tents still stood, but the sense of a new youth culture had vanished. There was no music and no campfires and the Peace Caravan had departed. All, that is, except for Peter.

"Oh, hi."

"Hi, how are you?"

"Fine. I stayed behind. Jeff and Susie are driving the Micro back. Everybody is with them. They'll be all right. I wanted to stay here, see if you needed anything."

"I'm okay, Peter, really I am. Have you seen Donny at all?"

"Him? Jesus, you know what they did to that girl and you want to know where *he* is?"

"Donny didn't do anything. Besides, I read the Marines tried to save her."

"If there hadn't been any Marines, Amy would still be here," Peter said obstinately, and then the two just looked at each other. He drew her close and hugged her and she hugged back.

"Thanks for hanging around, Peter."

"Ah, it's okay. How was the Coliseum?"

"Okay. Not so bad. They finally reduced charges, parading without a permit. They let us all go today."

"Well," he said. "If you want me to drive you to the Marine Barracks or something, I will. Whatever you want. I have a VW from a guy. It's no problem."

"I'm supposed to get married this week."

"That's fine. That's cool. Good luck and God bless. Let me see if I can help you in any way."

"I think I ought to hang here until I hear from Donny. I don't know what happened to him."

"Sure," said Peter. "That's a good idea."

The alert was finally cancelled at 1600 that afternoon, to the cheers and relief of the companies. It took an hour or so to actually stand down—that is, to return the rifles to the armory, to shed and repack the combat gear in its appropriate place in the lockers, to shed the utilities, bag them for the laundry, shower and shave. But by 1700, when the work was done, the captain at last released his men—the married to go home, the rest to relax in town or on base as they preferred, with only a few left on skeleton duty, such as duty NCO or armory watch.

That is, except for Donny.

He was done, and still in his cone of isolation, finally changing into civvies—jeans and a white Izod shirt—when a runner came from headquarters and said he was wanted ASAP. No, he didn't have to dress in the uniform of the day.

Donny returned to Captain Dogwood's office, where Bonson and Weber waited.

"Captain, we could take him to our offices. Or would you allow us to use yours?"

"Yes, sir, go ahead," said Dogwood, who wanted to get home to see his own wife and kids too. "Stay here. Duty NCO will lock up when you're finished."

"Thank you, Captain," said Bonson.

So Donny was alone with them at last. They were in civilian clothes this time, Weber looking like the Sigma Nu he'd undoubtedly been at Nebraska, and the dour Bonson in slacks and a black sport shirt, buttoned to the top. He looked almost like a priest of some sort.

"Coffee?"

"No, sir."

"Oh, sit down, Fenn. You don't have to stand."

"Yes, sir. Thank you, sir."

Donny sat.

"We want to go over your testimony with you. Tomorrow there'll be an arraignment, at the Judge Advocate General's Offices at the Navy Yard, nothing elaborate. It's simply a preliminary to an indictment and trial. Ten hundred. We'll send a car. Your undress blues will be fine; I've arranged with Captain Dogwood for you to be off the duty roster. Then I think we'll give you a nice bit of leave. Two weeks? By that time, we should be able to cut orders for your new stripes. Sergeant Fenn. How does that sound?"

"Well, I—"

"Tomorrow won't be hard, Fenn, I assure you. You'll be sworn in and then you'll recount how at my instruction you befriended Crowe and traveled with him into a number of peace movement functions. You'll tell how you saw him in the presence of peace movement strategists such as Trig Carter. You saw them in serious conversation, intense conversation. You needn't testify that you *overheard* him giving away deployment intelligence. Just tell what you saw, and let the JAG prosecutor do the rest. It's enough for an indictment. He'll have a lawyer, a JAG JG, who'll ask you some rote questions. Then it's over and done and off you go."

Bonson smiled.

"Clean and simple," said Weber.

"Sir, I just . . . I don't know what I can tell them. There were hundreds of people at those parties. I saw no evidence of *conspiracy* or deployment intelligence or—"

"Now, Donny," said Bonson, leaning forward and trying a smile. "I know this is confusing for you. But trust me. You're doing your country a great service. You're doing the Marines a great service."

"But I—"

"Donny," said Weber, "they knew. They *knew.*"

"Knew?"

"They knew we had Third Infantry committed in Virginia, that the DC National Guard was a complete fuckup, the 101st Airborne was stuck at Justice and the 82nd down at the Key Bridge and that the cops were frazzled beyond endurance after eighty straight duty hours. It was an elaborate game of chess—they move here, we countermove; they move there, we countermove—all set up to get them to that bridge where they'd be faced by United States Marines where the chances of a big-time screwup on television were huge. And that's just what they got: another martyr. Another catastrophe. The Justice Department humiliated. A propaganda victory of immense proportions. They're parading with Amy's name in London and Paris already. Give them credit, it was as skillful a campaign as there was."

"Yes, sir, but we tried to save her. The girl panicked. It had nothing to do with us."

"Oh, it had *everything* to do with you," said Bonson. "They wanted her going off the bridge and the Marines to take the fall. See how much better that is than the Washington Metro Police or some third-rate National Guard unit, most of whom'd be demonstrating themselves if they had the chance? No, they *wanted* a big scandal to be laid right at the Marines' feet and that's what they got! And Crowe gave it to them. Now, it is mandatory to get this fact before the public, to show that we were betrayed from within and to move swiftly to restore confidence in the system by eliminating the treason. And I can't think of a more edifying contrast for the American public than between Crowe, an Ivy League dropout with his fancy connections, and you, a decorated combat veteran from a small Western town doing his duty. It'll be very educational!"

"Yes, sir," said Donny.

"Good, good. Ten hundred. Look sharp, Corporal. You will impress the JAG officers, I know you will. You will inherit your own future, the future you and I have been working on, I know it."

"Yes, sir," said Donny.

They rose.

"All right, Weber, we're finished here. You relax, Fenn. Tomorrow is your big day, the beginning of the rest of your life."

"I'll get the car, sir," said Weber.

"No, I'll get it. You—you know; tell him what's cooking."

"Yes, sir."

Bonson left the two younger men alone.

"Look, Fenn, I'm the bad cop. I'm here to give you the bad news. I've got photos of you smoking grass with Crowe, okay? Man, they can really nail you with them. I mean big time. I told you this guy Bonson was cold. He is beaucoup cold, you know? So give him what he wants, which is another bad boy's scalp to hang up on his lodge pole. He's sent a bunch to the 'Nam, and he wants to send more. I don't know why, what he is driving at, but I know this: he will rotate your ass back to the Land of Bad Things and not ever even *think* about it again. He's got you cold. It's you or it's Crowe. Man, don't throw your life away for nothing, dig?"

"Yes, sir."

"Good man, Fenn. Knew you'd see it our way."

At 2300, Donny just walked out the front door of the barracks. Who was there to stop him? Some corporal in first platoon had duty NCO that night and he was scribbling in the duty logs in the first sergeant's office as Donny passed.

Donny walked to the main gate and waved at the sentry there, who waved him past. Technically, the boy was to look for liberty papers, but in the aftermath of an alert, such niceties of the Marine way had fallen aside. Donny just walked, crossed I Street, headed down the way, took a left, and there found, unbothered, his 1963 Impala. He climbed in, turned the key and drove away.

It didn't take him long to reach Potomac Park, site of the recently abandoned May Tribe. A few tents still stood, a few fires still burned. He left his car along the side of the road and walked into the encampment, asked a few questions and soon found the tent.

"Julie?" he called.

But it was Peter who came out.

"She's sleeping," he said.

"Well, I need to see her."

"It would be better if she slept. I'm watching out for her."

The two faced each other; both wore jeans and tennis shoes, Jack Purcells. But Donny's were white, as he washed them every week. Peter's didn't look as though he had washed them since the fifties. Donny wore a madras short-sleeved button-down shirt; Peter had some kind of tie-dyed T-shirt on, baggy as a parachute, going almost to his knees. Donny's hair was short to the point of neuroticism, with a little pie up top; Peter's was long to the point of neuroticism, a mass of curly sprigs and tendrils. Donny's face was lean and pure; Peter's wore a bristle of scraggly red beard and a headband.

"That's very cool," said Donny. "But I have to see her. I need her."

"I need her too."

"Well, she hasn't given you anything. She's given me her love."

"I want her to give me her love."

"Well, you'll have to wait awhile."

"I'm tired of waiting."

"Look, this is ridiculous. Go away or something."

"I won't leave her unguarded."

"Who do you think I am, some kind of rapist or killer? I'm her fiancé. I'm going to marry her."

"Peter," said Julie, coming out of the tent, "it's all right. Really, it's all right."

"Are you sure?"

Julie looked tired; still, she was a beautiful young woman, with hair the color of straw and a body as lean and straight as an arrow, and brilliance showing behind her bright blue eyes. Both boys looked at her and recommitted to her love again.

"Are you okay?" Donny asked.

"I was in the lockup at the Coliseum."

"Oh, Christ."

"It was fine; it wasn't anything bad."

"You killed a girl," said Peter.

"We didn't kill anyone. *You* killed her, by telling her being on that bridge mattered and that we were rapists and murderers. You made her panic; you made her jump. We tried to save her."

"You fucking asshole, you killed her. Now, you're a big tough guy and you can kick the shit out of me, but you killed her!"

"Stop screaming. I never killed anyone who didn't have a rifle and wasn't trying to kill me or a buddy."

"Peter, it's okay. You have to leave us alone."

"Christ, Julie."

"You have to leave us."

"Ahhh . . . all right. But don't say—anyhow, you're a lucky guy, Fenn. You really are."

He stormed away in the darkness.

"I never saw him so brave," said Julie.

"He loves you. So much."

"He's just a friend."

"I'm sorry I didn't get here earlier. We were on alert. There was a lot of shit because of Amy. I'm very sorry about Amy, but we didn't have a thing to do with it."

"Oh, Donny."

"I want to marry you. I love you. I miss you."

"Then let's get married."

"There's this thing," Donny said.

"This thing?"

"Yeah. By the way, I've technically deserted. I'm UA. Unauthorized absence. I'll be reported tomorrow at morning muster. They'll do something to me probably. But I had to see you."

"Donny?"

"Let me tell you about this thing."

And so he told it: from his recruitment to his attempts to enter into a duplicitous friendship with Crowe to his arrival at the party to his strange behavior that night until, finally, the action on the bridge, Crowe's arrest and tomorrow's responsibilities.

"Oh, God, Donny, I'm so sorry. It's so awful." She went to him and in her warmth for just a second he lost all his problems and was Donny Fenn of Pima County all over again, the football hero, the big guy that everybody thought so highly of, who could do a 40 in four-seven, and bench press 250, yet take pride in his high SATs and the fact that he was decent to his high school's lowliest creeps and toads and never was mean to anybody, because that wasn't his way. But then he blinked, and he was back in the dark in the park, and it was only Julie, her warmth, her smell, her sweetness, and when he left her embrace, it was all back again.

"Donny, haven't you done enough for them? I mean, you got shot, you lay in that horrible hospital for six months, you came back and did exactly what they said. When does it end?"

"It ends when you get out. I don't hate the Corps. It's not a Corps thing. It's these Navy guys, these super patriots, who have it all figured out."

"Oh, Donny. It's so awful."

"I don't work that way. I don't like that stuff at all. That's not me. Not any of it."

"Can't you talk to somebody? Can't you talk to a chaplain or a lawyer or something? Do they even have the right to put you through that?"

"Well, as I understand it, it's not an illegal order. It's a legitimate order. It's not like being asked to do something that's technically wrong, like shoot kids in a ditch. I don't know who I could talk to who wouldn't say, Just do your duty."

"And they'll send you back to Vietnam if you don't testify."

"That's the gist of it, yeah."

"Oh, God," she said.

She turned from him and walked a step or two away. Across the way, she could see the Potomac and the dark far shore that was Virginia. Above it, a tapestry of stars unscrolled, dense and deep.

"Donny," she finally said, "there's only one answer."

"Yeah, I know."

"Go back. Do it. That's what you have to do to save yourself."

"But it's not like I know he's guilty. Maybe he doesn't deserve to get his life ruined just because—"

"Donny. Just do it. You said yourself, this Crowe is not worth a single thing."

"You're right," Donny finally said. "I'll go back, I'll do it, I'll get it over. I'm eleven and days, I'll get out inside a year with an early out, and we can have our life. That's all there is to it. That's fine, that's cool. I've made up my mind."

"No, you haven't," she said. "I can tell when you're lying. You're not lying to me; you never have. But you're lying to yourself."

"I should talk to someone. I need help on this one."

"And I'm not good enough?"

"If you love me, and I hope and pray you do, then your judgment is clouded."

"All right, who, then?"

Who, indeed?

There was only one answer, really. Not the chaplain or a JAG lawyer, not Platoon Sergeant Case or the first sergeant or the sergeant major or the colonel or even the Commandant, USMC.

"Trig. Trig will know. We'll go see Trig."

Bitterly, from afar, Peter watched them. They embraced, they talked, they appeared to fight. She broke away. He went after her. It killed him to sense the intimacy they shared. It was everything he hated in the world—the strong, the handsome, the blond, the confident, just taking what was theirs and leaving nothing behind.

He watched them, finally, go toward Donny's old car and climb in, his mind raging with anger and counterplots, his energy unbearably high.

Without willing it, he raced to the VW Larry Frankel had lent him. He turned the key, jacked the car into gear and sped after them. He didn't know why, he didn't think it would matter, but he also knew he could not help but follow them.

CHAPTER SEVEN

Peter almost missed them. He had just cleared a crest when he saw the lights of the other car illuminate a hill and a dirt road beyond a gate, then flash off. His own lights were off, but there was enough moonlight to make out the road ahead. He pulled up to the gate and saw nothing that bore any signal of meaning, except a mailbox, painted white with the name WILSON scribbled on it in black. He was on Route 35, about five miles north of Germantown.

What the hell were they up to? What did they know? What was going on?

He decided to pull back a hundred yards, and just wait for a while. Suppose they ran in there, and turned around and collided with him on the road? That would be a total humiliation.

Instead, he decided just to watch and wait.

At the top of the hill, they turned the engine off. Below lay a farm of no particular distinction, a nondescript house, a yard, a barn. Propane tanks and old tractors, rusted out, lay in the yard; there was no sound of animals. The farm, in fact, looked like a Dust Bowl relic.

Yet something was going on.

Twin beams illuminated the yard, and Donny, with his unusually good eyesight, could make out a van with its lights on, a shroud of dust, and two men who were in the process of moving heavy packages of some sort out from the barn into the van by the light of the headlamps.

"I think that's Trig," Donny said. "I don't know who the other guy is."

"Shall we go down?"

Donny was suddenly unsure.

"I don't know," he said. "I can't figure out what the hell is going on."

"He's helping his friend load up."

"At this hour?"

"Well, he's an irregular guy. The clock doesn't mean much to him."

That was true; Trig wasn't your nine-to-fiver by any interpretation.

"All right," said Donny. "We'll walk down there. But you hang back. Let me check this out. Don't let them see you until we figure what's happening. I'll call you in, okay? I'm just not feeling good about this, okay?"

"You sound a little paranoid."

He did. Some hint of danger filled the air, but he wasn't sure what it was, what it meant, where it came from. Possibly, it was the mere strangeness of everything, the way nothing really made any sense. Possibly it was his own fatigue, raw after the many hours on alert.

They headed down the hill, and Donny detoured them around the house, until at last they came upon the two men from the rear. Donny could see them better now, both working in jeans and denim shirts. They were loading by wheelbarrow immensely awkward sacks of fertilizer into the van, packing it very full. AMMONIUM NITRATE, the sacks said. Dust that the wheelbarrow tires ripped up from the ground filled the air, floating in large, shimmering clouds, which shifted through the beams of the truck lights and in the yellower light that blazed from the barn door. It lit wherever it could, coating the truck, the men, everything. Both Trig and the other man wore red bandannas around their faces.

Pushing Julie back into the dark, Donny stepped out and approached, coughing at the stuff in the air as it filled his mouth and throat with grit. He stepped farther; nobody noticed him.

"Trig?" he called.

Trig turned instantly at his name, but it was the other man who reacted much faster, turning exactly to Donny, his dark eyes devouring him. He had a full, tangled web of blond hair, much thicker than Trig's, and was large and powerful next to Trig's delicacy. They looked like a poet and a stevedore standing next to each other.

"Trig, it's me, Donny. Donny Fenn." He stepped forward a little hesitantly.

"Donny, Jesus Christ, I didn't expect you."

"Well, you said to come on out."

"I did, yeah. Come on in. Donny, meet Robert Fitzpatrick, my old friend at Oxford."

"Halloo," said Robert, pulling off his own bandanna to show a smile that itself showed a mouthful of porcelain spades, a movie star's gleam of a smile. "So you're the war hero, eh? We've hopes for you, that we do! Need boyos like you for the movement. We'll stop this bloody thing *and* get the west field covered in horseshit and ammonium nitrate, if I'm a judge of things. Roll up your sleeves, boy, and get to work. We could use some back. Me goddamned pickup broke down and I'm stuck with this piece of shit to git the stuff out to the spreader. We're doing it at night to beat the heat."

"Robert, he's been on some kind of alert for seventy-two hours. He can't do manual labor," Trig said.

"No, I—"

"No, we're almost done. It doesn't matter."

"You left so suddenly."

"Ah, one more demonstration. I was worn out. What did it prove? I've lost my will for the movement."

"You'll get your will back, boyo," said the giant Fitzpatrick heartily. "I'll go get us a beer for the recharge. You wait here, Donny Fenn."

"No, no, I just had a thing I wanted to talk over with Trig."

"Oh, Trig'll steer you right, no doubt about it," he said, his voice light with laughter. "It's a drink I'll be gittin', Trig. You lads talk."

With that he turned to the house and headed in.

"So what is it, Donny?"

"It's Crowe . . . they arrested him. Violations of the Uniform Code of Military Justice. I'm supposed to testify against him in"—he looked at his watch—"about seven hours."

"I see."

"Maybe you don't. I was asked to spy on him. That was my job. That's why I got close to him. I was supposed to report to them on his off-base activities and try and put him with known members of the peace groups. That's why I was with him at the party that night; that's why I came to your party. I was ordered to spy."

Trig stared at him for a while, then his face broke into the oddest thing: a smile.

"Oh, that's your big secret? Man, that's *it*?" He laughed now, really hard. "Donny, wise up. You work for them. They can ask you to do that. If they say so, that's your duty. That's the game in Washington these days. Everybody's watching everybody. Everybody's got an agenda, a plan, an idea they're trying to push or sell. I don't give a damn."

"It's worse. They have some idea you were Weather Underground and you planned the whole thing. I mean, can you imagine anything so stupid? He was feeding you deployment intelligence so the May Tribe could humiliate the Corps."

"Boy, their imagination never fails to amaze me!"

"So what should I do, Trig? That's what I'm here to ask. About Crowe. Should I testify?"

"What happens if you don't?"

"They've got some pictures of me smoking dope. Funny, I don't smoke dope anymore, but I did to get in with him. They could send me to Portsmouth. Or, more likely, the 'Nam. They could ship me back for a last go-round, even though I'm short."

"They're really assholes, aren't they?"

"Yeah."

"But that's neither here nor there, is it? This isn't

about them. We know who *they* are. This is about you. Well, then it's easy."

"Easy?"

"Easy. Testify. For one reason, you can't let them get you killed. What would that prove? Who benefits from the death of Lochinvar? Who wins when Lancelot is slain?"

"I'm just a guy, Trig."

"You can't give yourself up to it. Somebody's got to come out on the other side and say how it was."

"I'm just . . . I'm just a guy."

People were always insisting to Donny that he was somehow more than he really was, that he represented something. He'd never gotten it. It was just because he happened to be good-looking, but underneath he was just as scared, just as ineffective, just as simple as anyone else, no matter what Trig said.

"I don't know," said Donny. "Is he guilty? That would matter."

"It doesn't matter. What matters is: you or him? That's the world you have to deal with. You or him? I vote him. Any day of the week, I vote him."

"But is he guilty?"

"I'm no longer in the inner circle. I'm sort of a roaming ambassador. So I really don't know."

"Oh, you'd know. You'd know. Is he guilty?"

Trig paused.

Finally he said, "Well, I wish I could lie to you. But, goddammit, no, no, he's not guilty. There is some weird kind of intelligence they have at the top; I just get glimmerings of it. But I don't think it's Crowe. But I'm telling you the truth: that doesn't matter. You should dump him and get on with your life. If he's not guilty of that, he's guilty of lots of other stuff."

Donny looked at Trig for a bit. Trig was leaning against the fender of the van. He lifted a milk carton and poured it over his head, and water gushed out, scraping rivulets in the dust that adhered to his handsome face. Trig shook his wet hair, and the droplets flew away. Then he turned back.

"Donny, for Christ's sake. Save your own life!"

Peter was no good at waiting. He got out of the car and walked along the shoulder of the road. It was completely dark and silent, unfamiliar sensations to a young man who'd spent so much time OCS—on city streets. Now and then he heard the chirp of a cricket; up above, the stars towered and pinwheeled, but he was not into stars or insects, so he noticed neither of these realities. Instead, he reached the gate, paused a moment, and climbed over. He saw before him a faint rise in the land, almost a small hill, and the dirt road that climbed it. He knew if a car came over the hill and he were standing on that road, he'd be dead-cold caught in the lights. So he walked a distance from the road, then turned to head up the hill, figuring he could then drop to the ground if Donny and Julie returned.

Gently, he walked up the hill, feeling as alone as that guy who had walked on the surface of the moon. He reached the top of the hill and saw the farmhouse below him. No sight of Julie but he saw Trig and Donny slouched on the fender of a van in the yard between the house and the barn, and they were chatting animatedly, relaxed and intimate. There was no sign of danger, no sign of weirdness: just two new friends bullshiting in the night.

But then small things began to seem off. What was Trig doing way out here? What was this place? What was going on? It connected with nothing in Peter's memory of Trig.

Puzzled, he stepped forward and almost tripped as he bumbled into something.

Two figures rose before him.

Oh, shit, he thought, for they wore suits and one of them carried a camera with a long lens.

Clearly they were feds, spying on Trig.

They had the pug look of FBI agents, with blunt faces

and crew cuts; one wore a hat. They did not look happy to be discovered.

"W-who are you?" Peter asked in a quavering voice. "What are you doing?"

"I don't think I can sell him out," said Donny.

"Donny, this isn't a Western. There are no good guys. Do you hear me? This is real life, hardball style. If it's you or Crowe, do not give yourself up for Crowe."

"I suppose that's the smart move," said Donny.

"So, there," said Trig. "I made your decision easy for you. All you have to do is cooperate with them. Come on, when the war is over, they'll reduce his sentence. He may never even serve a day. They'll work some deal, he'll get out and go on with the rest of his life. He won't even be upset."

Donny remembered that once upon a time, even Crowe had given him the same advice. *Roll over on me in a second, Donny, if it ever comes to that.* Somehow Crowe had known it would.

"Okay," he finally said.

"Do your duty, Donny. But think about what it costs you. Okay. Think about how you feel now. Then when you get out, do me one favor, okay? No matter what happens to me, promise me one thing."

Trig winced as if in pain in the hot light of the head-lights, though perhaps something had just gotten in his eye. There was an immense familiarity to that look, the strain on his face, the set of it, the clearness of vision. And . . . And what?

"Sure," Donny said.

"Open your mind. Open your mind to the possibility that the power to define *duty* is the power of life and death. And if people impose duty on you, maybe they're not doing it for your best interests or the country's best interests but for their own best interests. Okay, Donny? Force yourself to think about a world in which each man got to set his own duty and no one could tell anyone what to do, what was right, what was wrong; the only rules were the Ten Commandments."

"I—" stammered Donny.

"Here," said Trig. "I have something for you. I was going to mail it to you from Baltimore, but this'll save me the postage and the fuss. It's no big deal."

He went over to some kind of knapsack on the ground, fished around, and came out with a folder, which he opened to reveal a piece of heavy paper.

"Sometimes," he said, "when the spirit moves me, I'm even pretty good. I'm much better at birds, but I did okay on this one. It's nothing."

Donny looked: it was a drawing on a creamy page trimmed from that sketchbook Trig was always carrying, incredibly delicate and in a spiderweb of ink, that depicted himself and Julie as they stood and talked in the trees at West Potomac Park.

There was something special about it: he got them both, maybe not exactly as a photograph, but somehow their love too, the way they looked at each other, the faith they had in each other.

"Wow," said Donny.

"Wow, yourself. I dashed it off that night in my book. It was neat, the two of you. Gives me hope for the world. Now, go on, get the hell out of here, go back to your duty."

Trig drew him close, and Donny felt the warmth, the musculature, and maybe something else, too: passion, somehow, oddly misplaced but genuine and impressive. Trig was actually crying.

Over the shoulders of the two FBI agents, Peter saw Donny and Trig embrace, and then Donny stepped out of the light and was gone. He'd head to his car, which Peter now saw was but fifty or so yards away. He was screwed. Donny would see him here with the two feds, who showed no sign at all of moving, and he would have made an ass out of himself.

He felt despair rising in his gorge.

"I have to go," he said to the larger of the two plain-clothes officers.

"No," the man said back, and the other moved to embrace Peter, as if to wrestle him to the ground. Peter squirmed out of the man's grip, but he was grabbed and thrust to the ground.

The two men loomed over him.

"This is ridiculous," he said.

They seemed to agree. They looked at each other foolishly, not quite sure what to do, but suddenly one of them pointed.

Then the engine of Donny's car came to life and its lights flashed on.

The man with the camera pulled away from Peter, leaving the other, the bigger, to lean on him, and ran toward the gate.

"Well, did he help?" said Julie as they walked through the dark.

"Yeah," said Donny. "Yes, he did. He really did. I've got it figured out now."

"Should I go meet him?"

"No, he's in a very strange mood. I'm not sure what's going on. Let's just get out of here. I've got some things to do."

"What did he give you?"

"It's a picture. It's very nice. I'll show you later."

They walked through the dark, up the hill. Donny could see the car ahead. He had an odd tremor suddenly, a sense of not being alone. It was a freakish thing, sometimes useful in Indian country: that sensation of being watched. He scanned the darkness for sign of threat but saw nothing, only farmland under moon, no movement or anything.

"Who was that blond guy?" she asked.

"His pal Fitzpatrick. Big Irish guy. They were loading up to spread fertilizer."

"That's strange."

"He said they decided to do the hard part of the job in the cool of the night. Hell, it was only fertilizer. Who knows?"

"What was going on with Trig?"

"I don't know. He was, uh, *strange* is all I can call it. He had the same look on his face that the *Time* photographer got, when he was carrying that bleeding kid in from the cops in Chicago and his own head was bleeding too. He was very set, very determined, but somehow, underneath it all, very emotional. He seemed like he was facing death or something. I don't know why or what. It spooked me a little."

"Poor Trig. Maybe even the rich boys have demons."

"He wanted to hug. He was crying. Maybe there was something weirdo in it or something. I felt his fingers in my muscles and I felt how happy he was to be hugging me. I don't know. Very weird stuff. I don't know."

They reached the car, and Donny started it, turning on the lights. He backed into the grass, turned around and headed down the road to the gate.

"Jesus," he said. "Duck!" For at that moment a figure suddenly rose from a gulch. A man in a suit, but too far away to do anything. A camera came up. Donny winced at the bright beam of flash as it exploded his night vision. Fireballs danced in his head, reminding him of nighttime incoming Hotel Echo, but he stepped on the gas, gunned up the road and turned right, then really floored it.

"Jesus, they got our picture," he said. "A fed. That guy had to be FBI! Holy Christ!"

"My face was turned," said Julie.

"Then you're okay. I don't think he got a license number, because my rear plate illumination bulb is broken. He just got my picture. A lot of good that'll do them. A fed! Man, this whole thing is strange."

"I wonder what's going on?" she said.

"What's going on is that Trig's about to get busted.

Trig and that Fitzpatrick guy. We were lucky we weren't rounded up. I'd be on my way to the brig."

"Poor Trig," said Julie.

"Yes," said Donny. "Poor Trig."

The man let him up. He brushed himself off.

"I haven't *done* anything," Peter explained. "I've come to see my friends. You have no right to detain me, do you understand? I haven't *done* anything."

The man stared at him sullenly.

"I'm going now. This is none of your business," he said.

He turned and walked away. The agent had seemed genuinely cowed. He stepped away, awaiting a call, but none came. Another step filled him with confidence, but he didn't see or hardly feel the judo chop that broke his spine and, in the fullness of his tender youth and in the ardor of his love for his generation and its pure idea of peace, killed him before he hit the ground.

CHAPTER EIGHT

Donny reached DC around four in the morning, and he and Julie checked into a motel on New York Avenue, in the tourist strip approaching downtown. They were too tired for sex or love or talk.

He set the cheap alarm for 0800, and slept deeply until its ungentle signal pulled him awake.

"Donny?" she said, stirring herself.

"Sweetie, I've got some things to do now. You just stay here, get some more sleep. I paid for two nights. I'll call you sometime today and we'll decide what to do next."

"Oh, Donny." She blinked awake. Even out of sleep, with a slightly puffy face and her hair a rat's nest, she seemed to him quite uniquely beautiful. He leaned over and kissed her.

"Don't do anything stupid and noble," she said. "They'll kill you."

"Don't you worry about me," he said. "I'll be all right."

He dressed and drove the mile or so through the section of city called SE, passing Union Station, then left up the hill until he was in the shadow of the great Capitol dome, turning down Pennsylvania, then down Eighth. He arrived, found parking on a street just off the shops across from the barracks, locked the car and headed to the main gate.

From across Eighth Street, the little outpost of Marine elegance seemed serene. The officers' houses along the street were stately and magnificent; between them, Donny could see men on the parade deck in their modified blues, at parade practice, endlessly trying to master the arcane requirements of duty and ritual. The imprecations of the NCOs rose in the air, harsh, precise, demanding. The grass on which the young men toiled was deep green, intense and pure, like no other green in Washington in that hot, bleak spring.

Finally, he walked across the street to the main gate, where a PFC watched him come.

"Corporal Fenn, you've been reported UA," the PFC said.

"I know. I'll take care of it."

"I've been ordered to notify your company commander of your arrival."

"Do your duty, then, Private. Do you call Shore Patrol?"

"They didn't say anything about that. But I have to call Captain Dogwood."

"Go ahead, then. I'm changing into my duty uniform."

"Yes, Corporal."

Donny walked through the main gate, across the cobblestone parking lot and turned left down Troop Walk to the barracks.

As he went, he was aware of a strange phenomenon: the world seemed to stop, or at least the Marine Corps world. It seemed that whole marching platoons halted to follow his progress. He felt hundreds of eyes on him, and the air suddenly emptied of its usual fill of barked commands.

Donny went in, climbed the ladder well as he had done so many hundreds of times, turned left on the second deck landing and into the squad bay, at the end of which was his little room.

He unlocked his locker, stripped, slipped into flipflops and a towel and marched to the showers, where he scalded himself in water and disinfectant soap. He washed, dried, and headed back to his room, where he slipped on a new pair of boxers and pulled out his oxfords.

They could be better. For the next ten minutes he applied the full weight of his attention to the shoes, in regulation old Marine Corps fashion, until he had burnished the leather to a high gleam. As he finished the shoes, the tough professional figure of Platoon Sergeant Case came to hover in the door.

"I had to put you on UA, Fenn," he said, in that old Corps voice that sounded like sandpaper on brass. "Do you want me to Article Fifteen your young ass?"

"I was late. I had personal business. I apologize."

"You're not on the duty roster. They say you've got some legal obligations at ten hundred."

"Yes, Sergeant. In the Navy Yard."

"Well, I'll get you off report. You do the right thing today, Marine. Do you hear me?"

"Yes, Sergeant."

Case left him alone after that.

Though he hadn't been so ordered, and in fact didn't even know the uniform of the day, he decided to put on his blue dress A uniform. He pulled on socks and taped them to his shins so that they'd never fall, selected a pair of blue dress trousers from the hanger and pulled them on. He tied his shiny oxfords. He pulled on a T-shirt, and over it, finally, the blue dress tunic with its bright brass buttons and red piping. He pulled tight the immaculately tailored tunic, and buttoned up to that little cleric's collar, where the eagle, globe and anchor stood out in brass bas-relief. He pulled on a white summer belt, drawing it tight, giving him the torso of a young Achilles on a stroll outside Troy. His white summer gloves and white summer cover completed the transformation into total Marine.

The medals, reduced to ribbons, stood out on his chest—nothing spectacular, for the Marines are a dour bunch, not into show: only a smear of red denoting the very hot day when he'd slithered through rice water and buffalo shit with half the world shooting at him to pull a wounded PFC back into the world, to life, to possibility. The blur of purple was for the bullet that had passed through his chest a few weeks later. The rest was basically crap: a National Defense Ribbon, the in-service RSVN award, the Presidential Unit Citation for the overall III Marine Amphibious Force presence in the Land of Bad

Things, the Vietnamese Cross of Gallantry and expert marksman in rifle and pistol with second awards. It was no chest of fruit salad, but it did say, This man is a Marine, who's been in the field, who was shot at, who tried to do his duty.

He adjusted the white summer cover until it came low over his blue eyes, then turned and went to face Commander Bonson.

He left the barracks and headed toward the captain's office, where he was to be picked up. The XO wandered by and he snapped off a quick salute.

"Fenn, is that the uniform of the day?"

"For what I have to do, sir, yes, sir."

"Fenn— Never mind. Go ahead."

"Thank you, sir."

Two NCOs, including Case, watched him go. By the time he reached Troop Walk, by some strange vibration in the air, everyone knew he was in his full dress blues. The men, in their modifieds, watched him with suspicion, maybe a little hostility, but above all, curiosity. The uniform, of course, was not the uniform of the day, and for a Marine to strut out in so flagrant a gesture of rebellion was extremely odd; he could have been naked and caused less of a ruckus.

Donny strode down Troop Walk, aware of the growing number of eyes upon him. He had a fleeting impression of men running to catch a glimpse of him going; even, across the way, when he passed by Center House, the base's BOQ, a couple of off-duty first lieutenants came out onto the porch in Bermudas and T's to watch him pass by.

He turned into the parking lot, where a tan government Ford, with a squid driving, waited by the steps; he then turned left, climbed and walked across the porch and into the first sergeant's office, which led to Captain Dogwood's office. The first sergeant, holding a cup of coffee with *Semper Fi* emblazoned on the porcelain, nodded at him, as orderlies and clerks scurried to make way.

"They're waiting on you, Fenn."

"Yes, First Sergeant," said Donny.

He stepped into the office.

Captain Dogwood sat behind his desk, and Bonson and Weber, in their summer khakis, sat across from him.

"Sir, Corporal Fenn, reporting as ordered, *sir,*" Donny said.

"Ah, very good, Fenn," said Dogwood. "Did you misunderstand the uniform of the day? I—"

"Sir, no, *sir!*" Donny said. "Sir, permission to speak, *sir?*"

Another moment of silence.

"Fenn," said the captain, "I'd consider carefully before—"

"Let him speak," said Bonson, eyeing Donny without love.

Donny turned to face the man fully.

"Sir, the corporal wishes to state categorically that he will not testify against a fellow Marine on charges of which he has no personal knowledge. He will not perjure himself; he will not take part in any proceedings involving the Uniform Code of Military Justice. *Sir!*"

"Fenn, what are you pulling?" asked Weber. "We had an agreement."

"*Sir,* we never had an agreement. You gave me orders to investigate, which I did, against my better instincts and in contravention to every moral belief I have. I did my duty. My investigation was negative. Sir, that is all I have to say, *sir!*"

"Fenn," said Bonson, fixing him with a mean glare, "you have no idea what forces you're playing with and what can happen to you. This is no game; this is the serious business of defending the security of our nation."

"Sir, I have fought for our nation and I have bled for our nation. No man who hasn't has the right to tell me about defending our nation, whatever his rank, *sir!* Finally, sir, may I sincerely say, *sir,* you are an asshole and a creep and you haven't done one thing for the United

States of America, and if you want to meet me out back, let's go. Bring Weber. I'll kick his ass too!"

"Fenn!" said Dogwood.

"All right, Captain Dogwood," said Bonson. "I see this is the kind of Marine you have here at Eighth and I. I'm very disappointed. This reflects on *you*, Captain, and my report will so state. Fenn, if I were you, I'd start packing. Don't forget your jungle boots."

He turned and walked out.

"That was stupid, Fenn," said Weber.

"Fuck you, Weber, you ass-kissing creep."

Weber swallowed and turned to Dogwood.

"Restrict him to quarters. His orders will be cut by four."

Then he turned and walked out.

Dogwood went to the phone and talked in an intimate voice with someone. Then he hung up.

"Sit down, Fenn," said Dogwood, turning back to Donny. "Do you smoke?"

"No, sir."

"Well, I do." Shaking a little, he lit up a Marlboro and went to the door.

"Welch, get in here!"

Welch scurried in.

"Yes, sir."

"You have until four, Welch, to get liberty papers cut for Corporal Fenn; get 'em back here for my signature. Seventy-two hours. If you have to run over to personnel at Henderson Hall, you take my car and driver. Don't stop for traffic. Do you understand?"

"Uh, well, sir, I, it's highly irregular, I'm not—"

"You heard me, Welch," said the captain. "Now get going."

He turned back to Donny.

"Okay, Fenn, I can't save you from Vietnam, but I can get you some time off before you have to go if I can get your orders cut before Bonson's paperwork catches up with you."

"Yes, sir."

"You go change into civvies now. You be ready to take off as soon as possible."

"Yes, sir. I— Thank you, sir."

"Oh, just a moment. Yes, here she is."

A woman walked into the room, pleasant, in her late twenties. Donny recognized her from the picture on the desk as Dogwood's wife.

"Here, Mort," she said, handing an envelope over. She turned to Donny. "You must be very foolish, young man. Or very brave."

"I don't know, ma'am."

"Fenn, here. It's six hundred dollars, cash. It's all we had in our quarters. It'll take you and your girlfriend someplace for a few days."

"Sir, I—"

"No, no, go ahead, son. Take it. Enjoy yourself. Pay it back when you can. And when you get to the 'Nam, keep your ass down. That shithole isn't worth another Marine. Not a single one. Now go. Go, go, son. And good luck."

PART II

SNIPER TEAM
SIERRA-BRAVO FOUR

RSVN, I Corps
February–May 1972

CHAPTER NINE

The rain fell in torrents in I Corps. It was the end of the rainy season and no rainier season is rainier than the one in the Republic of South Vietnam. Da Nang, the capital of this dying empire, was wet, but some further hundred klicks out, wetter still, lay the fortified fire base a few of the Marines left in the Land of Bad Things called Dodge City, a ramshackle slum of sandbags, 105mm howitzers, S-shops, bunkers, barbed wire and filthy, open four-holers. It was the tail end of a lost war and nobody wanted to get wasted before the orders were cut that got these sad boys home.

But there were Marines even beyond Dodge City, out in Indian Country. There, in a tangle of scrub trees near the top of a hill identified on maps only by its height in meters—Hill 519—two of them cowered in the downpour, watching the drops accumulate on the rims of their boonie caps, gather and finally drop off, while the rain beat a cold tattoo against the ponchos that covered both of them and their gear.

One of them dreamed of home. It was Lance Corporal Donny Fenn, and he was getting very short. In May, his four-year enlistment was up; he was home free. He knew his DEROS by heart, as did every man in the 'Nam, the ones who first came in 1965, the ones who were still there: Date of Estimated Return from Overseas Service. Donny's was 07 May 1972. He was a two-tour guy, with a Purple Heart and a Bronze Star, and though he no longer believed in the war, he did believe, passionately, that he was going to make it. He had to.

On this wet morning, Donny dreamed of dry pleasures. He dreamed of the desert, from where he'd come, Pima County, Arizona, the town of Ajo, and the hot dry air that pulsed down from the Sonoras out of Mexico, dry as the devil's breath. He dreamed of baking in such a place, going back to college, on to law school. He dreamed of a house, of a family, a job. Most of all, he dreamed of his young wife, who had just written him, and the words were inscribed in his mind now as he sat in the downpour: "You keep your spirits high, Marine! I know you'll make it and I pray for that day. You are the best thing that ever happened to me and I cannot live without you, so if you get killed, I am going to be plenty angry! I might never talk to you again, I would be so mad."

He had written her back just before this boonie jaunt: "Oh, you sweet thang, I do miss you so. Things are fine here. I didn't know spiders could get big as lobsters or that it could rain for three solid months, but these are useful facts and will come in ever so handy back in the world. But the Sarge will keep me alive, because he's the smartest Marine that ever lived or breathed and he said if I got wasted, who the hell would he pick on and that would be no fun at all!"

Rolled into his hatband, swaddled in cellophane, was a picture of Julie, now out of her hippie phase, though she worked at the Tucson Veterans Hospital among the wounded from another war and was even talking of a nursing career now. In the picture, Julie's beauty was like a beam in the night for a man lost and starving.

A shiver rose through Donny's spine, a deep and relentless cold. The world had liquified: it was mud, fog or rain; no other elements existed. It was an almost incandescent world, whose low lights yielded no hint to time of day. The vapors simply floated in gray murk, a kind of universal declamation of misery.

Under his poncho he felt the coldness of one of the few M14s left in Vietnam, with a twenty-round magazine leaning into his leg, ready for instant deployment if Sierra-Bravo-Four were bounced, but that would never happen because the sergeant was so skilled at picking hides.

He carried two canteens, a 782-pack full of C-rats,

mostly barbecued pork, four M26 grenades, a Colt .45 automatic, an M-49 spotting scope, a black phosphate-bladed K-Bar, ten extra twenty-round 7.62 NATO mags, three Claymore mine bandoleers, one M57 electrical firing device, a canvas bag full of flares and a flare launcher, and, enemy of his life, bane of his existence, most hated of all objects on the face of the earth, a PRC-77 radio, fourteen pounds of lifeline to Dodge.

"Commo check," said the sergeant, who sat a few feet from Donny, gazing at the same rain-blasted, foliage-dense landscape, the plains and paddies and jungles and low, mean hills. "Get on the horn, Pork."

"Shit," said Donny, for deploying the radio meant moving, moving meant breaking the steamy seal the poncho had formed around his neck, which meant cold water would cascade down his neck into the sweaty warmth of his body. There was no colder place than Vietnam, but that was okay, because there was no hotter place, either.

Donny stirred in the tent of his poncho, got the Prick-77 up and on, knew its freak was preset accurately, and managed somehow, leaning it forward precariously, to let its four feet of whip antenna snap forward and out into the wet air.

He brought the phone to his ear up through his poncho and pushed the on-off toggle to ON. And, yes, a shivery blade of water sluiced down between his shoulder blades, underneath his jungle cammies. He shivered, said "Fuck" under his breath and continued to struggle with the radio.

The problem with the Pricks wasn't only their limited range, their dense weight, their line-of-sight operational capabilities but, more critically, their short battery lives. Therefore grunts used them sparingly on preset skeds, contacting base for a fast sitrep. He pressed SEND.

"Foxtrot-Sandman-Six, this is Sierra-Bravo-Four, over?"

He pressed RECEIVE, and for his efforts got a crackly

soup of noise. No big surprise, with the low clouds, the rain, and the terrain's own vagaries at play; sometimes they got through and sometimes they didn't.

He tried again.

"Foxtrot-Sandman-Six, this is Sierra-Bravo-Four, do you read? Is anybody there? Hello, knock, knock, please open the door, over?"

The response was the same.

"Maybe they're all asleep," he said.

"Naw," said the sergeant, in his rich Southern drawl, slow and steady and funny as shit, "it's too late to be stoned and too early to be drunk. This is the magic hour when them boys are probably alert. Keep trying."

Donny hit the send button and repeated his message a couple more times without luck.

"I'm going to the backup freak," he finally stated.

The sergeant nodded.

Donny spread the poncho so that he could get at the simple controls atop the unit. Two dials seemed to grin at him next to the two butterfly knobs that controlled them, one for megahertz, the other for kilohertz. He diddled, looking for 79.92, to which Dodge City sometimes defaulted if there was heavy radio traffic or atmospheric interference, and as he did, the radio prowled through the wave band of communications that was Vietnam in early 1972, propelled by the weird reality that it could receive from a far greater distance than it could send.

They heard a lost truck driver trying to get back to Highway 1, a pilot looking for his carrier, a commo clerk testing his gear, all of it crackly and fragmented as the signals in their varying strengths ebbed and flowed. Some of it was in Vietnamese, for the ARVN were on the same net; some of it was Army, for there were more soldiers than Marines left by fifty-odd thousand; some of it was Special Forces, as a few of the big A-camps still held out to the north or west; some of it was fire missions, permission to break off search, requests for more beer and beef.

Finally, Donny lit where he wanted.

"Ah, Foxtrot-Sandman-Six, this is Sierra-Bravo-Four, do you copy?"

"Sierra-Bravo-Four, Foxtrot-Sandman-Six here; yes, we copy. What is your sitrep, over?"

"Tell 'em we're drowning," said the sergeant.

"Foxtrot-Sandman-Six, we're all wet. Nothing moving up here. Nothing living up here, Foxtrot, over."

"Sierra-Bravo-Four, does Swagger want to call an abort? Over."

"They want to know, do you want to call an abort?"

The hunter-killer mission was slated to go another twenty-four hours before air evac, but the sergeant himself appeared to be extremely low on the probability of contact at this time.

"Affirmative," he said. "No bad guys anywhere. They're too smart to go out in shit like this. Tell 'em to get us the hell out of here as soon as possible."

"That's an affirmative, Foxtrot-Sandman-Six. Request air evac, over."

"Sierra-Bravo-Four, our birds are grounded. You'll have to park it until we can get airborne again."

"Shit, they're souped in," said Donny.

"Okay, tell 'em we'll sit tight and wait for the weather to break, but we ain't bringing home any scalps."

Donny hit SEND.

"Foxtrot, we copy. We'll sit tight and get back to you when the sun breaks through, over."

"Sierra-Bravo-Four, roger that. Out."

The radio crackled to silence.

"Okay," said Donny, "that about ties that one up."

"Yeah," said the sergeant, with just a hint of a question in his voice.

"Pork," he said after a second or two, "was you paying attention while you were going to the backup freak? You hear anything?"

The sergeant was like a cop who could understand and decipher the densest code or the most broken-up sound bits on the radio.

"No, I didn't hear a thing," said Donny. "The chatter, you know, the usual stuff."

"Okay, do me a favor, Pork."

He always called Donny "Pork." He called all his spotters Pork. He'd had three spotters before Donny.

"Pork, you run through them freaks real slow and you concentrate. I thought I heard a syllable that sounded like 'gent.' "

"Gent? As in *gent*-lemen prefer blondes?"

"You got a blonde, you should know. No, as in *ur*-gent."

Donny's fingers clicked slowly through the chatter on the double dials as a hundred different signals came and went in the same fractured militarese, made more incomprehensible by radio abbreviations, the tangle of codes and call signs, Alpha-Four-Delta, Delta-Six-Alpha, Whiskey-Foxtrot-Niner, Iron-Tree-Three, Rathole-Zulu-Six, Tan San Nhut control, on and on, *Good morning, Vietnam, how are you today, it's raining.* It meant nothing.

But the sergeant leaned forward, his whole body tense with concentration, unshivery in the wet, hardly even human in his intensity. He was a thin stick of a man, twenty-six, with a blond crew cut, a sunburn so deep it had almost changed his race, cheekbones like bed knobs, squinty gray squirrel-shooter's eyes, 100 percent American redneck with an accent that placed him in the backwoods of some underdeveloped principality far from sophisticated living, but with an odd grace and efficiency to him.

He had no dreams, not of desert, not of a farm or a city, not of home, not of hearth. He was total kick-ass professional Marine Corps lifer, and if he dreamed of anything, it was only of that harsh and bitter bitch Duty, whom he'd never once cheated on, whom he'd honored and served on two other tours, one as a platoon sergeant in sixty-five and another running long-range patrols up near the DMZ for SOG. If he had an inner life, he kept it to himself. They said he'd won some big civilian shooting tournament and they said his daddy was a Marine too, back in World War II, and won the Medal of Honor, but the sergeant never mentioned this and who would have the guts to ask? He had no family, he had no wife or girlfriend, he had no home, nothing except the Marine Corps and a sense that he had been produced by turbulent, hardscrabble times, of which he preferred not to speak and on whose agonies he would remain forever silent.

He was many other things, but only one of them mattered to Donny. He was the best. Man, he was good! He was so fucking good it made your head spin. If he fired, someone died, an enemy soldier always. He never shot if he didn't see a weapon. But when he shot, he killed. Nobody told him otherwise, and nobody would fuck with him. He was supercool in action, the ice king, who just let it happen, kept his eyes and ears open and figured it out so fast it made you dizzy. Then he reacted, took out any moving bad guys, and went about his business. It was like being in Vietnam with Mick Jagger, or some other legendary star, because everybody knew who Bob the Nailer was, and if they didn't love him, by God, they feared him, because he was also Death From Afar, the Marine Corps way. He was more rifle than man, and more man than anybody. Even the NVA knew who he was: it was said a 15,000-piastre bounty had been placed on his head. The sergeant thought this was pretty funny.

But in the end, it would kill him, Donny thought. The war would eat him up in the end. He would try one more brave and desperate thing, eager somehow to keep it going, to press himself even further, and it would, in the end, kill his heroic ass. He'd never hit his DEROS. For boys like this, there was no such thing as DEROS. Vietnam was forever.

He reminded Donny of someone but Donny hadn't figured it out. There was something about him, however, oddly familiar, oddly resonant. This had struck him before but he could never quite nail it down. Was it a teacher somewhere? Was it a relative, a Marine from his earlier tour or his time at Eighth and I? For a time, he'd thought it was Ray Case, his furious platoon sergeant there, but as he got to know Bob, that connection vaporized. Case was a good, tough, professional Marine, but Bob was a great Marine. They didn't make many of them like Bob Lee Swagger.

But who was he like? Why did he seem so familiar?

Donny shook the confusion out of his head.

Swagger sat under the poncho, the water dripping off his boonie hat, his eyes almost blank as he listened to the crackly tapestry of radio. He was as equally laden as Donny: the taped bull barrel of his M40 sniper rifle—really just a Remington 700 .308 Varmint with a Redfield 9X scope aboard—poked out from the neck of his poncho as he did what he could to keep the action and the wood, which would swell with moisture, dry. He also carried four M26 grenades, two Claymore bandoleers, an M57 electrical firing device, a .45 automatic, two canteens and a 782-pack full of C-rats (preferred poison: ham and powdered eggs), and seventy-two rounds of M118 Lake City Arsenal Match ammo, the 173-grain load used by Army and Marine high-powered shooters at Camp Perry. But he was a man who traveled well prepared; he had a Randall Survivor knife with a sawtooth blade, a Colt .380 baby hammerless in an aviator's shoulder holster under his camo utilities and, strapped to his back, an M3 grease gun and five thirty-round magazines.

"There," he said. "You hear it? Swear to Christ I heard something."

Donny had heard nothing in the murk of chatter; still, he slowed his diddling and redialed, watching the little numbers on the face crackle through the gap as he shifted them. Finally he lit on something so soft you could miss it entirely, and he only received it because it seemed to be right on the cusp of the megahertz click to another freak; if he took the tension off the knob, the signal disappeared.

But, raspy and distant, they did hear it, and the words seemed to define themselves out of the murk until they became distinct.

"Anyone on this net? Anyone on this net? How you read me? Over? Urgent, goddammit, over!"

There was no answer.

"This is Arizona-Six-Zulu. I have beaucoup bad guys all over the goddamn place. Anyone on this net? Charlie-Charlie-November, you there, over?"

"He's way out of our range," Donny said. "And who the hell is Arizona-Six-Zulu?" Donny wondered.

"He's got to be one of the Special Forces camps to the west. They use states as call signs. They call 'em FOBs, forward operating bases. He's trying to reach Charlie-Charlie-November, which is SOG Command and Control North at Da Nang."

But Arizona-Six-Zulu got a callback.

"Arizona-Six-Zulu, this is Lima-Niner-Mike at Outpost Hickory. Is that you, Puller? Can hardly read your signal, over."

"Lima-Niner-Mike, my big rig took a hit and I'm on the Prick-77. I have big trouble. I have bad guys all over the place hitting me frontally and I hear from scouts a main force unit is moving in to take my base camp out. I need air or arty, over."

"Arizona-Six-Zulu, neg on the air. We are souped in and everything has been grounded. Let me check on arty, over."

"I am Team Arizona base camp, grid square Whiskey Delta 5120-1802. I need Hotel Echo in the worst possible way, over."

"Shit, neg to that, Arizona-Six-Zulu. I have no, repeat no, fire support bases close enough to get shells to your area. They closed down Mary Jane and Suzie Q last week, and the Marines at Dodge are too far, over."

"Over, Lima-Niner-Mike, I am out here on my lonesome with eleven Americans and four hundred indigs and we are in heavy shit and I am running down on ammo, food, and water. I need support ASAP, over."

"I have your coordinates, Arizona-Six-Zulu, but I have no artillery fire bases operational within range. I will go to Navy to see if we can get naval gunfire in range and I will call up tac air ASAP when weather clears. You must hang on until weather breaks, Arizona-Six-Zulu, over."

"Lima-Niner-Mike, if that main force unit gets here before the weather breaks, I am dog food, over."

"Hang tight, Arizona-Six-Zulu, the weather is supposed to break by noon tomorrow. I will get through to Charlie-Charlie-November and we will get Phantoms airborne fastest then, over."

"Roger, Lima-Niner-Mike," said Arizona-Six-Zulu, "and out."

"God bless and good luck, Arizona-Six-Zulu, out," said Lima, and the freak crackled into nothingness.

"Man, those guys are going to get roasted," said Donny. "This weather ain't lifting for days."

"You got that map case?" said Swagger. "Let me see that thing. What were those coordinates?"

"Shit, I don't remember," said Donny.

"Well, then," said Bob, "it's a good thing I do."

He opened the case that Donny shoved over, went through the plastic-wrapped sheaves of operational territory 1:50,000s, and at last came to the one he wanted. He studied hard, then looked over.

"You know, goddamn, if I ain't a fool at map reading, I do believe you and I are the closest unit to them Special Forces fellows. They are west of us, at Kham Duc, ten klicks out of Laos. We are in grid square Whiskey Charlie 155–005; they are up in Whiskey Delta 5120-1802. As I make it, that's about twenty klicks to the west."

Donny squinted. His sergeant indeed had located the proper square, and the Special Forces camp would therefore have been, yes, about twenty klicks. But—there were foothills, a wide brown snake of river and a mountain range between here and there, all of it Indian Territory.

"I'm figuring," Bob said, "one man, moving fast, he might just make it before the main force unit. And those boys would have to move up through this here An Loc valley. You got into those hills, you'd have a hell of a lot of targets."

"Christ," said Donny.

"You just might slow 'em up enough so that air could make it in when the weather broke."

A cold drop of rain deposited itself on Donny's neck and plummeted down his back. A shiver rose from his bones.

"Raise Dodge again, Pork. Tell 'em I'm going on a little trip."

"I'm going too," said Donny.

Bob paused. Then he said, "My ass you are. I won't have no short-timer with me. You hunker here, call in extraction when the weather clears. Don't you worry none about me. I'll get into that camp and extract with Arizona."

"Bob, I—"

"No! You're too short. You'd be too worried about getting whacked with three and days till DEROS. And if you weren't, I would be. Plus, I can move a lot faster on my own. This is a one-man job or it's no job at all. That's an order."

"Sergeant, I—"

"No, goddammit. I told you. This ain't no goddamned game. I can't be worrying about you."

"Goddammit, I'm not sitting here in the fucking rain waiting for extract. You made us a team. You shoot, I spot targets, I handle security. Suppose you have to work at night? Who throws flares? Suppose it's hot and somebody has to call in air? Who works the map for the coordinates and the radio? Suppose you're bounced from behind? Who takes out the fast movers? Who rigs the Claymores?"

"You are fixing to git yourself killed, Lance Corporal. And, much worse, you are pissing me off beaucoup."

"I am not bugging out. I *will not* bug out!"

Bob's eyes narrowed. He suspected all heroism and self-sacrifice because his own survival wasn't based on any sense of them, but rather on shrewd professional combat skills, even shrewder calculation of odds and, shrewdest of all, a sense that to be aggressive in battle was the key to coming out alive on the other side.

"What are you trying to prove, kid? You been a hard-ass to prove something ever since I teamed with you."

"I'm not trying to *prove* anything. I want no slack, that's all. Zero fucking slack. I go all the way, that's all there is. When I get back to the world, maybe then it's different. But out here, goddamn it, I go all the way."

His fierceness softened Swagger, who'd coaxed many a boy through bad times with shit coming in, who'd gotten the grunts moving when the last thing they wanted to do was move, who never lost a spotter to a body bag and lost a hell of a lot fewer young Marines than some could say. But this stubborn boy perplexed him all the way, all the time. Only one of 'em who got up *earlier* than he did, and who never *once* made a mistake on the premission equipment checks.

"Donny, ain't nobody going to ever say you bugged out. I'm trying to cut you some room, boy. No sense dying on this one. This is a Bob show. This is what old Bob was put here to do. It ain't no college football game."

"I'm going. Goddamn, we are Sierra-Bravo-Four, and I am going."

"Man, you sure you were born in the right generation? You belong in the old breed, you salty bastard, with my dead old man. Okay, let's gear up. Call it in. I'm going to shoot us a goddamn compass reading to that grid square, and when we're done I'll buy you a steak and a case of Jack Daniel's."

Donny took the moment to peel off his boonie cap and pull out the cellophane-wrapped photo of Julie.

He stared at it as the raindrops collected on the plastic. She looked so dry and far away, and he ached for her. Three and days till DEROS. He would come home. Donny would come marching home again, hurrah, hurrah.

Oh, baby, he said to himself, oh baby, I hope you're with me on this one. Every step of the way.

"Let's go, Pork," sang Bob the Nailer.

CHAPTER TEN

After a time, Donny stopped hurting. He was beyond pain. He was also, ever so briefly, beyond fear. They traveled from landmark to landmark along Swagger's charted compass readings over the slippery terrain, the rain so harsh some time you could hardly breathe. At one moment he was somewhat stunned to discover himself on the crest of a low hill. When had they climbed it? He had no memory of the ascent. He just had the sense of the man ahead of him pulling him forward, urging him on, oblivious to both of their pains, oblivious also to fear and to mud and to changes in the elevation.

After a while they came to a valley, to discover the classical Vietnam terrain of rice paddies separated by paddy dikes. The dikes were muddy as shit, and in a few minutes, the going on them proved slow and treacherous. Swagger didn't even bother to tell him, he just lifted his rifle over his head, stepped off the break and started to fight through the water, churning up mud as he went. What difference could it make? They were so wet it didn't matter, but the water was thick and muddy and at each step the muddy bottom seemed to suck at Donny's boots. His feet grew heavier. The rain fell faster. He was wetter, colder, more fatigued, more desperate, more lonely.

At any moment, some lucky kid with a carbine and a yen to impress his local cadre could have greased them. But the rain fell so hard it drove even the VC and the main force NVA units to cover. They moved across a landscape devoid of human occupation. The fog coiled and rolled. Once, from afar, the vapors parted and they saw a village a klick away down a hill, and Donny imagined what was going on in the warm little huts: the boiling soup with its floating sheaves of bible tripe and brisket sliced thin and fish heads floating in it, and the thought of hot food almost made him keel over.

This is nothing, he told himself. Think of football. Think of two-a-days in August. No, no, think of games. Think of . . . Think of . . . Think of making the catch against Gilman High; think of third and twelve, we've never beaten them, but for some odd reason late in this game we're close but now we've stalled. Think of setting up at tight end instead of running back because you have the best hands on the team. Think of Julie, a cheerleader in those days, the concern on her face.

Think of the silliness of it all! It all seemed so important! Beating Gilman! Why was that so important? It was so silly! Then Donny remembered why it was important. Because it was so silly. It meant so little that it meant so much.

Think of going off the set, faking inside, then breaking on a slant for the sidelines as Vercolone, the quarterback, broke from his disintegrating pocket and began to rotate toward him, curling around, his arm cocked then uncocked as he released the ball. Think of the ball in the air. Think of seeing it float toward you, Vercolone had led you too much, the ball was way out of reach, there was no noise, there was no sensation, there was only the ball sliding past. But think of how you went airborne.

That was the strange thing. He did not ever remember leaping. It just happened, one of those instinct things, as the computer in your head took over your body and off you went.

He remembered straining in the air and, with his one hand stretched out to the horizon, the slap of contact as the ball glanced off his longest fingers, popped into the air and seemed to pause forever as he slid through the air by it, now about to miss it, but somehow he actually pivoted in air, got his chest out to snare it as it fell, then clasped his other hand against it, pinning it to him as he thudded to the ground and by the grace of a God who must love jocks, it did not pop out, he had caught it for a first down, and three plays later they scored and won the game, beating an ancient enemy for the first time in living memory.

Oh, that was so very good! That was so very good.

The warmth of that moment came flooding back across him, its meaningless glory warming and giving him just the slightest tingle of energy. Maybe he would make it.

But then he went down, floundering, feeling the water flood into his lungs, and he struggled, coughing out buffalo shit and a million paramecium. A harsh grip pulled him out and he shook like a wet dog. It was Swagger, of course.

"Come on," Swagger yelled through the din of pounding rain. "We're almost out of the paddies. Then all we got is another set of hills, a river and a goddamn mountain. Damn, ain't this fun?"

Water. According to the map, the river was called Ia Trang. It bore no other name and on the paper was a squiggly black line, its secrets unrevealed. As it lay before them in reality, however, it was swollen brown and wide, overspilling its banks, and was a swift, deadly current. The rain smashed against its turbulent surface like machine gun fire.

"Guess what?" said Swagger. "You just got a new job."

"Huh?"

"You just got a new job. You're now the lifeguard."

"Why?"

" 'Cause I cain't swim a lick," he said, with a broad smile.

"Great," said Donny. "I can't either."

"Oh, this one's going to be a pisser. Damn, why'd you insist on this trip?"

"I was momentarily deluded into thinking I was important."

"That kind of thinkin'll git you killed every damn time. Now, let's see if we can find some wood or something."

They ranged the dangerous bank of the river and in

time came to a bombed-out village. The gunships and Phantoms had worked it over pretty well; nothing could have survived the hell of that recent day. No structure stood: only timbers, piles of ash liquified to gunk in the pounding rain, craters everywhere, a long smear of burned vegetation where the napalm splashed through, killing everything it touched. A cooking pot lay on its side, speared by a machine gun bullet, so that it blossomed outward in jagged petals. The stench of the burning still clung to the ground, despite the rain. There were no bodies, but just out of the kill zone a batch of newly dug graves with now-dead Buddhist incense reeds in cheap black jars had been etched into the ground. Two were very, very small.

"I hope they were bad guys," said Donny, looking at the new cemetery.

"If we run this fucking war right," Swagger said, "we'd have *known* they was bad, because we'd have people on the ground, up close. Not this shit. Not just hosing the place down with firepower. Nobody should have to die because he's in the wrong place at the wrong time and some squid pilot's got some ordnance left and don't want to land on no carrier with it."

Donny looked at him. In five months of extreme togetherness, Bob had never said a thing about the way the war was waged, what it cost, who it killed, why it happened. His, instead, was the practical craft of mission and its close pal survival: how to do this thing, where to hide, how to track, what to shoot, how to kill, how to get the job done and come back alive.

"Well, nobody'll ever know, that's for goddamn sure," said Bob. "Unless you get out of this shit hole and you tell 'em. You got that, Pork? That's your new MOS: witness. You got that?"

Familiar again. Where was this from? What did this mean? What sounded so right about it, the same melody, slightly different instrument?

"I'll tell 'em."

" 'Cause I'm too dumb to tell 'em. They'll never listen to a hillbilly like me. They'll listen to you, boy, 'cause you looked the goddamn elephant in the eye and came back to talk about it. Got that?"

"Got it."

"Good. Now let's scare up some wood and build us Noah's ark."

They scrounged in the ruins and came up after a bit with seven decent pieces of wood, which Bob rigged together in some clever Boy Scout way with a coil of black rope he carried. He lashed his and Donny's rifles, the two 782-packs and harnesses, all the grenades, the map case, the canteens, the PRC-77, the flares and flare gun, and the pistols to it.

"Okay, you really can't swim?"

"I can sort of."

"Well, I can a bit, too. The deal is, you cling hard to this thing and you kick hard. I'll be on the other side. Keep your face out of the water and keep on fighting, no matter what. And don't let go. The current'll take you and you'll be one dead puppy dog and nobody'll remember your name till they inscribe it on some monument and the pigeons come shit on it. Ain't that a pretty thought?"

"Very pretty."

"So let's do it, Pork. You just became a submariner."

The water was intensely cold and stronger than Zeus. In the first second Donny panicked, floundered, almost pulled the rickety raft over and only Bob's strength on the other side kept them afloat. The raft floated diagonally across and the swiftness and anger of the river had it in an instant, and Donny, clinging with both desperate hands to the rope lashings Bob had jury-rigged, felt swept away, taken by it, the coldness everywhere. His feet flailed, touched nothing. He sank a bit and it gushed down his throat and he coughed and leaped like a seal, freeing himself.

It was all water, above and beneath, his chin in the

stuff, his eyes and face pelted by it as it fell from the gray sky at a brutal velocity.

"Kick, goddammit!" he heard Bob scream, and with his legs he began a kind of strangely rhythmic breast-stroke. The craft seemed to spurt ahead just a bit.

But there came a moment when it was all gone. Fog obscured the land and he felt he was thrashing across an ocean, the English Channel at the very least, a voyage that had forgotten its beginning and couldn't imagine its ending. The water lured him downward to its black numbness; he could feel it sucking at him, fighting toward his throat and his lungs, and it stank of napalm, gunpowder, aviation fuel, buffalo shit, peasants who sold you a Coke by day and cut your throat by night, dead kids in ditches, flaming villes, friendly-fire casualties, the whole fucking unstoppable momentum of the last eight years, and who was he to fight it, just another grunt, a lance corporal and former corporal with a shaky past, it seemed so huge, so vast, it seemed like history itself.

"Fight it, goddammit," came Swagger's call from the other side, and then he knew who Bob was.

Bob was Trig's brother.

Bob and Trig were almost the same man, somehow. Despite their differing backgrounds, they were the aristocrats of the actual, singled out by DNA to do things others couldn't, to be heroes in the causes they gave their lives to, to be always and forever remembered. They were Odin and Zeus. They were dangerously special, they got things done, they had an incredible vitality and life force. The war would kill them. That's why *both* had commanded him to be the witness, he now saw. It was his job to survive and sing the story of the two mad brothers, Bob and Trig, consumed in, devoured by, killed in the war.

Trig was dead. Trig had blown himself up at the University of Wisconsin along with some pitiful graduate assistant who happened to be working late that night. They found Trig's body, smashed and ruptured by the explosive. It made him famous, briefly, a freak of headlines:

HARVARD GRAD DIES IN BLAST; CARTER FAMILY SCION KILLS SELF IN BOMB BLAST; TRIG CARTER, THE GENTLE AVIAN PAINTER TURNED MARTYR TO THE CAUSE OF PEACE.

It had killed Trig, as Trig had known it would. That's what Trig was telling him that last night; now he understood. He *had* to make it back, to tell the story of Trig and his mad brother Bob, eaten, each in his own way, by the war. Would it ever be over?

Someone had him. He swallowed and looked, and Swagger was yanking him from the water to the shore, where he collapsed, heaving with exhaustion.

"Now hear this. The smoking light is now lit," said Bob.

From the wet river through the wet rain they finally reached the mountain. It wasn't a great mountain. Donny had seen greater mountains in his time in the desert; he'd even climbed some. Swagger said he was from mountain country too, but Donny had never heard of mountains in the South, or Oklahoma or Arkansas or whatever mysterious backwoods the sniper hailed from.

The mountain was dense with foliage over hard rock, wide open to observation from hundreds of meters out. Pick your poison.

"Oh, Christ," said Donny, looking at the steep slope. Time had no meaning. It seemed to be twilight but it could have been dawn. He looked upward and the water pelted him in the face.

"I want to get halfway up in the next two hours," Bob said.

"I don't think I can," gulped Donny.

"I don't think I can either," said Bob. "And, what's worse, if that goddamn main force battalion is in the area heading on that base camp, they're sure to have security out, just the thing to keep boys like us out of their hair."

"I can't do it," Donny said.

"I cain't do it neither," said Swagger. "But it's gotta be

done and I don't see no two other boys here, do you? If I saw two others, believe me, I'd send them, yessirree."

"Oh, shit," Donny said.

"Well, look at it this way. We only got where we got 'cause we came through full monsoon. We go back, when the rains dry up Victor C. gonna come out. He's gonna find us. He's gonna kill us. We weren't invited into his goddamn yard, and he's gonna be plenty pissed. So we gotta make that Special Forces base camp or we are going to die out here for sure. That's just about the size of that piece of shit and that's all there is to it!"

He smiled, not out of happiness or glee but possibly because he was too exhausted to do anything else.

"Wish I had a Dexedrine," he said. "But I don't believe in that shit. Came back from my second tour with a monkey the size of a ape on my butt. Had to work like hell to kill that furry bastard, too. Now, that wasn't much fun at all."

The man wasn't *in* Vietnam; in some sense he *was* Vietnam. He'd done it all: sniped, raided, taken hills, led recons, worked intel, advised ARVN units, run interrogations, done analysis, fought in a thousand firefights, killed who knew how many, visited hospitals, talked to generals. He was one part of his whole goddamned generation rolled into one. This was entirely new, but unsurprising: he'd been a speed freak. Maybe he'd done heroin, maybe he'd caught the clap, maybe he'd been tattooed, maybe he'd murdered prisoners. He *was* Trig, at least in the way that he'd done everything to win the war that Trig had done in his parallel universe to end it, a furious, relentless crusade, presaged on the obsolete notion that one man could make a difference.

"You remind me of a guy," Donny said.

"Oh, yeah. Some hillbilly on the radio. Lum or the other one, Abner? They come from my hometown."

"No, believe it or not, a peacenik."

"Oh, a commie. He has long hair and looked like

Jesus. His shit didn't stink, I bet. Mine does, but good, Pork."

"No. He was like you, a hero. He was bigger than the rest of us. He was a legend."

"To be a legend, don't you have to be dead? Ain't that part of the job description?"

"He is dead."

"He managed to get his ass wasted demonstrating against the war? Now, that do take some kind of genius level intelligence. And I remind you of him? Son, you must have the fever bad."

"He just wouldn't quit. There wasn't any quit in him."

"Yeah, well, there's plenty of quit in me, Pork. One more job, then I am going to quit for the rest of my life. Now, let's just git a move on."

"Which way?"

"We go up the switchbacks, they'll bounce us. Only one way. Straight up."

"Christ."

"We'll eat. Picnic time. It'll be the last meal you git till this is over or you get killed and you get a nice steak in heaven. Dump your C-rats and your canteens and your 782. Use your entrenching tool. Set it at the angle. We going to use it to pull our way up, you got that?"

"I don't—"

"Sure you do. Watch me."

Quickly and expertly, he shed himself of most of his gear; only the weapons remained. He fished a C-rat out of his dumped pack, and quickly used his can opener to whip up cold eggs and ham, which he gobbled quickly.

"Go on, chow time. Eat something."

Donny set out to do the same and in a few seconds was pulling down the barbecued pork, cold but flavorful.

"When we're done, you gimme the radio. I ain't carrying as much weight."

"I'll take your rifle."

"The hell you will. Nobody touches the rifle but me."

Of course. The basic rule. He remembered when

Swagger had come looking for him, sitting forlornly on outpost duty at a forward observation post his third week at Dodge City.

"You Fenn?"

"Uh, yeah. Uh, Sergeant—?"

"Swagger. Name's Swagger. I'm the sniper."

Donny had a momentary intake of breath. In the dark, he could hardly see him: just a fierce wraith of a man sheathed in darkness, speaking in a dense Southern accent. Bob the Nailer, the one with the 15,000-piastre bounty on his head and over thirty kills. Donny had the sense that all was quiet, that the other men had just willed themselves to nothingness out of fear or respect for Bob the Nailer. Though he could not see the sniper's eyes, Donny knew they burned at him, and ate him up.

"I just put my spotter on a medevac back to the world with a hole in his leg," said the sniper. "I'm looking for a replacement. You shot expert. You have the highest GCT at Dodge. You have twenty-ten vision. You done a tour, won a medal, so you been shot at some and won't panic. All that don't mean shit. You was at Eighth and I. That means you done the ceremonial stuff, which means you have a patience for detail work and a willingness to be an unnoticed part of a bigger team. I need that. You interested?"

"Me? I—"

"Good perks. I'll get you steak and all the bourbon you can drink. When we're in, we live like kings. I'll keep you off crap like night watch and ambush patrols and forward observation and shit-burning details. I'll get you R&R anywhere you want. Bad shit: A) You don't touch the rifle. Nobody touches the rifle. B) You don't do drugs. I catch you with a buzz on, I ship you home under guard and you'll spend two years in Portsmouth. C) You don't call nobody gook, dink, slope or zip. These are the very finest soldiers in the world. They are winning and they will win. We kill them, but by God, we kill them with respect. Those are the only three rules, but they ain't to be bent or even breathed hard on. Or, you can sit here in this shit hole waiting for someone to drop a mortar shell on your head. And somehow I got a feeling every shit detail, every shit patrol, every piece-of-crap garbage job that comes up, you're number one on the fuck list. I hope you like the stink of burning shit because you're going to smell a lot of it."

"Back in the world, I had some problems," said Donny. "I got a bad rap. I wouldn't 'cooperate.' "

"I figured it from your jacket. Some kind of infraction of orders? You lost your rating. Hey, kid, this ain't the world. This is the 'Nam, have you noticed? It don't mean shit to me, you got that? You do the jobs I give you one hundred percent and I'll back you one hundred percent. You may get killed, you will work hard, but you will have fun. Killing people is *lots* of fun. Now, you want in or what?"

"I guess I'm in."

Within thirty minutes, Donny had been relieved of duty and moved into the scout-sniper squad bay with S/Sgt. Swagger NCOIC—or, as some called him, NCGIC, Non-Commissioned God in Charge—and the only man whose word mattered anywhere in the world.

He had never broken one of the rules until now. He had weighed each M118 round Swagger carried against the one-in-a-million chance of an off-charge at Lake City; he had cleaned Bob's .45, .380 and grease gun and his own M14 and .45; he shined and dried the jungle boots; he laid out and assembled the gear before each mission; he polished the lens of the spotting scope; he checked the pins on the grenades, the plastic canteens for mildew; he hand-enameled the brass on the 872 gear dead black; he did laundry; he learned elevation, windage and range estimation; he kept range cards; he filled out after-action reports; he studied the operating area maps like a sacred text; he handled flank security and once killed two NVC who were infiltrating around Bob's position; he learned

PRC-77 protocol and maintenance. He worked like hell, and he had never broken one of the rules.

Only Bob touched the rifle. Bob broke it down after each mission, cleaned it to the tiniest crevice, scrubbed it dry, rezeroed it, treated it like a baby or a mistress. He and only he could touch or carry the rifle.

"It ain't I don't trust you. It ain't you drop it and it gets knocked out of zero and you don't tell me and I miss a shot and somebody, probably me, gets killed. It's just that the bedrock here is simple, clear, powerful and helps us both: nobody touches the rifle but me. Good fences make good neighbors. Ever hear that one?"

"I think so."

"Well, the rifle rule is my fence. Got that?"

"I do. Entirely, Sergeant."

"You call me sergeant around the lifers here in Dodge. In the field, you call me Bob or Swagger or whatever the hell you want. Don't call me sergeant in the field. One of them boys might be listening and he might decide to kill me because he heard you call me sergeant. Got that, Pork?"

"I do."

And he had never forgotten that rule or any of the rules, until now.

"I forgot," he said in the rain to Swagger. "About the rifle."

"Damn, Fenn, I was just getting to like you, too. I thought you'se going to work out," Bob said, needling him ever so gently. But then it was back to mission: "Okay, you done eating? You got your shit wired in tight? This is it. Over this hill, through their security and then sleep a bit. Comes morning we get to do some shooting."

Bob went first, down to soaked tiger camos and boonie cap, his rifle slung upside down on his back. He carried the M3 grease gun in one hand and the entrenching tool in the other, and he used the tool as a kind of hook, to sink into roots of trees or the tangles of vegetation to get himself up the steep incline a few more feet. He moved with slow, almost calm deliberation. The rain fell still in torrents in the darkening gloom, and it rattled off the leaves and against the mud. How could it rain so hard so long? Was God ending the world, washing away Vietnam and its sins, its atrocities, its arrogances and follies? It seemed that way.

Donny was fifty yards to the left, doing the same trick, but behind Swagger and working carefully not to get ahead. Bob was the eyes up front to the right; Donny's responsibility was behind and to the left, the flank he was on.

But he saw nothing, just felt the chill of the biting rain, and felt the weight of the M14, one of the last few left in the 'Nam. For this job, really, the plastic M16 would have been more ideally suited, but Bob hated the things, calling them poodle shooters, and wouldn't let a man in his unit carry them.

Every now and then Bob would halt them with a raised right hand, and both men would drop low to the ground, hidden in the foliage, waiting, clinging desperately against the incline. But each time whatever Bob had noticed proved to be nothing, a false alarm, and they continued their steady, slow climb.

Twice they crossed paths, switchbacks etched into the vegetation, and Bob waited for five minutes before allowing them out on the open ground even for the seconds or so that it exposed them.

The darkness was falling. It was harder and harder to see. The jungle, far from relaxing as they climbed, actually seemed to be getting denser. There was a time when Donny felt himself cut off entirely from Bob, and a shot of panic came to him. What if he got lost? What would he do? He would wander these ghostly mountains until they caught him and killed him, or he wore down and starved.

You boys ain't so tough, he heard from somewhere, and realized it was a mocking memory of a football coach somewhere back in his complicated athletic career.

No, we ain't so tough, he thought. We never said we were. We just tried to do our job, that was all.

But then he came out of the rubbery-smelling thorns that had swallowed him, and saw a figure to the right and recognized it for its caution and precision of movement to be Bob.

He started to rise—

No, no—

Bob's hand was up urgently, signaling him still and back. He froze and dropped on his belly low to the ground, even as Bob himself did the same.

He waited.

Nothing. No, just the sound of the rain, some occasional thunder, now and then a streak of distant lightning. It seemed so—

The next thing, he was aware of motion on his left. He did not move, he did not breathe.

How had Swagger seen them? How did he know? What gave them away? Another step and it was all over, but somehow, out of some trick of instinct or predator's preternatural nerve endings, Bob had stunned him into silence and motionlessness a second before they arrived.

Before him the men passed by, no more than ten feet away, sliding effortlessly through the foliage and the undergrowth. He could smell them before he could see them. They had the odor of fish and rice, for that was what they ate. They were small, bandy-legged guys, the pros of the army of the Republic of North Vietnam, a point man, a squad leader, a squad in file picking its way carefully through the jungle high above the last path, twelve of them. They were bent forward under beige rain capes and wore regulation dark green uniforms, those absurd pith helmets, and carried AK47s and complete combat gear—packs, canteens and bayonets. Three or four of them wore RPG-40s, the hellish rocket grenades, strapped to their backs.

He had never been so close to the actual enemy, they seemed almost magical, or mythological, somehow, the phantoms of so many nightmares at last given flesh. They terrified him. If he moved or coughed, it was over: they'd turn and fire, whole minutes before he could get his M14 into action. He had a bad thought of himself dying up here at the hands of these tough little monkey-men sliding so confidently through the rain and the jungle that were exhausting him.

Almost as if one were talking to him, he heard the silence breaking a few feet away.

"Ǎhn ỏi, múa nhiêu qúa?"

"Phải roi, chắc không có ngủỏi mỹ dêm naỳ," came the buddy's bitter answer, both voices propelled by the explosive lung energy of Vietnamese, so foreign to American ears and which sounded almost like belches.

"Bính sĩ ôi, dung nôi, nghê," came a sharp cry from the head of the unit, a sergeant, the same the world over and whatever the army, clamping down on his naughty grunts.

The patrol moved slowly along in the dying light and the falling rain, then slowly disappeared around a bend in the slope. But Bob held Donny still for a good ten minutes before giving the okay, excruciating seconds of death-like stillness in the cold and wet, which cramped the muscles and hurt the brain. But at last Bob motioned, and he slowly uncoiled and began to move up again.

Gradually Bob navigated his way over.

"You okay?"

"Yeah. How the hell did you see them?"

"The point man's canteen jingled against his bayonet. I heard it, that's all. Luck, man; it's better to be lucky than good."

"Who were they?"

"That's flank security from a main force battalion. That means we're getting close. They put out security teams when they move a big unit through, same as us. The sergeant had flashes for the Number Three Battalion. I don't know what regiment or nothing, but I think the biggest unit up this ways was the 324th Infantry Division.

Man, they close down that Special Forces camp tomorrow, the rain stays bad, they could get to Dodge City the day or so *after* tomorrow."

"Is this some big offensive?"

"There's several newly Vietnamized units there; it'd do 'em a lot of good to kick all that ARVN ass."

"Great. I wonder what they were saying."

"The first one says, Man, it's raining like *shit,* and his buddy says, Ain't no Americans coming out in this, and the sarge yells back, Hey, you guys, shut up and keep moving."

"You speak Vietnamese?" Donny said in wonderment.

"Picked up a little. Not much, but I can get by. Come on, let's get out of here. We got to rest. Big day tomorrow. We kick butt and take names. You bet on it, Marine."

CHAPTER ELEVEN

FOB Arizona was in bad trouble. Puller had lost nineteen men already and the VC had gotten mortars up close over to the west, and were pounding the shit out of them so that he couldn't maneuver, and that main force unit would be in tomorrow at the latest. But worse: he'd sent out Matthews with a four-man assault unit to take out the mortars and Matthews hadn't come back. Jim Matthews! Three tours, M/Sgt. Jim Matthews, Benning, the Zone, one of the old guys who dated all the way back to Korea, had done everything—gone!

The rage of it flared deep in Major Puller's angry, angry brain.

This wasn't supposed to be happening. Goddamn them, this wasn't supposed to be happening.

Kham Duc was way out on its lonesome, near Laos, where it had fed in cross-border recon teams for years, but was largely invulnerable because of the umbrella or air power, so the NVA didn't even bother with main force units close by. Where had this one come from? He was feeling very Custerlike, that sick moment when he suddenly realized he was up against hundreds, maybe thousands. And where the hell had this weather come from and how fast could this big-ass, tough-as-shit battalion get down here?

Oh, he wants us. He smells our blood; he wants us.

Puller's antagonist was a slick operator named Huu Co Thanh, a senior colonel, commanding, No. 3 Battalion, 803rd Infantry Regiment, 324th Infantry Division, Fifth People's Shock Army. Puller had seen his picture, knew his résumé: from a wealthy, sophisticated Indo-French family and even a graduate of the École Militaire in Paris before deserting to the North in sixty-one after revulsion at the excesses of the Diem regime, he had become one of their most able field grade military commanders, a sure general.

A mortar shell fell outside, close by, and dust shook from the rafters of the command post.

"Anybody hit?" he called.

"No, sir," came his sergeant's reply. "The bastards missed."

"Any word from Matthews?"

"No, sir."

Major Richard W. Puller pulled on his boonie cap and slithered out the dugout door to the trench and looked around at his shaky empire. He was a lean, desperate man with a thatch of gray hair, and had been in Fifth Special Forces since 1958, including a tour in the British Special Air Service Regiment, even seeing some counterinsurgency action in Malaysia. He'd been to all the right schools: Airborne, Ranger, Jungle, National War College, Command and Staff at Leavenworth. He could fly a chopper, speak Vietnamese, repair a radio or fire an RPG. This was not his first siege. He had been encircled at Pleiku in 1965 for more than a month, under serious bombardment. He'd been hit then: a Chinese .51-caliber machine gun bullet, which would kill most men.

He hated the war, but he loved it. He feared it would kill him but a part of him wanted it never to end. He loved his wife but had had a string of Chinese and Eurasian mistresses. He loved the Army but hated it also, the former for its guts and professionalism, the latter for its stubbornness, its insistence always of fighting the next war by the tactics of the old.

But what he hated most of all was that he had fucked up. He had *really* fucked up, gambling the lives of his team and all his indigs that the NVA couldn't get him during his window of vulnerability. He was responsible for it all, it was happening to them because it was happening to him. And nobody could save his ass.

The main gate was down, and where his ammo dump had been, smoke still boiled from the ground, rising to mingle with the low clouds that hung everywhere. The S-shops were a shambles as were most of the squad hootches, but a unit of VC sappers that had gotten into the compound the night before and actually taken over the Third Squad staging area and what remained of the commo shack had been finally dislodged in hand-to-hand with the dawn. No structure remained; most of the wire still stood, but for now, that was the mortar objective: to pound avenues into his defenses so that when Huu Co and his battalion got here, they wouldn't get hung up in the shit as they came over him, backed by their own mortars and a complement of crew-served weapons.

Puller looked up and caught rain in the eye and felt the chill of the mist. Night was falling. Would they come at night? They'd move at night, but probably not attack. At least not in force: they'd send probers, draw fire, try and get Arizona to use up its low supplies of ammo on bad or unseen targets, but mainly work to keep the defenders rattled and sleepless for the No. 3 Battalion.

Would the weather break? On the Armed Forces Net, the meteorological forecasts were not promising, but Puller knew they'd try like hell, and if they could get birds up, they'd get 'em up. But maybe the pilots were reluctant: who'd want to fly into heavy small-arms fire to drop napalm on a few more dinks when the war was so close to being over? Who'd want to die now, at the very tag end of the thing, after all the years and all the futility? He didn't know the answer to that one himself.

Puller looked down his front to the valley. He could see nothing in the gloom, of course, but it was a highway, and Huu Co would be barreling down it at the double time like a fat cat in a limousine, knowing they ran no danger from the Phantoms or the gunships.

"Major Puller, Major Puller! You ought to come see this, quick."

It was Sergeant Blas, one of his master sergeants who worked with the Montagnards, a tough little Guamese who had seen a lot of action on too many tours and also didn't deserve to get caught in a shit hole like FOB Arizona so late in a lost and fruitless war.

Blas led him through the trenches to the west side of the perimeter, crouching now and then when a new mortar shell came whistling their way, but at last they reached the parapet, and a Montagnard with a carbine handed Puller a pair of binocs.

Puller used them to peer over the sandbags, and saw in the treeline three hundred meters out something that was at first indecipherable but at last assembled itself into a pattern and then some details.

It was a stick and on the stick was Jim Matthews's head.

Three quicks and one slow. Three strongs. That was the rhythm, the slow steady pace of accomplishment over the long years and the long bleeding. Now, he was under pressure, great pressure, for one last quick. Far off, the diplomats were talking. There would be a peace soon, and the more they controlled when that peace was signed, the more they would retain afterward and the more they could build upon for a future, he knew, he would never see, but his children might.

He knew he would not survive. His children would be his monument. He would leave a new world behind for them, having done his part in destroying the terrible old one. That was enough for any father, and his life did not particularly matter; he had given himself up to struggle, to tomorrow, to the ten rules of the soldier's life:

1) Defend the Fatherland; fight and sacrifice myself for the People's Revolution.
2) Obey the orders received and carry out the mission of the soldier.
3) Strive to improve the virtues of a Revolutionary Soldier.
4) Study to improve myself and build up a powerful Revolutionary Army.

5) Carry out other missions of the Army.
6) Help consolidate internal unity.
8) Preserve and save public properties.
9) Work for the solidarity between the Army and the People.
10) Maintain the Quality and Honor of the Revolutionary Soldier.

All that remained was this last job, the American Green Beret camp at Kham Duc, at the end of the An Loc Valley, which must be eliminated in order to take more land before documents were signed.

Three quicks, one slow, three strongs.

Slow plan.

Quick advance.

Strong fight.

Strong assault.

Strong pursuit.

Quick clearance.

Quick withdrawal.

He had developed the plan over three years of operations, gaining constant intelligence on the E5 sector of administrative division MR-7, knowing that as the war wound down, it would do, it was explained to him by higher headquarters and as he himself understood, to make an example of one of the camps.

Quick advance. That is where No. 3 Battalion was now. The men were seasoned, toughened campaigners with long battle experience. They moved quickly from their sanctuary in Laos and were now less than twenty kilometers from the target, which was already under assault by local Viet Cong infrastructure under specific orders from Hanoi, and from whom he got combat intelligence over the radio.

The column moved in the classical structure of an army on the quick, derived not entirely from the great Giap, father of the Army, but also from the French genius Napoleon, who understood, when no one in history since

Alexander had, the importance of quickness, and who slashed across the world on that principle.

So Huu Co, senior colonel, had elements of his best troops, his sappers, running security on each flank a mile out in two twelve-men units per flank; he had his second best people, also sappers, at the point in a diamond formation, all armed with automatic weapons and RPGs, setting the pace, ready to deliver grenades and withering fire at any obstacles. His other companies moved in column by fours at the double time, rotating the weight of the heavy mortars among them by platoons so that no unit was more fatigued than any other.

Fortunately, it was cool; the rain was no impediment. The men, superbly trained, shorn of slackers and wreckers by long years of struggle, were the most dedicated. Moreover, they were excited because the weather was holding; low clouds, fog everywhere, their most feared and hated enemy, the American airplanes, nowhere in sight. That was the key: to move freely, almost as if in the last century, without the fear of Phantoms or Skyhawks screaming in and dropping their napalm and white phosphorous. That is why he hated the Americans so much: they fought with flame. It meant nothing to them to burn his people like grasshoppers plaguing a harvest. Yet those who stood against the flame, as he had, became hardened beyond imagination. He who has stood against flame fears nothing.

Huu Co, senior colonel, was forty-four years old. Sometimes, memories of the old life floated up before him: Paris in the late forties and early fifties, when his decadent father had turned him over to the French, under whose auspices he studied hard. But Paris: the pleasures of Paris. Who could forget such a place? That was a revolutionary city and it was there he first smoked Gauloise, read Marx and Engels and Proust and Sartre and Nietzsche and Apollinaire; it was there his commitment to the old world, the world of his father, began to crumble, at first in small, almost meaningless ways. Did the French have to be so nasty to their yellow guests? Did they have to take such pleasure in their whiteness, while preaching the oneness of man under the eye of God? Did they have to take such pleasure in rescuing bright Indochinese like himself from their yellowness?

But even still, he wondered now, Would I have followed this course had I known how hard it would be?

Huu Co, senior colonel, fought in seven battles and three campaigns with the French in the first Indochinese War. He loved the French soldiers: tough, hardened men, brave beyond words, who truly believed theirs was the right to master the land they had colonized. They could understand no other way; he lay in the mud with them at Dien Bien Phu in 1954, eighteen years ago, praying for the Americans to come and rescue them with their mighty airpower.

Huu Co, senior colonel, learned the Catholic God from them, moved south and fought for the Diem brothers in building a bulwark against the godless Uncle Ho. In 1955, he led an infantry platoon against the Binh Xuyen in violent street fighting, then later against the Hoa Hao cult in the Mekong and was present at the execution of the cult's leader, Ba Cut, in 1956. Much of the killing he saw was of Indochinese by Indochinese. It sickened him.

Saigon was no Paris either, though it had cafes and nightclubs and beautiful women; it was a city of corruption, of prostitutes, gambling, crime, narcotics, which the Diems not only encouraged but also from which they profited. How could he love the Diems if they loved silk, perfume, their own power and pomp more than the people they ruled, whom they yet felt themselves removed from and immensely superior to? His father counseled him to forgive them their arrogances and to use them as a vessel for carrying God's will. But his father never saw the politics, the corruption, the terrible way they abused the peasants, the remove from the people.

Huu Co went north in 1961, when the Diems' corruption had begun to resemble that of a city destroyed in the

Bible. He renounced his Catholicism, his inherited wealth and his father, whom he would never see again. He knew the South would sink into treachery and profiteering and would bring flame and retribution upon itself, as it had.

He was a humble private in the People's Revolutionary Army, he who had sat in cafes and once met the great Sartre and de Beauvoir at the Deux Maggots in the Fourteenth Arrondisement; he, a major in the Army of the Republic of South Vietnam, became a lowly private carrying an SKS and wanting to do nothing but his duty to the fatherland and the future and seek purification, but his gifts always betrayed him.

He was always the best soldier among them, and he rose effortlessly, though now without ambition: he was a student officer after two years, and his passage in the west and in the south, after six months' strenuous reeducation in a camp outside Hanoi, where he withstood the most barbarous pressures and purified himself for the revolutionary struggle, only toughened him for the decade of war that was to follow.

Now he was tired. He had been at war since 1950, twenty-two years of war. It was almost over. Really, all that remained was the camp called Arizona, and between himself and it, there stood nothing, no unit, no aircraft, no artillery. He would crush it. Nothing could stop him.

CHAPTER TWELVE

In the dream, he had caught a touchdown pass, a slant outside, and as he broke downfield all the blockers hit their men perfectly, and the defense went down like tenpins opening lanes toward the end zone. It was geometry, somehow, or at least a physical problem reduced to the abstract, very pleasing, and far from the reality which was that you ran on instinct and hardly ever remembered things exactly. He got into the end zone: people cheered, it was so very warm, Julie hugged him. His dad was there, weeping for joy. Trig was there also, among them, jumping up and down, and so was Sergeant Bob Lee Swagger, the sniper god, a figure of preposterous joy as he pirouetted crazily, laden with firearms and dappled in a war face of camouflage.

It was such a good dream. It was the best, the happiest, the finest dream he ever had, and it went away, as such things do, to the steady pressure of someone rocking his arm and the sudden baffling awareness that he was not there but here.

"Huh?"

"Time to work, Pork."

Donny blinked and smelled the wet odor of jungle, the wet odor of rain, and felt the wet cold. Swagger had already turned from him and was off making his arcane preps.

The dawn came as a blur of light, just the faintest smear of incandescence to the east, over the mountains on the other side of the valley.

In its way, it was quite beautiful in that low 0500 light: vapors of fog clung to the wet earth everywhere, in valleys and hollows and gulches, nestled thickly in the trees, and though it wasn't at present raining, surely it would rain soon, for the low clouds still rolled over, heavy with moisture. Still, so quiet, so calm, so pristine.

"Come on," whispered Swagger into Donny Fenn's ear.

Donny shook sleep from his eyes and put his dreams of Julie aside and reconfirmed his existence. He was on a hillside in heavy foliage above the An Loc Valley, near Kham Duc and Laos. It would be another wet day, and the weather had not broken, so there would be no air.

"We got to get lower," said Bob. "I can't hit nothing from up here."

The sergeant now wore the M3 grease gun on his back and in his hands carried the M40 sniper rifle, a dull pewter Remington with a thick bull barrel and a dull brown wooden stock. It carried a Redfield scope, and a Marine Corps armorer had labored over it, free floating the barrel, truing up the bolt to the chamber, glass-bedding the action to the wood, torquing the screws tight, but it was still far from an elegant weapon, built merely for effectiveness, never beauty.

Bob had smeared the jungle grease paint on his face, and under the crinkled brow of the boonie cap his visage looked primitive; he seemed a creature sprung from someone's worst dreams, some kind of atavistic war creature totally of the jungle, festooned with pistols and grenades, all smeared with the colors of nature, even his eyes gone to nothing.

"Here. Paint up and we'll get going," he said, holding the stick of camo paint out to Donny, who quickly blurred his own features. Donny gathered his M14 and the impossibly heavy PRC-77, his real enemy in all this, and began to ease his way down the slope with Bob.

It seemed they were lowering themselves into the clouds, like angels returning to earth. The fog would not break; it clung to the floor of the valley as if it had been enameled there. No sun would burn it away, not today at any rate.

Now and then some jungle bird would call, now and

then some animal shudder would ripple from the under-growth, but there was no sense of human presence, nothing metallic or regular to the eye. Donny scanned left, Bob scanned right. They moved ever so slowly, frustratingly slowly, picking their way down, until at last they were nearly to the valley floor and a field of waist-high grass, in the center of which a worn track had been beaten, by men or buffaloes or elephants or whatever.

From far away, at last, came some kind of unnatural noise. Donny couldn't identify it and then he could; it was the noise of men, somehow—nothing distinct, not breaking talk discipline—somehow become a herd, a living, breathing thing. It was No. 3 Battalion, still a few hundred yards away, gearing up for the last six or so klicks of quick march to the staging area for their assault.

Bob halted him with a hand.

"Okay," he said. "Here's how we do it. You got the map coords?"

Donny did; he had memorized them.

"Grid square Whiskey-Delta 5120–1802."

"Good. If the sky clears and the birds come, you'll have line of sight to them and you can go to the Air Force freak and you talk 'em in. They won't have good visuals. You talk 'em down into the valley and have 'em plaster the floor."

"What about you? You'll be—"

"Don't you worry about that. No squid Phantom jock is flaming me. I can take care of myself. Now listen up: that is your goddamn job. You talk to 'em on the horn. You're the eyes. Don't you be coming down after me, you got that? You may hear fighting, you may hear small arms; don't you fret a bit. That's my job. Yours is to stay up here and talk to the air. After the air moves out, you should be able to git to that snake-eater camp. You call them, tell them you're coming in, pop smoke, and come in from the smoke so they know it's you and not some NVA hero. Got that? You should be okay if I can hold these bad boys up for a bit."

"What about security? I'm security. My job is to help you, to cover your ass. What the hell good am I going to do parked up here?"

"Listen, Pork, I'll fire my first three shots when I get visuals. Then I'll move back to the right, maybe two hundred yards, because they'll bring heavy shit down. I'll try and do two, three, maybe four more from there. Here's how the game works. I pull down on a couple, then I move back. But guess what? After the third string, I ain't moving back, I'm moving forward. That's why I want you right here. I'll never be too far from this area. I don't want 'em to know how many guys I am, and they'll flank me, and I don't want 'em coming around on me. I guarantee you, they will have good, tough, fast-moving flank people out, so you go to ground about twenty minutes after I first hit them. They may be right close to you; that's all right. You dig in and sink into the ground, and you'll be all right. Just watch out for the patrols I know they'll call in. Them boys we saw last night. They'll be back, that I guarantee."

"You will get killed. You will get killed, I'm telling you, you cannot—"

"I'm giving you a straight order; you follow it. Don't give me no little-boy shit. I'm telling you what you have to do, and by God, you will do it, and that's all there is to it, or I will be one pissed-off motherfucker, Lance Corporal Fenn."

"I—"

"You do it! Goddammit, Fenn, you do it, and that's all there is to it. Or I will have you up on charges and instead of going home, you'll go to Portsmouth."

This was bullshit, of course, and Donny saw through it in a second. It was all bullshit, because if Swagger went into the valley without security, he was not coming back. He simply was not. That's what the physics of firepower decreed, and the physics of firepower were the iron realities of war. There was no appeal.

He was throwing his life away for some strangers in a camp he'd never see. He knew it, had known it all along.

It was his way. More like Trig: hungry to die, as if the war were so inside him he knew he could not live without it; there would be no life to go home to. He had kept himself hard and pure just for this one mad moment when he could take on a battalion with a rifle, and if he could not live, it was also clear that he would fight to the very end. It was as if he knew there would be no place for warriors in any other world, and so he may as well embrace his fate, not dodge it.

"Jesus, Bob—"

"You got it square?"

"Yes."

"You are a good kid. You go back to the world and that beautiful girl. You go to her and you put all this bad bullshit behind you, do you copy?"

"Roger."

"Roger. Time to hunt. Sierra-Bravo-Four, last transmission, and out."

And, with the sniper's gift for subtle, swift movement, Bob then seemed to vanish. He slithered off down the hill to the low fog without looking back.

Bob worked down through the foliage, aware that he was clicking into the zone. He had to put it all behind him. There could be nothing in his head except mission, no other memories or doubts, no tremor of hesitation to play across the nerves of his shooting. He tried to get into his war face, to *become,* in some way, war. It was a gift his people had; his father had won the Medal of Honor in the big one against the Japs, messy business on Iwo Jima, and then come home to get the blue ribbon from Harry Truman and get blowed out of his socks ten years later by a no-account piece of trash in a cornfield. There were other soldiers in the line too: hard, proud men, true sons of Arkansas, who had two gifts: to shoot and see something die, and to work like hogs the long hot day. It wasn't much; it's what they had. But there was also a cloud of melancholy attached to the clan—off and on, over the

Swagger generations back to that strange fellow and his wife who'd shown up in Tennessee in 1786 from who knew where, they'd been a line of killers and lonely boys, exiles. There was a blackness in them. He'd seen it in his father, who never spoke of war, and was as beloved as a man in a backwater like Blue Eye, Arkansas, could be, even more so than Sam Vincent, the county prosecutor, or Harry Etheridge, the famous congressman. But his father would have black dog days: he could hardly talk or stir; he'd sit in the dark, and just stare out at nothing. What was dogging him? The war? Some sense of his own luck? A feeling for the fragility of it? Memories of all the bullets that had been fired at him, and the shells, and how nothing had hit him in his vitals? That kind of luck had to run out, and Daddy knew it, but he went out anyway, and it killed him.

What could save you?

Nothing. If it was in the cards, by God, it was in the cards, and Daddy knew that, and faced up to it like a man, looked it in the eyes and spat in its black-cat face, until at last it reared up and bit him in a cornfield on the Polk County line.

Nothing could save you. Bob pressed on, sliding deeper into the fog. Odd how it clung, like clouds of wet wool; he'd never seen anything like it in the 'Nam, and this here was his third tour.

The fear began to eat at him, as it always did. Some fools said he had no fear, he was such a hero, but that only proved how little they knew. The fear was like a cold lump of bacon grease in his stomach, hard and wet and slick, that he could taste and feel at all times. You could not make it go away, you could not ignore it, and anybody who said you could was the worst damned kind of fool. Go on, be scared, he ordered himself. Let it rip. This may be it. But the one thing that scared him most of all wasn't dying, not really; it was the idea of not doing the job. That was something to fear in the heart. He would do the job, by God; that he would.

Trees. He slid through them, tree to tree, his eyes working, testing, looking for possibilities. A hide? A fallback? A line of movement not under fire? A good field of fire? Damn this fog, could he even see them? Could he read ranges, gauge the drop on the long shots? Cover or just concealment? Where was the sun? Nope, didn't matter, no sun.

A thin, cold rain had begun to fall. How would that affect the trajectory? What was the wind, the humidity? How wet was the stock of the rifle? Had it bloated and was now some little swollen knot rubbing secretly against the barrel, fucking up his point of impact? Had the scope sprung a leak, and was now a tube of fog, worthless, leaving him with nothing?

Or: were there NVA ahead? Had they heard him coming? Were they laughing as he bumbled closer? Were they drawing a bead even as he considered the possibility? He tried to exile the fear as he had exiled his own past and future, and concentrate on the mechanical, the aspect of craft that lay before him, how he would reload fast enough if it came to that, since the Remingtons didn't have no stripper clips and the M118 had to be threaded in one round at a time. Should he set up his two Claymores to cover his flanks? He didn't think he had time.

Help me, he prayed to a God he wasn't sure existed, maybe some old gunny up there above the clouds, just watching out for bad boys like him on desperate jobs for people who didn't even know his name.

He halted. He was in trees, had good tree cover, and good fog, a fallback to a hilltop, and then he could cut back the other direction. Professionally, he saw that this was it. A perfect choke point, with targets in the open, fog to cover him, a rare opportunity to get at the NVA in the open, lots of ammunition.

If this is it, by God, then this is it, he thought, settling in behind a fallen tree, literally slipping into a bush, as he squirmed to find a good position. He found his prone, and although he couldn't get one leg flat on the ground for the gouge of a rock or a stump, he got most of his body down, drawing stability from the earth itself. The rifle was back and in, left grip lightly on the forearm, sling tight as it ran from the wood, lashed around that forearm and headed tautly to the stock. Right hand on the small of the stock, finger still off the trigger. Breathing easy, trying to stay cool. Another day at the office. He was situated so no light would reflect off his lens. The trees around him would muffle and defuse the sound of the shots. In the first minutes, anyhow, no one would be able to figure out where the shots were coming from.

He slid his eye behind the scope, finding the proper three inches of relief. Nothing. It was like peering into a bowl of cream. Drifting whiteness, the outline of two or three scrub trees, no sense of the hills forming the other side of the valley, a slight downward angle into vertigo. Nothing stood out from which to estimate range.

He checked his watch: 0700 hours. They would be along soon, not moving quite so quickly because of the fog, but confident that it hid them and that in hours they'd be in possession of Arizona.

So come on, you bastards.

What are you waiting for?

Then he saw one. It was the hunter's thrill after the long stalk, that magical moment when the connection between hunter and hunted, fragile as a china horse, first establishes itself. Blood rushed through him: old buck fever. Everybody gets it when they see the beast they will kill and eat; that's how primordial it is.

I will not eat you, he thought, but by God I will kill you.

More emerged. Jesus Christ . . . the first thin line of sappers in cloth hats with foliage attached, rifles at the high port, eyes strained, at maximum alertness; more tightly bunched, an infantry platoon, battle ready, caped and pith-helmeted, chest web gear, green Bata boots and AKs, Type 56, and no other identifying insignia; the platoon leaders at the front; behind them in a tight little knot the staff, their ranks unrecognizable in the muddy uniforms.

You never saw this. A North Vietnamese infantry battalion moving at the half-trot through a choke point in tight formation, not spread out for four thousand meters or broken down and moving in cells to reassemble under dark. The pilots never saw it, the photos never got it. The NVA, goddamn their cold, professional souls, were too quick, too subtle, too disciplined, too smart for such movement. They moved at night, in small units, then reassembled; or they moved through tunnels, or in bomb-free Cambo or Laos, always careful, risking nothing, knowing surely that the longer they bled the American beast, the better their chances became. Possibly no American had seen such a thing.

The CO was pushing them hard, gambling that he could beat the weather, whack out Arizona and be gone. Speed was his greatest ally, the bleak weather his next. The rain fell harder, pelting the ground, but it did not stop the North Vietnamese, who seemed not to notice. Onward they came.

He snicked off the safety, and through the scope hunted for an officer, a radio operator, an ammunition bearer with RPGs, an NCO, a machine-gun team leader. The targets drifted before him, floating through the crucifer of the crosshairs. That he was about to kill never occurred to him; the way his mind worked, he thought only that he was about to shoot.

Finally: you, little brother. An officer, youngish, with the three stars of a captain lieutenant, at the head of an infantry platoon. He would go first; then, back swiftly, to a radio operator; then, swing left as you run the bolt, and go for the guy with the Chicom RPD 56, put him down, then fall back. That was the plan, and any plan was better than no plan.

The reticle of the Redfield scope wobbled downward,

bouncing ever so slightly, tracking the first mark, staying with him as the shooter took his long breath, hissed a half of it out, found bone to lock under the rifle, told himself again to keep the gun moving as he fired, prayed to God for mercy for all snipers, and felt the trigger break cleanly.

CHAPTER THIRTEEN

"**G**ooooooood morning, Vietnam," said the guy on Captain Taney's portable, "and hello to all you guys out there in the rain. Well, fellas, I've got some bad news. Looks like that old Mr. Sun is *still* AWOL. That's UA, for you leathernecks. Nobody's gonna stop the rain *today*. But it'll be great for the flowers, and maybe Mr. Victor Charles will stay indoors himself today, because his mommy won't let him outside to play."

"What a moron," said Captain Taney, Arizona's XO.

"The weather should break tonight, as a high pressure zone over the Sea of Japan looks like it's making a beeline for—"

"Shit," said Puller.

Why did he put himself through this? It would break when it would break.

Standing in the parapet outside his command bunker, he glanced around in the low light, watching the floating mist as it seethed through the valley that lay beyond.

Should he put an OP out there, so they'd know when the 803rd was getting close?

But he no longer controlled the hills, so putting an OP out there would just get its people all killed.

The rain began to fall, thin and cold. Vietnam! Why was it so cold? He had spent so many days in country over the past eight years but never had felt it this biting before.

"Not good, sir," said Taney.

"No, it isn't, Taney."

"Any idea when they'll get here?"

"You mean Huu Co? He's already here. He pushed 'em hard through the night and the rain. He's no dummy. He wants us busted before our air can get up."

"Yes, sir."

"You have that ammo report ready, Captain?"

"Yes, sir. Mayhorne just finished it. We have twelve thousand rounds of 5.56 left, and a couple more thousand .30 carbine rounds. We're way low on frags, seventy-nine rounds and belted 7.62. Not a Claymore in the camp."

"Christ."

"I've got Mayhorne distributing the belted 7.62, but we're down to five guns and I can't cover any approach completely. We can set up a unit of quickmovers with one of the guns to jump to the assault sector, but if he hits us more than one place at once, we screw the pooch."

"He will," said Puller bleakly. "That's how he operates. The pooch is screwed."

"You know, sir, some of these 'Yards have family here in the compound. I was thinking—"

"No," said Puller. "If you surrender, Huu Co will kill them all. That's how he operates. We hang on, pray for a break in the weather, and if we have to, go hand to hand in the trenches with the motherfuckers."

"Was it ever this bad in sixty-five, sir?"

Puller looked at Taney, who was about twenty-five, a good young Spec Forces captain with a tour behind him. But in sixty-five he'd been a high school hotshot; what could you tell him? Who could even remember?

"It was never this bad, because we always had air and there were plenty of firebases around. I've never felt so fucking on my own. That's what trying to be the last man out gets you, Captain. Let it be a lesson. Get out, get your people out. Copy?"

"I copy, sir."

"Okay, get the platoon leaders and the machine gun team leaders to my command post in fifteen and—"

They both heard it.

"What was that?"

"It sounded like a—"

Then another one came. A solitary rifle shot, heavy, obviously .308, echoing back and forth across the valley.

"Who the fuck is that?" Taney said.

"That's a sniper," said Puller.

They waited. It was silent. Then the third shot and Puller could read the signature of the weapon.

"He's not firing fast enough for an M14. He's shooting a bolt gun, and that means he's a Marine."

"A Marine? Way the hell out here in Indian Territory?"

"I don't know who this guy is, but he sounds like he's doing some good."

Then came a wild barrage of full automatic fire, the lighter, crisper sound of the Chicom 7.62X39mm the AKs fired.

Then the gunfire fell silent.

"Shit," said Taney. "Sounds like they got him."

The sniper fired again.

"Let's run the PRC-77 and see if we can pick up enemy radio intelligence," Puller said. "They must be buzzing about this like crazy."

Puller and his XO and Sergeant Blas and Y Dok, the 'Yard chieftain, all went down into the bunker.

"Cameron," Puller said to his commo NCO, "you think you've got any juice left in the PRC-77?"

"Yes, sir."

"Let's do a quick scan. See if you can get me enemy freaks. They ought to be close enough to pick up."

"Yes, sir. Sir, if air comes and we need to talk 'em in—"

"Air isn't coming today, Cameron. Not today. But maybe someone else has."

Cameron fiddled with the radio mast on the PRC-77, snapping a cord so that it flew free above the wood and dirt of the roof, then clicked it on, and began to diddle with the frequency dials.

"They like to operate in the twelve hundreds," he said. He pulled through the nets, not bringing anything up except static, the fucking United States Navy bellowing about beating the Air Force Academy in a basketball game and—

"Shit."

"Yeah," said Puller, leaning forward. "Can't you get us in a little tighter?"

"It's them, isn't it, sir?" asked Taney.

"Oh, yes, yessy, yessy, yessy," said the head man Y Dok, who wore the uniform of a major in the ARVN, except for the red tribal scarf around his neck, "yep, is dem, yep, is dem!" He was a merry little man with blackened teeth and an inexhaustible lust for war, afraid, literally, of nothing.

"Dok, can you follow?" asked Puller, whose Vietnamese was good but not great. He was getting odd words— *attack, dead, halt*—and he couldn't follow the verb tenses; they seemed to be describing a world he couldn't imagine.

"Oh, he say they under assault on right by platoon strength of marksmen. Snipers. The snipers come for them. *Ma my,* 'merican ghosts. He says most officers dead, and most machine gun team leaders also—*oh!* Oh, now he dead too. Y Dok hear bullet hit him as he talk. Good shit, I tell you, Major Puller, got good deaths going, oh, so very many good deaths."

"A platoon?" said Taney. "The nearest Marine firebase is nearly forty klicks away, if it hasn't rotated out. How could they get a platoon over here? And why would they send a platoon?"

"It's not a platoon," said Puller. "They couldn't—no, not overland, across that terrain, not without being bounced. But a team."

"A team?"

"Marine sniper teams are two-men shows. They can move like hell if they have to. Jesus, Taney, listen to this and be aware of the privilege you've been accorded. What you are hearing is one man with a rifle taking on a battalion-strength unit of about three hundred men."

"Dey say dey got him," said Y Dok.

"Shit," said Taney.

"God bless him," said Puller. "He put up a hell of a fight."

"Dey say, 'merican is dead and head man say, You

fellas get going, you got to push on to the end of the valley and de officer say, Yes, yes, he going to—*oh. Oh ho ho ho!*" He laughed, showing his blackened little teeth.

"No. No, no, no, no. He got dem! Oh, yes, he just killed man on radio. I hear scream. Oh, he is a man who knows the warrior's walk, dot I know. He got the good deaths, very many, going on."

"You can say that again," said Puller.

CHAPTER FOURTEEN

When the trigger broke, the North Vietnamese captain lieutenant turned as if to look at Bob just once before he died. All the details were frozen for a second: he was a small man, even by NVA standards, with binoculars and a pistol. An instant ago, he had been full of life and zeal. When the bullet struck him, it sucked everything from him and he stood with grave solemnity, colorless, as all the hopes and dreams departed him. If he had a soul, this would be where it fled to whatever version of heaven sustained him. Then it was over: with the almost stiff dignity of formal ceremony, he toppled forward.

Bob threw his bolt fast, tossing out the spent shell, but never breaking his eye relief with the scope, a good trick it only took a lifetime to master. In the perfect circle of nine magnifications, he saw the men who were his targets looking at one another in utter confusion. There was no inscrutability in their expression: they were dumbfounded, because this was not supposed to happen, not in the rain, in the fog, in the perfect freedom of their attack, not after their long night march, their good discipline, their toughness, their belief. They had no immediate theory to explain it. No, this was not possible.

Bob pivoted the rifle just a bit, found a new target, and felt the jolt as the rifle fired. Two hundred yards out and two tenths of a second later, the 173-grain bullet arrived at 2,300 odd feet per second. The tables say that at that range and velocity, it will pack close to two thousand foot-pounds of energy, and it hit this man, a machine gun team leader standing near his now dead commanding officer, low in his stomach, literally turning him inside out. That was what such a big bullet did: it operated on him, opening his intimate biological secrets to those around him, not a killing shot, but one that would bleed him out in minutes.

Quickly Bob found another and within the time it takes to blink an eyelash, fired for the third time and set that one down, too.

The North Vietnamese did not panic, though they could not hope to pick out Bob in the fog, and the muzzle blast was diffused; they only knew he was on the right somewhere. Someone calmly issued orders; the men dropped and began to look for a target. A squad formed to flank off to the right and come around. It was standard operating procedure for a unit with much experience and professionalism.

But Bob slithered away quickly, and when he felt the fog overwhelm him, he stood and ran ahead, knowing he had but a few seconds to relocate. Would they take the casualties and continue to march? Would they send out flanking parties; would they take the time to set up mortars? What will they do? he wondered.

He ran one hundred yards fast, slipping three new cartridges into the breech as he jounced along, because he didn't want to waste time loading when he had targets. That was shooting time, precious. He slipped down off the incline onto the valley floor and crouched as he moved through the elephant grass, an odd nowhere place sealed off by vapors. He came at last to the center of the track, and got a good visual without the grass: he was now three hundred yards away and saw only the dimmest of shapes in the fog. Sinking to a quick, rice-paddy squat, he put the glass to them, put the crosshairs on one, quartering them high to account for a little drop at that distance, and squeezed the trigger. Maybe he was shooting at a stump. But the blob fell, and when he quartered another, it fell too. He did that twice more, and then the blobs disappeared; they'd dropped into the grass or had withdrawn, he couldn't tell.

Now what?
Now back.

The flankers will come, but slowly, thinking possibly they're up against a larger force.

Not even bothering to crouch, he ran again, full force through the mist. Suddenly the NVA opened up and he dropped. But the sleet of firepower did not come his way and seemed more of a probing effort, a theoretical thing meant to hit him where, by calculation, he should be. He watched as tracers hunted him a good hundred yards back, liquid splashes of neon through the fog, so quick and gossamer they seemed like optical illusions. When they struck the earth, they ripped it up, a blizzard of splashy commotion. Then the firing stopped.

He dropped, squirmed ahead and came to a crook in a tree. Quickly he slipped four more rounds into the M40's breech, throwing the last one home and locking the bolt downward with the sensation of a vault door closing.

The rifle came up to him, and he seemed to have lucked into a thinner spot in the veil of fog, where suddenly they were quite visible. An officer was talking on the radio phone as around him men fanned out. Bob killed the officer, killed two of the men. Then he got a good shot at a man with four RPGs on his back squirming for cover, put the crosshairs onto a warhead and fired once. Force multiplier: the quadruple detonation ripped a huge gout in the earth, possibly driving others back, possibly killing some of them.

He didn't wait to count casualties, or even take a quick look at his results. He crawled again through the high elephant grass, the sweat pouring off him. He crawled for what seemed like the longest time. Tracer rounds floated aimlessly overhead, clipping the grass, making the odd *whup* sound a bullet fighting wind will make. Once, when the firing stopped, he thought he sensed men around him and froze, but nothing happened. When at last he found some trees so that he could go back to work, he discovered he was much farther back in the column. Before him, as the vapors drifted and seethed, were some men who seemed less soldiers than beasts of burden, so laden were they with their equipment. This was simple murder; he took no pleasure in it, but neither did he consider it deeply. Targets? Take them down, eliminate them, take them out. Numbly he did the necessary.

Huu Co, senior colonel, had a problem. It wasn't the firepower; there wasn't much firepower. It was the accuracy.

"When he shoots, brother Colonel," his officer told him, "he hits us. He is like a phantom. The men are losing their spirit."

Huu Co fumed silently, but he understood. In a frontal attack his men would stand and fight or charge into guns: that was battle. This was something else: the terrible fog, the mysterious bullets singing out of it with unerring accuracy, seeking officers and leaders, killing them, then . . . silence.

"Maybe there are more than one," someone said.

"I believe there are at least ten," someone else said.

"No," said Huu Co. "There is only one and he has only one rifle. It is a bolt-action rifle, so therefore he is an American Marine, because their army no longer uses bolt actions. One can tell from the time between the rounds, the lack of double shots or bursts. You must be calm. He preys on your fear. That is how he works."

"He can see through the fog."

"No, he cannot see through the fog. He is in the hills to the right, clearly, and as he moves, he encounters disparities in the density of the mist. When it is thin, he can see to shoot. Get the men down into the grass; if they stand they will be killed."

"Brother Colonel, should we continue to march? How many can he kill? Our duty lies at the end of the valley, not here."

It was a legitimate point, raised by Commissar Tien Phuc Bo, the political officer. Indeed, under certain circumstances, duty demanded that officers and men simply accept a high rate of casualty in payment for the importance of the mission. Rule No. 1: Defend the Fatherland; fight and sacrifice myself for the People's Revolution.

"But this is different," said Huu Co. "The fog makes it different, and his accuracy. Indiscriminate fire may be sustained as fair battle loss. The sniper presents a different proposition, both philosophically and tactically. If the individual soldier feels himself being targeted, that has disproportionate meaning to him and erodes his confidence. In the West they call it 'paranoia,' a very useful term, meaning overimaginative fear for the self. He will give himself up to a cause or a mission, in the abstract, but he will not give himself up to a man. It's too personal, too intimate."

"Huu Co is right," argued his executive officer, Nhoung. "We may not simply accept losses as we travel, for the weight becomes immense and when we reach our goal, the men are too dispirited. What then have we accomplished?"

"As you decide," said Phuc Bo. "But you may be criticized later and it will sting for many, many years."

Huu Co accepted the rebuke; he had been criticized in a reeducation camp in 1963 for nine long months, and to be criticized, in the Vietnamese meaning of the term, was excruciating.

Bravely, he thrust ahead.

"A man like this can inflict a surprisingly high number of casualties, particularly upon officers and noncommissioned officers, the heart of the Army. Without leadership, the men are lost. He can attrit our officer staff if we do not deal with him now and immediately. I want Second Platoon on the right, supported by a machine gun team on each end for suppressive fire. They are to maneuver on a sweeping movement, while the rest of the unit holds up in the high grass. I want radio contact with Company Number Two sappers, and recall them and assign them in the blocking role. They must move quickly. Latest reports say the weather will not break. We have some time and I prefer by far to maintain unit integrity than to push on at this time. We will take him in good time. Patience in all things; that is our way. Communicate with your leaders and the fighters. Now is not the time for rash action; this is a test of discipline and spirit."

"That is understood, sir."

"Then let's do our duties, brothers. I anticipate success within the hour and I know you will not let me down."

Donny lay in the high grass, working the spotting scope. But the range was too far, a good four hundred meters, and in the valley he just saw the drifting mist, and heard the gunfire.

He took his right eye away from the scope and looked out with both of them. Again, nothing. The shooting rose and fell, rose and fell, punctuated now and then by two or three heavy rifle cracks, Bob's shots. At one point some kind of multiple blast came. Had Bob fired a Claymore? He didn't know but he didn't think the sniper would have time, as he'd been moving this way and that through the hills.

He was well situated, half buried in a clump of vegetation, halfway up a hill, a little above the fog. He could see far to the right and far to the left, but he didn't think anybody could get the drop on him. He had a good compass heading to the Special Forces camp at Kham Duc and knew if he had to he could make it in two or three hard hours. He drank a little water from his one remaining canteen. He was all right. All he had to do was sit there, wait for air, direct the air, then get the hell out of there. If no air came, then he was to move under cover of nightfall. He was not to go into the valley.

He thought of a familiar remark scrawled in Magic Marker on Marine helmets and flak jackets: "Yea, though I walk in the Valley of Death, I shall fear no harm, because I am the meanest motherfucker in the valley!" Bravado, sheer, thumping bravado, chanted like an incantation, to keep the Reaper away.

I'm not going into the Valley of Death, he thought.

Those aren't my orders. I followed my orders, I did everything I was told, I was specifically ordered not to go into the Valley of Death.

He accepted that as both a moral and a tactical proposition as ordered by a senior staff NCO. No man could challenge that, nor would one want to or try to.

I am fine, he told himself. I am short, I am fine, I am three and days till DEROS. I have my whole goddamned life in front of me and no man can say I shirked or ducked or dodged. No one can ever wonder if my beliefs were founded on moral logic or my own cowardice. I have to prove nothing.

Then why do I feel so shitty?

It was true. He felt truly sick, angry at himself, almost to the point of revulsion. Down there Swagger was probably giving away his life and Donny had somehow missed the show. Everybody cared about *him*. Trig, too, had cared about *him*. What was so special about him that he had to survive? He had no writer's gift, he was not conversational or charismatic—no one could listen to him, he could be no witness.

Why me?

What's so special about my ass?

He heard them before he saw them. It was the *thup-thup-thup* of men running, coming at the oblique. He didn't jerk or move quickly and in an instant was glad he hadn't, for sudden moves like that get you spotted.

They passed about twenty-five meters ahead of him, in single file, fastmovers, stripped of helmets and packs and canteens, racing toward duty and combat. It was the twelve-man flanking patrol, recalled by radio to move on the sniper from behind.

He could see how it would work. They'd form a line and flankers would drive Bob into them, or they'd come upon him from the rear. In either event, Bob was finished.

If Donny'd had the grease gun he might have gotten all twelve in a single burst. But probably not; that was very tricky shooting. If he had a Claymore set up, he might have gotten them too. But he didn't. He had nothing but his M14.

He watched them go and they pounded along with grace, economy and authority. They disappeared into the fog.

I have my orders, he thought.

My job is the air, he thought.

Then he thought, Fuck it!, and got up to take them from behind.

They came as he thought they would, good, trained men, willing to take casualties, a platoon strength unit fanning through the high grass. Bob could make them out in the mist, dark shapes filing through the weaving fronds; he thought of a deer he'd once seen in a foggy cornfield back in Arkansas, and Old Sam Vincent, who'd tried to be a father to him after his own had passed, telling him to fight the buck fever, to be calm, to be cool.

He heard Sam now.

"Be cool, boy. Don't rush it. You rush it, it's over and you can't never get it back."

And so he was calm, he was death, he was the kind hunter who shot for clean kills and no blood trails, who was a part of nature himself.

But he wasn't.

He was war, at its cruelest.

He had never had this feeling before. It scared him, but it excited him also.

I am war, he thought. I take them all. I make their mothers cry. I have no mercy. I am war.

It was an odd thought, just fluttering through a mind far gone into battle intensity, but it could not be denied.

The platoon leader will be to the left, not in the lead, he'll be talking to his men, holding them together.

He hunted for a talking man and when he found him, he shot him through the mouth and ceased his talking forever.

I am war, he thought.

He shifted quickly to the man who'd run to the fallen officer and almost took him, but instead held a second, and waited for another to join him, grab him, take command, and turn himself to issue orders. Senior NCO.

I am war.

He took the NCO.

The men looked at each other, dead targets in his eyes, and in a moment of utter panic did exactly the right thing.

They charged at him.

He couldn't possibly take them all or even half of them, he couldn't escape or evade. There was only one thing to do.

He stood, war-crazed, face green-black with paint, eyes bulged in rage, and screamed, *"Come on you fuckers, I want to fight some more! Come on and fight me!"*

They saw him standing atop the rise, and almost en masse pivoted toward him. They froze, confronting him, a mad scarecrow with a dangerous rifle atop a hill of grass, unafraid of them. For some insane reason, they did not think to fire.

The moment lingered, all craziness loose in the air, a moment of exquisite insanity.

Then they ran at him.

He dropped and slithered the one way they would not expect.

Right at them.

He slithered ahead desperately, snaking through the grass, until they began to fire.

They paused a few feet from him, fired their weapons from the hip as if in some terrified human ceremony aimed at slaying the devil. The rounds scorched out, ripping the stalks above his head to land somewhere behind. It was a ritual of destruction. They fired and fired, reloading new mags, sending their bullets out to kill him, literally obliterating the crest of the hill.

He crawled ahead, until he could see feet and spent brass landing in heaps.

The firing stopped.

He heard in Vietnamese the shouts:

"Brothers, the American is dead. Go find his body, comrades."

"You go find his body."

"He is dead, I tell you. No man could live through that. If he were alive, he would be firing at us even now."

"Fine, go and cut his head off and bring it to us."

"Father Ho wants me to stay here. Somebody must direct."

"I'll stay, brother. Allow me to give you the privilege of examining the body."

"You fools, we'll all go. Reload, make ready, shoot at anything that moves. Kill the American demon."

"Kill the demon, my brothers!"

He watched as the feet began to move toward him.

Get small, he told himself. *Be very, very small!*

He went into a fetal position, willing himself into a stillness so total it was almost a replication of genuine animal death. It was a gift he had, the hunter's gift, to make his body of the earth, not upon it. He worried only about the smell of his sweat, rich with American fats, that could alert the wisest of them.

Feet came so close.

He saw canvas boots, and a pair of shower clogs.

They won this fucking war in shower clogs!

The two pairs of feet sloughed through the grass, each vivid in the perfection of its detail. The man in shower clogs had small, dirty, tough feet. The clogs were probably just an afterthought; he could fight barefoot in snow or on gravel. The other's boots were holey, torn, taped together, a hobo's comic footwear, something Red Skelton's Clem Kadiddlehopper might wear. But then the boots marched on, passing by, and Bob scooted ahead, slithering through the grass until he came to a fold in the earth. He rose, checked around, and saw nothing in the mist, and then raced off to the right, down the fold, toward the column, which had probably resumed its movement toward Arizona.

Then he crashed into the soldier.

NVA.

The two looked at each other for one stupid moment, Bob and this obvious straggler, the idiot who'd wandered away. The man's mouth opened as if to scream even as he fumbled to bring his AK to bear, but Bob launched at him in an animal spring of pure evil brutality, smashing him in the mouth with his skull, and driving downward on him, pinning the assault rifle to his chest under his own dense weight. He got his left hand about the man's throat, crushing it, applying the full pinning weight of his body while at the same time reaching for his Randall knife.

The man squirmed and bucked spastically, his own hands beating at Bob's neck and head. Then one hand dipped, also for a knife, presumably, but Bob rolled slightly to the left and drew his knee up and drove it into the man's testicles with all the force he could muster. He heard the intake of breath as the concussion folded his enemy.

Then he had the knife, and no impulse halted him. He drove it forward into the belly, turned it sideways so the cutting edge sliced into entrails, and drew it to the left. The man spasmed, fighting the pain, his hand flying to Bob's wrist, gagging sounds leaking from a constricted throat. Bob yanked the knife out and stabbed upward, feeling the blade sink into throat. He fought for leverage over the dying soldier, got himself upright and astride the heaving chest and drove the blade two or three more times into the torso, the man arching with each stroke.

He sat back. He looked about, saw the Remington a few feet away. He wiped the Randall blade on his camouflaged trousers, and slipped it back into the upside-down sheath on his chest. He checked quickly: two pistols, a canteen. He picked up the Remington but had no time to look for his hat, which had fallen off in the struggle. A lick of salty blood ran down from the point on his crown where he'd head-butted the North Vietnamese, and it arrived at the corner of his mouth, shocking him. He turned, looked at the man.

Why had it been so easy? Why was the man so weak?

The answer was obvious: the soldier was about fourteen. He'd never shaved in his life. In death, his face was dirty, but essentially undisturbed. His eyes were open and bright but blank. His teeth were white. He had acne.

Bob looked at the bloody package that had been a boy. A feeling of revulsion came over him. He bent, retched up a few gobs of undigested C-rat, gathered his breath, wiped the blood off his hands, and turned back to the path that lay ahead of him, which led to the column.

I *am* war, he thought; this is what I do.

Huu Co's political officer Phuc Bo was adamant. A stocky little man who'd been to Russian staff school, Phuc Bo had the blunt force of a party apparatchik, a man who lived and breathed the party and was a master of dialectics.

"Brother Colonel, you must move, despite the cost. To waste more time is to lose our precious advantage. How many can a single man kill? Can he kill more than forty, possibly fifty? That is well under a twenty percent casualty rate; that is entirely acceptable to the Party. Sometimes, the fighters' lives must be spent to accomplish the mission."

Huu Co nodded solemnly. Up ahead, sporadic fire broke out, but the column had bogged down again. There was no word from the flanking patrol and no word from the sappers who'd been recalled. Still, the American assailed them with well-aimed shots, cadre his particular specialty.

How did he know? Cadre wore no rank pins, carried few symbols of the ego of leadership such as riding crops, swords or funny hats. Leaders were indistinguishable from fighters, both in party theory and in actual practice. Yet this American had some instinct for command, and when he fired, he brought down leaders, not always but in high enough percentage to be disruptive.

"He is hitting our cadre, brother Political Officer. And what if we push on, and he robs us over the kilometers of our leadership? And we get to the objective and no leaders come forth and our attacks fail? What will the party say then? Whose ears will ring the most loudly with criticism?"

"Our fighters can produce leaders from amongst themselves. That is our strength. That is our power."

"But our leaders must be trained, and to squander them for nothing but the ego of a political officer who seeks the glory of seeing his column destroy an American fort late in an already victorious war may itself be a decision that is commented upon."

"I wonder, dear brother Colonel, if indeed there are not vestiges of Western humanitarianism, the sick decadence of a doomed society, still within your soul? You worry too much about such things as the petty lives of individuals when it is the movement of the masses and the forces of history and our objective that should be your concern."

"I am humble before my brother's excellent and perceptive critique," said the colonel. "I still believe in patience over the long journey, and that in patience lies virtue."

"Dearest Colonel," said the man, his face lighting with fire, "I have sworn to the commissar that the American fort shall fall. I therefore demand that you give the order to move forward without regard to—"

Phuc Bo stopped talking. It was difficult to continue without a lower jaw and a tongue. He stepped backward, the blood foaming brightly across his chest and gurgling from the hole that had been his mouth. Odd arguments came from him, so arcane and densely constructed they could not be followed. His eyes turned the color of an old two-franc coin and he died on his feet, falling backward into the high grass amid a splash of muddy water that flew up when he hit the wet ground.

Around the senior colonel, men dived for cover, but the senior colonel knew the American would not fire. He realized that he would be spared. In his way, the American was like a psychiatrist as much as a sniper, and he operated on the body of the people to remove the self-important, the vain, the overbearing. Political Officer Phuc Bo was an angry man and had been addressing his senior colonel aggressively, with brisk and dramatic hand movements and a loud voice, in the gestural vocabulary of superiority. Examining them, the American had assumed that it was he who was in command, it was he who was dressing down a naughty inferior. Thus the senior colonel's total lack of ego and presence had rendered him effectively invisible in the sniper's scope.

There was another shot; down the column, a sergeant fell, screaming.

The senior colonel turned, one man standing among many cowering men, and said conversationally to his XO, "Send out another platoon; I fear our antagonist has evaded the first. And keep the men low in the grass. We need not die for party vanity or some American's hunt for glory."

The order was sent.

The senior colonel turned back to the hills, where the American still hunted them.

You, sir, he thought in the language of his youth, forgotten all these years, you, sir, are *très formidable*.

Then he went back to considering how to kill the man.

Puller cursed the clouds. They were low, wet, dense, thicker than the blood on the floor of the triage tent, and they rewarded his anger with a burst of rain, which fell like gunfire slopping through the mud.

No air.

Not today, not with these low motherfuckers choking the earth. He looked back to his shabby empire of mud and slatternly bunkers and smashed squad hootches and blown latrines. A ragged curl of smoke still rose from where the dump had been blown yesterday. Tribesmen and cadre huddled behind parapets or ran from place to place, risking rifle fire. The mud smelled of buffalo shit and blood and the acrid tang of burned powder.

A mortar shell detonated nearby, and he dropped behind his own parapet, as a scream went up, "Medic! Goddammit, medic!" But there was no medic; Jack Deems, who'd been with him since sixty-five and was cross-trained both as a medic and a demolitions expert, a very good professional soldier indeed, was hit yesterday. Shot in the chest. Bled out screaming the names of his children.

Puller shivered.

Another mortar shell hit. Thank God the VC units only had 60-mms, which lofted a grenade-sized bit of explosive into Arizona, and could take out a man only if they scored a lucky, direct hit or they got him in the open and took him down with shrapnel. But when Senior Colonel Huu Co and his bad boys showed up, they'd have a weapons platoon with Chicom Type 53s in 82-mm, and those suckers were bad news. If they chose not to go for the direct kill, they could batter Arizona to pieces with that much throw-load, then move in and shoot the wounded. That would be it; then they'd fade into the hills. The whole front would go: it was exquisitely planned, just as American strength was ebbing but ARVN confidence not high enough, the temptation too huge to deny and therefore getting them out of their normal defensive posture for the first time since sixty-eight.

Puller looked again down the valley, which was shrouded in mist, and felt the bone-chilling rain on the back of his neck. He stared, as if he could penetrate that drifting, seething but altogether blank nothingness. But he could not.

Now and then a shot or two sounded, the heavy smack of the Marine's .308; it was always answered with a fusillade. That Marine was still at it.

Man, you are a tiger, he thought. Don't know you, brother, but you are one fucking tiger. You are the only thing between us and a complete screwing of the pooch.

"They no get him," said Y Dok.

"No," said Puller, wishing he could break a team out to bring in the sniper, but knowing he couldn't, and that it would be evil waste to try. "No, but they will, goddamn them."

Now they had him.

They were going to get him, but it was a question of when: early or late?

Where had these guys come from?

Then he knew.

They had to be the sapper unit out on flank security, brought back fast from out there. Probably Huu Co's best troops, real pros.

Bob lay on his belly on the crest of a small knoll, still as death, breathing in unmeasurable increments. Underneath him he was wedded to the Remington sniper rifle, whose bolt now gouged him cruelly in the stomach. He could see through the wavering scope and watched as they came for him.

Somehow, they knew this was his hill: it was some hunter's very good instinct. Then he realized: *they found the dead soldier in the gully and tracked me.* As he had moved through the wet elephant grass, he'd probably left a pattern of disturbance, where the grass was wiped clean, where the turf was trampled. Good men could follow much less.

Now they had him on this goddamned hill; it would be over in a few minutes. Oh, these guys were good.

They had spread out, and were moving up very methodically, two three-men elements of movement, two of cover. No more than three men, too widely spaced for three shots, were visible at any one moment, and then only for seconds. They were willing to give up one of the three to find him and take him out. Soldiers.

He knew he had to get to his grease gun; if they got close, and he was stuck with the Remington with one cartridge in the spout and a bolt-throw away from another shot, he was done.

Now it was his turn to move, ever so slowly, ever so noiselessly.

Learn from them, he instructed himself. Learn their lessons: patience, caution, calmness, freedom from fear, but above all the discipline of the slow move. He had a complicated thing before him: without making a sound, he had to reach back under his rain cape, release the sling of the M3, draw it forward around his body, ease open the ejection port cover and fingerhole the bolt back. Then and only then would he have a chance, but that destination was long minutes away.

The rain fell in torrents now, disguising his noise just a bit. But these were sharp, trained men: their ears would hear the sound of canvas rubbing on leather or metal sliding across flesh; or they would smell his fear, acrid and penetrating; or they would see his movement irregular against the steadier rhythms of nature.

Ever so slowly, he eased over to his side from his belly, an inch at a time, shifting his hand back over the crest of his body. Now he could hear them calling to each other: they spoke the language of birds.

"Coo! Coo!" came the call of a dove in a part of the south where there were no doves.

"Coo!" came the response, from the right.

"Coo!" came another one, clearly from behind. Now they *knew* he was here, for the trail had led up the hill but had not led down it; they had not cut across it. He was thoroughly cooked.

His fingers touched metal. They crawled up the grip of the grease gun, pawed, climbed up to the tubular receiver and found the sling threaded through its latch. His fingers struggled against the snap on the sling.

Oh, come on, he prayed.

These little fuckers could be tough; they could rust

shut or simply be tightly fitted and need too much lever-age to free up.

Why didn't you check it?

Agh!

Asshole!

He ordered himself to check the sling snap a thousand times if he ever got out of this fix, so that he would never, ever again forget.

Come on, baby. Please, come on.

With his fingers pulling, his thumb pushing, he battled the thing. It was so small, so absurd: twelve men were twenty-five yards away hunting him, and he was hung up on the cold, wet ground trying to get a fucking little—

Ah!

It popped, with a metallic click that he believed could be heard all the way to China.

But nobody cooed and he wasn't jumped and gutted on the spot.

The gun slid free and down his back, but he captured it quickly with his hand, and now withdrew it, very slowly, bringing it around, drawing it close to him, like a woman to treasure for the rest of his life. He smelled its oily magnificence, felt its tinny greatness. A reliable, ugly piece of World War II improvisation, it probably cost a buck fifty to manufacture from hubcaps and sleds and bikes picked up in scrap-metal drives in the forties. That's why it had such a cheap, toylike, rattly feel to it. With his fingers he deftly sprung the latch on the ejection port, then inserted a finger into the bolt hole that he had just revealed. With the finger he pushed back, felt the bolt lock, then let it come forward. He dropped down and drew the gun up to him.

"Coo! Coo!"

CHAPTER FIFTEEN

The message came by radio to the hasty command post dug into the side of a hill. It was from the sapper patrol on the right flank.

"Brother Colonel," gasped Sergeant Van Trang, "we have the American trapped on a hill half a kilometer to the west. We are closing on him even now. He will be eliminated within the quarter hour."

Huu Co nodded. Van Trang was a banty little north countryman with the heart of a lion. If he said such a thing was about to happen, then indeed it would happen.

"Excellent," said the colonel. "Out."

"There are no shots," his XO told him. "Not since the unfortunate Phuc Bo was martyred."

Huu Co nodded, considering.

Yes, now was the time. Even if he couldn't get the whole battalion through the pass, he could get enough men through to overwhelm Arizona. But he had every confidence in Van Trang and his sappers. They were the most dedicated, the best trained, the most experienced. If they had the American trapped, the incident was over.

"All right," he said. "Send runners to One, Two and Three companies. Let's get the men out of the grass, get them going. Fast, fast, fast. Now is the time for speed. We have wasted enough time and energy on this American."

The XO rapidly gave the orders.

Huu Co went outside. All around him, men rose from the grass, shook the accumulated moisture from their uniforms and formed up into loose company units. A whistle sounded from in front of the column. Behind Huu Co, with amazing swiftness, members of the combat support platoon broke down the hasty command post so that nothing remained, then they too went to their positions.

"Let's go," said Huu Co, and with a gaggle of support

personnel around him, he too began to move at the half-trot, ahead through the mist and the rain, to the end of the valley where the Americans were under siege.

The long train of men moved quickly, bending back the grass. Overhead, the blessed clouds still hung, low and dense, to the surface of the earth. No airplanes would come. He would make Arizona by nightfall, give the men a few hours' rest, then move them into position and, sometime after midnight, strike with everything he had, from three directions. It would be over.

From the right it came, at last: the sudden flurry of fire, the sound of grenade detonations, a few more shots and then silence.

"They got him," the XO said to him.

"Excellent," said Huu Co. "At last. We have triumphed. Frankly, between you and I, the American provided a great service."

"The political officer, Brother Co? I agree, of course. He loved the party too much and the fighters not enough."

"Such men are necessary," said Huu Co. "Sometimes."

"That American," said the XO. "He was some kind of fighter himself. If they were all like that, our struggle would be nowhere near its conclusion. I wonder what motivates a man like that?"

Huu Co had known Americans in Paris in the early fifties and then in Saigon in the early sixties. They had seemed innocent, almost childish, full of wonder, incapable of deep thought.

"They are not a serious people," he said. "But I suppose by the odds, every now and then you get one who is."

"I suppose," said the XO. "I'm glad we killed this one. I prefer the good ones dead."

He lay very composed, trying not to listen to his heart or to his mind, or to any part of his body, which yearned to survive. Instead he listened to nothing and tried to plan.

They are tracking you. They will come right to you. If you let them carry the fight, you will die. You must shoot first, shoot to kill, attack decisively. If you are aggressive you may stun them. They will expect fear and terror. Aggression is the last thing they expect.

He tried to lay it all out, under the knowledge that any plan, even a bad plan, is better than no plan.

Shoot the visible ones; spray till the mag empties; throw grenades; fall away to the left; fall back into better cover in the trees. But most of all: get off this hill.

They were very close, cooing softly to one another, having converged. They were patient, calm, very steady. Oh, these were the best. They were so professional. No problems. Getting the job done.

One suddenly stood before him. The man was about thirty, very tough looking, his face a blank. He held an American carbine. He seemed to have some trouble believing what lay before him on the ground.

Bob fired a five-round burst into his body, sending him down. He pivoted, rising, and in the same second saw others turning toward him. He swept the grease gun across them, a long, thudding burst, watching the bullets chop through the grass in a blizzard of spray, ensnare his opponents and take them down. Spent shells poured spastically from the breech of the junky little piece as it rattled itself dry. In the silence that followed, he heard the ping of grenade pins being pulled and frantically threw himself backward, rolling through the grass, feeling it lash and whip at him as he went, so glad he'd left the pack behind. The first grenade detonated about ten yards away and he felt the pain as several pieces of shrapnel tore at his arm and the side of his body that was exposed. But still he rolled and another grenade detonated, this one still farther away.

He came to a stop, could hear some hustling around, and pulled a grenade from his belt, pried the pin out and lofted it in the general direction of his enemies. As it exploded—was that a scream he heard?—he got a new magazine into the submachine gun, and though he had no targets, lost himself in the madness of firing. He emptied the magazine stupidly in a sustained blast, the gun thudding, the bullets fanning out to splash through the grass, atomizing stalks they struck, ripping sheets of mud spray from the earth.

Then he rolled backward and continued to propel himself down the hill. In one moment of repose, he got another magazine into the gun, but before he could see targets he heard the soft crush of something heavy landing nearby, and he went flat as a grenade detonated, sending a spout of earth high into the sky and numbing his eardrums. Now he heard nothing: his hearing was momentarily gone and his vision blurred. The left arm hardly worked; it had numbed out and he saw that it was bleeding badly.

Oh, shit.

Fire came at him from three points, short, professional bursts from AK47s. They probed, sending the rounds skirmishing after him in three vectors. He assumed that a few more were working around behind him.

That's it, he thought.

I buy it.

This is it.

Oh, fuck, I tried so hard. Don't let me chicken out here at the end. Oh, please, let me be brave.

But he wasn't brave. His anger melted. A profound sense of regret washed over him. So much he hadn't done, so much he hadn't seen. He felt the powerful pain of his own father's death upon him, and how, now that he was gone, no one would be left alive to mourn and miss Earl Swagger.

God help me, Daddy, I tried so goddamned hard. I just didn't make it.

A shot kicked up next to his face, stinging his neck with pricks of dirt. Another one buzzed by close. They were all shooting now, all of them that were left.

I ain't no hero, he thought.

Oh, please, God, please don't let me die here. Oh, I don't want to die, please, please, please.

But nobody answered and nobody listened and it was all over, it was finished. Bullets cracked past or hit nearby, evicting gouts of angry earth and pelting spray. He willed himself back, shrinking to nothingness, but there was only so far he could go. His eyes were shut. They had him. The next round would—

Three fast booming cracks, heavy and powerful. Then two more.

Silence.

"Swagger? Bob Lee? You all right?"

Bob lifted his head; about forty yards away, a young Marine stepped out of the elephant grass. Donny's boonie hat had fallen to his back and his hair was golden even in the gray light and the misty rain. He was an improbable black-and-green-faced angel with the instrument of his sergeant's deliverance, the U.S. Rifle M14, 7.62 MM NATO.

"Stay down," Bob called.

"I think I got 'em all."

"Stay down!"

In that second, two men fired at Donny but missed, the bullets pulling big spouts from the valley floor. Bob turned to watch their shapes scuttle away in the grass, and he walked bursts over both of them, until they stopped moving. He crouched, waiting. Nothing. No noise, just the ringing in his ears, the pounding of his heart, the stench of the powder.

After a bit, he went to them; one was dead, his arms thrown out, the blood congealing blackly as it pooled to form a feast for ants. The other, a few yards away, was on his back, and still breathed. He had left his AK 30 feet away as he'd crawled after taking the hits. But now, exhausted, he looked up at Bob with beseeching eyes. His face and mouth were spotted with blood, and when he breathed heavily, Bob heard the blood bubble deep in his lungs.

The hand seemed to move. Maybe he had a grenade or a knife or a pistol; maybe he was begging for mercy or deliverance from pain. Bob would never know, nor did it matter. Three-round burst, center chest. It was over.

Donny came bounding over.

"We got 'em all. I didn't think I could get here in time. Christ, I hit three guys in a second."

"Great shooting, Marine. Jesus, you saved this old man's fucking bacon," Bob said, collapsing.

"You're all right?"

"I'm fine. Dinged up a bit." He held out his bloody left arm; his side also sang of minor penetration in a hundred or so places. Oddly, what hurt the most was his neck, where the impacting NVA round had blown a handful of nasty dirt into the flesh and hair of his scrubby beard, and for some reason it stung like a bastard.

"Oh, Christ, I thought I was cooked. I was finished. Wasted, greased. Man, I was a gone motherfucker."

"Let's get the fuck out of here."

"You wait. I left the rifle up top. Just let me catch my breath."

He sucked down a few gulps of the sweetest air he'd ever tasted, then ran up the hill. The M40 lay where he had dumped it, its muzzle spouting a crown of turf, its bolt half open and gummed also with turf.

He grabbed it and ran back to Donny.

"Map?"

Donny fished it out of the case, handed it over.

"All right," Bob said, "he's sure got that column moving again. We've got to move on, pass them, and jump them again."

"There's not much light left."

Bob looked at his Seiko. Jesus, it was close to 1700 hours. Time flies when you're having fun.

"Fuck," he said.

He had a moment's gloom. No light, no shoot. They were going to get close enough to stage an assault in the dark, and all the snipers in the world wouldn't make a spit's worth of difference.

"Shit," he said.

But Bob's mind was so fogged with delirium, adrenaline and fatigue it wasn't processing properly. He had the vague sense of missing something, as if he'd left his IQ points up there on that ugly little hill. It was Donny who pulled another sack from around his waist, opened it, and out came what looked like a small tubular popgun and a handful of White Star illumination flares; the bag was heavy with the cartridges.

"Flares!" he said. "Can you shoot by flares?"

"If I can see it, I can hit it," Bob said.

They moved swiftly through the gloom, amid small hills, in the elephant grass, ever mindful they were paralleling the movement of the enemy main force in the valley, ever mindful that there were still scouting units out in the area. If and when the NVA discovered their dead recon team, they might send still other men after them.

They moved at the half-jog, through a fog of fatigue and pain. Bob's arm hurt desperately and he didn't have any painkillers, not even aspirin. His head ached and his legs felt withered and shaky. They followed a compass heading, reshooting it each time they moved around a hill. The elephant grass was tall and concealing, but it cut at them mercilessly. There wasn't much water left and even in the falling dark, Bob could see that the clouds hadn't broken, still hung low and close. A wicked, pelting rain started, delivering syringes of cold where it struck them. Soon the trip became pure blind misery, two hungry, dead-tired, filthy men running on faith and hope toward a destination that might not even exist.

Bob's mind slipped in and out; he tried to concentrate on the job ahead but it would not stay. At one point, he called a halt.

"I got to rest," he said.

"We been pushing pretty hard," Donny said.

Bob slipped down into the grass.

"You've lost a lot of blood."

"I'm okay. I only need a little rest."

"I got some water. Here, take some water."

"Then what'll you drink?"

"I don't need to shoot. I just fire flares. You need to shoot. You need the water."

"You'd think, all this fucking rain, the last thing we'd be is thirsty."

"I feel like I just played two football games without quarters or halftimes. Just two games straight through."

"Oh, man," Bob said, taking a big swig of Donny's water, feeling its coolness rush down his flaming throat.

"After this, I'm going to sleep for a month," said Donny.

"No, after this," said Bob, "you are going on R&R to be with your wife, if I have to go to the goddamned general and ass-kick him myself."

It was almost full dark. Somewhere birds were beginning to call; the jungle was close, just beyond the hill line. There was, however, nothing alive in view; once again, they seemed alone in the world, lost in the hills, stuck in a landscape of desolation.

Suddenly Bob's mind sped to other possibilities.

"I got a idea," he said. "You got tape? Don't you carry tape? I think I told you to—"

Donny reached into a bellows pocket of his cammies, pulled out a roll of gray duct tape.

"This would be tape, no?"

"That would be tape, yes. Okay, now . . . goddamn . . . the spotting scope. Don't tell me you dumped your spotting scope. You didn't leave that back with your gear, did you?"

"Fuck," said Donny, "I brought everything except a helicopter. Hmmm, sink, tent, Phantom jet, mess hall; oh, yeah, here . . ."

He pulled another piece of gear slung around his shoulder. It was a long, tubular green canvas carrying case, strapped at either end, which carried an M49 20X spotting scope, complete with a folded tripod. It was for glassing the really far targets.

He unslung it and handed it over.

"Now what?"

"Oh, just you watch."

Greedily, Bob bent to the scope case, unscrewed it and reached out to remove a dull-green metal telescope, disjointed slightly, with a folding tripod underneath. It must have cost the Marine Corps a thousand bucks.

"Beautiful, ain't it?" he asked. Then he rammed its delicate lens against Donny's rifle muzzle, shattering it into a sheet of diamonds. He reamed the tube out on the rifle barrel, grinding circularly to take out all the glass and the delicate internal mechanisms for focus adjustment. He unscrewed and threw away the tripod. Then he seized the canvas case, took out his Randall Survivor and began to operate.

"What are you doing?" Donny asked.

"You never mind, but you get my rifle cleaned up. No rules today. Hurry, Pork, we gotta get a goddamned move on."

Donny worked some rough maintenance on the gun, clearing the muzzle of mud and grass, scraping the dirt, and in a few minutes had it ready to shoot again. He looked back to see that Bob had sawed off one end of the scope case and cut a smaller hole through the other, giving him a green tube about twelve inches long.

Bob wedged the spotting scope tube back into the case.

"Here, you hold that goddamn muzzle up for me," he commanded, and, working swiftly, commenced to wedge the scope case and scope on the muzzle, then wrap yards of tape around the case and the muzzle, securing the case so that it projected a good eight inches beyond the muzzle.

It looked like some kind of silencer but Donny knew it wasn't a silencer.

"What is?"

"Field expedient flash suppressor," said Bob. "Flash is just powder burning beyond the muzzle. If you can lengthen the cover on the barrel, it'll burn up in there, not in the air, where it'll light me up like a Christmas tree. It's pretty flimsy and won't hold much more than a few dozen shots, but by God, I don't want them tracking my flash and hitting me with the goddamned kitchen sink. Now, let's mount out."

A last fast.

The troops were driven by duty and destiny. An extraordinary accomplishment, the long double-time march from Laos, the ordeal of the sniper in the valley, the victory over the man, and now, on to the Green Beret camp at Kham Duc. Battalion No. 3 was just a kilometer away from the staging point, maintaining good order, moving smartly.

Huu Co, senior colonel, glanced at his watch and saw that it was near midnight. They would be in place in another hour, and could use a little time to relax and gather themselves. Then the assault teams would stage and the weapons platoon would set up the 81mm Type 53s, and the last stage would commence. It would be over by dawn.

The weather wouldn't matter.

Still, it was holding beautifully for him. Above there was a starless night, gray and dim, the clouds close to the earth. In his old mind, his Western mind, he could believe that God himself had willed the Americans from the earth. It was as if God were saying, "Enough, begone. Back to your land. Let these people be."

In his new mind, he merely noted that his luck had held, and that luck is sometimes the reward for boldness. The Fatherland appreciated daring and skill; he had gambled and won, and the eventual fall of the Kham Duc camp would be his reward.

"It is good," said the XO.

"Yes, it is," said Huu Co. "When this is over, I will—"

But Nhoung's face suddenly lit up. Huu Co turned to wonder about the source of illumination.

A single flare hung in the sky beneath a parachute, bringing light to the dark night. As it settled the light grew brighter, and there was one lucid moment in which the battalion, gathered as it plunged toward its study, seemed to stand out in perfect clarity. It was a beautiful moment too, suffused with white light, gentle and complete, exposing the people's will as contained and expressed through its army, nestled between close hills, churning onward toward whatever tomorrow brought, unhesitatingly, heroic, stoic, self-sacrificing.

Then the shot rang out.

Puller dreamed of Chinh. His second tour. He hadn't planned to, it just happened; she was Eurasian, lived in Cholon, he'd been in the field eleven months and, suffering from combat exhaustion, had been brought back to MACV in Saigon, given a staff job, just to save him from killing himself. It was a safe job back then, sixty-seven, a year before Tet, and Chinh was just there one day, the daughter of a French woman and a Vietnamese doctor, more beautiful than he could imagine. Was she a spy? There was that possibility, but there wasn't much to know; it was brief, intense, pure pleasure, not a whisper of guilt. Her husband had been killed, she said, by the communists. Maybe it was so, maybe it was not. It didn't matter. The communists killed her one night on the road in her Citreon after she'd spent hours making love with him. She ran through an ambush they'd prepped for an ARVN official: just blew her away.

He dreamed of his oldest daughter, Mary. She rode horses and had opinions. She hated the Army, watched her mother play the game, suck up all the way through in the shit posts like Gemstadt or Benning, always making a nice home, always sucking up to the CO's wife.

"I won't have it," Mary said. "I won't live like that. What does it get you?"

His wife had no answer. "It's what we do," she finally said. "Your father and me. We're both in the Army. That's how it works."

"It won't work that way for me," she said.

He hoped it wouldn't. She was too smart to end up married to some lifer, some mediocrity who would go nowhere and only married her because she was the daughter of the famous Dick Puller, the lion of Pleiku, who'd taken a Chicom .51 in the chest and wouldn't even let himself be medevaced out and who died in the shitty little Forward Operations Base at Kham Duc a year after the war was lost, threw himself away for nothing that nobody could make any sense of.

Puller came awake. It was dark. He checked his watch. It would start soon, be over soon. He smelled wet sand from the soaked bags out of which the bunker was built, dirt and mud, gun oil, Chinese cooking, blood, the works, the complete total that was life in the field.

But he had an odd sensation: something was happening. He looked at his watch and saw that it was nearly midnight. Time to get up and—

"Sir."

It was young Captain Taney, who would probably also die tonight.

"Yeah?"

"It's—ah—you won't believe it."

"What?"

"He's still out there."

"Who?" Puller thought instantly of Huu Co.

"Him. Him. That goddamned Marine sniper."

"Does he have night vision?"

"No, sir. You can see it from the parapet. You can hear it. He's got flares."

He didn't get good targets. Not enough light. But in the shimmering glow of the floating flares he got enough: movement, fast, frightened, scurrying, the occasional hero who would stand and try and mount a rally, the runner who was sent to the rear to report to command, the machine gun team that peeled off to try and flank him.

The flares fired with a dry, faraway pop, like nothing else in the 'Nam. They lit at about three hundred feet with a spurt of illumination; then the 'chute would open and grab the wind, and they'd begin to float downward, flickering, spitting sparks and ash. It was white. It turned the world white. The lower they got the brighter it got, but when they swung in the breeze, they turned the world to a riot of shadows chasing each other through the dimness of his scope.

But still, he'd get targets. He'd fire at what his instincts told him was human, what looked odd in the swinging light, the sparks, the glow that filled the world, the crowd of panicked men who now felt utterly naked to the sniper's reach. The night belonged to Charlie, it was said. Not this night. It belonged to Bob.

They'd worked it right. No movement, not now. It was too dark to move and they'd get mixed up, get out of contact with one another and that would be that. Donny was on the hilltop, Bob halfway down. The bad guys were moving left to right beyond them, one hundred yards out, where the grass was shorter and there wasn't any cover. It was a good killing zone, and the first element of the column was hung up, pinned in the grass, believing that if they moved they would die, which was correct.

Donny would fire a flare and move a hundred steps or so on the hilltop, while Bob waited for the flare to get low enough to see the movement. Bob would fire twice, maybe three times in the period of brightest light. Then he'd move too, the same one hundred steps, through the grass, and set up again.

Forward; then they'd move back. They couldn't see one another, but they had the rhythm. They'd send people up after him, but not soon enough. They wouldn't be sure where the flares were coming from, because, God bless the little fireworks, they didn't trail illumination as they ascended.

Bob couldn't even see the reticle. He just saw the movement and knew where the reticle would be because that's where it always was, and he fired, the rifle cracking, its flash absorbed in the steel tube that surrounded the muzzle but would sooner or later have to give way. No one could yet see where the shots were coming from.

The flare floated, showering sparks. In its cone of light, Bob saw a man drop into vegetation and he put a bullet into him. He flicked the bolt fast, jacking out the spent case, and watched as another man came through the light to his fallen comrade, and he killed him too. The trick was the light; the flares had to be constant; there couldn't be a dark moment when there was no light because these guys would move on him then, and they'd be too close, too fast and it would be over.

It lasted for ten minutes; then, having planned it, Donny stopped firing and Bob stopped firing. They both fell back, met at the far side of the hill, and took off on the dead run, leaving behind the confusion. They moved on, looking for another setup.

"That'll slow 'em. It'll take 'em ten minutes to figure out we're gone. Then they'll get moving again. We should be able to hit them again. I want to set up on that side now. You watch me."

Donny had the M14 at high port, Bob's rifle was slung and he carried the M3 in his hands, though he was down now to two magazines. Both his handguns were cocked and locked.

"Okay, you ready?"

"I think so."

"You cover me if I take fire."

"Gotcha."

Bob stepped out of the grass onto the valley floor.

He felt so naked. He was all alone. The wind whistled, and once again it began to rain. The NVA must have been a half klick or so behind. Suddenly, the sky behind them lit up: an assault team had moved up to and taken the now empty hill on which they had situated. Grenade blasts rocked the night, and blades of the sheer light slashed from the concussion. Heavy automatic weapons fire followed: again, they were slaying the demon.

Bob got halfway across, then turned with his grease gun to cover, and called out for Donny to join him.

"Come on!" he shouted.

The boy came across the valley floor and passed Bob, and went to set up on the other side. Bob raced over. Quickly, they found another hill.

"You get on up there," Bob said. "When you hear me shoot, you fire the first flare. I'm going to open up further out this time. Meanwhile, you set up Claymores. I'm down to about twenty rounds and I want a fallback. If we get bounced, we'll counterbounce with the Claymores, then fall back. Set them up, and wait to pop flares. Password is . . . fuck, I don't know; make up a password."

"Ah—Julie."

"Julie. As in 'Julie is beautiful,' roger that?"

"Roger that."

"You hear movement coming to you and he don't sing out 'Julie is beautiful,' you go to Claymores, use the confusion to fall back and find a hide, then you wait until tomorrow and call in a bird after a while. Okay? There'll be a bird tomorrow. Got it?"

"Got it."

"If I don't make it back, same deal. Fall back, go to ground, call in a bird. They'll be buzzing all over this zone tomorrow, no problem. Now, how many flares you got?"

Donny did a quick check on his bag.

"Looks like about ten."

"Okay, when they're gone, they're gone. Then we're out of business. Fall back, hide, bird. Okay?"

"Check," said Donny.

"You all right? You sound kind of shaky."

"I'm just beat. I'm tired. I'm scared."

"Shit, you can't be scared. I'm scared enough for both of us. I got all the fear in the whole fucking world."

"I don't—"

"Just this last bad thing, then we are the fuck out of here, and I'm going to make sure you get home in one piece, I give you my word. You done yours. Nobody can say, He didn't do his. You done it all ten times over. You get to go home after this one, I swear to you."

There was an odd throb in his own voice that Bob had never heard before. Where did it come from? He didn't know. But somehow Bob had a blinding awareness that in some way, the life of the world now depended on getting Donny home in one piece. Donny was the world, somehow, and if he, Bob, got him killed out here for this shit, he would answer for all eternity. Very strange; nothing he'd ever felt before on any battlefield.

"I'm cool," Donny said.

"See you in a bit, Sierra-Bravo-Four."

Donny watched the sergeant go. The man was like some Mars or Achilles or something, so lost in the ecstasy of the battle that he somehow didn't want it to end, didn't want to come back. Once again, Donny had the odd feeling that he was destined to witness all this and tell it.

To whom?

Who would care? Who would listen? The idea of soldiers as heroes was completely gone. Now, they were baby killers or, if not that, they were fools, suckers, morons who hadn't figured out how to beat the machine.

So maybe that was his job: to remember the Bob Lee Swaggers of the world and, when the times somehow changed, the story could be retrieved and told. How one crazy Arkansas sumbitch, mean as a snake, dry as a stick, brave as the mountains, took on and fucked up an entire battalion, for almost nothing, really, except so that nobody would ever say of him, He let us down.

What made such a man? His brutal, hardscrabble childhood? The Corps as his home, his love of fighting, his sense of country? Nothing explained it; it was beyond explanation. Why was he so meaninglessly brave? What compelled him to treat his life so cheaply?

Donny made it to the top of the hill. It was a queer little empire, much smaller than the last hill, a little hump that overlooked the larger valley before it. Here is where they would fight.

He unstrapped his three Claymores bandoleers and took the things out, your basic M18A1 Directional Mine. Jesus, were these nasty little packages. About eight inches across and four inches tall, they were little convexes of plastic-sheathed C-4, impregnated with about seven hundred pieces of buckshot apiece. You opened a compartment, pulled out about one hundred meters of wire, unspooled it to your safe hole, and there crimped it to the Electrical Firing Device M57, which came packed in the bandoleer and looked like a green plastic hand exerciser. When you clamped it, you jacked a goose of electricity through the wire to the detonator, the pound and a half of C-4 went kaboom, and the seven hundred steel balls went sailing through the air at about two thousand miles an hour. For a couple of hundred feet, anything in their way—man, beast, vegetable or mineral—got turned to instant spaghetti. Just the thing for human wave attacks, night ambushes, perimeter defense or those annoying staff meetings, though the Marine Corps thoughtfully added the message FRONT TOWARD ENEMY for its dimmer recruits, so they wouldn't get mixed up in all the excitement and blow a nasty hole in their own lines.

Donny pulled down the folding scissors legs on each mine, made sure that the front indeed faced the enemy, and set up the three of them about sixty feet apart, atop the hill. There was some little technical business to be done involving blasting caps, shipping plug priming adaptors, the detonator well, wire crimped and so on. Then the wire was fed backward, where he used his entrenching tool to dig a quick, low hole, though he knew that if he ever had to go to the mines, it meant there were enough zips coming at them that whether he survived the backblast or not was kind of a moot point.

He took a last swig on his canteen and tossed it away.

He wished he had a C-rat left, but he'd left them back with most of his gear. Now, however, instead of the usual huge burden, he felt almost light-headed. He had no food, no canteen, no spotting scope, no Claymores. The only burden, beside his M14 magazines, was the goddamned PRC-77, tied tightly to his back by a couple of cruel straps. He even dared peel it off, and now felt really light. He felt like dancing. The freedom from the ache of going into battle with sixty pounds of gear and then twenty pounds of gear and now nothing was astonishing. He had trained himself to ignore the ache in his back; now it vanished. Cool, he thought, I get to die without a backache, first time in my career in the 'Nam.

Then the shot came, and Donny hastily pulled out his flare device, slipped a flare into the breech, screwed it shut and thrust it against the ground to fire. Like a tiny mortar, the flare popped out and hissed skyward, seeming to disappear. A second passed, then the night bloomed illumination as the flare lit, its 'chute opened and it began to float down into the valley, showering sparks and white. It was snowing light.

Bob was shooting now.

The last act had begun.

They were much closer than he anticipated. The scope was cranked down to three power so that he could get as clear and wide a view as possible. Still, they weren't targets so much as possibilities, squirms of movement that in their rhythm seemed human against the stiller spectacle of the natural world, though it was all made stranger yet by the rushing shadows the swing of the flare created as it descended.

He saw, he fired. Something stopped moving, or just went down. He'd had eighty rounds; he was down to less than twenty. *God, I killed some boys today. Jesus fucking Christ, I did some killing today. I was death today, I was the Marine Corps's finest creation, the stone killer, destroying all that moved before me.*

Something moved, he shot it, it stopped. Clearly the NVA couldn't locate him, and he was so close, and now the bossman had made a decision—to keep going, to take casualties, to make the rallying point for the attack on Arizona, to march through the minefields, as a Russian general had put it.

It was as though he were saying to Bob: You can't kill us all. We will defeat you through our willingness to absorb death. That is how we won this war; that is how we will win this battle.

He could hear sergeants screaming, *"Bi! Bi! Bi!"* meaning "go, go, go," urging the troops onward, but they could not see him because of his flash hider, the panic, the fear. The troops did not want to go, clearly. He'd gotten into their heads: that was the sniper thing; that was what was so terrible about the sniper. He was intimate and personal in a way which nothing else that kills in war can be; his humanness preys on your humanness, and it was hardest for even the most disciplined of troops to face.

He jacked out a round into the breech, fired, watched someone die. He fired again, quickly, in the fading light; then another flare popped, the light renewed and he saw more targets, so close it was criminal murder to take them, but that was his job tonight: he took them, reloaded, fell back through the high grass, emerged when another flare fired off, and killed some more. He was gone totally in the red, screaming urgency of his own head, not a man anymore, but a total killing system, conscienceless, instinctive, his brain singing with blood lust. It was so easy.

Xo Nhoung was gone. The bullet snuffed his life out in a second, drilling him through the neck with the sound of an ax hitting a side of raw beef. Nhoung died on his feet, and hit the ground a corpse. His soul flew away to be with his ancestors.

"We are dying! He can see us! There is no hope!" a young soldier screamed.

"Shut up, you fool," yelled Huu Co, yearning to reach to the sky and crush those blasphemous flares with his bare hands, then rip the skulls from the bodies of the sniper and his spotter.

"They're on the left this time," he screamed again, because he had seen the XO fall to the right, pushed by the impact of the bullet.

"On the left. Fire for effect, brothers, fire now, kill the demons!"

His troops began to open fire helter-skelter, without much thought, the lacy neon of the tracers jumping through the darkness like spiderwebs, ripping vaguely where they struck tree or vegetation, but the point of it was to calm them while he figured out what to do.

He stood. A flare lit over his head. He was in bold relief and the flare seemed to be falling directly toward him. The man next to him fell, stricken; the man behind him fell, stricken; He was in the cone of light; he was the target. It didn't matter. His life didn't matter.

"Number One assault platoon, advance one hundred meters to the left; Number Two assault platoon, provide covering fire during the movement; weapons platoon, set up mortar units to be ranged at 150 meters on the hill at 1000 hours to our front. Machine gun platoon, set up automatic weapons one hundred meters to the right."

He waited for the sniper to kill him.

But instead, an astonishing thing happened. No bullet came at all. The sniper lit a torch and began waving at him, as if to say, Here I am. Come kill me. He could see the man, surprisingly close, waving the torch.

"There he is; kill him! You see him. Kill him," Huu Co shouted.

As he came out of the grass, another flare popped, low this time, filling the night with white light. The spectacle was awesome through the scope, jacked up three times: he saw men run in panic, he saw the blind fire directed outward, he saw men in the center of the position yelling desperately.

Commanding officer, he thought.

Oh, baby, if I can do you, I can call this one a day!

Three men stood. The center of the scope found one and he pulled the trigger with—*damn!*—enough jerk so the shot went high and he knew he hit high, in the neck; in the perfect circle of the scope, his target sank backward, stiff and totaled. Bob cocked fast, but the flare died. He could hear nothing. The fire lashed outward pointlessly, unaimed, mere fireworks as if the terrified were trying to drive demons away.

Another flare popped: low and bright and harsh.

Bob blinked at the brightness of it, saw another man stand, fired, taking him down. As he pivoted slightly, he went past a second man to a third, fired quickly, hit him off center and put him down. Then he came back to the second man as he rushed through the bolt cycle.

Got you.

You're it.

You're the man.

He caught his breath, steadied himself. The flare seemed to be falling right toward this brave individual, and Bob saw that yes: this was him, whoever he was.

The officer alone stood, taking the full responsibility of the moment. He called directions so forcefully, Bob could hear the Vietnamese vowels through the noise of the fire. He was fortyish, small, tough, very professional looking, and on his green fatigues he wore the three stars of the senior colonel, visible only now because the light was so bright as the flare descended.

Bob took a second's worth of breath, noticing that in the brightness of the instant, the reticle had even materialized; the crosshairs stood out bold and merciless upon the colonel's chest, and in that second Bob took the slack out and with the *snap* of a piece of balsa wood shattering, the trigger went, the rifle recoiled, death from afar was sent upon its way.

But something was wrong; instead of a sight picture, Bob saw bright lights, bouncing balls of sheer incandescence, his night vision shattering as he blinked to clear but the world had caught on fire. Flames ate the darkness. It made no sense.

Then he realized what had happened. The jury-rigged suppressor, sustained in its nest of tape, had finally yielded to the hammering of muzzle blast and flash, slipped down into the trajectory of the bullet, deflected it and, exposed directly to the detonation of flash, the canvas exploded into flame. The rifle had become a torch signaling his location. He stared at it for an oafish moment, realized it was his own death, and threw the whole mad blazing apparatus away.

Now there was nothing left except the remotest possibility of survival.

He turned to flee, as bullets clipped about, whacking through the stalks. He was hit hard, on the back, driven to the earth. The pain was excruciating.

He saw it very clearly: *I am dead. I die now. This is it.* But no life sprung before his eyes; he had no sense of wastage, loss, recrimination, only sharp and abiding pain.

He reached back to discover not hot blood but hot metal. A bullet aimed for his spine had instead hit the slung M3 grease gun, driving it savagely into him, but doing him no permanent harm. He shucked the disabled weapon, and began to slither maniacally through the grass as the world seemed to explode around him.

He didn't know what direction; he just crawled, pathetically, a fool begging for life, so far from heroic it was ludicrous, thinking only one phrase like a mantra: *I don't want to die, I don't want to die, I don't want to die.*

He kept going, through his terror, and came at last to a little nest of trees, into which he dove and froze. Men moved around him in the darkness; shots were fired, but the action, after the longest time, seemed to die away, and he slipped in another direction.

He got so far when someone shouted, and then, goddamn them, the NVA fired their own flares. Theirs were green, less powerful, but they had more of them: the sky filled with multiple suns from a distant planet, sparky green, descending through green muck as if it were an aquarium.

In a moment of primeval fear, Bob simply turned and ran. He ran like a motherfucker. He ran crazily, insanely to escape the cone of light, but even as it promised to die, another blast of candlepower lit the night as another dozen or so green Chicóm flares popped.

This seemed to be the place. He ran upward, screaming madly, *"Julie is beautiful, Julie is beautiful!",* saw Donny rise above him with his M14 in a good, solid standing offhand and begin to fire on his pursuing targets very professionally. Bob ran to the boy, feeling the armies of the night on his butt, and dove into Donny's shallow hole.

"Claymores!" he screamed.

"They're not close enough!" Donny responded. Bob rose: more flares came, and this time a whole company seemed to be rushing at them to destroy them.

"Now!" he screamed.

"No!" screamed Donny, who had the three firing devices. Where had this kid got this much cool? He held them, the shots cracking up the hill, tracers flicking by, the green flares floating down, the screams of the rushing men louder and louder until he fell back, smiled and squeezed the three firing devices simultaneously.

CHAPTER SIXTEEN

Donny had three M14 mags left, with twenty rounds each; Bob had seven rounds in his .45, one loaded magazine, and seven rounds in his .380 with no extra magazines. Donny had four grenades. Bob had his Randall Survivor. Donny had a bayonet.

That was it.

"Shit," said Donny.

"We're cooked," said Bob.

"Shit," said Donny.

"I fucked up," said Bob. "Sorry, Pork. I could have led them away from here. I didn't have to come back up this hill. I wasn't thinking."

"It doesn't matter," said Donny.

The NVA scurried around at the base of the hill. Presumably they'd carried off their dead and wounded, but it wasn't clear yet what their next move would be. They hadn't fired any flares recently, but they were maneuvering around the hill, Bob supposed, for the last push.

"They may think we have more Claymores," he said. "But probably they don't."

It was dark. Donny had no flares. They crouched in the hole at the top of the hill, one facing east, the other west. The dead M57s with their firing wires lay in the hole too, getting in the way. The stench of C-4, oddly pungent, filled the air, even now, close to an hour after the blasts. Donny held his M14, Bob a pistol in each hand. They could see nothing. A cold wind whipped through the night.

"They'll probably set up their 81s, zero us, and take us out that way. Why take more casualties? Then they can be on their way."

"We tried," said Donny.

"We fought a hell of a fight," said Bob. "We hung 'em

up a bit. Your old dad up in Ranger heaven would be proud of you."

"I just hope they find the bodies, and my next of kin is notified."

"You ever file that marriage report?"

"No. It didn't seem important. No off-post living in the 'Nam."

"Yeah, well, you want her to get the insurance benefits, don't you?"

"Oh, she doesn't need the money. They have money. My brothers could use it for school. It's okay the way it is."

Nothing much to say. They could hear movement at the base of the hill, the occasional secret muttering of NCOs to their squads.

"I lost the picture," Donny said. "That's what bothers me."

"Julie's picture?"

"Yeah."

"When?"

"Sometime in the night. No, the late afternoon, when I went after that flank security unit. I don't remember. My hat fell off."

"It was in your hat?"

"Yeah."

"Well, tell you what, I can't git you out of here and I can't git you the Medal of Honor you deserve, but if I can git you your hat back, would you say I done okay by you?"

"You always did okay by me."

"Yeah, well, guess what? Your hat fell off your head, all right, but you been so busy, and now you're so tired you ain't figured out that you was wearing a cord around the hat to pull it tight in the rain. It's still there. It's hanging off your neck, across your back."

"Jesus!"

Donny reached around his neck and felt the cord; he drew it tight, pulled the hat up from around his back and removed it.

"Shit," he said, because he could think of nothing else to say.

"Go on," said Bob, "that's your wife; look at her."

Donny pulled at the lining of the hat and removed the cellophane package, unpeeled it and removed, a little curled and bent, slightly damp, the photograph.

He stared at it and could see nothing in the darkness, but nevertheless it helped.

In his mind, she was there. One more time. He wanted to cry. She was so sweet, and he remembered the three days they'd had. They got married in Warrenton, Virginia, and drove up to the Skyline Drive and rented a cabin in one of the parks. They spent each day going for long walks. That place had paths that ran along the sides of the mountains, and you could look down into the Shenandoahs or, if you were on the other side, into the Piedmont. It was green, rolling country, checkerboard farms, as far as you could see; beautiful, all right. Maybe it was his imagination, but the weather seemed perfect. It was early May, spring, and life was breaking from the crust of the earth with a vengeance, green buds everywhere. Sometimes it was just them alone in the world, high above the rest of the earth. Or was it just that all soldiers remember their last leave as special and beautiful?

"Here, look," said Donny.

"It's too dark."

"Go on, *look*!" he commanded, the first time he had ever spoken sharply to his sergeant.

Swagger gave him a sad look, but took the picture.

He looked at Julie, but saw nothing. Still, he knew the picture. It was a snapshot taken in some spring forest, and the wind and the sun played in her hair. She wore a turtleneck and had one of those smiles that made you melt with pain. She seemed clean, somehow, so very, very clean. Straw blond hair, straight white strong teeth, a tan face, an outdoorsy face. She *was* a beautiful girl, model or movie-star beautiful. Bob had a brief, broken moment when he contemplated the brute fact that no one nowhere loved him or would miss him or give a shit about his death. He had no one. A middle-aged lawyer in Arkansas might shed a tear or two, but he had his own kids and his own life and the old man would probably still miss Bob's father more than he'd miss Bob. That was the way it went.

"She's a great-looking young woman," Bob said. "I can tell she loves you a lot."

"Our honeymoon. Skyline Drive. My old captain gave me six hundred dollars to take her away when I got my orders cut. Emergency leave. He got me three days. He was a great guy. I tried to pay him back, but the letter came back, and it was stamped, saying he had left the service."

"That's too bad. He sounds like a good man."

"They got him too."

"Yeah, they get everyone in the end."

"No, I don't just mean 'them, they.' I mean a specific guy, with influence, who set about to purify the world. We were part of the purification process. I'd still like to look that guy up. Commander Bonson. Here's to you, Commander Bonson, and your little victory. You won in the end. Your kind always does."

Flarc. Green, high. Then two or three more green suns descending.

"Git ready," said Bob.

They could hear the *ponk-ponk-ponk* as a few hundred yards away, three 81mm mortar shells were dropped down their tubes. The shells climbed into the air behind a faint whistle, then reached apogee and began their downward flight.

"Get down!" screamed Bob. The two flattened into the mud of the shallow hole.

The three shells landed fifty meters away, exploding almost simultaneously. The noise split the air and the two Marines bounced from the ground.

"Ah, Christ!"

A minute passed.

Three more flares opened, green and almost wet, spraying sparks all over the place.

Bob wished he had targets, but what the hell difference did it make now? He lay facedown in the mud, feeling the texture of Vietnam in his face, smelling its smells, knowing he would never see another of its dawns.

Ponk-ponk-ponk.

The shells climbed, whispering of death and the end of possibilities, then descended.

Oh, Jesus, Bob prayed, oh, dear Jesus, let me live, please, let me live.

The shells detonated thirty meters away, triple concussions, loud as hell. Something in his shoulder began to sting even before he landed again in Vietnam, having been lifted by the force of the blast. Acrid Chinese smoke filled his eyes and nostrils.

He knew the drill. Somewhere a spotter was calling in corrections. Fifty back, right fifty, that should put you right on it.

Oh, it was so very near.

"I was a bad son," Donny sobbed. "I'm so sorry I was a bad son. Oh, please, forgive me, I was a bad son. I couldn't stand to visit my dad in the hospital, he looked so awful, oh, Daddy, I'm so sorry."

"You were a good son," Bob whispered fiercely. "Your daddy understood, don't you worry about it none."

Ponk-ponk-ponk.

Bob thought of his own daddy. He wished he'd been a better son too. He remembered his daddy pulling out in his state trooper cruiser that last night in the twilight. Who knew it was a last time? His mother wasn't there. His daddy put his hand out to wave to Bob, then turned left, heading back to Blue Eye, and would there go on out U.S. 71 to his rendezvous with Jimmy Pye and his and Jimmy's deaths in a cornfield that looked like any other cornfield in the world.

The explosions lifted them, and more parts of Bob seemed to go numb, then sting. This triple shot bracketed the position. This was it. They had them; they had merely to drop a few more shells down the tube and the direct hit would come out of statistical inevitability, and it would be all over. Fire for effect.

"I'm so sorry," Donny was sobbing.

Bob held him close, felt his young animal fear, knew there was no glory in any of it, only an ending, a mercy, and who would know they lived or died or fought here on this hilltop?

"I'm so sorry," Donny was sobbing.

"There, there," Bob said.

Someone fired an orange flare over on the horizon. It was a big one, it hung there for the longest time, and only far past the moment when reasonable men would have caught on did it at last dawn on them that it wasn't a flare at all, it was the sun.

And with the sun came the Phantoms.

The Phantoms came low, screaming in from the east, along the axis of the valley, their jet growls filling the air, almost splitting it. They dropped long tubes that rolled through the air into the valley beneath, and blossomed oranger than the sun, oranger and hotter than any sun, with the power of thousands of pounds of jellied gasoline.

"God!" screamed Bob. "Air! *Air!*"

They peeled off, almost in climbing victory rolls, and a second flight hammered down, filling the valley with its cleansing flame.

Then the gunships.

Cobras, not like snakes but like thrumming insects, thin and agile in the air: they roared in, their mini-guns screaming like chainsaws ripping through lumber, just eating up the valley.

"The radio," Bob said.

Donny rolled over, thrust the PRC-77 at Bob, who swiftly got it on, searched for the preset band that was the air-ground freak.

"Hit eight, hit eight!" Donny was screaming, and Bob found it, turned it on to find people looking for him.

"—Bravo-Four, Sierra-Bravo-Four, come in, please, immediate. Where are you, Sierra-Bravo-Four? This is Yankee-Niner-Papa, Yankee-Niner-Papa. I am Army FAC at far end valley; I need your position immediate, over."

"Yankee-Niner-Papa, this is Sierra-Bravo-Four. Goddamn, ain't you boys a sight!"

"Where are you, Sierra-Bravo-Four, over?"

"I am on a hill approximately two klicks outside Arizona on the eastern side of the valley; uh, I don't got no reading on it, I don't got no map, I—"

"Drop smoke, Sierra-Bravo-Four, drop smoke."

"Yankee-Niner-Papa, I drop smoke."

Bob grabbed a smoke grenade, pulled the pin, and tossed it. Whirls of angry yellow fog spurted from the spinning, hissing grenade, and fluttered high and ragged against the dawn.

"Sierra-Bravo-Four, I eyeball your yellow smoke, over."

"Yankee-Niner-Papa, that is correct. Uh, I have beaucoup bad guys all around the farm. I need help immediate. Can you clean out the barnyard for me, Yankee-Niner-Papa, over?"

"Wilco, Sierra-Bravo. Y'all hang tight while I direct immediate. Stay by your smoke, out."

In seconds, the Cobras diverted to the little hill upon which Bob and Donny cowered. The mini-guns howled, the rockets screamed; then the gunships fell back and a squadron of Phantoms flashed by low and fast, and directly in front of Bob and Donny, the napalm bloomed hot and bright in tumbling flame. The smell of gasoline reached their noses.

Soon enough, it was quiet.

"Sierra-Bravo-Four, this is Yankee-Zulu-Nineteen. I am coming in to get you."

It was the bird, the Huey, Army OD, its rotors beating as if to force the devil down, as it settled over them, whipping up the dust and flattening the vegetation. Bob clapped Donny on the back of the neck and pushed him toward the bird; they ran the twenty-odd feet to the open hatch, where eager hands pulled them away from the Land of Bad Things. The chopper zoomed skyward, into the light.

"Hey," Donny said over the roar, "it's stopped raining."

CHAPTER SEVENTEEN

E ven in the hospital, Huu Co, Senior Colonel, was criticized. It was merciless. It was relentless. It went beyond cruelty. Each day, at 1000 hours, he was wheeled
into the committee room, his burned left arm swaddled in
bandages, his head dopey with painkillers, his brain ringing with revolutionary adages with which nurses and doctors alike pummeled him in all his waking hours.

He sat stiffly in the heat, waiting as the painkillers
gradually diminished, facing faceless accusers from behind banks of lights.

"Senior Colonel, why did you not press on despite
your casualties?"

"Senior Colonel, who advised you to halt your progress and send units to deal with the American sniper?"

"Senior Colonel, are you infected with the typhus of
ego? Do you not trust the Fatherland and its vessel, the
party?"

"Senior Colonel, why did you waste time setting up
mortars, when a small unit could have kept the Americans
pinned, and you might have made your attack on the
Camp Arizona before dawn?"

"Senior Colonel, did Political Commissar Phuc Bo ar-
gue with you as to the best course of action before his
heroic death, and if so, why did you discount his advice?
Do you not know he spoke with the authority of the
party?"

The questions were endless, as was his pain.

They were also right in their implication: he had be-
haved unprofessionally, egged on by the demon of Western ego, whose poison was evidently deep in his soul,
unpurged by years of rigor and asceticism. He had allowed it to become a personal duel between himself and
the American who so bedeviled him. He had given up the

mission to kill the American, and failed at both, if intelligence reports could be believed.

He was in disgrace. No meaningful future loomed before him. He had failed because his heart was weak and his character flawed. Everything they said about him was true, and the criticism he received was not nearly enough punishment. They could not punish him more than he punished himself. He deserved the fury of hell; he deserved oblivion. He was a cockroach who had—

But then the strangest thing happened. Even as he endured yet another session, feeling the unbending wills of the political officers crushing against the fragility of his own pitiful identity, the doors were flung open and two men from the Politburo rushed in, handed an envelope to the senior inquisitioner, which the man tore open and read nervously.

Then his face broke into a huge smile of love and compassion. He looked at Huu Co as if he were looking at the savior of the people, the great Uncle Ho himself.

"Oh, Colonel," he brayed in the voice of such sugary sweetness it seemed nearly indecent, "oh, Colonel, you look so *uncomfortable* in that chair. Surely you would like a glass of tea? Tran, quickly, run to the kitchen, get the colonel a glass of tea. And some nice candy? Sugar beet? American chocolate? Hershey's, we have Hershey's, probably, if I do say so myself, with . . . *almonds.*"

"Almonds?" said the colonel, who, yes, far down, did in fact enjoy Hershey's with almonds.

Tran, who had an instant before been upbraiding the colonel for his stupidity, rushed out with the furious urgency of a lackey, and returned in seconds with treats and drinks and almond-studded Hershey bars for the new celebrity. In very short time, the committee had gathered around their new great friend and revolutionary hero, the colonel, and even old Tran himself pushed the colonel to the automobile in his wheelchair, inquiring warmly about the colonel's beautiful wife and his six wonderful children.

The committee waved good-bye merrily as the colonel

was driven away in a shiny Citreon by the two Politburo officers, who said nothing, but offered him cigarettes and a thermos of tea and did everything to assure his comfort.

"Why am I suddenly rehabilitated?" he asked. "I am a class traitor and coward. I am a wrecker, an obstructionist, a deviationist, a secret Western spy."

"Oh, Colonel," the senior of the men said, laughing uncomfortably, "you joke. You are so funny! Is he not a funny one? The colonel's wit is legendary!"

And Huu Co saw that this man, too, was terrified.

What on earth could be happening?

And then he knew. Only one presence in the Republic of North Vietnam could explain such a sea change: the Russians.

At their military compound, Soviet experts from GRU—Chief Intelligence Directorate—grilled him intently, though no effort was made to assign guilt. The men were remote and intense at once, in black SPETSNAZ combat uniforms without rank, though subtle distinctions on the team could be recognized. They never once mentioned politics or the revolution. He understood clearly: this wasn't preparation for a trial, it was an intelligence operation.

They were very thorough in their Western way. He talked them through it slowly, working first from maps and then, after the first day, from a scale model of the valley before Kham Duc, quickly built and painted with surprising accuracy. The conversations were all in Russian.

"You were . . . ?"

"Here, when the first shots came."

"How many?"

"He fired three times."

"Semiauto?"

"No, bolt action. He never fired quickly enough for semiauto, though he was very, very good with that bolt.

He may have been the fastest man with a bolt I've ever heard of."

The Russians listened intently, but it wasn't just the sniper that interested them; that was clear. No, it was the whole action, the loss of the sapper squad, the sounds of fire from the right flank, the presence of the flares. The flares, especially.

"The flares. You can describe them?"

"Well, yes, comrade. They appeared to be standard American combat flares, bright white, more powerful than our green Chinese equivalent. They hung in the air approximately two minutes and grew brighter as they descended."

They listened, taking notes, keeping elaborate charts and timelines, trying to reconstruct the event in painstaking detail. It was even clear they had interviewed other participants of the Kham Duc battle.

They forced him to no conclusions: instead, they seemed his partner in a journey to understanding.

"Now, Colonel," the team leader asked, a small, ratty man who smoked Marlboros, "based on what we've learned, I wonder if you'd venture a guess as to what happened. What is the significance of the flares, particularly given their location vis-à-vis the angle of most of the fire directed at you?"

"Clearly, there was another man. These American Marine sniper teams, they are almost always two-men operations."

"Yes," the team leader said. "Yes, that is what we think also. And interestingly enough, the ballistics bear you out. Some men were killed by 173-grain bullets, which is the American match target ammunition, which is the sniper's round. But we also recovered bodies with 150-grain slugs, which is the standard combat load of the M14. So clearly, one of the rifles was the Remington bolt action and the other the M14. Of course, that's different than the men killed by the forty-five-caliber submachine gun. We believe that was the sniper's secondary weapon."

The colonel was astounded: they had torn into this as if it were an autopsy, as if its last secrets must be exhumed. It was so important to them, as if their most precious asset were somehow at risk, and now they were committed totally to the destruction of the threat.

"Do you wish to know about these men?"

The colonel did, yes. But his own ego had to be conquered, for to learn about the men who had destroyed his battalion and his reputation and his future would be to further personalize the event and make it private, an obsession, an extension of his own life, as if its significance were him and not the cause.

"No, I think not. I care nothing for personality."

"Well spoken. But alas, it is now a necessity. It is part of your new assignment."

Well, wasn't this interesting? A new assignment under Russian sponsorship. What possibly could it mean?

And so it was that he learned of his primary antagonist, a man called Swagger, a sergeant, who had once won a great shooting championship and had done much damage to the cause of the Fatherland in his three tours in Vietnam and was even now prowling the glades in hunt of yet more victims.

They had a picture of him from something called *Leatherneck* magazine, and what he saw was what he expected. He knew Americans from Paris and from his time in Saigon with the puppets. This one was a type, perhaps exaggerated, but familiar. Thin, hard, resilient, braver even than the French, brave as any Germans in the Legion. Cunning, with that specially devious quality of mind that let him instinctively understand weakness and move decisively against it. Disciplined in a way the Americans almost never were. He would have made a brilliant party official, so tight and focused was his mind.

The picture simply showed a slit-eyed young man with prominent cheekbones, his leathery face lit with a grin. He held some ludicrous trophy thing in his arms; next to him was an older version of the same man, same slit eyes, close-cropped hair but with more vanity on his chest. "Sergeant Swagger accepts the congratulations of the Commandant after winning at Camp Perry," read the caption, translated into the Vietnamese. It was warrior's glee, the colonel knew; and he saw in those slit eyes the deaths of so many, and the remorselessness that had driven their executioner.

"For this one," he said, "the war is not a cause. It is merely an excuse."

"Possibly," said the Russian intelligence chief. "Perhaps even the war releases him to find his greatness. But do you not think he has a certain discipline? He is not profligate, he is not one of their criminals, like the Calleys and the Medinas. He has never raped or murdered in combat. He has no sexual weaknesses, a pathology associated with psychopathy."

"He is not a psychopath," Huu Co said. "He is a hero, though the line between them is thin, possibly fragile. He needs a cause to find his true self, that is what I mean. He is the sort who must have a cause to live. He needs something to humble himself in front of. Take that from him and you take everything."

"Very good. Here, here is more, here is what we have."

It was more on Swagger, culled from various American public resources. The package included, unbelievably, Marine records, obviously from a very sensitive source.

"Yes."

"Study this man. Study him well. Learn him. He is your new responsibility."

"Yes, of course. I accept. And what is the ultimate arrival of this project?"

"Why . . . his death, of course. His death and the death of the other one, too. They both must die."

He slept Swagger, he dreamed Swagger, he read Swagger, he ate Swagger. Swagger engaged and caused the rebirth of the Western part of his mind: he struggled to grasp principles like pride and honor and courage and how their existence sustained a corrupt bourgeoisie state. For such a state could not exist without the pure fire of such centurions as Swagger standing watch, ready to die, on the Rhines of its empires.

"Why me?" he asked the Russian. "Why not one of your own analysts?"

"What can our analysts know? You have been fighting these people since 1964."

"You have been fighting them since 1917."

"But ours is a distant fight, a theoretical fight. Yours is up close, close enough to smell blood and shit and piss. That's experience hard bought and much respected."

Then another day brought another surprise: reconnaissance photos, taken from a high-flying vehicle of some sort, of what appeared to be a Marine post in the jungles of some province of his own country.

"I Corps," said the Russian. "About forty kilometers from Kham Duc. One of the last American combat posts left in the zone. They call it Firebase Dodge City. A Marine installation. It is from here the American Swagger and his spotter mount their missions."

"Yes?"

"Yes, well, if we're to take him, it'll be on his territory. He'll always have the advantage, unless, of course, we can learn the terrain as well as he knows it."

"Surely local cadre . . ."

"Well, now, isn't that an interesting situation? Local cadre have been extremely inactive in that region for some months. This man Swagger terrifies them. They call him, in your language, *quan toi.*"

"The Nailer."

"The Nailer. Like a carpenter. The nailer. He nails them. At any rate, at the local cadre level, most combat operations have ceased. That is why Firebase Dodge City still exists, when so many other Marines have been shipped home. Because the Nailer has nailed so many people that nobody likes to operate in his area. What is the point? The war will be over soon, he will be recalled, that will be that. But we cannot let that be that, can we?"

But try as he might, Huu Co could not hate the American. It seemed pointless. The man was no architect of war, no policy designer; he clearly had no sadistic side to him, no tendency toward atrocity: he was merely an excellent professional soldier, of the sort all armies have relied upon for thousands of years. He had some extra gene for aggression, some extra gene for shooting ability, and that was it. He was a believer—or maybe not. The colonel remembered, from his other life, the Frenchman Camus, who said, "When men of action cease to believe in a cause, they believe only in action."

It didn't matter. Nor did it matter that he wondered what the delay was. Why were they not moving now, if this was so important? Why were they waiting, *what* were they waiting for? He applied himself to the problem, and set out to master the terrain in and around Firebase Dodge City.

It was situated on a hill, and the Americans had deforested for a thousand yards all around it with their Agent Orange. The camp was typical: he'd seen hundreds in his long years of war. Its tactical problems were typical, too. In many respects it was similar to the unfallen A-Camp Arizona. The doctrine was primitive, but usually effective: approach at night, rally in the dark, send in sappers to blow the wire, attack in strength. But for the killing of one sniper team, that was a different tactical problem. The team would probably exit at night, that is, if they weren't helicopter extracted. The trick would then be understanding from which point from the perimeter they would leave, and what would be their typical passage across the open zone. One could therefore hope to intercept them if one knew the terrain and the way Swagger's mind worked.

Studying the photos, Huu Co saw three natural paths away from the camp, through gulches, enfilades, natural depressions in the land, where men would travel to avoid being spotted. One would set an ambush at such points, yes. It would be possibly effective, a long stalk, luck playing the most likely role. But if for some reason, the Americans could be induced to leaving during the day, right, say, at first dawn, a good shooter might have a chance to hit them from a hill not quite fifteen hundred yards out. Oh, it was a long shot, a desperately long shot, but the right man might bring it off, much more effectively, say, than an ambush team, who's luck might be on or off.

But where would such a man be found? He knew the North Vietnamese certainly didn't have such a man. In fact, such a man, such a specialist might not exist, at least not effectively. Huu Co said nothing about his conclusions; the Russians did not ask him. And then one night, he was awakened roughly by SPETSNAZ troopers and informed that they had a journey to make.

He climbed into a shiny black Zil limousine in his dress uniform, among four or five Russians, all talking and laughing boisterously among themselves. They ignored him.

They drove into Hanoi, through darkened streets, down the broad but now empty boulevards, and by the ceremonial plazas where the American Phantoms were displayed. Banners flapped mightily in the wind: ONWARD TO VICTORY, BROTHERS and LONG LIVE THE FATHERLAND and LET US EMBRACE THE REVOLUTIONARY FUTURE. The Russians paid them no mind, and laughed, and talked of women and alcohol and smoked American cigarettes; they were like Americans in many ways, not an observant or respectful people, but men who took their own destiny so much for granted that they could be annoying.

After a time, Huu Co realized where they were going: unmistakably, they headed for the People's Revolutionary Airfield, north of Hanoi, passed through its wire defenses and guard posts with the wave of passes of the highest clearance, and sped not to the main building but to an out-of-the-way compound, which was heavily guarded by white men with automatic weapons, in the combat uniforms of SPETSNAZ, the hotshots who got all the sexy assignments and handled training for NVA cadre on certain dark, arcane secret arts.

The Zil parked, debarking its men, who escorted Huu Co inside, to discover an extremely comfortable little chunk of Russia, complete with televisions, a bar, elaborate Western furniture and the like. Also, many *Playboy* magazines lay about, and empty beer bottles, and the walls were festooned with pictures of blond women with large, gravity-defying breasts and no pubic hair.

Russians, thought Huu Co.

After a time, the little party went out to the tarmac, parked at the obscure end of a runway and awaited the arrival of someone designated Solaratov, whether a real name or a trade name, Huu Co was not informed. No rank, either; no first name. Just Solaratov, as if the name itself conveyed quite enough information, thank you.

Again, it was chilly, though no rain. The hot season was hard on them, but it had not arrived yet. In the emerging gray light, Huu Co stood a little apart from the crowd of bawdy, laughing Russian intelligence and SPET-SNAZ people, himself the solitary man, not a part of their camaraderie and unsure why his presence was required. Yet clearly, they wanted him here: he was seeing things possibly no North Vietnamese below the Politburo level had seen. Why? What was the meaning of it all?

The sound of a jet airplane asserted itself, low but insistent, coming in from the east, out of the sun. The plane flashed overhead, glinting in the rising light, revealing itself to be a Tupolev Tu-16, code-named by the Americans "Badger," a twin-engine, three-man bombing craft with a bubble canopy and sparkle of plastic at the nose. It wore combat drab, and its red stars stood out boldly against green camouflage. Its flaps were down and it peeled to the west, found a landing vector and set down on the main runway. It taxied for a distance, then began to head over toward the little party standing by itself on the runway.

The plane halted and its jet engines screamed a final

time, then died; a hatch door opened beneath the nose, just behind the forward tire of the tricycle landing gear, and almost immediately two aviators descended, waved to the crowd, then got aboard a little car that had come for them, while Russian ground crew attended to the airplane.

"Oh, he'll make us wait, of course," one of the Russians said.

"The bastard. Nobody hurries him. He'd make the party secretary wait if it suited his fucking purpose!"

There was some laughter, but after a while, another figure descended from the aircraft, climbing slowly down, then landing on the tarmac. He wore an aviator's black jumpsuit, but he was no aviator. He carried with him something awkward, a long, flat case; a musical instrument or something?

He turned to look at the greeters and his face instantly silenced them.

He was a wintry little man, late thirties, with a stubble of gray hair and a thick, short bull neck. His eyes were blue beads in a leather mask that was his grim face. He had immense hands and Huu Co saw that he was quite muscular for so short a fellow, with a broad chest and a spring of power to his movements.

No salutes were offered, no exchange of military courtesies. If he knew any of the Russians, he hid the information. There seemed nothing emotional about him at all, no sense of ceremony.

A man rushed to him to take the package he carried.

The little fellow silenced him with a vicious glare and made it apparent that he would carry the case, the severity of his response driving the man back into humiliated confusion.

"Solaratov," said the Russian intelligence chief, "how was the flight?"

"Cramped," said Solaratov. "I should tell them I only fly first class."

There was nervous laughter.

Solaratov walked by the colonel without noticing him, surrounded by sycophants and bootlickers. He actually reminded Huu Co of a figure that had been pointed out to him back in the late forties, in Paris, another man of glacial isolation whose glare quieted the masses, who nevertheless—or perhaps for that reason, indeed—attracted sycophants in the legions but who paid them no attention at all, whose reputation was like the cloud of blue ice that seemed to surround him. That one was named Sartre.

CHAPTER EIGHTEEN

Vietnam leaped up at him as if out of a dream: green, endless, crusted with mountains, voluptuous, violent, ugly, beautiful all at once. The Land of Bad Things. But also, in some way, the Land of Good Things.

Where I went to war, Donny thought. Where I fought with Bob Lee Swagger.

It wasn't a dream; it never had been. It was the real McCoy, as glimpsed through the dirty plastic of an aircraft dipping toward that destination from Okinawa, where grunts headed to the 'Nam touched down on the way back from R&R. Monkey Mountain loomed ahead on the crazed peninsula above China Beach, and beyond that, like downtown Dayton, the multiservice base and airstrip at Da Nang displayed itself in a checkerboard of buildings, streets and airstrips. Hills 364, 268 and 327 stood like dusty warts beyond it.

The C-130 oriented itself off the coastline, dropped through the low clouds and slid through tropic haze until it touched down at the ghost town that had once been one of the most populous cities of the world, the capital of the Marine country of I Corps, home of the ruling body of the Marine war, the III Marine Amphibious Force.

The palms still blew in the breeze, and around it the mountains still rose in green tropic splendor, but the place was largely empty now, its mainside structure shrunken to a few tempo buildings, an empty or at least Vietnamized metropolis. A few offices were still staffed, a few barracks still lived in, but the techies and the staffs and the experts who'd run the war in Vietnam were home safe except for the odd laggard unit, like the boys of Firebase Dodge City and a few others in the haphazard distribution of late-leavers across I Corps.

The plane finally stopped taxiing. Its four props ended

their mission with a turbine-powered whine as their fuel was cut off. The plane shuddered mightily, paused like a giant beast and went still. In seconds the rear door descended, and Donny and the cargo of twenty-odd short-timers and reluctant warriors felt the furnace blast of heat and the stench of burning shit that announced they were back.

He stepped into the radiance, felt it slam him.

"This fuckin' place will git me yet," said a black old salt, with a dozen or so stripes on his sleeve, and enough wound ribbons to have bled out a platoon.

"Ain't you short?" someone asked.

"I ain't as short as the lance corporal," he said, winking at Donny, with whom he'd struck up a bantering relationship on the flight over from Kadena Air Force Base on Okie. "If I was as short as him, I'd twist an ankle and head straight for sick bay."

"He's a hero," the other lifer said. "He ain't going in no sick bay."

The old black sarge pulled him aside.

"Don't you be takin' no bad-ass chances in the bush, you hear?" the man said. "Two and days, Fenn? Shit, don't git busted up. It ain't worth it. This shit-hole place ain't worth a thing if you ain't a career sucker gittin' the ticket punched one more time. Don't let the Man git you."

"I copy."

"Now git over to reception and git your grunt ass squared away."

"Peace," said Donny, flashing the sign.

The sergeant looked around, saw no one close enough to overhear or overlook, and flashed the sign back.

"Peace and freedom and all that good shit, bro," he said with a wink.

Donny hit reception with his sea bag, to arrange temporary quarters for the night and the soonest chopper hop back to Dodge City.

He felt . . . good. A week on Maui with Julie. Oh,

Christ, who wouldn't feel good? Could it have been any better? Swagger had slipped him an envelope as he'd choppered out after debriefing, and he'd been stunned to discover a thousand dollars cash, with instructions to bring none of it back. Why would Swagger do such a thing? It was so generous, so spontaneous—just a strange-ass way of doing things.

It was—well, a young man back from the war with his beautiful young wife, in the paradise of Hawaii, under a hot and purifying sun, flush with money and possibility and so short he could finally, after three years and nine months and days, see the end. See it.

I made it.

I'm out.

She said, "It's almost too cruel. We could have this and then you could get killed."

"No. That's not how it works. The NVA fights twice a year, in the spring and fall. They fought their big spring offensive, and now they're all stuck up in a siege around An Loc City, fighting the ARVN way down near Saigon. We're out of it. Nothing will happen in our little area. We're home free. It's just a question of getting through the boredom, I swear to you."

"I don't think I could stand it."

"There's nothing to worry about."

"You sound like the guy in the war movie who always gets killed."

"They don't make war movies anymore," he said. "Nobody cares about war movies."

Then they made love again, for what seemed like the 28,000th time. He found new plateaus from which to observe her, new angles into her, new sensations, tastes and ecstacies.

"It doesn't get much better than this," he finally said. "God, Hawaii. We'll come back here on our fiftieth anniver—"

"No!" she said suddenly, as sweaty as he and just as flushed. "Don't say that. It's bad luck."

"Sweetie, I don't need luck. I have Bob Lee Swagger on my side. He *is* luck itself."

That was then, this was now, and Donny stood at the bank of fluorescent-lit desks in a big green room that was reception until a buck sergeant finally noticed him, put down the phone and gestured him to the desk.

Donny sat, handed over his documents.

"Hi, I'm Fenn, 2-5-Hotel, back from R&R on sked. Here's my paperwork. I need a billet for the night and then a jump out to Dodge City on the 0600."

"Fenn?" said the sergeant, looking at the order. "All right, let me just check it out; looks okay. You're one of the guys in the Kham Duc?"

He entered Donny's return in the logbook, stamped the orders, adroitly forged his captain's signature and slipped them back to Donny, all in a single motion.

"Yeah, that was me. My NCO pulled in some favors and got me R&R'd out for ten days."

"You've been nominated for the Navy Cross."

"Jesus."

"You won't get it, though. They're not giving out big medals anymore."

"Well, I really don't care."

"They'll probably buck it down to a Star."

"I have a Star."

"No, a Silver."

"Wow!"

"Hero. Too bad it don't count for shit back in the world. In the old days, you could have been a movie star."

"I just want to make it back in one piece. I can pay to see movies. That's as close to movies as I want to get."

"Well, then, I have good news for you, Fenn. You got new orders. Your transfer came through."

Donny thought he misunderstood.

"What? I mean, there must be—What do you mean, *transfer*? I didn't ask for a transfer. I don't see what—"

"Here it is, Fenn. Your orders were cut three days ago. You been dumped in 1-3-Charlie, and assigned to battalion S-3. That's us, here in Da Nang; we're the administrative battalion for what's left of Marine presence. My guess is, you'll be running a PT program here in Da Nang for a couple of months before you DEROS out on the big freedom bird. Your days in the bush are over. Congratulations, grunt. You made it, unless you get hit by a truck on the way to the slop chute."

"No, see, I don't—"

"You go on over to battalion, check in with the duty NCO and he'll get you squared away, show you your new quarters. You're in luck. You won't believe this. We closed down *our* barracks and moved into some the Air Force vacated, 'cause they were closer to the airstrip. Air-conditioning, Fenn. Air-conditioning!"

Donny just looked at him, as if the comment made no sense.

"Fenn, this is a milk run. You got it made in the shade. It's a number-one job. You'll be working for Gunny Bannister, a good man. Enjoy."

"I don't want a transfer," Donny said.

The sergeant looked up at him. He was a mild, patient man, sandy blond hair, professional-bureaucrat type of REMF, the sort of sandy-dry man who always makes the machine work cleanly.

He smiled dryly.

"Fenn," he explained, "the Marine Corps really doesn't care if you want a transfer or not. In its infinite military wisdom, it has decreed that you will teach a PT class to lard-ass rear-echelon motherfuckers like me until you go home. You won't even *see* any more Vietnamese. You will sleep in an air-conditioned building, take a shower twice a day, wear your tropicals pressed, salute every shitbird officer that walks no matter how stupid, not work very hard, stay very drunk or high and have an excellent time. You'll take beaucoup three-day weekends at China Beach. Those are your orders. They are better orders than some poor grunt's stuck out on the DMZ or Hill

553, but they are your orders, nevertheless, and that is the name of that tune. Clear, Fenn?"

Donny took a deep breath.

"Where does this come from?"

"It comes straight from the top. Your CO and your NCOIC signed off on it."

"No, who *started* it? Come on, I have to know."

The sergeant looked at him.

"I have to know. I was Sierra-Bravo-Four. Sniper team. I don't want to lose that job. It's the best job there is."

"Son, any job the Marine Corps gives you is the best job."

"But you could find out? You could check. You could see where it comes from. I mean, it is unusual that a guy with bush time left suddenly gets rotated out of his firebase slot and stowed in some make-work pussy job, isn't it, Sergeant?"

The sergeant sighed deeply, then picked up the phone.

He schmoozed with whomever was on the other end of the line, waited a bit, schmoozed some more, and finally nodded, thanked his co-conspirator and hung up.

"Swagger, that's your NCO?"

"Yes."

"Swagger choppered in here last week and went to see the CO. Not battalion but higher, the FMF PAC CO, the man with three stars on his collar. Your orders were cut the next day. He wants you out of there. Swagger don't want you humping the bush with him no more."

Donny checked in with the PFC on duty at 1-3-Charlie, got a bunk and a locker in the old Air Force barracks, which were more like a college dormitory, and spent an hour getting stowed away. Looking out the window, he could not see a single palm tree: just an ocean of tarmac, buildings, offices. It could have been Henderson Hall, back in Arlington, or Cameron Station, the multiservice

PX out at Bailey's Crossroads. No yellow people could be seen: just Americans doing their jobs.

Then he went to storage to pick up his stowed 782 gear and boonie duds, and lugged the sea bag to supply to return it, but learned supply was already closed for the day, so he lugged the stuff back to his locker. He checked back in at company headquarters to meet his new gunny and the CO; neither man could be found—both had gone back to quarters early. He went by the S-3 office—operations and training—to look for Bannister, the PT NCO, and found that office locked too, and Bannister long since retreated to the staff NCO club. He went back to the barracks, where some other kids were getting ready to go to the movies—*Patton*, already two years old, was the picture—and then to the 1-2-3 Club for a night of dowsing their sorrows in cheap PX Budweiser. They seemed like nice young guys and they clearly knew who Donny was and were hungry to get close to him, but he said no, for reasons he himself did not quite understand.

He was tired. He climbed into the rack early, pulling clean, newly issued sheets around him, feeling the springiness of the cot beneath. The air conditioner churned with a low hum, pumping out gallons of dry, cold air. Donny shivered, pulled the sheets closer about him.

There were no alerts that night, no incoming. There hadn't been incoming in months. At 0100 he was awakened by the drunken kids returning from the 1-2-3 Club. But when he stirred, they quieted down fast.

Donny lay in the dark as the others slipped in, listening to the roar of the air conditioner.

I have it made, he told himself.

I am out of here.

I am the original DEROS kid.

I am made in the shade, I am the milk-run boy.

He dreamed of Pima County, of Julie, of an ordered, becalmed and rational life. He dreamed of love and duty. He dreamed of sex; he dreamed of children and the good life all Americans have an absolute right to if they work hard enough for it.

At 0-dark-30, he arose quietly, showered in the dark, pulled on his bush utilities and gathered up his 782 gear and headed out to the chopper strip. It was a long walk in the predawn. Above him, mute piles and piles of stars were humped up tall and deep like a mountain range. Now and then, from somewhere in this dark land, came the far-off, artificial sound of gunfire. Once some flares lit the horizon. Somewhere something exploded.

The choppers were warming up. He ducked into the operations shack, chatted with another lance corporal, then jogged to the Marine-green Huey, its rotors already whirring on the tarmac. He leaned in, and the crew chief looked at him.

"This is Whiskey-Romeo-Fourteen?"

"That's us."

"You're the bus to Dodge City?"

"Yeah. You're Fenn, right? We took you outta here two weeks back. Great job at Kham Duc, Fenn."

"Can you hump me back to the City? It's time to go home."

"Climb aboard, son. We are homeward bound."

CHAPTER NINETEEN

"You will crawl all night," Huu Co explained to the Russian. "If you do not make it, they will see you in the morning and kill you."

If he expected the man to react, once again, he was wrong. The Russian responded to nothing. He seemed, in some respects, hardly human. Or at least he had no need for some of the things humans needed: rest, community, conversation, humanity even. He never spoke. He appeared phlegmatic to the point of being almost vegetable. Yet at the same time he never complained, he would not wear out, he applied no formal sense of will against Huu Co and the elite commandos of the 45th Sapper Battalion on their long Journey of Ten Thousand Miles, down the trail from the North. He never showed fear, longing, thirst, discomfort, humor, anger or compassion. He seemed not to notice much and hardly ever talked, and then only in grunts.

He was squat, isolated, perhaps desolated. In his army, Huu Co's heroes were designated "Brother Ten" when they distinguished themselves by killing ten Americans: this man, Huu Co realized, was Brother Five Hundred, or some such number. He had no ideology, no enthusiasms; he simply was. Solaratov: solitary. The lone man. It suited him well.

The Russian looked across the fifteen hundred yards of flattened land to the Marine base the enemy called Dodge City, studying it. There was no approach, no visible approach, except on one's belly, the long, long way.

"Could you hit him from this range?"

The Russian considered.

"I could hit a man from this range, yes," he finally said. "But how would I know it was the right man? I cannot see a face from this distance. I have to hit the right man; that is the point."

The argument was well made.

"So then . . . you must crawl."

"I can crawl."

"If you hit him, how will you get out?"

"This time I'm only looking. But when I hit him, I'll wait till dark, then come out the same way I came in."

"They'll call in mortars, artillery, napalm even. It is their way."

"Yes, I may die."

"In napalm? Not pleasant. I've heard many scream as it ate the flesh from their bones. It's over in an instant, but I had the impression it was a long instant."

The Russian merely glared at him, no recognition in his eyes at all, even though they'd lived in close proximity for a week and had for days before that pored over the photos and the mock-up of Dodge City.

"My advice, comrade brother," said Huu Co, "is that you follow the depression in the earth three hundred meters. You move at dark, in maximum camouflage. They have nightscopes and they will be hunting. But the scopes aren't one hundred percent reliable. It'll be a long stalk, a terrible stalk. I can only hope you are up to it and that your heart is strong and pure."

"I have no heart," said the solitary man. "I am the sniper."

For the first recon, Solaratov did not take his case, which by now all considered a rifle sheath. He carried no weapons except a SPETSNAZ dagger, black and thin and wicked.

He left at nightfall, dappled in camouflage, looking more like an ambulatory swamp than a man. Behind his back, the sappers called him not the Solitary Man or the Russian but, with the eternal insouciance of soldiers, the Human Noodle, because the stalks were stiff like unboiled noodles. In seconds, as he slithered off through the elephant grass, he was invisible.

Huu Co noted that his technique was extraordinary, a mastery of the self. This was the ultimate slow. He moved with delicacy, one limb at a time, a pace so slow and deliberate it almost didn't exist. Who would have patience for such a journey?

"He is mad," one of the sappers said to another.

"All Russians are mad," said the other. "You can see it in their eyes."

"But this one is *really* mad. He's nuts!"

The sappers waited quietly underground, in elaborate tunnels built in the Year of the Snake, 1965. They cooked meals, enjoyed jury-rigged showers and treated the event almost like a furlough. It was a happy time for men who had fought hard, been wounded many times. At least six of them were Brothers Ten. They were shrewd, experienced professionals.

For his time, Huu Co studied the photographs or waited up top, hidden in the grass, using up his eyestrain to stare at the strange fort fifteen hundred yards off, which looked so artificial cut into the earth of his beloved country by men from across the sea with a different sensibility and no sense of history.

He waited, staring at the sea of grass. His arm hurt. He could hardly close his hand. When he grew bored, he snatched a book from his tunic, in English. It was *Lord of the Rings,* by J.R.R. Tolkein, very amusing. It took him away from this world but always, when Frodo's adventures vanished, he had to return to Firebase Dodge City and his deepest question: when would the sniper return?

The fire ants were only the first of his many ordeals. Attracted to his sweat, they came and crawled into the folds of his neck, tasting his blood, crawling, biting, feasting. He was a banquet for the insect world. After the ants, others were drawn. Mosquitoes big as American helicopters buzzed around his ears, lit on his face, stung him gently and departed, bloated. What else? Spiders, mites, ticks, dragonflies, the whole phyla drawn to the miasma of decay a sweating man produces in the tropics on a hot morning. But not maggots. Maggots are for the dead, and perhaps in some way the maggots respected him. He was not dead and, moreover, he fed the maggots much in his time on earth. They left him alone.

It wasn't that Solaratov was beyond feeling such things. He felt them, all right. He felt every sting, bite, prick or tweak; his aches and swellings and blotches and throbbings were the same as any man's. He had just somehow managed to disconnect the feeling part of his body from the registering part of his brain. It can be learned, and at the upper reaches of the performance envelope, among those who are not merely brave, willful or dedicated but truly among the best in the world, extraordinary things are routine.

He lay now in the elephant grass, approximately one hundred yards from the sandbag perimeter of Firebase Dodge City, just outside the double strands of concertina wire. He could see Claymore mines facing him from a dozen angles, and the half-buried detonators of other, larger mines. But he could also hear American rock and roll bellowing out of the transistor radios all the young Marines seemed to carry, and listening to it was his only pleasure.

"I can't get no satisfaction," someone sang with a loud raspy voice, and Solaratov understood: he could get no satisfaction either.

The Marines were unbearably sloppy. He had seen the Israelis from extremely close range in some of his ops and the British SAS and even the fabled American Green Berets; all were sound troops. These boys thought the war was over for them; they were worse than Cubans or Angolans. They lounged around sunbathing, played touch football or baseball or basketball, sneaked out to smoke hemp, got in fights or got drunk. Their sentries slept at night. The officers didn't bother to shave. Nobody dressed in anything resembling a uniform, and most spent the days in shorts, undershirts (or shirtless) and shower shoes.

Even when they went on combat patrol, they were loud and stupid. The point men paid no attention, the flank security drifted in toward the column, the machine gunner had his belts tangled around him, and his assistant, with other belts, fell too far behind him to do him any good in a fight. Clearly they had not been in a fight in months, if ever; clearly they expected no such thing to occur as they waited for the order to leave the country.

Once, a patrol stumbled right over him. Five men, hustling through the elephant grass on the way out for a night ambush mission, walked so close to him that if any had been even remotely awake, they would have killed him easily. He saw their jungle boots, big as mountains, just inches from his face. But two of the men were listening to radios, one was clearly high, one so young and frightened he belonged in school, and the platoon leader, stuck with these silly boys, looked terrified. Solaratov knew exactly what would happen; the patrol would go out a thousand yards and the sergeant would hunker them down in some high grass, where they'd sit all night, smoking and talking and pretending they weren't at war. In the morning the sergeant would bring them in and file a no-contact report. It was the kind of war fought by men who'd rather be anywhere except in the war.

Each night, Solaratov would relieve himself, hand-bury his feces, drink from his canteen and slowly, ever so slowly change position. He didn't care what was in the encampment, but he had to know by what routes an experienced man would make an egress on the way to a hunting mission. How would Swagger take his spotter out? Which part of the sandbag berm would they go over and from what latitudes was it accessible to rifle fire?

He made careful notes, identifying eight or nine spots where there appeared to be a lane through the wire and the Claymores and the mines, where an experienced man would travel efficiently; of course, conversely, the other

Marines would stay well clear of these areas. He read the land, looking for folds that led out of the camp to the treeline, or a progression of obstacles behind which two men, moving quickly, could transverse on the way to the job. They were the only two men still fighting the war; they were the only two men keeping this place alive. He wondered if the other soldiers knew it. Probably not.

Twice, he saw Swagger himself and felt the hot rush of excitement a hunter sees when his prey steps into the kill zone. But always, he cautioned himself to be slow, be sure, not to become excited; that caused mistakes.

From this vantage point, Swagger was a tall, thin, hard man, who always appeared parade-ground neat in his camouflaged tunic. Solaratov could read his contempt for the boys of Dodge City, but also his restraint, his disinterest, his commitment to his own duties that kept him apart from them. He was aloof, walking alone always: Solaratov knew this well—it was the sniper's way. The Russian also noted that when Swagger walked through the compound, even the loudest and most disgruntled of the Marines grew quickly still and pretended to work. He worked silently, and moved with economy of motion and style. But he was not going on missions for now, and seemed to spend much of his time indoors, in a bunker that was probably intelligence or communications.

On the last day, he saw him again, from an even closer vantage point. Solaratov had worked up until he was but fifty meters from the complex of huts where Swagger seemed to spend most of his time, in hopes of getting a good look into the face of the man he proposed to kill. By this time he was quite bold, convinced that the Marines were too narcissistic to notice his presence even if he stood and announced it through a bullhorn.

It was after the daily helicopter flight. The Huey dipped in fast, landed at the firebase's LZ, and a young man jumped out, even as the rotors still spun and kicked up a pall of dust; he disappeared into the complex but in time Solaratov saw him, this time with Swagger. It looked almost to be a fight. The two raged at each other, far from the others. If he were armed, it might have been a chance to take them both, but there was no escape and if he'd fired shots, even these childish troopers could have brought massive firepower to bear and gotten him. That wasn't the point: he wasn't on a suicide mission. He would never give himself up for an objective, unless there was no other way and the objective represented something that was his own passionate, deeply held conviction, not a job for another department, that he didn't fully trust to begin with.

So he just listened and watched. The two had it out. It was like a final confrontation between a proud father and his disappointing son or an upright son and his disappointing father. He could hear the anger and the betrayal and the accusation in the voices.

"What the fuck is wrong with you?" the older man kept screaming in the English that the Russian had studied for years.

"You cannot do this to me! You do not have the moral authority to do this to me!" the younger screamed back.

On and on it went, like a grand scene from Dostoyevsky. It was a mark of how each man was held in the respect of his comrades that no witnesses intruded, no officers interceded; their anger drove the young Marines, normally working hard on their suntans by this time, inside.

Finally, the two men reached some kind of rapprochement; they went back into the intelligence bunker, and after a while the young man left alone and went over to what must have been the living quarters, where he would bunk. He emerged an hour or so later, in full combat gear, with a rifle and a flack vest and went back to the intelligence bunker.

Solaratov knew: *At last, the spotter is back.*

There were no other sightings that day, and at nightfall, Solaratov finished his last canteen, rolled over and began the long crawl back to the tunnel complex in the treeline more than a thousand yards away.

"Senior Colonel, the Human Noodle is here!"

The call, from a sergeant, rocked Huu Co out of sleep. It was a good thing, too. As on most nights, he was reliving the moment when the American Phantoms came roaring down the valley and the napalm pods tumbled lazily from under their wings. They hit about fifty meters ahead of his forward position in the valley and bounced majestically, pulling a curtain of living flame behind them.

He arose swiftly and located the Russian, eating with gusto and lack of sophistication in the tunnel's mess hall. The Russian devoured everything in sight, including noodles, fish head soup, chunks of raw cabbage, beef, pork, tripe. He ate with his fingers, which were now coated with grease; he ate with perfect clarity and concentration, pausing now and then for a satisfying belch, or to wipe a paw across his greasy mouth. He drank too, glass after glass of tea and water. Finally, when he was done, he asked for vodka, which was produced, a small Russian bottle. He finished it in a single draught.

At last, he turned and faced the senior colonel.

"Now I wash, then I sleep. Maybe forty-eight hours. Then, on the third day, I will move out."

"You have a plan."

"I know when and where he'll leave, and how he'll move. It's in the land. If you can read the land, you can read the other man's mind. I'll kill them both three days from now."

For the first time, he smiled.

CHAPTER TWENTY

The Huey dipped low and landed in a swirl of dust. Quickly, the crew chief kicked off that run's supplies—a couple of crates of belted 7.62mm NATO, a couple more of 5.56mm NATO for the M16s, package of medical provisions, an intelligence pouch, a command pouch—nothing major, just the routine deliveries of war—and Donny.

The chopper zoomed upward, leaving him standing there in the maelstrom, choking.

"Jesus, you're back!"

It was a lance corporal in another platoon, a vague acquaintance.

"Yeah, they tried to fire me. But I love this place so much, I had to come back."

"Jesus Christ, Fenn, you had it *knocked*. Nobody ever got out of here early. The Man sends you to the world and you come back to this shit hole, short as you are? Man, you are fucked in the head!"

"Yeah, well."

"A hero," the lance corporal spat derisively, threw the intel and command packs around his shoulders and headed out to deliver the mail. The ammo would sit until someone had the gumption to gather it in.

Donny blinked, and took a fraction of a second to reorient. He knew he wanted to stay away from the command bunker and the old man; officially he had no standing, and he didn't want to face that shit until he faced Swagger. He went off to the scout-sniper platoon area, where Bob was king. But when he got there, two other NCOs told him Bob was now over in the intel bunker and he better get his young ass over there and get this squared away. One of them pointed out to him that he was officially UA from his new assignment in downtown Da Nang, and there'd be hell to pay.

Donny navigated through the S-shop area of the base, a warren of sandbagged bunkers with crudely stencilled signs, until at last he came to S-2, next to commo, a low structure from which flew an American flag. He ducked into it, feeling the temp drop a few degrees in the dark shadow, smelled the mildew of the rotting burlap bags that comprised the bunker's walls, saw maps and photos hung on a bulletin board and two men hunched over a desk, one of whom was most definitely Swagger and the other of whom was a first lieutenant named Brophy, the company intelligence honcho and sniper employment officer.

Swagger looked up, down, then back in a hurry.

"What the fuck are you doing here?" he said fiercely.

"I'm back, ready for duty, thanks very much. I had a wonderful time. Now I've got a tour to finish and I'm here to finish it."

"Lieutenant, this here boy is UA from Da Nang. He'd better get his young ass back there or he'll finish up in the brig. You put him on report, or I will. I want him gone."

Swagger almost never talked to officers this way, because of course like many NCOs he preferred to allow them the illusion that they had something to do with running the war. But he no longer cared for protocol, and the officer, a decent-enough guy but way overmatched against a legend, chose discretion over valor.

"You work it out with him, Sergeant," he said, and beat a hasty advance to the rear.

"I want you out of here, Fenn," growled Swagger.

"No damn way."

"You are too goddamn short. You will be out there thinking about humping Suzie Q instead of humping I Corps and you will get your own and my ass greased. I've seen it a hundred times."

"You recommended me for the Navy Cross! Now you're firing me?"

"I had a heart-to-heart with my closest pal, Bob Lee Swagger, and he told me you are black poison in the field. I want you running a PT program somewhere. You go home, you git out of 'Nam. I fired you. You're a Marine and you follow orders and those are your orders!"

"Why?"

"Because I say so, that's why. I'm sniper team leader and NCOIC of scout-sniper platoon. It's my call. It ain't your call. I don't need your permission."

"Why?"

"Fenn, you are getting on my damn nerves."

"I'm not going until you tell me why. Tell me why, goddammit. I earned that much."

Swagger's eyes narrowed-up, tight like coin slots in a Coke machine.

"What is with you?" he finally asked. "I've had three spotters before you, good boys all of them. But no one like you. You didn't have *no* limits. You'd do *anything* I goddamned asked you to. I don't like that. You don't have no sense. If I had to think about it, I'd say you were trying to get yourself killed. Or trying to prove something, which amounts to the same goddamn thing. Now you come clean with me, goddammit. What's going on in that head of yours? Why the hell are you out here?"

Donny looked away.

He thought a bit, and finally decided to spit it out.

"All right, I'll tell you. You can't tell anyone. It's between you and me."

Swagger stared hard at him.

"I knew a guy named Trig. I mentioned him to you. Well, he was a star peacenik, but a real good guy. A hero, too. He was willing to give his life to stop the war. Well, I hate the war too. Not only for all the reasons everyone knows, but also because it's killing people we can't afford to lose. Like Trig. It'll kill you, too, Sergeant Swagger. So I'm going to stop it. I will chain myself to the White House gate if I have to, I will throw my medals back on the Senate steps if I have to, I will blow myself up in a building. It's so fucking evil, what we are doing to these people and to ourselves. But I cannot let anybody say I quit, I bugged out, I shortcut my duty. They can have no doubts about me. So I will fight the war full-bang dead out till the day I DEROS and then I will fight full-bang dead out against it!"

He was screaming, sweating, like an insane man. He'd flared up, big as life, larger than Bob, stronger than him, menacing him for the first time, inconceivable until it happened. He stepped back now, relaxing.

"Jesus," said Swagger, "you think I give a fuck what you think about the war? I don't give a shit about politics, I'm a Marine. That's all I care about."

He sat back.

"All right, I'll tell you what's going on, finally. You have earned that. I'll tell you why I want you out of here. There's somebody out there."

"Huh? Out there? Out where?"

"There, in the bush, some new bird. That's why I've been huddling with Brophy. It was bucked down from headquarters. There's a guy out there, and he's hunting for me. He's a Russian, we think. The Israelis have a very good source in Moscow and they got a picture of a guy climbing into a TU-16 for the normal intel run to Hanoi. They knew him, because he'd trained Arab snipers in the Bekaa Valley and they tried to hit him a couple of times, but he was too goddamn smart. Our people think he worked Africa too, lots of stuff in Africa. He may have been in Cuba. Anywhere they got shit to be settled, he's the one to settle it. Anyhow, his name has something to do with 'Solitary' or 'Single,' something like that. He may be a championship shooter named T. Solaratov, who won a gold medal in prone rifle at the sixty Olympics. Then NSA got a radio intercept a week or two back. One NVA regional commander talking to another, about this *Ahn So Muoi*, as they call it. They have this thing called Brother

Ten, which is an award and a nickname they call someone who's killed ten Americans. It's as close in their language as they come to the word *sniper*. Anyhow, in this intercept, the officers were jawing about the 'White Brother Ten' moving down the trail to our province. White sniper, in other words. They got this special guy, this Russian, he's coming after me and anybody I'm with."

"Jesus," said Donny, "you really pissed them off."

"Fuck 'em if they can't take a joke," Bob replied. "And here's the new joke. I'm going to kill this guy. I'm going to nail him between the eyes and we'll send the word back to them very simply: do not fuck with the United States Marine Corps."

Donny suddenly said, "It's a trap! It's a trap!"

"That's right. I'm going to play cat-and-mouse with him; only, he thinks he's the cat, when he's the mouse. We want this bird swollen with confidence, thinking he's the cock of the walk. It's all a big phony show so we can get him to hit me in a certain way, only, I ain't gonna be there, I'm gonna be *behind* his sorry ass and I will drill him clean, and if I can't drill him, I will call in gunships with so much smoke there won't be nothing left but cinders. Now, that is dangerous work and it don't seem to me it has one thing to do with being a grunt in Vietnam. That is why I want your young ass out of here. You ain't getting killed in anything this personal. This is between me and this Solitary Man. That's it."

"No. I want in."

"No way. You're out of here. This ain't your show. This is about me."

"No, this is about the Kham Duc. I was at Kham Duc. He wants to take us for Kham Duc. Swell, then he wants to take me. I'll go against him. I'm not afraid of him."

"You *are* an idiot. I'm scared shitless."

"No, we have the advantage."

"Yeah, and what if he zeros me out in the bush, and you're left alone? You against him, out in the bad, bad bush. The fact that you're married, got a great future, had a great war, done your duty, won some medals, all that don't mean shit. He don't care. He just wants to ice you."

"No, I will be there. Forget me. You *need* another man. Who are you taking, Brophy? Brophy isn't good enough, no one here is good enough. I'm the best you got, and I'll go with you and we'll fight this goddamn thing to the end, and *nobody* can say about me, oh, he had connections, he got off easy, his sergeant got wasted but he got a cush job in the air-conditioning."

"You are one screwed-up kid. What do I say to Julie if I get you wasted?"

"It doesn't matter. You're a sergeant. You can't think like that. You only think of the mission, okay? That's your job. Mine is to back you up. I'll run the radio, back you up. We'll get this asshole, then we'll go home. It's time to hunt."

"You asshole kid. You think you want to meet this guy? Okay, you come with me. Come on, I'll introduce you two boys."

Swagger pulled him out of the S-2 bunker and out toward the perimeter.

"Come on, scream a little at me!"

"Huh?"

"Scream! So he notices us and gets an eyeful. I want him to know we're back and tomorrow we're going out again."

"I don't—"

"He's out there. I guarantee you, he's out there, in the grass, a hundred meters or so away, but don't look at him."

"He can—"

"He can't do shit. If he shoots from this close, we'll call in artillery and napalm. The squids'll soak his ass in burning gas. And he knows it. He's a sniper, not a kamikaze. The challenge ain't just gunning me, no sir. It's gunning me and going back to Hanoi to eat grilled pork, fuck a nice gal, and going home on the seven o'clock bus to

Moscow. But he's there, setting up, planning. He's reading the land, getting ready for us, figuring how to do us, the motherfucker. But we're going to bust his ass. Now, come on, yell."

Donny got with the program.

CHAPTER TWENTY-ONE

The Russian finally opened his case, quickly assembled the parts with an oily clacking sound, until he had built what appeared to be a rifle.

"The Dragon," he said.

Huu Co thought: does he think I'm a peasant from the South, soaked in buffalo shit and rice water?

He of course recognized the weapon as a Dragunov, the new Soviet-bloc sniper weapon as yet unknown to Vietnam. It was a semiauto, in the old Mosin-Nagant 7.62 x 54 caliber, a ten-round magazine, a mechanism based on the AK47's, though it had a long, elegant barrel. It wore a skeletal stock that extended from a pistol grip. A short, electrically illuminated four-power scope squatted atop the receiver.

The sniper inserted the match rounds into the magazine, then inserted the magazine into the rifle. With a snap, he threw the bolt, chambering a round, flicked the safety on, then set the rifle down. Then he set to wrap the rifle in a thick tape to obscure the glint of its steel and the precision of its outline. As he wound, Huu Co talked to him.

"You do not need to zero?"

"The scope never left the receiver, so no, I don't. In any event, it won't be a long shot, as I have planned it. Possibly two hundred meters at the longest. The rifle holds to four inches at two hundred meters and I always shoot for the chest, never the head. The head shot is too difficult for a combat situation."

He was fully dressed. He wore a ghillie suit of his own construction, and was well tufted with a matting of beige strips identical in color to the elephant grass. His hat was tufted too, and under it, he'd painted his face in combat colors, a smear of ochre and black and beige.

"Sundown," came a cry from above.

"It's time," said Huu Co.

The sniper rose and threw a large pack over his back, the rifle strap diagonally over his shoulder, and with a soft swaying as of many different feathers, like some exotic bird, he walked to the ladder and climbed out of the tunnel.

He rose in the dusk, and Huu Co followed him. It was but a few hundred feet to the treeline and the long crawl down the valley toward the American firebase.

"You have this planned?" Huu Co asked. "I need to know for my report."

"Well planned," said the Russian. "They'll go out just before sunrise, over their berm and through their wire. I can tell you exactly where, because it's the one place where they're higher; there aren't any subtle rises in the ground. They'll continue in the rising light on a north-northwest axis, then turn to the west. When the sun is full, they'll have a last few hundred meters to go through the grass toward the north. I've examined their own after-action reports. Swagger runs his missions the same each time, but what varies is where he'll operate. If he's headed south, toward Kontum, he'll go toward the Than Quit River. If he heads north, toward the Hai Van Peninsula, then he'll go toward Hoi An. And so forth. In any event, that small rise out there, that's his intersection. Which way will he turn from there? I'm betting tonight it's toward the north, because he worked the west when he headed out toward Kham Duc. It's the north's turn. I'll set up behind him; that is, between himself and the firebase. He'll never expect shots from that direction. I'll take them both when they come out from behind the hill. It'll be over quickly; two quick rounds to the body, two more when they're down. Nobody from the base camp can reach me by the time I'm back here, and I've got a good, clean escape route with two fallbacks, if need be."

"Well thought out."

"And so it is. That's what I do."

There was little left to say. The sappers gathered around the banty little Russian, clapped him on the back, embarrassing him. Night was coming quickly, all was silent, and in the far distance the firebase stood like a sore on the flank of a woman.

"For the Fatherland," Huu Co said.

"For the Fatherland," chimed the tough sappers.

"For survival," said the sniper, who knew better.

The last briefing was at sundown. Donny faced himself. Or rather, the man who would be himself, a lance corporal named Featherstone, roughly his own size and coloring. Featherstone would wear Donny's camouflaged utilities, carry his 782 gear complete to Claymores and M49 spotting scope, and the only M14 that could be found in the camp. Featherstone, and Brophy similarly tricked out as Bob Lee Swagger, were bait.

Featherstone, a large, slow boy, was not happy at this job; he had been volunteered for it by virtue of his similarity to Donny. Now he sat, looking very scared, in the S-2 bunker, amid a slew of officers and civilians in various uniforms. Everybody except Featherstone seemed very excited. There was a kind of partylike atmosphere, long absent from Firebase Dodge City.

Bob went to the front of the group, as they sat down, and addressed the primary players: Captain Feamster, who was CO here at Dodge City; an intelligence major who represented the Marine Corps's higher interest, in from Da Nang; an army colonel who'd choppered in from MACV S-2; an Air Force liaison officer; and a civilian in a jumpsuit with a Swedish K submachine gun who radiated Agency from all his pores. A map of the immediate area had been rigged on a large sheet of cardboard, reducing the clearing around Dodge City to its contours and landforms and the base itself to a big X at the bottom.

"Okay, gentlemen," Bob started, and no officer in the room felt it peculiar to be briefed by a staff sergeant, or at least this staff sergeant, "let's run this through one more time to make sure everybody's on the same page in the hymn book. The game starts at 2200, when Fenn and I, dressed in black and painted up like black whores, head out. It's approximately thirteen hundred yards to what I'm designating Area 1. That's where, based on my reading of the land and this guy's operating procedure as the files from Washington reveal, I think he's going to operate. Fenn and I will set up about three hundred yards from his most probable shooting zone. I don't want to get too close; this bird has a nose for trouble. At 0500 Lieutenant Brophy and Lance Corporal Featherstone roll over the berm at the point designated Roger One."

He pointed to it on the map.

"Why there, Sergeant?"

"This guy has eyeballed Dodge City, believe you me, and maybe from as close as this bunker. He's been here. He knows where the best place to get quickly into this little dip here is"—he pointed—"which gives you close to half mile of nearly unobserved terrain."

"Do you know that for a fact?" asked the leg colonel.

"No, sir, I do not. But before this problem came up, it's where I took my teams out ninety percent of the time, unless we choppered somewhere. He'll know that, too."

"Carry on, Sergeant."

"From there, the lieutenant and Featherstone follow the route I have indicated." He addressed the two of them directly. "It's very important you stay there. He can't get a good shot at you, because he can't get close enough, but he'll know you're there. He'll start tracking you about five hundred yards out, but you're still too far out to shoot. He don't have a rifle that he can trust to make that far a shot; plus, he wants you out of sight of camp when he hits you, so that he'll have time to make his get-out."

"How do we know he just won't take them out, then fade?" asked the Air Force major.

"Well, sir, again, we don't. But I been all over that ground. I don't think he can get a shot when they're in the gulch. That's why they have to be right careful to stay there, to move slowly. Now, about one thousand yards out, you got a little-bitty bit of hill. It's Hill Fifty-two, meaning it ain't but fifty-two meters high. It's hardly a tit. You wouldn't give it a squeeze on Saturday night."

"I would," said Captain Feamster, and everybody laughed. "I may go do it now, in fact!"

After they settled down, Bob continued.

"Sir, when y'all git behind that hill, you go flat. I mean, you dig in, you stay put. He's going to watch you come, he'll be set up on the other side, where you come out to high ground and make your decision which way you're going to turn the mission. You stay put. Now, it may take some time. This bird's patient. But, you disappearing suddenly, he's going to get annoyed, then irritated. He'll move. Maybe just a bit, but when he moves, we put the glass on him, I quarter him and waste his ass."

"Sergeant Swagger?" It was Brophy.

"Sir?"

"Do you want us to move out in support after you engage him?"

"No, sir. I don't want no other targets in the zone. If I see movement, I may have to shoot without ID. I'd hate it to be you or Featherstone. Y'all just go to earth once you get behind that hill, then move back under cover of the choppers, if we have to call in choppers."

"Sounds good."

"This sucks," Featherstone whispered bitterly to Donny. "I'm going to get smoked, I know it. It isn't fair. I didn't sign up for this shit."

"You'll be okay," Donny said to the shaky man. "You just walk, then dig in and wait for help. Swagger's got it figured."

Featherstone shot him a look of pure hatred.

"Anyhow," continued Swagger at the front of the bunker, "I take him when he rises to move. If I don't get a solid hit or if I get a miss, that's when I signal Fenn, who's sitting on the PRC-77. You've checked out the radio?"

"Of course," said Donny.

"At that moment I signal, Fenn's on the horn with you Air Force boys."

It was the Air Force major's turn.

"We've laid on a C-130 Hercules call-signed Night-Hag-Three, holding in orbit about five klicks away, just off Than Nuc. We can have Night Hag there in less than thirty seconds. The Night Hag brings major pee: four side-mounted Vulcan twenty-mm mini-guns and four 7.62 NATO mini-guns. It can unload four thousand rounds in less than thirty seconds. It'll turn anything in a thousand square yards to tenderized hamburger."

"That's better than napalm or Hotel Echo, sir?"

"Much better. More accurate, more responsive to ground direction. Plus, these guys are really good. They've been on these suppression missions for years. They can pinwheel over a zone just above stalling speed like a gull floating over the beach. Only, they're pumping out lead all the while. They bring unbelievable smoke. The snake eaters love them. You know the napalm problem. It can go any way, and if the wind catches it and takes it in your direction, you got a problem."

"Sounds good," said Bob.

"Sergeant Swagger?"

It was the CIA man, who'd brought the Solaratov documents.

"Yes, sir, Mr. Nichols?"

"I'm just asking: is there any conceivable way you could take this man alive? He'd be an incomparable intelligence asset."

"Sir, I should say, hell, yes, I'll try my damndest, and we'll share whatever we git with our friends who've cooperated with us. But this bastard's tricky and dangerous as hell. If I get him in the scope, I have to take him out. If he gets away, we go to gunships. That's all."

"I respect your honesty, Sergeant. It's your ass on the line. But let me tell you one thing. The Sovs have a new sniper rifle called the Dragunov, or SVD. He might have one."

"I've heard of it, sir."

"We've yet to shake it out. Even the Israelis haven't uncovered one. Be very nice if you brought that out alive."

"I'll give it my best, sir."

"Good man."

Donny was supposed to get a last few hours of sleep before he geared up, but of course he couldn't. So much ran through his mind, and he lay in the bunker, listening to music coming from the squad bays a few dozen meters away.

CCR was banging out something from last year on somebody's tape deck. It sounded familiar. Donny listened.

> Long as I remember, the rain been coming down,
> Clouds of mystery falling, confusion on the
>   ground,
> Good men through the ages, trying to track the
>   sun,
> And I wonder, still I wonder, who'll stop the
>   rain?

It had some kind of anti-war meaning, he knew. The rain was war, or had become war. Some of these kids had known nothing but the war; it had started when they were fourteen and now they were twenty and over here and it was still going on. It was coming for them, they'd get caught in the rain, that's why the song was so popular to them. Kids had picked it up in DC last year and it was everywhere. He knew Commander Bonson had heard it.

He thought of Bonson now.

Bonson came back to him. Navy guy, starchy, duty-haunted, rigid, black-and-white Bonson. In his khakis. His beard dark, his flesh taut and white, his eyes glaring, set in rectitude.

He remembered the look on Bonson's face when he

told him he wasn't going to testify against Crowe. Man, that may have been worth it, that one moment, let Solaratov grease my ass, it was worth it, the way his jaw fell, the way confusion—no, clouds of mystery, confusion on the ground—came into his eyes. He could not process it. He could not accept that someone would turn his little plan over. Someone would actually tell him to go fuck off, derail his little train.

Donny had a nice dream of it all, the moment of soaring triumph he'd felt.

Oh, that's just the beginning, he thought. I will get back to the world and we will see what became of Commander Bonson, what his crusade got him. What goes round, comes round. You put shit out in this world, somehow you get it back. Donny believed that.

Now, sleep was impossible. He rose, restless, bathed in sweat. He had another three hours to kill before they mounted out.

He rose, left the bunker and wandered for a bit, not sure where he was going, but then realizing he did in fact have a destination. He was in grunt city, among the line Marines, the proles of 2-5-Hotel, who really were Firebase Dodge City.

He saw a shadow.

"You know where Featherstone would be?"

"Two hootches back. Oh. You. The hero. Yeah, he's back there, getting ready to get his ass wasted in the grass."

The anger Donny felt surprised him. What the hell was *this* all about? Why was everybody so pissed at *him*? What had he done?

Donny walked back, dipped into the hootch. Four bunks, the fraternity squalor of young men living together, the stink of rotting burlap, the shine of various Playmates of the Month pinned to whatever surface would absorb a tack and, of course, the smell, sweet and dense, of marijuana.

Featherstone sat amid a dark circle of fellow martyrs,

all stoned. He was so still and depressed he seemed almost dead. But it was clear he wasn't the ringleader here; another Marine was doing all the talking, a bitter rant about "We don't mean shit," "It's all a game," "Fucking lifers just getting their tickets punched," that sort of thing.

Donny butted in.

"Hey, Featherstone, you wanna go light on that stuff. You may have to move fast tomorrow; you don't want that shit still in your head."

Featherstone didn't seem to hear him. He didn't look up.

"He's gonna be dead tomorrow. What difference does it make?" the smart guy said. "Who invited you here, anyhow?"

"I just came by to check on Featherstone," said Donny. "He ought to pull himself out of this funk or he's gonna get wasted, and if you guys claim to be his buds, you ought to help him."

"He's gonna get zapped tomorrow, no matter what. We who are not about to die salute him."

"Nothing's going to happen to him. He's going to go for a walk, then hide in the bush. A plane will come and shoot the fuck out of a zone 250 yards ahead of him. He'll probably get a Bronze Star out of it and go back to the world a hero."

"Nobody cares about heroes back in the world."

"Well, he just has to keep his head. That's—"

"Do you even know what this is all about?"

"Yes."

"What is it?"

"I can't tell you. Classified."

"No, not the shit about the Russian sniper. That's just shit. You know what this is *really* about?"

"What are you talking about?"

"It's about the championship."

"The what?"

"The championship," said the man, fixing Donny in a bitter, dark gaze.

"Of what?"

"Of snipers."

"What?"

"In 1967, a gunny named Carl Hitchcock went home with ninety-three kills. The most so far. Now along comes this guy Swagger. He's in the fifties till that stunt you pulled off in the valley. They gave him credit for thirty-odd kills. I hear he's up to eighty-seven in one whack. Now, he gets six more, he ties. He gets seven more, he's the champ. It doesn't mean shit to me and it doesn't mean shit in the world, but for these lifers, let me tell you, something like that gets you noticed and you end up the fucking command sergeant major of the whole United States Marine Corps. So what if a couple of grunts get wasted to get you your last few kills? Who the fuck cares about that?"

"That's shit," said Donny. He looked at his antagonist's name, saw that it was one Mahoney, and then recalled, yes, another college guy, Mahoney, always riding the line, dozens of Article 15s, angry and pissed off and just desperate to get out of there.

"It's not shit. It's how military cultures operate if you knew anything about it at all."

"I've been with Swagger in the bush for six months. I've never, *ever* seen him claim credit for a kill. I record the kills in a book, as per regs. I have to do that; it's the rule. The sniper employment officer writes up the kills. I just write down what I see. Swagger's never asked me to claim kills for him. He doesn't give a shit about that. On top of that, the number thirty-seven or whatever is completely made up; he had eighty rounds, he probably hit seventy-five of those, if he missed at all. The record doesn't mean a thing. That's a load of crap."

"He just likes the killing. Man, he must like to squeeze that little trigger and watch some gook dot go still. It's as close to being God as you can get. There's something so psychotic about it, you—"

Donny hit him, left side of the face, hard. It was stupid. In seconds, he was down, pinned, and somebody kicked him in the head, and his eyes filled with stars. He squirmed and yelped, but more body blows came, and he felt the pressure of many hands pressing him down, and still more punches driving through. At last someone pulled his antagonists off him. Of course it was the pacifist Mahoney.

"Settle down, settle down," Mahoney screamed. "Man, you'll get lifers in here, and we are cooked!"

Donny's head flared. Someone had really nailed him.

"You assholes," he said. "You fucking crybaby assholes, you're going to get your buddy wasted for nothing except your own sense of victimization. You have nothing to be sorry about. You made it. You're golden."

"All right, all right," said Mahoney, holding the swelling that distended his face, "you hit me, they hit you, let's call it even. No one on staff has to hear about this."

"Man, my fucking head aches," said Donny, climbing to his feet.

"You're not going to tell on anyone, are you, Fenn? It was just tempers. We all get fucked if you tell."

"Shit," said Donny. "My goddamn head hurts."

"Get him an aspirin. You want a beer? We have some Vietnamese shit, but I think there's a couple of Buds left. Get him a Bud. Good, cold Bud."

"No, I'm all right."

He looked at them, saw only dark faces and glaring eyeballs.

"Look, let's forget all about this shit, but just get *him*"—Featherstone, who still sat, zombielike, on the cot—"straight for tomorrow. Okay? He can't be fucked up out there; he'll get killed."

"Yeah, sure, Fenn, no problem."

"And let me tell you guys something, okay? You kicked the shit out of me, now you listen."

Some eyes greeted his angrily in the low light, but most looked away. It was hot and rank with sweat and the odor of beer and marijuana.

"You guys may say Swagger is a psycho and he likes to kill and all that shit. Fine. But have you noticed how come we never get hit and our patrols don't get ambushed? Have you noticed we haven't had a KIA in months? Have you noticed our only wounded are booby traps, and they're almost never fatal, and there's almost no ambushes? Hasn't been an ambush in months, maybe years. You know why that is? Is it because they love you? Is it because they know you're all peaceniks and dope smokers and you flash the peace sign and all you are saying is give peace a chance? Is that why?"

No voices answered his. His head really hurt. He had been whacked good. His vision was blurry as shit.

"No. It has nothing to do with you. Nobody gives a fuck about you. No, it's because of *him*. Of Swagger. Because the NVA and Victor Charles, they fear him. They are scared shitless of him. You say he's psycho, but every time he drops one of them, you benefit. You live. You survive. You're living on the goddamn time he buys for you by putting his ass in the grass. He's your guardian angel. And he'll always wear the curse of being the killer, the man with the gun, while you guys have the luxury of not getting your pretty little hands dirty. He'll always be on the outside because of his kills. He takes the responsibility, he lives with it, and you guys, you worthless assholes, you'll go back to the world on account of it, and all you can do is call him psycho. Man, have you ever heard of *shame*? You all ought to be ashamed."

He turned and slipped out into the night.

The Russian lay motionless in the high grass, on a little crest maybe twelve hundred yards out from the firebase. In the dark, he could see nothing except the steady illumination of guard post flares, one fired every three or four minutes, and the occasional movement of the Marines from hootch to hootch in the night, as sentries changed. There was no sense whatsoever of anything wrong.

He was still tired from the nearly five hours of crawling, but felt himself beginning to rally as the energy flooded back into him. He looked at his watch. It was 0430. The Dragunov was before him in the grass; it was time.

Deftly, he rolled over a bit, unstrapped the pack, pulled it off his back and opened it. He took out a large cylindrical object, an optical device, mounted to an electronics housing. It was Soviet issue, PPV-5, a night-vision telescope, too clumsy to be mounted on a rifle but fine for stable observation. He set it into the earth before him, and his fingers found the switch. As a rule, he didn't trust these things: too fragile, too awkward, too heavy; worse, one grew wedded to them, until they destroyed initiative and talent; worse still, one lost one's night vision to them.

But this time, the device was the perfect solution to the tactical problem. He was concealed, but at great range; he had to know exactly when and if the sniper team left in the hour before dawn, so that he could move to his shooting position and take them as they emerged from behind the hill. If they didn't come, he'd simply spend the day there, waiting patiently. He had enough water and food in the pack to last nearly a week, though of course each day he'd be weaker. But today, it felt good.

Through the green haze of the device, which crudely amplified the ambient light of the night, he saw the camp in surprising detail. He saw the lit cigarettes of smoking sentries, he saw them sneak out into the night for marijuana or to defecate in the latrine, or to drink something—beer, he guessed. But he knew where to look. At the sandbag berm nearest to the intelligence bunker, there was a crease at the base of the hill that led this way directly. He'd even been able to spot the zigzag in the concertina there, and the gap in the preset Claymore mines, and the prongs of the other anti-personal mines buried in the approach zone. It was a path, where men could move and get out of the camp. This is where it would come, if it would come at all.

The first signal was just a flick of bright light, as the

flap on a bunker was momentarily pushed aside, letting the illumination inside escape to register on Solaratov's lens. Solaratov took a deep breath, and in another second, another brief flash came. As he watched, two men, heavily laden, moved to the sandbag berm and paused.

He watched. He waited. If only he had a rifle capable of hitting at fifteen hundred yards! He could do it and be done. But no such weapon existed in his own or his host country's inventory. Finally a man rose, peered over the edge of the berm, then pulled himself over it and fell the three-odd feet to the ground. He snaked down the dirt slope to a gully at the base. In time, another Marine duplicated the efforts, though he was a larger, more ponderous man. He too fell to the ground, but gracelessly; then he rolled down the dirt embankment and joined his leader.

The two hesitated in their next move, watching, waiting. The leader lifted his rifle—yes, it had a scope—and searched the horizon for sign of an ambush. Making none out, he lowered the weapon and spoke to the assistant. The assistant rose unsteadily from cover, and began to move ever so slowly through the mines and the Claymores, finding gaps in the wire exactly where they should be and slipping through them. His leader followed him, and when both were free of the approach zone, the leader stepped forward and, moving at a slow, steady, hunched pace, began to work his way down the draw. Solaratov watched them until they disappeared.

They come, he thought.

He flicked off the scope, and began to slither through the grass toward his shooting position.

Around 0630 the suns began to rise. There were two of them, both orange, both shimmery, both peering over the edges of the earths, just beyond the far trees. Donny blinked hard, blinked again. His head ached.

"You okay?" Swagger hissed, lying next to him.

"I'm fine," he lied.

"You keep blinking. What the hell is going on?"

"I'm fine," Donny insisted, but Swagger looked back into that patch of yellow grass and undulating earth he had designated Area 1.

Of course Donny wasn't fine. He thought of a book he once read about bomber pilots in World War II and a soldier who saw everything twice. He was seeing everything twice. But he didn't scream "I see everything twice" like that guy did.

He had a simple concussion, that was all, not enough to sickbay him or bellyache him out of any job in the Corps—except, of course, this one. The spotter was eyes, that was all he was.

"What the hell happened to you?"

"Huh?"

"What the hell happened to you. You're swole up like a grapefruit. Someone bang you?"

"I fell. It's nothing."

"Goddamn you, Fenn, this is the one fucking day in your life when you cannot have goddamn fallen. Oh, Christ, you got double vision, you got pain, you got dead spots in your vision?"

"I am fine. I am roger to go."

"Bullshit. Goddammit."

Swagger turned back, furiously. He lay in blazing concentration on the ridge, his sniper rifle before him, gazing through a pair of binoculars, sweeping Area 1. Donny blinked, wished he had a goddamn aspirin and put his eye to the M49 spotting scope planted in the earth before him.

Using one eye resolved the double-image problem, but not the blur. It didn't matter that he looked only with his best eye; there was still only a smear of visual information, like a television set without an aerial, getting mostly fuzz.

The right thing to do: say, Sarge, I have blurred vision. Sorry, I'm not worth shit out here. Let's call an abort before they get into range and—

"Shit!" said Bob. "They are moving too fast, they have panicked, they gonna be here in ten seconds."

Donny looked back and saw four—actually two—camo boonie hats just above the fold in the earth that took them out of sight. Something *was* wrong. They were moving too fast, almost running. The pressure of living a few seconds in a sniper's scope had gotten to them. They were headed in a beeline like half-milers for the hill and the comfort it supposedly provided.

"He'll know that ain't me. *Goddammit!*"

"What do we do?" said Donny, sickly aware that the situation had passed beyond his meager ability to influence, and full of images of that scared Featherstone, called to be a hero by nothing more than freak physical similarity, running to stop the shit from dribbling out his ass and the poor lieutenant, unable to yell, stuck with him, trailing behind, knowing that if he let him get away, Solaratov would take him down in a second.

"Fuck," said Bob, bitterly. "Get back on the scope. Maybe he'll bite anyhow."

Hmmmm. The sniper considered.

Why are they moving so fast? They have a long journey ahead of them, and they know there is much less chance of being observed if they move slowly than if they run.

He watched them, now about five hundred yards out, rushing pell-mell along the gully, almost out of sight.

Possibly they want to get into the shelter of the trees before full daylight?

No, no, not possible: they've never operated like that before. Therefore there are two possibilities: A) they know a man is out here and they are scared or B) they are bait, they are pretenders, and the real sniper is already out here, looking in my direction for some kind of movement, at which point he sends a bullet crashing my way.

Of the two possibilities, he had no favorites. His preference was not to overinterpret data. It was always to pick the worst possibility, assume that it was correct and counterreact.

Therefore: I am being hunted.

Therefore: where would a man be to get a good shot at me?

He turned and to the east, about three hundred yards away, made out a low undulation in the shine of the rising sun, not much, really, but just enough elevation to give a shooter a peek into this sea of grass here in the defoliated zone.

He looked at the sun: he'd be behind the sun, because he'd not want its reflection on his lens. Therefore, yes, the ridge.

But if he turned in that direction and put his own glass upon it, then he'd clearly get the reflection and the bullet. Therefore, he had to move to the north or south to get a deflection shot into them.

Slowly, he began to move.

"No, goddammit," said Bob.

"No, what?"

"No, he ain't biting. Not at them two birds. Shit!"

He paused, considering.

"Should we pull back?"

"Don't you get it, goddammit? We ain't hunting him no more. He's hunting us!"

The information settled on Donny uncomfortably. He began to feel the ooze and trickle of sweat down his sides from his pits. He glanced about. The world, which had seemed so benign just a second ago, now seemed to seethe with menace. They were alone in a sea of grass. The sniper, if Bob no longer believed him to be in Area 1, could therefore be anywhere, closing in on them even now.

No, not yet. Because if he read the fake sniper team moving too fast, he would not have had enough time to react and get out of there. He would still be an hour by low crawl away.

"Shit," said Bob. "Which way would he go?"

"Hmmmm," bluffed Donny, with no real idea of an answer.

"If he figures them guys is fake, and he looks around, about the only place we could be to shoot at his ass would be here, on this little ridge."

"Yeah?"

"Yeah, so to git a shot at our asses, how's he going to move? He going to try and flank us to the left or the right? What do you think?"

Donny had no idea. But then he did.

"If the treeline equals safety, then he'd go that way, wouldn't he? To his right. He'd put himself closer to it, not closer to Dodge City."

"But maybe that's how he'd figure we'd think, so he'd figure it the other way?"

"Shit," said Donny.

"No," said Bob. "No, you're right. Because he's on his belly, remember? This whole thing's gonna play out on bellies. And what he's looking at is an hour of crawling in the hot sun versus two hours. And being a half hour from the treeline is a hell of a lot better than being three hours from it. He'd have to go to the west, right?" He sounded as if he had to convince himself.

"It would take a lot of goddamn professional discipline," he continued, arguing with himself. "He'd have to make up his mind and cut free of his commitment to the only targets he's got. Man, he's got a set of nuts on him if he can make that decision."

He seemed to fight the obvious for a bit. Then he said, "Okay, Area One ain't it no more. Designate Area Two on your map, being the coordinates of a five hundred by five hundred grid square one thousand yards left. His left. Make it north-northeast. Give me them coordinates."

Donny struggled to get the map out, then struggled with the arithmetic. He worked it out, coming up with a new fire mission, hoping the dancing numbers his eyes were conjuring up were correct, scrawling them in the margins of the map. He had the sinking sensation of failing a math test he'd never studied for.

"Call it in. Call it in now, so we don't have to fuck with it later."

"Yeah."

Donny unleashed the aerial to vertical, then took the handset from its cradle, snapped on power, checking quickly to see that the PRC was still set on the right frequency.

"Foxtrot-Sandman-Six, this is Sierra-Bravo-Four, over."

"Sierra-Bravo-Four, this is Foxtrot-Sandman-Six, send your immediate, over."

"Ah, Foxtrot, we're going to go from Area One to new target, designated Area Two, over."

"Sierra, what the hell, say again, over."

"Ah, Foxtrot, I say again, we think our bird has flown to another pea patch, which we are designating Area Two, over."

"Sierra, you have new coordinates, all after? Over."

"Correct, Foxtrot. New coordinates Bravo-November-two-two-three-two-two-seven at zero-one-three-five-Zulu-July-eight-five. Break over."

"Wilco, Romeo. I mark it," and Foxtrot read the numbers back to him.

"Roger, Foxtrot, on our fire mission request. Out."

"Copy here, and out, Sierra," said the radio.

Donny clicked it off.

"Good," said Bob, who'd been diddling with a compass. "I make a route about five hundred yards over there to a small bump. That's where we'll go. We should be on his flank then. Assuming he goes the way I figure he's going."

"Got you."

"Get your weapon."

Donny grabbed his rifle, which was not an M14 or even an M16 or a grease gun. Instead, because of the short order in which the job was planned, it was the only scoped rifle that could be gotten quickly, an old fat-barreled M70 Winchester target rifle, with a rattly old Unertl Scope, in .30-06, left in the Da Nang armory since the mid-sixties.

"Let's go," Bob said.

CHAPTER TWENTY-TWO

Only bright blue sky above, and swaying stalks of the grass. The Russian crawled by dead reckoning, trusting skills it had taken him years to develop. He moved steadily, the rifle pulling ever so gently on his back. It was 0730 according to the Cosmos watch on his wrist. He wasn't thirsty, he wasn't angry, he wasn't scared. The only thing in his mind was this thing, right now, here. Get to elevation five hundred yards to the right. Look to the left for targets that in turn will be looking for targets to their front. Two of them: two men like himself, men used to living on their bellies, men who could crawl, who could wait through shit and piss and thirst and hunger and cold and wet. Snipers. Kill the snipers.

He came after a time to a small knoll. He had been counting as he moved: two thousand strokes. That is, two thousand half-yard pulls across the grass. His head hurt, his hands hurt, his belly hurt. He didn't notice, he didn't care. Two thousand strokes meant one thousand yards. He was there.

He shimmied up the knoll, really more of a knob, not four feet high. He set himself up, very carefully, flat on the crest, well shielded in a tuft of grass. He checked the sun, saw that it was no longer directly in front of him and would not bounce off his lens. He brought the Dragunov up, slipped it through the grass close to his shoulder and his hand, a smooth second's easy capture and grasp. Then he opened his binocular case and pulled out a pair of excellent West German 25X's. He eased himself behind their eyepieces and began to examine a world twenty-five times as large as the one he left behind.

The day was bright and, owing to the peculiarity of the vegetation in the defoliated zone and the oddities in the rise and fall of the land, he saw nothing but an ocean of yellow elephant grass, some high, some low and thread-bare, marked here and there by a rill of earth. He felt as if he were alone on a raft in the Pacific: endless undulation and ripple, endless dapple of shadow, endless subtle play of color, endless, endless.

He hunted methodically, never leaping ahead, never listening to hunches or obeying impulses. His instinct and brain told him the Marines would be five hundred yards ahead of him, on an oblique. They would seek elevation; their rifle barrels would be hard and flat and perfect against the vertical organization of the world. He found the low ridge where by all rights they should have been sited, and began to explore it slowly. The 25X lenses resolved the world beautifully; he could see every twig, every buried stone, every stunted tree, every stump that had survived the chemical agent all those years ago, every small hill. Everything except Marines.

He put the glasses down. A little flicker of panic licked through him.

Not there. They are not there. Where are they, then? Why aren't they there?

He considered falling back, trying another day. It was becoming an uncontrollable situation.

No, he told himself. No, just stay still, stay patient. They think you are over there, and you are over here. After a bit their curiosity will get the best of them. They are Americans: hardy, active people with active minds, attracted to sensations, actions, that sort of thing. They haven't the long-term commitment to a cause.

He will move, he thought. He was looking for me, I was not there, he will move.

Blackness.

Somewhere in his peripheral, a flash of black.

Solaratov did not turn to stare. No, he kept his eyes where they were, fighting the temptation to crank them around and refocus. Let his unconscious mind, far more effective in these matters, scan for them.

Blackness again.

He had it.

To the right, almost three hundred yards away. *Of course. He's flanking me to my right.*

Slowly, he turned his head; slowly, he brought up the binoculars.

Nothing. Movement. Nothing. Movement.

He struggled with the focus.

The unnatural blackness was a face. The Marine sniper had blackened it at night, for his long crawl into position; he'd shed his black clothes, and now wore combat dapple camouflage, but *he had made a mistake*. He had forgotten to take off his face paint. Now, black against the dun and yellow of the elephant grass, it stood out just the slightest bit.

Solaratov watched, fascinated. The man low-crawled two strokes, then froze. He waited a second or two, then low-crawled another two. His face, its features masked by the paint, was a study in warrior's concentration: tense, drawn, almost cracked with intensity. His rifle was on his back, wearing a tangle of strips for its own camouflage.

He tried to deny it, but Solaratov felt a flare of pleasure as intense as anything in his life.

He laid the binoculars down, and raised the rifle to his shoulder, finding the right position, rifle to bone to earth, finding the grip, finding the trigger, finding the eyepiece.

Swagger crawled through his scope. The crosshairs quartered his head. The Russian's thumb took the safety off and he expelled half a breath. His finger began its slow squeeze of the trigger.

"Goddamn," Bob said.

"What is it?" Donny said behind him.

"It's thinned out here. Goddamn. Less cover."

Donny could see nothing. He was lost in elephant grass; it was in his ears, his nose, in the folds of his flesh. The ants were feasting on him. He heard the dry buzz of flies drawn to the delicious odor of his sweat and blood—

he'd been cut a hundred or so times by the blades of the grass.

Ahead of him were the two soles of Bob's jungle boots.

"Shit," Bob said. "I don't like this one goddamn bit."

"We could just call in the Night Hag. She'd chew the shit out of all this. We'd pop smoke so she wouldn't whack us up."

"And if he ain't here, he knows we got him, and he's double careful or he don't come back at all and we never know why he came and we don't git us a Dragunov. Nah."

He paused.

"You still got that Model Seventy?"

"I do."

"All right. I want you to reorient yourself to the right. You squirt on ahead; see that little hummock or something?"

"Yeah."

"You set up on that, you scope it out for me. If you say it's okay, I'm going to shimmy on over there, to where it's thick again. I'll set up over there and cover for you. Fair enough?"

"Fair enough," said Donny. He squirmed around, took a deep breath and wiggled ahead.

"Damn, boy, I hope he ain't in earshot. You're grunting louder than a goddamn pig."

"This is hard work," Donny said, and it was.

He got up to the hummock, peered over it. He saw nothing.

"Go to the M49?"

"Nah. Don't got time. Just check it with your Unertl."

Donny slipped his eye behind the scope, which was a long, thin piece of metal tubing suspended in an odd frame. When you zeroed this old thing, it had external controls, which meant the whole scope moved, propelled this way and that by screws for windage and elevation. It had been assembled sometime back in the early forties, but rumor said it had killed more than its share of Japs,

North Koreans and VC. It wasn't even a 7.62mm NATO but the old Springfield cartridge, the long .30-06.

The optics were great. He scanned the grass as far as he could see, and saw no sign of human presence. But the blur had not gone away. He was aware he was missing fine detail. He squeezed the bridge of his nose with his fingers, and nothing improved. No, nothing out there, nothing that he could see.

"It looks clear."

"I didn't ask how it looked. I asked how it was."

"Clear, clear."

"Okay," said Bob. "You keep eyeballing."

The sergeant began to creep outward, this time at an even slower rate than before. He crawled slowly, ever so slowly, halting each two pulls forward, going still.

Donny returned to his scope. Back and forth, he swept the likely shooting spots, seeing nothing. It was clear. This was beginning to seem ridiculous. Maybe they were out here in the middle of nothing, acting like complete idiots. The bees buzzed, the flies ate, the dragonflies skittered. He couldn't keep his eye behind the scope for very long because it fell completely out of focus. He had to blink, look away. When would the call come from Bob that he was all right?

The trigger rocked back, stacked up and was on the very cusp of firing.

Where is the other one?

His finger came off the trigger.

There were two. He had to kill them both. If he fired, the other might take him or, seeing his partner with his head blown open, simply slide back farther into the grass and disappear. He'd call in air, possibly, and Solaratov would have to get out of the area.

Where was the other one?

He looked up from the scope. He realized he could see the sniper because for some odd reason, the grass was thinner there. The other one would be nearby, covering, as he was vulnerable. He would be vulnerable for only a few more seconds.

A plan formed in Solaratov's mind: Find the spotter. Kill the spotter. Come back and kill the sniper. It was possible because of the semiautomatic nature of the weapon and the fact that the distance was under three hundred meters.

He returned to the scope and very carefully began to crank backward, looking for another black face against the dun and the tan of the vertical thickets of stalks. He came back a bit more, no, nothing, nothing . . . and there! An arm! The arm led to a body, which led to the form of another prone man hunched over a rifle—he took a gasp of air, a little spurt of pleasure—and then continued up the trunk to the torso to discover that it was indeed a man but he was not a spotter, he was another sniper, and his rifle was pointing exactly at him. At Solaratov.

The man fired.

Donny looked up from his scope. His head ached. When would the call come from Bob? God, he needed an aspirin. He glanced about, seeing nothing, only the endless grass.

A dragonfly flashed close by. It was odd how their wings somehow caught the sunlight and threw a reflection just like—

Donny went back to the scope.

He was so close!

The sniper was less than three hundred yards away—or rather, the snipers, for there was a smear of enemy, blurry in the haze of Donny's concussion, well sunk in the grass. The man was bent into his rifle, moving slowly, tracking, and with a start, Donny realized he had located Swagger.

Kill him! he ordered himself. *Shoot! Do it now!*

The crosshairs seemed to quarter the head. He squeezed the trigger.

He lost his sight picture as the pressure increased. He squeezed harder. Nothing happened.

The safety, the safety. He reached for where it should have been, that nub in front of the trigger, but it wasn't there. That's where it was on an M14. On an M70, it was up on the bolt housing. He took his eye off the scope, looked for the flange that was the safety, and snapped it forward. He ducked to the scope, saw the man had turned and the rifle's muzzle was coming . . . right at him.

He jerked at the trigger and the rifle fired.

Bob crawled forward. Only a few more yards and then he was into the higher grass and

The shot, so unexpected, sounded like a drumbeat against his own ears. He froze—lost it, the great Bob Lee Swagger—and had a moment of twisted panic.

What? Huh? Oh, Christ!

Then he picked himself up, ran like a son of a bitch for the higher grass, waiting to get nailed and trying to sort it out.

"He's there! I saw him!" Donny screamed, and instantly from three hundred yards out, an answering shot sounded. It struck near Donny, blowing a big puff of dirt into the air.

Donny fired back almost instantly and Bob looked, saw the puff of dust where his shot hit.

"Get down!" he screamed, now terrified that Donny would take a shot in the head. He dove into the brush, righted himself, squirmed until he could see the dusty bank.

He threw the rifle to his shoulder, put his eye to the glass and saw . . . nothing.

"He's there!" Donny screamed again, but Bob could see nothing. Then a shot cracked out, seeming to come from the left, and he swung his rifle just a bit, saw some dust in the air from the disturbance of muzzle blast, and fired. He cycled, fired again, fast as he was able to, not seeing a target but hoping one was there.

"Get down!" he screamed again. *"Get down and call Foxtrot for air!"*

He worked the bolt, but could not see the sniper in the dust that floated in the grass in the area Donny had identified. Where was he? *Where was he?*

Donny edged back a bit and the second shot blasted the earth just a few inches from his face. *Ow!* The dirt blossomed as if a cherry bomb had detonated, and a hundred tiny flecks of grit bit him; he blinked, slid back even farther. He could hear Bob screaming but he couldn't make the words out. He thought: the radio. Call air. Get air.

But then Bob fired, fired again, and it filled Donny with courage. He squirmed up over the other side of the hummock, going to a left-handed shooting position. He couldn't throw the bolt from here, not easily, but a lot less of him stuck out, and that pleased him.

Where is he? Where are you, motherfucker?

Through the scope, he saw nothing, just dust hanging in the air, the slow wobble of grass signifying recent commotion but nothing to shoot at all.

He scanned left and right a few yards, didn't see a damned thing. He had this idea that he, not Bob, would be the one who brought the Russian down. Images from a forgotten boyhood book played suddenly through his mind: that would be like Lieutenant May getting the Red Baron instead of salty old pro Roy Brown. A gush of excitement came to him and a spurt of intense pleasure.

Where was he?

We can take him under fire from two sources, he realized. We can take this motherfucker.

"Air!" he heard Bob scream.

Yes, air. Get the Night Hag in here, smoke this fucker, blow him to—

On a wide scan, he saw him, much farther back, crawling away desperately.

Got you!

He put the crosshairs on the bobbing head, not a

shape so much as a suggestion in the blur of his vision. He tried to find the center, quartered it with the scope, felt in supreme control, felt the trigger rock against his finger, stack up just a tiny bit and then surprise the hell out of him when the shot occurred.

The man's rifle leaped, his hat popped off and he rolled over into the grass, still.

"I got him!" he screamed. *"I hit him!"*

"Air," Bob screamed. "Get us air!"

Donny let the rifle slide away, drew the PRC off his back and hit the on switch.

"Foxtrot, this is Sierra-Bravo, flash, I say again, flash, flash. We have contact, over."

"Sierra-Bravo, what are your needs? Are you calling air, Sierra-Bravo?"

Suddenly Bob was next to him, snatching the handset from him.

"Foxtrot, get us Night Hag superfast. I'm designating Area Two for the strike, bring in Night Hag, I say again, immediate, Area Two, Area Two."

"She is coming in, Sierra-Bravo; watch your butt, over."

"I got him!" Donny said.

"I am popping smoke to designate my position for Night Hag, over," said Bob. He grabbed a smoker off his belt, yanked the pin and tossed it. It spun and hissed and torrents of green smoke began to pour out of it.

"Sierra-Bravo-Four, this is Night Hag, I eyeball green smoke, over," a new voice on the net declared, even as they heard the roar of engines rising.

"That is correct, Night Hag, we are buttoning up, out."

Bob pulled Donny down and close to the hummock.

A shadow passed over them and Donny looked up and saw the great plane as it flashed overhead, began to bank. It seemed huge and predatory, its engines beating at the air. It was pitch black, an angel of death, and it banked to the right, raising a wing, presenting the side of its fuselage to the earth it was about to devastate.

The eight mini-guns fired simultaneously, tongues of gobbling flame streaking from the black flank, the sound not of guns firing quickly, but just a steady, screaming roar.

"Jesus," said Donny. He thought of worlds ending, of the end of civilization, of Hiroshima. This sucker brought heat. He couldn't imagine it.

The thousands of rounds poured from the guns to the earth, each fifth one a tracer, and the guns fired so fast it seemed they fired nothing but tracers. The bullets didn't strike the earth so much as disintegrate it. They pulverized, raising clouds of destruction and debris. The air filled with darkness as if the weather itself had turned to gunfire. It was a locust plague of lead that devoured that upon which it settled. Earlier versions of this baby had been called Puff the Magic Dragon, but they only had one gun. With eight, Night Hag could put a mythological hurt on the world. She just ate up Area 2 for what seemed like years but was in reality just a few seconds. She had only thirty seconds worth of shooting time, she ate so fast.

The plane pivoted as if tethered, the roar of its engines huge as it curled above them, then again its eight guns fired and again the ground shook and a blizzard of debris flew from the earth. Then it straightened out, climbed slightly and began to describe a holding pattern.

"Sierra-Bravo-Four, that's my best trick, over."

"Night Hag, should be sufficient, good work. Foxtrot, you there, over?"

"Sierra, this is Foxtrot."

"Foxtrot, let's move the teams out. I think we got him. I think we nailed him."

"Sierra-Bravo-Four, Wilco and good job. Out."

Huu Co, senior colonel, and the sappers watched the airplane hunt the sniper from the relative safety of the treeline. It was quite a spectacle: the huge plane wheeling, the thunderous streams of fire it brought to the defoliated zone, the rending of the earth where the bullets struck.

"Oh, the Human Noodle will be turned to the human sieve by that thing," one of the men said.

"Only the Americans would hunt a single man with an airplane," said another.

"They would send an airplane to fix a toilet," someone else shouted, to the laughter of some others.

But Huu Co understood that the sniper was dead, that the outlaw Swagger had once again prevailed. No man could withstand the barrage, and what came later, when, in the immediate aftermath of the airplane, when its dust still hung in the air, five jeeps suddenly burst from the fort and came crashing across the field, stopping right where two American snipers suddenly emerged from hiding a little to the east of the devastated area.

The men began to work methodically with flamethrowers. The squirts of flame spurted out, and where they touched, they lit the grass. The flames rose and spread, and burned furiously, as black, oily smoke rolled upward.

"The Human Noodle has now been roasted," someone said.

The flames burned for hours, out of control, rolling across the prairie of the defoliated zone, blazing vividly, as more and more men from the post came out in patrols, set up a line, and began to follow the flames. Soon enough, a flight of helicopters flew in from the east and began to hover over the field. They were hunting for a body.

"They will probably eat him if they can find him."

"There won't be enough left. They could put him in soup."

Though the Russian was a chilly little number, Huu Co still had a moment's melancholy over his fate. The airplane made war so totally; it was the most feared weapon in the American arsenal of superweapons. How horrible to be hunted by such a flying beast and to feel the world disintegrating around you as the shells exploded. He shivered a bit.

The Americans picked through the blasted field for

some time, until nearly nightfall, at one time finding something that excited them very much—Huu Co watched through his binoculars, but could not make it out—until finally retreating.

"Brother Colonel, shall we retreat?" his sergeant wished to know. "There is clearly nothing left for us here."

"No," said the colonel. "We wait. I don't know for how long, but we wait."

It was a lance corporal from First Squad who found the Dragunov.

"Whooie!" he shouted. "Lookie here. Gook sniper rifle."

"Corporal, bring that over here," called Brophy. "Good work."

The man, pleased to be singled out, came over with his trophy and turned it over to Brophy.

"There's your rifle," Bob said to the CIA man, Nichols.

The command team crowded around the new weapon, something no one had seen before. Like a kid unwrapping a Christmas present, Nichols wrapped the camouflage tape off the weapon.

"The legendary SVD. That's the first one we've recovered," said Nichols. "Congratulations, Swagger. That's not a small thing."

Donny just looked at it, feeling nothing, his head pounding from the stench of the gasoline and the oily smoke. It was a crude-looking thing, not at all sleek and well machined.

"Looks like an AK got stuck in a tractor pull," Bob said. He handled the weapon, looked it over, worked the action a few times, looked through the scope, then became bored with it and passed it on to other, more eager hands.

He moved away from the crowd, and watched with narrowed eyes and utter stillness as the Marines probed the burn zone while others set up flank security, under the CO's direction. Meanwhile Hueys and Cobra gunships hovered about the perimeter.

"Do you think he got away?" Donny finally asked him.

"Don't know. Them flames could have burned him up. Six or seven twenty-mm shells could have blown him to pieces, and the flames charred what meat was left off the bone. He could be indistinguishable from the landscape, I suppose. I just don't know. I didn't see any blood trails."

"Wouldn't the flames have burned the blood?"

"Maybe. I don't know."

"I'm pretty sure I hit him."

"I think you did too. Otherwise, I'd be a dead monkey. I'm going to put you in for another medal."

"I didn't do anything."

"You saved my bacon," said Bob. He seemed somehow genuinely shaken, as if he'd somehow learned today that he could die. Donny had never seen him quite like this.

"Man, I could use me a bottle of bourbon tonight," the sergeant added. "I could use it real bad."

Donny nodded. He had invested totally in the idea that he had shot the white sniper. He re-created it in his mind: the crosshairs on the head, the jerk of the trigger, the squirm of the man as if hit, the flying hat, the leap and twist of his rifle, then stillness. It felt like a hit, somehow. Everything about it felt good. But the rifle hadn't been found in the rough area where memory told him the sniper had been when he'd taken his shot.

And, he had the terrifying feeling, unconfessed to anyone, that maybe in the blur of his concussion—gone now—he'd zeroed incorrectly and killed a phantasm, not the real thing. He couldn't bring himself to express this, but it filled him with the blackest dread.

"I don't see how he could have gotten away," Donny said. "Nothing could stand up to it and nobody's that lucky."

"No way he could have stood up to it. If he was in the

middle of it, he was wasted, no doubt about it at all. But—was he in the middle of it?"

That was the question and Donny had no answer. He and he alone had seen the sniper, but by the time the plane was done chewing the world up, and he looked again, that world had changed: it was tattered, eviscerated; the grass was flattened; dust hung in the air. Then the flamethrower teams worked it over, and it burned and burned. Hard to figure now exactly where he'd been, what he'd seen, where it had been.

"Well, we'll see," said Bob. "Meanwhile, you come by tonight and we'll have us a drink or two."

Swagger was drunk. He was so drunk the world made no sense at all to him, and he liked it that way. The bourbon was like a nurse's hand on his shoulder in the middle of the night, when he awoke screaming in the Philippines after having gotten hit on his first tour, really messed up through the upper lung. The nurse had touched him and said, "There, there, there."

Now the bourbon said, "There, there, there."

"Fucking good stuff," Bob said. "The fucking-A best."

"It is," said Donny, smoking a giant cigar he'd gotten from somewhere. There were some others too: Brophy and Nichols of the CIA, Captain Feamster, the always mild XO, the company gunny—Firebase Dodge City's inner circle, as it was, drunk as skunks in the intel bunker. Somewhere Mick Jagger was blaring out over an eight-track, the one about satisfaction.

"Well, we got some satisfaction today, goddamn," said Feamster, an amiable professional who would never make bird colonel.

"We did, we did," confirmed the XO, who would make brigadier, because he agreed with everything that was said by anybody above him in rank.

A couple of other sergeants made faces at the XO's fawning, but only Swagger caught it.

"Goddamn right," he said to make the officers go away, and after a bit they did.

He took another taste. Prairie fire. Crackling. The sense of merciful blur; the world again full of possibility.

Now it was Nichols's turn to pay homage.

The CIA officer wandered over shyly, and said, "You know, it was a great day."

"We didn't get no head on the wall," said Bob.

"Oh, the Russian's dead, all right," said Nichols. "Nobody could live through that. No, but what I'm talking about is the rifle."

The rifle? thought Donny.

Oh, yeah. The *rifle*.

"You know how long we've been looking for that rifle?" Nichols turned and looked at Donny, who puffed on his cigar, took another swallow of bourbon and answered with a goofy smile.

"Well," said Nichols, "we've been looking since 1958, when Evgenie Dragunov drew up the plans at the Izhevsk Machine Factory. Some of our analysts said it would revolutionize their capacities. But others said, no, it was nothing."

"Looks like a piece of Russian crap to me," said Bob. "I don't think them guys know shit about building a precision rifle. They ain't got no Townie Whelans or no Warren Pages or no P. O. Ackleys. They just got tractor drivers in monkey suits."

Donny couldn't tell if Swagger, out of some obscure sense of need, was putting on the earnest, ambitious intelligence officer or not.

"Well, whatever," said Nichols. "Now we don't have to wonder. Now we'll be able to tell. And do you know what that means?"

"No."

"Nothing here. This shit is over and it never meant shit to the Russians except as a way to bleed us dry. They wouldn't even send Dragunovs to the 'Nam, that's how low on the priority list it was. The Dragunov was a higher priority than Vietnam to them."

This didn't play well with Swagger, and a darkness came over his face, but the CIA man didn't notice and kept on yapping.

"No, Russia's interested in Europe. That's where all the Russian divisions are. Now, with the Dragunovs coming down to platoon level in the next few years, and reaching the other Warsaw Bloc countries after that, what does that mean for our tactics? What level of precision fire can they bring against us if they move? Are they committing to sniper warfare in a big way? That'll have a great deal to do with our dispositions, our troop strength, our alignments, our relationships to our allies and the general thrust of NATO policy over the next few years. Dammit, you gave it to us! *No one* could get one, *no one* could buy one, they were *nowhere* except under lock and key, and old Bob Lee Swagger goes out in the bad bush and brings one back alive. Goddamn, it was a good day!" His eyes were bright and happy. He wasn't even drunk.

"Right now, it's been shipped priority flash to Aberdeen in Maryland for thorough testing at the Army Weapons Lab. They'll wring it out like you won't believe. They'll make that rifle sing!"

"A real feather in your cap," said Donny.

"A victory for our side. One of damn few of late. You did a hell of a job, Swagger. I'll see this goes into your record. I'll see phone calls are made, the right people are informed. You are a piece of action, my friend. But I will say one damned thing. You must have really *pissed* them off if they were willing to engage you with a Dragunov. Man, they want you all the ways there are. If you want, I can let it be known your expertise is invaluable and we can get you on the next flight to Aberdeen, Sergeant, on that team. No need to get iced, if they try again."

"I got a few months yet till my DEROS, Mr. Nichols. It's just fine, thanks."

"Think it over. Chew on it in your mind. You could be

TDY Aberdeen Proving Ground the day after tomorrow. Baltimore? The Block? Those beauties up there? Blaze Starr? A damn fine town, Baltimore. A man could have himself some fun there, you know. A hell of a lot finer than Dodge City, I Corps, RSV-fucking-N!"

"Mr. Nichols, I extended and I have a tour to serve. I got four months and days till DEROS."

"You are hard-core, Swagger. The hardest. The old Corps, the hardest, the best. Well, thanks, and God bless. You are a piece of action!"

He wandered away.

"You should do that," said Donny.

"Yeah, clap in Baltimore and hanging out with a bunch of soldiers with long hippie hair and unshined boots. No thanks. Not for me, goddammit."

"Well, at least we're heroes," said Donny.

"Today. They'll forget all about it in a few hours, when they sober up. That's a headquarters man for you. Your basic REMF."

He took another deep swallow of the bourbon.

"You sure you should be drinking that much?"

"I can hold my liquor. That's something the Swagger boys was always good at."

"Boy, I'll say."

"You know, I want to tell you something," he finally said. "Your gal. She is, goddammit, the prettiest goddamn woman I ever saw. You are one lucky boy."

"I am," said Donny, grinning like a monkey, taking a great slug of bourbon, then a draught on the cigar, expelling the smoke like vapors of chemwar.

"Here, I got something I want to show you."

"Yeah?"

"Yeah. I've showed you the photo. Look at this."

He reached into his pocket and drew out a folded sheaf of heavy paper and delicately unfolded it.

"It was that Trig guy. He was an artist. He did it."

Bob looked at it unsteadily in the flickering light. It was a creamy piece of paper, very carefully torn along one edge. But it wasn't the paper that caught Bob's eyes, it was the drawing itself. Bob didn't know a goddamned thing about art, but whoever this bird was, he had something. He really caught Donny in a few lines; it was as if he loved Donny. Somehow you could feel the attraction. The girl was next to him and the artist's feelings toward her were more complex. She was beautiful, hopelessly beautiful. A girl in a million. He felt a little part of himself die, knowing he'd never have a woman like that; it just wasn't in the cards. He'd be alone all his life, and maybe he preferred it that way.

"Hell of a nice picture," said Bob, handing it back.

"It is. He really got her. I think he was in love with her too. Everybody who sees Julie falls in love with her. I am so lucky."

"And you know what?" said Swagger.

"No, uh-uh."

"She is a damned lucky woman, too. She's got you. You are the best. You are going to have a happy, wonderful life back in the world."

Bob lifted the bottle, took two deep swallows and handed the bottle to Donny.

"You're a hero," said Donny. "You'll have a great life, too."

"I am finished. When you opened up on that bird, it come to me: you don't want to be here, you want to live. You gave me my life back, you son of a bitch. Goddamn, I owe no man not a thing. But I owe you beaucoup, partner."

"You are drunk."

"So I am. And I got one more thing for you. You come over here and listen to me, Pork, away from these lifer bastards."

Donny was shocked. He had never heard the term "lifer" from Bob's lips before.

Bob drew him outside.

"This ain't the booze talking, okay? This is me, this is

your friend, Bob Lee Swagger. This is Sierra-Bravo. You reading me clear, over?"

"I have you, Sierra, over."

"Okay. Here it is. I have thought this out. Guess what? The war is over for us."

"What?"

"It's over. I'm telling you straight. We go out on three missions a week, see, but we don't *go* nowhere. We go out into the treeline and we lay up for a couple of days. We don't take no shots, we don't go on no treks, no long wanders; we don't set up no ambushes. No, sir, we lay up in the tall grass and relax, and come in, like all the other patrols. You think I don't know that shit is going on? Nobody in this shit hole is fighting the war and nobody is fighting back in Da Nang. S-2 Da Nang don't give a shit, Captain Feamster don't give a shit, USMC HQ RSVN don't give a shit, WES PAC don't give a shit, USMC HQ Henderson Hall don't give a shit. Nobody wants to die, that's what it's all about. It's over, and if we get fucking wasted, we are just throwing our lives away. For nothing, you hear what I'm saying? We done our bit. It's time to think about number one. You hear what I'm saying?"

"Yeah, you'll do that till I DEROS out of here back to the world, then you'll go out on your own, and get more kills and go back to your job. You'll have to because by then the gooks will be getting very fucking bold and you'll be afraid they'll hit this place and take all these worthless assholes down, and you'll get hosed for them, and if that isn't the biggest waste there ever was, I don't know what is."

"No, I won't."

"Yeah, you will. I know you."

"No way at all."

"All right, I'll do this on one condition."

"I'm your goddamned sergeant. You can't 'one condition' me."

"On this one I can. That is: I go to Nichols, tell him you want on that Aberdeen team, but you got stuff to do first, and you can't go till a certain date. On the date I DEROS, you go to Aberdeen. Is that fair? That's fair! Goddamn, that's fair, that's what I want!"

"You young college smart-ass hippie bastard."

"I'll go get him now. Okay? I want to hear you make that statement to him, then I'll do this."

Bob's eyes narrowed.

"You ain't never outsmarted me before."

"And maybe I won't ever again, but by God, this is the night I do! Ha! Got you, Swagger! At last. Got you."

Swagger spat into the dust, took a swallow. Then he looked at Donny and goddamn if the silliest goddamn thing didn't happen. He smiled.

"Go get Mr. CIA," he said.

"Wahoo!" shrieked Donny, and went off to find the man.

The days passed. The sappers relaxed and treated the mission as a leave, a time for restoring hard-pressed spirits, catching up on correspondence with loved ones, renewing acquaintanceship with political and patriotic principles that could be lost in the heat of combat. They lounged in the tunnel complex on the edge of the defoliated zone two thousand yards from Dodge City, enjoying the amenities.

At night, Huu Co sent them on probing patrols, nothing aggressive, just simply to make certain the Americans at Dodge City weren't up to anything. He directed: no engagements, not at this time. So the tiny men in the dun-colored uniforms with the patience of biblical scholars simply waited and watched. Waited for what?

"Senior Colonel, the Human Noodle is not coming back. No man could survive that. We had best return to base camp and a new mission. The Fatherland needs us."

"My instructions," Huu Co told his sergeant, "are from the highest elements of the government, and they are to support and sustain our Russian comrade in any way possible. Until I determine that mission is no longer viable, we shall stay."

"Yes, sir."

"Long live the Fatherland."

"Long live the Fatherland."

But privately, he had grave doubts. It was true: no man could stand up to the intensity of the air attack with those fast-firing guns, and no man, particularly, could stand up to the flames from the American flamethrowers, a ghastly weapon that he believed they would never use against enemies of their own racial grouping.

And of course this: another failure.

Not his, surely, but failure has a way of spreading itself out and tainting all who are near it. He had led the mission, he had helped plan it, he had organized it. Was his heart not pure enough? Was he still infected with the virus of Western vanity? Was there some character defect that attended to him and him alone that caused him to continually misjudge, to make the wrong decision at the wrong time?

He rededicated himself to the study of Marxism and the principles of revolution. He read Mao's book for the four hundredth time, and Lao-tzu's for the thousandth. He buried his grief and fear in study. His eyes ate the hard little knots of words; his mind grappled with their deeper meanings, their subtexts, their contexts, their linkages to past and present. He was a hard taskmaster to himself. He gave himself no mercy, and refused to take painkillers for his crippled hand and its caul of burn. Only his dreams betrayed him. Only in his dreams was he a traitor.

He dreamed of Paris. He dreamed of red wine, the excitement of the world's most beautiful city, his own youth, the hope and joy of a brilliant future. He dreamed of crooked streets, the smell of cheese and pastry, the taste of Gauloises and *pommes frites;* he dreamed of the imperial grandeur of the place, of its sense of empire, the confidence with which its monuments blazed.

It was on one such night, as he tossed on his pallet, his semiconscious mind rife with bright images out of Lautrec, that the hands of a whore imploring him to her bed became the hands of his sergeant, beckoning him from sleep.

He rose. It was dark; candles had burned low. The man led him from his chamber, down earthen tunnels, to the mess hall. There, in the dark, a squat figure sat hunched over a table, eating with unbelievable gusto.

The sergeant lit a candle and the room flickered, then filled with low light.

It was the white sniper.

CHAPTER TWENTY-THREE

They lay in the high grass, or in the hills under the scrubby trees and bamboo, watching and tracking but never shooting.

A VC squad moved into the zone of fire, four men with AKs, infiltrating farther south. Easy shots; he could have taken two and driven the other two into the high grass and waited them out and taken them, too. But farther south was only ARVN, and Bob figured it was a Vietnamese problem, and the ARVNs could handle it or they could handle the ARVNs, depending. Another time, a VC tax collector clearly blew his cover and was making his rounds. It was an easy shot, 140-odd yards into a soft target. But Bob said no. The war was over for them.

They lay concealed or they tracked, looking for sign of big bodies of men, of units moving into position for an assault on Firebase Dodge City, whose immediate environs they patrolled. There was nothing. It was as if a kind of enchantment had fallen over this little chunk of I Corps. The peasants came out and resumed work in their paddies, the farmers went back to furrowing the hills with their ox-pulled plows. The rainy season was over. Birds sang; now and then a bright butterfly would skitter about. Above, fewer contrails marred the high sky, and if you flicked across the FM bandwidths on the PRC-77, you could tell that the war had wound way down; nobody was shooting at anything.

Two weeks into it, orders came for Bob, assigning him TDY to Army Weapons Lab, Aberdeen Proving Ground, Aberdeen, Maryland. He was slated to leave the day after Donny's DEROS. Feamster told him since he was so short and enemy activity so quiet and nothing coming down from Battalion S-2, he and Donny didn't have to go out anymore, but the two said they'd do it anyway, looking for signs of an assault but not for kills. Feamster may have gotten it; that was okay by him. He said that word of turning Dodge City over to ARVN forces was imminent—"Vietnamization," they called it—and the whole unit would be DEROSed back to the States before the summer came, no matter where the guys were in their tours.

"This is pretty cool," said Donny.

Bob just grunted and spat.

Solaratov slept for two days solid and then rose and came to see Huu Co. The story of his escape went untold. He made no report. How he had survived, where he had gone, what he had suffered, all of it went unrecorded and no one dared ask him. A medic attended his burns, which were severe but not debilitating, and he never complained or winced. He seemed disconnected from the agonies of his body. He had one trophy. It was his SPETSNAZ field cap, a floppy, beige thing that looked like a deflated beret or an American sailor hat that had been run over by a tank. It had two holes in it on the left side of the crown, an entrance wound and an exit wound. How could his head have survived such a thing? He had no comment but liked to wiggle his fingers through the two holes at the sappers, who would dash away in confusion.

On the morning he came to Huu Co, he said, "These people are very good. Good craft, good tactics, very well-thought-out planning. I was impressed."

"How did you possibly survive?"

"Not a remarkable story. Luck, guile, courage, the usual. Anyhow, I am not prepared to give up the mission."

"What do you require of us?"

"I will never maneuver close enough, I see that now. Plus, of course, I lost my weapon, much to my embarrassment. I hope it perished in the flames or was destroyed by cannon fire."

He frowned; failure in his profession was not an acceptable outcome.

"But, no matter. I have certain requirements for a new weapon. I will be shooting at over a thousand yards. I can do it no other way, that is, unless I want to die myself, and I prefer not to."

"Our armorers are dedicated to their jobs, but I doubt we have a weapon capable of such accuracy."

"Yes, I know. Nor, frankly, do we. But you must have some small cache of American weapons, no? Your intelligence people would maintain an inventory? It's common for guerrillas to turn the enemy's weapons against himself."

"Yes."

"Now, I will give you a very specific type of American weapon. It must be found and delivered here within two weeks. It has to be this exact weapon; with no other would I have a chance."

"Yes."

"But that is not all. You must also contact the Soviet SPETSNAZ unit at the airfield; they will be required to acquire certain components from outside Asia. These are very specific also; no deviation can be allowed. There is a place where such a list can be filled out in just a few seconds, and they will have access to capabilities to do so."

"Yes, comrade. I—"

"You see, it's not merely the rifle. The rifle is only part of the system. It's also the ammunition. I have to construct ammunition capable of the task which I have in mind."

He handed over the list, which was in English. Huu Co did not recognize the rifle by type, nor the list of "ingredients," which appeared to be of a chemical or scientific nature. He did recognize one word, but it had no meaning to him: MatchKing.

The sniper worked with care. He studied the reconnaissance photos of the area, discussed the topography once again with Huu Co, trying to find the right combination of elements. He worked very, very carefully. After devising theories, he went to test them, exploring the area at night and spending his days hidden in the grass, trying to learn what there was to learn.

This time he never went near the base. He was acclimatizing himself to the very long shots, and hunting for a shooting position. He finally found one on a nameless hill that, by his judgment, was close to fourteen hundred yards from the base, but it offered the most generous angle into the encampment, with the least drop, the least exposure to wind pressure, the most favorable light in the early morning, when such a thing would take place, and it was also sited immediately to the north of the original ambush site, a gamble, but a calculated one. Solaratov reasoned that on general principle alone, the American sniper team would be reluctant to go out the same way as the one that had almost gotten them killed. But they would consider going out the opposite side too obvious. Therefore, on their missions they would either leave above, to the north, or below, to the south. He had a one-in-two chance of encountering them, and in the days that he waited, he saw them leave the post three times. Tiny dots, so far away. Hardly human.

Fourteen hundred yards. It was a hellaciously long shot. It was a shot nobody had any business trying to make. Beyond six hundred yards, the margin of error shrinks to nothing; the play of the elements increases exponentially. You would need more power than the Dragunov's 7.62 X 54 round; you would need more power than any round available under normal circumstances in either the North Vietnamese or the American inventory, because war had become a thing of light, fast-firing weapons that kill by firepower, not accuracy. He had contempt for such a philosophy. It was the philosophy of the common untrainable man, not of the elite professional who masters all the variables in his preparation and who has genius-level skill at his task. War nowadays no longer demanded special men but ordinary men—lots of them.

He lay on the hill, trying to will himself into the mental state necessary. He had to be calm, his eyesight perfect, his judgment secure. He had to dope the wind, the mirage, the temperature, the angle of travel of the targets, his bullet's trajectory, the time in flight, everything. At this range, it was not like rifle shooting; it was like naval gunfire, for the bullet would have to rise in high apogee and describe an arc across the sky, and float downward with perfect, perfect placement. There were not but a dozen men in the world who could take such a shot with confidence.

He watched, through binoculars: the Marines far off scuttled about behind their berm, making ready to depart, confident that for them the war was almost over. And for two of them, it was.

Finally: the rifle. It came almost at the end of the two-week period, and not without difficulty. It had been a trophy in the People's Museum of Great Struggle in downtown Hanoi; thousands of schoolchildren had looked upon it with great horror as part of their political education. It demonstrated the evil will of the colonialists and the capitalists, that they took such great pains to construct the devil's own tool. In this, it was very useful indeed, and it took Russian intervention at the highest levels to have it withdrawn from the permanent exhibit. A special sapper unit was ordered to transport it down the Trail of Ten Thousand Miles to Huu Co's little hidden post on the outskirts of the defoliated zone of Firebase Dodge City.

The Russian broke it down, for the first step to mastering a rifle is to master what makes it work. He studied the system, the cleverness of it, the robustness of it, the rise and fall of springs, the thrusting of rods, the gizmo of the trigger group. It was ingenious: overengineered in the American fashion, but ingenious. This one had been crudely accurized with flash hider, a fiberglass bedding for the action in the stock, a wad of leather around the comb to provide a nest for the cheek in relation to the scope, which was a mere four-power and, Solaratov saw, the weakest element in the system, attached to the rifle parallel to but not above the barrel, creating problems in parallax that had to be mastered. But his main focus of interest was that trigger group, a mesh of springs and levers that could be pulled whole from the receiver group. He broke it down to the tiniest component, then carefully polished each engagement surface to give the piece a crisper let-off.

At this point, the box of "components" came from the Soviet intelligence service. They were the easiest mission requirements to acquire: a Soviet asset had merely gone to a Southern California gun store and purchased them, for cash; they had been shipped to the Soviet Union via diplomatic pouch and to North Vietnam by the daily TU-16 flight. To look at them was to see nothing: these were actually reloading tools, which looked like steel chambers of mysterious purpose, and green boxes of bullets, cans of powder, DuPont IMR 4895, tools for resizing the case, pressing in new primers, reinserting the bullet. He knew that no military round could deliver the accuracy he needed and that it would take great attention to detail and consistency.

He took the entire rig for a day's march to the north, and there, out of the eyes of Westerners and Vietnamese alike except for a security team of sappers and the ever-curious Huu Co, he set up a fourteen-hundred-meter range, shooting at two close targets, white silhouettes that were easy to see and would not be moving like they would on the day of his attempt.

The scope was small and had an ancient, obsolete reticle: a post, like a knife point, rising above a single horizontal line. Additionally, it did not have enough elevation to enable him to hit out to fourteen hundred meters, close to three times the rifle's known efficiency, though well within the cartridge's lethal capability. He hand-filed shims from pieces of metal and inserted them within the scope rings to elevate the scope higher, and tightened the assembly with aircraft glue so that it would hold to a thousand-yard zero over the course of his testing.

He worked with infinite patience. He seemed lost in a world no one could penetrate. He seemed distracted to an absurd degree, almost catatonic. His nickname, "the Human Noodle," took on added comic meaning as he entered a zone of total vagueness that was actually total concentration. He seemed to see nothing.

Gradually, increment by increment, he managed to walk his shots into the target. Once he was on the target, he began hitting regularly, primarily through mastery of trigger control and breathing and finding the same solid position off a sandbag. The sandbag was the important feature: it had to be just so dense, packed so tight, and it had to support the rifle's forestock in just such a way. Infinitely patient micro-experimentation was gradually revealing the precise harmony among rifle and load and position and his own concentration that would make his success at least possible.

Finally, he took to having the sappers present the targets from over a berm, so that he could see them for just the second they'd be visible. He'd teach himself to shoot fast. It went slowly and he burned out the sappers with his patience, his insistence on recleaning the rifle painstakingly every sixteen rounds, his demand that all his ejected cartridges be located and preserved in the order that they were fired. All the time he kept a notebook of almost unreadable pedantry as he assembled his attempts.

"For a sniper, he is a very dreary fellow," the sergeant said to Huu Co.

"You want a romantic hero," said Huu Co. "He is a bureaucrat of the rifle, infinitely obsessed with microprocess. It's how his mind works."

"Only the Russians could create such a man."

"No, I believe the Americans could too."

Finally, the day came when the Russian hit his two targets in the kill zone twice in the same five seconds. Then he did it another day and then another, all at dawn, after lying the night through on his stomach.

"I am ready," he announced.

CHAPTER TWENTY-FOUR

The sandbags were the hardest. He had grown almost superstitious about them. He would let no one touch them, for fear of somehow shifting the sand they concealed and altering irrevocably their inner dynamics.

"The Human Noodle has gone insane," someone said.

"No, brother," his comrade responded. "He has always been insane. We are only noticing it now."

The sandbags were packed with the care of rare, crucial medicines, and transported back to the tunnel complex in the treeline, with the Human Noodle watching them with the concentration of a hawk. He literally never let them out of his sight; the rifle and its scope, strapped inside a gun case and more or less suspended and shockproofed by foam rubber pellets taken from American installations, bothered him much less than the sandbags.

That held true for his gradual setup as well. He began with the sandbags, examining them minutely for leaks, for some alteration of their density. Finding none, he convinced himself he was satisfied, and made the sappers delicately transport them to the treeline. There he had rigged a kind of harness, a flat piece of wood to be tied to his back when he was prone, upon which the sandbags themselves were to be tied.

"I hope he isn't crushed," said Huu Co, genuinely alarmed.

"He could suffocate," said his sergeant.

Ever so delicately, weighted down under the nearly one hundred pounds of sand—two forty-pound bags and a ten-pound bag—the Russian began his long crawl to the shooting position, which was a good two thousand yards from the tunnel complex far from the burned zone. It took six hours—six back-breaking, degrading hours of slow, steady crawl through the grass, suffering not merely from back pain but from the crushing fear of his utter helplessness. A man under a hundred pounds of sand, crawling into enemy territory. What could be more ridiculous, more pathetic, more poignant? Any idiot with a rifle could have killed him. He had no energy, his senses were dulled by the pain in his back and the breathless smash of the huge bags on his back. He crawled, he crawled, he crawled, seemingly forever.

He made it, somehow, and crawled back, just before the first light of dawn, looking more dead than alive. He slept all day, and all the next day, because his back still ached.

On the third day, again he crawled, this time with the rifle and a batch of his specially constructed cartridges. It was much easier. He made it to the small hill well before dawn and had plenty of time to set up.

He loaded the rifle, tried to find some sense of relaxation, tried to will himself into the sort of trance he knew he needed. But he never could quite relax. He felt tense, twitchy. Twice, noises startled him. His imagination began to play tricks on him: he saw the great black plane hovering overhead, and felt the earth open up as it fired. He remembered crawling desperately, his mind livid with fear, as the world literally exploded behind him. You could not crawl through such madness; there was no "through." He crawled and crawled, the explosions ringing in his ears, dumbstruck that he had chosen to crawl in the right direction. And what was the right direction?

"If he's out there, he's dead now," he heard one Marine say to another.

"Nothing could come through *that,*" said the other.

They were so close! They were ten feet away, chatting like workers on a lunch break!

Solaratov willed himself to nothingness. Like an animal he ceased to consciously exist. He may not even have been breathing, not as normal humans would define it, anyhow. His pulse nearly stopped; his body temp dropped; his eyes closed to slits. He gave himself up to the earth totally and let himself sink into it and would not let his body move a millimeter over the long day. Marines walked all around him, once so close he could see the jungle boots. He smelled the acrid stench of the burning gasoline when they used the flamethrowers and he sensed first their joy, when they recovered the rifle he had abandoned in panic, and then their irritation, when no body itself could be located. The body was right there, almost under their feet; it still breathed!

Movement!

The flash of movement recalled him from that day to this one. Through his binoculars he could see movement just behind the berm in the predawn light, though it was so far away. The rifle was set into the bags, firmly moored, sunk into sand so dense and unyielding it was almost concrete, the heel of its butt wedged just as tightly into the smaller bag. He squirmed behind it, felt himself pouring himself around the rifle, not moving it a hair, so perfectly was it placed. His eye went to the eyepiece.

Again, he saw movement: a face, peering out?

Up, down, then up again, then down.

His finger touched the trigger, his heart hammered.

Here, after so long, the long hunt was over.

No.

He watched them rise, the shooter, then the spotter, rolling over the sandbag berm so far away, gathering themselves in a gulch at its bottom, and then heading out.

Infinite regret poured through him.

You were afraid to shoot.

No, he told himself. You were not able today. You were not in the zone. You could not have made the shot.

It was true.

Better to let them go and gamble that sometime soon he'd have another opportunity than to rush and destroy all the work he'd invested and all the hopes and responsibilities riding on his shoulders.

No. You did the right thing.

Not months anymore. Not even days. Donny was down to a day.

One more day.

And he would spend it processing out. Then a wake-up, and the chopper would arrive at 0800 the day after tomorrow and at 0815 it would leave and he would be on it. He'd be back to Da Nang in an hour, processed out by 1600, on the freedom bird by nightfall, home eighteen hours later.

DEROS.

Date of estimated return from overseas. How many had dreamed of it, had fantasized about it? For his generation, the generation of men sent to do a duty they didn't quite understand, and that made them especially hated in their own country, this was as good as it got. There would be no parades, no monuments, no magazine covers, no movies, no one waiting to call them heroes. You only got DEROS, your little piece of heaven. You earned it the hard way, and it wasn't much, but that's what you got.

What a feeling! He'd never felt anything quite like it before, so powerful and consuming. It went deep into his bones; it touched his soul. No joy was so pure. The last time, after getting hit, there'd been only the fear and the pain and the long months in a crappy hospital. No DEROS.

This time, within twenty-four hours: DEROS.

"Hey, Fenn?"

He looked up. It was Mahoney, the ringleader in the anti-Swagger mutiny, under whose auspices he'd gotten kicked in the head by somebody.

"Oh, yeah," said Donny, rising from his cot.

"Hey, look, I wanted to come by and tell you I was sorry about that thing that happened. You're an okay guy. It turned out all right. Shake my hand on it?"

"Yeah, sure," said Donny, who always found it impossible to hold a grudge.

He took the other lance corporal's hand, shook it.

"How's Featherstone?"

"He's cool. He's down to one and days; he'll rotate back to the world. Me, too. Well, two and days, then my ass is on the golden bird."

"You may not even have to make it that far. I hear the ARVN are going to take over Dodge City, and you guys'll be rotating out early. You won't even have to see your DEROS."

"Yeah, I heard that too, but I don't want to count on anything the Marine Corps wants to give me. I'm still locked onto DEROS. I make DEROS and I'm home free. Back to city streets, NYC, the Big Apple."

"Cool," said Donny, "you'll have a good time."

"I'd ask you what it felt like to be so short and I'd buy you a beer, but I know you want to go to bed and make tomorrow come earlier. All that processing out." It was company policy that no man went into the field on his last day.

"Well, sometime back in the world, you can buy me a beer and we'll have a big laugh over this one."

"We will. You're staying in, right? You're not going out with Swagger tomorrow."

"Huh?"

"You're not going out with Swagger tomorrow?"

"What are you talking about?"

"I saw him hunched up with Feamster and Brophy and a couple of the lifer NCOs in the S-2 bunker. Like he was going on a mission."

"Shit," said Donny.

"Hey, you sit tight. If they didn't ask you, you don't got to go. Just be cool. Time to take the golden bird back to the land of honeys and Milky Ways."

"Yeah."

"Go in peace, bro."

"Peace," said Donny, and Mahoney dipped out of the hootch.

Donny lay back. He checked his watch. It was 2200 hours. He tried to forget. He tried to relax. Everything was cool, everything was calm, he was home free.

But what the fuck was Swagger up to?

It ate at him. What deal was this?

It bothered him.

He can't go out. He promised.

Shit.

He rose, slipped out the hootch and walked across the compound to the dark bunker of the S-2 shop, where he found Bob, Feamster and Brophy bent over maps.

"Sir, permission to enter," he said, entering.

"Fenn, what the hell are you doing here? You should be checking your gear to turn in to supply tomorrow," said Feamster.

"Is something going on with Sierra-Bravo-Four?"

"Sierra-Bravo-Four is going back to the world; that's what's going on with Sierra-Bravo-Four," said Bob.

"Looks like a mission briefing to me."

"It ain't nothing that concerns you."

"That's a map. I see route markers pinned on it and coordinates penciled in. You going on a job, Sierra-Bravo?"

"Negative," said Bob.

"You are too," said Donny.

"It ain't a goddamn thing. Now, you git your young ass out of here, got that? You got work you should be doing. This ain't no time for screwing off, even if you're down to a day and a wake-up."

"What is it?" Donny said.

"Nothing. No big deal."

"Sir?"

"Sergeant," said Feamster, "you ought to tell him."

"It's a rinky-dink recon, that's all, a one-man thing. We haven't covered the north in a couple of weeks. They could have infiltrated in, gone through the trees and have set up in the north, a few klicks out. I'm just going to mosey out to see if I cut tracks to the north. A couple klicks out, a couple klicks in. I'll be back by nightfall."

"I'm going."

"My ass, you are. You have to spend tomorrow processing out. *Nobody* goes into the field on the last day."

"That's right, Fenn," said Captain Feamster. "Company policy."

"Sir, I can process out in an hour. Just this one last mission."

"Christ," said Swagger.

"I'll worry about it all the way back."

"Man, can't you take no slack at all? *Nobody* goes out with just a wake-up left. It's a Marine Corps policy."

"It is, my ass. It's the same deal, a guy to spot, a guy to talk on the radio. A guy to work security if it comes to that."

"Christ," said Swagger. He looked over at Feamster and Brophy.

"It really is a two-man job," said Brophy.

"If we go, we go. Full field packs, Claymores, cocked and locked. I would hate to get caught short on the last day."

"Cocked and locked, rock and roll, the whole goddamn nine yards," Donny said.

"When did you take over this outfit?"

"I'm only doing my job."

"You are a stubborn crazy bastard and I hope that poor girl knows what a hardhead she's looped up with."

At 0-dark-30, Donny rose and found Bob already up. He slipped into his camouflages for the last time, pulled the pack on. Canteens ready. Claymores ready. Grenades ready. He painted his face jungle green and brown. Last time, he told himself in the mirror. He smiled, showing white teeth against the earthy colors.

He checked his weapons: .45, three mags, M14, eight mags. There was a ritual here, a natural order, checking one thing then the next, then checking it all again. It was all ready.

He crawled from his hootch, went to the S-2 bunker, where Bob, similarly accoutred except that he had the

Remington rifle instead of an M14, waited, sipping coffee, talking quietly with Brophy over the map.

"You don't have to go, Fenn," said Bob, looking over to him.

"I'm going," said Donny.

"Check your weapons, then do a commo check."

Donny examined his M14, pulling the bolt to seat a round in the chamber, then letting it fly forward. He put the safety on, then took out the .45, ascertained that the mag was full but the chamber empty, as Swagger had instructed him to carry the piece. He ran the quick commo check, and all systems were functioning.

"Okay," said Bob, "last briefing. Up here, toward Hoi An. We go a straight northward course, through heavy bush, across a paddy dike. We should hit Hill 840 by 1000 hours. We'll set up there, glass the paddies below in the valley for a couple of hours, and head back by 1400 hours. We'll be in by 1800 at the latest. We'll stay in PRC range the whole time."

"Good work," said Brophy.

"You all set, Fenn?" Bob asked.

"Gung ho, *Semper Fi* and all that good shit," said Donny, at last strapping the radio on, getting it set just right. He picked up his M14 and left the bunker. The light was beginning to seep over the horizon.

"I don't want to go out the north," said Bob. "Just in case. I want to break our pattern. We go out the east this time, just like we did before. We ain't never repeated ourself; anybody tracking us couldn't anticipate that."

"He's gone, he's dead, you got him," said Brophy.

"Yeah, well."

They reached the parapet wall. A sentry came over from the guard post down the way.

"All clear?" Swagger asked.

"Sarge, I been working the night vision scope the past few hours. Ain't nothing out there."

Bob slipped his head over the sandbags, looked out into the defoliated zone, which was lightening in the rising sun. He couldn't see much. The sun was directly in his eyes.

"Okay," he said, "last day-time to hunt."

He set his rifle on the sandbag berm, pulled himself over, gathered the rifle and rolled off. Donny made ready to follow.

How many days now? Four, five? He didn't know. The canteen had bled its last drop of water into his throat yesterday before noon. He was so thirsty he thought he'd die. He hallucinated through the night: he saw men he had killed, he saw Sydney, where he won the gold, he saw women he had fucked, he saw his mother, he saw Africa, he saw Cuba, he saw China, he saw it all.

I am losing my mind, he thought.

Everything was etched in neon. His nerves fired, his stomach heaved, he had starvation fantasies. I should have brought more food. Something in his blood sugar made him twitch uncontrollably.

This would be the last day. He could stand it no more.

The days were the worst. There was no shield from the sun and it had burned his body red in slivers, between the brim of his soft cap and his collar. The backs of his hands were now so swollen he could hardly close them.

But the nights were no better: it got cold at night and he shivered. He was afraid to sleep because he might miss the Americans on their way out. So he stayed awake at night and slept during the day, except that it was too hot to sleep well. The insects devoured him. He'd never leave this cursed chunk of bare ground in the most forgotten land in the world. He could smell his own physical squalor and knew he was living beyond the bounds of both civilization and sanitation. He was putting himself through the absolute worst for this job. Why was he here?

Then he remembered why he was here.

He looked at his watch: 0600. If they were going on a mission today, this was the time they'd go.

Wearily, he brought the binoculars to his eyes, and

peered ahead. He had to struggle with the focus and he lacked the strength to hold it steady.

Why didn't I take that shot when—

Movement.

He blinked, unbelieving, feeling the sense of miracle a hunter feels when after the long stalk he at last sees his game.

There was motion down there, though it was hard to make out in the low light. It looked like the movement of men from the bunkers toward the berm but he could not be sure.

He abandoned the binoculars, shifted left and squirmed behind the rifle, trying his hardest not to jar its placement. He poured himself around it, half mounting the sandbag into which the toe of its butt was jammed, his fingers finding the grip, his face swimming up toward the spot weld, feeling the jam of his thumb against his cheekbone.

He looked through it, saw nothing, but in a second his focus returned.

He could see motion behind the berm, a small gathering of men.

It was an unbearably long shot, he now saw, a shot no man had the right to take.

The wind, the temperature, the humidity, the distance, the light: it all said, You cannot take this shot.

Yet he felt a strange calm confidence now.

All his agonies vanished. Whatever it was inside him that made him the best was now fully engaged. He felt strong, purposeful. The world ceased to exist. It gradually bled away as he gave himself to the circle of light before him, his position perfect, the right leg cocked just to the right to put some tension in his body, tightening his *Adductor magnus* but not too much, his hands strong and steady on the rifle, the spot weld perfect, no parallax in the scope, the butt strong against his shoulder; it was all so perfect. He controlled his breath, exhaling most of it, holding just a trace of oxygen in his lungs.

Reticle, he thought.

His focus went to the ancient reticle, to the dagger point that stood up just beyond the horizontal line that bisected the circle of light, and watched now, in amazement, as, like a phantasm springing from the very earth itself, a man came over the berm, dappled in camouflage, face painted, but even from this far, far distance recognizable as a member of his own rare species.

He did not command himself to fire; one cannot. One trusts the brain, which makes the computations; one trusts the nerves, which fire the processed information down their networks and circuits; one trusts that little patch of fingertip that alone on the still body must be responsive.

The rifle fired.

Time in flight: one full second. But the bullet would arrive far before the sound of it did.

The scope stirred, the rifle cycled lazily, called another cartridge into its chamber and settled back, all before, ever so lazily, the green man went down.

He knew the second would come fast and that to hit him he had to do the nearly unthinkable. Fire before he saw him. Fire on the sure knowledge that his love would propel him after his partner, just hit, the knowledge that the bullet must be on its way before the man himself had even decided what he must do.

But Solaratov knew his man.

He fired just a split second before the second man jumped into view, arms extended in urgent despair, and as the man climbed, the bullet traveled its long parabola, rode its arc, rising and falling as the man himself was squirming desperately over the berm, and when it fell, it met him exactly as he landed on the ground and lurched toward his partner and it took him down.

PART III

HUNTING IDAHO

*The Sawtooth Mountains
Earlier this year*

Chapter Twenty-five

The black dogs were everywhere. They yipped at him at night, preventing him from sleeping; they haunted his dreams with their infernal racket; they made him wake early, crabby, bitter, spent.

Were they dreams from bad old times? Or were they just the generalized melancholy that attends a man who begins to understand he can never be what he was before he reached fifty, that his body and eyesight and gift of feel and stamina were on the decline? Or were they from some deep well of grief, once opened impossible to shut down?

Bob didn't know. What he knew was that he awoke, as usual, with a headache. It was not yet dawn, but his wife, Julie, was already up, in the barn, saddling the horses. She clung to her habits even during his dark times. Ride early, work hard, never complain. What a woman! How he loved her! How he needed her! How he mistreated her!

He felt hungover, but it was a dream of post-alcoholic pain. He had not allowed liquor to touch his lips since 1985. He didn't need it. He'd lost close to a decade and a half to the booze, he'd lost a marriage, a batch of friendships, half his memories, several jobs and opportunities; he'd lost it all to the booze.

No booze. He could do it. Each day was the first day of the rest of his life.

Lord, I need a drink, he thought today, as he thought every day. He wanted it so bad. Bourbon was his poison, smooth and crackling, all harsh smoke and glorious blur. In the bourbon, there was no pain, no remorse, no bad thoughts: only more bourbon.

The hip hurt. Inexplicably, after many years of near painlessness, it had begun to ache all over again. He had to see a doctor about it, and stop gobbling ibuprofen, but he could not, somehow, make himself do it.

"It hurts," his wife would say. "I can tell. You don't complain, but your face is white and you move slowly and you sigh too much. I can tell. You have to see somebody."

He answered her as he answered everybody these days: a sour grimace, a furious stubbornness, then wintry retreat behind what she once called the wall of Bobness, that private place he went, even in the most public of circumstances, where nobody, not even his wife and the mother of his only child, was admitted.

He went and stood naked under a shower, and let its heat pound at him. But it did not purify him. He emerged in as much pain as he had entered. He opened the medicine cabinet, poured out three or four ibus and downed them without water. It was the hip. Its pain was dull, like a deep bone bruise, that throbbed, and lighted the fire of other pains in his knees and his head and his arms. He'd been hit in so many places over the years: his body was a lacework of scars that testified to close calls and not a little luck.

He pulled on ancient jeans and a plaid shirt, and a pair of good old Tony Lamas, his oldest friends. He went down to the kitchen, found the coffee hot and poured himself a cup. The TV was on.

Something happening in Russia. This new guy everybody was scared of, an old-fashioned nationalist, they said. Like the czars in the nineteenth century, he believed in Russia over everything. And if he got control, things would get wobbly, since they still had so many rockets and atomic warheads, and were only a few hours' work from retargeting America's cities. There was an election coming up in a couple of months; it had everybody worried. Even the name was scary. It was Passion. Actually, it was Pashin, Evgeny Pashin, brother of a fallen hero.

It made Bob's headache worse. He thought Russia had fallen. We'd stood up to them, their economy had collapsed, they'd had their Vietnam in Afghanistan, and it had all fallen apart on them. Now they were back, in some new form. It didn't seem fair.

Bob didn't like Russians. A Russian had hit him in the hip all those years ago, and started this run of bad luck that, just recently he thought he'd beaten down, but then it had returned, ugly and remorseless.

Bob finished the coffee, threw on a barn jacket and an old beat-up Stetson and went out of the bright warm kitchen into the predawn cold, looking like an old cowboy who'd been to his last roundup. A grizzle of beard clung to his still sunken jaws and he felt woozy, a beat behind, his mind filled with cobwebs and other junk.

Just enough of the mountains were visible in the rising light. They stirred him still, but only just. They were so huge, caped in snow, remote, unknowing, vaster by far than the mountains he had grown up in back in Arkansas. They promised what he needed: solitude, beauty, freedom, a place for a man who went his own ways and only got himself into deep trouble when he got involved with other men.

He saw the barn, heard the snuffle and rasp of horses, and knew that Julie and Nikki were saddling up for their morning ride, a family ritual. He was late. His horse, Junior, would be saddled too, so that he could join them at the last second. It was not right: to earn the right to ride a horse, you should saddle it yourself. But Julie let him sleep for those rare moments when he seemed to do so calmly. She just didn't know what nightmares lay inside his calm sleep.

He looked about for his other enemy. The landscape, high in the mountains but still a good mile from the snow, was barren. He saw only the meadows, where some cattle drifted and fed, miles of dense trees, and the rugged crinkles of the passes as they led to openings in the peaks that were the Sawtooths.

But no reporters. No agents. No TV cameras, Hollywood jockeys, slick talkers with smooth hair and suits that fitted like cream on milk. He hated them. They were the worst. They had exiled him from a life he had loved.

It began when Bob, at the insistence of a good young man who reminded him a bit of his wife's first husband, Donny Fenn, had urged him to return to Arkansas to look into the matter of the death of Earl Swagger, his father, in 1955. Things got complicated and hairy fast; some people tried to stop him and he had to shoot back. No indictments were ever handed down as no physical evidence could be located and nobody in Polk County would talk to outsiders. But some rag had gotten wind of it, linked him to another set of events that took place a few years before that, and taken a picture of him and his wife, Julie, as they'd walked out of church back in Arizona some months later. He woke up the next Wednesday to discover that he was AMERICA'S DEADLIEST MAN and that he had STRUCK AGAIN. Wherever ex-Marine sniper Bob Lee Swagger hangs his hat, men die, it pointed out, relating his presence to a roadside shootout that left ten men, all felons, dead, and the mysterious deaths of three men, including an ex-Army sniper, in the remote forest, and recalling that some years earlier he had briefly been a famous suspect in the shooting of a Salvadorian archbishop in New Orleans, until the government dropped the charges for reasons that were to this day unclear. Why, he had even married the widow of a Vietnam buddy, the paper reported.

Time and *Newsweek* picked it up and for a few weeks there, Bob had the worst kind of fame his country could offer: he was hounded by reporters and cameras wherever he went. It seemed many people thought he held the keys to a fortune, that he knew things, that he was glamorous, sexy, a natural-born killer, which, by some odd current loose in America, made him, in the argot, "hot."

So here he was, on a ranch that was owned by his wife's father's estate as an investment property, living essentially on charity, without a penny to his name except for a piddling pension and no way of making one. The future was unsettled and dark; the peace and quiet and good living he had achieved seemed all gone. *Where am I going to get the money? My pension ain't enough, by a damn sight.* Though it had never been expressed, he had become convinced that his wife secretly wished he'd do something with the one asset he owned, his "story," which many people believed was worth millions.

He walked toward the barn, watching the sun just begin to smear the sky over the mountains. The black dogs came upon him and overpowered him halfway between the structures. That was his name for them: the sense that he was a worthless failure, that everything he touched turned to shit, that his presence hurt the two people he cared about the most, that everything he'd done had been a mistake, every decision wrong, and anybody who'd gone along with him had ended up dead.

The dogs came fast and hard. They got their teeth into him good, and in seconds, he was no longer in the barnyard under the mountains where a red sun was about to pull itself up and light the world with the hope of a new day, but in some other, dank, foul place, where his own failures seemed the most prominent landform, and the only mercy was bourbon.

"Well, Mister, nice of you to join us," called Julie.

He looked at his wife, at her smile, which continued to dazzle him if even now there seemed a layer of fear behind it. He had seen her first on a cellophane-wrapped photograph that a young man had carried in his boonie cap in Vietnam, and maybe he had fallen in love with her in that second. Or maybe he fell in love with her the second the young man died and she was the only part of him still alive. Still, it took long years, many of them soaked in bourbon, before he'd finally met her and, by the odd twists that his life seemed always to take, ended up being the lucky jerk she took as her second husband. Yet now . . . was it falling apart on him?

"Daddy, Daddy," yelled Nikki, eight, running to meet him. She grabbed his blue-jeaned leg.

"Howdy, honey, how's my girl this morning?"

"Oh, Daddy, you know. We're going to ride up to Widow's Pass and watch the sun come across the valley."

"We do that *every* morning. Maybe we ought to find a new place."

"Honey," said Julie. "She loves that view."

"I'm only saying," Bob said, "it might be nice to change. Forget it. It don't mean a thing."

He had more edge in his voice than he'd meant. Where had it come from? Julie shot him a hurt look at his harsh words, and he thought, Well, that's fine, I deserve that, and he had himself in control, everything was fine, he was fine, it was—

"I do get tired of riding the same goddamn place every goddamn morning. You know, there are *other* places to ride."

"All right, Bob," she said.

"I mean, we can ride there, no problem. Is that where you want to ride, sweetie? If that's where you want to ride, that's fine."

"I don't care, Daddy."

"Good. That's where we'll ride."

Who was talking? He was talking. Why was he so mad? Where was this coming from? What was going on?

But then he had himself back and he was fine again and it would be—

"And why the hell is she riding English? You want her to be some fancy person? You want her to go to little shows where she wears some red jacket and helmet and jumps over fences and all the fags clap and the rich people come and drink champagne, and she learns her old man, who don't talk so good and swears a mite, he ain't up to them folks who ride English, he's just an old farm boy from shit-apple Arkansas? Is that what you want?"

He was yelling. It had come on so fast, so ugly, it had just blown in, a squall of killing anger. Why was he so mad these days? It made him sick.

"Bob," his wife, Julie, said with slow, fake sweetness,

"I just want to widen her horizons. Open up some possibilities."

"Daddy, I *like* English. It's more leg than stirrup; it doesn't hurt the horse."

"Well, I don't know nothing about English. I'm just a cop's kid from Hick Town, Arkansas, and I didn't go to no college, I went into the Marine Corps. Nobody ever gave me nothing. When I see her riding like that—"

He bellowed for a while, as Julie got smaller and smaller, and Nikki began to cry and his hip hurt and his head ached and finally Junior spooked.

"Oh, fuck it!" he said. "What the hell difference does it make?" and stormed back to the house.

He'd left the TV on, and sat before it, nursing his fury, angered by the terrible unfairness of it all. Why couldn't he support his family? What could he have done different? What could he do?

After a bit, he turned and watched the two of them ride out through the fence and head up toward Widow's Pass.

Good, that was fine. They could do that. He was better off alone. He knew where he wanted to go. He stood, raging with fury, and though it was early, turned and walked to the cellar door, went down into it. He'd meant to set up a shop here, where he could reload for next hunting season and work out some ideas he had for wildcat cartridges, new ways to get more pop out of some old standards. But somehow he'd never found the energy; he didn't know how long they'd be here, he didn't know if—

He went instead to the workbench, where a previous occupant had left a set of old, rusty tools and nails and such, and reached around to grab what was stashed there. It was a bottle, a pint of Jim Beam, subtly curved like a Claymore, with its black label and white printing.

The bottle had weight and solidarity to it—it felt serious, like a gun. He hefted it, went to the steps and sat down. The cellar smelled of damp and rot, for this was wet country, snowy in the winter and ripe for floods in the spring. He'd been so long in dry country, this all seemed new. Its smell was unpleasant: mildew, perpetual moisture.

He held the bottle in his hand, examined it carefully. Shifting it ever so slightly sent the cargo inside sloshing this way and that, like the sea at China Beach, where he'd gone on R&R one time or another, but he couldn't say on which of his three tours.

His hand closed around the cap of the bottle, its seal still pristine. Just the slightest twist of his hand could open it, much less strength than that required to kill a man with a rifle, which he had done so many times.

He looked carefully at the thing. He waggled it just a bit, feeling the slosh of the fluid. Its brownness was clear and butterscotchy; it beckoned him onward.

Yes, do it. One sip, just to take the edge off, to make the bad pictures go away, blunt the worries about money and prying reporters and TV cameras, to retreat to some sacred, private land of blur and wobble and laughter, where only good times are remembered.

Drink to the lost. Drink to the boys. Drink to the dead boys of Vietnam, drink to poor Donny. Drink to what happened to Donny and how Donny haunted him, how he had married Donny's wife and fathered Donny's child and done what could be done to resurrect Donny, to keep Donny still on this earth.

Yes, drink to Donny, and all the boys killed before their time for Veet Nam to stop commu-nism.

Oh, how the bottle called him.

Fuck this, he thought.

I have a wife and a daughter and they are out on the range without me, and so I had best get to them. That is one thing left I can do.

He put the bottle back and climbed the stairs. His hip hurt, but what the fuck. He headed for the barn, his horse, and his wife and daughter.

CHAPTER TWENTY-SIX

They rode up through the meadow, found the track through the pines and followed that, always trending upward. The air was cool, though not really cold, and the sun's presence in the east, over the mountains, gave the prospect of warmth.

Julie nuzzled her coat closer, tried to cleanse her thoughts of trouble and put her anger at her husband and what had happened to their life behind her. Her daughter, the better rider, galloped ahead merrily, the ugliness of the scene in the barn seemingly forgotten. Nikki rode so well; she had a gift for it, a natural affinity for the horses, and was never happier than when she was out in the barn with the animals, tending them, feeding them, washing them.

But Nikki's happiness was also somewhat illusory. As they neared the treeline and the ride across the high desert toward Widow's Pass and the trip to overlook the far valley, she drifted back to her mother.

"Mommy," she said, "is Daddy sick?"

"Yes, he is," said Julie.

"Is he going to be all right?"

"Your father is as strong as ten horses and he has faced and beaten many enemies in his long and hard life. He'll beat this one, too."

"What is it, Mommy?" Nikki asked.

"It's a terrible disease called post-traumatic stress disorder. It has to do with the war he was in. He was in heavy fighting and many of his very close friends were killed. He was strong enough to put that behind him and build us a very fine and happy life. But sometimes there are things that just can't be kept away. It's like a little black dog has escaped from the secret part of his brain and come out. It barks, it bites, it attacks. His old wounds are hurting, but also his memory keeps recalling things he thought it had forgotten. He has trouble sleeping. He is angry all the time and doesn't know why. He loves you very, very much, though. No matter what happens and how he acts, he loves you very much."

"I hope he's all right."

"He will be. He needs our help, though, and he needs the help of a doctor or something. He'll understand that eventually and get some help, and then he'll be better again. But you know what a stubborn man he is."

The two rode on in silence.

"I don't like it when he yells at you. It scares me."

"He's not really yelling at me, honey. He's yelling at the men who killed his friends and the men who sent him over there to fight that war and then walked away from it. He's yelling for all the poor boys who got killed and never came back to the lives they deserved and were forgotten."

"He loves you, Mommy."

"I know he does, honey. But sometimes that's not enough."

"He'll be all right."

"I believe he will be, too. He needs our help, but he needs mostly to help himself, get some medication, find a way to take advantage of his very special skills and knowledge."

"I can ride Western. I don't mind."

"I know. It's not about that, really. It's about how mad he is at things he can't stop. We just have to love him and hope that he sees how important it is to get some help."

They were out of the trees. The high chaparral was desolate, rock strewn, clustered with primitive forms of vegetation. Ahead, in the shadow of the snowcaps, the cut in the earth between mountains that was called Widow's Pass beckoned, and beyond it, after a course on a shelf of dirty rock and broken slope, a precipice from which could be seen as much beauty as has been put on earth. Julie loved it and so did Nikki. Bob loved it too. They rode here nearly every morning; it got the day off to a fine start.

"Oh, here we go, baby. Be careful."

The track was tricky, and Julie was speaking more to herself than to her nimble daughter or to her daughter's horse, the better athlete of the two animals.

She felt the tension come into her; this was delicate work and she wished her husband were here. How had they ended up like this?

Nikki laughed.

When the noise came, it didn't shock or surprise the sniper. He had waited in the dawn for targets before. He knew it had to come, sooner or later, and it did. It didn't fill him with doubt or regret or anything. It simply meant: time to work.

The noise was a peal of laughter, girlish and bright. It bounced off the stone walls of the canyon, from the shadow of a draw onto this high plain from close to a thousand yards off, whizzing through the thin air.

The sniper wiggled his fingers, finding the warmth in them. His concentration cranked up a notch or so. He pulled the rifle to him in a fluid motion, well practiced from hundreds of thousands of shots in practice or on missions.

Its stock rose naturally to his cheek as he pulled it in, and as one hand flew to the comb, the other set up beneath the forearm, taking the weight of his slightly lifted body, building a bone bridge to the stone below. He found the spot weld, the one placement of cheek to stock where the scope relief would be perfect and the circle of the scope would throw up its image as brightly as a movie screen. He cocked one knee halfway up toward his torso to build a muscular tension into his position, as he had been trained to do.

The child. The woman. The man.

"Hey, there!"

She turned at the voice to see her husband riding toward her and her heart soared.

But then it subsided: it was not Bob Lee Swagger but the neighboring rancher, an older widower named Dade Fellows, another tan, tall, leathery coot, on a chestnut roan he controlled exquisitely.

"Mr. Fellows!"

"Hello, Mrs. Swagger. How're you this morning?"

"Well, we're just fine."

"Hello there, honey."

"Hi, Dade," said Nikki. Dade was an occasional hanger-on at the ranch, welcome for his knowledge of the area, his sure way with animals and guns.

"Y'all haven't seen a dogie or two up this way? My fence is down and I'm a little short. They're so stupid, they might have come this way."

"No, it's been completely quiet. We're riding through the pass to see the sun come across the valley."

"That is a sight, isn't it?"

"Would you care to join us?"

"Well, ma'am, I've got a full day and I'd like to find my baby cows. But, hell, why not? I ain't seen the sun rise in quite a while. I'm up too early."

"You work too hard, Mr. Fellows. You should slow down."

"If I slow down, I might notice how old I got," he laughed, "and what a shock that would be! Okay, there, Nikki, you lead the way. I'll follow your mother.

Nimble Nikki took her big chestnut along the climbing path, and it rose between the narrow canyon walls until they seemed to swallow her. Then she sunk into shadow where the pass was really deep. Julie was close behind, and as her eyes adjusted to the dark, she saw her daughter break clear, into the light. At the end of the enfilade was a shelf of land that ran along the mountainside for half a mile, gently trending upward, and then it reached a vantage point on the far valley.

Nikki laughed at the freedom she felt when she emerged, and in a second had freed her horse to find its own pace; it preferred speed and began to gallop. A fear rose in Julie's heart; she could never catch the girl, nor stay up with her if she had to, and she felt the urge to call out, but suppressed it as pointless, for there was no stopping Nikki, a natural-born hero like her father. The eight-year-old galloped ahead, the horse's bounding grace eating up the distance to the vantage point.

Julie then came into the light and saw that, safely, Nikki had slowed to a walk as she neared the precipice. She turned back and called, "Come on, Mr. Fellows! You'll miss it."

"I'm coming, ma'am," he yelled back at her.

She cantered ahead, feeling the rise of the mountains on either side but also the freedom of the open space ahead of her. Its beauty lightened her burden and the mountains looked down solemn and dignified and implacable. She approached Nikki, even as she heard Fellows coming up behind her, driving his horse a bit harder.

"Look, Mommy!" Nikki cried, holding her horse tight between her strong thighs, leaning forward and pointing out.

Here, there was no downslope beyond the edge, just sheer drop, which afforded a vista of the valley beyond, the ridge of mountains beyond that as the sun crested them. The valley was green and undulating, thatched with pines, yet also open enough to show off, sparkling in the new sun, its creeks and streams. Across the way there was a falls, a spume of white feathery water that cascaded down a far cliff. Under the cloudless sky and in the pale power of the not yet fully risen sun, it had a kind of storybook quality to it that was, even if you'd seen it a hundred-odd times, breathtaking.

"Ain't that something?" said Fellows. "That is the true West, the one they write about, yes, sir."

Swagger had aged, as all men do, even as the sniper himself had aged. But he was still lean and watchful and there was a rifle in the scabbard under his saddle. He looked dangerous, like a special man who would never panic, who would react fast and shoot straight, which is exactly what he was. His eyes darted about under the hood of his cowboy hat. He rode like a gifted athlete, almost one with the animal, controlling it unconsciously with his thighs while his eyes scanned for signs of aggression.

He would not see the sniper. The sniper was too far out, the hide too carefully camouflaged, the spot chosen to put the sun in the victim's eyes at this hour so that he'd see only dazzle and blur if he looked.

The crosshairs rode up to Swagger, and stayed with the man as he galloped along, finding the same rhythm in the cadences, finding the same up-down plunge of the animal. The shooter's finger caressed the trigger, felt absorbed by its beckoning softness, but he did not fire. He knew the range perfectly: 742 meters.

Moving target, transversing laterally left to right, but also moving up and down through a vertical plane. By no means an impossible shot, and many a man in his circumstances would have taken it. But experience told the sniper to wait: a better shot would lie ahead, the best shot. With a man like Swagger, that's the one you took.

Swagger joined his wife, and the two chatted, and what Swagger said made her smile. White teeth flashed. A little tiny human part in the sniper ached for the woman's beauty and ease; he'd had prostitutes the world over, some quite expensive and beautiful, but this little moment of intimacy was something that had evaded him completely. That was all right. He had chosen to work in exile from humanity. Seven hundred thirty-one meters.

He cursed himself. That's how shots were blown, that little fragment of lost concentration which took you out of the operation. He briefly snapped his eyes shut, absorbed the darkness and cleared his mind, then opened them again to what lay before him.

Swagger and his wife had reached the edge: 722 meters. Before them would run a valley, unfolding in the sunlight as the sun climbed even higher. But what this meant to the sniper is that at last his quarry had ceased to move. In the scope he saw a family portrait: man, woman and child, all at nearly the same level, because the child's horse was so big it put her up with her parents. They chatted, the girl laughed, pointed at a bird or something, seethed with motion. The mother stared into the distance. The father, his eyes still seeming watchful, relaxed just the tiniest bit.

The crosshairs bisected the square chest.

He stroked the trigger and the gun jarred and as it came back in a fraction of a second, he saw the tall man's chest explode as the Remington 7mm Magnum tore through it.

It was a moment of serene perfection, until she heard a sound that reminded her somehow of meat dropping on a linoleum floor—it had a flat, moist, dense reverberation to it, somehow—and at that same instant felt herself sprayed with warm jelly. She turned to see Dade's gray face, his eyes lost and locked on nothingness as he fell backward off his horse. His chest had been somehow eviscerated, as with an ax, its organs exposed and spewing blood in torrents, his heart decompressing with a pulsing jet of deoxygenated, almost black liquid spurting in an arc over the precipice. He hit the ground, in a cloud of dust, landing with the solidity of a sack of potatoes falling off a truck as his horse panicked and bucked, hooves flailing in the air. As a nurse, from too many nights in a reservation ER, Julie was no stranger to blood or to what mysteries lay inside of bodies, but the transformation was so instantaneous that it shocked her, even as, from far off, the report of a rifle shot finally arrived.

The sound seemed to unlock her brain from the paralysis into which it had blundered. She knew in the next nanosecond that they were under fire, and in the nanosecond after that her daughter was in danger, and she found the will to turn and yell "Run!" as loud as possible, and yanked hard to the left on her reins, driving her horse into Nikki's to butt it about.

My daughter, she thought. *Don't kill my daughter.*

But like hers, Nikki's reflexes were fast and sure, and the girl had already reached the same conclusion, reeled her horse to the left, and in another second, both horses were free of the ruckus caused by Dade's plunging animal.

"Go!" shrieked Julie, kicking and lashing her horse with the reins. The animal churned ahead, its long legs bounding over the dirt toward the narrow enfilade of the pass. She was to the left of and a little behind Nikki, that is, between Nikki and the shooter, which is where she wanted to be.

The horses thundered along, careering madly for safety, and Julie was bent over the neck of hers like a jockey, but she could not keep up with Nikki's, which, a stronger animal with a much lighter load, began to gun away and ahead, exposing the child.

"Nikki!" she screamed.

Then the world went. It twisted into fragments, the sky was somehow beneath her, dust rose like a gas, thick and blinding, and she felt herself floating, her heart gathering fear for the knowledge of what would come next. The horse screamed piteously and she slammed into the ground, her head filling with stars, her will scattering in confusion. But as she slid through the dust and the pain, feeling her skin rip and something in her body shatter, and the horse scampered away, she looked to see that Nikki had halted and was circling around toward her.

She rose, astounded that she could move through all the fire that was eating her skin, and had a moment when she noticed the blood pouring across her shirt. She staggered, went to one knee, but then rose again, and screamed at Nikki, *"No! No! Run! Run!"* waving her away desperately.

The girl pulled up, confused, the fear bright on her face.

"Run for Daddy!" Julie screamed, then turned herself

and began to scramble for a ravine to the right, a copse of rough vegetation and tough little trees, hoping that the shooter would follow her and not the girl.

Nikki watched her mother run toward the edge of the shelf, then turned herself, lashed the horse, felt it churn into a gallop. The dust of the slashing hooves floated everywhere, clotting her breathing, and the tears on her face matted up with it, but she stayed low and whipped the horse and whipped it again, and though it neighed in pain, whipped it still a third time, gouging it with her English boots, and in seconds, the dark shadows of the enfilade covered her and she knew she was safe.

Then she heard a shot.

CHAPTER TWENTY-SEVEN

He fired and the sight picture at the moment of ignition—the stout, heroic chest quadrisected perfectly by the crosshairs zeroed exactly for a range of seven hundred meters—told him instantly that he had hit. As the scope came back, he saw red from the falling body, just a fraction of a second's worth, but square in the full chest, until it was lost in the dust.

Then he shifted to the woman but—

He was astonished by the swiftness with which the woman responded. His whole shooting scenario was based on her utter paralysis when her husband's chest exploded. She would be stupefied and the next shot would be easy.

The woman reeled her horse about almost instantaneously and he was astounded at how much dust floated into the air. You cannot anticipate everything, and he had not anticipated the dust. He had no shot for almost a second, and then, faster than he could have begun to imagine, she and the child were racing hellbent and crazed toward the pass and safety.

He had a momentary flash of panic—never before had such a thing happened!—and took his eye from the scope to get an unimpeded visual on the fleeing woman. She was much farther away than he had figured; the angle was oblique, dust floated in the air. Impossible shot! Only seconds remained as she and the girl raced toward the pass.

He fought his terror, and instead let the rifle sit, and picked up his secret advantage in all this, a set of Leica binoculars with a laser range finder, since unknown distance shooting is almost pointless, and he put the glasses on her to see the readout as it shot back to him, straight and true. She was now 765 meters, now 770, racing away.

His mind did the computations as he figured the lead, all while setting the binocs down and reacquiring the rifle, flipping through a bolt throw with the shell ejecting cleanly to the right. A lifetime's experience and a gift for numbers told him he had to shoot a good nine meters ahead of her—no, no, it would be nine if she were preceding at an exact ninety degrees, but she was on the oblique, more like forty-five or fifty degrees, so he compensated to seven meters. A mil-dot—that is, one of a series of dots etched into the crosshairs—in the scope, at this range, was about thirty inches, so when he went back to the rifle, he led her six mils and a mil high, that is, putting her just inside the edge of the solid part of the horizontal crosshair. Impossible shot! Incredible shot! Close to eight hundred meters on a fast-mover at the oblique away from him in heavy dust.

The rifle jolted in recoil and came back to reveal a ruckus of disturbance. He could see nothing. The horse was down, then up, bucking and kicking in fury, dust floating in the air.

He cycled the bolt again.

Where was she? The child was forgotten but that was not important.

He searched the dust, then put the rifle down and seized the binoculars, which would give him a much bigger field of vision.

Where was she? Had he hit her? Was she about? Was she dead? Was it over? He waited for centuries, and without oxygen. But now, there she was, hit—he could see the blood on her blue shirt—and stiff with the pain of the fall. But she had not gone into shock, was not surrendering and, like many who discover themselves in mortal circumstances for the first time, giving up to lie and wait for the final blow. Heroically she moved away from the horse and the dust to the edge.

Soft target. Giving herself up for the girl, who didn't matter.

She was at the edge.

He put the binoculars squarely on her and had just a glimpse of her face, only the fleetest impression of her beauty. A melancholy closed upon him, but his heart was strong and hard and he put it away. He pressed a button to fire a spurt of smart laser at her and it bounced back and he looked to the readout and got a range of 795 meters, and knew he'd have to hold dead center of the first low vertical mil-dot.

He set the binocs down, went back to the rifle and saw her at the edge, just standing there, daring him to concentrate on her while the daughter vanished into the shadows of the pass. The woman's foolish courage sickened him. Her dead husband's insane courage sickened him.

Who were these people? What right did they have to such nobility of spirit? Why did they consider themselves so special? What gave them the right? He put the center of the first mil-dot below the horizontal crosshair on her.

The hatred flared as he pulled the trigger.

The rifle jolted. Time in flight was about a second, maybe a little less. As the 175 grains of 7mm Remington Magnum arched across the canyon, tracing an invisible parabola, unstoppable and tragic, he had the briefest second to study her. Composed, calm, on two feet, defiant even at the end, holding her wound. Then she disappeared as, presumably, the bullet struck her. She tumbled down and down, raising dust, until she vanished from sight.

He felt nothing.

He was done. It was over.

He sat back, amazed to discover the inside of his jacket soaked with sweat. He felt only emptiness, just like the last time he'd had this man in his scope—only the professional's sense of another job being over.

He put the scope back on the man. Clearly he had been eliminated. The gravity of the wound, its immensity, its savagery, was apparent even from this distance. But he paused. So resilient, so powerful, such an antagonist. Why take the chance?

It felt unclean, as if he were dishonoring someone who might be as great as himself. But he again yielded to practicality: this wasn't about honor among snipers but doing the job.

He threw the bolt, ejecting a shell, and put the crosshairs squarely on the underside of the chin, exposed to him by the man's supine, splayed position. This would drive a bullet upward through the brain at eighteen-hundred feet per second. A four-inch target at 722 meters. Another great shot. He calmed himself, watched the crosshairs still, and felt the trigger break. The scope leaped, then leaped back; the body jerked and again there seemed to be a cloud, a vapor, of pinkish mist. He'd seen it before. The head shot, evacuating brains in a fog of droplets. The fog dissipated. There was nothing more to see or think.

He rose, threw the rifle over his shoulder. He gathered the equipment—the ten-pound sandbag was the heaviest—and recased the binoculars. He looked about for traces of himself and found plenty: scuffs in the dust, the three ejected shells, which he scooped up. He grabbed a piece of vegetation from the earth and used it to sweep the dust of his shooting position, rubbing back and forth until he was convinced no sign of his having been there existed. He threw the brush down into the canyon before him, and then set out walking, trying to stay on hard ground so as to leave no tracks.

He climbed higher into the mountains, expertly and without fear. He knew it would be hours at the least before any kind of police reaction to his operation could be commenced. His problem now would be the remote possibility of running into random hunters or hikers, and he had no wish to kill witnesses, unless he had to, which he would do without qualm.

He walked and climbed for several hours, finally passing over the crests and descending to rough ground. He hit his rendezvous spot by three and got out the small transmitter and sent his confirmation.

The helicopter arrived within an hour, flying low from the west. The evac was swift and professional.

He was done.

Chapter Twenty-eight

Bob rode up through the trees and across the barren, high desert to the mountains. He loped easily along, trying to calm himself, wondering if he could make it before the sun rose fully. The black dogs seemed to have gone back to their kennel. They kept no schedule, nothing set them off; they were just there some days and not some others. Who knew? Who could tell, who could predict?

He tried to think coherently about his future. Clearly he could not stay here much longer, because the weight of living off his in-laws was more than he could bear. It turned all things sour and made him hate himself. But he doubted he could get started in his profession, which was running a lay-up barn for horses, not until he sold his spread in Arizona and had the money to invest in an upgraded barn and other facilities. Plus, it would mean getting to meet the local vets, getting them to give him referrals. Maybe the place was already crowded with lay-up barns.

He could sell his "story." Too bad old Sam Vincent wasn't around to advise him, but Sam had come to a sorry end in that Arkansas matter which even now Bob had his doubts about starting up. It got a lot of people killed, for not much but the settling of forgotten scores. He had some shame left in him for that thing. Maybe scores weren't worth it.

But if Sam wasn't around, who could he trust? The answer was, nobody. He had an FBI agent friend in New Orleans and a young writer still struggling with a book, but not yet having had any success. Who could he approach? The jackals of the press? No, thank you, ma'am. They turned him off beaucoup.

No, the "story" thing wasn't any solution to his problems, not without the advice of somebody he trusted. That left shooting. He knew his name was worth something in that world—some fools considered him a hero, even, like his father, a blasphemy he couldn't begin to even express—and the idea of making that pay somehow sickened him. But if he could pick up work at a shooting school, where they taught self-defense skills to cops and military personnel, maybe that could bring in some money and some contacts. He thought he knew some people to call. Maybe that would work. At least he'd be among men who'd been in the real world and knew what it meant to both put out and receive fire. He tried to imagine such a life.

The sound was clear and distinct, though far off. No man knew it better than he.

Rifle shot. Through the pass. High-velocity round, lots of echo, a big-bore son of a bitch.

He tensed, feeling the alarm blast through him, and had a moment of panic as he worked out that it was possible the shot had come from exactly where Julie and Nikki ought to be. In the next split second he realized he didn't have a rifle himself and he felt broken and useless.

Then he heard a second shot.

He kicked Junior and the horse bolted ahead. He raced across the high desert toward the approaching mountains, his mind filling with fear. Hunters, who happened to get a good shot at a ram or an antelope in the vicinity of his women? Random shooters, plinkers? But not up this high. Maybe there was some trick of the atmosphere, which made the sound of the shots travel from miles away, up through the canyons, and it only now reached him and was meaningless. He didn't like the second shot. A stupid hunter could shoot at something wrong, but then he wouldn't shoot again. If he shot again, he was trying to kill what he was shooting at.

There was a third shot.

He kicked the horse, bucking a little extra speed out of it.

Then he heard the fourth shot.

Christ!

Now he was really panicked. He reached the darkness of the pass but had a moment's clarity and realized the last thing he should do would be to race out there, in case someone was shooting.

As he slowed the animal down to a walk, he saw Nikki's horse, its saddle empty, come limping toward him.

A stab of pain and panic shot through his heart. *My baby? What has happened to my baby? Oh, Christ, what has happened to my baby?*

A prayer, not one of which had passed his lips in Vietnam, came to him, and he said it briefly but passionately.

Let my daughter be all right.

Let my wife be all right.

"Daddy?"

There she was, huddled in the shadows, crying.

He ran to her, snatched her up, feeling her warmth and the strength of her young body. He kissed her feverishly.

"Oh, God, baby, oh, thank God, you're all right, oh, sweetie, what happened, where's Mommy?"

He knew his wild-eyed fear and near loss of control were not helping the girl at all, and she sobbed and shuddered.

"Oh, baby," he said, "oh, my sweet, sweet baby," soothing her, trying to get both himself and her calmed down, back in some kind of operational zone.

"Honey? Honey, you have to tell me. Where's Mommy? What happened?"

"I don't know where Mommy is. She was behind me and then she wasn't."

"What happened?"

"We were looking at the sunrise across the valley. Mr. Dade was there. Suddenly he blew up. Mommy screamed, the horses bucked, and we turned and rode for safety. Mommy was—oh, Daddy, she was right behind me. Where's Mommy, Daddy? Oh, Daddy, what happened to Mommy?"

"Okay, sweetie, you have to be brave now and get a hold of yourself. We are going to have to ride out of here soon. You have to settle down and be calm. I'm going to go look for Mommy."

"No, Daddy, no, please don't go, he'll kill you too!"

"Honey, now, you be calm. I will take a look-see. You stay here in the shadows. When you feel up to it, gather your horse and get Junior's reins. We will be riding like hell out of here very shortly. All right?"

His daughter nodded solemnly through her tears.

Bob turned, whipped off his hat, and slithered along the wall of the pass toward the light. As he neared it, he slowed . . . way . . . down. Fast movement would attract the eye, draw another shot if the bad boy was still scoping. Swagger thought he wouldn't be. Swagger thought he'd hit his primary and his secondary and the girl couldn't figure in anything, and so he was beating it to higher elevations or his pickup or whatever. Who knew? That had to be figured out later. The issue now was Julie.

He edged ever so slowly toward the light, at last setting himself so that he had a good vantage point. Some dust still hung in the air, but the sun was bright now. He could see poor Dade about one hundred-odd yards away, right at the edge. From Dade's broken posture alone it was clear the old man was finished, but a monstrous head wound testified to no possibility of survival. Bad work. Expanding bullet, presumably fired in through the eye or something, a cranial vault explosion, gobbets of brain and blood flung everywhere.

He looked about for a sign of his wife, but there was none. He saw her horse over in the shade, calm now, chewing on some vegetation. He looked about for a hide in case she had gotten to one, but there were no rocks or bushes thick enough to conceal or protect her. That left the edge; he tried to recall what lay beyond the edge, and built an image of a rough slope littered with scrub vegetation and rocks, down a few hundred feet to a dense mess of pines where the creek ran through. Was that right, or was it some other place?

He thought to call, but held back.

The sniper hadn't seen him yet.

There really wasn't a decision to be made. He knew what had to be done.

He slipped back to where Nikki, who had now collected herself, stood with the two horses.

"Do you have any sense of where the shots came from, sweetie? Did you hear them at all?"

"I only remember the last one. As I was riding and had reached the pass. It came from behind."

"Okay," he said. If the shot came from "behind," that probably meant he was shooting from across the canyon, on the ridgeline that ran anywhere from two hundred meters to one thousand meters away. That jibed with the position of Dade's body, too. Whatever, it meant the shooter was cut off from where they were by the gap between the mountains and wouldn't be able to reach them from here on out, unless he came after them. But he wouldn't come after them. He'd fall back, get to safe ground, hit his escape route and be out of here.

"All right," he said, "we are getting the hell out of here and beelining straight for home, where we'll call the sheriff and get him and his boys in here."

She looked at him, stricken.

"But, Mommy—she's out there."

"I know she is, honey. But I can't get her now. If I go out there, he may shoot me, and then what have we got?"

He didn't think he would be. He had worked it out to the next logical step: whoever had done the shooting, his target was not Dade Fellows but Bob Lee Swagger. Someone had reconned him, planned the shot, knew his tendencies and lay in wait from a safe hide a long way off. It was a sniper, Bob felt, another professional.

"She might be hurt. She might need help bad."

"Listen to me, honey. When you are shot, if it's a bad hit, you die right away, like poor Mr. Dade. If it ain't hit you seriously, you can last for several hours. I saw it in Vietnam; the body is very tough and it'll fight on its own for a long time, and you know how tough Mommy is! So there's no real advantage to going to Mommy right now. We can't risk that. She's either already dead or she's going to pull through. There's nothing in between."

"I—I want Mommy," said Nikki. "Mommy's hurt."

"I want Mommy, too," said Bob. "But sweetie, please trust me on this one. We can't help Mommy by getting ourselves killed. He may still be there."

"I'll stay," said Nikki.

"You're such a brave girl. But you can't stay. We have to get out of here, get the state cops and a medical team here fast. Do you understand, baby girl? That's what's best for Mommy, all right?"

His daughter shook her head; she was not convinced and nothing would ever convince her but Bob knew in his Marine heart that he had made the right decision—the tough one, but the right one.

CHAPTER TWENTY-NINE

It had to happen sooner or later and he was glad it happened sooner. It had to be gotten out of the way.

"Mr. Swagger," said Lieutenant Benteen, the chief investigator of the Idaho State Police, "would you mind stepping over here for a second, sir?"

Bob knew what was coming. As he stood on the escarpment, two and a half hours had passed since the shooting. His daughter was with a female state police detective and a nurse back at the house; here, an investigation team and coroner's team worked the crime site, while below a team of sheriff's deputies struggled through the trees and underbrush for a sign of Julie Swagger. Across the gorge, detectives and deputies looked for evidence of the shooting site, ferried there by a state police helicopter that idled on that side of the gap.

"I figured you would be talking with me," said Bob. "You go ahead. Let's get it done with."

"Yes, sir. You know, when a wife is killed it's been my experience that ninety-eight percent of the time, the husband is somehow involved, if he didn't do the thing himself. Seen a lot of that."

"Sure, it figures."

"So I have to ask you to account for your whereabouts at the time of the shooting."

"I was on the other side of the pass, riding up to join my wife and daughter. We usually go out for an early morning ride. Today we had words, and I let the girls go alone. Then I got mad at myself for letting my damn ego seem so important, so I went after them. I heard four shots and rode like hell, to find my baby girl in the shadows of the pass. I looked out and saw poor Dade. I decided the best thing was to get Nikki back to the house, where I called you all and you know the rest."

"Did it occur to you to look for your wife?"

"It did, but I had no medical supplies and I didn't know if the shooter was around, so I thought it best to get the girl out of here and call in the sheriff and a medical team."

"You are, sir, I believe, a marksman of some note."

"I am a shooter, yes. I was a Marine sniper many years ago. I won the big shoot they hold in the east back in 1970. The Wimbledon Cup, they call it. Not for tennis, for long-range shooting. Also, I have been in some scrapes over the years. But, sir, can I point a thing out?"

"Go ahead, Mr. Swagger."

"I think you'll find them shots came from the other side of the gap. That's what my daughter said, and that's what the indication of Dade's body said. Now, there ain't no way I could have fired those shots from over there and gotten to my daughter over here in a very few seconds. There's a huge drop-off, then some rough country to negotiate. I was with my daughter within thirty seconds of the last shot. You can also see the tracks of my horse up here from the ranch house, and no tracks that in any way connect me with what went on over there. And finally, you have surely figured out by now that poor Dade is gone because whoever pulled the trigger thought he was hitting me."

"Duly noted, Mr. Swagger. But I will have to look into this further, to let you know. I will be asking questions. I have no choice."

"You go ahead. Do I need a lawyer?"

"I will notify you if you are considered a suspect, sir. That's how we do it out here."

"Thank you."

"But you were a shooter who used a rifle with a scope? And if I don't miss my best guess, this was a pretty piece of shooting with just such a rig."

"Possibly. I don't know yet."

"This couldn't be some sniper thing? Some other

sniper? Maybe someone getting even with you for something in your past?"

"I don't know, sir. I have no idea at all."

The lieutenant's radio crackled and he picked it up.

"Benteen here, over."

"Lieutenant, I think we found it. Got a couple of shells and some tracks, a coffee thermos and some messed-up ground. You care to come and look?"

"I'll hop right over, Walt, thanks." He turned to Bob. "They think they found the shooting position. Care to look at it, Mr. Swagger? Maybe you can tell me a thing or two about this sort of work."

"I would like to see it, yes, sir. There's no word on my wife?"

"Not yet. They'll call as soon as they know."

"Then let's go."

Of course the chopper was a Huey; it was always a Huey and Bob had the briefest of flashbacks as the odor of aviation fuel and grease floated to his nose. The bird rose gracefully, stirring up some dust, and hopped the canyon to the ridgeline on the other side and set its cargo down.

Bob and the lieutenant jumped out and the bird evacuated. A hundred yards away and up, a state policeman signaled and the two men followed a rough track up to the position. There, the younger cop stood over a little patch of bare ground. Something glittered and Bob could see two brass shells in the dust. There were some other marks and scuffs, and a Kmart thermos.

"This appears to be the spot," said the young officer.

"Maybe we'll get prints off the thermos," Benteen said.

Bob bent and looked at the marks in the earth.

"See that," he said, pointing to two circular indentations in the dust right at the edge of the patch. "Those are marks of a Harris bipod. The rifle rested on a Harris bipod."

"Yeah," said the cop.

Bob turned and looked back across the gulf to where Dade's body still rested under a coroner's sheet. He gauged the distance to be close to two hundred meters dead on, maybe a little downward elevation but nothing challenging.

"A hard shot, Mr. Swagger?"

"No, I would say not," he said. "Any half-practiced fool could make that shot prone off the bipod with a zeroed rifle."

"So you would look at this and not necessarily conclude that it's a professional sniper's work."

"No. In the war we did most of our shooting at four hundred to eight hundred meters, on moving targets. This is much simpler: the distance is close, his angle to the target was dead on, the target was still. Then he misses the other two shots he takes at my wife, or at least he didn't hit her squarely. Then he comes back and hits the old man in the head as he lays dead in the dirt. No, as I look at this, I can't say I see anything that speaks of a trained man to me. It could have been some random psycho, someone who had a rifle and the itch to see something die and suddenly he sees this chance and his darker self gets a hold of him."

"It's been known to happen."

"Yes, it has."

"Still, it would be a mighty big coincidence, wouldn't it? That such a monster just happens to nail your wife? I mean, given who and what you were?"

"As you say, such things have been known to happen. Let's take a look at the shell."

"Can't pick it up till we photo it," said the younger man.

"He's right. That's procedure."

"Okay, you mind if I squat down and get a look at the head stamp?"

"Go ahead."

Bob bent down, brought his eyes close to the shell's rear end.

"What is it?" asked Benteen.

"Seven-millimeter Remington Mag."

"Is that a good bullet?"

"Yes, sir, it is. Very flat shooting, very powerful. They use them mainly in hunting over long distances. Rams, 'lopes, elk, the like. Lot of 'em in these parts."

"A hunter's round, then. Not a professional sniper's round."

"It is a hunter's round: I've heard the Secret Service snipers use it, but nobody else."

He stood, looked back across the gap. Bipod marks, circular, where the bipod sat in the dust, supporting the rifle. Two 7mm Remington Mag shells. Range less than two hundred meters, a good, easy shot. Nearly anyone could have made it with a reasonable outfit. Now what was bothering him?

He didn't know.

But there was some oddness here, too subtle for his conscious mind to track. Maybe his unconscious brain, the smarter part of him, would figure it out.

He shook his head, to himself, mainly.

What is wrong with this picture?

"I wonder why there's only two shells," said Benteen, "if he fired four times. That would be two missing."

"Only one," said Bob. "He may not have ejected the last shell. As for the third shell, maybe it caught on his clothes or something, or he kicked it when he got up. Or it was right by him and he picked it up. That's not surprising. The shells are light; they get moved about easily. You can never find all your shells. I wouldn't pay too much attention to that."

Was that it?

"Good point," said the elderly officer.

But then the radio crackled again. Old Benteen picked it off his belt, listened to the stew of syllables, then turned to Bob.

"They found your wife."

CHAPTER THIRTY

S he would live. She lay encased in bandages. The broken ribs, five of them, were difficult; time alone would heal them. The shattered collarbone, where a bullet had driven through, missing arteries and blood-bearing organs by bare millimeters, would heal with more difficulty, and orthopedic surgery lay ahead. The abraded skin from her long roll down the mountainside, the dislocated hip, the contusions, bruises, muscle aches and pains, all would heal eventually.

So now she lay heavily sedated and immobile in the intensive care unit of the Boise General Hospital, linked to an EKG whose solid beeping testified to the sturdiness of her heart despite all the fractures and the pain. Her daughter sat on her bed, flowers filled the room, two Boise cops guarded the door, the doctor's prognostication was optimistic and her husband was there for her.

"What happened?" she finally said.

"Do you remember?"

"Not much. The police have talked to me. Poor Mr. Fellows."

"He was in the wrong place at the wrong time. I am very sorry about that."

"Who did this?"

"The police seem to think it was some random psycho in the hills. Maybe a militia boy, full of foolish ideas, or someone who just couldn't handle the temptation of the rifle."

"Have they caught anybody?"

"No. And there were no distinguishable prints on a cheap thermos they recovered. They really don't have much. A couple of shells, some scuffs in the dust."

She looked off. Nikki was coloring steadily, a big Disney book. The scent of flowers and disinfectant filled the room.

"I hate seeing you here," Bob said. "You don't belong here."

"But I am here," she said.

"I've asked Sally Memphis to come up and stay with you. She's a couple of months pregnant but she was eager to help. I called Dade Fellows's daughter, and she said her father has a ranching property over in Custer County, remote and safe in a valley. When you get better, I want Sally to move you up there. I want you and Nikki protected."

"What are you talking about?"

"Nikki, honey, why don't you go get a Coke?"

"Daddy, I don't want a Coke. I just had a Coke."

"Well, sweetie, why don't you get *another* Coke. Or get Daddy a Coke, all right?"

Nikki knew when she was being kicked out. She got up reluctantly, kissed her mother and left the room.

"I haven't told the cops," he said, "because they wouldn't get it and they couldn't do anything about it. But I don't think this is a wandering Johnny with a rifle. I think we got us a big-time serious professional killer and I think I'm the boy he's after."

"Why on earth?"

"There could be many reasons. As you know, I have been in some scrapes. I don't know which of 'em would produce this. But what that means is until I get this figured out, I believe you are in more danger around me than less. And I need freedom. I need to get about, to look at things, to get some items sorted out. This guy's got a game going on me; but now I have the advantage because for a few days more he won't know he missed me. I have to operate fast and learn what I can in the opening."

"Bob, you should talk to the FBI if you don't think these Idaho people are sophisticated enough."

"I don't have anything they'd recognize yet. I have to

develop some evidence. I'd just get myself locked in the loony bin."

"Oh, Lord," she said. "This is going to be one of your *things,* isn't it?"

There was a long moment of quiet. He let the anger in him rise, then top off, then fall; then he began to hurt a little.

"What do you mean, 'things'?"

"Oh, you have these crusades. You go off and you get involved in some ruckus. You don't talk about it but you come back spent and happy. You get to be alive again and do what you do the best. You get to be a sniper again. The war never ended for you. You never *wanted* it to end. You loved it too deeply. You loved it more than you ever loved any of us, I see that now."

"Julie, honey, you don't know what you're saying. You're on painkillers. I want you to be comfortable. I'm just going to look into some things for a while."

She shook her head sadly.

"I can't have it. Now it's come to my daughter. The war. It killed my first husband and now it's come into my life and you want to go off and fight it all over again, and my daughter, who is eight, had to see a man die. Do you have any idea how traumatizing that is? No child should have to see that. Ever."

"I agree, but what we have is what we have and it has to be dealt with. It can't be ignored. It won't go away."

He could see that she was crying.

"Get some help," she finally said. "Call Nick; he's with the FBI. Call some Marine general; he'll have connections. Call one of those writers who's always wanting to do a book with you. Get some help. Take some money from my family's account and hire some private guards. Don't be Bob the Nailer anymore. Be Bob the husband and Bob the father, Bob the man at home. I can't stand that this is in our life again. I thought it was over, but it's never over."

"Sweetie, I didn't invent this. It's not something I

thought up. Please, you're upset, you had a terrible experience, you're in what we call post-traumatic stress syndrome, where it keeps flashing before your eyes and you're angry all the time. I've been there. Time is going to heal you up, your mind as well as your body."

She said nothing. She looked at Bob, but wasn't seeing him any longer.

"But I have to deal with this. Okay? Just let me deal with this."

"Oh, Bob—"

She started to cry again.

"I can't lose you, too. I can't lose *both* you and Donny to the same war. I can't. I can't bear it."

"I just have to look into this. I'll be careful. I know this stuff; I can work a lot faster alone and you'll be safer without me there at all. Okay?"

She shook her head disconsolately.

"You have to answer me a question or two, please. All right?"

After a bit, she nodded.

"You went over this with the cops, only they won't let me see the report. But they don't have a clue. He's already got them outfoxed. Now, I'm assuming no two shots followed upon each other closely. Is that right?"

She paused again, thinking, and then at last yielded. "Yes."

"There must have been at least two seconds between shots?"

"It felt like less than that."

"But if he hits Dade in the chest, then he hits you in the collarbone, and you're forty, fifty yards away, it took him some time to track and fire. So it had to be at least two, maybe three seconds."

"You won't put Nikki through this?"

"No. Now—he hits you moving. I'm guessing you were really galloping, right?"

"Yes."

"That's a pretty good shot."

He sat back, his respect slightly increased. An oblique fast-mover, at two hundred yards.

"Why does he hit you in the collarbone and not in the full body?"

"It's my right collarbone, not my left one," she said. "That means he was aiming at my back, dead center. What I remember is the horse seemed to stumble forward just a bit, and the next second it was like somebody hit me in the shoulder with a baseball bat. The second after that I was down; there was dust everywhere. Nikki came back to me. Somehow I got up. I was afraid he'd shoot at her, so I yelled at her. Then I ran away from her so that he'd shoot me instead."

"It still makes no sense. If he's two hundred yards out, then the time in flight is so minimal he hits the sight picture he sees, and he don't shoot if he don't see the right sight picture. You're *sure* the horse stumbled?"

"I felt it. Then, whack, and I was down, there was dust everywhere, the horse was crying."

"Okay. Next, I heard four shots fired. One into Dade, the knock-down shot, the third shot, then the fourth into Dade's head."

"Thank God I never saw that."

"But there was a third shot?"

"I think so. But I went off the edge."

"You *jumped* off the edge? You weren't knocked down?"

"I jumped."

"God. Great move. Right move, great move, smart move. Guts move. Guts move. That gets you a medal in the Marine Corps."

"It was all I could think to do."

"So he did take a third shot. He *was* shooting at you. Man, I cannot figure why he is missing. Why is he missing? You jump, but at two hundred meters or less, with a seven-millimeter Remington Mag, what he sees is what he gets. He *can't* miss from that range. Maybe he's not so good."

"Maybe he's not."

"Maybe the cops are right. It's some psycho."

"Maybe it is. But that would cheat you out of your crusade, wouldn't it? So it can't be a psycho. It's got to be a master sniper."

He let her hostility pass.

"Another thing I can't figure is how come he's shooting at you at all? You'd think once he did me, it's over. That's it. Time to—"

But then something came into his mind.

"No. No, I see. He has to hit you, because he knows exactly how quickly you could get back to the ranch and a phone and that's cutting it too close. Nikki's not a problem, she's probably not together enough to think of that. But he has to do you to give himself the right amount of time to make his getaway. He's figured out the angles. I can see how his mind works. Very methodical, very savvy."

"Maybe you're dreaming all this up."

"Maybe I am."

"But you want the man-to-man thing. I can tell. You against him, just like Vietnam. Just like all the other places. God, I hate that war. It killed Donny, it stole your mind. It was so evil."

But then Nikki came back with a Coke for her dad and a nurse came in with pills and their time alone was finished.

CHAPTER THIRTY-ONE

The wind howled; it was cloudy today, and maybe rain would fall. Bob's horse, Junior, nickered nervously at the possibility, stamped, then put his head down to some mountain vegetation and began to chew.

Bob stood at the shooter's site. It was a flat nest of dust across an arroyo, not more than two hundred meters from where Dade had been shot and maybe 280 from where Julie fell. If he had had a range finder, he would have known the range for sure, but those things—laser-driven these days, much more compact than the Barr and Stroud he'd once owned—cost a fortune, and only wealthy hunters and elite SWAT or sniper teams had them. It didn't matter; the range was fairly easy to estimate from here because the body sizes were easy to read. If you know the power of your scope, as presumably this boy would, you could pretty much gauge the distance from how much of the body you got into your lens. That worked out to about three hundred yards, and then it was a different matter altogether: you entered a different universe when the distances were way out.

Why did you miss her? he wondered. She's running away, she's on the horse, the angle is tough; the only answer is, you're a crappy shot. You're a moron. You're some asshole who's read too many books and dreamed of the kick you get looking through the scope when the gun fires, and you see something go slack. So you do the old man, then you swing onto the racing woman, her horse bounding up and down, and it's too much shot for you. You misread the angle, you misread the distance, you just ain't the boy for the job.

Okay. You fire, you bring her down. There's dust, and then she emerges from the dust, running toward the edge. She *wants* you to shoot her, so you concentrate on her, not the girl. You've really got plenty of time. There's no rush, there's no up-down plunge as there would be on a horse; it's really a pretty elementary shot.

But you miss again, this time totally.

No, you ain't the boy you think you are.

That added up. That made sense. Some asshole who thought too much about guns and had no other life, no family, no sane connection to the world. It was the sickening part of the Second Amendment computation, but there you had it: some people just could not say no to the godlike power of the gun.

But how come there ain't no tracks?

Apparent contradiction: he's not good enough to make the shot, but he is good enough to get out cold without any stupid mistakes, like the print of his boot in the dust, which would at least narrow it down a bit. Yet he leaves two shells and a thermos. Yet all three are clean of prints. How could that be? Is he a professional or not? Or is he just a lucky amateur?

Bob looked at the bipod marks, still immaculate in the dust, undisturbed by the process of making plaster casts of them. They would last until the rain, and then be gone forever. They told him nothing; bipod, big deal. You could buy the Harris bipod in any gun store in America. Varmint shooters used them and so did police snipers. Some men used them when they took their rifles to the range for zeroing or load development, but not usually: because the bipod fit by an attachment to the screw hole in which the front swing swivel was set. That meant the screw could work lose under a long bench session and that it could change the point of impact much more readily than a good sandbag. Some hunters used them, but it was a rarity, because you almost never got a prone position in the field, so the extra weight was not worth it. Some men used them because they thought they looked cool. Would that be our guy?

He stared at imprints of the legs, trying to divine a

meaning from their two, neat square images. No meaning arrived. Nothing.

But contemplating the bipod got him going in another direction: What's he see? Bob wondered. What's he see from up here?

So he went to the prone and took up a position indexed to the marks in the dust. From there he had a good, straight-on view of Dade's position, yes; and the shot—with the stable rifle, the sun behind you, the wind calm as it was at that point in the day—it was just a matter of concentrating on the crosshairs, trusting the rig, squeezing the trigger and presto, instant kill. You threw the bolt, and no more than a few seconds later you had the woman.

He now saw how truly heroic Julie had been. Nine-hundred-ninety-nine out of a thousand inexperienced people just freeze on the spot. Sniper cocks, pivots a degree or so, and he has a second kill. But bless her brilliant soul, she reacted on the dime when Dade went down, and off she went with Nikki. He had to track her.

Bob had a thought here. What happens if the point where she was hit wasn't within pivot range of this spot? What happens if there's some impediment? But there wasn't. It was an easy crank, an arc of about forty degrees, nothing in the way, you just track her, lead her a bit and pull the trigger.

Why did he miss?

Bob thought he had it.

He probably didn't keep the rifle moving as he pulled the trigger. That's why he hits her behind the line of her spine, he's centered on her, but he stops when he fires, and the bullet, arriving a tenth of a second later, drills her trailing collarbone.

That made a sort of sense, though usually when you were tracking a bird or a clay with a shotgun and you stopped the gun, you missed the whole sucker, not just hit behind on it. Maybe the birds moved faster. On the other hand, the range was a lot farther than any wing or clay shooting. On the third hand, the velocity of the rifle bullet was much faster.

There were so many goddamned variables.

He sat back.

Used to be pretty goddamned good at this stuff, he thought. Used to have a real talent for understanding the dynamics of a two- or three-second interval when the guns were in play.

None of this made any goddamned sense, not really, and he had no way of figuring it out and his head ached and it was about to rain and destroy the physical evidence forever and Junior nickered again, bored.

Okay, he thought, rising, troubled, facing the fact that he had not really made any progress. He turned to go back to the horse and his empty house and his unopened bottle of Jim Beam and—

Then he saw the footprint.

Yeah, the cops missed a footprint, that's likely.

He looked more closely and saw in a second that it was his own footprint, a Tony Lama boot, size 11, the one he was wearing, yes, it was his goddamned own. A little hard to ID because he'd turned and sort of stretched it out and—

That was it.

There it was.

He turned back, quickly, and stared at the bipod imprints.

If he has to *pivot* the bipod, the bipod marks would be distorted. They'd be rounded from the fast, forceful pivot as he followed her, and one would inscribe an arc through the dust. But these bipod marks were squared off, perfectly.

Bob looked at them closely.

Yes: round, perfect, the mark of the bipod resting in the dust until the rain came and washed it away.

He saw it now: this was a classic phony hide. This hide was built to suggest the possibility that a screwball did the shooting. But our boy didn't shoot from here. He shot from somewhere else, a lot farther out.

Bob looked at the sky. It looked like rain.

He rode the ridgeline for what seemed like hours, the wind increasing, the clouds screaming in from the west, taking the mountains away. It felt like fog, damp to the skin. Up here, the weather could change just like that. It could kill you just like that.

But death wasn't on his mind. Rather, his own depression was. The chances of finding the real hide were remote, if traces remained at all. When the rain came, they would be gone forever. Again he thought: nicely thought out. Not only does the phony hide send the investigation off in the wrong direction, it also prevents anyone from seeing the real hide until it is obliterated by the changing weather. So if he does miss something, the weather takes it out.

Bob was beginning to feel the other's mind. Extremely thorough. A man who thinks of everything, will have rehearsed it in his mind a hundred times, has been through this time and time again. He knows how to do it, knows the arcane logic of the process. It isn't just pure autistic shooting skill, it's also a sense of tactical craft, a sense of the numbers that underlie everything and the confidence to crunch them fast under great pressure, then rely on the crunching and make it happen in the real world. Also: stamina, courage, the guts of a burglar, the patience of a great hunter.

He knew we came this way. But some mornings we did not. He may have had to wait. He was calm and confident and able to flatten his brain out, and wait for the exact morning. That was the hardest skill, the skill that so few men really had. But you have it, don't you, brother?

A sprinkle of rain fell against his face. It would start pounding soon and the evidence would be gone forever.

Why didn't I think this through yesterday? I'd have had

him, or some part of him. But now, no, it would be gone. He's won again.

He searched for hides, looking down from the trail into the rough rocks beneath. Every so often there'd be a spot flat enough to conceal a prone man, but upon investigation, each spot was empty of sign. And as he rode, of course, he got farther out. And from not everywhere on the ridge was the shelf of land visible where both Dade and Julie could be hit in the same sweep.

So on he went, feeling the dampness rise and his sense of futility rise with it. He must have missed it, he thought, or it's already gone. Damn, he was a long way out. He was a *long way out.* He was getting beyond the probable into the realm of the merely possible. Yet still no sign, and Junior drifted along the ridge, over the small trail, tense at the coming rain, Bob himself chilled to the bone and close to giving up.

He couldn't be out this far!

He rode on even farther. No sign yet. He stopped, turned back. The target zone was miniature. It was far distant. It was—

Bob dismounted, let Junior cook in his own nervousness. He'd thought he'd seen a little point under the edge of the ridge, nothing much, just a possibility. He eased down, peeking this way and that, convinced that, no, he was too far out, he had to go back and look for something he had missed.

But then he saw something just the slightest bit odd. It was a tuft of dried brush, caught halfway down the ridge. Wind damage? But no other tufts lay about. What had dislodged it? Probably some freak accident of nature . . . but on the other hand, a man wiping away marks of his presence in the dust, he might just have used a piece of brush to do it, then tossed the brush down into the gap. But it caught, and as it dried out over the two days, it turned brown enough so a man looking for the tiniest of anomalies might notice it.

Bob figured the wind always ran north to northwest

through this little channel in the mountains. If the wind carried it, it would have come off the cliff just a bit farther back. He turned and began to pick his way back in that direction and had already missed it when, looking back to orient himself to the tuft of bush, he noticed a crevice and, peering into it, he looked down to see just the tiniest, coffin-sized flatness in the earth, where a man could lie unobserved and have a good view of the target zone.

He eased down, oriented himself to where Dade had died and Julie fell. He was careful not to disturb the earth, in case any scuff marks remained, but he could see none. At last he turned to get his best and first look at the killing zone from the shooting site.

Jesus Christ!

He was eight hundred, maybe a thousand meters out.

The killing zone was a tiny shelf far off at the oblique.

There were no features by which he could get an accurate distance-by-size estimation, and even on horseback, the targets would have been tiny. The scope wouldn't have blown them up too much, either: too big a scope would have amplified the wobble effect until a sight picture was simply unobtainable and, worse, it would have had too small a breadth of vision at this range. If he lost contact with his targets, he might never have gotten them back in time. He had to be shooting a 10X, nothing bigger than a 12X, but probably a 10.

That's some shooting. That's beyond good; that's in some other sphere. Careful, precise, deliberate, mathematical long-range shooting is very good shooting. Knowing instinctively how far to lead a moving target in the crux of the fraction of the second you've got, knowing it automatically, subconsciously . . . that is *great* shooting. Man, that is so far out there, it's almost beyond belief. He knew of one man who could hit that shot, but he was dead, a bullet having exploded his head in the Ouachitas. There might be two or three others but—

He now saw too why the shooter had missed the kill on Julie.

He didn't make a mistake: he had the shot perfectly. He was just betrayed by the physics of the issue, the bullet's time in flight. When he fired, he had her dead to rights. But it takes a second for the bullet to travel that long arc, to float down on her; and there's plenty of time, even in that limited period, for her to alter her body movement or direction enough to cause the miss. That's why Dade is at least an easier shot. He's not moving, to say nothing of at the oblique, on horseback galloping away as Julie was.

Bob sat back. His head ached; he felt dizzy; his heart beat wildly.

He thought of another man who might have done this. He'd buried the name and the memory so far it didn't usually intrude, though sometimes, in the night, it would come from nowhere, or even in the daylight it would flash back upon him, that which he had tried to forget.

But he had to find out. There had to be a sign. Somehow, some way, the shooter would have left something that only another shooter could read.

Oh, you bastard. Come on, you bastard. Show me yourself. Let me see your face, this once.

He forced himself to concentrate on the hardscrabble dirt before him. He felt a raindrop, cold and absolute, against his face. Then another. The wind rose, howling. Junior, made restive, whinnied uncomfortably. The rain was moments away. He looked and he could see it, a gray blur hurtling down from the mountains. It would come and destroy. The sniper had planned for it. He was brilliant, well schooled in stratagems.

But who was he?

Bob leaned forward; he saw only dust. Then, no, no, yes, yes, he leaned forward even farther, and up front, where the dust had clearly been swept clean, he saw very small particulate residue. Tiny beads of it, tiny grains. White sand. White sand from a sandbag, because a great shooter will go off the bag, prone.

The rain began to slash. He pulled his jacket tight. If

the sandbag was here—it had to be, to index the rifle to the killing zone—then the legs were splayed this way. He bent to where they'd have been, hoping for the indent of a knee, anything to leave a human mark of some sort. But it was all scratched out, and gone, and now the rain would take it forever.

The rain was cold and bitter. It was like the rain of Kham Duc. It would come and wipe anything away.

But then he went down farther, and amid the small and meaningless dunes, he at last found what he had yearned for. It was about two inches of a sharp cut in the dust, with notches for the thread holding sole to boot. Yes. It was an imprint of the shooter's boot, the edge of the sole, the tiny strands of thread, the smoothness of the contour of the boot itself, all perfectly preserved in the dust. The shooter had splayed his foot sideways, to give him just the hint of muscular tension that would tighten his muscles up through his body. It was an adductor muscle, *Adductor magnus.* That was the core of the system, as isolated by a coach who'd gotten so far into it he'd worked out the precise muscles involved.

That was Russian. A shooting position developed by the coach A. Lozgachev prior to the fifty-two Olympics, where the Eastern Bloc shooters simply ran the field. In sixty, someone else had been coached by A. Lozgachev and his system of the magic *Adductor magnus* to win the gold in prone rifle.

T. Solaratov, the Sniper.

CHAPTER THIRTY-TWO

It was late at night. Outside, the wind still howled, and the rain still fell. It was going to be a three-day blow. The man was alone in a house that was not his own, halfway up a mountain in a state he hardly knew at all. His daughter was in town, close to her injured mother, in the care of a hired nurse until an FBI agent's wife would arrive.

In the house, there was no sound. A fire burned in the fireplace, but it was not crackly or inviting. It was merely a fire and one that hadn't been tended in a while.

The man sat in the living room, in somebody else's chair, staring at something he had placed on the table before him. Everything in the room was somebody else's; at fifty-two, he owned nothing, really; some property in Arizona that was now fallow, some property in Arkansas that was all but abandoned. He had a pension and his wife's family had some money, but it wasn't much to show for fifty-two years.

In fact, what he had to show for those fifty-two years was one thing, and it was before him on the table.

It was a quart bottle of bourbon: Jim Beam, white label, the very best. He had not tasted whiskey in many years. He knew that if he ever did, it might kill him: he could wash away on it so easily, because in its stupefying numbness there was some kind of relief from the things that he could not make go away in any other way.

Well, sir, he thought, tonight we drink the whiskey.

He had bought it in 1982 in Beaufort, South Carolina, just outside Parris Island. He had no idea why he was there: it seemed some drunken journey back to his roots, the basic training installation of the United States Marine Corps, as if nothing existed before or after. It was the end of an epic, seven-week drunk, the second week of which his first wife had fled for good. Not many memories of the time or place could be recalled, but he did remember staggering into a liquor store and putting down his ten-spot, getting the change and the bottle and going out, in the heat, to his car, where what remained of his belongings were dumped.

He sat there in the parking lot, hearing the cicadas sing and getting set to crack the seal and drown out his headache, his shakes, his flashbacks, his anger in a smooth brown tide. But that day, for some reason, he thought to himself: maybe I could wait just a bit before I open it up. Just a bit. See how far I can get.

He had gotten over twelve years out of it.

Well, yes, sir, tonight is the night I open it up.

Bob cracked the seal on the bottle. It fought him for just a second, then yielded with a dry snap, slid open with the feeling of cheap metal gliding on glass. He unscrewed the cap, put it on the table, then poured a couple of fingers' worth into a glass. It settled, brown and stable, not creamy at all but thin, like water. He stared at it as if in staring at it he could recognize some meaning. But he saw the futility, and after a bit raised it to his lips.

The smell hit him first, like the sound of a lost brother calling his name, something he knew so well but had missed so long. It was infinitely familiar and beckoning, and it overpowered, for that was the way of whiskey: it took everything and made everything whiskey. That was its brilliance and its damnation too.

The sip exploded on his tongue, hot with smooth fire, raspy with pouring smoke, with the totality that made him wince. His eyes burned, his nose filled, he blinked and felt it in his mouth, sloshing around his teeth. Even at this last moment it was not too late, but he swallowed it, and it burned its way down, like a swig of napalm, unpleasant as it descended, and then it hit and its first wave detonated, and there was fire everywhere.

He remembered. He forced himself to.

Last mission. Donny was DEROS. He should have

been outprocessing. No, the little bastard, he couldn't let anything alone. He had to be so perfect. He had to be the perfect Marine. He had to go along.

Why did you let him?

Did you hate him? Was there something in you that wanted to see him get hit? Was it Julie? Was it that you hated him so fiercely because he was going back to Julie and you knew you'd never have her if he made it?

Donny hadn't made it. Bob did have Julie. He was married to her, though it took some doing. So in a terrible sense he had gotten exactly what he desired. He had benefited. Hadn't seemed so at the time, but the one Johnny who came out of the fracas with more than he went into it was he, himself, Gy.Sgt. Bob Lee Swagger, USMC (Ret.).

Don't think, he warned himself. Don't interpret; list. List it all. Dredge it up. He had to concentrate only on the exactness of the event, the hard questions, the knowable, the palpable, the feelable.

What time was it?

0-dark-30, 0530, 06 May 72. Duty NCO nudges me awake, but I am already conscious and I have heard him come.

"Sarge?"

"Yeah, fine."

I rise before the sun. I decide not to wake Donny yet; let him sleep. He's DEROS tomorrow, on his way back to the world. I check my equipment. The M40 is clean, having been examined carefully the night before both by myself and the armorer. Eighty rounds of M118 7.62mm NATO Match ammunition have been wiped and packed into pouches on an 872 harness. I slip into my shoulder holster for my .380; over that I pull on my cammies, I lace and tighten my boots. I darken my face with the colors of the jungle. I find my boonie cap. I slip into the 782 gear, with the ammunition, the canteens, the .45, all checked last night. I take the rifle, which hangs by its sling, off the nail in the bunker wall, slide five M118s into it, closing the bolt to drive the top one into the chamber. I pull back to put on safe, just behind the bolt handle. I'm ready to go to the office.

It's going to be a hot one. The rainy season is finally over, and the heat has come out of the east, settling like a mean old lady on us poor grunts. But it's not hot yet. I stop by the mess tent, where somebody's already got coffee going, and though I don't like the caffeine to jimmy my nerves, it's been so quiet of late I don't see any harm in having a cup.

A PFC pours it for me into a big khaki USMC mug, and I feel the great smell, then take a long, hard hot pull on it. Damn, that tastes good. That's what a man needs in the morning.

Sitting in his living room, the fire burning away, Bob took another sip on the whiskey. It, too, burned on the way down, then seemed to whack him between the eyes, knock him to blur and gone. He felt the tears come.

06 May 1972. 0550.

I head to the S-2 bunker and duck in. Lieutenant Brophy is already up. He's a good man, and knows just when to be present and when not to be. He's here this morning, freshly shaved, in starched utilities. There seems to be some sort of ceremonial thing going on.

"Morning, Sergeant."

"Morning, sir."

"Overnight your orders came through on the promotion. I'm here to tell you you're officially a gunnery sergeant in the United States Marine Corps. Congratulations, Swagger."

"Thank you, sir."

"You've done a hell of a job. And I know you'll be bang-up beaucoup number one at Aberdeen."

"Looking forward to it, sir."

Maybe the lieutenant feels the weight of history. Maybe he knows this is Bob the Nailer's last go-round. Three tours in the 'Nam with an extension for the last one, to give him nineteen straight months in country. He wants to observe it properly and that satisfies me. In some way, Brophy gets it, and that's good.

We go over the job. We work the maps. It's an easy one. I'll go straight out the north side, over the berm and out to the treeline. Then we work our way north toward Hoi An, through heavy bush and across a paddy dike. We go maybe four klicks to a hill that stands 840 meters high and is therefore called Hill 840. We'll go up it, set up observation and keep a good Marine Corps eyeball on Ban Son Road and the Thu Bon River. I'm done killing: it's straight scout work. I'm here for firebase security, nothing else. Along those lines, we plan to look for sign of large-body troop movements, to indicate enemy presence, on the way out and the way back.

The lieutenant himself types up the operational order and enters it in the logbook. I sign the order. It's official now.

I tell the clerk to go get Fenn. It's 0620. We're running a little late, because I've let Fenn sleep. Why did I do this? Well, it seemed kind. I didn't want to break his balls on the last day. He really isn't needed until we leave the perimeter, as the mission has been well discussed and briefed the night before; he knows the specs better than I do.

He shows up ten minutes later, the sleep still in his eyes, but his face made-up green, like mine. Someone gets him some coffee. The lieutenant asks him how he's doing. He says he's fine, he just wants to get it over with and head back to the world.

"You don't have to go, Fenn," I say.

"I'm going," he says.

Why? Why does he *have* to go? What is driving him? I never understood it then; I don't understand it now. There was no reason, not one that ever made no sense to me. It was the last, the tiniest, the least significant of all the things we did in the 'Nam. It was the one we could have skipped and oh, what a different world we'd live in now if we had.

Bob threw down another choker of bourbon. Hot fire. Napalm splashes, the whack between the eyes. The brown glory of it.

"Check your weapons," I tell Fenn, "and then do commo."

Donny makes certain the M14 is charged, safety on. He takes out his .45, drops the mag, sees that the chamber is empty. That's the way I've told him to carry it. Then he checks out the PRC-77, which of course reads loud and clear since the receiving station is about four feet away. But we do it by the numbers, just like always.

"You all set, Fenn?" I ask.

"Gung ho, Semper Fi and all that good shit," says Donny, at last strapping the radio on, getting it set just right, then picks up the weapon, just as I pick mine up.

We leave the bunker. The light is beginning to seep over the horizon; it's still cool and characteristically calm. The air smells sweet.

But then I say, "I don't want to go out the north. Just in case. I want to break our pattern. We go out the east this time, just like we did before. We ain't never repeated ourself; anybody tracking us couldn't anticipate that."

Why did I say that? What feeling did I have? I did have a feeling. I know I had one. Why didn't I listen to it? You've got to pay attention, because those little things, they're some part of you you don't know nothing about, trying to reach you with information.

But now there was no reaching back all these years; he had made a snap decision because it felt so right, and it was so wrong. Bob finished the glass with a last hot swig, then quickly poured another one, two fingers, neat, as on so many lost nights over so many lost years. He held it before his eyes as the blur hit him, and almost laughed. He didn't feel so bad now. It was easy. You could just dig it out that simply, and it was there, before him, as if recorded on videotape or as if, after all these years, the memory somehow *wanted* to come out at last.

"He's gone, he's dead, you got him," says Brophy,

meaning, The white sniper is gone, there's nobody out there, don't worry about it. He should have been dead, too. We cooked his ass in 20mm and 7.62. The Night Hag sprayed him with lead. The flamethrower teams barbecued him to melted fat and bone ash. Who could live through that? We recovered his rifle. It was a great coup, waiting to be studied back at Aberdeen by none other than yours truly.

But—why did we believe he was dead? We didn't find no body, we only found the rifle. But how could he have survived all that fire, and the follow-up with the flamethrowers and then the sweep with grunts? No one could have survived that. Then again, this was a terrifically efficient professional. He didn't panic, he'd been under a lot of fire, he'd taken lots of people down. He kept his cool, he had great stamina.

"Yeah, well," I tell the lieutenant.

We reach the eastern parapet wall. A sentry comes over from the guard post down the way.

"All clear?" I ask.

"Sarge, I been working the night vision scope the past few hours. Ain't nothing out there."

But how would he know? The night vision is only good for a few hundred yards. The night vision tells you nothing. It simply means there's nobody up close, like a sapper platoon. Why didn't I realize that?

He took another dark, long swallow. It was as if something hit him upside the head with a two-by-four, and his consciousness slipped a little; he felt his bourbon-powered mellowness battling the melancholy of his memory as it presented itself to him after all these years.

I slip my head over the sandbags, look out into the defoliated zone, which is lightening in the rising sun. I can't see much. The sun is directly in my eyes. I can only see flatness, a slight undulation in the terrain, low vegetation, blackened stumps from the defoliant. No details, just a landscape of emptiness.

"Okay," I say. "Last day: time to hunt." I always say this. Why do I think it's so cool? It's stupid, really.

I set my rifle on the sandbag berm, pull myself over, gather the rifle and roll off.

I land, and there's a moment there where everything is fine, and then there's a moment when it isn't. I've done this hundreds of times before over the past nineteen months, and this feels just like all those times. Then time stops. Then it starts again and when I try to account for the missing second, it seems a lot has happened. I've been punched backwards, come to rest against the berm itself. For some reason my right leg is up around my ears. I can make no sense of this until I look down and see my hip, pulped, smashed, pulsing my own blood like a broken faucet. Somewhere in here I hear the crack of the rifle shot, which arrives just a bit after I'm hit.

It makes no sense at all and I panic. Then I think: motherfuck, I'm going to die. This fills even my hard heart with terror. I don't want to die. That's all I'm thinking: I don't want to die.

There's blood everywhere, and I put my fingers on my wound to stanch it, but the blood squirts out between them. It's like trying to carry dry sand; it slips away. I can see bone, shattered. I feel the wet. Again an odd second where there is no pain and then the pain is so heavy I think I'll die from it alone. I'm thinking of nothing but myself now: there's no one in the world but me. A single word forms in my head, and it's *morphine.*

Bob looked into the amber bourbon, so still, so calm. The wind rushed outside, cold and harsh. He heard himself screaming, *"I'm hit!"* from across the years, and saw himself, hip smashed, blood pouring out. And he knew what happened next.

He took a swallow. It landed hard. He was quite drunk. The world wobbled and twisted, fell out of and back into focus a dozen times. He was crying now. He hadn't cried then but he was crying now.

"No!" he screamed, but it was too late, for the boy had

leaped over the berm too, to cover his sergeant, to inject morphine, to drag the wounded man to cover.

Donny lands and at that precise moment he is hit. The bullet excites such vibration from him as it crashes through that the dust seems to snap off his chest. There's no geyser, no spurt, nothing; he just goes down, dead weight, his pupils slipping up into his head. From far off comes the crack of that rifle. Is there something familiar in it? Why does it now seem so familiar?

The sound of it played in his ears: crisp, echoless, far away, but clear. Familiar? Why familiar? Rifles and loads all have their signature, but this one, what was it? What about it? What information did it convey? What message did it carry?

"Donny!" I cry, as if my cry can bring him back, but he's so gone there's no reaching him. He collapses into the dust a foot or so from me with the crash of the uncaring, and how I do it I don't know, but I somehow squirm to him and hold him close.

"Donny!" I scream, shaking him as if to drive the bullet out, but his eyes are glassy and unfocused, and blood is coming out of his mouth and nose. It's also coming out of his chest, pouring out. No one ever gets how much blood there is: there's lots of it, and it comes out like water, thin and sloppy and soaking.

His eyelids flutter but he's not seeing anything. There's a little sound in his throat, and somehow I have him in my arms and now I'm screaming, *"Corpsman! Corpsman!"*

I hear machine gun fire. Someone has jumped to the berm with an M60 and is throwing out suppressive fire, arcs and arcs of tracers that skip out across the field, lifting the dirt where they hit. A 57mm recoil-less rifle fires, big booming flash, that blows a mushroom cloud into the landscape to no particular point, and more and more men come to the berm, as if repulsing a human-wave attack.

Meanwhile, Brophy has jumped, and he's on both of us, and there are three or four more grunts, pressing against us, firing out into the emptiness. Brophy hits me with morphine, then hits me again.

"Donny!" I scream, but as the morphine whacks me out, I feel his fingers loosening from my wrist, and I know that he is dead.

Bob hit the bottle again, this time dispensing with the glass. The fluid coursed down. His mind was now almost thoroughly wasted. He couldn't remember Donny anymore. Donny was gone, Donny was lost, Donny was history, Donny was a name on a long black wall. Were there even any photos of him? He tried to recall Donny but his mind wouldn't let him.

Gray face. Unfocused eyes staring at eternity. The sound of machine gun fire. The taste of dust and sand. Blood everywhere. Brophy jacking the morphine in. Its warmth and spreading, easing numbness. I won't let go of Donny. I must hold him still. They're trying to pull me away, over the berm. The blackness of the morphine taking me out.

I sleep.

I sleep.

Days pass, I'm lost in morphine.

I'm finally awakened by a corpsman. He's shaving me. That is, my pubic region.

"Huh?" I say, so groggy I can hardly breathe. I feel inflated, creamy with grease, bound by weight.

"Surgery, Gunny," he says. "You're going to be operated on now."

"Where am I?" I ask.

"The Philippines. Onstock Naval Hospital, Orthopedic Surgery Ward. They'll fix you up good. You been out for a week."

"Am I going to die?"

"Hell, no. You'll be back in the Major Leagues next season."

He shaves me. The light is gray. I can't remember much, but somewhere underneath it there's pain. Donny? Donny's gone. Dodge City? What happened to Dodge

City? Brophy, Feamster, the grunts. That little place out there all by itself.

"Dodge?"

"Dodge?" he asks. "You ain't heard?"

"No," I say, "I been out."

"Sure. Bad news. The dinks jumped it a few days after you got hit. Sappers got in with grenades. Killed thirty guys, wounded sixty-five more."

"Oh, fuck."

He shaves me expertly, a man who knows what he's doing.

"Brophy?" I say.

"I don't know. They got a lot of officers; they hit the command bunkers. I know they got the CO and a bunch of grunts. Poor guys. Probably the last Marines to die in the Land of Bad Things. They say there'll be a big investigation. Careers ended, a colonel, maybe even a general will go down. You're lucky you got out, Gunny."

Loss. Endless loss. Nothing good came out of it. No happy endings. We went, we lost, we died, we came home to—to what?

I feel old and tired. Used up. Throw me out. Kill me. I don't want to live. I want to die and be with my people.

"Corpsman?" I grab his arm.

"Yeah?"

"Kill me. Hit me with morphine. Finish me. Everything you got. Please."

"Can't do it, Gunny. You're a goddamned hero. You've got everything to live for. You're going to get the Navy Cross. You'll be the Command Sergeant Major of the Marine Corps."

"I hurt so bad."

"Okay, Gunny. I'm done. Let me give you some Mike. Only a little, though, to make the pain go away."

He hits me with it. I go under and the next time I awake, I'm in full traction in San Diego, where I'll spend a year alone, which will be followed by a year in a body cast, also alone.

But now the morphine hits and thank God, once again, I go under.

The light awakened him, then noise. The door cracked open and Sally Memphis walked in.

"Thought I'd find you here."

"Oh, Christ, what time is it?"

"Mister, it's eleven-thirty in the morning and you ought to be with your wife and daughter, not out here getting drunk."

Bob's head ached and his mouth felt dry. He could smell himself, not pleasant. He was still in yesterday's clothes and the room had the stench of unwashed man to it.

Sally bustled around, opening window shades. Outside, the sun glared; the three-day blow had lasted only one and then was gone. Idaho sky, pure diamond blue, blasted through the windows, lit by sun. Bob blinked, hoping the pain would go away but it wouldn't.

"She was operated on at seven A.M. for her collarbone. You should have been there. Then you were supposed to pick me up at the airport at nine-thirty. Remember?"

Sally, who had just graduated from law school, was the wife of one of Bob's few friends, a special agent in the FBI named Nick Memphis who now ran the Bureau's New Orleans office. She was about thirty-five and had acquired, over the years, a puritan aspect to her, unforgiving and unshaded. She was going to start as an assistant prosecutor in the New Orleans district attorney's office that fall; but she'd come here out of her and her husband's love of Bob.

"I had a bad night."

"I'll say."

"It ain't what it appears," he said feebly.

"You fell off the wagon but good, that's what it appears."

"I had to do some work last night. I needed the booze to get where I had to go."

"You are a stubborn man, Bob Swagger. I pity your beautiful wife, who has to live with your flintiness. That woman is a saint. You *never* are wrong, are you?"

"I am wrong all the time, as a matter of fact. Just don't happen to be wrong on this one. Here, lookey here."

He picked up the uncapped bottle of Jim Beam, three-quarters gone, and walked out on the front porch. His hip ached a little. Sally followed. He poured the stuff into the ground.

"There," he said. "No drunk could do that. It's gone, it's finished, it won't never touch these lips again."

"So why did you get so drunk? Do you know I called you? You were hopeless on the phone."

"Nope. Sorry, don't remember that."

"Why the booze?"

"I had to remember something that happened to me long ago. I drunk for years to forget it. Then when I got sober finally, I found I disremembered it. So I had to hunt it out again."

"So what did you learn on your magical mystery tour?"

"I didn't learn nothing yet."

"But you will," she said.

"I know where to look for an answer," he finally said.

"And where would that be?"

"There's only one place."

She paused.

"Oh, I'll bet this one is rich," she said. "It just gets better and better."

"Yep," he said. "I don't never want to disappoint you, Sally. This one is really rich."

"Where is it?"

"Where a Russian put it. Where he hid it twenty-five years ago. But it's there, and by God, I'll dig it out."

"What *are* you talking about?"

"It's in my hip. The bullet that crippled me. It's still there. I'm going to have it cut out."

CHAPTER THIRTY-THREE

It was dark and the doctor was still working. Bob found him out back of the Jennings place, down the road from the Holloways, where he'd had to help a cow through a difficult birth. Now he was with a horse called Rufus whom the Jennings girl, Amy, loved, although Rufus was getting on in years. But the doctor assured her that Rufus was fine; he would just be getting up slower these days. He was an old man, and should be treated with the respect of the elderly. Like that old man over there, the doctor said, pointing to Bob.

"Mr. Swagger," said Amy. "I'd heard you'd left these parts."

"I did," he said. "But I came back to see my good friend Dr. Lopez."

"Amy, honey, I'll send over a vitamin supplement I want you to add to Rufus's oats every morning. I bet that'll help him."

"Thank you, Dr. Lopez."

"It's all right, honey. You run up to the house now. I think Mr. Swagger wants a private chat."

" 'Bye, Mr. Swagger."

"Good-bye, sweetie," said Bob, as the girl skipped back to the house.

"Thought those reporters chased you out of this place for good," the doctor said.

"Well, I did too. The bastards are still looking for me."

"Where'd you go to cover?"

"A ranch up in Idaho, twenty-five miles out of Boise. Just temporarily, waiting for all this to blow over."

"I knew you were something big in the war. I never knew you were a hero."

"My father was a hero. I was just a sergeant. I did a job, that's all."

"Well, you ran a great lay-up barn. I wish you'd come back into the area, Bob. There's no first-class outfit this side of Tucson."

"Maybe I will."

"But you didn't come all this way to talk about horses," said Dr. Lopez.

"No, Doc, I didn't. In fact, I flew down this afternoon. Took the two-ten American from Boise to Tucson, rented a car, and here I am."

Bob explained what he wanted. The doctor was incredulous.

"I can't just do that. Give me a reason."

"I am plumb tired of setting off airport alarms. I want to get on an airplane without a scene."

"That's not good enough. I have an oath, as well as a complex set of legal regulations, Bob. And let me point out one other thing. You are not an animal."

"Well," said Bob, "actually I am. I am a Homo sapien. But I know you are the best vet in these parts and you have operated on many animals, and most of 'em are still with us today. I remember you nursed Billy Hancock's paint through two knee operations, and that old boy's still roaming the range."

"That was a good horse. It was a pleasure to save that animal."

"You never even charged him."

"I charged him plenty. I just never collected. Every few months, Billy sends me ten or fifteen dollars. It should be paid up by the next century."

"Well, I am a good horse, too. And I have this here problem and that's why I come to you. If I go to VA, it could take months for the paperwork to clear. If I go to a private MD, I got a passel of questions I have to answer and a big operating room to tie up and weeks to recover, whether I need it or not. I need this thing now. Tonight."

"Tonight!"

"I need you to go in on local, dig it out, and sew me up."

"Bob, we are talking about serious, invasive work. It would take any normal man a month to recover, under intensive medical care. You won't be whole again for a long time."

"Doc, I been hit before. You know that. I still come back fast. It's a matter of time. I can't tell you why, but I'm under the gun on time. I have to find something out so I can go to the FBI. I need a piece of evidence. I need your help."

"Oh, Lord."

"I know you did a tour over there. It's a thing guys like us have in common. We ought to help each other when we can."

"No one else will, that's for sure," said Dr. Lopez.

"You was a combat medic and you probably saw more gunshot wounds and worked on more than any ten MDs. You know what you're doing."

"I saw enough of it over there."

"It's a nasty thing to fire a bullet into a man," said Bob. "I was never the same, and now that I am getting old, I feel my back firing up because of the damage it did to my structure. And the VA don't recognize pain. They just tell you to live with it, and cut your disability ten percent every year. So on I go, and on all of us go with junk in us or limbs missing or whatever."

"That war was a very bad idea. Nothing good ever came out of it."

"I copy you there. I wouldn't be here if I didn't have no other choice. I need that bullet."

"You are a fool if you think what I can offer you is as safe as modern hospital medicine."

"You dig the bullet out and put in the stitches. If you don't do it, I'll have to do it myself and that won't be pretty."

"I believe you would, Bob. Well, they say you are one tough son of a bitch. You better be, because you're going to need every bit of tough to get through the next few days."

Bob lay on his back, looking at the large mirror above him. The ugliness of the entrance wound was visible; he hated to look at it. The bullet had hit him almost dead on at a slight downward angle, plowed through skin and the tissue of his sheathing *gluteus medius* muscle, then shattered the platelike flange of the hip bone, deflecting off to plunge down the inside of his leg, ripping out muscle as it went. The bullet hole was unfilled: it was that alone and nothing else—a channel, a void, an emptiness in his hip that plunged inward, surrounded by an ugly pucker of ruined flesh.

"No false hip?" said Dr. Lopez, feeling at it, examining it carefully.

"No, sir," said Bob. "They patched it up with bone grafts from my other shin and screws. On cold days, them screws can light up, let me tell you."

"Did it break a leg, too?"

"No, sir, it just tore up tissue traveling down the leg."

The doctor probed Bob's inner thigh, where a long dead patch described the careening bullet's terrible passage through flesh. Bob looked up, away, feeling the acute humiliation of it. The doctor's operating theater was immaculately clean, though out of scale to human bodies, as its most usual patients were horses with leg or eye problems. Except for the two of them, it was deserted.

"Well, you're lucky," Dr. Lopez said. "I was afraid it still might be hung up in the mechanics of the hip. If that had happened, you were out of luck. I couldn't take it out without permanently crippling you."

"I am lucky," said Bob.

"Yeah," the doctor said, "I can feel it here, nested in the thigh, down close to the knee. I know what happened. They had to screw your hip together with transplants; the deep, muscular wound of the bullet didn't matter to them. They didn't even bother to look for it. They just sewed it up. They were trying to keep you alive and ambulatory, not make sure you could get through airport metal detectors."

"You can get it?"

"Bob, this is going to hurt like hell. I have to cut through an inch of muscle, get down close to the femur. I can feel it in there. You will bleed like a dog on the roadway. I will sew you up, but you will need a good long rest. This isn't a small thing. It isn't a huge thing, but you ought to spend at least a couple of weeks off your feet."

"You cut it out tonight. I'll sleep here and be gone in the morning. You give me a good pain shot and that will be that."

"You are a hard case," said the doctor.

"My wife says the same."

"Your wife and I bet anyone that ever met you. All right, you sit back. I'm going to wash you up, then shave you. Then I'll go scrub, and we'll give you a painkiller and we'll do what's gotta be done."

Bob watched with a numb leg and an odd feeling of dislocation. The doctor had put an inflatable tourniquet around the upper leg to cut down on blood loss. Then he'd wrapped his leg in a sterile Ace bandage, and now he cut through it, a horizontal incision with a scalpel an inch deep and three inches long into the lower inside of his right thigh. Bob felt nothing. The blood jetted out in a spurt, as if an artery had been snipped, but it hadn't, and as the initial jet was soaked up by the bandage, the new blood crept back to seep out of the ugly gash.

He'd seen so much blood, but the blood he remembered was Donny's blood. Because the bullet had shattered his heart and lungs, it had gotten into his throat fast and he'd gagged it out. There was so much, it overcame his pipes and found new tunnels out of which to surge: it came from his nose and mouth, as if he'd been punched in the face. Donny's face was ruined, taken from them all by the black-red delta as it fanned from the center of his face down to his chin.

The doctor tweaked and squeezed the incision, opening it as one would a coin purse; then he took a long probe and inserted it into the wound and began to press and feel.

"Is it there?"

"I don't have it—yeah, yeah, there it is, I ticked against it. It seems to be encapsulated in some scar-type tissue. I'd guess that's standard for an old bullet."

He removed the probe, now sticky with blood, gleaming in the bright light of the operating theater, and set it down. Picking up a new scalpel, he cut more deeply; more blood flowed.

"I'm going to have to irrigate," he said through his mask. "I can't see much; all that damn blood."

"They will do that on you, won't they?" said Bob.

Lopez merely grunted, squirted a blast of water into the wound, so that it bubbled.

It was so strange: Swagger could feel the water as pressure, not unpleasant, even a little ticklish; he could feel the probe, could almost feel as the pincers tugged at the bullet. The sensations were precise, the doctor tugging at the thing, which was evidently quite disfigured and jammed into some tissue and wouldn't just pop out as a new bullet would. Bob felt all these details of the operation. He saw the opening in his leg, saw the blood, saw the doctor's gloved fingers begin to glow with blood, and the blood begin to spot his surgeon's gown and smock.

But he felt nothing; it could have been happening to someone else. It was unrelated to him.

At last, with a tiny tug, Lopez pulled the bloody pincers out of the wound and held the trophy up for Bob to see: the bullet was crusted in gristle, white and fatty, and the doctor cut it free with his scalpel. It had mangled when it had met his bone, its meplat collapsing into its body, so that it was deformed into a little flattened splat, like a mushroom, oddly askew atop the column of what remained. But it hadn't broken into pieces; it was all there, an ugly little twist of gilding metal sheathing lead, and its original aerodynamic sleekness, its missileness, was still evident in the twisted version. He could see striations running down it, where the rifle's grooves had gripped it as it spun through the barrel so long ago on its journey toward him.

"Can you weigh it?"

"Yeah, right, I'll *weigh* it and then I'll *wax* it, and then I'll *gift-wrap* it while you quietly bleed to death. Just hold your horses, Bob."

He dropped the bullet into a little porcelain tray, where it tinkled like a penny thrown into a blind man's cup, then went back to Bob.

"Please weigh it," said Bob.

"You ought to be committed," the doctor said. He irrigated the wound again, poured in disinfectant and inserted a little sterile plastic tube, for drainage. Then he quickly and expertly sewed it up with coarse surgical thread. After finishing, he restitched with a finer thread. Then he bandaged the wound, wrapped an inflatable splint around it and blew hard until the splint held the leg stiff, nearly immobile. Then he loosened the Velcro on the tourniquet and tossed it aside.

"Pain?"

"Nothing," said Bob.

"You're lying. I felt you begin to tense five minutes ago."

"Okay, it hurts a bit, yeah."

Actually, it now hurt like hell. But he didn't want another shot or anything that would drug him, flatten him, keep him woozy. He had other stuff to do.

"Okay," said the doctor. "Tomorrow I'll rebandage it and remove the tube. But it'll relieve the pressure tonight. Now—"

"Please. I have to know. Weigh it. I have to know."

Dr. Lopez rolled his eyes, took the porcelain cup to a table where a medical scale was sitting, and fiddled and twisted.

"All right," said the doctor.

"Go on," said Bob.

"It's 167.8 grains."

"Are you sure?"

"I'm very sure."

"Christ!"

"What's wrong?"

"This thing just got so twisted it don't make no sense at all."

He slept dreamlessly for the first time in weeks in one of Doc Lopez's spare bedrooms; the pain woke him early, and the unbearable stiffness in the leg. The doctor redressed the wound, then replaced the inflatable splint.

"No major damage. You ought to be able to get around a little bit."

He had some crutches lying around, and advised Bob to seek professional medical help as soon as possible. Bob could not walk or bathe, but he insisted on going to the airport, on the power of ibuprofen and will alone. White-faced and oily with sweat, he was pushed to the ten-fifteen plane in a wheelchair by a stewardess, and used the crutches to get aboard. He got to enter the plane early; it was like being important.

No one was seated next to him, as the flight was only half full. The plane took off, stabilized and eventually coffee was brought. He took four more ibus, washed them down with the coffee, then at last took out his grisly little treasure in its plasticine envelope.

Well, now, ain't you a problem, brother, he thought, examining the little chunk of metal, mushroomed into the agony of impact, frozen forever in the configuration of the explosion it had caused against his hip bone.

One hundred sixty-eight grains.

Big problem. The only 168-grain bullet in the world in 1972 was American—the Sierra 168-grain MatchKing, the supreme .30-caliber target round then and, pretty much, now. He was expecting a 150-grain Soviet bullet, for the

7.62mm x 54, as fired in either a Dragunov or the old Mosin-Nagant sniper rifle.

No. This boy was working with an American handload, as the 168-grainers weren't used on manufactured bullets until the services adopted the M852 in the early nineties. Nor was it the 173-grain match American bullet, loaded equally into the M72 .30-06 round or the M118 7.62 NATO round.

No. American handload, tailored, planned, its last wrinkle worked out. A serious professional shooter, at the extended ranges of his craft. That meant this was a total effort, even to somehow obtaining American components in RSVN to get the absolute maximum out of the system. Why?

He tried to think it out.

T. Solaratov has lost his Dragunov. The field-expedient choice would then be an American sniper rifle, presumably available in some degree within the NVA supply system; after all, half their stuff was captured.

Bob bet it was an M1-D, the sniper version of the old M1 Garand rifle that the GIs won World War II with.

The more he thought about it, the more sense it made, up to a point. Yes, that would explain the almost subconscious *familiarity* of the sound signature. In his time, he'd fired thousands of rounds with an M-1. It had been his first Marine rifle, a solid, chunky, robust, brilliantly engineered piece of work that would never let you down.

This is my rifle, this is my gun.
This is killing, this is for fun.

Every recruit had marched in his underwear around the squad bay some indeterminate number of hours, a ton of unloaded M1 on his shoulder, Parris Island's sucking bogs out beyond the wire, his dick in his left hand, that primitive rhyme sounding in his ears under the guidance of a drill instructor who seemed like a God, only crueler and tougher and smarter.

Yeah, he thought, he uses a Garand rifle with a scope, he works out the load with the best possible components, he takes me down, he's the hero.

Looking at the striations imprinted in the copper sheathing of the bullet by its explosive passage up the barrel that day, he guessed closer examination by experts would prove them to be the mark of a rifling system that held to ten twists per inch, not twelve, for that would prove the bullet was fired from a match grade M1 and not an M14. He saw the logic in that, too. It made sense to choose a .30-06 over a .308 because downrange the .30-06, with its longer cartridge case and higher powder capacity, would deliver more energy, particularly beyond a thousand yards. It really *was* a long-range cartridge, as so many deer had found out over the years; the .308 was a mere wannabe.

But here's where he hit the wall.

If in fact he decided to go with the .30-06 cartridge, then why the hell wouldn't he have used a Model 70T, a bolt gun? That was the Marine sniper rifle of the first five years of the war. There *had* to be plenty of those still around; hell, even Donny had come up with one of them in that one shot at Solaratov they'd had.

Why would the Russian use the less accurate, considerably more problematic semiauto instead of one of the most classic sniper rifles in the world? Carl Hitchcock, the great Marine sniper of 1967, with his ninety-two kills, he'd used a 70T, with a sportsman's stock and an 8X Unertl externally adjusted scope. That would be the rifle to use. What the hell was this Russian bird up to?

Could it be: no Model 70s available?

Well, he could check out combat losses through friends in the Pentagon, but it seemed impossible that the Russian wouldn't be able to pick up a Model 70. He could probably have gotten one of Bob's own Model 700 Remingtons if he'd wanted it.

What was there about the M1 that made it mandatory for the Russian's selection?

It was indeed a very accurate rifle. Maybe he'd wanted the semiauto capacity to bracket the target, to put three or four shots into the area fast, in hopes that one would hit.

Nah. Not at that range. Each shot had to be precise.

The problem with the Garand as a sniper rifle was it was at its best with national match iron sights. It ruled in service rifle competition in which telescopic sights were not permissible. But the weapon became difficult when a scope was added, because its straight-down topside en bloc loading and straight-up ejection made it impossible to mount the scope over the axis of the bore. Instead, through a complicated system never really satisfactory, the M1 had worn a parallel scope, one mounted a little to the left of the action. That meant at a given range, the scope was intersecting the target but it was not on the same axis as the bore, which made rapid computation very difficult, particularly when the target was not exactly zeroed, or moved, or some such.

Yet he chose this rifle.

What the hell was going on?

Bob mulled, trying to make sense of it all.

He had the feeling of missing something. There was a thing he could not see. He could not even conceive of it.

What am I missing?

What in me prevents me from seeing it?

I can't even conceive it.

"Sir?"

"Oh, yes?" he said, looking up at the flight attendant.

"You'll have to put up your lap tray and straighten your seat back. We're about to land at Boise."

"Oh, yeah, sorry, wasn't paying any attention."

She smiled professionally, and he glimpsed out the windows to see the Sawtooths, the down-homey little Boise skyline, and the airfield, named after a famous ace who'd died young in war.

CHAPTER THIRTY-FOUR

Bob drove to the hospital straight from the airport. During a brief gap in the power of the ibuprofen, his incision began to knit in truly exquisite pain. He knew bruising would start by tomorrow and the thing would be agonizing for weeks—but he didn't want to stop.

He drove through the quiet, bright streets of Boise, as unpretentious a town as existed anywhere, and finally reached the hospital where the crutches got him in, the ibuprofen got him beyond the agony again and an elevator got him to his wife's room, outside of which his daughter and Sally Memphis waited.

"Oh, hi!"

"Daddy!"

"Sweetie, how are you?" he said, gathering up his daughter and giving her a big hug. "Oh, it's great to see my gal! Are you okay? You doin' what Sally says?"

"I'm fine, Dad. What's wrong with you?"

"Sweetie, nothing. Just a little cut on my leg, that's all," he said, as Sally shot him a disbelieving look.

He chatted with his daughter for a bit and with Sally, whose response to him was cool. It seemed that Julie was sleeping now, but there hadn't been any real complications from the surgery. They thought she'd get out sometime soon and Sally had made arrangements to go to the small ranch in Custer County as Bob had planned. She agreed with him that it was a safe security arrangement, at least until the situation clarified.

Finally, Julie awakened and Bob went in to his wife.

Her torso was in a full-body cast that supported the arm on the side where the collarbone had been shattered. His poor girl! She looked so wan and colorless and somehow shrunken in the cast.

"Oh, sweetie," he said, rushing to her.

She smiled but not with a lot of force or enthusiasm and asked how he was and he didn't bother to answer her, but instead went on about her, caught up on her medical situation, checked on the security arrangements, finally told her he thought he was on to something.

"I could tell; you're all lit up."

"It's a long story. There's something I can't figure out, and I need help."

"Bob, how can I help you? I don't know anything. I've told you everything I know."

"No, no, I don't mean about it. I mean about me."

"Now you've lost me."

"Honey, I got this thing I have to figure out. It doesn't make no sense to me. So either it's wrong, or I am wrong. If it's wrong, there's nothing I can do about it. If it's me that's wrong, then I can figure it out."

"Oh, Lord. I get shot and it's all about you."

He let the cut simmer, not responding.

Finally he said, "I'm very sorry you got hit. I'm very happy you survived. You should concentrate on how lucky you were to make it through, not how unlucky you were. You handled yourself well, you took control, you were a hero. You got your life, you got your daughter, you got your husband. It ain't no time to be angry."

She said nothing.

"It ain't about me. It's about us. I have to figure this thing out."

"Can't you let the police, the FBI do it? They're all over the place. That's their job. Your job is to be here with your family."

"I have a man hunting me. The more around you I am, the more danger you're in. Don't you see that?"

"So you'll be off again. I knew it. You weren't there when I got shot, you weren't there when I lay in that gulch for three hours, you weren't there when I was operated on, you weren't there when I came out of the operation, you haven't been taking care of your daughter, you're evidently not going with us to the mountains, I hear you've been drinking, you've obviously been in some kind of fight or something, because of the terrible way you're limping and the way your face is completely sheet-white, and all you want to do is go off again. And . . . somehow, you're *happy.*"

"I wasn't in a fight. I had a bullet cut out of my leg, that's all. It's nothing. I'm sorry," he said. "This is the best way, I think."

"I don't know how much of this I can take."

"I just want this to be over."

"Then stay here. Stay here, with us."

"I can't. That puts you in danger. He'll know soon enough, if not yet, that I wasn't the man he hit. So he'll come back. I have to be able to move, to operate, to think, to defend myself. Not only that, if he comes after me again, and you're there again, do you think I can defend you? Nobody can defend you. Let him come after me. That's what he was trained to do. Maybe I can get him, maybe not, but I sure as shit ain't going to let him go after you."

"Bob," she said. "Bob, I called a lawyer."

"What?"

"I said, I called a lawyer."

"What is that supposed to mean?"

"It means I think we ought to separate."

Certain moments, you just feel your chest turning to ice. It just freezes solid on you. You have trouble breathing. You swallow, there's no air, then there's no saliva in your mouth. Your ears hammer, your head aches, blood rushes through your veins, pumping crazily. You're that close to losing it. It had never happened to him when the shit was flying in the air and people were dying all around him, but it happened now.

"Why?" he finally said.

"Bob, we can't live like this. It's one thing to say we love each other, we have a family, we take care of each other. It's another when you go off every so often and I hear rumors that people are dead and you won't talk about it. It's another when you're so angry all the time you won't talk or touch me or support me and you snap at me all the time. I can just make so many excuses to our daughter. But then the next thing, the worst thing, the war comes into our house and I'm shot with a bullet and my daughter sees a man die before her very eyes. And then you go off again. I love you, Lord, I love you, but I cannot have my daughter going through that again."

"I'm—I'm very sorry, Julie. I didn't see how hard this was on you."

"It's not just the violence. It's that you somehow *love* it so. It's that it's always in you. I can see it in your eyes, the way you're always searching the terrain, the way you're never quite relaxed, the way there's always a loaded gun close at hand, the way you drive me out. You're not a sniper anymore; that was years ago. But you're still over there. I can't compete with the war in Vietnam; you love her more than us."

Bob breathed heavily.

"Please, don't do this to me. I can't lose you and Nikki. I don't have anything else. You're all I value in this world."

"Not true. You value yourself and what you became. Secretly, you're so happy to be Bob the Nailer, different from all men, better than all men, loved and respected or at least feared by all men. It's like a drug addiction. I feel that in you, and the angrier you get and the older you get, the worse it becomes."

He could think of nothing to say.

"Please don't do this to me."

"We should be apart."

"Please. I can't lose you. I can't lose my daughter. I'll do what you want. I'll go with you to the mountains. I can change. I can become the man you want. You watch me! I can do it. Please."

"Bob, I've made up my mind. I've been thinking about this for a long time. You need space, I need space. The shooting business just makes it more important. I have to get away from you and get my own life, and get away from the war."

"It's not the war."

"It *is* the war. It cost me the boy I loved and now it's cost me the man I loved. It cannot take my daughter. I've thought all this through. I'm filing for separation. After I recover, I'm returning to Pima County and my family. We can work out financial details. It doesn't have to be bad or ugly. You can always see Nikki, any time, unless you're off at war or in the middle of a gunfight. But I just can't have this. I'm sorry it didn't work out any better, but there you have it."

"I'll go. Just promise me you'll think it over. Don't do anything stupid or sudden. I'll take care of this business—"

"Don't you see? I can't have you taking care of this business and getting yourself killed. I can't lose someone else. It almost killed me the first time. You think you had it hard in your traction and your VA hospital? Well, I *never* came back. There isn't a day I don't wake up and not remember what it felt like when the doorbell rang and it was Donny's brother, and he looked like hell and I knew what was happening. It took me ten, maybe twenty years to get over that and I only just barely did."

He felt utterly defeated. He could think of nothing to say.

"I'll go now," he said. "You need to rest. I'll say good-bye to Nikki. I'll check on you, stay in contact. That's okay, isn't it?"

"Yes, of course."

"You be careful."

"We'll be all right."

"When this is all over, you'll see. I'll fix it. I can do that. I can fix myself, change myself. I know it."

"Bob—"

"I know I can."

He bent and kissed her.

"Bob—"

"What?"

"You wanted to ask me what was wrong with you. Why you couldn't figure something out?"

"Yes."

"I'll tell you why. It's because of the great male failing of your age. Vanity. You're publicly modest but privately insanely proud. You think everything is about you, and that blinds you to what is going on in the world. That's your weakness. You have to attack your problem without ego and vanity. Approach it objectively. Put yourself out of it."

"I—"

"It's the truth. I've never told you that, but it's the truth. Your anger, your violence, your bravery; it's all part of the same thing. Your pride. Pride goeth before the fall. You cannot survive unless you see through your pride. All right?"

"All right," he said, and turned to leave.

Here I am, right back where I started from, he thought.

The room was shabby, a motel on the outskirts of Boise, not a chain but one of those older, forties places on a road that had long since been surpassed by other, brighter highways.

I am slipping, he thought. I am losing everything.

The room smelled of dust and mildew. Every surface was slightly warped wood, the bathroom was only nominally clean, the lightbulbs were low-wattage and pale.

I drank a lot of bourbon in rooms like this, he thought.

He was here on more or less sound principles. The first was that by this time, whoever had been trying to kill him surely realized he had missed and was back on the hunt again. Therefore the ranch house, with its clothes, its life, was out. He knew that place and to go there was to get yourself killed, this time for real, with no poor old Dade Fellows to stop the bullet.

So, after doubling back and crossing his own tracks a dozen times, and setting up look-sees for followers and finally satisfying himself nobody was onto him yet, he was here. Paid cash, too. No more credit cards, because whoever this bird was working for, he might have a way of tracking credit cards. No more phone calls except from public phones.

What he needed now was a gun and cash, like any man on the run. The cash he knew he could get. He had $16,000 left from a libel case the late Sam Vincent had won for him years ago, and he'd moved it from a cache in Arkansas to a cache here in Idaho. If he was clear again tomorrow, he would get it.

A gun was another problem. He felt naked without one, and the gun laws here in Idaho weren't troubling yet, but there was still that goddamn seven-day wait by national law. He could head back to his property, where his .45 Commander was stored away, but did he really want to carry it on a daily basis? Suppose he had to take an airline or wandered into a bank with a metal detector? Sometimes it was more trouble than it was worth. Besides, how could he shoot it out against a sniper with a 7mm Remington Magnum with a .45? If the white sniper found him, it was over, that was all.

Bob sat back, turning the TV on by remote, discovering to his surprise that it worked. The news came on.

Bob paid no attention. It was just white noise.

His head ached. He held a bottle in his hands, between his legs as he lay on the bed, on a thin chintz bedspread. Jim Beam, $9.95 at the Boise Lik-r-mart, recently purchased. There were water spots on the ceiling; the room stank of ancient woe, of raped girlfriends and beaten wives and hustled salesmen. Cobwebs fogged the corners; the toilet had a slightly unwholesome odor to it, like heads he'd pissed in the world over.

I am losing it, he thought.

He tried to press his brain against the riddle again.

He felt if he could get that, he would have something.

Why, all those years ago, did Solaratov use an M1 rifle, a much less accurate semiauto? It appeared to be one of those mysteries that had no solution. Or, even worse, the answer was mundane, stupid, boring: he couldn't get a bolt gun, so he settled for the most accurate American rifle available, an M1D Sniper. Yes, that made perfect sense but . . .

. . . but if he could get an M1D, he could get a Model 70T or a Remington 700!

It don't make no goddamn sense!

It doesn't have to make sense, he told himself. Not everything does. Some things just can't be explained; they happen in a certain way because that's the way of the world.

Bob looked at the bottle again, his fingers stole to the cap and the plastic seal that kept the amber fluid and its multiple mercies from his lips, and yearned to crack it and drink. But he didn't.

Won't never touch my lips again, he remembered telling someone.

Liar. Lying bastard. Talking big, not living up to it.

He tried to lose himself in what was on the tube. The news, some talking head from Russia. Oh, yeah, it sounded familiar. Big elections coming up, everybody all scared because some joker who represented the old ways was in the lead and would carry the day, and the Cold War would start up all over again. The guy was this Evgeny Pashin, handsome big guy, powerful presence. Bob looked at him.

Thought we won that war, he said to himself.

Thought that was one we did okay in, and now here's this guy and he's going to take over and restore Russia and all the missiles go back into the silos and it's the same old crock of shit.

Man, there was no good news anywhere, was there?

He was feeling powerfully maudlin. He yearned for his old life: his wife, his lay-up barn, the sick animals he was so good at caring for, his perfect baby daughter, enough money. Man, had it knocked.

It all was taken away from him.

He turned the TV off and the room was quiet. But only for a moment. A couple of units down, somebody was yelling at somebody. Somewhere outside, a kid was crying. Other TVs vibrated through the walls. Traffic hummed along. Looking out the window he saw the buzz of neon, blurry and mashed together, from fast food joints and bars and liquor stores across the way.

Man, I hate to be alone anymore, he thought.

That's why Solaratov will get me. He likes *being alone. I* lived *alone for years, I* fought *alone. But I lost whatever edge I had.*

I want my family. I want my daughter.

The lyrics of some old rock and roll song sounded in his ears, moist, rich, poignant.

Black is black, he heard the music, *I want my baby back.*

Yeah, well, you ain't going to get her back. You're just going to sit here until that fucking Russian hunts you down and blows you away.

Ceiling, discolored. Cobwebs, mildew, the sound of other people's grief over the traffic and me stuck by myself with no goddamn way in hell to figure out what I got to figure out.

You think everything is about you and that blinds you to the world, his wife had told him.

Yeah, as if she would know. She really never did get him, he thought bitterly.

His hand involuntarily cranked on the bottle top and he heard it crack as the seal broke. He opened the bottle, looked down into the open muzzle. He knew a form of doom lay behind that muzzle. It was like looking down the barrel of a loaded rifle, the incredible temptation it had to some weak and deranged people, because to look down it was to look straight into death's own eye. So it was with the bottle for an ex-drunk. Look into it, take what it has to offer and you are gone. You are history.

He yearned for the strength to throw it out but knew he didn't have it. He raised the bottle to his lips, wise with the knowledge that he was about to die, and brought the bottle—

You think everything is about you.

Bob stopped. He considered something so fundamental he'd not seen it before, but suddenly it seemed as big as a mountain: his assumption that Solaratov came to Vietnam to kill him and had returned to Idaho to kill him.

But suppose it wasn't about him?

What could it be about, then?

He tried to think.

The sniper had a semiauto.

He could fire twice, fast.

He had to take them both to make sure of hitting one.

But suppose I wasn't the one he had to hit.

Well, who else was there?

Only Donny.

Could it be about . . . Donny?

CHAPTER THIRTY-FIVE

He awoke early, without a hangover, because he had not been drunk. He looked at his watch and saw that it was eight here, which meant it was eleven in the East.

He picked up the phone, then called Henderson Hall, United States Marine Corps Headquarters, Arlington, Virginia. He asked to be connected to the Command Sergeant Major of the Corps, got an office and a young buck sergeant, and eventually got through to the great man himself, with whom he'd served a tour in Vietnam in sixty-five and run into a few odd, friendly times over the years.

"Bob Lee, you son of a bitch."

"Howdy, Vern. They ain't kicked you out yet?"

"Tried many a time. It's them pictures I got of a general and his goat."

"Those'll git a man a long way."

"In Washington, they'll git you all the way."

The two old sergeants laughed.

"So anyhow, Bob Lee, what you got cooking? You ain't written a book yet?"

"Not yet. Maybe one of these years. Look, I need a favor. You're the only man that could do it."

"So? Name it."

"I'm flying to DC this afternoon. I need to look at some paperwork. It would be the service jacket of my spotter, a kid that got killed in May 1972."

"What was his name?"

"Fenn, Donny. Lance corporal, formerly corporal. I have to see what happened to him over his career."

"What for? What're you looking for?"

"Hell, I don't know. I got something to check out involving him. What it is, I don't know. It's come up, though."

"Didn't you end up marrying his widow?"

"I did, yeah. A terrific lady. We're sort of on the outs now."

"Well, I hope you get it straightened out. This may take me a day or so. Or maybe not. I can probably get it, if not from here, from our archives, out in Virginia."

"Real fine, Sergeant Major. I appreciate it much."

"You call me when you get in."

"I will."

Bob hung up, hesitated, thought about the booze he did not drink and then dialed the Boise General Hospital and eventually was connected to his wife's room.

"Hi," he said. "It's me. How are you? Did I wake you?"

"No, no. I'm fine. Sally took Nikki to school. There's nobody around. How are you?"

"Oh, fine. I wish you'd reconsider."

"I can't."

He was silent for a while.

"All right," he finally said, "just think about it."

"All right."

"Now I have something else to ask."

"What?"

"I need your help. This last little thing. Just a question or two. Something you would know that I don't."

"What?"

"It's about Donny."

"Oh, God, Bob."

"I think this may have something to do with Donny. I'm not sure, it's just a possibility. I have to check it out."

"Please. You know how I hate to go back there. I'm over that now. It took a long time."

"It's a nothing question. A Marine question, that's all."

"Bob."

"Please."

She sighed and said nothing.

"Why was he sent to Vietnam? He had less than thirteen months to serve. But he had just lost his rating. He was a full corporal and he showed up in 'Nam just a lance corporal. So he had to be sent there for punitive reasons. They did that in those days."

"It *was* punitive."

"I thought it was. But that doesn't sound like Donny."

"I only caught bits and pieces of it. I was only there at the end. It was some crisis. They wanted him to spy on some other Marines who they thought were slipping information to the peace marchers. There was this big screwup at a demonstration, a girl got killed, it was a mess. He was ordered to spy on these other boys and he got to know them, but in the end, he wouldn't. He refused. They told him they'd ship him to Vietnam, and he said, Go ahead, ship me to Vietnam. So they did. Then he met you, became a hero and got killed on his last day. You didn't know that?"

"I knew there was something. I just didn't know what."

"Is that a help?"

"Yes, it is. Do you know who sent him?"

"No. Or if I did, I forgot. It was so long ago."

"Okay. I'm going back to DC."

"What? Bob—"

"I'll only be gone a few days. I'm flying out there. I've got to find out what happened to Donny. You listen to Sally; you be careful. I'll call you in a few days."

"Oh, Bob—"

"I've got some money, some cash. Don't worry."

"Don't get in trouble."

"I'm not getting in any trouble. I promise. I'll call you soon."

There it was: WES PAC.

He remembered the first time he had seen it, that magic, frightening phrase, when the orders came through for that first tour in 1965: WES PAC. Western Pacific, which was Marine for Vietnam. He remembered sitting outside the company office at Camp Lejeune, North Carolina, and thinking, Oh, brother, I am in the shit.

"That's it," said the sergeant major's aide.

"That's it," said Bob.

He sat in the anteroom in Henderson Hall, with the tall, thin young man with hair so short it hardly existed and movements so crisp they seemed freshly dry-cleaned.

"We got it this morning from Naval Records Storage Facility, Annandale. Sergeant Major used lots of smoke. He served with the CO's chief petty officer on the old Iowa City."

"You'll tell him I appreciate it."

"Yes, sir. I'm sniper-rated, by the way. Great school, out at Quantico. They still talk about you. Understand you fought a hell of a fight at Kham Duc."

"Long time ago, son. I can hardly remember it."

"I heard of it a hundred times," said the young sergeant. "I won't ever forget it."

"Well, son, that's kind of you."

"I'll be in my office next door. You let me know if you need anything else."

"Thank you, son."

The jacket was thick, all that remained of FENN, DONNY J.'s almost, but not quite four years in the Marine Corps. It was full of various orders, records of his first tour in the Nam with a line unit, his Bronze Star citation, his Silver Star nomination for Kham Duc, travel vouchers, shot records, medical reports, evaluations going back to Parris Island in the far-off land of 1968 when he enlisted, GCT results, the paper trail any military career, good, bad or indifferent, inevitably accumulates over the passage of time. There was even a copy of the Death in Battle report, filled out by the long-dead Captain Feamster, who only survived Donny a few weeks until the sappers took out Dodge City. But this one sheet, now faded and fragile, was the one that mattered; this was the one that sent him to the Nam.

HEADQUARTERS, USMC, 1C-MLT: 111
1320.1
15 MAY 1971

SPECIAL ORDER: TRANSFER

NUMBER 1640–71
REF: (A) CMC LTR DFB1/1 13 MAY 70
    (B) MCO 1050.8F

1. IN ACCORDANCE WITH REFERENCE (A), EFFECTIVE 22 AUGUST 70, THE PERSONNEL LISTED ON THE REVERSE HEREOF ARE TRANSFERRED FROM THIS COMMAND TO WES PAC (III MAF) FOR DUTIES SPECIFIED BY CO WES PAC (III MAF).

2. PRIOR TO TRANSFER, THE COMMANDING OFFICER WILL ASSIGN AS PRIMARY THE MOS SHOWN FOR EACH INDIVIDUAL IN ACCORDANCE WITH THE AUTHORITY CONTAINED IN EXISTING REGULATIONS.

3. TRAVEL VIA GOVERNMENT PROCURED TRANSPORTATION IS DIRECTED FOR ALL TRAVEL PERFORMED BETWEEN THIS COMMAND AND WES PAC (III MAF) IN ACCORDANCE WITH PARAGRAPH 4100, JOINT TRAVEL REGULATIONS.

4. EACH INDIVIDUAL LISTED ON THE REVERSE HEREOF IS DIRECTED TO REPORT TO THE DISBURSING OFFICER WITHIN THREE WORKING DAYS AFTER COMPLETION OF TRAVEL INVOLVED IN THE EXECUTION OF THESE ORDERS FOR AN AUDIT OF REFUNDS.

It was signed OF Peatross, Major General, U.S. Marine Corps, Commanding, and below that bore the simple designation DIST: 'N' (and WNY, TEMPO C, RM 4598).

Bob had received just such a document three times, and three times he'd come back from it, at least breathing. Not Donny: it got him a name inscription on a long black wall with bunches of other boys who'd much rather have been working in factories or playing golf than inscribed on a long black wall.

Bob turned it over, not to find the usual computerized list of lucky names but only one: FENN, DONNY, J., L/ CPL 264 38 85 037 36 68 01 0311, COMPANY B, MARINE BARRACKS WASHINGTON DC MOS 0311.

The rest of the copy was junk, citations of applicable regulations, travel information, a list of required items all neatly checked off (SRB, HEALTH RECORD, DENTAL RECORD, ORIG ORDERS, ID CARD and so on), and the last, melancholy list of destinations on the travel subvoucher, from Norton AFB in California to Kadena AFB on Okinawa to Camp Hansen on Okinawa and on to Camp Schwab before final deployment to WES PAC (III MAF), meaning Western Pacific, III Marine Amphibious Force. Donny's own penmanship, known so well to Bob from their months together, seemed to scream of familiarity as he looked at it.

Now what? he thought. What's this supposed to mean?

He tried to remember his own documents and scanned this one for deviations. But his memory had faded over the years and nothing seemed at all different or strange. It was just orders to the Land of Bad Things; thousands and thousands of Marines had gotten them between 1965 and 1972.

There seemed to be nothing: no taint of scandal, no hint of punitive action, nothing at all. In Donny's evals, particularly those filed in his company at the Marine Barracks, there were no indications of difficulty. In fact, those recordings were uniformly brilliant in content, suggesting an exemplary young man. A SSGT Ray Case had observed, as late as March 1971, "Cpl. Fenn shows outstanding professional dedication to his duties and is well-respected by personnel both above and below him in the ranks. He performs his duties with thoroughness, enthusiasm and great enterprise. It is hoped that the Corporal will consider making the Marine Corps a career; he is outstanding officer material."

Bob knew the secret language of these things: where praise is the standard vocabulary, Case's belief in Donny clearly went beyond that into the eloquent.

Even Donny's loss of rating order, which demoted him from corporal to lance corporal, dated 12 May 71, was empty of information. It carried no meaning whatsoever: it simply stated the fact that a reduction in rank had occurred. It was signed by his commanding officer, M. C. Dogwood, Captain, USMC.

No Article 15s, no Captain's Masts, nothing in the record suggesting any disciplinary problems.

Whatever had happened to him, it had left no records at all.

He stood up and went to the door of the sergeant major's aide.

"Is there a personnel specialist around? I'd like to run something by him."

"I can get Mr. Ross. He worked personnel for six years before coming to headquarters."

"That'd be great."

In time the warrant officer arrived, and he too knew of Bob and treated him like a movie star. But he scanned the documents and could find nothing at all unusual except—

"Now this is strange, Gunny."

"Yes, sir?"

"Can't say I ever saw it before."

"And what is that, Mr. Ross?"

"Well, sir, on this last order, the one that sent Fenn to Vietnam. See here"—he pointed—"it says 'DIST: "N." ' "

That means, distribution to normal sources, i.e. the duty jacket, the new duty station, Pentagon personnel, MDW personnel and so forth, the usual grinding wheels of our great bureaucracy in action."

"Yes, sir."

"But what I see here is odd. In parentheses '(and WNY TEMPO C, RM 4598).'"

"What would that mean?"

"Well, I'd guess Washington Naval Yard, Temporary Building C, Room 4598."

"What's that?"

"I don't know. I was twelve in 1971."

"Any idea how I could find out?"

"Well, the only sure way is to go to the Pentagon, get an authorization, and try and dig up a Washington Naval Personnel logbook or phone book or at least an MDW phone book from the year 1971. They might have one over there. Then you'd just have to go through it entry by entry—it would take hours—until you came across that designation."

"Oh, brother," said Bob.

The next night, Bob drove his rented car out to a pleasant suburban house in the suburbs of America and there had dinner with his old pal the Command Sergeant Major of the United States Marine Corps, his wife and three of his four sons.

The sergeant major grilled steaks out on the patio while the two younger boys swam in the pool and the sergeant major's wife, Marge, threw together a salad, some South Carolina recipe for baked beans and stewed tomatoes. She was an old campaigner herself and Bob had met her twice before, at a reception after he had been awarded the Distinguished Service Cross for Kham Duc— 1976, four years after the incident itself, a year after he finally left the physical therapy program and the year he decided he could no longer cut it as a Marine—and the next year, when he did retire.

"How's Suzy?" she asked, and Bob remembered that she and his first wife had had something of an acquaintanceship; at that point, he'd been higher in rank than the man who was hosting him.

"Oh, we don't talk too much. You heard, I went through some bad times, had a drinking problem. She left me, and was smart to do it. She's married to a Cadillac dealer now. I hope she's happy."

"I actually ran into her last year," Marge said. "She seemed fine. She asked after you. You've had an adventurous few years."

"I seem to have a knack for trouble."

"Bob, you won't get Vern's career in any trouble? He retires this year after thirty-five years. I'd hate to see anything happen."

"No, ma'am. I'll be leaving very shortly. My time here is done, I think."

They had a nice dinner and Bob tried to hide the melancholy that seeped into him; here was the life he would have had if he hadn't gotten hit, if Donny hadn't gotten killed, if it all hadn't gone so sour on him. He yearned now for a drink, a soothing blur of bourbon to blunt the edge he felt, and he recalled a dozen times on active duty when he and this man or a man just like this man had spent the night recalling sergeants and officers and squids and ships and battles the world over, and enjoying immensely their lives in the place where they'd been born hard-wired to spend it, the United States Marine Corps.

But that was gone now. Face it, he thought. It's gone, it's finished, it's over.

That night they went to a baseball game, Legion Ball, where the youngest boy, a scholarship athlete at the University of Virginia, got three hits while giving up only two as pitcher over the game's seven innings. Again: a wonderful America, the best America—the suburbs on a spring evening, the weather warm, the night hazy, baseball, family and beer.

"Do you miss your wife?" asked the sergeant major's wife.

"I do, a lot. I miss my daughter."

"Tell me about her."

"Oh," said Bob, "she's a rider. She's a great horse-woman. Her mother has her riding English in case she decides to come east for college."

And off he went, for twenty uncontrollable minutes, missing his daughter and his wife and the whole thing even more. *Black is black,* he thought, *I want my baby back.*

The game was over and in triumph everybody went back to the sergeant major's house. Beer was opened, though Bob had Coke; some other senior NCOs came over and Bob knew a few, and all had heard of him. It was a good time; cigars came out, the men moved outside, the night was lovely and unthreatening. Then finally a young man showed up, trim, about thirty, with hard eyes and a crew cut, in slacks and a polo shirt. Bob understood that he was the sergeant major's oldest boy, a major at Quantico, in the training command, back recently from a rough year in Bosnia and before that an even nastier one in the desert.

Bob was introduced and they chatted and once again he encountered a young man who loved him. What good did it do if his own family didn't? But it was nice, all the same, and eventually the talk turned to his own day. He'd spent it in the DOD library in the Pentagon, where the sergeant major's pass had got him admitted, going painfully through old phone books, trying to find out what this office was.

"Any luck?" asked the sergeant major.

"Yeah, finally. Room 4598 in Tempo C in the Washington Navy Yard, it was the location of an office of the Naval Investigative Service."

"Those squid bastards," said the Command Sergeant Major.

"At least now I've got a name to go on," Bob said.

"The CO was some lieutenant commander named Bonson. W. S. Bonson. I wonder what became of him."

"Bonson?" said the gunny's son. *"Ward* Bonson?"

"I guess," said Bob.

"Well," said the young officer, "he shouldn't be too hard to find. I served a tour with the Defense Intelligence Agency in ninety-one. He was in and out of that shop."

"You knew him?"

"I was just a staff officer," he said. "He wouldn't notice or remember me."

"Who is he?" asked Bob.

"He's now the deputy director of the Central Intelligence Agency."

CHAPTER THIRTY-SIX

He watched through binoculars as the car, a black Ford sedan, arrived at 6:30 A.M. and picked up the occupant of 1455 Briarwood, Reston, Virginia. Bob followed at a distance. The lone passenger sat in the back, reading the morning papers as the car wound its way through the nearly empty streets. It progressed toward the Beltway, then followed that road north, toward Maryland; at the George Washington Parkway it surged off, westward, until it reached Langley, and then took that otherwise unremarkable exit. Bob languished back, then broke contact as the car disappeared down the unmarked road that led to the large installation that was unnamed from the road but which he knew to be the headquarters of the Central Intelligence Agency.

Instead, he drove back to Reston and relocated the house. He parked on the next court over—it was in a prosperous unit of connected townhouses—and slid low into the seat. It took almost two hours before he figured the pattern. There were two security vehicles, one a black Chevy Nova and the other a Ford Econoline van. Each had two men in them, and one or the other showed up every forty minutes, pausing on the street in front of the house and on the street in back. At that point, one of the men walked around back, bent in the weeds and checked something, presumably some sort of trembler switch that indicated if any kind of entry had been made.

Bob marked the address and drove to the nearest convenience store. There, he called the fire department and reported a fire in the house two down on the court. By the time he got back, three trucks had arrived, men were stomping in bushes, two cop cars with flashing light bars had set up perimeter security—it was a carnival. When the black Nova arrived, an agent got out, showed credentials, conferred with the police and firemen, then went to Bonson's door, unlocked it and went in to check the house and secure it. He went around back to reset the trembler switch.

Bob went, found a place for lunch, then came back and parked a court down the line. He checked his watch to make certain neither of the patrol vehicles was expected, then walked back to Bonson's house, where he knocked on the door. No answer came and, after a bit, he used his credit card to pop the door and slipped inside.

An alarm immediately began to whine. He knew he had sixty seconds to defuse it. The sound of the device enabled Bob to find it in ten seconds, which left fifty. Without giving it a lot of thought, Bob pressed 1-4-7 and nothing happened. The alarm still shrilled. He then hit 1-3-7-9 and the alarm ceased. How had he known? Not that difficult: most people don't bother with learning numbers; they learn patterns that can easily be found in the dark, or when they are tired or drunk, and 1-4-7, the left-hand side of the nine-unit keypad, is the simplest and the most obvious; 1-3-7-9, the four corners, is the second most obvious. He waited a bit, then slipped out the back and found the trembler switch attached to an electric junction outside the house. It blinked red to indicate entry. With his Case knife, he popped the red plastic cone off the bulb, unscrewed the bulb, then squeezed and compressed the red cone to get it back on. Covering his tracks in the loam, he reentered the house. Soon enough the CIA security team rechecked the house on their rounds, but when the agent got out to check the trembler indicator, he did not get close enough to note the jimmied bulb. He was tired. He'd been through a lot. He returned to the truck.

Like his codes, Bonson's home was plain. The furniture was spare but luxurious, mostly Scandinavian and leather, but it was not the home of a man whose pleasures included pleasure. It was banal, expensive, almost featureless. One room was a designated office, with a computer terminal, awards and photos on the wall that could have been of any business executive except that they showed a furiously intense individual who could not broadcast ease for a camera but always seemed angry or at least focused. He was usually pictured among other such men, some of them famous in Washington circles. His house was clean, almost spotless. A University of New Hampshire bachelor's and a Yale law degree hung on the wall. Nothing indicated the presence of hobbies except, possibly, a slightly fussy fondness for gourmet cooking and wines in the kitchen. But it was the house of a man consumed by mission, by his role in life, by the game he played and dominated. No wife, no children, no relatives, no objects of sentimentality or nostalgia; seemingly no past and no future; instead, simplicity, efficiency, a one-pointed existence.

Bob poked about. There were no secrets to be had, nothing that could not be abandoned. The closet was full of blue suits, white shirts and red striped ties. The shoes were all black, Brooks Brothers, five eyelets. He appeared to have no casual wear, no blue jeans, no baseball caps or sunglasses or fishing rods, no guns, no porno collections, no fondness for show tunes or electric trains or comic books. There were huge numbers of books—contemporary politics, history, political science, but no fiction or poetry. There was no meaningful art in the home, nothing soiled, nothing that spoke of uncertainty, irrationality or passion.

Bob sat and waited. The hours clicked by, then the day itself. It turned to night. It got later. Finally, at 11:30 P.M., the door opened and the lights came on. Bob heard a man hanging up his raincoat, closing the closet. He walked into the living room, took off his suit coat, loosened a tie and unbuttoned his collar. He had his mail, which included some bills and the new issue of *Foreign Policy*. He turned on a CD stereo player, and light classical oozed out of the speakers. He mixed himself a drink, went to the big chair and sat down. Then he saw Bob.

"W-who are you? What is this?"

"You're Bonson, right?"

"Who the hell are you!" Bonson said, rising.

Bob rose more pugnaciously, pushed him back into the chair, hard, asserting physical authority and the willingness to do much harm fast and well. Bonson's eyes flashed fearfully on him, and read him for what he was: a determined, focused man well-versed in violence. He recognized instantly that he was overmatched. He got quiet quickly.

Bob saw a trim fifty-seven-year-old man of medium height with thinning hair slicked back and shrewd eyes. The suit pants and shirt he wore fit him perfectly and everything about him seemed unexceptional except for the glitter in his eyes, which suggested he was thinking rapidly.

"The false alarm; yeah, I should have figured. Do you want money?"

"Do I look like a thief?"

"Who are you? What are you doing here?"

"You and I have business."

"Are you an agent? Is this something over a vetting or an internal security report or a career difficulty? There are channels and procedures. You *cannot* do yourself any good at all with this kind of behavior. It is no longer tolerated. The days of the cowboys are over. If you have a professional problem, it must be dealt with professionally."

"I don't work for your outfit. At least not for thirty years or so."

"Who are you?" Bonson said, his eyes narrowing suspiciously as he tried to click back to his file on thirty years ago.

"Swagger. Marine Corps. I done some work for y'all up near Cambodia, sixty-seven."

"I was in college in 1967."

"I ain't here about 1967. I'm here about 1971. By that time, you was a squid lieutenant commander, in NIS.

Your specialty was finding bad boy Marines and having them shipped to the 'Nam if they didn't do what you said. I asked some questions. I know what you did."

"That was a long time ago. I have nothing to apologize for. I did what was necessary."

"One of those boys was named Donny Fenn. You had him shipped from Eighth and I to 'Nam, even though he was under his thirteen. He served with me. He died with me on the day before DEROS."

"Jesus Christ—*Swagger!* The sniper. Oh, now I get it. Oh, Christ, you're here for some absurd revenge thing? I sent Fenn to 'Nam, he got killed, it's my fault? That is probably how your mind works! What about the North Vietnamese; don't they have something to do with it? Oh, please. Don't make me laugh. Another cowboy! You guys just don't get it, do you?"

"This ain't about me."

"What do you want?"

"I have to know what happened back then. What happened to Donny. What was that thing all about? What did he know?"

"What are you talking about?"

"I think the Russians *tried* to kill him. I think it was him they were targeting, not me."

"Ridiculous."

"There was no Russian involvement?"

"That's classified. High top-secret. You have no need to know."

"I'll decide what's ridiculous. I'll decide what I need to know. You talk, Bonson, or this'll be a long evening for you."

"Jesus Christ," said Bonson.

"Finish your drink and talk."

Bonson took a swallow.

"How did you find me?"

"I shook your Social Security number out of your service records. With a Social Security number you can find anybody."

"All right. You could have made an appointment. I'm in the book."

"I prefer to talk on my terms, not yours."

Bonson rose, poured himself another bourbon.

"Drink, Sergeant?"

"Not for me."

"Fair enough."

He sat down.

"All right, there was Russian involvement. Tertiary, but definite. But Fenn could not have known a thing. He knew nothing that would make him valuable enough for the Russians to target. I went over that case, over and over it. Believe me, he could not have known a thing."

"Tell me the fucking story. I'll decide what it means."

"All right, Swagger, I'll tell you. But understand I am only doing so under what appears to be threat of physical duress, because you have threatened me. Second, I prefer to tape this conversation and the terms under which it took place. Is that fair?"

"It's already being taped, Bonson. I saw your setup."

"You don't miss much. You'd make a good field man, I can tell."

"Get to the fucking story."

"Fenn. Big handsome kid, good Marine, from Utah, was it?"

"Arizona."

"Yes, Arizona. Too bad he got hit, but a lot of people got hit over there."

"Tell me about it," said Bob.

Bonson took a drink of his bourbon, sat back, almost relaxing. A little smile came across his face.

"Fenn was nothing. We were after someone much bigger. If Fenn had played his part, we might have gotten him, too. But Fenn was a hero. I never counted on that. It didn't seem there were any heroes left at that time. It seemed it was a time where every man looked after his own ass. But not Fenn. God, he was a stubborn bastard! He really ripped me a new asshole. I could have had him up on charges for insubordination! He might have spent the next ten years in Portsmouth instead of—well, instead."

Bob leaned forward.

"You don't say nothing about Donny. I won't listen to any lip on Donny."

"Oh, I see. We can't tell the truth, we just worship the dead. You won't learn anything that way, Sergeant."

"Go on, goddammit. You are pissing me off."

"Fenn. Yes, I used Fenn."

"How?"

"We had a bad apple named Crowe. Crowe, we knew, had contacts within the peace movement, through a young man named Trig Carter, a kind of Mick Jagger type, very popular, connected, highly thought of."

The name sounded familiar.

"Trig was bisexual. He had sex with boys. Not always, not frequently, but occasionally, late at night, after drinks or drugs. The FBI had a good workup on him. I needed someone who fit the pattern. He liked the strong, farmboy type, the football hero, blond, Western. That's why I picked Fenn."

"Jesus Christ."

"It worked, too. Fenn started hanging out with Crowe and in a few nights, Carter had glommed onto him. He was an artist, by the way, Carter."

Bob remembered a far-off moment when Donny showed him a drawing of himself and Julie on heavy paper. It was just after they got Solaratov, or so they thought. But maybe not. It all ran together. But he remembered how the picture thrummed with life. There was some lust in it, as Bonson suggested. It was so long ago.

"Carter had a very brilliant mind, one of those fancy, well-born boys who sees through everything," Bonson continued. "But he was just another run-of-the-mill amateur revolutionary, if I recall, until 1970 and 1971, when he burned out on the protests and took a year in England.

Oxford. That's where we think it happened. Why not? Classical spy-hunting ground."

"What are you talking about?"

"We believed that the peace movement had been penetrated by Soviet Intelligence. We had a code intercept that suggested they were active at Oxford. We even knew he was an Irishman. Except he wasn't an Irishman. He only played one on TV."

He smiled at his little joke.

"We think this guy was sent to Oxford to recruit Trig Carter. Not recruit; it wasn't done that crudely. No, it would have been subtler. Whoever he was, he was straight Soviet professional, one of their very best. Smart, tough, funny, a natural gift for languages, the nerves of a burglar. He was the Lawrence of Arabia of the Soviet Union. Man, he would have been a prize! Oh, Lord, he would have been a prize!"

"You never got him?"

"No. No, he got away. We never got a name on him or anything. We don't know what his objective was. We don't know what the operation was all about. It was my call; I fucked up. We had him somewhere in the DC area. But we never quite got him. Fenn was supposed to give us Crowe, who'd give us Carter, who'd give us the Russian. Classic domino theory! A Soviet agent working the peace movement beat! God, what a thing that would have been! That would have been the goddamed white buffalo."

"How did he get away?"

"We lost time with Fenn; the case against Crowe wouldn't stand. We lost a day, we never nabbed Trig. We almost had him at a farm in Germantown, but by the time we found it, there was nobody there. We missed him at his mother's outside Baltimore; she wouldn't tell us a thing. He was gone, disappeared. The next thing—"

"Trig was killed. I remember Donny mentioning it. He was killed in a bomb blast."

"Under the math lab at the University of Wisconsin.

Yes, he was. And we never found hide nor hair of anybody else. Whoever he was, he got away clean."

"If he existed."

"I still believe he existed."

"What a waste!"

"Yes, and some poor graduate student working late on algorhythms got wasted too. Two dead."

"Three dead. Donny."

"Donny. I didn't send him to 'Nam to die, Swagger. I sent him to 'Nam because it was my duty. We were fighting a clever, subtle, brilliant enemy. We had to enforce discipline in our troops. You were an NCO; you know the responsibility. My war was much subtler, much harder, much more stressful."

"You don't look like you done so bad."

"Well, it ruined my Navy career. I was passed over. I read the writing on the wall, went to law school. I was a corporate lawyer on my way to a partnership and high six figures. But the agency took an interest in me and decided it had to have me, and so in 1979, I took an offer. I haven't looked back since. I'm still fighting the war, Swagger. I've lost a few more Donny Fenns along the way, but that's the price you pay. You're out of it, I'm still in it."

"All right, Bonson."

"What is this all about?"

"We always heard the man who made the shot on me—on us—was a Russian."

"So? They had advisers over there in all the branches. Nothing remarkable."

"It was said this guy flew in special. Your own people were involved, because they wanted the rifle he had, an SVD Dragunov. We didn't have one until then."

"I suppose. That's not my area. I can check records. What does this have to do with *today*?"

"Okay, so four days ago, someone makes a great shot on an old cowboy in Idaho. Blows him so far out of the saddle hardly nothing left. Seven hundred-odd meters, crosswind. He wings a woman with him."

"So?"

"So," Bob said, "the woman was my wife. The old man should have been me. Luckily, it wasn't. But . . . he was trying for me. I examined the shooting site. I don't know much, but I know shooting, and I'll tell you this Johnny was world-class and he employed Soviet shooting doctrine, which I recognize. Maybe it's not, but it sure seems like the same guy is on my track now as was on it then."

Bonson listened carefully, his eyes narrowing.

"What do you make of this?" he said.

"Donny *knew* something. Or they thought he did. Same difference. So they have to take him out. They think the war will do it, but he's a good Marine and it looks like he's going to come out all right. So they *have* to take him. They send in this special man, mount this special operation—"

"Weren't you some kind of hero? Weren't you especially targeted?"

"I can only think what I done in Kham Duc alerted them to Donny's whereabouts. It made good cover, too. The Russians wouldn't care a shit about how many NVA some hillbilly dusted in a war that was already won. We always thought they requested the sniper; no, now I think the Russians *insisted* on the sniper."

"Hmmm," said Bonson. "That's very interesting."

"Then a little while ago, I got famous."

"Yes, I know."

"I thought you might."

"Go on."

"I get famous and they get to worrying. Whatever it was he knew, maybe he would have told me. So . . . they have to get me. It's that simple."

"Hmmm," said Bonson again. His face seemed to re-assemble itself into a different configuration. His eyes narrowed and focused on something far away as behind them, his mind whirred through possibilities. Then he looked back to Swagger.

"And you don't know what it is?"

"No idea. Nothing."

"Hmmmmm," said Bonson again.

"But what I don't get—there is no more Soviet Union. There is no more KGB. They're gone, they're finished. So what the fuck does it matter now? I mean, the regime that tried to kill me and did kill Donny, it's gone."

Bonson nodded.

"Well," he finally said, "the truth is, we really don't know what's going on in Russia. But don't think the old Soviet KGB apparatus has just gone away. It's still there, calling itself Russian now instead of Soviet, and still representing a state with twenty-thousand nuclear weapons and the delivery systems to blow the world to hell and gone. What is going on is a political tussle over who makes the decisions—the old-line Soviets, the secret communists? Or a new nationalist party, called PAMYAT, run by a guy named Evgeny Pashin. There's an election coming, by the way."

"So I heard."

"That election will have a lot to do with whose Russia it will be in the next twenty-five years and what happens to those twenty-thousand nukes—and to us. It's very complicated, rather dangerous, and it's not at all improbable that there's some kind of Russian interest in this business you've spoken of."

Bob's eyes narrowed as he considered this.

"You're thinking. I can tell. What do you intend to do? That is, if I don't swear out charges for breaking and entering?"

"You won't," said Bob. "Well, to find out what happened to Donny, I guess I have to find out what happened to Trig. I guess I'll follow that trail. I have to solve this if I have any chance of nailing this guy who's hunting me. If I keep moving, keep him away from my family, it may work out."

"This is very interesting to me, Swagger. I want to follow up on this. I can get you people. A team. Backup, shooters, security people. The best."

"No. I work alone. I'm the sniper."

"Look, Swagger, I'm going to give you a phone number. If you get in trouble, if you learn something, if you get in a jam with the law, if anything happens, you call that phone and the person will say 'Duty Officer' and you say, ah, think up a code word."

"Sierra-Bravo-Four."

"Sierra-Bravo-Four. You say 'Sierra-Bravo-Four' and you will get my attention immediately and you will be stunned at what I can do for you and how fast. All right?"

"Fair enough."

"Swagger, it's too bad about Fenn. The game can be rough."

Bob didn't say anything.

"Now go on, get out of here."

"I should beat the shit out of you for what you did to Donny. He was too good to use that way."

"I did my job. I was a professional. That's all there is to it. And if you ever do strike me, I will use the full authority of the law to punish you. You don't have the right to go around hitting people. But if you do, Swagger, remember: not the face. Never the face. I have meetings."

CHAPTER THIRTY-SEVEN

Bob wondered what it would be like to be born in a house like this one. It was not really in Baltimore, but north of Baltimore, out in what they called the Valley, good horse country, full of rolling hills, well packed with lush green vegetation, and marked with fine old houses that spoke not merely of wealth but of generations of wealth.

But no houses as fine as this house. It was at the end of a road, which was at the end of another road, which was at the end of still another road. It had a dark roof and many complexities, and was red brick swaddled in vine, with all the trim white, freshly painted. Beyond it lay acres of rolling paradise, mostly apple orchards; but the house itself, tall and dignified and a century old, could have been another form of paradise. The oak trees surrounding it threw down a network of shadows. A cul-de-sac announced a final destination outside it, and off to the right were formal gardens, now somewhat overgrown.

Bob parked the rented Chevy, adjusted the knot on his tie and walked to the door. He knocked. After a while the door opened and a black face, ancient as slavery, peeked out.

"Yes, sir?"

"Sir, I am here to talk to Mrs. Carter. I spoke to her on the phone. She invited me out."

"Mr. Stagger?"

"Swagger."

"Yes, come in."

He stepped into the last century, hushed, now threadbare. It smelled of mildew and old tapestries, a museum without a sign in front of it or a guidebook. He was escorted through silent corridors and empty rooms with elegant, dusty furniture and under the haunted gaze of illustrious predecessors until he reached the sunroom, where the old lady sat in a wicker chair, looking out fiercely on her estate. Beyond, from this vantage, the windows displayed a view of a formal garden and a long, sloping path down through the apple trees.

"Mrs. Carter, ma'am?"

The old woman looked up and gave him a quick, bright once-over, then gestured him to the wicker sofa. She was about seventy, her skin very dark with too much Florida tan, her eyes very penetrating. Her hair was a ducktail of iron gray. She wore slacks and a sweater and had a drink in her hand.

"Mr. Swagger. Now, you wish to talk about my son. I have invited you here. Your explanation of why you wanted this discussion was frankly rather vaporous. But you sounded determined. Do you care about my son?"

"Well, ma'am, yes, I do. About what happened to him."

"Are you a writer, Mr. Swagger? He has been mentioned in several dreadful books and even got a whole chapter in one of them. Awful stuff. I hope you are not a writer."

"No, ma'am, I'm not. I have read those books."

"You look like a police officer. Are you a police officer or a private detective? Is this some paternity suit? Some snotty twenty-five-year-old now says Trig was his father and he wants the bucks? Well, let me tell you, those bucks aren't going to anybody except the American Heart Association, Mr. Swagger, so you can forget that idea right now."

"No, ma'am. I'm not here about money."

"You're a soldier, then. I can see it in your bearing."

"I was a Marine for many years, yes, ma'am. We would never say soldier. We were Marines."

"My husband—Trig's father—fought with Merrill in Burma. The Marauders, they called them. It was very rigorous. His health broke; he saw and did terrible things. It was very unpleasant."

"Wars are unpleasant things, ma'am."

"Yes, I know. I take it you fought in the one my only son gave up his idiotic life to end?"

"Yes, ma'am, I was there."

"Were you in the actual fighting?"

"Yes, ma'am."

"Were you a hero?"

"No, ma'am."

"I'm sure you're merely being modest. So why *are* you here, if you're not writing a book?"

"Your son's death is somehow tied up with something that hasn't yet been answered. It's also tied up, I think, with the death of that young man I mentioned earlier, another Marine. I just have a glimmer of it; I don't get it yet. I was hoping you could tell me what you knew, that maybe in that way there could be some understanding."

"You said on the phone you didn't think my son killed himself. You think he was murdered."

"Yes."

"Why?"

"I don't yet know."

"Do you have any evidence?"

"Circumstantial. There seems to be some level of intelligence involvement in this situation. He may have seen something or someone. But it seems clear to me that there were spooks involved."

"So my son wasn't a moron who blew himself up for nothing except the piety of the left and the sniggering contempt of the right?"

"That would be my theory, yes, ma'am."

"What would be more of your theory? Where is this heading?"

"Possibly he was used as a dupe. Possibly he was murdered, his body left in the ruins to make it look like it was a protest thing. His body would make that almost certain."

She looked hard at him.

"You're not a crank, are you? You look sensible, but

you're not some awful man with a radio show or a news-letter or a conspiracy theory?"

"No, ma'am."

"And if you do come to understand this, what would you do with that understanding?"

"Use it to stay alive. A man is trying to kill me. I think he's also a spook. If I'm to stop him, I have to figure out why he's after me."

"It sounds very dangerous and romantic."

"It's a pretty crappy way to live."

"Well, if you went into most houses in America and laid out that story, you'd be dismissed in a second. But my husband spent twenty-eight years in the diplomatic corps, and I knew spooks, Mr. Swagger. They were malicious little people who were capable of anything to advance their own ends. Theirs, ours, anyone's. So I know what spooks do. And if the spooks of the world killed my son, then the world should know that."

"Yes, ma'am," said Bob.

"Michael," she called, "tell Amanda Mr. Swagger is staying for lunch. I will show him around the house and then afterwards he and I will have a long talk. If anybody comes looking to kill him, please tell the gentleman we are not to be disturbed."

"Yes, ma'am," said the butler.

"It is exactly as it was," she said, "on that last day."

He looked around. The studio had been built out back, in what had once been servants' quarters. The house was small, but its walls had been ripped out, leaving one huge raw room with red brick walls, a gigantic window that looked down across the orchards. It still smelled of oil paint and turpentine. Dirty brushes stood in old paint cans on a bench; the floor was spotted with paint drops and dust. Three or four canvases lay against the wall, evidently finished; one more was still on the easel.

"The FBI went through this, I guess?" Bob asked.

"They did, rather offhandedly. I mean, after all, he was dead by that time."

"Yes, ma'am."

"Come look at this one. It's his last. It's very interesting."

She took Bob to a painting clamped rigidly on an easel.

"Rather trite," she said. "Yet I suppose it was the correct project for him to express his anxieties."

It was, unbelievably, a bald eagle, with the classic white head, brown, majestic body stout with power, anchored to a tree limb by clenching talons. Bob looked at it, trying to see what was so different, so alive, so painful. Then he had it: this wasn't a symbol at all, but a bird, a living creature. It had obviously just survived some ordeal, and the gleam in its eyes wasn't the predator's gleam, the winner's smug beam of superiority, but the survivor's dazed, traumatic shock. It was called the thousand-yard-stare in the Corps, the look that stole into the eyes after the last frontal had been repulsed with bayonets and entrenching tools. Bob saw that the talons which gripped this tree branch were dark with blood and that the bird's feathers, low on its stout body, were spotted with blood. He bent closer, looked more carefully. It was amazing how subtly Trig got all the components: the slight sense of the blood spots being heavier, moist against the fluff of the other feathers.

He looked at the bird's single visible eye: it seemed haunted by horrors unforgotten, its iris an incredibly detailed mix of smaller color pigments that were different in color yet formed a whole, a living whole. Bob could sense the muscles twitching under its netting of feathers, and the breath coming heavily to it after much exertion.

"That boy was in one hell of a fight," he said.

"Yes, he was."

"Did he work from models? It ain't like no eagle I ever saw. You'd have to be out in the wild and just seen the bird after it got out of a mix-up to get that look."

"Or, possibly, see it in a man's face, and project it onto a bird's. But he'd been out West. He'd been all over, doing his paintings. He'd been all over the world, to Harvard, in a war, in every major peace demonstration, on committees, and the illustrator of a best-selling book by the time he was twenty-five."

"Is he using the eagle as his country?"

"I don't know. Possibly. I suspect that such a bird would be less alive, more rigid. This bird is too alive to be symbolic. Maybe it's his own revulsion for bloodshed he's displaying. I don't see much heroic about that bird; I see a shaken survivor. But I don't think you can know too much from it."

"Yes, ma'am," said Bob.

"For some reason, he *had* to finish this painting. Or finish the bird. He showed up late, in a pickup truck. He was dirty and sweaty. I asked him what he was doing? He said, 'Mother, don't worry, I can handle it.' I asked him what he was doing here. He said he had to finish the bird.

"Then he came out here and he painted for seven straight hours. I had seen the preliminary sketches. It was different, conventional. Good, but nothing inspired. On that last night, this is the one place he had to go, the one thing he had to do."

"Can you tell me about him? Was he different after he got back from England? What was going on with him, ma'am?"

"Did something happen to him? Is that what you're asking?"

"Yes, ma'am. The intelligence officer I spoke to about all this said that the security services monitoring him believed he'd changed in England."

"They kept a watch on all the bad boys, didn't they?"

"They sure tried."

They walked outside, where a few more rustic pieces of furniture languished. She sat.

"He was burnt out by seventy. He'd been marching since sixty-five. I think like all the young people then, it was more of a party than a crusade. Sex, drugs, all that. What young people do. What we would have done in the forties if we hadn't had a war to win. But by seventy, I had never seen him so low. All the marching, the jail sentences, the times he was beaten up, the people he'd seen used up: it seemed to do no good. There was still a war, boys were still getting killed, they were still using napalm. He was traveling, also painting; he had a place in Washington, he was everywhere. He spent four months in jail in 1968 and was indicted two more times. He was very heroic, in his way, and if you believed in his cause. But it wore him out. And there was the problem with Jack. That is, his father, who was forced by circumstance and perhaps inclination to accept the government's view of the war. His father was still in the State Department and was, I suppose, actively engaged in planning some aspect of the war. Jack and Trig had been so close once, but by the end of the sixties they weren't even talking. He once said to me, 'I never thought that decent, kind man who raised me would turn out to be evil by every value I hold dear, but that's what has happened.' Rather a cruel judgment, I thought, for Jack had always loved and supported Trig, and I think he felt Trig's alienation more painfully than anyone. I do know that Trig's death ultimately killed Jack, too. He died three years later. He never really recovered. He was a casualty of that war, too, I suppose. It was such a cruel war, wasn't it?"

"Yes, ma'am. You were telling me about 1970. Trig goes to England."

"Yes, I was, wasn't I? 'I need to get out of here,' he said. 'I have to get away from it.' He took a year at the Ruskin School of Fine Art at Oxford. Do you know Oxford, Mr. Swagger?"

"No, ma'am," said Bob.

"He really was a wonderful artist. I think it had more to do with his decision just to get out, though, than with any particular artistic need."

"Yes, ma'am."

"Well, somehow, for some reason, it worked. He came back more excited, more dedicated, more passionate and more compassionate than I'd seen him since 1965. This was the early winter of 1971. He had evidently made some personal discoveries of a profound nature over there. He met some kind of mentor. I believe the name was Fitzpatrick, some charismatic Irishman. The two of them were going to end the war, somehow. It was so uncharacteristic of Trig, who was so cautious, so Harvard. But whatever this Fitzpatrick had sold him on, it somehow transfigured Trig. He came back obsessed with ending the war, but also obsessed with pacifism. He had never formally been a pacifist before, though he was never an aggressive or a brutal young man. But now he formally believed in pacifism. I felt he was on the verge of something, possibly something great, possibly something tragic. I felt he was capable of dousing himself with gasoline on the Pentagon steps and setting himself aflame. He was dangerously close to martyrdom. We were very worried."

"Yet he was planning something else. He obviously was planning the bombing."

"Mr. Swagger, let me tell you what has haunted me all these years. My son was incapable of taking a human life. He simply would not do it. How he ended up dynamiting a building with a man inside it is beyond my capacity to understand. I understand that it was meant to be a 'symbolic act of defiance,' against property and not against flesh. Yet another man was killed. Ralph Goldstein, a young mathematics teaching assistant, a name largely lost to history, I'm afraid. You see it in none of the books about my son's martyrdom, but I got a wretched note from his wife, and so I know it. I know it by heart. He was another wonderful young man, I'm sorry to report. But Trig would not have killed anyone, not even by accident. The accounts that portray him as a naive idiot are simply wrong. Trig was an extremely capable young man. He would not have blown himself up and he would not have blown up the building without checking the building. He was very thorough, very Harvard in that way. He was competent, completely competent, not one of those dreamy idiots."

Bob nodded.

"Fitzpatrick," he said, then over again. "Fitzpatrick. There's not a record, a photo of Fitzpatrick, anything solid."

"No . . . not even in the sketchbook."

"I see," said Bob.

It took several seconds before he made the next connection.

"Which sketchbook?" he asked.

"Why, Trig was an artist, Mr. Swagger. He had a sketchbook with him always. It was a kind of visual diary. He kept one everywhere. He kept one at Oxford. He kept one here, during his last days. I still have it."

Bob nodded.

"Has anybody seen it?"

"No."

"Mrs. Carter, could—"

"Of course," the old lady said. "I've been waiting all these years for someone to look at it."

CHAPTER THIRTY-EIGHT

The thing was dirty. Thick and motheaten, it had the softness of old parchment, but also of filth: the lead of pencil and the dust of charcoal lay thick on every page. To touch it was to come away with stained fingertips. That gave it an air of tremendous intimacy: the last will and testament or, worse, a reliquary of Saint Trig the Martyr. Bob felt somehow blasphemed as he peered into it, pausing to mark the dates on the upper right hand of the cover: "Oxford, 1970—T. C. Carter III."

But it had this other thing. It was familiar. Why was it familiar? He looked at the creamy stock and realized that it was in this book Trig had drawn his picture of Donny and Julie, then ripped it out to give to Donny. Bob had seen it in Vietnam. The strange sense of a ghost chilled him.

He turned the first pages. Birds. The boy had drawn birds originally. The first several pages were lovely, lively with English sparrows, rooks, small, undistinguished flyers, nothing with plumage or glory to it. But you could tell he had the gift. He could make a single spidery line sing, he could capture the blur of flight or the patience of a tiny, instinct-driven brain sedate in its fragile skull as the creature merely perched, conceiving no yesterday or tomorrow. He caught the ordinariness of birds quite extraordinarily.

But soon his horizons expanded, as if he were awaking from a long sleep. He began to notice things. The drawings became extremely casual little blots of density where out of nothing Trig would suddenly decide to record "View from the loo," and do an exquisite little picture of the alley out back of his digs, the dilapidated brickiness of it, the far, lofty towers of the university in the distance; or, "Mr. Jenson, seen in a pub," and Mr. Jenson would throb to life, with veins and carbuncles and a hairy forest in his nose. Or: "Thames, at the point, the boathouses," and there it would be, the broad river, green in suggestion, the smaller river branching off, the incredible greenness of it all, the willows weeping into the water, the high, bright English sun suffusing the whole scene, although it was a miniature in black pencil, dashed off in a second. Still, Bob could feel it, taste it, whatever, even if he didn't quite know what it was.

Trig was losing himself in the legendary beauty of Oxford in the spring. Who could blame him? He drew lanes, parks, buildings that looked like old castles, pubs, rivers, English fields, as if he were tasting the world for the first time.

But then it all went away. The vacation was over. At first Bob squinted. He could not understand as he turned to the new page; the images had a near abstraction to them, but then they gradually emerged from the fury of the passion-smeared charcoal. It was the girl, the child, reduced to shape, running out of the flames of her village, which had just been splashed in American fire. Bob remembered seeing it: the war's most famous, most searing image, the child naked and exposed to the fierce world, her face a mask of shock and numbness yet achingly alive. She was shamelessly naked, but modesty meant nothing, for one could see the cottage-cheesey streaks where the napalm had burned her, as it had incinerated her family behind her. Even a man whose life has been saved by napalm had a sickening response to that image: Why? he wondered now, all the years later. Why? She was just a child. We didn't fight it right, that was our goddamn problem.

He put the book down, looked off into the long darkness. The black dogs were outside now, ready to pounce. He needed a drink. His head hurt. His throat was dry. Around him, in the empty studio, the birds danced and perched. The eagle fixed him with its panicked glare.

When will this shit be over? he wondered and went back to the sketchbook.

Trig too had had some kind of powerful emotional reaction. He'd given himself over to flesh. The next few pages were husky boys, working-class studs, their muscles taut, their butts prominent, their fingers naturally curled inward by the density of their forearms. There was even one drawing of a large, uncircumsized penis.

Bob felt humiliated, intrusive, awkward. He couldn't concentrate on the drawings and rushed forward, skipping several pages. At last the season of sex was over; the images changed to something more noble. Trig seemed stricken with admiration for a certain heroic figure, a lone man sculling on the river. He drew him obsessively for a period of weeks: an older man, Herculean in his passions, his muscles agleam but in a nonsexual way, just an older athlete, a charisma merchant.

Was this Fitzpatrick, or some other lost love? Who would know, who could tell? There wasn't even a portrait of the face by which the man could be recognized. But the pictures had somehow lost their originality, become standard. The hero had arrived, from a Western, or out of the Knights of the Round Table, or something. Bob could feel the force of Trig's belief in this man.

The drawings went on, as the weeks passed, and as Trig's excitement mounted. He was actually happy now, happier than he'd been. The explosion became a new motif in his doodling; it took him but a few tries, and suddenly he got quite good at capturing the violence, the sheer liberation of anarchistic energy a blast unleashed, and its beauty, the way the clouds unfurled from the detonation's center like the opening of a flower. But that was all: there was no horror in his work, no fear that any man who's been around an explosion feels. It was all theory and beauty to Trig.

The final drawing was of a shiny new TR-6.

Bob closed the book and held it up to the light and saw a kind of gap running along the spine of the book suggesting that something was missing. He reopened it and looked carefully and saw that, very carefully, the last few pages had been sliced out.

He left the studio and walked back to the big house, where the old lady nursed a scotch in the study.

"Would you care for a drink, Mr. Swagger?"

"A soda. Nothing else."

"Oh, I see."

She poured him the soda.

"Well, Sergeant Swagger. What do you think?"

"He was a wonderful artist," Bob said. "Can't ask for more, can you?"

"No, you can't. I made a mistake just then, didn't I?"

"Yes, ma'am."

"I called you sergeant. You never told me your rank."

"No, ma'am."

"I still know a fool or two in State. After you called me, I called a man. Just before you arrived, he called back. You were a hero. You were a great warrior. You were everything that my son could never understand."

"I did my job, somehow."

"No, you did more than your job. I heard about it. You stopped a battalion. One man. They say it may never have been done in history, what you did. Amazing."

"There was another Marine there. Everybody forgets that. I couldn't have done it without him. It was his fight as much as mine."

"Still, it was your aggressiveness, your bravery, your willingness to kill, to take on the mantel of the killer for your country. Is it difficult to live with?"

"I killed a boy that day with a knife. Now and then I think of that with sorrow."

"I'm so sorry. Your heroism aside, nothing good came of that war, did it?"

"My heroism included, nothing good came of that war."

"So tell me; why did my son die? You of all men might know."

"I'm no expert in these matters. It ain't my department. But it looks to me like he was picked up by a pro. Someone who knew his weaknesses, had studied him, who knew of his troubles with his father and played on them. He's in the drawings as a heroic rower. I can feel Trig's love for him. He may be this Fitzpatrick. Trig was *different*, you said. When he came back?"

"Yes. Excited, committed, energetic. Troubled."

"He had to finish that painting?"

"Yes. Is there a message in the painting?"

"I don't know. I don't understand it either."

"But you think he was innocent of murder? That would be so important to me."

"Innocent of first-degree murder, yes, I do. The death of that man may have been unintended. If so, it would have been second-degree murder, or some form of manslaughter. I won't lie to you. He may be guilty of that."

"I appreciate the honesty. Trig will have to face his own consequences. But at least someone believes he wasn't a murderer and an idiot."

"I don't know what was really going on yet. I can't figure what it was about, why it happened, what the point was. It seemed to have no point, not then, not now, and what's happening to me would then have no point. Maybe I'm completely wrong about all this and am just off on a wild goose chase, because I'm under a lot of pressure. But tell me . . . are you aware that the last few pages in the sketchbook are missing? The American pages?"

"No. I had no idea."

"Do you have any idea where they might be?"

"No."

"Is it possible they're here?"

"You're free to look. But if they were here, I think I would have found them."

"Possibly. Did he have a place, a favorite spot around here?"

"He loved to bird-watch at a spot in Harford County.

Out near Havre de Grace, overlooking the Susquehanna. I could show you on a map. For some reason that was a spot especially alive with birds, even the occasional Baltimore oriole."

"Could you show me on the map?"

"Yes. Do you think the pages are there?"

"I think I'd better look, that's all I know."

Bob drove through the failing light across Baltimore County, then north up I-95 until he passed into Harford County and turned off on a road that led him to Havre de Grace, a little town on the great river that eventually formed the Chesapeake Bay.

He didn't know what he was looking for, but there was always a chance. If Trig ripped those sketches out, he probably wanted to destroy them. But there was just a shred of the other possibility: that he learned something that scared him, that he saw something he didn't understand, that he had begun to see through Robert Fitzpatrick. He was frightened, he didn't know what to do. He came here to paint; because of some passionate psychological, stress-induced oddness or other, he had to finish the painting of a bird. He did, then he decided to remove the late sketches and hide them. He could have hid them anywhere, sure—but his mind worked a certain way, it was organized, pure, concise, it dealt frontally with problems and came up with frontal solutions. So: hide the sketches. Hide them in a place away from the house, for surely investigators will come to the house. Hide them where I will never forget and where someone tracking me sympathetically could find them. Yes, my "spot." My place. Where I go to relax, to chill, to cool down, to watch the birds gliding in and out across the flat, silent water. It made a species of sense: he could have driven to this upcoming spot, wrapped the sketches in plastic or screwed them into a jar, hid them somehow, buried them, planted them under a rock, in a cave.

Trig, after all, had traveled the wilderness on his birding quests. He'd been to South America, to Africa, all across the remote parts of the United States, its deserts, its mountains. So he knew field craft; he was adroit in the out-of-doors, not some helpless idiot. His mother even said so: he was *competent,* he got things done, he handled them.

So what am I looking for?

A mark, a possible triangulation of marks, something. Bob tried to think it through, and reminded himself that such a sign, if it had been cut into the bark of a tree, say, would have been distorted horizontally in twenty-odd years' growth. It would be wide, not high, as trees grow from the top.

He drove for a time along the river's edge. It was a huge flat pan of water here, though back beyond the town the land rose to form bluffs and he could see huge bridges spanning them. A train crossed one, an orange bullet headed toward New York. Beyond that was a superhighway.

At last he came to the site Trig's mother had designated on the map, and he knew immediately he would have no luck. He saw not geese and ducks but golden arches, and where a glade by the river had once been, uniquely attractive to birds the region over, now a McDonald's stood. A clown waved at him from behind the bright bands of glass that marked the restaurant. He was hungry, he parked, walked around a few minutes, and realized it was hopeless. That site was forever gone, and whatever secrets it may or may not have concealed, they had been plowed under in the process of making the world safe for beef.

He went in, had a couple of burgers and an order of fries and a Coke, then went back to his car to begin the long drive to his motel room near the airport, during which time he hoped to settle the puzzlement of his next move.

It was here that he noticed the same black Pathfinder

that had preceded him up I-95. But it peeled off, to be replaced by a Chevy Nova, teal and rusty, and then, three exits down, when it disappeared, by a FedEx truck.

He was being followed, full-press, by a damned good team.

CHAPTER THIRTY-NINE

Bonson financed the operation out of a black fund he and three other senior executives had access to, because he didn't want it going through regular departmental vetting procedures, not until he knew where it was leading and what it might uncover. He operated this way frequently, it was always better to begin low-profile and let the thing develop slowly, undistored by the pressures of expectation.

He picked his team with great care too, drawing on a tempo manpower pool of extremely experienced people who were kept on retainer for just such ad hoc, high-deniability missions. He ended up with three ex-FBI agents, two former state policemen, a former Baltimore policewoman and a surprisingly good surveillance expert cashiered by the Internal Revenue Service.

"Okay," he told them in the safe house in Rosslyn, Virginia, the agency maintained as a staging area for emergency ops, "don't kid yourself. This guy is very, very experienced. He has been in gunfights and battles his whole life. He operated as a recon team leader for SOG for a long year up near and inside Cambodia in sixty-seven. He was an immensely heroic sniper who may be the only man in history to have stopped a battalion by himself, in seventy-two. If you look at the dossier I've distributed, you see that he's been involved in dust-ups ever since then: some business in New Orleans in ninety-two and then, two years ago, he spent some time in his hometown in Arkansas and the state death-by-shooting rate skyrocketed. This is a very, very salty, competent individual. He is strictly at the top of the pyramid.

"So let me repeat: your job is to monitor him, to report his activities, to tap into his discoveries, but that is all. I want this understood. This is not an apprehension; it's no kind of wet work. Is that clear?"

The team nodded, but there were questions.

"Commander, do you want his lines tapped?"

Bonson hesitated. That would be helpful. But it was illegal without a court order and you never knew how these things would end up playing out. His career was his most important possession.

"No. Nothing illegal. This isn't the old days."

"We might be able to make a nice acoustic penetration on him in the old lady's place."

"If you can get that, fine. If not, that's okay, too."

"If he burns us, do we disengage?"

"No, you go to backups. That's why I want six cars, not the usual four. You stay in radio contact. I'll be monitoring in the control van. Each hour I'm going to broadcast a frequency change, to cut down on the possibility of him countermonitoring us."

The team understood immediately how unusual this was. Under normal circumstances, no executive at Bonson's level would serve as case officer on an operation. It was like a brigadier general taking over a platoon.

"Are we armed?"

"No, you are not armed. If you should unexpectedly encounter him, if he should make you and turn you out, you go into immediate deniability. You deny everything; you all have fake IDs. If you have to, you go to jail without compromising operational security. I do not want him knowing he's being watched."

Notes were taken, procedures written down. Bonson discussed call signs, probable routes he'd take to the old woman's house north of Baltimore, that sort of thing. But then—

"One last thing: this man claims he is also being hunted by a former Russian sniper. I tend to believe him, though his record would incline him toward paranoia. But we have to take the sniper as a real, not an imaginary threat. So let's assume that sniper has no idea where he is and thinks he's still in Idaho. But he's an enormously resourceful man. If the Russian is farther ahead of the game than I have even begun to suspect, and you encounter him, you fall back and contact me immediately and, if no other option exists, you may have to move aggressively. You may have to risk your lives to save Swagger, in that eventuality."

"Jesus Christ."

"Swagger knows something. Or he has the power to figure it out. He's a key, somehow, to something very deep and troubling. He cannot be lost. He still has work to do for his country. He doesn't know it yet, but he's still got a mission."

"Commander, could you tell us what this is about?"

"The past. Old men's dreams, young men's deaths. The spy that never was but is again. Ladies and gentlemen, we're on a mole hunt. We're after the one that got away."

In Boise, Solaratov's first move was to call the hospital, asking to speak to Mrs. Swagger. Mrs. Swagger had checked out of the hospital two days earlier. Where had she gone and in whose care had she been left? The hospital operator wasn't permitted to release such information. What was her doctor's name? Again, no answer.

Late that afternoon, Solaratov parked his rented car in a national park that provided access to the Sawtooth National Forest, and, outfitted as any hiker, began the seventeen-mile trek along the ridgeline that ultimately left national property and deposited him nine hundred yards above Swagger's ranch house. He set up a good spotting position, well hidden from casual hikers, of whom there were likely to be none, and equally invisible from the meadows and pastures that stretched beneath him. He settled in to wait.

He waited two full days. The house was absolutely

empty. Even the livestock had been sent elsewhere. In the middle of the second night, he came down off the ridge and penetrated, using a lock pick to spring the locks. Then, making certain the shades were drawn, he explored the house using a powerful flashlight for six hours, a thorough, professional examination as he sought some clue as to where the Swagger family had gone to cover. But on the first pass, the house yielded nothing. The Swaggers had vanished.

The home was orderly, jammed with books on the subject of war, very clean. The little girl's room was the messiest, but only by a small margin. The living room was messy too, but it was a superficial mess, a one-day job, not the accrual of weeks of untidiness, and he could see where someone had spent a long night on the sofa. He found an empty bottle of bourbon in the garbage under the sink.

One ordinary hunting rifle, a Model 70 in .308, more a useful tool in this part of the country. A lightly customized .45 Colt Commander. No precision rifles. Swagger had seemed to leave that behind him. There was a study, where someone had done a lot of reading, but that was about all. He looked for family account books or financial files, in hopes that such would yield another possibility, but again, he found nothing.

It appeared to be hopeless. He was wondering what to do next. He went outdoors, carefully locking the door behind him, and went over to the garbage cans by the side of the house, still in the cart by which they would be hauled to the road twice a week. He opened one can and found it empty, but the second produced a last green plastic bag, knotted with yellow plastic ribbon at the top; it hadn't been picked up or even set out. Perhaps the garbage contract had been cancelled when the family decamped.

He took the bag to the barn, sliced it open with his Spyderco, and went through the materials very carefully. Not much: old yogurt cups, the bones of steaks and chops and chickens eaten carefully, used paper towels, tin cans, an ice cream package, very sticky, coffee grounds, the usual detritus. But then: something crinkled, a yellow Post-It tab. Very carefully he unrolled it and saw what it revealed.

"Sally M.," it said. "American 1435, 9:40 A.M."

Chapter Forty

Bob took his time driving back from the McDonald's, letting his baby-sitters enjoy their presumed advantage over him. He went back to his motel room just outside the airport, called Mrs. Carter and told her that he hadn't found anything at the site but that he had some other ideas to pursue and he would certainly keep her informed.

He went out, got some dinner and caught a movie at a suburban mall, a stupid thing about commandos who fired and never missed and who took fire and never got hit, just to eat up the time. When he got out of the film it was 2300, which meant in London it was 0600 tomorrow. That was fine. Instead of returning immediately to his car, he walked around the strip mall until he found a pay phone, well aware that at least two cars of watchers were in the lot, eyeballing him.

Using his phone card, he placed an overseas call to the American embassy in London, getting a night-shift receptionist; he asked to be transferred to the embassy Marine guard detachment, was passed on to the duty NCO and asked for the NCOIC, Master Sergeant Mallory, who should be up and about, and in a few seconds Mallory came to the line.

"Mallory, sir."

"Jack, you remember your old platoon sarge, Bob Lee Swagger?"

"Jesus Christ, Bob Lee Swagger, you son of a bitch! I ain't spoke to you in thirty years, since I medevaced out of the 'Nam. How the hell are you, Gunny? You done some great things in your third tour."

"Well, I am okay, still kicking around on a pension, no bad problems."

"Now what in hell is this all about? You bringing a

missus to London and want a place to stay? I got an apartment and you can camp there all you want."

"No, Jack, it ain't that. It's an S-2 thing."

"You name it and it's yours."

"It's not a big thing, a little favor."

"Fire when ready, Gunny."

"Now, I'm thinking that with your embassy security responsibilities, you have probably made contact with folks in the British security apparatus."

"I deal with Scotland Yard and the two MI's all the goddamn time. We got two officers over here, but, shit, you know officers."

"Do I ever. So, anyhow, you got a good NCO-type in Six or Five you know?"

"Jim Bryant, used to be a color sergeant in SAS. He now handles embassy coordination in security for MI-6. I meet with him all the goddamn time, especially when we have people coming in that present security problems."

"Good, counted on that. Now, here's the thing. In 1970, a guy named Fitzpatrick operated in Great Britain, but I think he was a Russian agent, or a Russian-hired agent. I don't know who the hell he was or what he did or what became of him, but it would be goddamned helpful for me to find out. Could you run that by your pal and see what shakes out? Their intel people would have the shit on him if anybody did."

"Gunny, what's this all about?"

"Old business. Very old business that's come around and is biting me in the ass."

"Okay, I'll give it a run. If it's in there and it ain't real top-secret or whatever, Jim Bryant can nose it out for me. I'll get back to you soonest. What's your time frame?"

"Well, I'm about to sack out now. It's getting close to midnight over here."

"I'll give Jim a call and get to him as soon as possible. You got a number?"

"Let me call you. What's a good time?"

"Call me at 1800 hours my time. That would be, what, 1100 yours?"

"That's it."

"Get me direct at 04-331-22-09. Right to my office; don't go through the embassy switchboard."

"Good man."

"You got me on that chopper, Gunny. Wouldn't be here if you hadn't. I owe you this one."

"Now we're even, Jack."

"Out here."

"Out," said Bob.

He went back to his car and drove to the motel. His room had been expertly tossed and everything replaced neatly, including the cap on his toothpaste tube. But they'd been here, he could tell. They were watching him.

He undressed, showered and turned the lights out. It would be more comfortable in here than out there.

He went to breakfast at a Denny's the next morning, went for a little walk, watching the campers struggle to stay unseen, and precisely at 1100, put his long-distance call through to London.

"Mallory here."

"Jack."

"Howdy, Gunny."

"Any luck?"

"Well, yes and no."

"Shoot."

"This Fitzpatrick is more rumor or innuendo than actual operator. The Brits know he operated here around that time, but that info came late, from decoded radio intercepts after he'd gone on to his next duty station, wherever the hell that was. But there was no way of covering him through their regular ways of watching, which means he didn't operate out of an embassy or a known cell."

"Is that strange?"

"As in, very strange."

"Ummmm," said Bob.

"So they have no photos. Nobody knows what he looks like. Nobody really knows who he was, whether he was a recruited Irishman or a native-born Russian citizen. They do say that when the Russians go abroad, they tend more than not to impersonate Irishmen, because there's a correspondence between the accents. In other words, a Russian can't play an Englishman in England or an American in America, but they've got a good record of playing an Irishman in England or America. The Russian phonetic *ah* sound is very similar in tongue placement to the *ae* of the classic Irish accent."

"So they think he's Russian?"

"Ah, they can't say for sure. That seems to be the best possible interpretation. The file has been dead for nearly fifteen years. Poor Jim had to drive all the way out to a records depository to even find the goddamn thing."

"I see."

"They only have some radio transmissions and some defector debriefings."

"What would they be?"

"Ah, a guy came over in seventy-eight and then another came over in eighty-one, both low-level KGB operatives, in political trouble, afraid they were going to get an all-expenses-paid TDY to the gulags. They gave up everything they had: a funny thing, you know, the Russians are all worried about confusing issues so they 'register' work names, code names, the like; they got so many agencies, they want to make sure nobody uses the name and things get all fouled up. The work name 'Robert Fitzpatrick' was one item in the registry that both these guys gave up. But here's the odd part."

"Okay."

"According to these guys, to both of 'em, he wasn't in the First Directorate. That's the KGB section that specializes in foreign operations, recruitments, penetrations, that sort of thing."

"The straight-up spies."

"Yeah, you know, hiring informants, getting pictures, running networks, working out of embassies, that sort of thing. The usual KGB deal."

"So what was he?"

"According to these clerks, the work name 'Robert Fitzpatrick' was the property of GRU."

"And what was that?"

"GRU is Russian military intelligence."

"Hmmm," said Bob again, unsure what this information could possibly mean. "He was army?" he finally asked.

"Well, yes and no. I asked Jim too. It seems GRU was uniquely tasked with penetration of strategic targets. That is, missiles, nuke delivery systems, satellite shit, that whole shebang. All the big atomic spies, like the Rosenbergs, like Klaus Fuchs, all them guys—they were GRU. This guy Fitzpatrick would be interested—I mean, if he existed, if he was Russian, if this, if that—he'd be doing something that was global, not local. He'd be trying to get inside our missile complexes, bomb plants, research facilities, the satellite program, anti-missile research."

"Shit," said Bob, seeing the thing just twist out of his control. "Man, I don't know crap about that and I'm much too old to learn."

"Plus you got your other problem; the Soviet Union broke up, all these guys went who-knows-where. Some are still working for Russian GRU, some are working for KGB or other competing organizations with different agendas, some for the Russian mafia, some for all these little republics. If it was hard to understand then, it don't make no sense now."

"Yeah. Anything else?"

"Gunny, that's it. It ain't much. A possible name, a suggestion of possible affiliation. Man, that's all they got."

"Christ," said Bob. He searched his memory for anything that he had learned about Trig that touched on any issue of strategic warfare, but came up blank. It was all Vietnam, the war, that sort of thing.

"Sorry I wasn't any help."

"Jack, you were great. I'm much obliged."

"Talk to you."

"Out here."

"Out."

Bob put the phone down, more confused than ever. He felt everything was now hopelessly twisted out of his slender ability to grasp it. The "strategic" business had him buffaloed. Where the hell did *that* come from? What did it mean?

He called Trig's mother and got her right away.

"Have you learned anything, Sergeant Swagger?"

"Well, maybe. It turns out the fellow's name is Robert Fitzpatrick. The rower."

"Yes. The Irishman."

"Yeah, him. The British think he was a Russian agent, but not the sort that would be interested in the peace movement or anything like that. They think his mission would have been nuclear warfare, missiles, that sort of thing. Is there anything in Trig's life that would touch on that?"

"Good heavens, no. I mean, I assume the conventional peace movement wisdom on strategic warfare was simply 'Let's ban the bomb and everything will be peachy,' but it wasn't an issue, not at all. They were fighting to stop the war that was going on, the war they saw on television, the war that threatened *them*."

"Your husband was in the State Department. Did he have any connection with any of this?"

"Not at all. He was in the counselor service. We served in a number of embassies abroad representing American interests but never had a thing to do with the missiles or that sort of thing. He finished up his career managing an economic research project."

"A brother, a sister?"

"My brother is the famous Yale ornithologist; two of Jack's are dead, one a doctor, the other a lawyer in New York; the third, a survivor, manages the family money; my sister is three times divorced and lives in New York, spending money and trying to look younger."

"All right."

"You'll get it. Eventually, Sergeant Swagger, you'll figure it out."

"I think I'm out of my league this time, ma'am. I will keep working on it, though."

"Good luck."

"Thanks."

He hung up, stumped. He opened the phone book, found a commercial shooting range called On Target over near the airport. There, he rented a stock .45 and spent an hour shooting holes in a target at twenty-five yards while his campers cooled their heels outside in the parking lot.

When he emerged, the food choices weren't great: Popeyes Fried Chicken, a Pizza Hut, a Subway and, down the road a bit, a Hardee's. He decided on Subway, and was walking toward it when he realized what it had to be and where he had to go next.

Bonson was flagged down after the 3 P.M. meeting by his secretary, who said there was an urgent call from Team Cowboy. He took it in his office.

"He burned us."

"Shit."

"He knew we were there all along."

"Where did he go?"

"He slipped us so easily it was pathetic. Went into a Subway bathroom, never came out."

"Subway, where, in DC or Baltimore?"

"No, the sandwich shop. On Route 175 near Fort Meade. Went in, never came out. We waited and finally checked it out. He was long gone. His rental car was still there in the parking lot, but he was long gone."

"Shit," said Bonson.

Where has the cowboy gone? What does he know?

CHAPTER FORTY-ONE

S olaratov knew the one sound rule that held true the world over: to catch a professional, hire a professional.

This meant that in his time he had worked with criminals of all stripe and shape, including mujahideen skyjackers, Parisian strong-arm men, Angolese poachers and Russian mafioso. But never a seventeen-year-old boy, with dreadlocks, a baseball cap backward on his head and a pair of trousers so baggy they could contain three or four editions of his thin, wiry body. He wore a T-shirt that said: JUST DO IT.

They met in an alley in the dockside section of New Orleans. And why New Orleans? Because the origin of "Sally M's" flight on the Post-It slip was that city.

The boy sashayed toward him with an abundance of style in his bopping walk that was astounding: he pulsed with rhythm and attitude, contrapuntal and primary, his eyes blank behind a pair of mirror-finish glasses.

"Yo, man, you got the change?"

"Yes," said Solaratov. "You can do this?"

"Like fly, Jack," said the boy, taking the envelope, which contained $10,000. "You come this way, my man."

They walked down sweltering alleys, where the garbage, uncollected, stank. They passed sleeping men wrapped around bottles and now and then other crews of tough-looking youths dressed almost identically to Solaratov's host, but with this young gangster in command, nobody assaulted them. Then they turned into a backyard and made their way into a decrepit slum dwelling, went up dark, urine-soaked stairs and reached a door. It was locked; the boy's quick hands flew to his pockets and came out with a key. The lock was sprung; Solaratov followed him into a decrepit room, then through another door to an inner office where possibly a million dollars' worth of computer equipment blinked and hummed.

"Yo, Jimmy," said another boy who was watching a bank of TV monitors that commanded all approaches to the computer room. He had a shorty CAR-15 with a thirty-round mag and a suppressor.

"Yo," responded Jimmy, and the sentry moved aside, making room for the master.

Jimmy seated himself at a keyboard.

"Okay," he said. "M. You said M, from New Orleans, receiving phone calls from Idaho, is that it?"

"Yes, that's it."

"Cool. Now what we do, see, we got to get into the phone company's billing computer. All that takes is a code."

"I have no code."

"Not a problem. Not a problem," said Jimmy. He called up a directory, and learned the code.

"How do you know?"

"My peoples regularly be going Dumpster diving, man. We hit the Dumpsters behind the phone company three times a week. A week don't go by we don't git their code memos. Yeah, here it is, a simple dial-in."

The computer produced the mechanized tones of dialing, then announced LINKED and produced what Solaratov took to be the index of its billing system, with a blinking cursor requesting an order.

"This is the FAC," said the boy, "Southern Bell's facilities computer. Gitting into this one is easy. No problem. Kiddie shit."

He asked the computer to search for calls received in the greater New Orleans area from Idaho's 208 area code, and the machine obediently rifled its files and presented a list of several hundred possibilities over the past week.

"Memphis," said Solaratov. "Our information says the husband once had a friendship with a New Orleans–area federal agent named Memphis. My guess is 'Sally M.' is this agent's wife, come up to Idaho to take care of the woman. She would call home from wherever she's hiding. That is my thinking. She—"

"Don't tell me too much, man. Don't want to know too much. Just want to find you your buddy. Okay, Memphis."

"Memphis," said Solaratov, but by that time the boy had it up. A Nicholas C. Memphis, 2132 Terry Drive, Metarie, Louisiana, telephone 504-555-2389.

"Now we cooking," said the boy. "I'll just ask Mr. FACS to locate and—"

He did so; a new set of numbers popped onto the screen.

"—there's your billing address and service records. Now let's see."

He looked.

"Yes, yes, yes. Your friend Mr. Memphis, he got calls from outside Boise beginning late afternoon May fourth—"

Solaratov knew this as the date of the shooting.

"Three, four calls from—"

"That number is not important. That is the ranch house number."

"Hey, man, I done told you, I don't want to know *nothing*."

"Go on, go on."

"Then nothing, then the last three days, one call a night from 208-555-5430."

"Can you locate the source of that call?"

"Well, let's see, we can git the F-1, which is the primary distribution point and that turns out to be . . ."

He typed and waited.

"That turns out to be the Bell Substation at Custer County, in central Idaho, near a town called Mackay."

"Mackay," said Solaratov. "Custer County. Central Idaho. Is there an address?"

"No, but there's an F-2: 459912."

"What's that?"

"That's the secondary distribution point. The pole."

"The pole?"

"Yeah, the pole nearest wherever they are. That be the pole that the phone wire is directly wired to. It can't be more than one hundred feet away from the house, probably closer than that. They got all the poles labeled, man. That's how Ma Bell do it."

"Can I get an address on that?"

"Not here. I don't have access to their computer from here. What you got to do is go to that little phone substation and break in somehow. You got to get into their computer or their files and get an address for F-2 459912. That'll put you there, no problem."

"I can't do computers. You come with me. You do it. Much money."

"Yeah, me in Idaho, with the dreads and the 'tude. That'd be rich. Man, them whiteboy five-Os arrest me for how I be *looking*. No, man: you got to do it yourself. You want that address, you break in. It ain't no big deal. You may even get it out of the Dumpster. But you break in, you check the files, you find the F-2 listings. You might even find a map with the F-2s designated, you dig? Ain't no big thing, brother. I ain't shitting you."

"You could call, no? Bluff them into giving you information?"

"Here, no sweat. In any big city in America, no sweat. You can social engineer the shit out of these boys. But out there: they hear a brother in a place where there ain't no brothers, I think you got problems. I don't want to risk blowing your caper, man. What I'm telling you, it's the best way, it really is. You'll see; you be chilling in no time."

Solaratov nodded grimly.

"You can do it, man. It ain't a problem."

"No problem," Solaratov said.

CHAPTER FORTY-TWO

In the graduate degree ceremony at the Massachusetts Institute of Technology, 132 men and women were awarded their Ph.D's in assorted academic and scientific specialties. But only one received the Ball Prize as the Institute Scholar, for only one was the ranking member of the class.

He was a tall young man, prematurely bald, of surprising gravity and focus. He took his degree—"Certain Theories of Solar Generation As Applied to Celestial Navigation" was his dissertation—in quantum physics from the dean and was asked to speak some words, and when he assumed the podium, his remarks were short.

"I want to thank you," he said, "for the chance you have given me. I have been a scholarship student since my undergraduate years and even before that. I came from a poor family; my mother worked hard, but there was never enough. But institutions such as this one—and Yale University and Harvard University and Madison High School—were kind to me and doors were opened. Without your generosity I could not be here and I am honored by that, and by your faith in me. I only wish my parents could be here to share this moment. They were good people, both of them. Thank you very much."

He stepped down to polite applause and went back to his place in line as the ceremony—interminable to an uninvested outsider—went on hour after hour. It was a hot day and cloudless in Boston. The Charles River was smooth as blackened, ancient ivory; a thin veil of clouds filtered the sun, but did nothing to help the heat. The Orioles were in town, to play the Red Sox in a four-game series; the president had just announced a new attempt to curb welfare growth; the international news was grave—the Russian election had the pundits worried, with everybody's favorite bad guy leading by a seemingly unassailable margin—and the stock market was up four points. None of this meant anything to the tall man in the khaki suit who sat in the last row of the graduation ceremony.

He waited impassively as the minutes churned by until at last the crowd broke up and families rejoined, old friends embraced, the whole litany of human joy was re-enacted. He walked through the milling people toward the podium and at last he spotted his quarry, the young man who was the Ball Prize winner.

He watched him; the young man accepted the attentions he had earned somewhat passively and seemed not to respond to them with a great deal of enthusiasm. He accepted the embraces of colleagues and professors and administrators, but after a while—surprisingly quickly, as a matter of fact—he was alone. He took off his cap and hung his gown over his arm to reveal a nondescript, almost shabby suit, and began to leave. He had, in fact, the look of a loner, the boy who's ever so rarely at the center but prefers to blur through the margins of any situation, is uncomfortable with eye contact or attempts at intimacy, and will lose himself readily enough in the arcane, be it quantum physics, Dungeons & Dragons or sniper warfare. It was a quality of melancholy.

Bob intercepted him.

"Say there," he said, "just wanted to tell you that was a damned nice little talk you gave there."

The boy was not so mature that he didn't appreciate a compliment, so an unguarded smile crossed his face.

"Thanks," he said.

"What's next for you?"

"Oh, the prize thing is an automatic year at Oxford as a research fellow. I leave for England tomorrow. Very exciting. They have a good department, lots of provocative people. I'm looking forward to it. Say—excuse me, I didn't catch your name."

"Swagger," Bob said.

"Oh, well, it's nice to talk to you, Mr. Swagger. I've, uh, got to be going now. Thanks again, I—"

"Actually, it's not just coincidence, me running into you. It took some digging to find you."

The young man's eyes narrowed with hostility.

"I don't give interviews if this is some press thing. I have nothing to say."

"Well, see, the funny thing is, I ain't here about you. I'm here about your dad."

The boy nodded, swallowed involuntarily.

"My father's been dead since 1971."

"I know that," said Bob.

"What is this? Are you a cop or anything?"

"Not at all."

"A writer? Listen, I'm sorry, the last two times I gave interviews to writers, they didn't even *use* the stuff, so why should I waste my—"

"No, I ain't a writer. Fact is, I pretty much hate writers. They always get it wrong. I never encountered a profession that got more wrong than being a writer. Anyhow, I'm just a former Marine. And your dad's death is mixed up in some business that just won't go away."

"More on the great Trig Carter, eh? The great Trig Carter, hero of the left, who sacrificed his life to stop the war in Vietnam? Everybody remembers him. There'll probably be a movie one of these days. This fucking country, how can they worship a prick like him? He was a killer. He blew my father to little pieces, and crushed him under a hundred tons of rubble. And nobody gives a fuck. They think Trig is the big hero, the victim, the martyr, because he came from a long line of Protestant swine and sold out to anybody that would have him."

But then his bitterness vanished.

"Look, this isn't doing any good. I never knew my father; I was less than a year old when he was killed. What difference does it make?"

"Well," said Swagger, "maybe it still makes a little. See, I was struck by the same thing as I looked into this. There ain't nothing about your father nowhere. Excuse my grammar, I never had a fancy education."

"Overrated, believe me."

"I do believe you on that one. Anyhow, he's the mystery man in this affair. Nobody wants to know, nobody's interested."

"Why is this of interest to you? Who cares?"

"I care. Maybe your father wasn't the poor guy in the wrong place at the wrong time, like everybody says. Maybe he was more important than people think. That's a possibility I'm looking at. And maybe the folks who pulled the strings are still around. And maybe I'm interested in looking into this and maybe I'm the only man who cares about your dad—"

"My mother was a saint, by the way. She taught, tutored, worked like hell to give me the chances I had. She died my freshman year at Harvard."

"I'm very sorry. You were a lucky young man, though, who had parents who cared and sacrificed."

"Yes, I was. So you think—you have some conspiracy theory about my father? Do you have a radio show or something?"

"No, sir. I'm not in this for the money. I'm just a Marine trying to get some old business straightened out. Believe it or not, it connects with the death of still another member of that generation, a boy who died in Vietnam. That was another great loss for his family and our country."

"Who are you?"

"I was with that boy when he died. May seventh, 1972. He bled out in my arms. This is something I been working on a long time."

"Um," said the boy.

"Look, I know you're busy. You must be. But I was

hoping you'd have a cup of coffee with me. I'd like to talk about your dad. I want to know about him."

"He was quite a guy," the boy said. "Or so I hear." He looked at his watch. "Hell, why not? I have nothing else to do."

CHAPTER FORTY-THREE

Bonson was debriefing the team in the Rossyln safe house. It was not a happy time.

"I *warned* you he was good. You people were supposed to be the best. What the hell went on?"

"He *was* good. He was professional. He read us, burned us and turned us when it suited him," came the answer. "Sometimes people are just too good and they can do that to you. That's all."

"All right, let's go through it again, very carefully."

For what seemed the tenth time, the team narrated their one day of adventures with Bob Lee Swagger, where he'd been, what they'd learned, how indifferent to them he seemed, how swiftly and effectively he had slipped them.

Bonson listened carefully.

"Usually there's a moment," one of the ex-FBI agents said, "when you can tell you've been burned. There was nothing like that this time. He just disappeared."

"I figure he made it out back, cut through the neighborhood behind us and called a cab from another little shopping center about a mile away. Or maybe he went up to the roof and waited until nightfall and slipped away."

"You didn't see him interact with anybody?"

"Nobody."

"He had no contacts?"

"He made those phone calls."

"We did get that, sir."

The agents had written down the numbers of the phone booths and through them tracked the destinations of the calls, which turned out to be the American embassy in London, first the general number, and the next day the office of the Marine NCOIC of the embassy guard.

"We could have inquiries made."

"No, no, I know what he was asking about. He's very smart, this guy. He looks like Clint Eastwood and talks like Gomer Pyle and yet he's got a natural gift for this sort of thing. He's very—"

It was at this time an earnest young man entered the room.

"Commander Bonson," he said, "Sierra-Bravo-Four is on the phone."

Bonson looked about himself, stunned, then took the phone and waited for the switchboard to route it to him.

"Bonson."

"Sierra-Bravo-Four here," he heard Swagger's voice.

"Where the hell are you?"

"You didn't tell me about the baby-sitters."

"It's for your own good."

"I work alone. I made that clear, Bonson."

"We don't do it that way anymore. You have to come in. You have to come under control. It's the only way I can help you."

"I need some questions answered."

"Where are you? I can have you picked up in an hour."

There was a pause.

"I'm outside, asshole."

"What?"

"I said, I'm outside, with a cellular I picked up at the Kmart a few minutes ago."

"How did—"

There was a clang as something hit the window.

"I just threw a rock at your window, asshole. Good thing it wasn't an RPG; you wouldn't last long in a war, asshole. I rented another car and followed the baby-sitters you had staking out *my* car back to your place. Now, let me in and let's start talking."

Swagger came in, past the team whom he had so adroitly outmanaged.

"All right, people, get out of here. I'll talk to him."

"Do you need security, Commander?" said an ex-state cop, correctly reading the anger in Bob's body.

"No. He'll see reason. He knows this isn't a pissing contest between him and this team, right, Swagger?"

"You just answer my questions and we'll see what's what."

The men and women he had vanquished slid out of the room and then Bonson took him into another one, neatly set up as an operational HQ with computer terminals and phone banks. A few technicians worked the consoles.

"Okay, everybody on break," Bonson called.

They too left. Bob and Bonson sat down on a beat-up sofa.

"I got the name of your Russian."

"All right," said Bonson.

"His name was Robert Fitzpatrick; he was affiliated with GRU, according to the Brits. But they don't have nothing on him, what he was up to."

"Swagger, good. Damn, you are an operator. I'm impressed. So what did you do with this? Where did you go?"

"You'll find out when I put it all together, which I ain't done yet, but I have some ideas. What have y'all got on this guy? I need to find out who he was or is, what became of him, what this is all about. He had the Brits buffaloed. They only found out he was operating in their country after he was long gone."

"Fitzpatrick," said Bonson. "Fitzpatrick was a recruiter. That was his specialty. He was one of those seductive, smooth presences who just gulled people into doing what he wanted, and they never, ever knew he was persuading them. You see, that's what's interesting about him. I don't think Trig was his only project. I think he may have recruited others, and whatever his business with Trig was, it wasn't the main reason he came to the United States."

"What was he doing?"

"He was recruiting a mole."

"Man," said Bob, "this shit is getting fucked up. Secret-agent crap, like some paperback novel. I do not want to be a part of this shit. My mind don't work that way."

"Nevertheless, that was his great gift, his special talent. We know a little more about him than the Brits—and the timing works out right."

"What do you mean?"

"For the past twenty years, the Agency has been in a curious down cycle. It seems to have had an enormous fund of bad luck. Every once in a while we smoke somebody out. In the early eighties, there was a guy named Yost Ver Steeg. A little later there was Robert Howard. Early in the nineties, we finally caught onto Aldrich Ames. And we think, well, that's it, we're clean at last. But somehow it never quite pans out that way. It never does. We're always a little behind, a little slow, a little off. They're always a little ahead of us. Even after the breakup, they've stayed strangely ahead of us. I'm convinced he's here. I can *feel* him. I can *smell* him. He's someone you'd never believe, someone totally secure. He's not in it for the money; he's not so active he's obvious. But he's here, I know it, goddammit, and I will catch him. And I know this goddamn 'Fitzpatrick' recruited him in the year 1971 when he was in this country. And, goddammit, I just missed him that year. I was a couple of hours slow, because your pal Fenn wouldn't roll over for me."

"So what happened to Fitzpatrick?"

"Disappeared. Gone. We have no idea. He was never serviced out of an embassy, never had a cut-out, any of the classic ploys of the craft. We never cut into his phone network. He was entirely a singleton. We don't know who serviced him. We don't even know what he looks like. We never got a photo. But it is provocative that suddenly all this is active again. Why would that be? Your picture goes in the paper and suddenly they're out to kill you?"

"But my picture has been in the paper before. It's

been on the cover of *Time* and *Newsweek.* They couldn't miss that. So what's different this time?"

"That's a great question, Sergeant. I can't answer it. I even have a team of analysts working on it back at Langley and so far they have come up with nothing. It makes no sense. And to make it more complicated, Fitzpatrick may not even be working for the Russians, or for the old Soviet communist regime, which is still there, believe me. He may be working against it now. It's a tough call, I'll tell you, but I guarantee it's simple underneath. Mole. Penetration of the Agency. The notification of your existence, something coming active over there, your elimination to prevent—what? I don't know."

Something didn't quite add up. There was some little thing here that didn't connect.

"You look puzzled," said Bonson.

"I can't figure it out," said Bob. "I'm getting a little alarm. Don't know what it is. Something you said—"

Photograph.

"You don't know what Fitzpatrick looks like?"

"No. No photos. That's how good he was."

What is wrong?

"Why aren't there any photos?"

"We never got close enough. We were never there. We were always behind him. It took too long, I told you. I was trying to set up a—"

Photograph.

"There is a photograph."

"I don't—"

"The FBI has a photograph. The FBI was *there.*"

"We're not on the same page. The FBI was *where*?"

"At the farm. The farm in Germantown in 1971. Trig had told Donny where it was. My wife went out there with Donny the night he was trying to decide whether or not to give up Crowe. He was looking for Trig for guidance. She saw Fitzpatrick. She said the FBI was there, and when she and Donny left, they got their picture. They were on the hill above the farm. They were about to bust Trig."

"The FBI was not there. The FBI was back in Washington with Lieutenant Commander Bonson trying to figure out where the hell everybody had gone to."

"There were agents there. They got a picture of Donny and Julie leaving the farm. She told me that less than a week ago."

"It wasn't the FBI."

"Could it have been some other security agency, moving in on Trig, unaware of the—"

"No. It didn't work that way. We were together."

"Who was there?"

"Call your wife. Find out."

He pushed the phone toward Bob, who took out the small piece of paper on which he had written the number of the ranch house in Custer County.

He dialed, listened as the phone rang. It was mid-afternoon out there.

After three rings, he heard, "Hello?"

"Sally?"

"Oh, the husband. The missing husband. Where the hell have you *been*? She is in great discomfort and you have not called in days."

"I'm sorry, I've been involved in some stuff."

"Bob, this is your *family*. Don't you understand that?"

"I understand that. I'm just about to come home and spell you and everything will be happy. She did separate from me, you remember."

"You still have responsibilities," she said. "You are not on vacation."

"I am trying to take care of things. How's Nikki?"

"She's fine. It's snowing. They say there's going to be a bad snowfall, one of those late spring things."

"It's June, for God's sake."

"They do things by their own rules in Idaho."

"I guess so. Is Julie able to come to the phone? It's important."

"I'll see if she's awake."

He waited and the minutes passed.

At last another extension clicked on, and his wife said, "Bob?"

"Yes. How are you?"

"I'm all right. I'm still in a cast, but at least I'm out of that awful traction."

"Traction sucks."

"Where are you?"

"I'm in Washington right now, working on this thing."

"God, Bob. No wonder my lawyer couldn't find you."

"I'll be home soon. I just have this thing to deal with."

She was silent.

"I had to ask you something."

"What?"

"You told me that when you and Donny left that farm, you were photographed, right? Some guys were in the hills, monitoring the situation, and they got a photo."

"Yes."

"You're sure?"

"Of course I'm sure. Why would I make something like that up?"

"Well, you might have it mixed up with something else."

"It was very straightforward. Donny knew where the farm was; we drove out there. We found Trig and some big blond guy he said was Irish. We left after Donny talked to Trig. We got to our car, got in, and this guy came out of nowhere and took our picture. That's it."

"Hmmm," he said. He put the phone down. "She says yes, definitely, there was a picture taken."

"What did the guy look like?"

Bob asked her.

"Guy in a suit. Heavy-set, blunt, I guess. I didn't get a good look. It was dark, remember? Cops. FBI agents."

"Just cops," Bob said.

"Don't you see," said Bonson. "Some kind of Soviet security team. Covering for Fitzpatrick."

Yes, Bob thought. That made sense.

"And that was everybody that was out there?" he asked.

"Well . . . Peter, Peter Farris."

"Peter?" Bob asked. *Peter?* Something rang in his head from far away.

"I don't know that he was there."

"Who was Peter?" he asked, struggling to remember. He thought he could recall Donny mentioning a Peter somewhere some time or other and had a bad feeling.

"He was one of my friends in the movement. He thought he was in love with me. He may have followed us out there."

"You don't know?"

"He disappeared that night. His body was found several months later. I wrote Donny about it."

"Okay," said Bob, "I'll call you as soon as I get back, and we can work this out however you want. You're safe in all this snow?"

"We may be snowed in for a few days, it's so isolated. But that's okay; we have plenty of food and fuel. Sally's here. It's not a problem. I feel very safe."

"Okay," he said.

"Good-bye," she said.

"That was a dead end," he said, after hanging up.

Peter, he thought. Peter is dead. Peter disappeared that night. Yet something taunted him. He remembered other words, spoken directly to him: *It's not about you this time.*

"Well, it's another good bit of circumstantial that the Russians had committed to a major operation, and they were running high-level security on it."

Then a thought just sort of fluttered through Bob's mind.

"It is odd," he noted, "that of all the people that went to that farm—Trig, a kid named Peter Farris, Donny—they're all dead. In fact, they all died within a few months of that night."

"Everybody except your wife."

"Yeah. And—"

Except my wife, he thought.

Except my wife.

Bob stopped, caught up suddenly. Something snapped into perfect focus. It wasn't there, then it was; there was no coming into being, no sense of emergence: it was just indisputably there, big as life.

"You know—" started Bonson.

"Shut up," said Bob.

He was silent another second.

"I get it," he said. "The picture, the timing, the target."

"What are you talking about?"

"They killed everyone except Julie. They didn't know who Julie was but they had a picture of her. The picture they got that night. But Donny never officially recorded his marriage with the Marine Corps. So there were no records of who she was. She was a mystery to them. Then, when my picture was on *Time*'s cover over that business in New Orleans, it didn't matter, it meant nothing. I didn't even know Julie yet. But two months ago, my picture runs again in *Time*. And the *National Star,* when I'm famous again for a weekend. It was snapped by a tabloid photographer as we were coming out of church, Julie and I. It's not my picture they're interested in, or even me. That story told how I had married the widow of my spotter in Vietnam."

He turned to Bonson.

"It's Julie. They're trying to kill Julie. They have to kill everyone who was at that farm and saw Fitzpatrick with Trig loading that truck. This whole thing isn't about killing me. It's about killing Julie. He fired at what he thought was me first in the mountains because I was armed. He had to take the armed man first. But *she* was the target."

Bonson nodded.

Bob picked up the phone, dialed quickly. But the line was out.

Chapter Forty-four

The snow didn't scare Solaratov. He had seen snow before. He had lived and hunted in snow. He had trekked the mountains of Afghanistan above the snowline with a SPETSNAZ team hunting for mujahideen leadership cadres. The snow was the sniper's ally. It drove security forces under cover, it grounded air cover and, best of all, it covered tracks. The sniper loved snow.

It fell in huge, lofty feathers, a wet, lush snow from a dark mountain sky. It adhered and quickly covered the earth and drove most people to shelter. The weatherman said it would snow all night, a last blast of winter, unusual but not unheard of. Twelve, maybe twenty inches of it, endless and silent.

He drove through already thinning traffic and had no trouble finding the Idaho Bell outstation that had been the F-1—primary distribution point—for the phone calls from remote rural Custer County to Nick Memphis's New Orleans address. It was a low, bleak building, built to modern American standards without windows. The happy Bell sign stood outside; inside, it was dark, presumably working entirely by robotics. To one side stood a phalanx of transformers, fenced off and marked with fierce DANGER signs, which produced a nexus of wires that rose to poles to shunt the miracle of communication around Custer County. A small parking lot was empty. Out back, a cyclone fence sealed off what appeared to be a sort of motor pool, where six vans with IDAHO BELL emblazoned on them were parked next to what looked like a sheet-metal maintenance garage. But it was dark too. Even better, the building was far from downtown, such as "downtown" was, along a country road that would now not be much traveled.

Still, he did not dare park in the lot, for that lone car

on a dark night could attract some attention. He drove several hundred yards into a small development of houses, where some cars were parked along the street, and pulled in, turning the engine off. He waited in darkness, as the snow fell silently on the hood of the car, soon veiling the windshield. He opened the door, got out, slipped it shut without a slam, for the noise would have seemed even louder in the quiet.

It was an easy walk, between two dark houses, across a field, and then next to the Cyclone fence. He looked for sign of an alarm or electrification or notice of a dog. There was none. Taking a pair of wire cutters from the pocket of his parka, he used the massive strength in his forearms to cut the cyclone and bend back an entrance to the wire. He slithered through. He slipped between vans, around the garage, and felt his way along the back of the phone building until he found a metal door. He looked about for signs of an alarm and, finding none, took from his pocket a leather envelope of lock picks. The lock was a simple but solid pin tumbler; he took the two tools he would need, the tension tool and the feeler pick, and set to work. He inserted the tension tool. It was a matter of delicate feel, the tension tool holding the pins down, the feeler tool locating them one by one along the shear line of the cylinder and pushing them back until he felt a slight thump, signifying that he'd gotten all the pins aligned. The cylinder turned; the door sprang open.

He stepped inside, pulled out a pair of glasses with a small, powerful flashlight mounted to them and began to explore the building.

It didn't take long. He found a map on the wall in what appeared to be the bullpen for the Bell linemen and took it down. It seemed to be Custer County as broken down into phone zones. Indeed, as he searched it in the illumination of the flashlight, he quickly noted small circles denoted along the roads that were numbered in integer sequences similar to the one he'd uncovered in New Orleans. These would be the secondary distribution points for the calls, the F-2s.

He had a powerful impulse just to flee with the map, but it was stiff and large, and carrying it across the field back to the car would be very difficult. Instead, he began a patient search, zone by zone, of the chart, searching for the magic numbers 459912. Again, it took some time, but at last, along a mountain road high in the Lost River range, he found the pole; it stood in a valley near a rectangle that clearly denoted a ranch house. From the crush of elevation contours close by, he understood that it stood under the mountains, giving him a perfect angle for a killing shot. He carefully copied the map onto a sheet of paper, which he would later compare with the exhaustive maps he had already acquired as he set up his approach to the target area.

He had the map hung on the wall again when he heard sounds. He fought the urge to panic and slipped down the wall until he found a desk behind which he could hide. He switched off his light, and took a Glock 19 out of his shoulder holster under the heavy parka.

The lights came on at that moment, and he heard the sound of a man walking to a desk, sitting down and fiddling with papers, sighing with the approach of a night's duty. The man picked up the phone and dialed a number.

"Bobby? Yeah, I want the guys in. Grace is already on the way. The state cops told me they got downed lines near Sunbeam Dam and I want somebody to check the meadow there at Arco; those suckers *always* go down. I'll start calling the A-line, you start calling the B's. Yeah, I know, I'm pissed too. This late. Oh, well, buddy, you wanted to be in management, that means long nights and no overtime. But free coffee, Bobby."

The man hung up.

Solaratov faced reality. In minutes the room would fill up with linemen come in to work the unexpected weather emergency. He was in a tenuous situation as it was, only undiscovered because the supervisor was so focused on his labors. When the others arrived, he would soon be discovered; even if he could hide, he'd be pinned for hours as the long night's repair effort was coordinated and executed.

"Mrs. Bellamy? This is Walter Fish at work. Is Gene there? Yes, ma'am, we're recalling the workforce; please wake him. That's right, ma'am. Thanks very much."

Walter Fish bent over his phones and was making another call when the shadow of Solaratov fell across him. He looked up; a bafflement fell across his features that transfigured almost instantaneously into a reflexive Western smile, and then became a mask of panic.

Solaratov shot him in the face, below the left eye, with a 147-grain Federal Hydra-Shock. The gun popped in his hand, cycled, spitting a shell across the room. Fish jerked backward as if in a different, a faster, time sequence. His brain tissue sprayed the wall behind him, and a small gouge of plaster blew out where the bullet exited the skull and plunked into the wall.

Solaratov turned and looked for the ejected shell; he spied it across the room, under a desk, and went quickly to pick it up. When he arose, he faced a woman in the doorway, with a thermos in one hand, still wrapped up babushkalike against the weather. Her features became unglued at the horror she saw and her eyes opened like quarters. Solaratov shot her in the chest but missed the heart. She staggered backward, spun and began to stagger down the hall, screaming, "No, no, no, no, no, no!"

He stepped into the hall, locked the Glock in both hands, acquired the nightlit front sight and shot her in the base of the spine. She went down, her hand reaching convulsively back to touch the wound itself. Why did they do that? They always did that. He walked to her; she still moved. He bent, put the muzzle to the back of her head and fired again. The muzzle flash ignited her hair. It blazed with an acrid, chemical stench, then extinguished itself, producing a vapor of smoke, and Solaratov realized she'd been wearing a wig of some artificial substance.

Now there was no time to pick up shells. He walked swiftly down the corridor, found the door and slipped out the back. Thank God it was still snowing heavily; in seconds, minutes at the most, his tracks would be gone.

He went across the field, the pistol still hot in his hand. He had no sense of shame or doubt or pain; he was the professional and he did what was necessary, the hard thing always, and kept going. But it shook him nevertheless: the look on the poor man's face in the second before the bullet blew through his cheekbone; and the woman who could only scream "No, no, no, no" as she rushed along the corridor.

It seemed to put a curse on his enterprise. He was not superstitious and he was too experienced by far to consider such nontechnical elements as having any meaning; still, it didn't feel right.

CHAPTER FORTY-FIVE

Bonson had promised Bob that he could surprise him with how much he could do and how quickly, and now he made good on that statement.

He picked up the phone and dialed a certain number and said, very calmly, "Duty officer, this is Deputy Director Bonson, authenticating code Alpha-Actual-Two-Five-Nine, do you acknowledge?"

When the man on the other end did so, Bonson said, "I am hearby declaring a Code Blue Critical Incident. Please notify the Fifth Floor and set up a Domestic Crisis Team. I want two senior analysts—Wigler and Marbella. I want my senior analysts from Team Cowboy. I want some people from computer division. I want to lay on air ASAP; I'm at 2854 Arlington Avenue, in Rosslyn. We will make our way to the *USA Today* building for pickup. I'd like that in the next five minutes."

He waited, got the reply he wanted.

"I also want an FBI HRT unit put on alert and ready to coordinate with our liaison ASAP. This may involve a shooting situation and I want the best guys. Do you copy?"

Getting his last acknowledgment, he hung up.

"Okay," he said, turning to Bob, "we have to get a ride to the newspaper building, and the chopper will pick us up. We'll be in Langley inside fifteen minutes and put our best people to work in twenty. I can have a security team on-site in four hours."

"Not if it's snowing," said Bob.

"What?"

"She said it was snowing. That's going to close the whole thing down."

"Shit," said Bonson.

"It won't shut him down," said Bob. "Not this boy.

He's been in the mountains. He hunted the mountains for years."

"It may be premature to worry," said Bonson.

"No, he'll go as soon as he can. He won't wait or goof around or take a break. He's got a job to do. It's the way his mind works. He's very thorough, very committed, very gifted, very patient, but when he sees it, he'll go for it instantly. He's been hunting her as I've been hunting him. And he's much closer."

"Shit," said Bonson again.

"Call them back and get them working the area. We're going to need maps, weather, satellite tracking, maybe. It's Custer County, about five miles outside of Mackay, Idaho, in the center of the state, in the Lost River Range. It's north of Mackay, off Route Ninety-three, in the foot-hills of the Lost River, as I understand it."

"That's good," said Bonson, and turned to make the call.

A half hour later they got the bad news.

"Sir," said a staff assistant with the grave face of a junior officer carrying the news no one wanted to hear, "we got some real problems out there."

"Go ahead," said Bonson, trailing along in Bob's wake into a room that could have been any meeting room in any office building in America but just happened to be in the headquarters of the Central Intelligence Agency in Langley, Virginia.

"There's a freak front moving in from Canada across central Idaho. The weather service people say it'll dump sixteen, eighteen inches on the place. Nothing's moving there; the roads will be closed until they can be plowed, and they can't be plowed until morning. Nothing's flying either. That area is totally sealed off. Nobody's going any-where."

"Shit," said Bonson. "Notify FBI. Tell them to stand down."

"Yes, sir, but there's more."

"Go ahead."

"We have been in contact with Idaho State Police authorities. Just to make things worse, there's been a double homicide at the phone company. A supervisor and his secretary, coming on to run the snow emergency shift, were shot and killed. Whoever did it got completely away. Nothing was stolen, nothing taken. Maybe it was domestic, but they say it looked like a professional hit."

"It's him," said Bob. "He's there. He probably had to get the final location out of the phone company files or something. He got surprised by these two people and he did what he had to do."

"Cold," said Bonson. "Very cold."

"I'll tell you what we need real fast," said Swagger. "We need an extremely good workup on the terrain there. Let's figure out, given the time of the shootings, if he'd have a chance at making it on foot to a shooting position. Where would he dump his car, how far would he have to go, what kind of speed could an experienced mountain operator be expected to make? Then double that, and you'll know what this guy is doing. What time will he make it there? Where would he likely set up? He'd want the sun behind him, that I know."

"Get cracking," said Bonson.

Nikki watched the snow.

"It's pretty," she said. "But I never knew it could snow in *June*."

"That's the mountains," said Aunt Sally. "It snows when it *wants* to."

"When we get back to Arizona," said her mother from the sofa, "you'll never see snow again, I promise."

"I think I like snow," said Nikki, "even if you can't ride in it."

She watched in the fading light as the world whitened. Outside, she could see a corral and beyond that the barn. There were no animals way up here, so there was nothing to worry about. The highway was about a half mile away, and it was her job to follow the long dirt road each day and check the solitary mailbox that stood where Upper Cedar Road, that high, lonely ribbon of dirt which connected them to Route 93, passed by.

But the mountains dominated what she could see. The house was in a high meadow, surrounded by them. Mount McCaleb was the closest, a huge brute of a mountain; it loomed above them, now unseen in the driving snow. Farther to the north was Leatherman Peak; farther to the south, Invisible Mountain. These were the peaks of the Lost River Range, dominated farther toward Challis by Mount Borah, the highest in Idaho. There was the sense of their presence, even though they were invisible. On an evening like this, it was much darker; you could feel them through your bones, dark and solid, just beyond the veil of the seen.

"Brrrr," Nikki said. "It looks so cold out."

"This snow'll be gone by the end of the week," Aunt Sally said. "That's what they said on the radio. Unseasonable cold front from Canada, but it'll be in the seventies by Monday. It'll melt away. Maybe it'll cause some flooding. It does feel like midwinter, doesn't it?"

"It does," said Nikki's mommy, who was at least ambulatory now. Her left arm and collarbone were secured in a half-body cast, but the abrasions and cuts had healed enough so that she could move about. She wore a bathrobe over jeans. She looked thin, Nikki thought.

"You know what?" said Aunt Sally, who with her spunky personality and Southern accent had quickly become Nikki's favorite person in the whole wide world, "I think it's a soup night. Don't you girls? I mean, snow, soup, what else goes together better? We'll do up some nice Campbell's tomato with crackers, and then we'll settle down and watch a video. Not *Born Free,* though. I cannot sit through that again."

"I love *Born Free,*" said Nikki.

"Nikki, honey, let's let Aunt Sally pick the movie tonight. She's a little tired of *Born Free.* So am I."

"Welllllll . . . ," Nikki considered.

"What about *Singin' in the Rain*?"

"That's a good one."

"What is it?" said Nikki.

"A musical. About these people who worked in old-time movies and how much fun they had. There's a lot of great singing and dancing."

"A man dances in the rain," said Sally.

"Ew," said Nikki. "Why would he do *that*? It's *stupid*."

Solaratov worked the maps by comparing his crude drawing with the U.S. Geologic Survey maps he had back in his motel room just north of Mackay. He tried to work quickly because he knew it would be a matter of time before the police began checking motels for strangers, and who knew if anybody had seen him come in half an hour after the murders? But at the same time, too much haste was no help at all. He tried to find the zone: that smooth place in his mind where his reflexes were at their best, his brain most efficient, his nerves calmest. He pushed his brain against the whirling topographic patterns of the map, located Route 93 and traced the path from his drawing to the map. He saw that the ranch house site was farther out 93, at the Mackay Reservoir. But there you turned right, drove across the flats and began to climb up FR 127, an "unimproved road," by the map symbol, which mounted the Lost Rivers and penetrated them, following Upper Cedar Creek. There was a natural fold in the rise of the mountains as the road went deeper, and at the end of that stood the ranch, surrounded on three sides by Mount McCaleb, Massacre Mountain and Leatherman Peak. The mountains were represented on the map by dizzying twirls of elevation lines, and the denser they were the more sheer the rise. He saw that the fast way in would be along Route 93, but that would not work, for the road was now officially closed, barely passable, and probably being monitored by the police. Who else would be driving through such a storm on such a night except a murderer fleeing the scene of his crime?

But he was a mere few miles from the south slope of Mount McCaleb, and the way was well marked, as it followed Lower Cedar Creek. The creek, protected from drifting snow by the furrow it had cut in the earth, would not be frozen this quickly, but it might be low, and no snow would adhere to it. Therefore, it might be surprisingly easy walking, even in the dark. When he got to McCaleb, he'd climb about two thousand feet—the slope didn't turn sheer for another five thousand feet—and could then just follow the ridge around and site himself above the ranch house. Again, the drifting snow could make it difficult, but he knew that on promontories, the snow doesn't drift or collect; in fact, that way might be easy too. He calculated the trip would take about six or seven hours; plenty of time to set up, lase the range, and get to his soft target in the morning, when the sun was due to break through. Then he could fall back, continue around McCaleb toward Massacre Mountain deeper into the Lost River Range, call in his helicopter, and be in another state by noon, leaving nothing but an empty motel room and a truck rented under a pseudonym.

He picked up his cellular and called.

"Yes, hello," came the answer.

"Yes, I've located the target," he said, and gave them the position. "I am moving out tonight to set up."

"Isn't it snowing, old man?"

"That's good. The snow doesn't mean a thing to me. I've seen snow before."

"All right. What then?"

"I'll be completing the deal sometime tomorrow morning whenever the client becomes visible. The husband isn't around. She'll be the one whose arm is in the cast. I'll execute cleanly, then fall back through the mountains about two miles and scale a foothill between McCaleb and Massacre. You have the map? You are following me?"

"Yes, we have it."

"Your helicopter pilot can navigate to that point?"

"Of course. If the sun is out, he'll have no problem."

"I'll call when the deal is closed. He'll be flying from . . . ?"

"You don't need to know, old man. He's relocated close to your area. We're in contact with him."

"Yes, I'll call when I reach the area of the pickup. When I see him, I'll pop smoke. I have smoke. He can come in and take me out—and then it's done."

"And then it's done, yes."

The working party met at 2330 with the best available intelligence. It felt so familiar, like a battalion operations meeting: stern men with dim but focused personalities, a sense of hierarchy and urgency, the maps on the wall, too many Styrofoam cups of coffee on the table. It reminded Bob of a similar meeting twenty-six years earlier, where the CIA and Air Force and S-2 Brophy and CO Feamster had met with him and Donny as they mapped their plans to nail Solaratov then.

"All right," said the map expert, "assuming he's located somewhere in the greater Mackay area and the roads are closed and he's going to go in overland, it's actually well within an experienced man's range, if he knows where he's going, he has good harsh-weather gear and he's determined."

"What time?"

"Oh, he can make it well before light. If he finds an exposed ridge, he won't have much snow accumulation, given a fair amount of wind. If he gets a tailwind, it could actually help him, though we don't have the wind-tendency dope in yet. He'd almost certainly make it before light. He could set himself up without much difficulty. I don't know where—"

"He'll be to the east," Swagger said. "He'll want the sun behind him. He won't want any chance of the light hitting his lens and reflecting down into the target area."

"How soon can Idaho State Police or park rangers make it in?" asked Bonson, who was running this show with glaring ferocity. He was apparently something of a legend in these precincts, Bob could tell; all the others deferred to him and at the same time were subtly eager for his attention and his approval. Bob had seen it in staff briefings a thousand times.

"Probably not till midmorning. They can't helicopter in; they can't navigate with snow mobiles or tracked vehicles at night."

"Can't they walk in?" said Bonson. "I mean, if Solaratov can walk, why can't they?"

"Well, sir," said the analyst, "don't forget they have a civil emergency on their hands. They're going to have people stuck along highways in snowdrifts for fifty miles each way, they're going to have accidents, frostbite, wires down, messed-up communications, hypothermia, the whole shebang of a public safety emergency. Sir, you could call the governor and get him to divert some people; that might work. But I don't know how it would play in—"

"It doesn't matter," said Bob. "If he runs into cops or rangers, he'll just kill them too and go on about his business. It's not a problem for him. These guys have no idea what they're up against. He can take them out, take out my wife, then escape and evade for weeks until pickup. That's how good he is. That's what his whole life has been about."

"Sir, with all due respect," said the young analyst, "I'd like to make a point which I'd be more comfortable making in private. But I have to make it here and now, so I hope Sergeant Swagger will understand that it's not about personalities, it's about responsibilities."

"Go ahead," said Swagger. "Speak freely. Say what has to be said."

"Well, sir," said the young analyst, "I have to think that it might be wise to concede the Russian his mission. We ought to be thinking about contingency plans for taking him down on the out route. He's an incredible asset. The information he has! Our first priority ought to be to take him alive and absorb the casualties—"

"No!" boomed Bonson, like Odin throwing thunderbolts. "Sergeant Swagger's wife is obviously in possession of valuable knowledge. You'd let that go? They think she's important enough to run this high-risk, maximum-effort mission, and you're going to let them get her? And you're saying to Sergeant Swagger here, we're just going to let your wife die? It's more important that we get some information on old ops? We'll just let him do his little thing, then we'll pick him up in the afternoon?"

"Sir, I'm trying to be realistic. I'm sorry, Sergeant Swagger. I get paid to call them as I see them."

"I understand," said Bob. "It ain't a problem."

"How fast could we get FBI HRT in there, or Idaho State Police SWAT?" asked Bonson again.

"It's a no-go for stopping the shot," said the analyst. "It just can't happen. We can't get people in there fast enough. Man, this guy's really caught some breaks!"

Bonson turned to him.

"I am not willing to concede him his mission. I absolutely am not. Will one of you bright young geniuses solve this problem? That also is what you're paid for."

"I'm just thinking out loud, but you could target the sniper's likely location with cruise missiles," someone said. "They're very accurate. You'd have a pretty good chance of—"

"No, no," someone else said, "the cruises are low-altitude slow-movers, with not a lot of wing to give them much maneuverability. They'd never get through the inclement weather. Plus, they have to read landforms to navigate and we don't have time to program them. Finally, the nearest cruises are on a nuclear missile frigate in San Diego. There's no mission sustainability in the time frame."

"Could we smart bomb?"

"The infrared could see through the clouds, but the

landforms in the mountains are so goddamned confusing that I don't see how he could pinpoint the target area."

"No, but that's promising," said Bonson. "All right, Wigler, I want you to run a feasibility study, and I mean instantaneously."

Wigler nodded, grabbed his coffee and raced out.

It was quiet. Bob looked at his watch. Midnight. Solaratov was well on his way. Six, maybe seven hours till daylight out there. He'd take his shot, Julie would join Donny and Trig and Peter Farris, and whatever secret she had would be gone forever. Maybe they could take Solaratov alive. But that was an illusion too. He'd have an L-pill. He was a professional. There was no way to stop him or take him. He was going to win. Again.

Then Bob said, "There is one way."

The banks of the creek shielded the shallow lick of water and Solaratov built a good rhythm as he plunged along, as if on a sidewalk that led to the mountains. He wore night-vision goggles, which lit the way for him as he walked through green-tinted whiteness, following the course of the creek bed as it wound along the flats. The wind howled; the snow cut down diagonally, gathering quickly or swirling.

But he felt good. He wore a Gore-Tex parka over a down vest, mountain boots, mountain pants, long underwear, a black wool knit cap. The boots, expensive American ones by Danner, were as comfortable as any he'd ever worn, much nicer than the old Soviet military issue. He had a canteen, a compass, forty rounds of hand-loaded ammunition, the 7mm Remington, the Leica range-finding binoculars, his night-vision goggles, and the Glock 19 in its shoulder holster with a reloaded fifteen-round magazine, and two other fifteen-rounders hanging under his other shoulder. He'd improvised a snow cape from the motel room sheets.

After two hours of steady pumping, he reached the place where the creek bed petered out as it went underground. Above him soared the lower heights of Mount McCaleb, barren and swept with snow and light vegetation. The mountains were too new, too arid to hold much life. He looked upward at the hardscrabble escarpment. Then he looked back across the flats into the center of the valley.

It was if the world had ended in snow. There was a foot of it everywhere and it had closed down everything. No lights, no sign of civilization or even human habitation stood against the whiteness of the landscape and its hugeness and emptiness, even in the green wash of the ambient light.

Solaratov had a brief moment of melancholy: this was the sniper's life, was it not? This, always: loneliness, some mission that someone says is important, the worst weather elements, the presence of fear, the persistence of discomfort, the rush always of time.

He began to climb. The wind howled, the snow slashed. He climbed through the emptiness.

"I'll bet this is good," said Bonson.

"HALO," said Bob.

"HALO?" asked Bonson.

"He'd never make it," said the military analyst. "He'd have no idea what the winds would do. The terrain is impossible; the drop would probably kill him."

"I didn't say *he*," said Bob. "I wouldn't ask another man to do it. But I'd do it."

"What the hell is HALO?" asked Bonson.

"High Altitude, Low Opening."

"It's an airborne insertion technique," said the young man. "Highly trained airborne operators have tried it, with mixed success. You go out very high. You fall very far. It's sort of like bungee jumping, without the bungee. You fall like hell, and in the last six hundred feet or so, the chute deploys. You land hard. The point is to fall through radar. You're falling so fast you don't make a parachute signature on radar. Most Third World radars can't even pick up a falling man. But I've never heard of anyone doing it in the mountains in a blizzard at night. The winds will play havoc all the way down; you have no idea where the hell you'd wind up. You could be blown sideways into a face. SOG tried it in 'Nam. But it never worked there."

"I was in SOG," said Bob. "It didn't work there because the problem was the linkup after the drop. We never could figure out how to reassemble the team. But here there ain't a team. There's only me."

"Sergeant, there's real low survivability on that one. I don't think this dog hunts."

"I'm airborne qualified," said Bob. "I did the jump course at Benning in sixty-six, when I was back from my first tour."

"That was thirty years ago," someone pointed out.

"I've made twenty-five jumps. Now, you guys have terrific avionics for night navigation. You got terrific computers. You can pinpoint the drop location and you can get there easily enough by flying above the storm. You can plot a drop point where the odds of my landing in the appropriate area are very high. Right?"

The silence meant assent.

Then someone said, "Instead of a smart bomb, we send a smart guy."

"Here's the deal. You get me there, over the storm. I'll fall through the blizzard. I can't chute through it, but I can cannonball through it and my deviation won't be that bad. I can open 'way low, to minimize wind drift, maybe as low as three hundred feet. If you liaise up an Air Force jet and a good crew, you can have me there in six hours. I can't think of another way to get a countersniper on the ground in that circumstance. When I'm on the ground, you can triangulate me with a satellite and I can get an accurate position and I can move overland and get there in time."

"Jesus," said Bonson.

"You owe me, Bonson."

"I suppose I do," said Bonson.

"Sergeant Swagger, there's not one man in a hundred who could survive that."

"I been *there* before, sonny," said Swagger.

"Get Air Force," said Bonson. "Get this thing set up."

Swagger had one more thing to say.

"I need a rifle. I need a *good* rifle."

CHAPTER FORTY-SIX

G o down and shoot her, he thought.

Go down now, kick in the door, kill her and be out of here before the sun is up. It's all over then. No risk, no difficulty.

But he could not.

He stood on a ridge, about five hundred yards from the ranch house, which was dark and hardly visible through the whirling snow. Its lights were out and it stood in the middle of a blank, drifted field of white. It was a classical old cowboy place from the Westerns Solaratov had seen in the Ukraine and Bengal and Smolensk and Budapest: two-storied, many-gabled, clapboarded, with a Victorian look to it. A wisp of smoke rose from the chimney, evidence of a dying fire.

He hunched, looked at his Brietling. It was 0550; the light would rise in another few minutes and it would probably be light enough to shoot by 0700, if the storm abated. But what would bring them out? Why wouldn't they stay in there, cozy and warm, drinking cocoa and waiting for time to pass? What would bring them out?

The child would, the girl. She'd have to frolic in the snow. The two women would come onto the porch and watch her. If she was as bold and restless as he knew her to be—he'd seen her ride, after all—she'd be up early and she'd have the whole house up.

Yet still a voice spoke to him: *go down now, kill the woman, escape deeper into the mountains and get out, go home.*

But if he went down, he'd have to kill them all. There was no other way. He'd have to shoot the child and the other woman.

Do it, he thought.

You have killed so many, what difference does it make? Do it and be gone.

But he could not force himself to. That was not how his mind worked, that was not how he had worked in the past; that, somehow, would bring him unhappiness in the retirement that was so close and the escape from his life.

Do it, the smart part of himself said.

Nyet, he answered in Russian. *I cannot.* He was *tselni,* which is a very Russian term for a certain kind of personality. It is a personality that is bold and aggressive and fearless of pain or risk. But it is in some way one piece, or seamless: it has no other parts, no flexibility, no other textures. He was committed to a certain life and as stubborn in the mastering of it as a man could be; he could not change now. It was impossible.

I cannot do it, he thought.

Instead, as he moved along the ridge, he at last located the spot he wanted, where he could see onto the porch yet was still far enough to the east that the sun would be behind him, and would not pick up on his lens. He squatted, took off the Leica ranging binoculars and bounced a laser shot off the house to read the range. It was 560 meters. Using a 7mm Remington Magnum at a velocity of 3010 feet per second and a 175-grain Sierra Spitzer Boat-tail bullet developing muzzle energy of over two thousand foot-pounds would drop about forty-five inches at that range, a fantastic load-velocity combination, untouchable by any .308 in the world. But he knew that to compensate, he'd still have to hold high, that is, to aim not with the crosshair but the second mil-dot beneath it in the reticle. That would put him nearly dead on, though he might have to correct laterally for windage. But it was usually calm after a blizzard, the wind spent and gone. Remember, he cautioned himself: account for the downward angle in your hold.

He visualized, a helpful exercise for shooters. See the woman. See her standing there. See the second mil-dot covering her chest, how rock steady it is, how perfect is the range, how easy the shooting platform. Feel the trigger with the tip of your finger, but don't think about it. Don't think about anything. Your breathing has stopped, you've willed your body to near-death stillness, there's no wind, you put your whole being into that mil-dot on the chest, you don't even feel the rifle recoil.

The bullet will reach her before the sound of it. It'll take her in the chest, a massive, totally destructive shot—still over eighteen hundred pounds of energy—that explodes her heart and lungs, breaks her spine, shorts out her central nervous system. She'll feel nothing. The secrets locked into her brain will be locked there forever.

And that's it. It's so easy, then. You fall back, about four miles, and you call in the helicopter on the cellular. He'll be on you in twenty minutes for evacuation. No police or civil authority will reach this place until midafternoon at the earliest, and you'll be far gone by that time.

He slipped down behind a rock to take himself out of the gusting wind. He settled in to nurse himself through the coldness that lay ahead. But it would not be a problem, he knew. He had beaten that one a long time ago.

The dark of the plane was serene, cocoonlike. Swagger was geared up. He wore jump boots, some kind of super-tight jumpsuit and was struggling to get his chute straps tightened. He was quite calm. It was Bonson who was nervous.

"We're getting close," Bonson said. "Altitude is thirty-six thousand feet. The computers have pinpointed a dropping point that should put you down in the flat just northwest of the Mackay Reservoir, about a mile or so from the location of the house. If you carry farther you'll go into the Lost River Mountains, see, *here.*"

He pointed to the map, which clearly showed the Thousand Springs Valley that ran northwest by southeast through central Idaho, cut by the Big Lost River between the Lost River range and the White Knob Mountains.

"The chute will deploy at five hundred feet and you

should land softly enough. You'll just have to make it across the flatlands under the cover of dark, get into the house, warn the targets, and if you have to, engage him."

"If I get the shot, I'll take it."

"That's fine. Our priority here is your wife. She's the target of this mission, so thwarting him is what counts. As soon as it's flyable, I've got a squad of air policemen heloing in from Mountain Home to set up a defensive perimeter, and park rangers and Idaho State Policemen ready to go into the mountains after this guy. If you get the shot, take it. But, man, if we could get him alive and her alive, we'd have—"

"Forget it," Swagger said. "He's a professional. He killed two people already. He won't be taken alive. The rest of his life in a federal prison is no life for this guy. He'd take the L-pill, laughing at you as he checked out."

"Maybe so," said Bonson.

Swagger finished with the parachute; it seemed okay, with the preset altitude-sensitive deployment device.

That was the tricky part. The altitude sensor read altitude from a predetermined height above sea level so that it was set to pop the chute five hundred feet over the flatland; if he drifted into the mountains, the chute might not pop at all before he hit some gigantic vertical chunk of planet. The Air Force people had explained this to him, and told him that, more than anything, was why this was so foolhardy. The computers could read the wind tendencies, compute his weight, the math of his acceleration, add in the C-130's airspeed and determine a spot where the trajectory would be right, navigate the bird to that spot and tell him when it was time to go. But the jump wouldn't be in a computer, it would be in the real world, unpredictable and unknowable; a gust of tailwind, some tiny imperfection, and he'd be dead and what good would that do?

The plane was making about 320 miles an hour, after a government Lear jet had zoomed them from Andrews to Mountain Home in less than five hours, during which time he and Bonson had been on the radio with various experts trying to work out the details.

They landed at Mountain Home and were airborne again in ten minutes.

Bob checked his electronics and other gear, all secured in a jump bag that was tethered to his ankle. In it, a cold-weather arctic-pattern camouflaged Gore-Tex parka and leggings had been folded. He also had a new Motorola radio, MTX-810 Dual Mode portable, with microprocessor and digitized, a tenth the weight of the old PRC-77 and with three times the range, which would keep him in contact with a network; it was linked to his belt, and secured to his head by a throat mike, sound-sensitive, so all he had to do was talk and he was on the net. He also had a Magellan uplink device to read the Global Positioning System satellites, which orbited overhead broadcasting a mesh of ultra-accurate signals, similarly digitized and microprocessor-driven, which could enable him to chart his position in milliseconds if he should wander off track. He had night-vision gear, the latest things; M912A night-vision goggles from Litton with two 18mm Gen II Plus image-intensifier assemblies, which provided three times the system gain of the standard AN/PVS-5A.

He had a Beretta 92 in a shoulder holster under his left arm, a 9mm mouse gun shooting a lot (sixteen) of little cartridges not worth a damn, but nobody had .45s anymore, goddamn their souls.

And he had a rifle.

Taken from the Agency's sterile weapons inventory, it appeared to be some Third World assassination kit of which the rifle was but one part. The rifle lay encased in a foam-lined aluminum case, the Remington M40A1, Marine-issue, in .308, with its fiberglass stock, its free-floated barrel, its Unertl 10X scope. It would shoot an inch at one hundred yards, no problem; and two boxes of Federal Premium 168-grain MatchKing boattailed hollowpoints.

He'd examined it closely and saw that the proprietary shooter had taped a legend to the butt stock.

"Zeroed at 100 Yards," it said. And under that: "200 yards: 9 klicks up; 300 yards: 12 klicks up; 400 yards: 35 klicks up; 500 yards: 53 klicks up."

"Okay," said Bonson, leaning close, "let's check commo."

"Just a goddamn second," said Bob, trying to guess the range he'd be shooting at.

What the fuck, he thought, and started clicking, fifty-three times.

"Come on, let's check commo," said Bonson again. Clearly the tools of the trade at this basic level did not much interest Bonson; they may even have frightened him. But there were other devices cut into the padded foam of the case; one was an SOG knife in a kydex sheath, a dark and deadly thing; another was leather-encased sap, just the thing for thumping sentries as you got to your hide; and still another, so discreet in its green canvas M7 bandoleer and therefore complete with firing device and wiring, was the M18A1 anti-personnel mine known as the Claymore, so familiar from Vietnam and just the thing for flank security on some kind of assassination mission outside Djakarta.

He had a moment when he wondered if he should have junked all this shit, but as it was all going into the parapack, and would be tethered to his leg, he decided not to worry about it. He locked the case up.

"Come on," said Bonson for a third time, "let's check commo."

"We just checked commo."

"Yeah, I'm nervous. You okay?"

"I'm fine, Commander."

"Okay, I'm going to run up to the cockpit and check with the pilots."

"Got you."

He turned and walked up the big ship's dark bay to the cabin, cracked a door and leaned in.

Back here it was dark, with a few red safety lamps lit, and the subtle roar of the big engines chewing through air on the other side of the fuselage. It felt very World War II, very we-jump-tonight, strangely melodramatic.

Here I am again, he thought.

Here I go. Face some other motherfucker with a rifle. Been here before.

But he did not feel lucky tonight. He felt scared, tense, rattled, keeping it hidden only because poor Bonson was so much more rattled.

He looked at the end of the bay, where the big ramp was cranked up. In a few minutes, it would yawn open into a platform and he would get a signal and he would step out, and gravity would take him. He'd fall for two minutes. Maybe the chute would work and maybe it wouldn't. He wouldn't know until it happened.

He tried to exile his feelings. If you get mad, you get excited, you get careless, you get dead. Don't think about all that shit. You just do what has to be done, calmly, professionally, with a commitment to mission and survival. Don't think about the other man. It's what has to be done. It's the only thing that makes sense.

He tried not to think of Julie or of the man who'd come across time and space to kill her for what she didn't even know she knew. He tried not to think of his ancient enemy and all the things that had been taken from him by the man. He tried not to think of larger meanings, of the geopolitics of it all, of the systems opposed to each other, and himself and the other, as mere surrogates. He exiled all that.

"Sarge?"

He turned; it was a young air crewman, a tech sarge who looked about fifteen.

"Yeah?"

"You got your parachute on upside down."

"Oh, Christ," said Bob.

"You haven't been to jump school, have you?"

"Saw a guy parachute in a movie once. Ain't it the same thing?"

The kid smiled.

"Not quite. Here, let me help you."

It took just a few seconds for the young NCO to have him geared up correctly.

Yeah, that made sense. It felt much better; now it fit right, it was okay.

"You need oxygen, too, you know. There's no air to breathe this high."

"Yeah, they told me."

The kid had a helmet for him, a jet pilot thing with a plastic face shield, an oxygen mask and a small green tank. The tank was yet another weight on the belt over his jumpsuit, and the tube ran up to the helmet, which fit close around his skull and supported it in plastic webbing.

"I feel like a goddamned astronaut," Swagger said.

It was nearly time.

Bonson came back.

Behind them, with a shriek of frigid wind, the ramp door of the Hercules opened. It settled downward with an electrical grind, and outside the dark sky swirled by.

Bonson hooked himself up to a guy wire so he wouldn't be sucked out. The tech sarge gave Bob a last go-round, pronounced him fit and wished him well. With the ramp down, there was no oxygen and so they were all on oxygen. He felt the gush of air into his lungs from the clammy rubber mask around his mouth, under the face plate. He tasted rubber.

Bob and Bonson edged down the walkway to the yawning rear of the aircraft. The wind rose, howled and buffeted them; the temperature dropped. Bob felt the straps of the chute, the weight of the jump bag tethered to his ankle, the warmth of the jump helmet. Outside he could see nothingness with a sense of commotion.

"You cool?" said Bonson over the radio.

Bob nodded. He was too old for this. He felt weighed

down with the rifle, the optics gear, the boots, the helmet, the parachute, all of it too much, all of it pulling on him.

"You got it? You just cannonball when you go out. You fall, you fall, you fall, then the thing opens up automatically. You can stabilize with the risers on the left or the right of the chute. I don't need to tell you. You've done it before."

Again, Bob nodded, as Bonson went ahead nervously into his own microphone.

"No problem. You get there, you save the women, you'll be all right. And we get Solaratov, no problem. We've got it all set up. As soon as the weather breaks, another team goes in, it's all taken care of."

Another nod.

"Okay, they're saying thirty seconds now."

"Let's go."

Bob moved slowly toward the gap in the rear of the plane. There was no sense of anything; just blackness beyond the ramp.

"Okay, get ready," said Bonson.

Bob paused in the buffeting torrent of black air. He was scared.

"Go!" said Bonson, and Bob stepped forward and off, into nothingness.

Nikki awoke early, before first light. It was a habit she could not break, partially because of her own pulsating energies but also because she had for so long awakened then to feed the horses.

Today, there were no horses to feed, but there was a whole new world of snow to explore.

She threw a bathrobe on over her pajamas and stepped into her moccasins and went downstairs. The fire was sleepy, so she threw a log onto it, and amid a spray of sparks, it began to stir to life. Then she went to the doorway, cracked it open. A wintry blast howled through, and yes, it was still snowing, but not as hard. She got the door open and crept out on the porch, pulling her bathrobe tight.

The world was lost in snow. Its natural shapes were blurred and softened. It was everywhere; on the fences, drifting over them; in strange hills that had been bushes; mounded on the roof of the barn and on the woodpile. She had never seen so much snow in her life.

The children who had once lived here had a sled; she'd seen it in the barn. She knew where she'd go, too. Off to the left, not too far, there was a slope, not a steep one but just enough to get up some good momentum.

She looked through the darkness to the mountains of the east, invisible in the slanting, falling snow. But she could feel a change coming somehow. She couldn't wait for daylight. She couldn't wait!

Solaratov watched the child through his night-vision goggles, a far-off figure in a field of green in the bottom of the aquarium that was the world of electronically amplified ambient light. Excited by the temptations of snow, she'd come early and stood, outside on the porch, a little green blob. Then she reached down and cupped a clutch of snow into a neat little ball, and threw it out into the yard.

The waiting was at last over. He pushed up the NV goggles, and took up the Leica range finder. He put the ranging dot on her and pressed the button, sending an invisible spurt of laser out to bounce off her and back, trailing its logo of data. Five hundred fifty-seven, it said in the display superimposed on the right of the image.

Five hundred fifty-seven meters. He thought for a second, computing drift and drop, and then lifted the rifle to place the mil-dot beneath the crosshairs on her. It felt obscene to target a child like this, but he had to familiarize himself with the sensations.

The dot blotted out her heroic little chest. His muscles, though stiff, remained hard, and he locked the rifle under a bridge of bone to the earth, and held the dot there with the professional shooter's discipline. No wobble, no tremble, nothing to betray fear or doubt. His finger touched the trigger. Were he to will it, four and a half pounds of pressure and she would leave the earth forever.

He put the rifle down, glad that he still had energy.

Clearly now, it was just a matter of time.

He knew something was wrong immediately.

Instead of curling his body into a cannonball, he flailed, feeling panic and fear. He had never fallen before, and the sense of no control completely stunned him. It was no question of courage, just his limbic system; he was suddenly unmanned by the sense of utter helplessness. The wind hammered at him like fists; his body planed and fluttered and he tried to bring his ankles up to his wrists but he could get nothing to work against the power of the air rushing up at him at hundreds of miles an hour.

He screamed but there was no sound, because he screamed into an oxygen mask. But it was a scream, nevertheless, mad and ripped from his lungs like a physical thing, like an animal. He heard it rattling around in his helmet.

He had never screamed before in a hundred or a thousand fights. He had never screamed at Parris Island or any of the places where he'd had to kill or die. He had never screamed on the nights before action, in contemplation of what might happen on the next day, and he never screamed the day after, in contemplation of the horrors that he had seen or caused or had just missed him. He'd never screamed in grief or rage.

He screamed.

The scream was pure fury boiling out of his soul, unstoppable but lost in the hugeness of the air pressure.

He fell through darkness, feeling lost and powerless and, above all, vulnerable.

Don't let me die, he thought, all commitment to mission, all dedication to justice, all sense of fatherhood gone. He fell screaming in complete treason to everything he thought he believed in, his arms clawing at the air, his legs pumping, the sense of weightlessness almost rendering him useless.

Don't let me die, he thought, feeling tears on his face under the Plexiglas of the helmet, gasping for breath. *Please don't let—*

The parachute shuddered open with a bang; he could simply sense it mutating strangely on his back, and the next split second, he was slammed into something that felt like a wall but was only air as the chute filled and grabbed him from doom. He could see nothing in the blackness, but he knew the ground was close and then, far before it should have happened, he whacked into it and felt his head fill with stars and concussion and confusion, as his body went hard against the ground. He staggered to his feet, trying to find the release lever for the chute in case it filled with air and pulled him away. He could not; it puffed and began to drag him, and the Plexiglas before him splintered; his face began to sting and bleed. His arm was numb. The equipment bag banged over the rocks as he slid along and seemed to rack his leg a couple of extra inches. He clawed at the harness, and then it popped open and the harness somehow rid itself of him, as if he were unwanted baggage, and deposited him in the snow as it went its merry way.

Oh, Christ, he thought, blinking, feeling pain everywhere. He looked around and saw nothing at all recognizable. He struggled to pop off his helmet, and felt just a second's worth of air until the air turned frozen. He pulled a white watch cap from his pocket and yanked a snow mask down from its folds. He pulled the equipment bag over, opened it and got the parka and the leggings on. The warmth comforted him. Then he yanked out the night-vision goggles, fiddled for the switch and looked around.

Oh, Christ, he thought.

Nothing was as it seemed. He was on a slope, not a

flat; there was no ranch house ahead because in the most obvious possible way there was no *ahead*.

There was only down, barren and remote.

He was way up.

He was lost in the mountains.

CHAPTER FORTY-SEVEN

Julie was dreaming. In the dream she and Bob and Donny were at a picnic somewhere in the green mountains by a lake. It felt very real, but was still clearly a dream. Everybody was so happy, much happier than they'd ever been in their conscious lives. Bob and Donny were drinking beer and laughing. Her father was there, too, and Bob's father, Earl, who'd been killed way back in 1955, and she was cooking hamburgers on a grill and all the men were drinking beer and laughing and tossing a ball around and flirting with Nikki.

Maybe it wasn't a dream. Maybe it had begun as a dream, something spun out of her subconscious, but now she was aware that she was controlling it, and somehow trying to keep it alive, to make it last longer as she hung in a gray zone just between wakefulness and sleep. Peter was there too. Earnest, decent, dedicated Peter Farris, who'd loved her so, his ardency poignant. He looked strange because Bob and Donny were so Marine-straight with their short, neat hair and Peter was the complete hippie, with a splotchy purple tie-dyed T-shirt, a headband, his hair a mess, a sad little Jesus beard. Peter's feelings got very hurt because he felt so powerless next to the two stronger men, and that somehow made him more poignant. He loved her so! Donny apologized, because it wasn't in him to hurt anybody's feelings. Bob was just watching them, Mr. Southern Cracker Alpha Male, amused by their silly youthfulness, and his dad and her dad were having a good laugh, though what a state trooper and a heart surgeon, one dead in 1955, the other in 1983, would have had to talk about was anybody's guess.

And there was someone else.

He was by himself, a graceful young man, also amused

by the manhood convention here on the shores of the Gitche Gumee or wherever it was, and it took her a while to figure out who he was, and then at last she knew it was Trig.

She'd seen him twice, no, three times. She'd seen him that night when Peter had dragged her to that party in Georgetown and he lived in that funny little place with all the bird paintings, and she'd seen him when he'd driven Donny out in the red Triumph to find her at West Potomac Park just before the last big May Day demonstration, and she saw him again, three nights later, at the farm in Germantown, where he and that Irishman were loading bags of fertilizer into the truck.

Trig: another of the lost boys of the Vietnam War. All of them were linked in some terrible chain, forever changed, forever mutilated. Nobody ever came back from that one. No one got home free. Donny, dead on DEROS. Peter, smashed, somehow, and found with a broken spine months later. Trig, blown to pieces in Madison, Wisconsin. And Bob, the only survivor but maybe the most hurting of them all, with his black-dog moods and his lost years and his self-hatred and his need to test himself against gunfire again and again and again, as if to finally earn the death he yearned for so intently and join his friends. Death or DEROS: which would come to Bob Lee Swagger first?

"Mommy?" her daughter asked her.

"Oh, honey," she said, but it was not in the dream, it was here in the dark, warm bedroom.

Julie blinked and came out of it. No, it wasn't a dream. It couldn't have been a dream. It was too real to be a dream.

"Mommy, please, I want to go ride the sled."

"Oh, Lord, honey, it's—"

"Please, Mommy."

She turned and looked at the clock. It was close to seven. Outside, just the faintest hint of light pressed through the margins of the shade.

"Oh, baby," she said, "it's so *early*. The snow's going to be around for a long, long time."

The deep ache in her body was there and the awkwardness conferred by the arm cast. She hadn't taken a painkiller since last night, halfway through *Singin' in the Rain* when her baby girl had fallen asleep on her lap.

"Please, Mommy. I'll go get Aunt Sally."

"Don't you *dare* wake Aunt Sally. God bless her, she's earned her escape from the Swaggers and all their problems. I'll get up, baby. Just give me a moment or two."

"Yes, Mommy. I'll go get dressed."

The child ran out.

So early, thought Julie. So damned early.

He tried the GPS receiver. Nothing happened. Eventually it lit up but the LCD produced a rattle of red digitized gibberish. Evidently it had banged too hard when the bag hit the ground and was out of whack. He turned on the radio, and heard through his earphones, "Bob One, Bob One, where are you, we have lost contact; goddammit, Swagger, where are you?"

He spoke: "Bob Control, this is Bob One, do you copy?"

"Bob One, Bob One, we have lost contact. Bob One, where are you?"

"Do you copy, Bob Control, do you copy? I am sending, does anybody hear me?"

"Bob One, Bob One, please notify control, we have lost contact."

Shit!

He ripped the thing off and threw it in the snow. The next thing to check was the rifle. He opened the case, gave it a once-over, saw that it seemed okay, but he doubted it. The same harsh impact that had screwed the electronics might have knocked the scope out of zero. There was no way to know except in the shooting. He couldn't shoot now so there wasn't a thing to do except hope that Unertl built the scope real nice and tight and that it would stand up where the other stuff didn't.

He stood. Pain rocked him, and he had a flash where he thought he might lose it, faint, and die under the snow. They'd find him next year. It would be in all the newspapers.

Fuck me if I can't take a joke, he thought.

He looked about. In one direction lay only an endless sea of snowy mountains. That couldn't be the way, and by God, yes, beyond the mountains at the horizon was just the faintest smear of light, signifying the east.

He appeared to be on the highest one. He knew the overflight went on a northwest-southeast access, aiming to put him into the flats below the mountains and the ranch. If he had overshot his mark, the deviation was longitudinal, not latitudinal; that would put him on Mount McCaleb, theoretically on its northwest slope. Down below, say six thousand feet, that would be where the ranch was. He couldn't see; the valley in that direction was lost in a strata of cloud, which closed it off like a lost world. He could see only peaks across a gap that he took to be a valley.

He slung the rifle over his shoulder, checked his compass and set off down the slope.

The land was barren, without vegetation, as if in some recent time a nuclear bomb had cleaned out all the life. The snow lay in undulating forms, sometimes thick and difficult, other times surprisingly light. Twice he tripped on rocks unseen under the smooth white crust.

Flakes still fell, stinging his eyes. But the fierce wind had died and no snow devils whirled up to defy him. He couldn't even hear the wind. He went downhill at an angle, almost galloping, feeling the boots bite into the stuff, trying to find a rhythm, a balance between speed and care. He was breathing hard and inside his parka began to sweat. He came to a rock outcropping and detoured around it.

Occasionally, he'd stop, flip down the night-vision goggles, and see—nothing. Ahead and below, the clouds lingered like a solid wall, impenetrable. The goggles resolved the cloud mass as green, only partially distinct from the green of the snow up here, and amplified the light so much that distinctions could hardly be made, and no valley could yet be seen through them: only an infinity of green, cut now and then by a black scut of rock.

It occurred to him that he might have completely misfigured. He could be anywhere, just heading foolishly down to some empty, remote valley where there would be no highway, no ranch, no Julie, no Sally, no Nikki. Just empty Western space, as Jeremiah Johnson had found it.

Then what?

Then nothing.

Then it's over. He'd wander, maybe hunting a little. He'd live, certainly, but in three days or a week, under a growth of beard, he'd emerge to find a different world, without a wife, with a bitter, orphaned daughter, with everything he'd worked for gone, all his achievements gone. Solaratov gone back to Moscow for blintz and borscht, with a nice reward in his pocket.

Just go, he thought.

Just push it out, think it through and do it.

He looked over his shoulder and got more bad news: it was getting lighter.

He raced the day downhill.

A light came on. Upstairs.

Solaratov stirred.

He was not cold at all. He rolled over, cracking fingers and joints, fighting the general numbness that his body had picked up in its long stay on the ground.

A shawl of snow cracked on his back as he moved, splitting and falling from him. He'd picked up the last inch. That was all right, he knew. A man can actually last in snow much longer than a rifle can.

The rifle was more problematical. Lubrication can solidify in the cold, turn to gum, destroy the trigger pull, catch in the next cycle of the bolt. The gasses don't burn as hot, so the bullet flies to a new point of impact, unpredictable. The scope stiffens somehow, comes out of zero. His breath could fog on it, obscuring his vision. Nothing works quite as well. There were a hundred reasons why a good shot could go bad.

He opened the Remington's bolt, slid it backward. No impediment marked the smoothness of the glide: no, the oil had not gummed in any way.

He pushed it ever so slowly forward until it would go no farther, then pushed the bolt handle downward two inches, feeling the bolt lock in place.

Without assuming the position to shoot, he put his hand around the pistol grip of the rifle, threaded a finger through the trigger guard, felt the curvature of the trigger. His finger caressed it through the glove. Without consciously willing it, his trigger finger squeezed ever so slightly, feeling a dry twig of resistance for an instant, and then the trigger broke with the precision of a bone-china teacup handle snapping off. Perfect: four and a half pounds, not an ounce more, not an ounce less.

He pulled the rifle to him and examined the muzzle where the Browning Optimizing System was screwed to a precise setting to control barrel vibration. The setting was perfect and tight.

Next, he slipped his glove off, unzipped his parka, reached inside the many layers until he reached his shirt, where he'd stored twenty rounds in a plastic case. Close to his heart. Close to the warmest part of him. He opened the box and removed four. Then he carefully returned the box to the pocket, to preserve the warmer environment. He opened the bolt and slid the cartridges, one by one, into the magazine. This somehow always pleased him. It was the heart of the issue of the rifle: the careful fit of round to chamber, the slow orchestration of the bolt syncopating this union, then vouchsafing it with the final, camming lockdown that felt solid as a bank vault.

No safety. Never used safeties. Didn't believe in them.

If you used safeties, it meant you didn't trust yourself. If you gave yourself up to the whim of mechanics, you begged trouble. You just kept your finger off the trigger until you were on target. That's how it worked.

Solaratov blew on his hand, pulled the glove on, then shifted his vision downhill to the house.

In the slightly intensified light of the rising dawn, the house was more distinct. The upstairs light remained on, but now one downstairs had been added. Its orange glow suffused the night. Because of the angle he could see one of the windows but the others were shielded by the rake of the porch roof. Behind that visible window, now and then a figure moved. It would be the woman, would it not, preparing breakfast? Making coffee, scrambling eggs, pouring milk for cereal for the child.

But which woman? The FBI agent's wife? Or the sniper's wife? That's why he couldn't send a shot into the shadow and be gone. Suppose it was the wrong woman? He could not afford another failure and, worse, he would never, ever again come upon conditions so totally in his favor.

Do not rush, he told himself. Do not move until you are sure.

The light rose, eventually, though second by second one could detect no difference. Now the day had gone from black edging to pewter to pewter edging to gray. The clouds were still low, though no snow was falling; no sun today. It would be hours before anyone could helicopter in, hours beyond that before they could come overland, except by snowmobile, and what point was there to that? By that time he'd be far, far away from the scene of the crime.

Telephone!

Of course! That last detail, the one you forgot, the one that could get you killed.

He fires, kills the woman and retreats. But the other woman sees her dead in the snow, and quickly picks up the phone and calls the sheriff's office. Deputies nearby on snowmobiles are reached by radio. They could get here in minutes; they'd zoom up the slope and quickly find his tracks. They'd call in his location. Other deputies would be dispatched. He'd end up in some half-baked last stand in this godforsaken chunk of America, brought low by a hayseed with a deer rifle who was a part-time deputy sheriff or forest ranger.

His eyes went back to the house, explored it carefully until at last he found the junction of the phone wires where they left the pole that ran along the road and descended to the house. His eyes met an astonishment!

The line was already down! The snow had taken the line down!

Now *there* was an omen! It was as if the God he had been taught not to believe in had come to his aid, not merely by bringing in the storm to cover his tracks but by breaking the phone line! Was God a communist?

He smiled just the littlest bit.

He looked back. A sudden slash of orange light flicked across the snow, as the front door opened.

He watched as a little girl ran off the porch and dived into a pile of snow. He could hear her laughter all the way up here. There was no other sound.

Then, standing on the edge of the porch, he saw the woman.

He was in the soup now.

The cloud was everywhere, visibility sunk to nothing. He was in the cloud and felt its penetrating moisture. Wetness gathered on his parka, glazing the white arctic-warfare pattern. His eyelashes filled with dampness. It gleamed off the pewter-colored rifle barrel.

The night-vision goggles were worthless now: engaged, they simply produced green blankness.

Throw them, he thought. Dump them. Complete shit!

But instead he pushed them up on his head; what would happen if he came out of it and needed them to negotiate rocks or something?

Instead he groped onward, the rifle hanging on his shoulder, trying desperately to keep up speed. But now the ground was rockier and he couldn't see far enough to choose the right paths through the descending gullies, the twisty snow-clogged passage between rocks, the increasing tufts of vegetation bent into nightmare forms by the thick, wet snow. His own breath blossomed before him, foamy and betraying.

He fell. The snow jammed into his throat, got down inside the parka. His leg hurt like hell. A shiver ran down his body.

Get up, goddammit!

He climbed back to his feet, remembering another dark day of fog and wet. That was so long ago; it seemed to have happened in some other lifetime. That day he'd been so electric, so animal, so tiger; his reflexes were alive, and in a secret way he now realized, he loved it all.

Now he felt old and slow. His limbs were working out of coordination. The cold and the wet fought him. His leg hurt, particularly his hip. A slow sting had begun inside his thigh and he realized that his impact had reopened the incision above his knee where Solaratov's bullet had nestled all these years in its capsule of scar tissue.

The rage came again, a hot red tide, a frenzy of mutilating hatred.

God help me, he prayed.

God help the sniper.

He raced downward, coming across a clear spot, and thought for just a moment he might be out of it, but saw in the next second it was only an illusion.

Snow!

In the gray light of dawn the snow was like a giant mound of softness. She thought of ice cream, vanilla, in big white piles everywhere, thick enough to grab her body and support her when she threw herself into it. She tasted it and received only messages of coldness and texture, which in the next fraction of a second became cold water, amazingly.

She giggled in delight.

"Mommy! It's fun!"

"Honey, don't go far. I can't get you yet. The sun will be up in a few minutes."

"Wheeeeeeee! I want to sled."

"No, baby, not yet. Wait till Aunt Sally is up. If you get hurt, I can't reach you."

She struggled through the snow, which reached her knees, not listening a bit. The sled was in the barn. She knew where, exactly. The barn was empty but the sled leaned against the wall, beyond the eight stalls, in a feed ing pen. It was an old sled—she could see it exactly in her mind—with rusty red runners and a battered wooden flat-bed. She should have gotten it last night when they said it would snow!

"Nikki!" her mother called.

Nikki turned back and saw her mother, standing on the edge of the porch, wrapped in a great parka over her immobilizing cast, her hand shielding her eyes from the snippets of snow the wind occasionally caught and flung.

"Nikki! Come back."

Her mother stood there.

Is it her?

Goddammit, is it her?

The woman stood rooted to the front of the porch. Against his finger, the trigger was a tease.

The mil-dot had her centered perfectly, and no tremor came to his arm. His position was superb. *Adductor magnus* was firm, anchoring him to the earth. He was four pounds away from the end of the war. No cold, no fear, no tremor, no doubt, no hesitation.

But . . . *is it her?*

He had only seen her through his scope at 722 meters for one second: he couldn't tell. She was wrapped in a coat, and one hand held it secured. Possibly that meant the other hand was immobilized in a cast; possibly it meant nothing. That's how you wore a coat if you didn't want to put it on and button it. Any person would wear it that way.

The woman ducked back. She was gone.

He exhaled.

"Wheeeeeeeeeeee!" came the far-off sound of the child.

"Wheeeeeeeeeeee!"

It was so far away, light, dry, just the smallest of things. Maybe a freak twist of wind blew it up to him or the kindness of God.

But there it was: *my child.*

He'd know it anywhere—the throaty timbre, the vitality, the heroism. Spirit. Goddamn, did that girl have some spunk. *Got it from her granddad; now there was a man with spunk!*

She was to the left somewhere, very far away. In that direction he could see nothing except rougher ground.

Fuck it, he thought.

He unslung the rifle and with a swift open-and-shut cocked it, jacking one of Federal's primo .308s into the spout.

He ran. He ran. He ran.

He dashed through the rocks, building momentum, his legs fighting the splash of snow that each one's energy unleashed. It ate at his heart and lungs, all the work, and his breath came in dry spurts, wrapped in a sheath of pain. Still, he pressed, he ran, and when he came out of the rocks, the slope dropped off closer to vertical and he had to slow up to keep from falling, almost leaping down through the snow, his momentum again building, right on the tippy edge of control.

Then suddenly he was out of it.

The day lightened as the cloud disappeared and before him stretched a valley filled with snow, like a vast bowl of off-color vanilla ice cream, still only gray in the rising illumination. He saw a house, telephone poles signaling a road, a corral with only the tips of the posts visible in the blanket of white, a barn itself laden with the stuff, all pretty as a greeting card—and his child.

She was a few yards in front of the porch, dancing.

"Wheeeeeeeeccccc!" she screamed again, her voice powerful and ringing.

Bob saw that he was on a ridge to the far side of the horseshoe of elevation that surrounded the place on three sides.

He saw lights in the house, a warm slash of brilliance from an open door and, on the porch now, something else moved and came out.

He saw her, standing on the steps, a parka wrapped about her, his wife. Nikki threw a snowball at her and she ducked and there was just a moment when her coat fell open and slipped and he could see the cast on her left arm.

He turned and flopped to the ground, finding prone, building the position, trying to slow the pounding of his heart.

The sniper. Find the sniper.

It was her. She ducked, the coat came open, then she shuddered it back onto her shoulders. But her left arm was immobilized in plaster.

Yes. Now.

He squirmed, making minute corrections. He didn't rush. What was the point of rushing?

There was nothing in the world except the woman standing there in her coat.

Five hundred fifty-seven meters.

Hold two dots below the reticle, that is, two dots high, to account for the bullet's drop over the long flight and the subtle effects of gravity over the downward trajectory.

Concentrate.

It's just another soft target, he thought, in a world full of soft targets.

He expelled a half breath, held the rest in his lungs. His body was a monument, *Adductor magnus* tight. The mil-dots didn't move: they were on her like death itself. The rifle was a chastised lover, so still and obedient. His mind emptied. Only the trigger stood between himself and the end of the war. It was a four-and-a-half-pound trigger, and four pounds were already gone.

Bob scanned the ridge as it curved away from him, knowing his man would set up to the east to keep the sun to his back. The scope was 10X, which was big enough to give him a little width of vision. God, why didn't he have binoculars? Binoculars would—

There he was.

Not him, not the man, but the rifle barrel, black against the white snow, sheltered near a boulder. The rifle was still, braced on one hand in a steady, perfect prone. In the lee of the rock, Bob knew Solaratov was making his last-second corrections, nursing his concentration to the highest point.

Long shot. Oh, such a long shot.

He steadied, prayed, for he knew the man was ready to fire.

It was close to a thousand meters. With a rifle he'd never zeroed, whose trigger was unknown to him.

But only a second remained, and his crosshairs found the rifle barrel, then rose above it based on his instinctive guesstimate of the range.

Is it right? Is this it?

Oh shit, he thought.

Time to hunt, he thought, and fired.

CHAPTER FORTY-EIGHT

Bonson felt a huge blast of utter, scalding frustration shudder through him. Agh! Ugh! Umf! This is where your major strokes came from: some little fritz in the brain and, in the blink of an eye, you're fried. His blood pressure felt dangerously high. He wished he had somebody to smack or kill. His muscles tightened into brick; redness flashed in his mind. His teeth ground against one another.

He spoke again into the microphone.

"Bob One, Bob One, this is Bob Control, come in, come in, *goddammit,* come in!"

"He isn't there, sir," said the tech sergeant, who was in the radio bay with him. "We've lost him."

Or the fucking cowboy's on his own, Bonson thought.

"Okay, switch me through to the larger net."

The sergeant dialed the new frequency on the console of the radio.

"Ah, Hill, this is Bonson, are you there?"

"Yes, sir," spoke his second in command from Mountain Home Air Force Base. "The whole team is in. We're in good shape."

"You've liaised with the state police?"

"Yes, sir. I have a Major Hendrikson on standby."

"Okay, here's the deal. We've lost contact with our asset. Tell this major to get state police helicopters in there as soon as possible. Sooner, if possible."

"Yes, sir, but the word I'm getting is that nobody's flying into those mountains until at least ten A.M. There's still real bad weather. And these guys are spread pretty thin."

"Shit."

"I did talk to Air Force. We can get some low-level radars set up on three surrounding mountains by 1200, assuming they can move in by 1000, and we can get good position on any incoming helos. If this Russian plans to exit by helo, we'll nab him."

"This guy's the best in the world at escape and evasion. He's worked mountains before. Swagger knew that. If Swagger doesn't get him, he's gone. It's that simple."

The man on the other end was silent.

"Goddamn, I hate to be beat by him! I *hate* it," said Bonson to nobody in particular. He ripped off his earphones and threw them against the fuselage of the plane; the plastic on one of them cracked and a piece spun off and landed at his feet. He stomped it into the floor, grunting mightily.

The sergeant happened to look away at precisely that moment, as the navigator came back to get some coffee from the thermos in the radio bay, and the two aviators locked eyes. The sergeant rolled his eyes, pointed his finger at his head and rotated it quickly, communicating in the universal language of human gesture a single idea: screwball.

The navigator nodded.

Julie knew at once it was a shot. The supersonic crack was sharp and trailed a wake of echo as it bounced off the sheltering hills.

"Nikki! Get in here! Now!" she screamed.

The little girl turned, paused in confusion, and then there was another one, like the snap of a whip, and Nikki ran toward her. Both recognized it from the time they'd been shot at so recently.

"Come on, come on!" yelled Julie, and she grabbed her daughter, pulled her into the house, locked the door.

She heard another shot, from a different location; an answering shot.

Men were trying to kill each other nearby.

"Get downstairs," she said to her daughter. "Now! And don't come up, no matter what, until you hear the police."

The girl ran into the cellar. Julie grabbed a phone, and found at once there was no dial tone. It was dead.

She looked outside and could see nothing except the hugeness of the snow, now lightening as full dawn approached. She heard no more shots.

She ran upstairs, and found Sally groggily wandering down the hall.

"Did you—?"

"Someone's shooting," Julie yelled.

"Jesus," Sally said. "Did you call the police?"

"The line's down or dead or something."

"Who—?"

"I don't know. There's two of them. Come on, we have to get into the basement."

The two women ran down the stairs, found the door into the cellar and descended into near darkness.

The cellar windows had been snowed in and only diffuse light showed through them. It was cold.

"Mommy," said Nikki. "I'm scared."

"I'm scared too," said Julie.

"I wish Daddy was here."

"I do too," said Julie.

"Now, you get in the corner," said Sally. "I'll figure out some way to block the door, just in case. I'm sure it's just hunters or something."

"No," said Julie. "They were shooting at each other. They're not hunters. They're snipers."

"I wish Daddy were here," said Nikki again.

Snow showered across Solaratov and his mind came out of its deep pool of concentration to recognize the familiar cloud of debris a high-velocity round delivers when it strikes, and the next split second the whipsong of the rifle crack reached him as it shattered the sound barrier.

Under fire.

The left.

The left.

Another detonation spewed snow into the sky.

Under fire.

He tore himself from the scope, looked to the left to see nothing, because of the shielding rock. But he knew from the sound that the man had to be on the rim of the ridge.

He looked back into the valley to just catch the little girl as she dipped under the porch roof, and in another split second heard the door slam.

Damn!

They were gone.

Who was shooting at him?

He realized now he was invisible to the shooter, else he'd be dead. The shooter could not see him behind his rock.

He knew too the man now had the rock zeroed, knowing full well that Solaratov would have to come around it to return fire.

He felt no fear. He felt no curiosity. He felt no disappointment, he felt no surprise. His mind did not work that way. Only: Problem? Process. And, solution!

Instead of rising to come around the rock, he backed, low as a lizard, through the snow, trusting that the man's scope would be so powerful that its field of view would be narrow and that the whiteness of his camouflage would also shield him from recognition.

He squirmed backward as low in the snow as a man could be, sliding through the stuff as if he were some kind of arctic snake. He canted his head as he backed, and as he slid out from behind the rock, he saw his antagonist, a disturbance ever so slight along the line of the ridge that could only be a man hunched over a rifle, desperately looking for a target. He studied and was sure he saw it move or squirm or something.

What was the distance? He pivoted on the ground, finding a good angle to the target, splaying his legs, coming into that good, solid prone. *Adductor magnus.* In the scope, yes, a man, possibly. In white. Another sniper. Low on the ridge. He watched his crosshairs settle, telling himself not to hurry, not to rush, not to jerk. He couldn't get a clear sight picture and he didn't have time to shoot a laser at the target to get its distance. He pivoted slightly, found a bush coned in snow, which he took to be of three feet girth. By covering it in the scope with mil-dots and racking through the math—the black mass covered two dots; multiply the assumed one meter in height by one thousand and divide by two to get the approximation of a thousand yards: say, less than a thousand but more than nine hundred yards he held four dots high. With greater concentration and less art, he steadied himself, pivoted to find the disturbance that had to be the man but was not really clear, felt his finger on the trigger but did not think about it, and let it decide itself, as if it had a brain, what to do next, and then it fired.

A geyser of snow erupted seven feet to the right of Bob, followed by the whipcrack of sound. Windage. The Russian had the range but there was some crosswind and the 7mm hadn't quite the weight to stand up to it. It had drifted ever so slightly. But how could Solaratov have read wind if he were shooting across the raw space of the valley? He wouldn't make that mistake again.

But quickly he'd understand that, cock again and shoot.

Bob squirmed back, feeling himself sliding a little off the edge of the ridge, and in the next split second, another eruption blew a hole in the surface of the planet, a big spout of flung snow and rock frags. It hit exactly where he'd been but just barely was no longer.

Oh, this motherfucker is so good. This motherfucker won't make another mistake.

Bob slid back farther.

No shots had gone toward the house. For a little while, at least, his wife was safe. He knew she'd have the sense to head to the cellar with Nikki and Sally and lock up and wait.

Meanwhile he had but one choice. That was to low-crawl along the ridge and hope that its tiny incline was enough to shield him from Solaratov's vision. Solaratov would realize he couldn't go up or down, he'd never go toward him; he could only fall back around the mountain until he disappeared around it, and could then get up and move to cover and set up an ambush. Solaratov would go up; elevation was power in this engagement. Whoever reigned on high, reigned, because he'd have the angle into a target where the other man would have nothing.

That was the plan: to get out of this area of dangerous vulnerability, move like hell when safe and find a good hide. Solaratov would have to come around the mountain to get him, but he'd come around high. Bob knew he'd get a good shot, maybe only one, but he knew he could make it.

He tried to calculate the differences between his .308 168-grain round and the Russian's 7mm Remington Magnum. The Magnum flew four hundred feet per second faster with almost a thousand pounds more muzzle energy; it shot so much flatter. The Russian, if he were under five hundred yards, could hold just a bit over him and pull the trigger, not worrying about drop. So he'd have to stay at least five hundred yards ahead, because the slight drop, plus the windage, would be his best defense.

He turned back, squirmed to the lip of the ridge, but could see nothing except the quiet house far below and the ridgeline running around the base of the mountain.

But he was coming. The Russian was coming. The Russian was hunting him.

Solaratov studied the situation. He looked across the horseshoe through his Leica binoculars at the ridge where he'd spotted the other shooter and understood the man couldn't go up or down, for both would expose him and he'd be dead in a second. He could only crawl desperately away, round the flank of the mountain, and try and set up in the mountain's next cove, waiting for a shot.

He shot a laser over and the readout told him the

range was about 987 meters. He calculated the drop to be about forty-two inches from his five hundred-yard zero, which was four dots high on the mil-dot reticle. Now that he'd solved the distance, he felt confident. But there was one other thing left to do.

He pulled the rifle down, and quickly unscrewed the BOSS nozzle, which controlled barrel vibrations. He reached inside his jacket and removed an AWC suppressor. It was a long black tube of anodized aluminum packed with "baffles," sound-absorbent material, like steel wool, and washers called "wipes"; it would reduce the 460-dB level of the gas exploding out of his muzzle by trapping it and bleeding it off, down to under a hundred db's, approximately the sound of a BB gun. From long distance, in the cone of the suppressor's pattern, that sound would be not merely significantly quieter but also more diffuse. There'd be no signature to reveal his position. Anyone on the receiving end would hear only the crack of the bullet as it broke the sound barrier, but nothing from the rifle's muzzle that could pinpoint a location. That meant he could shoot at his antagonist but his antagonist could not locate him by sound to shoot back. The downside: it changed his zero somewhat. How much? He'd have to reckon visually and make adjustments as he fired. He still felt that with the range finder, the suppressor gave him significant tactical advantage. He carefully screwed the suppressor tight to the muzzle.

He knew one other thing, because he had studied the topographical maps: that once his antagonist got around the mountain, he would be in for a surprise. The elevation was much steeper. There were no ridges as there were here fronting the valley. He'd have no place to hide. He'd be in the open.

Solaratov knew the wise move would be to scamper upward to gain further advantage of height. As he had the initiative at this point, he probably had a good four- or five-minute window of time where he could ascend, slide over one of the lesser hills of Mount McCaleb, and then shoot down upon his antagonist.

But he also knew that is exactly how the man's mind would work; that's how he'd figure it and he himself, once under shelter, would ascend quickly to try and prevent the Russian from gaining the height advantage.

But none of this mattered. The objective was the woman. The higher Solaratov got, the farther from the woman he got. It wasn't about some man-on-man thing, some sniper duel, some engagement of vanity. That was his advantage. The other man—it had to be Swagger— meant nothing to him. Solaratov's ego was uninvested; what had happened all those years back in Vietnam was totally disconnected from today, and that itself was a significant advantage.

Thus Solaratov made his plan: he would drop back a few yards behind the shield of an enfilade and then descend in freedom to the valley floor. He'd have a dangerous period of vulnerability as he went across the valley floor, but with his snow skills and his understanding of the other man's fear, he knew the other man would be busy setting up a hide in the next fold for a man he thought would ascend to fight.

Instead, the Russian would work from the ground and shoot uphill. He'd find cover in a treeline or behind rocks, he'd scope the distance, and he'd put his silent shots onto the antagonist, precise and perfect.

Swagger would not even know where the shots came from. He'd hear nothing. He'd be driven back until he was out of cover, and then he'd die.

Then, thought Solaratov, I'll backtrack, get into the house and do the women. Witnesses. I'll have to kill them all.

Bob squirmed in a last desperate burst of energy and came around the mountain. There is no lower or more degrading mode of transportation than the low crawl, and he had crawled enough in his time. His elbows and knees ached from the endless banging against the rock. Snow had gotten into his mouth and down his neck. Now at last: some kind of safety.

He paused, breathing hard, feeling wet with sweat. At least Solaratov had not gotten above him to fire down on him as he crawled.

His mouth was dry, his body heaved for oxygen that he could not replenish fast enough. His heart hammered like a drum beaten by a madman. His focus rolled in and out. But with a surge of will, he settled down. He pulled himself up the mountain and peeked back over some rocks at the valley he'd left behind.

Nothing.

No sign of Solaratov. The house lay undisturbed far below, in a huge field of undisturbed snow. The rock along the ridgeline where the Russian had set up now appeared deserted.

Bob picked up the rifle and used its scope to scan the mountain above. If he were Solaratov, that's what he would have done: climbed, worked around, always trying to get the elevation.

But he saw nothing; there was no snow in the air, no sign of disturbance. Putting the scope down, he tried to will himself into a kind of blankness, by which his subconscious, peripheral vision might note something his front-on, focused eyes might not, and send him a signal of warning. But he saw nothing; no movement registered on the slopes before him or the flatness beneath. He drew back.

Had Solaratov gone low, tried to get to the house and finish the job? Doubtful; he'd be exposed too long, and at any moment a shot could take him. He rethought it: yes, he has to come after me. His first priority is to eliminate the threat, because he is not on a kamikaze mission, he's no zealot. He's a professional. It only makes sense for him if he can escape; that means he's got an escape route, a fallback route, everything.

He will come.

He will hunt me.

Bob looked up. The slope of the mountain increased until it disappeared into fog, which was really cloud. Solaratov would get up there, come down by some magic and shoot down upon him.

He backed around, looking for a place to set up a hide.

The news was not good.

The ridge on which he perched, like a shelf that traced the jagged contours of the mountain, gave out 250 yards ahead; or, rather, it ran into a ravine, where a gash had been cut in the mountain, a long, ragged scar left by some ancient natural cataclysm. Now it was full of vegetation and rocks, all pristine with snow. But beyond the gap, there was nothing. The mountain slope was smooth and bare, offering no protection at all.

He looked up. It was too steep to climb at this point, though maybe beyond the gap he could engineer some elevation.

He looked down into a sector of valley. The floor was covered with snow-humped trees and brush, all bent into extravagant postures and made smooth under the weight of their white burden. It was a sculpture garden, a winter wonderland, a theme park, beautiful and grotesque and delicate at once, the frail tracery of the lesser branches all bearing their inch of white stuff. It looked quite poetic from six hundred yards up, but if you got caught down there, you'd never be able to move out.

There was really no choice. He had to get to the gash and take up a position in the rocks. He'd get one good shot at Solaratov, who would probably work his way down from above. Solaratov would have the advantage of elevation, but he wouldn't know where to look. He'd have to scout and he'd have to expose himself when he looked.

That's when I get him, Bob thought, wishing he believed it.

Then he noticed: it had begun to snow. Flakes cascaded down again, fluting and canting in the wind, a screen of them, dense and unyielding.

Visibility closed in.
Bob didn't like this a bit.

It was snowing. Solaratov, breathing hard, found a trail inside the scruffy vegetation that edged the mountain, where the overhanging leaves had cut down on snow accumulation. He almost ran, skirting the flat of the valley, staying off its exposure, staying away from the house for now. He knew that Bob could not see him from any elevation, through the snow-bearing branches. He probably wouldn't even look in the right direction.

Solaratov came around a curve of the valley, edged to the treeline and went hunched behind a fallen log that was somehow suspended by its branches. The snow fell gently around him out of the gray light. There was no sound at all in the world.

He read the land, looking for natural hides where an experienced man would go to ground. It was not a difficult problem, for the mountainside was largely featureless there, with only sparse vegetation to distract the eye. In fact the whole little war between them had been distilled to its most nearly abstract: two men in white in a white, cold world in white mountains of extreme elevation, hunting each other, going for whatever little edge of experience and luck they could find. Whoever read the problem better would win: it had nothing to do with courage or, really, even marksmanship. It would come down to this one thing: who was the better practitioner of the sniper's skills?

He could see a kind of gash in the mountainside ahead of him and realized that his quarry, coming around the edge, would have no choice but to seek refuge at its top.

He picked up his binoculars and scanned. He could see nothing but the rocks under their packing of snow. Visibility was not bad, though blurred by the falling snow.

He's up there. He's got to be.

He triggered a laser to the top of the gash, bounced it off a rock, and read the range in the readout: 654 meters.

Known distance. Upward. He did the math quickly and knew where to hold, computing in the uphill angle. He'd shoot from the center of the third mil-dot; that would put him there, crudely but close enough. And he felt his nearness to the mountain would shield the bullet from the predations of the wind; it wouldn't drift laterally.

He hunted patiently, looking for target indicators, for some implication that his prey was alive and hiding, and had not circled behind him. The rocks were everywhere, a kind of garden of stone humped in snow. He looked for disturbances in the snow, for sign of a man who'd crawled, upending the crust of white. But he could not see that for the angle.

What is his sign?
What is the sign?

Then he knew: the man's breath. It will rise like fog, maybe just a vapor, but it will show. It has to show. He has to breathe.

It was the slightest thing. Was it really there, or an optical illusion? But no, there it was: a slight curl through the snow, the suggestion of atmospheric density. It could be a man's breath leaking out as he huddled motionlessly in the rocks, awaiting his prey as he scanned upward.

Yes, my friend. There you are, he thought, slowly picking out the pattern of the arctic warfare camouflage, snow dappled with a little dead brown vegetation.

The man was on his belly, nestled behind rocks, in a little collection of them at the very top of the gash. He lay with the sniper's professional patience, totally engaged, totally calm. Solaratov could not see the rifle, but he saw the man.

There you are, he thought. There you are.

He again fired a laser at him: exactly 658 meters. He had the target.

He fixed markers in his mind's eye—a stand of snow-laden pines—put the binoculars down, raised the rifle and went to the scope. Of course it was not nearly so powerful as the binocs, and its field of vision was much smaller. But he found the pines, tracked down, waited, and yes, found the little trail of vapor that marked his prey.

He settled in, looking for the target. He could see just a half an inch of camouflaged parka above the rock, probably the upper surface of the prone back. He settled on this target, centering it on the third dot.

Should I fire?

I may not quite have enough of him visible to drive into the blood-bearing inner organs. I might just wound him.

My zero might be way off.

But then: so what? I have a suppressor.

He will not know where I am shooting from.

He will have to move as I bring him under fire.

He won't know if I'm above him or below him.

He'll have to move; I can chase him across the ravine. He'll run out of rocks. I'll have him.

He exhaled his breath, commanded his senses, felt the slow tick and twitch of his body as he made minute corrections, waited until the total rightness of it all fell across him.

The trigger broke, and with its odd, tiny sound, the rifle fired.

Bob lay quietly in the rocks. Above him a screen of snowy pines shielded him somewhat but left him with a good view of the direction he'd come. With the most discipline his body could invent, he scanned three zones: the first was the ridge, right where it came around the mountain; the next was a crop of rocks perhaps sixty meters above that; and the next was a notch in the mountain, perhaps two hundred meters up, that swam into and out of visibility as the cloud permitted. Solaratov would appear at one of those places as he came high around the mountain, with the idea of shooting downward.

Methodically he moved his eyes between them, the first, the second, the third, waiting.

Well, I did it, he tried to tell himself. I got him away

from my wife. In a little while they'll be here. He'll come, I'll get my shot, it'll be over then.

But he did not feel particularly good about it all. There was no sense of anything except unfinished business and that now, all these years later, it was his time.

I die today, came the message, insistent and powerful. *This is the day I die.*

He'd finally run up against a man who was smarter, a better shot, had more guts. Couldn't be many in the world, but by God, this was one.

The snow was falling more heavily now. It pirouetted downward from the low gray sky, and as he looked back to the house, still barely visible, he could hardly see it. It looked like it would snow for hours. That was not good. The longer it snowed, the longer it would take for help to arrive. He was on his own. He, and his ancient enemy.

Where is he?

It was making him nuts.

Where is—

A tremendous pain came across his back, as though someone had stood over him and whacked him, hard, with a fireplace poker.

Bob curled in the pain and knew instantly that he'd been hit. But no shock poured through him and took him out of his brain as it had when he'd been hit before. Instead a powerful spasm of fury kicked through him, and he knew in a second that he wasn't hit seriously.

He drew his legs up and at that moment the odd *BE-OWWWWWW!* of a bullet singing off a rock exploded just to his right, an inch above his skull.

He's got me, he thought, listening as the crack of the bullet snapping the sound barrier arrived.

But where was the muzzle blast?

There was no muzzle blast.

Suppressor, he thought. The motherfucker has a suppressor.

The sniper could be anywhere. Bob lay behind his rack of stones, waiting. No other shot came. Clearly he was completely zeroed but not quite visible enough for a good body or head shot.

Bob was almost paralyzed. No place to run, zeroed, completely outfoxed. Completely faked out.

He tried to run through the possibilities. Clearly Solaratov was not at one of the three places that Bob had determined. He'd gotten around somehow, and Bob believed him to be below, given the one shot that had ricocheted off the stone that shielded his head. The round had struck from downslope. If Solaratov were above him, it would be all over. The Russian had outthought him by descending into the valley and was now shooting upward. Bob tried to remember what was down there, and recalled a little patch of snow-packed forest. Somewhere the sniper was down there, but without a sound signature to locate him, he was effectively invisible.

Do something.

Sure: but what?

Move, crawl.

He has you.

If you move he kills you.

Checkmate. No moves possible. Caught in the rocks, trapped.

Then he realized that the Russian was but a few hundred yards from the house where the undefended women hid. After he killed Bob, it would take him five minutes to finish the job. Since it would be close-range work, he could leave no witnesses.

It was almost over now.

The Russian could see the man cowering behind the rocks and could sense his fear and rage and the closing in of his possibilities.

He filled with confidence. He had not fired twice but three times. The first shot landed about four feet above his target. That was the new zero. Swagger had not even noticed it. Quickly he dialed in the correction, fired again.

He hit him! The next shot barely missed him. But he knew: he had him!

It occurred to him to move ever so slightly, find a better shooting position and try and drive the killing shot home. But he had such an advantage now, why worry about it? Why move, not be able to shoot, just when the man is so helpless, has already been hit, is presumably leaking blood and in great pain.

The rifle rested on the tree trunk; he was comfortable behind it, sure that he was invisible from the ridge. The reticle was steady; he knew the range. It was merely a matter of time, of so little time.

What can he do?

He can do nothing.

Bob tried to clear the rattle from his head.

In the field, what would I do?

Call in artillery.

Call in smoke.

No artillery.

No smoke.

Throw a grenade.

No grenade.

Fire the Claymore.

No Claymore. The Claymore was in the case three thousand feet up the mountain. He wished he had it now.

Call in a chopper.

No chopper.

Call in tactical air.

No tactical air.

But a word caught somewhere in his mind.

Smoke.

No smoke.

It would not go away.

Smoke.

You move under smoke. Under smoke he cannot see you.

There is no smoke.

Why would the word not leave his head? Why would it not go away? *Smoke.*

What is smoke: gaseous chemicals producing a blur of atmospheric disturbance.

There is no smoke.

Smoke.

There is no—

But there was snow.

Snow, agitated, could hang in the air like smoke. Plenty of snow. Snow all around.

He turned to his right to face a wall of snow. Above him, on a precipice, more snow. The snow that had fallen silently through the night and even now glided down from the heavens.

Solaratov loves snow. He knows snow.

But Bob saw now that above him, several hundred pounds of the stuff rested on the branches of a pine, which had turned it into some kind of upside-down vanilla cone. In fact, several of the trees were above him. The snow fell and caught on them in the gray mountain light. He could almost feel them groaning, yearning for some kind of freedom.

He reached out with his rifle barrel but could touch none of it.

But then the plan formed in his mind.

He edged to his side, making certain to keep his body profile low behind the rocks, so that Solaratov would not get the last shot free. His right hand crept across the parka, unzipped it, and he reached inside and removed the Beretta.

He steeled himself.

It was instinct shooting, unaimed fire, but his reflexes at this arcane pistol skill had always been quite good. He threaded his other wrist through the sling of the Remington M40, to secure it for his move.

He thumbed back the hammer. He looked at each of his targets.

He took a deep breath.

So do it, he thought.
So do it!

Something was happening.

A series of dry popping cracks reached Solaratov's ears, far away, but definitely coming off the mountain.

What?

He looked hard through the scope, not daring to take it from the trapped man. He thought he saw a flash, the flight of something small through the air, a disturbance in the snow, and quickly came up with the idea of an automatic pistol, but what was he doing, trying to signal men in the area? Who could be in the area?

But in the next second his question was answered. He was shooting into the snow-laden pines above him, striking their trunks and driving the impact vibrations out their limbs, shooting fast so that the vibrations accumulated in their effect, and almost astonishingly, the snow loads of four pines yielded and slid down the mountain toward the supine man, where they hit and exploded into a fine blast of powder, a sheet of density that momentarily took his sight picture away from him.

Where is he?

He put the scope down because he could never find the man in the narrow width of vision, and saw him, rolling down the mountain a good fifty feet from the commotion he'd stirred.

Solaratov brought the rifle up fast, but couldn't find the man, he was moving so quickly. At last he located him and saw that he had gotten a full fifty meters down the hill.

He picked up the good moving sight picture, fired quickly, remembering to lead on the moving target, but the bullet impacted behind the target, kicking up a huge geyser of snow.

Of course! The range had changed subtly; he was still holding for 654 meters, and the range was probably down to six hundred or so.

By the time he figured this out, the man had come to rest in the rocks below, and was now much better situated behind them, having picked up some maneuverability and the position to shoot back.

Goddamn him! he thought.

With a thud he caught on something, taking his breath away. He had come to rest in a new nest of rocks fifty meters downslope. The snow still hung in the air, and in his desperate fall-run, it had gotten into his parka and down his neck. But in the complete uncoordination of the moment, he made certain he was behind cover. He breathed hard. He hurt everywhere, but felt warmth pouring down the side of his face, and reached up to touch blood.

Had he been hit?

No: the fucking night-vision goggles, totally worthless but forgotten in the crisis, had slipped down his head crookedly, and one strap cut a wicked gash in his ear. The cut stung. He grabbed the things and had an impulse to toss them away. What was the point now?

But maybe Solaratov wasn't sure where he was now, nestled behind a slightly wider screen of rocks. He looked and saw he had a little more room to move from rock to rock.

Maybe he could even get a shot off.

But at what?

And then he saw that the slope dropped off intensely and, worse, the rocks had run out.

This is it, he thought.

This is as far as I go.

What did I get out of it?

Nothing.

His ear stung.

"They've moved," Sally said. "Now they're behind the house. You can hear the shots are over there."

"Are we going to be all right?" asked Nikki.

"Yes, baby," Julie said, holding her daughter close.

The three were in the cellar of the house, and Sally had spent the past few minutes jamming old chairs, trunks and boxes against the door at the head of the steps, just in case someone came looking for them with bad intentions.

The cellar smelled of mold and faded material, and spring floods that had soaked everything some years back. It was dirty and dark, only meager light coming through snow-covered windows.

There was one other door, to the outside, one of those slanted wood things that led down three steps to them. Sally had piled up more impediments to that passageway, but there was no way of really locking the doors. They could only forestall things.

"I wish we had a gun," said Nikki.

"I wish we did too," said Sally.

"I wish Daddy was here," said Nikki.

Bob had a rare moment of visual freedom, a long, clean look into the stunted snow-covered trees at the base of the mountain. But he could see nothing, no movement, no hint of disturbance.

Then a bullet sang off the rock an inch beyond his face, kicking a puff of granite spray into his eye. He fell back, stifling a yell, and felt the telltale numbness that indicated some kind of trauma. But only for a second; then it lit into raw, harsh but meaningless pain, and he winced, driving more pain into the eye.

Goddamn him!

Solaratov had seen just the faintest portion of head exposed and he was on it that fast, putting a bullet an inch shy of the target. An inch at six hundred-odd meters. Could that son of a bitch shoot or what?

Swagger felt his eye puff, his lid flare, and he closed it, sensing the throb of pain. He touched the wounded sector of his face: blood, lots of it, from the stone spray, but nothing quite serious. He blinked, opened the eye, and saw hazily out of it. Not blind. Trapped but not blind, not yet.

The guy was so good.

No ranging shots; he got the range right every single time, had Bob pinned and eyeballed.

No goddamn ranging shots.

Solaratov had an odd gift, a perfect gift for estimating distance. It made the package complete. Some men had it, some didn't. Some could learn it with experience, some couldn't. It was in fact the weakest part of Swagger's own game, his ability to estimate range. It had cost him a few shots over the years because he lacked the natural inclination to read distances while possessing in spades all the shooter's other natural gifts.

Donny had a gift for it; Donny could look and tell you automatically. But Bob was so lame at it, he'd once spent a fortune on an old Barr & Stroud naval gunfire range finder, a complex, ancient optical instrument that with its many lenses and calibration gizmos could eventually work the farthest unknown distance into a recognizable quantity.

"Some day they'll make 'em real small," he remembered telling Donny at one lost moment or other.

"Then you won't need a go-fer like me," Donny had said with a laugh, "and I can sit the next war out."

"Yes, you can," Bob had said. "One war is enough."

An idea flirted with him. From where? From Donny? Well, from somewhere over the long years. But it wasn't solid yet: he just felt it beyond the screen of his consciousness, unformed, like a little bit of as-yet-unrecognizable melody.

This guy is so good. How can he be so good?

Donny had the answer. Donny wanted to tell him. Donny knew up in heaven or wherever he was, and Donny yearned somehow to tell him.

Tell me! he demanded.

But Donny was silent.

And down below Solaratov waited, scoping the rocks,

waiting for just a bit of a sliver of a body part to show so he could nail it, and then get on with business.

He is so good.

He made great shots.

He hit Dade Fellows dead on, he hit Julie riding at an oblique angle flat out at over eight hundred meters, he was just the—

That scene replayed in his mind.

What was odd about it, he now saw, was how featureless it had been. A ridge on a mountain, with a wall of rock behind it, very little vegetation. It had been almost plain, almost abstract.

So?

So how did he range it?

There were no guidelines, no visual data, no known objects visible to make a range estimate, only the woman on the horse getting smaller as she got farther away on the oblique.

How did he know where to hold, when her range changed so radically after the first shot?

He must be a genius. He must just have the gift, the ability to somehow, by the freakish mechanics of the brain, to just know. Donny had that. Maybe it's not so rare.

But then he knew. Or rather Donny told him, reaching across the years.

"You idiot," Donny whispered hoarsely in his ear, "don't you see it yet? Why he's so good? It's so *obvious.*"

Bob knew then why the man had shot at him as he fell but missed. The range had changed; he estimated the lead and got it slightly wrong and just missed. But once his target was still, he knew *exactly* the range. And that's how he could hit Julie. He knew *exactly.* He solved the distance equation, and knew how far she was and where to hold to take her down.

He has a range finder, Bob thought. The son of a bitch has a range finder.

———

Solaratov looked at his watch. It was just past 0700. The light was now gray approaching white, a kind of sealed-off pewter kind of weather. The snow was falling harder and a little breeze had kicked up, tossing and twisting the flakes, pummeling as they rotated down. The wind got under the crack of his hood, where his flesh was sweaty, and cut him like a scythe. A little chill ran up his spine.

How long can I wait? he wondered.

Nobody was flying in for yet another few hours, but maybe they could get in with snowmobiles or plow the highway and get in that way.

A sudden, uncharacteristic uneasiness settled over him.

He made a list:

1.) Kill the sniper.
2.) Kill the woman.
3.) Kill the witnesses.
4.) Escape into the mountains.
5.) Contact the helo.
6.) Rendezvous.

An hour's worth of work, he thought, possibly two.

He kept on the scope, the rifle cocked, his finger riding the curve of the trigger, his mind clear, his concentration intense.

How long can I stay at this level?

When do I have to blink, look away, yawn, piss, think of warmth, food, a woman?

He pivoted on the fulcrum of the log, running the scope along the ridge of rocks, looking for target indicators. More breath? A shadow out of place? Some disturbed snow? A regular line? A trace of movement? It would happen, it had to, for Swagger wouldn't be content to wait. His nature would compel action and then compel doom.

He can't see me.

He doesn't know where I am.

It's just a matter of time.

He tried to figure out a range finder. How do the goddamn things work? His old Barr & Stroud was mechanical, like a surveyor's piece of equipment, with gears and lenses. That's why it was so heavy. It was a combination binocular and adding machine: completely impractical.

But no modern shooter would have such a device: too old, too heavy, too delicate.

Laser. It has to work off a laser. It has to shoot a laser to an object, measure the time and make a sure, swift calculation off of that.

Lasers were everywhere. They used them to guide bombs, aim guns, operate on the eye, remove tattoos, imitate fireworks. But what kind of laser was this one?

Off the visible spectrum, since it projected no beam, no red dot.

Ultraviolet?

Infrared?

How could it be brought into the visible spectrum?

It's a kind of light. *How do I see it?*

One idea: light being heat, if he could get Solaratov to project it through an ice mist, its heat would burn tracks in the snow. Then he could shoot back down the tracks and . . .

But that was absurd. Besides involving setting up some complex linkage of actions, any one of which could catch him a 7mm Magnum through the lungs, he didn't even know if it would work.

Idea two: get Solaratov to shoot the laser through a piece of ice. It would bend, and send back some faulty reading. He would over- or undercompensate, miss and . . .

Insane. Unworkable.

Think! Think, Goddammit. How do I see it?

And then it occurred to him.

Would I see it on night vision? Would I see it in my goggles? Would they register it?

He picked them up where they lay, half in, half out of the snow, slid the harness over his skull, pulled the goggles down and snapped them on. They yielded a green dense landscape, as if the world had ended in water. The seas had risen. Green was everywhere. Nothing else was clear.

How can I get him to lase me again?

He knew. He had to move one more time, change the range.

Solaratov would go to his laser range finder.

If it works, it'll be like a neon sign in the green, saying I AM THE SNIPER.

Now something was happening.

He saw puffs of breath rising above a certain accumulation of boulders, signifying some kind of physical exertion. He watched and one of the rocks seemed somehow to tremble.

Is he moving the rock?

Why would he move the rock?

But in the same second, as he steadied himself, as the rock wobbled truly erratically, seemed to pause, and then tumbled ever so majestically forward, pulling a score of smaller rocks with it, uncurling a shroud of snow as it fell, he knew.

He's trying to bury me, Solaratov thought.

He's trying to start an avalanche, to send tons of snow down the mountain and bury me.

But it wasn't going to work. Avalanche snow, Solaratov knew, was old snow, its structure eroded by melt, its moisture mostly evaporated, so that it was dry and treacherous, a network of unsafe stresses and fault lines. Then and only then could a single fracture cut out its underpinnings and send it crashing down. This avalanche would never go anywhere. The snow was too wet and new; it might fly a bit, but it wouldn't build. It would peter out a few hundred yards down.

On top of that, clearly the man didn't even know where he was. Even now, as the rocks and their screen of snow tumbled abortively down the hill, not picking up energy but losing it, they were on no course toward himself, but more or less to the right about one hundred yards. The falling snow simply could not reach him.

He almost chuckled at the futility of it, remembering that his quarry was a jungle fighter, not a man of the mountains.

The rocks tumbled, trailing snow, but down the slope where the angle flattened, they lost their energy and rolled to a halt.

Solaratov watched them tumble, then brought the rifle back to bear on the original line of rocks. As he was shifting it upward, he thought he made out a white shape sloshing desperately through the snow.

He rose above it, came back, could not quite find it and then did track it quickly, but never quite got the fraction of line between third and fourth mil-dots precisely on it.

He saw that Swagger had moved, literally floundering his way downhill to this new position. So? He was a few dozen meters closer? Now he had less maneuverability. What possible difference did it make? He had made his last mistake.

The game, Solaratov thought, is almost over.

He put down his rifle, picked up the binoculars and prepared to shoot a laser, just to verify the distance to the new position.

Bob came to the halted rocks and hit them with a whack, but couldn't stop to acknowledge the pain. Instead he pulled himself up, put his head and shoulders over the top, flicked the night-vision goggles down as he snapped them on and peered desperately into the void. He knew he was violating every rule in *U.S. Marine Corps Sniping*

FMFM1-3B, which tells snipers never, ever to look over an obstacle, for that makes you too obvious to counterfire; no, you drop to your haunches and look around it. But he didn't have the time.

There was no definition in the green murk, no shape, no depth, nothing but flat, vaguely phosphorescent green. He scanned, registered this nothingness, but was too intense to feel much in the way of despair, even if he knew he was hung out over the lip of the rock and that Solaratov could take him in an instant.

He waited. A second, then another, finally a third yanked by like trains slowed by the sludgy blood his heart pumped.

Nothing.

Maybe the laser wasn't visible in the spectrum of the goggles. Who knew of such stuff? Maybe the laser ranging device was part of some advanced scope he knew nothing about, and it would announce itself, but be followed in another nanosecond by close to 1,500 foot-pounds of Remington 7mm Magnum arriving to erase him from the earth.

Maybe he's not there. Maybe he's moved, he's working his way up another slope, he's flanked me, and now he's just taking his time.

Two more seconds dribbled by, each encapsulating a lifetime, until Bob knew he could wait no longer, and as he began to duck back into a world of zero possibility, here it came, at last.

The yellow streak was like a crack in the wall of the universe. It pinged right at him from nothingness and lasted but an instant, but there it was, a straight line as the shooter below measured the distance to the shooter above.

Bob locked the source of the brief beam into his muscle memory and his sense of time and space. He could not move a muscle, an atom; he could not disturb the rigidity of his body, for it all depended on holding that invisible point before himself in the infinity of his mind as he brought the rifle up in one smooth, whipping motion and in to his shoulder and did not move his head to find the scope but moved the scope to that precise lock of his vision.

The scope flew before him and he saw nothing, even as his hands locked around the pistol grip and his finger found the curve of the trigger, caressed its delicacy, felt and loved its tension and sought to be one with it. He felt no tension, not now: here was the rest of his life; here was everything.

And as he flung away the goggles with a toss of his head, here was his ancient enemy. Bob saw the sniper, swaddled behind a horizontal trunk, his shape barely recognizable in the swirl of pewter-to-white dappling of the snow and his arctic warfare camouflaging, only the line of the rifle rising as it came toward Bob, hard and regular.

So many years, he thought, as he closed his focus down until he saw only the harsh cruciform of the reticle, made a slight correction to shoot lower to compensate for the downward angle, and then, without willing it as the reticle became such a statement of clarity it seemed to fill the whole universe, the trigger went and he fired.

You never hear the one that gets you.

Solaratov was on his target, racing through the excitement of knowing that at long last he had him, but he hesitated for just a second to compute the new range. And then he realized that the man above was aimed—incredibly—at him.

He felt no pain, only shock.

He seemed to be in the center of an explosion. Then time stopped, he was briefly removed from the universe, and when he was reinserted into it, he was not an armed man with a rifle boring in on a target but a supine man in the cold snow, amid a splatter of blood. His own breath spurted out raggedly, white cloud and red spray sending broken signals upward.

Someone was drunkenly playing a broken accordion or

a damaged pipe organ nearby. The music had no melody, was only a whine with a slight edge or buzz to it. Sucking chest wound. Left side, left lung gone, blood pouring out both exit and entrance wounds. Blood everywhere.

Internal damage total. Death near. Death coming. Death at last, his old friend, come to pick him up.

He blinked, disbelieving, and wondered at the alchemy by which such a result could have been engineered.

His life flashed and fled, dissolved in a blur, went away and came back.

He thought: I'm gone.

He wondered if he had the strength to gather the rifle, find a position and wait for the man until he bled to death, but the man would not be foolish.

He thought next of how the mission had redefined itself.

To kill the man who had killed him meant nothing. There was no escape. The only option left was: failure or success.

He pulled himself up, saw the house five hundred yards away through the snowy trees and felt he could make it. He could make it, for the shooter would now lay low, unsure as to whether or not the sniper was dead.

He could make it to the house, get in, and with that little Glock pistol finish the job that had killed him.

That would be his legacy in the world: he finished the last job. He did it. He was successful.

Finding the strength somewhere, amazed at how clear it all seemed, he headed off, bleeding, in a winter wonderland.

Swagger lay close to the rock for a minute or so, recalling the sight picture: the reticle, swollen in the intensity of his focus so that it was big and bold as a fist, held low on the covering tree because you hold low when shooting downward, so that the bullet would hit center chest, a nice big target. But it's tricky: the rifle was zeroed for five hundred yards, according to his shooter's instructions, but maybe the man who zeroed it held it slightly differently than he did; maybe there was a twig, a branch slightly unresolved in the 10X power of the scope. Maybe there was a wind he didn't feel, a sierra blowing around the contour of the mountain.

But the sight picture was as perfect as it could be. It was held where it should be held, and if he had to call the shot, he'd call it a hit.

He edged around the right, squinting out. He tried to find the shooting site of his enemy, but it was much harder to see from this angle. Instead, he scanned back and forth in what he determined was the proper sector, and saw nothing, no movement, no anything. He finally found the fallen tree he was convinced had supported his enemy, but there was no sign of him, there was no sign of disturbance in the snow. A spot, a little farther back, could have been blood, but it was impossible to tell. It could also have been a black stone, a broken limb.

He lowered the rifle, slipped down the nightscope lenses and watched in the murk for a while. It stayed green, uncut by the flick of a laser.

Did I hit him?

Is he dead?

How much time should I give him?

A dozen scenarios instantly occurred to him. Maybe Solaratov had moved to a fallback position. Maybe he had moved laterally. Maybe he was even advancing on him. He might even be headed now toward the house, certain he had Bob trapped.

That last seemed the most logical. After all, the job was to hit the woman, not Swagger. Swagger's death had no real meaning; Julie's had all the meaning.

And if he were seen, he'd kill witnesses too.

Bob took a deep breath.

Then he pushed himself up, scuttled down a few yards, turned angles obliquely, dodged, jumped, found cover. He tried to make himself difficult to hit, knowing he could not make himself impossible to hit.

But no shot came.

From his new cover his angle was lower, so his view of the valley was less distinct. He could only see a bit of the flatland through the snowy trees, and could see nothing moving on it, approaching the house. But his target would be camouflaged, moving at angles, dropping, easily evading him.

His heart was beating rapidly. There was no breath left in his lungs. The planet seemed scorched dry of oxygen.

He pulled himself out and moved at the assault again.

He fell twice in the snow and almost blacked out the second time. And when he looked up, the house seemed no closer.

His mind raced; it would not stay where he put it. He thought of sight pictures, of men going limp against reticles, of long stalks in mountains and jungles and cities. He had hunted in them all and been victorious in them all.

He thought of the crawl with the sandbag, the long, slow crawl outside the American fort and the earlier moment when they had him, and then the large black plane, like a vulture, hung in the air for just a split second before its guns pulverized the universe.

He thought of the times he'd been hit: over the years, it amounted to no less than twenty-two wounds, though two were blade wounds, one inflicted by an Angolan, one by a mujahideen woman. He thought of thirst, fear, hunger, discomfort. He thought of rifles. He thought of the past and the future, which was running out quickly.

He rose the last time, and stumbled through the snow, which fought him. It was not cold. The snow still fell, harder now, in swirls and pinwheels, dancing in the wind, the heavy damp flakes of Eastern European cities.

Where am I?

What has happened?

Why has it happened?

But then he was at the house.

All was silent.

He bent to the storm cellar door, pulled hard, even as he reached inside his coat and drew out the Glock pistol.

A nail seemed to hold him back. He felt the door want to yield but hang up. He pulled harder, finding strength somewhere in the backwash of his mind, and with a crack, the nail gave and he pulled the door open. It revealed three cement steps down into a dark entrance that looked jammed with clutter.

He slid by the door and stepped down into the darkness, aware only marginally that he had made it. He felt clear-eyed, suddenly, recommitted to his purpose, certain of what he must do.

He kicked his way through the impediments: a sawhorse, a bicycle, bed springs, boxes of old newspapers, and as he got through he felt the door slam shut behind him, sealing him off in the darkness. He took another step, kicking things aside, looking and waiting for his vision to clear. He smelled moisture, mildew, rot, old leather and paper, decaying material, ancient wood.

Then he could see them.

They were over against the far wall, huddled under the steps, two women and a girl clutching each other, crying.

Swagger made it into the treeline. This is where he needed a pistol, a short, handy, fast-firing weapon with a lot of firepower. But the Beretta was somewhere up the mountain, buried under a ton of snow.

He carried the rifle like a submachine gun in the low assault position, poking through the woods as he closed from the flank on the sniper's hide.

He paused, waiting, listening. There was no sound, no sense of life at all in the haunted place. Branches and bushes distended by heavy, moist, fresh snow stood out in extravagant shapes like a display of modern art. Through the gray, the snow fell, swirling.

Bob's breath rose above him, then parted. He advanced slowly. If the sniper was here, he was well hidden, completely disciplined.

He could see the fallen tree, and then made out the disturbance in the snow where the man had supported himself while shooting upward.

Bob slid as silently as he could on the oblique through the heavy trees, trying to shake no snow loose, and at last came to the site, paused a second, then stepped behind the cover to put his rifle muzzle on the man. But nobody was there. He heard only his own harsh breath heaving in the cold.

The blood told the story.

Solaratov had been hit bad. His rifle lay in the snow; the ranging binoculars were there too. A raspberry sherbet marked where he'd bled most profusely, driven to the ground by the impact of the .308.

Got him! Bob thought, but the moment of exultation never fully developed, for in the next seconds he read the tracks and the blood trail and saw that the man, seriously wounded but nothing like dead, had moved back through the trees toward the house.

At that moment he heard a bang, which could have been a shot, but it wasn't. He turned and saw through the trees the house and a little puff of flung snow. That helped identify the sound. It had been the sound of a heavy cellar door closing, and when it had slammed shut, it had vibrated free a cloud of snow.

He's in there with my family, Bob thought.

He had a rooted moment of terror. It felt like ice sliding down through his body, smooth and unbearably cold, numbing all the organs it brushed as it rushed through him.

But some part of his brain refused to panic, and he saw what he must do.

He raced to pick up the 7mm Remington Magnum, for the three hundred extra feet of velocity and the five hundred extra pounds of energy and, throwing aside his parka, ran, ran like a fool on fire or in love, not toward the house, which was too far, but for a good, straight-in angle on the door.

They heard the door creak as someone tried to pull on it.

"Oh, God," said Sally.

"Over here," instructed Julie.

She grabbed her daughter, and with the younger woman they fled to the back of the cellar, but only as far as the brick wall. There was no escape, for the stairwell up was jammed with junk to keep the same man out.

They fell back and cowered when the door cracked open, then was yanked wide, filling the dark space with light, destroying their adjusted vision.

He lumbered wheezily down the steps, kicking the junk aside like an enraged, drunken father home late from a night with the boys, come home to beat his wife. It stirred something deep in Julie, a memory of dread long buried, never examined. The cellar door slammed behind him, and he kicked more stuff aside until he came into the center of the room.

He blinked, waiting for his eyes to adjust, but he was everything they could possibly fear: a muscular gray savage dressed in white, except that a profuse smear of blood had irrigated a raggedy delta from a source on his chest, leaking down to his trousers and his boots.

He had a gray, blunt face, a crew cut and wintry little eyes. He smiled madly, and blood showed on his teeth. He coughed, and it erupted from his mouth. He seemed barely conscious, seemed almost to fall, but he stopped, caught himself and looked at them fiercely. He was insane with pain, his eyes lit weirdly, his whole body trembling.

The gun muzzle played across them all.

She stepped out.

The killer laughed for some strange reason, and another spurt of blood came from his mouth down to splash on his chest. His lungs were full of blood. He was drowning in it. Why wouldn't he fall?

He lifted the pistol until it pointed into her face.

Julie heard her baby crying, heard the intake of Sally's breath and thought of her husband and the man she'd loved before, the only two men she could ever love. She closed her eyes.

But he did not fire.

She opened them.

He had fallen halfway, but then he pulled himself up, and thrust the gun at her, his eyes filling with mad determination.

Bob ran until he had a good angle into the door.

He'll stop. He has to wait for his eyes to adjust.

He saw it. The man would step into the darkness and pause as his eyes adjusted. He'd be there, just beyond the door, for the length of time it took his pupils to adjust. With Solaratov, that interval would be a second or so.

He dropped to one knee, braced the rifle on his leg, found the good shooting position. It was five hundred yards if it was an inch, but that had to be the zero on the rifle, for Solaratov had come so close to him so often.

Without thinking, he wrapped the sling tight about his left, supporting arm as he slipped into a good Marine Corps position, feeling a bite of pain from the opened wound, but leaning through it. He took three breaths, building up his oxygen, and looked for his natural point of aim as something in him screamed *Faster! Faster!* and another part cooed *Slower, slower.* He laid the crosshairs dead-center on the door, just a patch of gray wood smeared with snow, and prayed for the extra oomph of the 7mm to do its thing.

He had one moment of clarity, and at the subliminal level willed all he knew of shooting into the effort: the relaxation of the finger, trained over the hard years; the discipline of the respiratory cycle, and the rhythm of deeper and shallower exhalation; the cooperation of rods and cones in the back wall of the eye, the orchestration of pupil, eye and lens, and the overall guidance and wisdom of the retina; but most of all, that deep, willed plunge into stillness, where the world is gray and almost gone, yet at the same time sharp and clear.

Nothing matters, the man coached himself when things mattered most.

And then it was gone as the rifle fired, kicked against him, blowing the sight picture to nothing but blur, and when he came back on target he saw a mushroom of snow mist floating from the vibes where the bullet had blasted through the wood.

The pistol settled down; she saw the hugeness of its bore just feet away from her and then felt—

Splatter in her face, a sense of mist or fog suddenly filling the air, a meaty vapor.

Mixed into this sensation was a sound which was that of wood splitting.

In it too was a grunt, almost involuntary, as if lungs gurgled, somehow human.

She found herself wet with droplets that proved to be warm and heavy: blood.

The sniper transfigured before her. What had been the upper quadrant of his face had somehow been pulped, ripped open, revealing a terrible wound of splintered bone and spurting blood. One eye looked dead as a nickle; the other was gone in the mess. Even as these details were fixing themselves in her memory, he fell sideways with a thump, his head banging on the cement floor, exposing the ragged entry wound in the corresponding rear quadrant of the skull, where the bones now seemed broken and frail.

A single light beam came through the cellar door where the bullet had passed.

She looked down, saw the stumpy little man fallen like a white angel into a red pool, as his satiny blood spread ever wider from his ruined face.

She turned to her daughter and her friend, who regarded her with mouths agape, and horror, more than relief, registering in both their eyes.

Then she spoke with perfect deliberation:

"Daddy's home."

CHAPTER FORTY-NINE

He had not fired a second time because he had no more ammunition. But in another second, the cellar door had been flung open and he recognized Sally, leaping to signal him that it was over.

By the time Bob got to the house, three Air Force Hueys and a state police helicopter had landed and more were on their way. Then another Air Force job, a big Blackhawk, arrived and disgorged still more staff. It almost looked like an advanced firebase when the war was at its hottest, the way the choppers kept ferrying people in.

He got the news immediately: everybody was all right, though medics were attending them. The sniper was dead.

His own wounds were tended: an emergency technician resewed, with anesthetic, the gash in his thigh that had opened up under the pressure of all the moving and jumping, and then picked stone and bullet fragments out of his face and eye for half an hour, before disinfecting, then covering the raw cuts with gauze. Nothing appeared to have hit the eye proper; more shooter's luck.

There was little to be done about the back wound. It had penetrated his camouflage and grazed the flesh of his back, scoring both burn and bruise. But other than disinfectant, only time and painkillers would make it go away.

A cop wanted to take a statement, but Bonson pulled rank and declared the ranch a federal crime site, until corroborating FBI agents could chopper in within the hour from Boise. In the cellar, a state police crime team worked the body of the dead sniper, hit twice, once through the left lung, once in the back of the head.

"Great shooting," said a cop. "You want to take a look at your handiwork?"

But Swagger had no desire to see the fallen man. What

good would it do? He felt nothing except that he'd seen enough corpses.

"I'd rather see my daughter and my wife," he said.

"Well, your wife is being treated by our medical people. We've got to debrief her as soon as possible. Mrs. Memphis is with Nikki."

"Can I go?"

"They're in the kitchen."

He walked through a strange house full of strangers. People talked on radios, and computers had been set up. A squad of uninteresting young people hung about, talking shop, clearly agitated at the prospect of a big treat. He remembered when Agency people were all ex-FBI men, beefy cop types, who carried Swedish Ks and liked to talk about "pegging gooks." These boys and girls looked like they belonged in prep school, but they sure made themselves at home, with the instant insouciance of the young.

He walked through them, and they parted, and he could feel their wonder. What would they make of him: his kind of war was so far from their kind it probably made no sense.

He found Sally in the kitchen, and next to her, there was his baby girl. These were the moments worth living for. Now he knew why he bothered to survive Vietnam.

"Hi, baby!"

"Oh, Daddy," she said, her eyes widening with deep pleasure. He felt a warmth in his heart so intense he might melt. His child. Through it all, after it all, his own: flesh, blood, brains. She flew to him and he absorbed her tininess, felt her vitality as he picked her up and hugged her passionately.

"Oh, you sweet thing!" he sang. "You are the sweetest thing there is."

"Oh, Daddy. They say you shot the bad man!"

He laughed.

"You never mind that. How are you? How's Mommy?"

"I'm fine, I'm fine. It was scary. He came into the basement with a gun."

"Well, he won't bother you no nevermore, all right?"

She clung to him. Sally fixed him with her usual gimlet eye.

"Bob Swagger," she said, "you are a mean and ornery piece of work, and you aren't much of a husband or a father, but by God, you do have a gift for the heroic."

"I can see you're still my biggest fan, Sally," he said. "Well, anyhow, thanks for hanging around."

"It sure was interesting. How are you?"

"My back hurts," he said. "So does my leg and my eye. I am plenty hungry. And there're too goddamned many young people out there. I hate young people. How is she?"

"She's fine. We're all fine. Nobody was hurt. But only just barely. Another tenth of a second and he would have pulled that trigger."

"Well, to hell with him if he can't take a joke."

"I'll leave you two alone."

"See if you can get one of these Harvard kids to fix some coffee."

"They probably don't do coffee, and there isn't a Starbucks around, but I'll see what I can manage."

And so he sat with his baby daughter in the kitchen and caught up on the news and told her about the superficiality of his wounds and made a promise he hoped he'd now be able to keep: to return with her and her mother to Arizona, and resume the good life they had together.

In half an hour a young man came to him.

"Mr. Swagger?"

"Yes?"

"We're going to have to debrief your wife now. She's asked that you be present."

"All right."

"She's very insistent. She won't talk unless you're there."

"Sure, she's spooked."

"This way, sir."

Sally came back to take care of Nikki.

"Sweetie," he said to his daughter, "I'm going to go with these people to talk to Mommy. You stay here with Aunt Sally."

"Daddy!"

She gave him a last hug, and he now saw how deeply she'd been traumatized. The war had come to her: she'd seen what few Americans ever saw anymore—combat death, the power of the bullet on flesh.

"Sweetie, I'll be back. Then this'll be over. It'll be fine, you'll see."

They took him upstairs. The Agency team had set up in a bedroom, pushing aside the bed and dresser and installing a sofa from the living room and a group of chairs. Cleverly, they weren't arranged before the sofa, as if to seat an audience, but rather in a semicircle, as if in a group counseling session. Tape-recording equipment had been installed, and computer terminals.

The room was crowded and hushed, but finally, he saw her. He walked through the milling analysts and agents, and found her, sitting alone on the sofa. She looked composed now, though her arm was still locked in its cast. She'd insisted on dressing and wore some jeans and a sweatshirt and her boots. She had a can of Diet Coke.

"Well, hello there," he said.

"Well, hello yourself," she said with a smile.

"You're okay, they say."

"Well, it's a little bothersome when a Russian comes into your house and points a gun at you and then your husband blows half his head away. I'm damn lucky to have a husband who could do such a thing."

"Oh, I'm such a big hero. Sweetie, I just pulled a trigger."

"Oh, baby."

He held her tight and it was fine: his wife; he'd slept next to her for years now, the same strong, tough beautiful woman, about as good as they made them. Her smell was achingly familiar. Strawberries, she smelled of strawberries always. He first saw her in a picture wrapped in cellophane that came from a young Marine's boonie hat. The rain was falling. There was a war. He fell in love with her then and never came close to falling out in all the years since.

"Where did you come from?" she said. "How did you get here so fast?"

"They didn't tell you? Damn idiot me, I got me a new hobby. I parachuted through the storm. Pretty exciting."

"Oh, Bob."

"I never been so scared in my life. If I'd had clean underwear, I'd have pissed in the ones I was wearing. Only, I didn't have no clean underwear."

"Oh, Bob—"

"We'll talk about all that stuff. That's up ahead."

"What in hell is this all about?" she finally asked. "He came for *me*? That's what these people say."

"Yeah. It has to do with something that happened a long time ago. I have it half figured. These geniuses think they know all the answers, or they can figure them. You up to this?"

"Yes. I just want it over."

"Then we'll get it all straightened out, I swear to you."

"I know."

"Bonson?"

Bonson came over.

"She's ready."

"That's terrific, Mrs. Swagger. We'll try and make this as easy as possible. Are you comfortable? Do you want anything? Another Coke?"

"No, I'm fine. I want my husband here, that's all."

"That's fine."

"Okay, people," Bonson said in a louder voice, "we're all set. The debriefing can begin."

He turned back to her.

"I have two lead analysts who'll run this. They're both

psychologists. Just relax, take your time. You're under no pressure of any sort. This is not adversarial and it has no legal standing. It's not an interrogation. In fact, we'll probably share things with you that you are not security-cleared to hear. But that's all right. We want this to be easy for you, and for you not to sense reluctance or authority or power or discretion on our part. If you can, try and think of us as your friends, not your government."

"Should I salute?" she said.

Bonson laughed.

"No. Nor will we be playing the national anthem or waving any flags. It's just a chat between friends. Now, let us set up things for you, so you have some idea of a context in which this inquiry is taking place, and why your information is so vital."

"Sure."

It began. The crowd settled, the kids obediently found chairs, and Julie sat relaxed on the couch. There were no harsh lights. One of the questioners cleared his throat, and began to speak.

"Mrs. Swagger, for reasons as yet unclear to us, factions within Russia have sent an extremely competent professional assassin to this country to kill you. That's extraordinarily venturesome, even for them. You probably wonder why, and so do we. So in the past seventy-two hours, we've been poring through old records, trying to find something that you might know that would make your death important to someone over there. May I begin by assuming you have no idea?"

"Nothing. I've never talked knowingly to a Russian in my life."

"Yes, ma'am. But we've put this into a larger pattern. It seems that three other people in your circle in the year 1971 were also killed under circumstances that suggest possible Soviet or Russian involvement. One is your first husband—"

Julie gasped involuntarily.

"This may be painful," Bonson said.

Bob touched her shoulder.

"It's all right," she said.

The young man continued, "Your husband, Donny Fenn, killed in the Republic of South Vietnam 6 May 1972. Another was a young man who was active with you in the peace movement, named Peter Farris, discovered dead with a broken neck, 6 October 1971, dead for several months at the time. And the third was another peace demonstrator of some renown, named Thomas Charles 'Trig' Carter III, killed in a bomb blast at the University of Wisconsin 9 May 1971."

"I knew Peter. He was so harmless. I only met Trig once . . . twice, actually."

"Hmmmm. Can you think of a specific circumstance that united the four of you? Marine, peace demonstrators, 1971?"

"We were all involved in one of the last big demonstrations, May Day of that year. The three of us as demonstrators, Donny as a Marine."

"Julie," said Bonson, "we're thinking less of an ideological unification here and more of a specific, geographic one. A time, a place, not an idea. And a private place, too."

"The farm," she finally said.

There was no sound.

Finally, Bonson prompted her.

"The farm," he said.

"Donny was distraught over an assignment he'd been asked to do."

Bob looked at Bonson and saw nothing, just the face of a smooth, professional actor in the role of concerned intelligence executive. No flicker of emotion, grief, doubt, regrets: nothing. Bonson didn't even blink, and Julie, remembering nothing of him and his role in what had happened, went on.

"He believed this Trig, of whom he thought so highly, might have some idea what he should do with his ethical dilemma. We went to Trig's house in DC but he wasn't there. Donny remembered that he was going out to a farm near Germantown. I think Peter may have followed us. Peter thought he was in love with me."

"What did you see on that farm?" asked the young analyst.

She laughed.

"Nothing. Nothing at all. What can have been so important about it?"

"We'd like to know."

"There was a man. An Irishman named Fitzpatrick. He and Trig were loading fertilizer into a van. It was very late at night."

"How clearly did you see him?"

"Very. I was just out of the light, maybe fifteen, twenty-five feet away. I don't think he ever saw me. Donny, for some reason, wanted me to stay back. So he and Trig and this Fitzpatrick talked for a few minutes. Then Fitzpatrick left. Then Donny and Trig talked some more and finally hugged. Then we left. There was some kind of agent in the hills. He got our picture—Donny's and mine—as we drove away. Donny's mostly. I was ducking. And that's it."

"That's it."

"Do you remember Fitzpatrick?"

"I suppose."

"Do you think you'd be able to describe—"

"No," said Bonson. "Go straight to the pictures."

"Mrs. Swagger, we'd like to have you look at some pictures. They're pictures of a variety of politicians, espionage agents, lawyers, scientists, military, mostly in the old Eastern Bloc, but some are genuinely Irish, some English, some French. They're all in their forties or fifties, so you'll have to imagine them as they'd have been in 1971."

"Yes," she said.

"Just take your time."

One of the kids walked across the room and handed her a sheaf of photographs. She flipped through them slowly, stopping now and then to sip on her Coke can.

"Could I have another Coke?" she asked at one time. Somebody raced out.

Bob watched as the gray, firm faces slid by, men possibly his own age or older, most of them dynamic in appearance, with square, ruddy faces, lots of hair, the unmistakable imprint of success.

They were hunting for a mole, he realized. They thought that somehow—was this Bonson's madness?—this Fitzpatrick had implanted someone in the fabric of the West, prosperous and powerful, but that his heart still belonged to the East, or what remained of it. If they could solve the mystery of Fitzpatrick, they could solve the mystery of the mole.

Bob felt an odd twist of bitterness. *That* war, the cold one, it really had nothing to do with the little hot dirty one that had consumed so many men he had known and so wantonly destroyed his generation. Who'll stop the rain? It wasn't even about the rain.

"No," she said. "He's not here, I'm sorry."

"Okay, let's go to the citizens."

Another file of photos was provided.

"Take your time," said one of the debriefers. "Remember, he'll be heavier, balder, he may have facial hair, he—"

"Mel, I think Julie understands that," said Bonson.

Julie was quiet. She flipped through the pictures, now and then pausing. But another pile disappeared without a moment of recognition. Another pile was brought, this time designated "security nationals."

She had a possible, but paused, and then it too went to the discards, though into a separate category of "almosts."

But then, finally, there were no more pictures.

"I'm sorry," she said.

The disappointment in the room was palpable.

"Okay," Bonson finally said. "Let's knock off for a while. Julie, why don't you take a break? Maybe a walk, stretch your legs. We'll have to do it the hard way."

"What does that mean?" she asked. "Drugs? Torture?"

"No, we'll get you together with a forensic artist. He'll draft a drawing from your instructions. We'll get our computers to run a much wider comparison on a much wider database. Mel, be sure to get the 'almosts' too. Have Mr. Jefferson factor those in too. That'll get us another bunch of candidates. We've got food. Would you care for some lunch or a nap or something?"

"I'm fine. I think I'd like to check on my daughter."

She and Bob walked downstairs and found Nikki— asleep. She was stretched across Sally's lap, snoozing gently, pinning Sally with her fragile weight.

"I can't even get up," said Sally.

"I'll take her."

"No, that's okay. These child geniuses got the cable running. The remote even works now. It didn't. See."

She held up the little device and punched a few buttons and the picture flicked across the channels: Lifetime, CNN, Idaho Public TV, HBO, the Discovery Channel, ESPN, CNN Headline N—

"My God," said Julie. *"Oh, my God."*

"What?" Bob said, and from around the house, others looked in, came to check.

"That's him," said Julie. "My God, yes, fatter now, healthier; yes, that's him. That's Fitzpatrick!" She was pointing at the television, where a powerful, dynamic man was giving an impromptu news conference in a European city.

"Jesus," said one of the kids, "that's Evgeny Pashin, the next president of Russia."

The second meeting was smaller, more informal. It was after lunch, prepared in an Air Force mess tent set up outside the house.

Surprisingly good, nourishing food, too. More to the point, someone had come up with a nice batch of Disney videos for Nikki, that is, when she got back from a sledding diversion with three state troopers.

Now, Julie and Bob sat upstairs with a much smaller contingent, the inner circle, as it were.

"Julie," said Bonson, "we're going to discuss the meaning of this right here, before you and your husband. That's because I want you on the inside now, not on the outside. I'm drawing the two of you in. You're not civilians. I want you to feel like you're part of the team. You will, in fact, both be paid as agency consultants; we pay well, you'll see."

"Fine," she said. "We could use the money."

"Now, I'm not even going to ask you if you're sure. I know you're sure. But I have to say: this guy has been on TV a lot lately. Can you explain why it's only now that you recognize him?"

"Mr. Bonson, have you ever been a mother?"

There was some laughter.

"No," he admitted.

"Have you ever been the wife to a somewhat melancholy yet incredibly heroic man, particularly as he's feeling his life has been taken from him by some unnecessary publicity and we had to move from one location to another?"

"No, no, I haven't," said Bonson.

"Well, I was both, simultaneously. Does that suggest to you why I wasn't watching much TV?"

"Yes, it does."

"Now, today, you take me back. You force me to think about faces. I pick several faces that are somewhat similar in structure to his. I'm working on re-creating that face in my own mind. Do you see?"

"Yes."

"The points are all well made," Bonson said. "Well then, let's throw it open for general discussion. Can someone tell me what possible meaning this has?"

"Sir, I think I can explain the sequencing."

"Go ahead," said Bonson.

"In 1971, four people saw Pashin operating undercover in this country as this Fitzpatrick. That is, really interfaced with him in commission of his duties. Three were eliminated quickly. But they had no ID on the fourth, and as I recollect, according to official Marine Corps records, Mrs. Swagger's first marriage to Donny Fenn was unrecorded."

"That's right," said Julie. "I received no benefits. It didn't matter to me. I didn't want anything to do with the Marine Corps. Although I ended up marrying it."

"But," continued the analyst, "they have a bad picture of her, the one they got at the farm. They can't ID it. It haunts them over the years. The decades pass. SovUn breaks up. Pashin is no longer GRU, he's part of PAMYAT, the nationalist party. He begins his political career. He's handsome, heroic, the brother of a martyred nationalist hero, has lots of mafia backing; he's scaring the old-line commies, he's within a few weeks of winning an election and control of twenty thousand nukes. Then, two months ago, a picture of Bob Lee Swagger appears in *The National Star* and subsequently in *Time* and *Newsweek,* who call him 'America's most violent man.' If you recall: it was a picture snapped by a *Star* photographer of Bob coming out of church in Arizona, with his wife. *Her* picture appears in the national media. And it contains the information that Bob is married to his spotter's widow. Donny's widow, the woman who got away, who's been haunting them all these years. The last survivor of that night on the farm. Suddenly, it becomes clear to PAMYAT and all the interests betting on Pashin that one witness from his undercover days still exists and can still put him on that farm. All right? So . . . from that point on, they have to take her out, and her husband's gaudy past certainly provides a kind of pretext."

"That's sequencing," said Bonson. "Fine, good, it makes sense. It's a theory that fits. But still . . . why?"

"Ah, he was involved with a famous peace demonstrator in blowing up a building."

"So?"

"Well . . ."

Bonson argued savagely, trying to compel the young man to a next leap. "It's widely known he had an intelligence background. It's known in some circumstances that the peace movement had some East Bloc involvement. Actually, that might *help* his candidacy in today's Russia. I don't understand why the same security mandates would be operational twenty-seven years later. They were protecting assets *then*. What can they be protecting now? Ideas, anybody?"

None of the senior people had any.

"Well, then, we're sort of stuck, aren't we?" said Bonson. "It's very interesting, but we still don't—"

"Should I explain it to you now, or do you want to yammer on a bit?" asked Bob.

"You ain't got it yet, Bonson," said Bob. "You still bought into the cover story. You still look at the cover story and you don't see the real story. And all your smart boys, too."

"Well, Sergeant," said Bonson evenly, "then go ahead. You explain the real story."

"I will. You missed the big news. There was a bomb explosion at the University of Wisconsin 9 May 1971 all right. A kid named Trig Carter blew himself up protesting the war in Vietnam. Maybe most of you are too young to remember it, but I do. He gave his life to peace. He was a rich kid, could have had anything, but he gave his life up for his ideals. They even wrote books about him. He may have been brave, too. I don't know.

"But the one name you won't find in that book or in any other books about the peace movement or the history of our country in 1971 is the name Ralph Goldstein. Anybody here recognize it?"

There was silence in the room.

"That's the big story. Ralph Goldstein was the doctoral student who was killed that night in the University of

Wisconsin Math Center. Jewish boy, twenty-seven, married, from Skokie, Illinois. Went to the University of Illinois, Chicago Circle campus, not a very impressive school compared to the fancy schools where Trig Carter went. He didn't know nobody. He just did his work and tried to get his degree and do his research. Smart as a whip, but very obscure. Never went to no demonstrations, smoked no dope, got no free love, or nothing. I did something nobody has yet done: I went and talked to his son, now himself a very bright kid. I hope nobody don't blow him up."

He could feel their eyes on him. He cracked a little smile. All the pointy heads, listening to *him*.

"But Ralph Goldstein had published a paper in *Duke Higher Mathematics Quarterly,* which he called 'Certain Higher Algorhythmic Functions of Topographical Form Reading in Orbital Applications.' Don't mean a thing to me. But guess what? We now got about 350 satellites in orbit watching the world because Ralph Goldstein figured out the math of it. He was only a grad student, and he himself didn't even know it, but he'd been picked to join the staff at the Satellite Committee at the Johns Hopkins Advanced Physics Lab in Maryland, where they did all the high-power number crunching that made the satellite program possible. Okay, so what his death meant practically was it took us three extra years to get terrain-recognition birds in the air. If it matters, that's three years where the Sovs upgraded their own satellite program, and closed a gap in the Cold War. That's three more years that kept them in the race. Which one of you geniuses or experts can tell me which part of Soviet staff was responsible for strategic warfare?"

"GRU," came the reply.

"That's right. And what was Pashin?"

"GRU."

"That's right. So guess what? His job wasn't to stop the war in Vietnam. He didn't give a shit about the war in Vietnam, or about Trig Carter or about nothing. It was to kill a little Jewish guy in an office in Madison, Wisconsin, who was just about to put the Americans way ahead in the Cold War. Kill him in such a way that no one would ever, in a hundred years, think it had to do with the Russians. Kill him in such a way that no one would even think about his death but only about the death of the man who killed him. To make him an extra in his own murder. That was Pashin's mission: it was straight GRU wet work, a murder job. Trig Carter and the peace movement were just part of the props."

He could hear them breathing heavily in the room, but no one spoke.

"And don't you see the cynicism in it, the goddamned motherfucking brilliance? They *knew* this country so goddamn well. They just *knew* that when any of you Ivy League heroes looked at that data, you couldn't see past Trig, because, no matter which side he was on, he was one of you. *That* would be the tragedy, and the fog it would release in your little pea fucking brains would keep you from ever figuring it out. It takes an outsider, someone who ain't been to no college and doesn't think the word Harvard or Yale means shit in this world. It takes gutter-trash rednecks who you all pay to do the dirty work with the rifles so you can sit in your clubs and make ironic little jokes. Or plan your little wars that the Swaggers and the Fenns and the Goldsteins have to go fight."

The silence lasted for a long moment.

Then finally, Bonson spoke: "Class anger aside, does this make any sense to you Skull and Bones boys?"

It took a while, but finally someone said, almost laconically, "Yeah, it makes perfect sense. It even explains why it's happening now. It puts them in a desperate situation. They—that's PAMYAT, the old GRU security bunch hiding behind nationalism and financed by mob money—have to keep this information quiet. They couldn't take a chance that just as he's closing in on the presidency, their man is revealed as a murderer of American nationals on American soil. That would make it impossible for him to work with any American president or with big American corporations. That information has to be buried at all costs. Their lives, their futures, their party depend on it. They *had* to eliminate the last witness, particularly as Pashin's fame is getting bigger and bigger."

"Sir," said someone else, "I think we could game out some very interesting tactical deployment for this information. We might have a hand ourselves in determining who their next president is."

"Okay," said Bonson, "you game it out. But I want it going in one direction. I want to kill this motherfucker."

PART IV

BACK TO THE WORLD

The Present

CHAPTER FIFTY

The snow didn't last. It melted on the third day after it had fallen, causing floods in the lowlands, closing roads, wrecking bridges, creating mud slides. But on Upper Cedar Creek it was a serene day, with blue skies, eastern zephyrs and creeks full of sparkling water. The pines shed their cloak of snow; the grass began to emerge, green and lush, and seemingly undamaged by the ordeal.

By now the excitement was over. Bonson had departed with a handshake the previous morning, after ensuring that a quickly convened Custer County grand jury found no culpability in the death by misadventure of one Frank Vborny, of Cleveland, Ohio, as the fake identification documents read in the dead sniper's pocket. Ballistics confirmed that indeed Mr. Vborny had shot and killed two innocent people in the Custer County Idaho Bell substation in Mackay; obviously a berserker, he next attacked a house that was luckily rented out by a gun owner, who was able to defend himself. The gun owner's name was never published but that was all right, and in Idaho most people took satisfaction from the moral purity of the episode and its subtle endorsement of the great old Second Amendment, a lesson most Westerners felt had been forgotten in the East.

Up in the mountains, the state police had pulled out, the helicopters and all the young men and women had gone back to wherever it was they came from, and there was little sign that they'd been there.

Bob and Julie had a check, in the odd sum of $146,589.07, and had no idea how that exact figure had been selected. It was from the Department of the Treasury, and the invoice banally read, "Consultancy," with the proper dates listed and his Social Security number.

The last of the security team left, the rifle and recovered Beretta were returned, the foam case with its cargo marked officially as "operational loss," and Sally had taken Nikki for a walk down to the mailbox on Route 93, when he at last had an opportunity to talk to his wife.

"Well, howdy," he said.

"Hi," she said. Doctors had examined her after her ordeal; she was in fine shape, her collarbone knitting properly. She seemed much stronger now, and was able to get about better. Sally would soon be leaving.

"Well, I have some things to say. Care to have a listen?"

"Yes."

"You know we have some money now. I'd like to git on back to Arizona and restart the business. Joe Lopez says they seem to miss me down there. It was a good business and a good life."

"It *was* a good life."

"I went a little crazy there. I put everybody through a lot. I wasn't very grown-up about my troubles. That's all in the past now. And what I learned was how important my family was. I want my family back. That's the only thing I want. No more adventures, no more screwing around. That's all finished."

"It wasn't your fault," she said. "It had nothing to do with you. It was all about me. How could I blame you for anything? You saved all—"

"Now, now," he said. "No need for that. I thought all this out. I just want the old life back. I want you to be my wife, I want my baby girl to be fine, I want to work with the horses and take care of y'all. That's the best life there is, the only life I've ever wanted. I get these bad moods. Or I used to; I hope I'm over that. If I had some ghosts, they ain't walking out of the cemetery no more. So . . . well, what do you say? Will you let me come back?"

"I already called the lawyer. He recalled the separation request."

"That's great."

"It'll be good," she said. "I think we should use some

of that money and go on a nice vacation. We should close up the house here, the house outside of Boise, but then go to some warm island for two weeks. Then we can go back to Arizona. R&R."

"God, does that sound like a plan to me," he said with a smile. "There's only one last little thing. Trig's mother. She was very helpful and she told me that if I ever learned anything about the way her son died, I should tell her. Tell her the truth. I still feel that obligation. So in a couple of months or so, when all this dies down, when we're back, I may take a bit of time and head back there to Baltimore."

"Do you want us to come with you?"

"Oh, it ain't worth it. I'll just fly in, rent a car, fly back. It'll be over quicker 'n' you can believe. No sense putting no trouble to it or taking Nikki away from her riding. Hell, I may drive instead of flying, save some money that way."

He smiled. For just a second she thought there might be something in his eyes, some vagrant thought, some evidence of another idea, another agenda; but no, not a thing could be seen. They were depthless and gray and revealed nothing except the love he felt for her.

Little by little, life for the Swagger family reassembled itself toward some model of normality. Even the big news of a spectacular murder in Russia failed to make much of a stir. Bob just watched a little of it on CNN, saw the burning Jeep Cherokee and the dead man in the back, and when the hysterical analysts came on to explain it all, he changed channels.

Sally stayed until they moved back to Boise, and then Bob drove her to the airport.

"Once again," she said at the gate, "the great Bob Lee Swagger triumphs. You killed your enemies, you got your wife and family back. Can't keep a good man down."

"Sally, I got 'em all fooled but you, don't I? You see clean through me."

"Bob, seriously. Pay attention to them this time. I

know it's easy to say, but you have to let the past go. You're married, you have a wonderful, brave, strong wife and a beautiful little girl. That's your focus."

"I know. It will be."

"There's no more old business."

"Is that a question or a statement?"

"Both. If there's one little thing left, let it go. It doesn't matter. It can't matter."

"There's nothing left," he said.

"You are one ornery sumbitch," she said. "I swear, I don't know what that woman sees in you."

"Well, I don't neither. But she's pretty smart, so maybe she knows something you and I don't."

Sally smiled, and then turned to leave, good friend and soldier to the very end. She winked at him, as if to say, "You are hopeless."

And he knew he was.

When the cast came off a little later, and Julie was back among the supple, the family flew to St. John, in the U.S. Virgins for two glorious weeks. They rented a villa just outside Cruz Bay on the little island, and each morning took a taxi to the beautiful Trunk Bay beach, where they snorkeled and lay in the sand and watched the time pass ever so slowly as they turned browner and browner. They were a handsome family, the natural aristocrats of nature: the tall, grave man with gray eyes and abundant hair, and his wife, every bit as handsome, her hair a mesh of honey and brown, her cheekbones strong, her lips thin, her eyes powerful. She had been a cheerleader years ago, but she was if anything more beautiful now than ever. And the daughter, a total ball of fire, a complete kamikaze who always had to be called in, who pushed the snorkeling to its maximum, who begged her father to let her scuba or go water- or para-skiing.

"You got plenty of time to break your neck when you're older," he told her. "Your old mommy and I can't keep up with such a thing. You have to give us a break. This is our vacation, too."

"Oh, Daddy," she scolded, "you're such a *chicken.*"

And when she said that, he did an imitation of a chicken that was clearly based on a little real time in the barnyard, and they all laughed, first at how funny it was but second at the idea that a man of such reserve could at last find some way to let himself go, to be silly. An astonishment.

At night, they went into town and ate at the restaurants there. Bob never had a drink, didn't seem to want one. It was idyllic, really too good. It reminded Julie just a bit of an R&R she'd had with Donny in Hawaii, just before . . . well, just before.

And Bob seemed to relax totally too. She'd never seen him so calm, so at ease. The wariness that usually marked his passage in society—a feeling for terrain and threat, a tendency to mark escape routes, to look too carefully at strangers—disappeared. And he never had nightmares. Not once did he awake screaming, drenched in cold sweat, or with the shakes, or with that hurt, hunted look that sometimes came into his eyes. His scars almost seemed to disappear as he grew tanner and tanner, but they were always there, the puckers of piebald flesh that could only be bullet wounds: so many of them. One of the Virgin Islanders stared at them once, then turned to say something to one of his colleagues, in that musical, impenetrable English of theirs, so fast and full of strange rhythms, but Julie heard the word "bombom mon," which she took to mean "boom-boom man," which she in turn took to be "gunman."

But Bob appeared not to notice. He was almost friendly, his natural reserve blurred into something far more open and pleasant to the world. She'd never quite seen him like this.

There was only one night when she awoke and realized he wasn't in bed with her. She rose, walked through the dark living room, until she found him on the deck, under a tropic night, sitting quietly. Before them was a slope of trees, a hill and then the sea, a serene sheet of glass throwing off tints of moonlight. He sat with utter stillness, staring at a book, as if it had some secret meaning to it.

"What is that?" she asked.

"This? Oh, it's called *Birds of North America* by Roger Prentiss Fuller."

She came over and saw that he was gazing at a section on eagles.

"What are you thinking about?" she asked.

"Oh, nothing. This book has some pretty pictures. Kid who painted them really knew his birds."

"Bob, it's so unlike you."

"I was just curious, that's all."

"Eagles?"

"Eagles," he said.

They returned to Arizona and with the money, Bob was able to upgrade the barn, hire two Mexican assistants, buy a new pickup and reintroduce himself to the Pima County horsey set. In just a little bit of time, they had patients—seven, eight, then ten horses in various states of healing, all ministered to with tender care. His lay-up barn became a thriving concern after a while, mostly on the basis of his own sweat, but also because people trusted him.

Nikki went back to school but she rode every day, English style, and would start showing on the circuit's junior level the next spring, her coach insisted. Julie resumed working three days a week at the Navajo reservation clinic, helping the strong young braves mend after fights or drinking bouts, helping the rickety children, doing a surprising amount of good in a small compass.

No reporters ever showed; no German TV crews set up in the barnyard; no young men came by to request interviews for their books; no gun show entrepreneurs offered him money to stand at a booth and sell autographs; no writers from the survivalist press wanted to write admiring profiles. He and the war he represented seemed once again to have disappeared. No part of it remained, its wounds healed or at least scarred over.

One night, Bob sat down and wrote a letter to Trig Carter's mother. He told her he was planning a trip east some time in weeks to come and, as he said, he'd like to stop by and share with her what he had learned about the death of her son.

She wrote back immediately, pleased to hear from him. She suggested a time, and he called her and said that was fine, that's when she should look for him.

He loaded his new pickup with gear and began the long trip back. He drove up to Tucson, to the veterans cemetery there, and walked the ranks of stones, white in the desert sun, until at last he came to:

Donny M. Fenn
Lance Corporal
U.S.M.C.
1948–1972

Nothing set it apart. There were dozens of other stones from that and other wars, the last years always signifying some violent eddy in American history: 1968, 1952, 1944, 1918. A wind whistled out of the mountains. The day was so bright it hurt his eyes. He had no flowers, nothing to offer the square of dry earth and the stone tablet.

He'd been in so many other cemeteries; this one felt no different at all. He had nothing to say, for so much had been said. He just soaked up the loss of Donny: Donny jumping over the berm, the vibration as the bullet went through him, lifting the dust from his chest; Donny falling, his eyes going blank and sightless, his hand grasping Bob's arm, the blood in his mouth and foaming obscenely down his nose.

After a while—he had no idea how long—he left, got back in the truck and settled in for a long pull across

Arizona, New Mexico, Texas, Oklahoma and on to the East.

The last part of the trip took him to the Virginia suburbs of Washington, DC, where once again he bunked with an old friend who had become the Command Sergeant Major of the United States Marine Corps. As a few months before, he fell in with cronies, both still on active duty or recently retired, men of his own generation and stamp, leathery, sinewy men who bore the career imprint of the Corps. There were a few loud nights at the CSM's house in the suburbs, the whole thing slightly more celebrative.

It was the next day that he called Mrs. Carter and told her he'd be up the next night. She said she couldn't wait.

He hung up and waited on the line for the telltale click of a wiretap. He didn't hear it, but he knew that meant nothing: there were other methods of penetration.

Now, he thought, only this last thing.

CHAPTER FIFTY-ONE

Bob drove carefully through the far reaches of Baltimore County, at sunset. It was as he remembered, the beautiful houses of the rich and propertied, of old families, of the original owners of America—people who rode English. At last he turned down a lane and drove under the overhanging elms until he found Trig's ancestral home.

He pulled in, once again momentarily humbled by the immensity of the place, its suggestion of stability and propriety and what endured in the world. At last he got out, adjusted his tie and went to the door.

It was September now, turning coolish at night here in the East. The leaves hadn't yet begun to redden but there was nevertheless a definite edge in the air. Things would change soon: that was the message.

He knocked; the old black butler answered, as before.

He was led through the same halls of antiques, paintings of patriots, exotic plants, dense Oriental rugs, damask curtains, lighting fixtures configured to represent the flicker of candles. Since it was darker, there wasn't quite the sense of the threadbare that had been so evident his first time out here.

The old man led him into the study, where the woman waited. She stood erect as the mast of a ship—the family had owned shipping once, of course, as well as railroads, oil, coal and more. She was still stern, still rigid, still had that iron-gray uplift to her hair. She was demurely dressed in a conservative suit, and he could see, even more now, that at one time she must have been a great beauty. Now an air of tragic futility attended her. Or maybe it was his imagination. But she'd lost a son and a husband to a war that the husband said was worth fighting and the son said wasn't. It had broken her family apart, as it had broken apart so many families. No family was immune, that was the lesson: not even this one, so protected by its wealth and property.

"Well, Sergeant Swagger, you look as if you've become a movie star."

"I've been working outdoors, ma'am."

"No, I don't mean the tan. I have sources still, I believe I told you. There's some news afoot about your heroics in Idaho, how you disconnected some terrible conspiracy. I'm sure I don't understand it, but the information has even reached the society of doddering State Department widows."

"They say we were able to get some good work done, yes, ma'am."

"Are you congenitally modest, Sergeant? For a man so powerful, you are so unassuming you seem hardly to be there at all."

"I'm just a polite Southern boy, ma'am."

"Please sit down. I won't offer you a drink, since I know you no longer drink. A club soda, a cup of coffee or tea, a soft drink, something like that?"

"No, ma'am, I'm fine."

They sat across from each other, in the study. One of Trig's birds observed them; it was a blue mallard.

"Well, then, I know you came here to tell me something. I suppose I'm ready to hear it. Will I need a drink, Sergeant Swagger? A great shot of vodka, perhaps?"

"No, ma'am, I don't believe so."

"Well, then, go ahead."

"Ma'am, I have satisfied myself on this one issue: I don't believe no way your son would have killed another human being and I don't believe he killed himself. I think he was duped by a professional Soviet agent—rather, Soviet in those days. Your son was sort of charmed into—"

"What a quaint euphemism. But I have to tell you I'm aware of my son's homosexual leanings. You believe it was a homosexual thing?"

"I don't know, ma'am. That's not my department. I

only know the result, that somehow he was snookered into assisting in what was represented as an act of symbolic violence as a way of reenergizing the peace movement. But the Russian operator, he didn't give a tinker's dam about the peace movement. He was only interested in your boy's fame and reputation as a masking device for the mission's real target, Ralph Goldstein, who was working on satellite topography–reading technologies and seemed on the verge of a breakthrough the Russians felt would put them way behind in the Cold War."

"It was only about murder, in the end. And some other boy was the target?"

"Yes, ma'am."

"So my poor Trig wasn't even the star of his own murder?"

"No, ma'am."

"Well, he'd been the star of so many other things, I don't suppose it matters."

"My guess is, he had begun to have doubts; perhaps he even tried to back out, or go to the FBI or something. Possibly there's some record of his doubts in his missing sketches. But it appears I won't never see them. He was killed, probably with a judo chop to the back of the neck. That was their specialty in those days. In fact, everybody who saw this agent was killed, at some effort, including another peace demonstrator named Peter Farris, a Marine named Donny Fenn, and later attempts were made on my wife, who had seen the agent with Trig. She was married to Donny Fenn at the time. I believe Ralph Goldstein was killed in the same way. Their bodies were put in the building and it was detonated. It goes down into the books as a violent fool and a math geek. But the books are always wrong. It was something entirely different; kids used by older, smarter, far more ruthless men, then thrown away for a momentary strategic advantage. It was a war, but the cold one, not the hot one."

"The one we won."

"I suppose we did."

"What happened to the Russian?"

"Well, our intelligence people found out a way to turn the information against him. I don't know much about it, but he's dead. They had it on CNN. You could see the burned bodies in the back of the Jeep."

"That nasty boy?"

"That one."

"And the man who was trying to kill you?"

"Well, he wasn't trying to kill me. He was trying to kill my wife. He was stopped," Bob said. "And he ain't never coming back."

"Were you responsible?"

Bob just nodded.

"Do you know what you are? Sergeant, you're a sacred killer. All societies need them. All civilizations need them. It is to the eternal shame and the current damnation of this country that it refuses anymore to acknowledge them and thinks it can get by without respecting them. So let an old bat speak a truth: you are the necessary man. Without you it all goes away."

Bob said nothing. Speculation on his place in the nature of things was not his style.

The old lady sensed this, and asked for an accounting of the politics of the affair, the details of history. He gave it, succinctly enough.

"Odd, isn't it? As you've explained it, after it's all counted up and all the accounts are settled, the one party to it all that could be said to benefit is the old Russian communist apparatus. It's kept them from going under another few years. And who can tell what that'll mean? The cruel irony of history, I suppose."

"I wouldn't know about that, ma'am. They were very happy, the intelligence people, that they were able to stop this fellow Pashin. He was their real target. My wife was his, but he was ours, and we got him first."

"Well, anyway: you've provided a measure of serenity to my life. My son wasn't a fool; he was overmatched by professionals, who've been punished. Justice isn't much, but it helps the nights go easier."

"Yes, ma'am. I agree."

"Sometimes you don't even get that, so one must be very grateful for what one does get."

"Yes, ma'am."

"Now . . . I know you weren't working for me, you were never my employee. But the one power I still have in the world is to satisfy myself through my checkbook. I would very much enjoy getting it out now and writing a nice big, fat one."

"Thank you," he said. "That's not necessary."

"Are you sure?"

"I am."

"Soon there'll be college expenses."

"Not for a while. We're doing fine."

"Oh, I hope I haven't spoiled things by bringing up money."

"No, ma'am."

"Well, then—"

"There is one thing, though."

"Name it."

"The painting."

"The painting?"

"The eagle after the fight. I don't know a thing about art and I don't know a thing about birds, but I'd be honored to have that. It has some meaning to me."

"You felt your breast stir when you saw it?"

"Well, something like that."

"Then you shall have it. Come with me, Sergeant Swagger."

She led him forthrightly out of the room, commanded the old butler to get a "torch"—a flashlight—and led Bob in the butler's uncertain illumination to the studio. Their breaths plumed in the frosty air. She opened the door, found a switch and the birds flashed to life, still and majestic.

"These are worth quite a lot of money to connoisseurs

of the macabre, I expect," she said. "But the eagle . . . it's so atypical, and also unsigned. Would you want a certificate of authenticity? It might seem pointless now, but when your daughter goes to school, it could mean the difference between buying one year at Radcliffe or four years."

"No, ma'am," he said, walking to the painting. "I just want it for what it is."

He stood before it, and felt its pain, its distraught, logy mind, its survivor's despair.

"I wonder how he got so much into it," she said.

He unscrewed the painting from the easel, where it had been clamped since May of 1971. It was unframed, but the canvas was tacked stoutly to a wood backing.

"I hope you'll let me pay for the framing," said the old woman. "That at least I can do."

"I'll send you the bill," he said.

He wrapped the painting carefully in some rags, making certain not to disturb the elegant depth of the crusted pigment, and put the whole package delicately under an arm.

"All set," he said.

"Sergeant Swagger, again, I can't thank you enough. You've made my dotage appreciably better, to no real gain of your own."

"Oh, I gained, Mrs. Carter. I gained."

The team watched him from far off, through night-vision binoculars. It had been a long stakeout until he showed, longer still since he was in there. Where had he been all afternoon? Still, it didn't matter. Now it was going to happen.

Swagger turned his truck around, pulled out, drove down the lane, and by the time he got back to Falls Road, the number-one van had moved into position, not behind his turn, as amateurs will do, but before it, letting him overtake them, and falling into position from behind that way, without attracting notice.

Swagger pulled around the van, scooted ahead and settled into an unhurried pace.

"Blue One, this is Blue Two," said the observer into his microphone. "Ah, we have him picked up very nicely, no problems. I have Blue Three behind me, you want to run this by management?"

"Blue Two, management just got here."

"You stay on him, Blue Two, but don't rush it," came the impatient voice any of them knew as Bonson's. "Play in the other van if you think you're in danger of being burned. Don't be too aggressive. Give me an update—"

"Whoa, isn't this interesting, Blue One. He didn't do the beltway. He just stayed on Falls Road on the way into Baltimore."

"Doesn't that become Eighty-three?" asked Bonson.

"Yes, sir, it does. Goes straight downtown."

"But his motel is out at B-W."

"That's the credit card data. He had something with him, some kind of package. Maybe he's going to do something with it."

"Got you, Blue Two, you just stay on him."

They watched as Bob drove unconsciously into downtown Baltimore on the limited access highway that plunges into that city's heart. He passed Television Hill with its giant antennae, and the train station, then the *Sun*, and finally the road drifted off its abutments to street level and became a lesser boulevard called President Street just east of downtown.

"He's turning left," said Blue Two. "It's, uh, Fleet Street."

"The map says he's headed towards Fells Point."

"What the hell is he doing there? Is he starring in a John Waters movie?"

"Cut the joking on the net," said Bonson. "You stay with him. I'm coming in; be in town very shortly."

The men knew Bonson and his radio team were in a hangar at B-W Airport, less than twenty minutes south of town this time of night, assuming there was no backup at the tunnel.

Bob turned up Fleet, and the traffic grew a bit thicker. He did not look around. He did not notice either the white or the black vans that had been on him since the country.

He passed through Fells Point, jammed with cars, kids, scum and bars, presumably the shady night town of the city, and kept on driving. Another mile or two and he turned on the diagonal down a beat-up street called Boston.

"Blue One, this is Blue Two. The traffic is thinning out. He's headed out Boston toward the docks. I'm going to stay on Fleet, run a parallel, and let Blue Three close on him, just to be safe."

"Read you, Two," said the observer in the second van.

There was no way Swagger could tell, now that the van which had been closest to him sped away down another road and the unseen secondary vehicle closed the gap, that he was under surveillance. More important, he exhibited nothing in his driving that demonstrated the signature of a surveillee who'd burned his trackers: he didn't dart in and out of traffic, he didn't signal right, then turn left, he didn't turn without signaling. He just drove blandly ahead, intent on his destination.

But once he passed two large apartment buildings on the right, at the harbor's edge, he began to slow down, as if he were looking for something.

It was a kind of post-industrial zone, with ruined, deserted factories everywhere; oil-holding facilities for off-loading by tankers; huge, weedy fields that served no apparent purpose at all but were nevertheless Cyclone-fenced. There was little traffic and almost no pedestrian activity; it was a blasted zone, where humans may have worked during the day, but deserted almost totally at night.

The number-two van was a good three hundred feet behind him when he turned right, down another street—it was called South Clinton Street—that seemed to veer closer to the docks. The van didn't turn; it went straight, after its observer notified the first vehicle, which had run parallel down Boston, and itself turned right on the street Bob had turned down.

"Two, I have him," said the observer.

"Cool. I'll roam a bit, then take up a tail position."

"That's good work," said Bonson, over the net. "We're going to lose you now. We're going through the tunnel."

"I'll stay on him, Blue One."

"Catch you when we get out of the tunnel."

The first van maintained about a four hundred-foot gap between itself and Swagger's truck, which now coursed down desolate South Clinton Street. Off to the right, a giant naval vessel, under construction, suddenly loomed, gray and arc-lit for drama and security. Bob passed it, passed a bank, a few small working men's restaurants, then stopped by the side of the road.

"Goddammit," said Two. "Burned. Goddammit."

His own driver started to slow, but he was exceedingly professional.

"No, just keep driving. Just drive by him. Don't eyeball him as you pass him, don't even *think* about it; he'll feel you paying attention. I'm dropping out of sight."

The driver continued at the same speed, while the observer dropped into the seat well, knowing that a single driver was much less of a giveaway signature for a tail job. And he hit the send button.

"Blue Three, do you read?"

"Yeah, I'm past the Boston-South Clinton Street exchange, just pulled over."

"Okay, he's stopped. We're going to pass him; you come on by and pull off a long way down. He's on the right. Don't use your lights. Go to night vision and monitor his moves."

The lead vehicle sped around the curve, passed several mountains of coal ready for loading on the right.

He pulled off when he was out of sight of the parked man.

"Two, this is Three. I'm in position and I've got him in my night lenses. He's just sitting there, waiting. I think he's turned off his engine. No, no, he's turned off his lights, now he's pulling ahead, he's turning in—now I've lost him."

"Okay, he's gone to ground."

"Sitrep, people," came the voice of Bonson, who had just cleared the tunnel and was now on this side of the harbor.

"Sir, he just pulled into a yard or something in the warehouse district down by the docks. Just off Boston. We have him under observation."

"I'm right at Boston Street here. Do we go east or west off of Ninety-five?"

"You go west. Go about a mile and turn left again, on South Clinton Street. I'm off by the side of the road just around that turn, lights off, left side of the road. Two is on the other side, around the curve. We're both about a half mile away from where he's gone to rest."

"Okay, let's meet one at a time in two-minute intervals two hundred yards this side, my side, of the location. You go first, Three, then you Two, from the other side, then I'll join you. Keep your lights on in case he's looking out. If he saw unlit vehicles, he could go ballistic."

"Sir, I honestly don't think he's seen a damned thing. He was off in his own world. He wasn't even looking around when he stopped. He's just looking for some deserted place."

"We'll know in a few minutes," said Bonson, just as his car turned left and pulled in behind one of the vans.

Bob parked to the left of the silent, corrugated-metal building, as far back and out of sight as he could. He paused, waiting. He heard no sounds; there was no night watchman. The place was some kind of grain storage facility, again for loading cargo ships, but no ship floated in the water. He could see the shimmering lights on the flat, calm water, and beyond that the skyline of the city, spangled in illumination. But here, there was nothing except the rush of cars from the tunnel exit nearby, a separate world sealed off by concrete abutments.

He got out, taking the wrapped painting, a powerful flashlight and a heavy pair of wire cutters with him, and headed to the warehouse. It was padlocked. But where the lock was strong, the metal fastener that secured door to wall was not, and the wire cutters made quick work of it. The lock fell, still secure, to the ground, wearing a little necklace of sheared steel. He pulled the door open, stepped into a space that in the darkness appeared to be cut by bins, now mostly empty. The dust of grains—wheat mostly, though he smelled soya beans too—filled the air.

He walked, his shoes echoing on the bricks, until at last he came to the center of the room. He stopped by a pillar and a drain, then turned on the light. The beam skipped across the empty building, finding nothing of interest but more emptiness, dramatic shadows, fire extinguishers, light switches, closets, crates. He went and got a crate, pulled it into the center and set it down. Finally, he set the light on the floor, aimed back toward where he had left the package. It cast a cold white eye on the painting.

He walked over, and leaned into the circle of light.

Slowly, he peeled the rags away, until at last the painting stood exposed. He examined it carefully, saw how the tacks held the canvas to the backing. He took out his Case pocketknife, and very slowly used its blade to scrape at the paint.

It was thick and cracked easily, falling to the ground in chunks and strips. He scraped, destroying the image of the eagle, pulling at the paint, watching it flake in colored chunks downward. In a minute or so, he came to a ridge under the paint, and ran the knife blade along it until he reached a corner. It was the top of a heavy piece of paper, and it had been literally buried under the heavy oil pigmentation of the image.

With the blade, he pried the corner loose enough to get a grip on, set the knife down and very carefully pulled the sheet of paper free. It cracked off the canvas. As he finally freed it, there was a kind of soft, slipping sound: paper, sliding loose, fluting down to land with a rattle on the dirty floor. He set the backing down and bent there in the harsh light to see what secrets he had unlocked.

It was the last few sketches from Trig's book. Bob began to shuffle through them, finding images of a campus building in Madison, Wisconsin, portraits of people at parties in Washington, crowd scenes of big demonstrations. There was a portrait of Donny. It must have been made about the time he did the scene of Donny and Julie, which Bob had seen in Vietnam. He brought those days vividly to life, and Bob began to feel his passion—and his pain.

CHAPTER FIFTY-TWO

One man had gone ahead and returned with a report. "He's in there with a flashlight, reading some pages or something. I can't figure it out."

"Okay," said Bonson. "I think I know what he's got. Let's finish this, once and for all."

The guns came out. The team consisted now of five men besides Bonson. They were large men in crew cuts in their late forties. They were tough-looking, exuding that alpha-male confidence that suggested no difficulty in doing violence if necessary. They looked like large policemen, soldiers, firemen, extremely well developed, extremely competent. They drew the guns from under their jackets, and there was a little ceremony of clicks and snaps, as safeties came off and slides were eased back to check chambers, just in case. Then the suppressors were screwed on.

Bonson led them along the road, into the lot and up to the old grain warehouse. Above, stars pinwheeled and blinked. Water sounds filled the night, the lapping of the tides against ancient docks. From somewhere came a low, steady roar of automobiles. He reached the metal door and through the gap between it and the building proper, he could see Bob in the center of the room, sitting on a crate he'd gotten from somewhere, reading by the light of a flashlight. The painting was on the floor, somehow standing straight, as if on display, and Bob was leaning against a thick pillar that supported the low ceiling. Bonson could see that the image had somehow been destroyed, yielding a large white square in its center.

What is wrong with this picture, he asked himself.

He studied it for a second.

No, nothing. The man is unaware. The man is lost.

The man is unprepared. The man is defenseless. The man is the ultimate soft target.

He nodded.

"Okay," he whispered.

One of the men opened the door and he walked in.

Bob looked up to see them as their lights flashed on him.

"Howdy," he said.

"Lights," said Bonson.

One of the men walked away, found an electrical junction and the place leaped into light, which showed the rawness of industrial space, a gravel floor, the air filled with dust and agricultural vapors.

"Hello, Swagger," said Bonson. "My, my, what's that?"

"It's the last sketches from Trig Carter's book. Real damn interesting," said Bob, loudly.

"How'd you find it?"

"What?"

What was wrong with his ears?

"I said, 'How did you find it?' "

"When I thought about his last painting, I figured it, pretty close. The reason the painting was so different was his clue: his way of saying to those who came after him, 'Look this over.' But no one ever came. Not until me."

"Nice work," said Bonson. "What's in it?"

"What?"

What was wrong with his ears?

"I said, *'What's in it?'* "

"Oh. Just what you'd expect," said Bob, still a bit loud. "People, places, things he ran into as he began to prepare his symbolic explosion of the math building. A couple of nice drawings of Donny."

"Trig Carter was a traitor," said Bonson.

"Yeah?" said Bob mildly. "Do tell."

"Give it over here," said Bonson.

"You don't want to see the drawings, Bonson? They're pretty damned interesting."

"We'll look at them. That's enough."

"Oh, it gits better. There's a nice drawing of this Fitzpatrick. Damn, that boy could draw. It's Pashin; everybody will be able to tell. That's quite a find, eh? That's *proof*, cold, solid dead-on proof the peace movement was infiltrated by elements of Soviet intelligence."

"So what?" said Bonson. "That's all gone and forgotten. It doesn't matter."

"Oh, no?" said Bob. "See, there's someone else in the drawing. Poor Trig must have grown extremely suspicious, so one day, late, right after the big May Day mess, he followed Fitzpatrick. He watched him meet somebody. He did. He watched them deep in conversation. And he recorded it."

Bob held it up, a folded piece of paper, the lines that were Pashin brilliantly clear.

Bob unfolded the rest of the drawing.

"See, Bonson, here's the funny part," said Bob, loudly. "There's someone else here. It's you."

There was a moment of silence. Bonson's eyes narrowed tightly, and then he relaxed, turned to his team and smiled. He almost had to laugh.

"Who are you, Bonson?" Swagger asked, more quietly now. "Really, I'd like to know. I had some ideas. I just couldn't make no sense of them. But just tell me. Who are you? What are you? Are you a traitor? Are you a professional Soviet agent masquerading as an American? Are you some kind of cynic playing the sides against each other? Are you in it for the money? Who are you, Bonson?"

"Kill him?" asked one of the men on the team, holding up a suppressed Beretta.

"No," said Bonson. "No, not yet. I want to see how far he's gotten."

"Finally it makes sense," Bob said. "The great CIA mole. The big one they've been hunting all these years. Who makes a better mole than the head mole hunter?

Pretty goddamned smart. But what's the deal? Why did no one ever suspect you?"

He could sense that Bonson wanted to tell him. He had probably never told anyone, had repressed his reality so deep and imposed such discipline on himself that it was almost not real to him, except when it needed to be. But now at last, he had a chance to explain.

"The reason I was never suspected," he said finally, "was because *they* recruited me. I never went to them. They offered me a job when I left the Navy, but I said no. I went to law school, I spent three years on Wall Street, they came after me three more times, and I always said no. Finally—God, it took some discipline—finally I said yes."

"Why did they want you so much?"

"Because of the NIS prosecutions. That was the plan. I sent fifty-seven young men to Vietnam, Marines, naval seaman, even a couple of junior officers. I reported on dozens more that I turned up in the other services, and many of them went, too. There was never a better secret policeman anywhere, one with less mercy and more ambition. They could see how fierce I was. I was so good. I was astonishing. They wanted me so bad it almost killed them, and I played so hard to get it still amazes me. But that was our plan from the beginning."

His face gleamed with vanity and pride. This was his great triumph, the core of his life, what made him better than other men, his work of art.

"Who are you, Bonson? Who the fuck are you?"

"The only time I ever came out on a wet operation was that one night when that idiot Pashin showed up without a driver's license. You needed a driver's license to buy that much ammonium nitrate, even in Virginia! That idiot. GRU begged the committee for help, and I had the best identity running, so I drove down to Leesburg and bought it. I met him in the restaurant to tell him where it was secured. He was a brilliant operator, but in little practical things like that he was stupid."

"And you were unlucky. Trig the human camera had followed him."

"I always worried about that. That was my one moment of vulnerability. But now, you've taken care of that for me."

"Who are you?" said Bob. "You have to tell me that."

"I don't have to tell you anything. I can kill you and I'm forever secure."

"In seventy-one, you were the source of deployment intelligence, weren't you?"

"You bet I was," said Bonson. "I invented chaos. It was the best professional penetration in history, the way I orchestrated it."

"You killed the little girl on the bridge, right? Amy Rosenzweig, seventeen. I looked it up. I saw how much trouble it caused."

"Oh, Swagger, goddamn, you are smart. We picked her up, shot her up and dropped her into the crowd. It was a massive dose of LSD. She never knew what hit her. My friend Bill here"—he indicated a man on his team—"did it. She freaked and went over. God, what a stink it caused; it almost wrecked the credibility of the U.S. government in that one thing. The *pressure* it caused."

"Those are your boys, aren't they, your security team? Which of 'em killed poor Peter Farris?"

The five men in suits arrayed around Bonson glowered at him. They had hard eyes, glittering with pure aggression, and taut, professional faces. Their pistols were in their hands.

"That was Nick."

"Who got the picture of Donny and my wife?"

"That was Michael. You'd like them, Swagger. They're all ex-NCOs in the Black Sea Marines and SPETSNAZ. They've been with me for a long time."

"Who blew the building in Wisconsin?"

"That was a team job."

"And when you were running the mission against Solaratov, you were really running it against PAMYAT.

Against Pashin, who was now a nationalist, and if he wins the presidency it sets you guys back even farther. You always knew Pashin was Fitzpatrick, but you had to find a way to get that information to us without compromising your position. You turned everything inside out, so that in the end, the American government was working in the interests of the communist party. The Cold War never ended for you, right?"

"It never will. History runs in cycles. We're in retreat now, largely underground. But we've been underground before. We started underground. We have to eliminate our enemies in Russia. First Russia, then the world, as the great Stalin understood. We'll be back. This great, rich, fat country of yours is about to explode at the seams; it'll destroy itself and I'll help it. I should get the directorship shortly. From there, politics. The very interesting part of my plan is just about to start happening."

"Who are you?" boomed Bob.

Why was he talking so loud?

"I'll tell you. But first, you satisfy me: when did you know?"

"I began to suspect at the meeting when the kid wanted to let Solaratov take out Julie and nab him on the way out. That was the smart move; even I knew that. But you said no, you couldn't do that to me. Fuck you, that was never you. You could send anybody down. I knew that about you from what you done to Donny. So when you say you could never do that, I knew you was lying. You had to stop Solaratov. That was your first mission."

"Smart," said Bonson. "Smart, smart, smart."

"It gets me thinking. In seventy-two, you guys must have been shitting because you let the most important witness to Pashin and Trig get away. You couldn't track him because a good officer gave him liberty and then he was on his way back to Vietnam. He has to be killed, not only to protect Pashin, but to protect you. So . . . how do the goddamn Russians know where he is and what he's doing in Vietnam? How can they target him? That's a very tough piece of info to come by, and their whole plan turns on it. They had to have someone inside. Someone had to get into naval personnel and figure out where the boy was. Somebody had to target him. Solaratov was only the technician. You was the shooter."

Bonson stared at him.

"Funny, how when you make the breakthrough, it all kind of swings into shape," Bob said. "It all makes some kind of sense. Your last mistake: how *fast* the information got to Moscow, got to higher parties in PAMYAT, to destroy Pashin's presidential thing. Man, that was fast work. You're telling me the Agency is that fast? No way. Had to be some inside thing, someone who just had to make a phone call. Damn! And everybody keeps saying, 'Ain't it funny the communist party really benefits from all this?' Yeah, the real joke is, through you, the communist party is running all this. Who are you?"

"You are smart," said Bonson. "You just weren't quick enough, were you?"

"Who are you?" repeated Bob.

"You'd never believe this, but I'm history. I'm the future. I'm mankind. I'm hope. I'm the messiah of what must be."

He smiled again, a pure pilgrim of his own craziness.

"Not even Solaratov believed that shit," said Bob.

"All right, I'll tell you," said Bonson. "And then I'll kill you. This is a great privilege for you."

"Who are you?"

"You'd know the original family name, or you could dig it up. It's in some books. My parents were working-class Americans and fervent members of the American Communist Party. In 1938, the year I was born, they were asked to drop out and go underground for the committee. Of course they agreed. It was the greatest honor they'd ever been paid. So they renounced the party, turned on all their friends and spent the next fifteen years working as couriers, cut-outs, bag men for the atom bomb spies. They serviced the Rosenbergs, Alger Hiss, Klaus Fuchs, the whole brilliant thing we ran in this country. They were heroes. My father was a great man. He was greater than your father, Swagger. He was greater, braver, stronger, tougher, more resilient than your father. He was the best and my mother was a saint."

Bonson's eyes shown with tears as he recalled the beauty of his mother.

"You know the rest. NSA decrypts finally gave them away. My father hung himself in a holding tank on Rikers Island. My mother got me out, and then poisoned herself as the agents were coming up the stairs to arrest her. They were heroes of the Soviet Union! They gave it all to the revolution. Someone in the network got me out of the country, and by the following Tuesday I was in Moscow. I was fourteen years old and totally American, a Yankees and Giants fan, with an IQ of 160 and an absolute commitment to bringing down the system that murdered my parents. I was trained for six years. When I reinfiltrated I was already a major in the KGB. I'm now a three-star general. I have more decorations than you'll ever dream about. I am a hero of the Soviet Union."

"You're a psychopath. And there ain't no Soviet Union," said Bob.

"Too bad you won't be around to see how wrong you are."

The two ancient enemies faced each other in silence.

Finally Bonson said, "All right. That's enough. Kill him."

The team raised their pistols. The suppressed 9mm bores looked at Bob. There was complete silence.

"Any last words?" asked Bonson. "Any message for the family?"

"Last words?" said Bob. "Yeah, three of 'em: front toward enemy."

He turned his hand over to show them what it held and Bonson realized in an instant why hc had been speaking so loudly. Because he was wearing earplugs. He held the M57 electrical firing device, the green plastic clapper with a wire running down to the painting, behind which stood on its silly little set of tripods an M18A1 anti-personnel mine, better known as a Claymore. One or two, the faster, may have tried to fire, but Bob's reflexes were faster still as he triggered the demolition.

The one and a half pounds of plastic explosive encased in the mine detonated instantly, and a nanosecond later the seven hundred ball bearings, a blizzard of steel, arrived upon them at close to four thousand feet per second. The mine did what the mine was supposed to do: it took them out.

It literally dissolved them: their upper bodies were fragmented in one instant of maximum, total butchery. They exploded as if they'd swallowed grenades and become part of the atmosphere.

As for Bob, he saw none of this. The pillar, as planned, saved his life by blocking the force of the concussion. The earplugs saved his eardrums. But a pound and a half of plastic explosive is no small thing. He felt himself pulled out of his body, and his soul went sailing through the air until it struck something hard, and his mind filled with a bright fog, an incandescent emptiness. He blacked out for a minute or two.

No police arrived. The waterfront is a place of odd noises from unspecified localities: freighters' horns, the rumble of trucks, backfires and an almost total night-emptiness of human life. The sound of the blast was just another unexplained aural phenomenon in a city full of unexplained aural phenomenon.

When Bob pulled himself out of his fog, he tasted blood. He smelled it too. The blood he tasted was his own: his nose bled and both his ears rang like firebells, despite the plugs. He felt pain. He thought he'd broken his arm, but he hadn't, although he'd bruised it deeply. He picked himself up, saw flashbulbs prance through the air as his short-circuited optic nerves sputtered ineffectively. He blinked, staggered, sat, pulled himself up, blinked again and then beheld the horror.

The blood he smelled was theirs, and much of it, atomized, still floated in waves in the air, lit by flickering lights. There had been six of them: now there were three legs left standing, though no two belonged to any one of the men. What remained of Ward Bonson, deputy director of the CIA for counter-intelligence, Wall Street lawyer, three-star general in the KGB and a hero of the Soviet Union, was applied to the punctured metal of the wall behind him, mixed completely with the remains of the men who'd served him so ably over the long years. No one would have the heart—or the stomach—to separate them. It was a pure hose job.

Small fires burned everywhere in the smoky space. The sketches had been scattered about. Slowly, Bob gathered them up, then went to the largest of the fires.

He knelt, and one by one fed them into the hungry fire. It gobbled them, and he watched them seized, then curl to delicacy as they were blackened and devoured, then transfigure again into crispy ash, which fragmented and floated away in the hot current.

In the way his mind worked, he thought he saw the souls of those three lost boys, his friend Donny and Donny's friend Trig and Trig's victim, Ralph, somehow released to rise and float free, DEROS at last.

He picked up the fingerprinted M57 and dropped it into his pocket for later disposal, his last physical connection to the fate of Bonson and his team. Then he rose and walked out, turning for one last glimpse at the slaughterhouse he had created and the end of all complications of his violent life.

He thought: *Sierra-Bravo-Four. Last transmission. Out.*

He walked into the night air, sucked in its freshness, headed to his truck and, though he ached and bled, knew it would be best to start the long drive west. It was time to rotate back to the world.

Acknowledgments

T he author would like to begin by making certain readers understand that the foregoing in no way advances
a claim for his own heroism, which is, of course, nonexis-
tent. He was not a Marine sniper nor even a Marine; he
never went to Vietnam but served as the least efficient
ceremonial soldier in the 1st Battalion (Reinf.), Third Infantry, in Washington, DC, 1969–1970. His own war story:
he was present at the occupation of the Treasury Building.
It was very boring. And once he cut his lip on some barb
wire at Camp A.P. Hill in Virginia.

Readers will also recognize that I've seized events
from Vietnam, fictionalized them and reinserted them in
a bogus time frame for my own dramatic purposes. That
includes inventing an extra year of Marine ground combat. Most Marine units left RSVN in 1971; I was stuck
with 1972 because I chose that year without doing a lick of
research when I was writing *Point of Impact,* the first of
the Bob Lee Swagger books, many years back. In earlier
books, I also set the action near An Loc, which turns out
to be close to Saigon, and nowhere near I Corps, where
the Marines served. So in a belated attempt at the illusion
of accuracy, I've deemphasized An Loc and moved the
location of Bob and Donny's fight in the rain up to I
Corps, near the Special Forces camp at Kham Duc.

I've also simplified the complicated events in Washington over the first four days of May 1971 into a single
night, put the massacre of Firebase Mary Ann—my
Dodge City—in a different year and ascribed it to a different service, and invented my own 'Nam jargon under the
license of telling stories, not writing history. In fact, one of
the few things recounted in this book that actually happened was the great catch that Donny remembered making against Gilman High School. It *was* made against

Gilman, a prep school not in Arizona but Baltimore, by my son Jake Hunter, in Boys' Latin's victory over Gilman in 1995.

I should add that I've made a good-faith effort to reconcile events of this book with events previously referred to in *Point of Impact* and *Black Light*. Alas, far too many times events were irreconcilable, so you'll simply have to trust my assertion that in other books things happened *that* way, but in this book they happen *this* way.

But where I've made up much, I've also talked with many people who had firsthand knowledge of the kind of events I describe. They're all good men and deserve no blame for my inaccuracies or the ends to which I've put information that they earned the hard way.

Ed DeCarlo, retired Army CSGT, and Alvin Guyton, retired Gy. Sgt., USMC, both good buddies from On Target Shooting Range, where I spend vast amounts of time and money, shared Vietnam memories and data with me. Ed was a radio operator and briefed me on the intricacies of the PRC-77 and map reading; Alvin, a recon Marine, lent me tons of reference material and even loaned me copies of his orders to Vietnam on which to base my version of Donny's, and tried to make me feel Marine culture well enough to imagine it. Two of the usual suspects, Weyman Swagger and John Feamster, offered their usual supplies of endless labor, commentary and suggestion, each reading the manuscript with a great deal of precision. Lenne Miller, another Vietnam vet and an old college friend, was equally generous with time and observation. My brother Tim Hunter sent me a terrific letter of constructive criticism. Jeff Weber not only lent me his name for one of the characters but also read the manuscript and offered good advice. Bob Lopez came up with a crucial idea at a crucial moment. J. D. Considine, the pop-music critic of *The Baltimore Sun,* my old paper, drew up a compilation tape of 1971 hits, to whose accompaniment this book was written. Mike Hill was very helpful. Bill Phillips, an ex-Marine officer, Vietnam vet and author of *The Night of Silver Stars,* read the manuscript carefully and helped me sort out Army jargon and replace it with Marine, but if I've called it a latrine somewhere instead of a head, it's my fault, not Bill's. Tim Carpenter, of Bushnell's, explained the subtleties of infrared ranging devices to me. Dave Lauck, of D&L Sports in Gillette, Wyoming, and author of *The Tactical Marksman,* ran his fine professional eye over the manuscript, to my great benefit. Kathy Lally and Will England, the *Sun's* Moscow correspondents, gave me tips and data on that city for a chapter that was ultimately cut. Warrant Officer Joe Boyer of the Marine Barracks took me on a prowl through that installation and patiently answered my questions. Jean Marbella, of my old paper and my new life, was her usual fabulous self and listened to me prattle on about titles and narrative issues late into the night. John Pancake, arts editor of my new paper, *The Washington Post,* just smiled every time I told him I was leaving early to work on the book. David Von Drehle, editor of the *Post's* Style section, was equally generous in letting me disappear when I deemed it necessary. Steve Proctor, of the *Sun,* had instituted a similar policy in my many years there, and he too should be recognized and thanked.

Former Green Beret Don Pugsley wrote to me at great length about communications procedures from A camps. Charles H. "Hap" Hazard, a *Sun* artist and former Army intelligence enlisted man, translated a lot of stuff into Vietnamese for me, very helpfully. Dr. Jim Fisher introduced me to Dr. Charlie Partjens, an orthopedic surgeon, who discussed the physical realities of an old bullet with me. Bill Ochs, former Army sergeant, discussed something of far more intensity: the trauma of his own hip wound, acquired in action in RSVN. I really appreciate his willingness to let a stranger invade his privacy like that.

I should also thank authors who have come before me. Peter R. Senich, the Thucydides of sniper warfare, came out with *The One-Shot War,* a history of Marine sniper operations in Vietnam, just as I was beginning. Then Michael Lee Lanning and Dan Cragg published *Inside the VC and the NVA,* which was very helpful for tough little Huu Co, senior colonel. Of course I've drawn from Charles Henderson's *Marine Sniper,* and Joseph T. Ward's *Dear Mom: A Sniper's Vietnam,* as well as the standard history texts. I never spoke to any Marine snipers, however, because I needed to be free to envision Bob Lee Swagger as I wanted him to be, warts and all.

Last, in the professional realm, I must thank my brilliant, wonderful agent Esther Newberg of ICM and my great editor, Bill Thomas, of Doubleday. And something finally for the book's dedicatee, John Burke, who was the great Carlos Hathcock's spotter in Vietnam, and didn't make it to DEROS. I never knew him but his story so moved me that I had to find a way to cast it into a book, and he became my Donny Fenn. So in a way this whole thing—this book and the three that proceeded it—all came from his sacrifice. Thanks, Marine.

© John Earle

Stephen Hunter is the author of eight novels, including the national bestsellers *Black Light,* *Dirty White Boys,* **and** *Point of Impact,* **with over three million copies in print. He is also the chief film critic for** *The Washington Post* **and the author of a collection of criticism,** *Violent Screen.* **He lives in Baltimore, Maryland.**